IN THE WAKE OF THE WICKED

V.B. LACEY

FICTION & FATE PRESS

THE VERIDIAN EMPIRE BOOK 1

IN THE WAKE OF THE WICKED

Exclusive Digitally Signed Edition

V. B. LACEY

AUTHOR'S NOTE

This book has scenes depicting a traumatic birth scene, blood magic, brief animal cruelty, violence, on-screen death, traumatic flashbacks, derealization, mild choking, brief mention of violence toward children, and mentions of physical assault.

Please be mindful of these and other possible triggers.

———

To those who have ever been told you aren't enough,
let
them
watch
you
fly.

———

THE VERID
ILUZE
CHAMPIONS RUN
LAKE LEZNEM
THE TEMPLE
CELESTRIA
FEYWOOD FOREST
ARCANE APOTHECARY
FEYWOOD
LUNA PORT
AVONIGE OCEAN
MYSTHELM

...IAN EMPIRE
EMBERFELL
LIGHTSWORN ACADEMY
ELDERTIDE OCEAN
EMBERFELL PORT
GUARDIAN RANGE
SCARRE RIVER
VERIDIA CITY
DRAKORUM
GOVERNOR'S HOUSE
TENEBRA
MISTWOOD MOUNTAINS
TRAINING GROUNDS
SHADOWMERE WASTELANDS

VERIDIA CITY
NORTH SECTOR
WEST SECTOR
WESTHAVEN
CENTRAL SECTOR
THE PALACE
RIDGEMORE
EAST SECTOR
SOUTH SECTOR
ARIS COTTAGE

"There is a poison in the fang of the serpent, in the mouth of the fly and in the sting of the scorpion; but the wicked man is saturated with it."
- Chanakya

PROLOGUE

In the stillness of the palace, a scream ripped through the air.
Footsteps clattered against stone, and the door flew open
with a *bang*.

"Emperor Aris!" the midwife shouted, summoning him to the
bed with a bloody rag. The frayed ends of her gray hair clung to the
nape of her neck, sweat rolling down her forehead. Her hands were
steady as she knelt over the bed in the center of the room.

A half dozen healers and servants rushed past, but Branock
Aris focused on his wife. His breath caught at the white sheets
beneath her, soaked in red, her eyes bloodshot and her wavy
blonde tresses tied back with a strap of leather. Tendrils of it were
plastered to her sweat-slicked skin. And in her arms—

"It's a girl," his wife told him, a smile lighting her tired eyes.

Branock dropped to his knees at the side of her bed. "Evadine,"
he whispered, heart pounding in his chest. "She's...she's beautiful."
His voice was laced with awe as he took in the sight of his wife and
daughter, whose little eyes were scrunched closed and tiny fingers
were poking out from the blanket wrapped tightly around her.
"Why did you not call for me?"

"There was no time, Your Majesty," the midwife explained.

"Her labor came quickly. I was barely able to get here myself before she began to push."

He looked at Evadine. "A girl." He repeated her words and leaned forward to kiss the baby's forehead, then Evadine's. "You did so beautifully, my love," he rasped.

His wife's eyes met his, full of joy despite the exhaustion that lined every feature. A smile formed on her lips. She opened her mouth to reply when her gaze became unfocused and her eyes rolled into her head.

Branock's heart lurched to his throat. "Evadine?" He gripped the back of her neck, his thumb brushing over her cheek. "Evadine, open your eyes."

When she slumped in his hold, he frantically turned to the midwife. "What's happening? What's wrong with her?"

A second healer swiftly took the baby girl from Evadine's limp arms. The head midwife lifted the blanket at Evadine's feet, her eyes widening. "I think...there is another baby, Your Majesty."

Pulse rushing, stomach churning, he gasped, "*Another?*"

Ignoring him, she hastily motioned to her assistant, who moved to Evadine's head and placed a flask of smelling salts beneath her nose. Within moments, Evadine roused, confusion lighting her face as she found Branock's eyes.

He couldn't believe the words about to come out of his mouth. Taking a deep breath, he said, "There's a second baby, my love. You're going to have to be strong one more time."

Her lips parted. "A *second?* How—"

Her question turned to a moan as a labor pain swept through her. She flung her head back in anguish, and a healer hurried to place a cold cloth on her forehead.

"I'm going to need you to push when I say," the midwife directed gently to Evadine, who grasped Branock's hand tighter. His wife clenched her teeth and slammed her eyes shut. Branock watched in horror as blood continued to soak the bed and the midwife's hands.

Too much blood.

"It's time—push, Your Majesty," the midwife commanded. Another cry tore from Evadine's throat, making Branock's chest constrict. He kissed her whitened knuckles as the midwife instructed her each time to keep pushing. Evadine whimpered and fell against the headboard, eyes fluttering.

"Evadine—Eva, one more push and it will all be over." He brushed a strand of hair away from her face. Meeting his eyes, she gritted her teeth, and he sensed her body clenching, another shriek clawing up her throat.

"Some—something's wrong, Bran," Evadine gasped, her hold on his hand tightening even further. Her face screwed in anguish as she tried to push again, more blood flooding the foot of the bed. "I can't—I can't—" Her words were forced and stammered, the vise-like grip on his fingers slowly loosening as her head dropped to her shoulder.

"No!" he roared, leaping to his feet and facing the midwife. "Get it *out of her*!"

The midwife strained to keep her voice calm. "I'm so sorry, Your Majesty, but I—I think the baby is breached. It isn't ready."

"Then *get* it ready," Branock snarled. "This is killing her!"

"We're trying, sir, but—" The midwife paused, indecision warring across her features as her eyes flitted back and forth.

He didn't have time for this. His *wife* didn't have time for this. "Whatever it is, tell me," he said, suddenly weak in the knees. "Tell me how to save them."

The midwife swallowed. "Your Majesty, I fear we are going to have to use other means to deliver this baby, and I don't know if both of them will survive."

The words rang through his mind, his vision graying as his heart hammered in his chest.

Never had he felt such distress. Such helplessness. It consumed him, wrapped around his throat and pulled. *I don't know if both of them will survive.* He knew what Evadine would want—save the baby. Save their child.

But he could not lose his Eva. This was not a choice he could make in a thousand lifetimes.

And so, he wouldn't.

He knew what he had to do.

Striding out the door, he found the nearest servant. "Get Theodore," he commanded. The young man stood to attention, blinking rapidly at the request. "*Theodore Gayl*," Branock repeated angrily. "I don't care if you have to drag him from his bed—get me Theodore Gayl. *Now!*"

Back inside the room, the midwife threw him a sharp look. "What are you doing, Your Majesty?"

"What I must to save my wife and child."

She opened her mouth to argue further, but she must have seen the determination in his eyes, for she turned her attention to the healers and began doling out quick instructions.

Branock strained his ears for the sound of footsteps coming down the hall, clenching and unclenching his fist as he kept his eyes on his wife, whose face was now leached of color.

She was running out of time.

He knew the risks, knew the chance he was taking by calling the Alchemist. But he didn't have a choice.

Finally, a knock sounded on the door, then was thrown open by the servant boy and a man following close on his heels. His long, greasy black hair hung past his pale neck, a wrinkled robe thrown on in haste over his night clothes. Theodore Gayl's piercing eyes took in the scene and met Branock's, sending a shiver down his spine. Those eyes shocked him every time he saw them. One of dark blue, one of pure white. Theodore's forehead wrinkled as he tilted his head, and Branock knew he understood without words. His wisdom, his intuition, went far beyond his mere thirty years of life.

"Your Majesty, I don't know what you think I can help with, but—"

"Save them, Gayl. My wife *and* the baby. I know you can—

you're the most powerful Alchemist this empire has seen in centuries."

Theodore's eyes flicked back to Evadine. The midwife had taken her position at the foot of the bed again, a sharp blade in her hand readying to cut into the skin at Evadine's stomach. Branock could feel his heartbeat in every inch of his body. *There wasn't enough time.*

Theodore took a step toward him. "Sir, what you ask is—"

"I don't *care*, Gayl! Look at her!"

The man swallowed. "The cost will be great." His voice was low, hesitant.

"Then I will pay it," Branock said, gripping Theodore's arm. "Whatever it is, I will pay the price. Just...save my family, Theodore. I beg you."

Theodore held his gaze for a second. Two. Branock's chest caved in until finally, the man gave a curt nod and knelt at Evadine's side.

Branock's eyes fell shut in relief, a heavy breath leaving his lips.

The midwife's blade sank into Evadine's stomach, flaying the skin open on either side. As Branock watched her hands dip inside his wife, soaked in blood, Theodore Gayl's murmured words reached his ears. His mouth moved faster than Branock could comprehend, whisperings of power flowing from between his lips. The air was heavy with the cloying taste of magic, blood, and the herbs Gayl had pulled from his pocket and now clutched in his fist. Something red leaked from the man's clenched hand, but Branock was too focused on his Evadine to care.

Branock stumbled to the other side of the bed, eyes on his wife's pale, lifeless expression, when the midwife exclaimed, "It's a boy!"

But the babe...the babe would not cry.

The emperor's heart shattered at the realization, unsure where to draw his attention—on his Eva, his bride, slowly fading from this world, or his son, struggling to draw breath.

His head snapped to Theodore, whose face was screwed in concentration. "Why is it not *working*?" he hissed.

The midwife sucked in a breath. "Your Majesty, this is dark magic you're attempting—"

"Silence!" he roared, but his anger swiftly turned to despair. "What choice do I have?"

Suddenly, Theodore's eyes snapped open, the blue and white fixed intently on Branock. "This will be a far greater burden than you are prepared to bear."

Branock gritted his teeth. "I will decide what I can and cannot bear. *Do it*, Gayl. I will not ask again."

Without hesitation, Theodore clapped his bloody hands together, his chanting growing louder as a current of power flowed through him. It felt like the air had been siphoned from the room, pulled tight as a bow string, the tension stretching and stretching until Branock was sure he would burst. His breath was shallow, his mind muddled.

With a snap, a bolt of magic erupted from Theodore, sending Branock stumbling.

The cry of not one, but *two* babes rang in his ears.

He quickly righted himself and reached for the healer holding his daughter, his gaze frantically searching for the other—

There, by the window. Safe. His son was safe.

But something caught his attention in the sky beyond the window.

His mouth fell open.

A red mist descended from the heavens, draping itself like a blanket over the land. He staggered to the sill. His breath fogged the glass as he peered through the dim moonlight. The red cloud coated the thin line of forests outside his palace grounds, coasting down to meet the tips of the buildings of Veridia City, the trees and gardens, the streets and houses. It settled into the ground and dissipated, gone almost as quickly as it had appeared.

He blinked away his disbelief.

"What was—"

"The cost, Your Majesty," Theodore said from behind him. Branock whirled, his stomach leaping into his throat.

Evadine.

She still lay unconscious as the midwife and a healer sewed the incision together, but the color had returned to her cheeks, her breaths now deep and even.

"Sh-she's alive," he breathed. "Both of them." He took Theodore's hands in his own. "Thank you, Gayl. I don't know how I can ever repay you."

"You have no idea what this has done, Your Majesty." Theodore stared into Branock's eyes. "What you have unleashed upon your empire."

Branock's heart stuttered. He wet his lips, a sour lump forming in his throat. "What do you mean?"

"The price of this kind of magic runs deep, Branock." Theodore extracted himself from Branock's grasp, glancing at both of the crying babes and their sleeping mother. "But it is not you who will pay it."

Branock's eyes strayed to the view of his land outside the window, terror gripping him.

What had he done?

I

ROSE

TWENTY-SEVEN YEARS LATER

I slid my hand beneath the counter, feeling around the boxes of metal tins. I knew what each contained simply by touch—I could find anything in this apothecary with my eyes closed. Rounded edges: *lavender stems*. Chip on the corner: *shredded stinging nettle*. Ripped label: *lemon balm*. None of which I needed.

Ah. There it was.

Square tin, still smooth and undented. Hardly touched. *Foxglove.*

"Can we hurry it along, please?" the customer asked impatiently. I peeked over the counter to see her anxiously looking behind her shoulder to the window leading outside, as if preparing to duck if anyone glimpsed her darkening the doorsteps of my shop.

I bit back a retort and swiftly opened the lid to the tin, pinching the crushed purple petals between my thumb and forefinger, then brought it to the counter and sprinkled them into the tea blend. Shooting the young woman a saccharine smile, I sifted the mixture together, tied the bag with twine, and held it out.

"Here you go, Madeline. That should help you get some more sleep."

She snatched the bag from my grip so fast one would think I'd burned her. "What's in it, again?" she demanded.

I cleared my throat. "Valerian root, chamomile, and a dash of lavender."

She nodded, satisfied, and dropped several coins onto the counter before turning on her heel and quickly exiting the shop, her red curls bouncing. I waited till the door to the apothecary shut before rolling my eyes.

"*You're welcome,*" I muttered.

The sound of heavy footsteps bounding through the back door reached my ears, followed by something slamming into wood. I held in a chuckle. *Typical Beau.*

Lurching beneath the counter, I shoved the box of foxglove out of sight and rearranged the other tins to cover it.

"Was that Madeline I heard?" my cousin Beau asked, his voice breathless as it broke on the girl's name.

"Yes," I replied, wiping my hands on my apron.

He came into view, his mop of brown hair disheveled as if he'd hurriedly tried to flatten it. His gray eyes darted toward the door and he craned his long, gangly neck, trying to catch a peek of the girl retreating. "Did—did she ask about me?"

I pinched the bridge of my nose, holding back a sigh. "Beau, honestly, after what she did to you, you *still* want to talk to her?"

A week ago, I'd found my sixteen-year-old cousin trudging through the dark streets of Feywood during a thunderstorm. He was soaked to the bone and his skin was ice cold, chills racking his entire body, but he didn't seem to care. His eyes were dull and distant. An alarm had swept through me like a tidal wave at the sight.

He was supposed to be with Madeline, the girl he'd been seeing for quite some time, yet he looked like he'd been wandering for *hours.*

When I'd found out what had happened, I almost ran through the streets to her house in a blind rage. Beau had stumbled upon his girlfriend in bed with another man—an older boy from town. Instead of showing guilt at being caught in the act, Madeline had *laughed*. She'd thanked Beau for putting on a good show, but now that she was eighteen, she didn't need him as a cover for her relationship with the older man.

Three days later, she'd publicly announced her engagement.

Beau had been a wreck ever since.

Today, he'd appeared slightly more like his normal self—chipper and easily distracted—until now, with the familiar red curls of his first heartbreak growing distant in the shop window. She hadn't been able to get out of the apothecary fast enough, more than likely to avoid an awkward encounter with Beau, but I knew that wasn't the only reason.

My cousin's face drooped. "I know, I know. I guess I just...I miss her." His dejection made me all the more pissed at the girl. "What did she come in for, anyway?" he asked.

"A sleeping tonic."

He raised an eyebrow. "Then why are your fingers purple?"

I looked down to see the slight colored tinge the foxglove had left on my fingers. *Fates*.

Beau groaned. "Rose, what did you do this time?"

Irritation boiled inside me, hot and acidic. "She cheated on you and used you for months, then broke your heart to run off and get married. This is the *least* of what she deserves."

"Thanks for the reminder." Beau ran his hand along his chin and the thin patch of scruff that had recently begun to grow in. "Is that *foxglove*? How much did you give her?"

I shrugged. "Enough to make her have an uncomfortable couple of nights. She'll be fine."

Beau wagged his head disappointedly. In that moment, he looked so much older, so much like my uncle, that it softened my anger. Sometimes I forgot he wasn't my annoying little cousin anymore, running between my legs and following me everywhere I went. He was becoming a man who could take care of himself. He didn't need me to play the coddling sister figure, as much as I wished I could always protect him from the Madelines of the world.

Rubbing the fabric of my apron between my fingers, I took a deep breath. "I just wanted to look out for you. I'm sorry, Beau."

Beau's gray eyes—so bright they appeared silver—pierced into me, and he gave a little snort. "No, you're not, but I guess you did it for a good reason."

A small smirk played at the corner of my mouth. I edged closer to him. "So, you're saying—"

"*No*, I'm not saying it's okay for you to poison people."

"*But*...you still love me?" I finished with a grin as I lunged to ruffle the top of his shaggy, light brown hair—several shades lighter than my own raven locks. He batted me away with a laugh, his long arms able to keep me away, unlike when he was younger.

"Yes, I still love you," he agreed, dodging my attacks. "Maybe next time, love me a little less, yeah? I don't know, put a potion in her soap that makes her skin turn green or something. *Don't* try to kill her."

I stopped in my tracks. The soap idea wasn't half bad. "I wasn't trying to kill her," I said, giving him a quick pat on the head before grabbing a rag to wipe down the counter. I motioned to the drawer next to Beau that contained the store's money bag. "Since you're here, mind counting down for me? I'm about ready to close."

He nodded and began separating the coins from the bag to take stock of our earnings for the day. My aunt and uncle—Beau's parents—had owned the shop, the Arcane Apothecary, for nearly twenty years now. My own parents had started it before then, but when my mother died during childbirth and my father had followed five years later, my aunt and uncle adopted me and took over the shop. I grew up learning the ways of the apothecary alongside my younger cousin. It was the only life I'd ever known— stable and comfortable, if not sometimes a bit...lonely. Like I was living a life meant for someone else.

Four years ago when I turned twenty-one, I'd decided to move to the small apartment above the shop instead of continuing to take up space in Uncle Ragnar and Aunt Morgana's household. They had done so much for me, and while they claimed me as their own, I'd always felt like a burden. Something thrust into their hands out of necessity. Out of pity. They loved me, of course, and were the only parents I'd known for the majority of my life. But they'd given me sixteen years at that point—it had been *my* turn to make something of myself.

I'd been running the Arcane ever since. Beau helped where he could, and it was still under Ragnar and Morgana's name—until I saved enough to properly buy it from them. But it was *mine*. Every stained glass window, every dusty nook, every wooden shelf lined with vials and herbs, tonics and bobbles. I'd found my purpose in the shadows of these shelves, the magic of my Alchemist blood singing each time I opened the doors.

If only the town felt the same way.

Morgana and Ragnar were respected in our province of Feywood, one of six in the Veridian Empire. The Arcane had always been a renowned establishment—the best shop for Alchemists to stock up on their herbs, try new potions, and buy basic remedies they didn't have the time or desire to brew themselves. But business had been steadily declining over the past couple of years. Once it had become obvious that *I* had taken over, the whispers started and the sales slowed.

I had *cursed blood*, they said. It seemed wherever I went, darkness wasn't far behind. An orphan with parents who died such tragic deaths, the little girl who couldn't make friends, the young woman with a penchant for toeing the line between acceptable and indecent, conventional and peculiar, righteous and wicked.

These people had condemned me before I could string full sentences together. Never mind the fact that I made the *best* healing poultices in the province, that my protection charms were second to none, and that Morgana and Ragnar had dedicated two decades of their lives to this place. The citizens here were superstitious to a fault. If they saw something wrong with you, something *other*, they distanced themselves as much as possible. I hated that the Arcane was suffering because of it. I hated that it was *my* fault.

"Sales were a little down today," Beau said with a shrug as he finished counting.

And I hated that it still hurt, every time.

"But we have a couple specialty orders that came in earlier," he continued. "I wrote them down and put them next to your Grimoire." He gave me a sheepish look. "I hope that's okay."

I pursed my lips but stayed quiet. An Alchemist's Grimoire was incredibly private, and while I knew my cousin didn't mean any harm, the idea of someone seeing into my spells—my *mind*, my magic—set me on edge.

He must have seen the look on my face, for his eyes widened. "I'm sorry, Rosie," he said, using his childhood nickname for me. "I didn't look, I just set the paper down and walked away."

"It's fine," I said curtly, crossing to the front door and locking it. Before I could return to the counter, however, a body slammed into the wood on the other side. Beau shouted in alarm behind me, and I heard something crash. He must've knocked over one of the glass jars.

I reached into the pocket of my brown skirt to grab a stem of amaranth, my favorite protection charm. Slowly, I unlocked the door and turned the handle, heavy breaths reaching my ears through the crack in the wood.

"Rose, is that you? It's Bethaly. I've got a delivery. Quick, this time—I can't stay long."

I exhaled at the familiar voice, pulling the door open all the way to reveal a young woman with shoulder-length, curly brown hair, golden skin, and a purple travel cloak sweeping around her ankles in the brisk Feywood evening. Her chapped lips broke into a grin, the dimples on her cheeks bursting to life.

"Sorry I didn't make it earlier. Had a little trouble getting through the forest," she said breathlessly.

"We're closed, Beth," I said with a *tsk*, crossing my arms. "Deliveries need to be made during operating hours."

"Oh, shut up and come here." She dropped her bag and enveloped me in a hug, which I returned warmly, letting my false grumpiness fall away.

After a moment, I stiffened, feeling eyes from the street watching us. "Get in before someone says something," I said, leading her into the shop, both of us lugging her bags of supplies to the counter.

Bethaly was from Celestria, our neighboring province to the northwest. Celestria was home to many flowers, herbs, and various natural ingredients we didn't have here in Feywood, and Beth was one of the few permitted to cross the border between the two to make routine deliveries. Fifteen years ago, the current emperor—Emperor Gayl—had established a law requiring one to have a special permit to enter another province, whether it was for trade, personal reasons, or other business. We were no longer free to travel among the empire, as our ancestors had been able to.

Another law the *mighty* Emperor Gayl put into place to divide us further. Just the thought of him sitting on his gilded throne watching the rest of the empire regress made anger boil beneath my skin.

Beth had been working with us for several years and over the course of time, had become one of my dearest friends. We didn't see each other as often as I'd like, but whenever she had to travel here for extended periods of time, she always stayed with me.

We had to be careful, though. Tension between the provinces had been growing ever since Gayl had enacted his law, and was now at an all-time high. Many people here wouldn't like the idea of me having such close ties with a Celestrian—or any foreigner to Feywood, for that matter.

I was already an outcast in my own province. I didn't need to give them a reason to hate me even more.

"That should be all of it," Beth said, heaving one of the bags onto the counter. "The guards took forever letting me through the forest. You know how border checks go when we get this close to the Decemvirate." She rolled her eyes in annoyance.

A chill went down my spine at the mention of the upcoming tournament, but I shook it off. "What good are those Strider abilities if you can't make it on time? Can't you *magick* yourself here from the border?" I joked, wiggling my fingers at her.

She scoffed. "I wish. It would be so much easier if I could just"—she winked at me, and in the next breath, disappeared from sight and reappeared right behind Beau—"snap my fingers and be here."

My cousin yelped. "I hate it when you do that," he said with a huff, his cheeks turning bright red as he began pulling tin canisters from Beth's bag. Those with the magic of Celestria, like Beth, were called Striders. Their power allowed them to magically transport themselves from one space to another. She loved using her abilities to tease Beau.

"You're just jealous." Beth grinned, ruffling his hair. He shoved her off and ducked away from her reach.

"Someone's moody," she remarked. "How are things going with that girl? The *older woman*." Beth shimmied her shoulders at Beau.

I winced as the color drained from his face.

"What?" Beth glanced between the two of us. "What happened?"

"I'll tell you later," I muttered, clearing space and reaching for the second bag of supplies.

"We're over," Beau said gloomily. "Madeline's getting married."

Beth's dark eyebrows shot straight into her forehead. "*What?* Girl moves on fast. Fates, I'm sorry, Beau," she said, frowning. "Want us to go cut off her hair or something?"

I snorted. "And this is why we're friends."

"Yeah, Rose already poisoned her," Beau added, a small smile breaking through the storm clouds.

And I'd do it again. I'd do anything for the few people in this world I cared about.

"That's our Rose," Beth said with a chuckle. "What about your father, Beau? How's he doing with the tournament?"

The playfulness in the room immediately dissipated, leaving behind a strain that made me cringe. I silently cursed at the way Beau's face tightened, his shoulders caving in.

The Decemvirate, a tournament that occurred every ten years among the six provinces of the Veridian Empire, was set to take place in two weeks at the capital of Veridia City. Legend has it that long before the empire became what it was today, the small island —now our capital—had been bestowed with untapped magic by the Fates, the three ancient beings believed to guide our way and dole out futures as they saw fit. They took the components that made up their essence, their purpose, and split the magic into six potent forms: light and dark, power over mind and power over nature, ability to change and move forward.

Nobody knew *why* the Fates chose this land to inhabit their magic so long ago, only that it was powerful.

And anything that powerful breeds conflict.

Over three hundred years ago, after the War of Beginnings when our Veridian Empire conquered the Kingdom of Mysthelm to the south in order to lay claim to this power, the Decemvirate was created as a way to divide the six types of magic among the provinces. Each of the six provinces selected a single challenger to compete, and all of them traveled to the island city for an exhibition of their skills through various tasks. Based on their performance, the challengers were allowed to select which strand of magic their people received: the ability to create and bend light, to wield shadows, to cast illusions, to practice spellcrafting, to shift into an animal form, or to transport from one place to another.

But it didn't stop there.

People began to realize the magic slowly lost its strength. After several years, their power took more effort to perform and wasn't nearly as effective as it once was. The reigning emperor sought to ensure he and his people didn't lose their magic entirely. According to history records, the three Fates appeared to him and told him of a ritual that could be performed to increase its power—but only every ten years.

He decided to structure this power ritual after the original Decemvirate. A tournament to replenish magic among the provinces in the same way it had been given in the beginning. The province with the challenger that performed the best in a series of magical tests received the highest tier of magic, and so on, until the sixth and final challenger—whose province received barely a fraction of the others. The magic would then dwindle for ten years until the next Decemvirate rolled around, and it started all over again.

This time, the challenger from our province of Feywood was Ragnar Gregor. Beau's father and my uncle.

He was, undoubtedly, the most prestigious and skilled Alchemist in all of Feywood. It was no wonder he was selected to compete, even though he was nearing fifty years of life and past what most would consider his prime. It was an *honor*, of course. A *privilege* to represent your province and have the chance to bring home the strongest of magic to your people.

I ground my teeth together.

It made me sick.

The Decemvirate was a hoax. Instead of making magic equally available to *all* provinces, it had been turned into nothing more than pageantry. A political scheme that had since been egged on by decades and decades of emperors who used it as a way to leash the people into doing their bidding. To turn the provinces against one another in the name of *competition* while keeping them in line. Who *wouldn't* obey every command when the future of their magic was at stake?

Since my uncle was a challenger this year, we would soon be leaving for the capital, and it had become harder and harder to deny the reality of what we were about to face. It wasn't uncommon for challengers to die in the Decemvirate, to face horrifying torment and danger. No matter how much he tried to hide it, I could tell Beau was *terrified* for his father. I was, as well, although I was used to locking my fears far beneath the surface.

Locking *anything* far beneath the surface.

Before I could attempt to inject some levity into the conversation, Beau responded with a heated, "We're not supposed to talk about our challenger with you. You're a *Strider*." Then he grabbed the store's money pouch and sulked off to the back room.

Beth blinked at me. "What did I say?"

"He's just..." I sighed, shaking my head. "He's got a lot going on. Don't take it personally—he didn't mean it like that."

Beau wasn't wrong; talk amongst provinces about their respective challengers *was* frowned upon. Some provinces, like Drakorum to the far east and Iluze to our north, weren't above sending spies to the others to scope out the competition. There was a rumor that in the last Decemvirate ten years ago, one of the Shifters from Drakorum had snuck into a neighboring province and poisoned their challenger before he could compete.

These people were cutthroat and cunning, unafraid to do what it took to win. Even if I despised the tournament, part of me understood. When the leader of our empire pitted the provinces against each other, what else could be expected? We adapted, or we lost.

And losing wasn't an option.

Feywood hadn't won the Decemvirate in seven decades, and our magic was hanging on by a thread. I felt the effects of it every day; the extra effort it took to perform simple spells, the way my mind was more sluggish after using too much magic, the number of people who came into the shop needing healing potions because they could no longer make their own.

This tournament and its cruelty was the price of that magic, I supposed. But it shouldn't be. Not when *every* emperor for the last three centuries could have put an end to it, could have decided to replenish the magic *equally* and without conditions, yet continued to keep up this spectacle. All for the sake of maintaining power and wealth—the Decemvirate brought hordes of inter-province commerce to the capital, lining the emperor's coffers with gold from all the visiting spectators.

Money and magic. The only things our dear leaders cared about.

I gripped a tin of crushed dandelion leaves from the bag so tightly that the thin material dented with a *crunch*.

Beth's brows pinched. "How are *you* doing with everything?" she asked. "Have you decided if you're going with them to the capital or staying here?"

A strand of dark hair fell across my eyes, and I blew it away, releasing some pent-up tension. "I'm going. Morgana keeps trying to convince me not to, but I found someone to watch the shop for the month. It's probably my only chance to ever travel outside of Feywood. I can't pass that up, you know?"

Beth finished laying out all of our new supplies on the counter, then buckled the straps on her bags. "I've always wanted to visit the capital, but I can't say I'm jealous. You need to be careful, Rose. I know we were both only fifteen the last time the Decemvirate came around, but this one feels...different." Her shoulders shivered. "I can tell. I see it in all the provinces I deliver to. Things are getting worse—fights breaking out in streets, border guards not letting us cross over, whispers of the stronger provinces wanting to expand into the weaker ones. And Emperor Gayl doesn't seem to care. As long as he gets his precious Decemvirate, the people can do whatever they want. And the challengers this year..." Beth trailed off, then grabbed my hand, her hazel eyes shadowed with worry. "Ragnar needs to be ready. *All* of you do. I've heard the one from Iluze in particular is a piece of work."

A sliver of dread slid down my spine, but I shoved it away and squeezed her hand. "We'll be careful, Beth. I promise."

She looked like she wanted to say more, but at that moment, Beau reappeared. "I put the money up and recorded everything for the day," he said, moodiness still lining his voice.

"Great." I straightened. "I'm going to go check those orders you left out for me. Can you help Beth put the supplies where they need to go?"

"Yeah, sure," he mumbled. I covered my mouth to hide a smile and shared a look with Beth.

She winked at me before cheerily saying, "So, Beau, there's this pretty girl I deliver to a few streets away…"

This time, I didn't bother hiding my laugh as I walked into the back room.

2

ROSE

To anyone else, the back room of the Arcane, which doubled as extra storage space and my personal workshop, was in desperate need of organization. But to me, it was perfect, orderly chaos.

A rickety wooden shelf stretched to the ceiling on the left wall, reinforced over the years by several rods of metal. It housed dozens of supply bins—empty glass vials, parchment for labels, bags, twine, candles. The back wall contained most of the gardening tools and a door leading to our greenhouse. That was where my Aunt Morgana liked to spend most of her time—she had a natural green thumb, and I was more than happy to hand her the reins. Herbs and spellcasting were her strong suit. She grew and nurtured the various plants we needed for the Arcane's most sought after herbal remedies, and once harvested, I sorted through them and replenished our stock.

Most nights, I stayed up far too late experimenting with new potions and spells, feeling a sort of freedom and comfort under the solace of the moon. Along with filling up my own Grimoire, I'd inherited both of my parents' when I turned sixteen. Even after nine years, I still found hidden treasures buried deep in the fading pages.

My gaze drifted to the right wall of the room, where my work table and shelves resided. On the table beneath a layer of stray moss, candles, and basil leaves rested both mine and my mother's Grimoires, hers flipped to a page in the center full of her notes. I'd fallen asleep the night before with my cheek plastered to the thin parchment.

An involuntary pang shot through my chest at the sight.

I'd never known my mother. Never felt her arms wrapped around me, never heard a soothing lullaby from her lips, never looked into her green eyes or saw the curl of dark hair. Aunt Morgana often told me how much I resembled her, and I had a small portrait of her and my father in the locket around my neck, but it did little to fill the hole that had been carved from my life.

Because of my life. Because she had died giving birth to *me*.

Reading her spells and potions, following each dip and curve of her letters…it was the closest I'd ever get to knowing her. To seeing her. It was like she was speaking to me, even now, eager for me to learn the magic she'd held so close to her heart.

The backs of my eyes prickled and I blinked the sudden emotion away, burying it beneath my weathered layers.

A chilly burst of wind ruffled the ends of my raven hair. A shiver crawled across my skin as a few leaves flew through the open window above my desk, sending seeds and crushed petals sprawling. I crossed to the window, surprised I'd been careless enough to leave it open, and quickly jerked it down.

The beginning of autumn was approaching, and in Feywood, that meant strong winds, brisk nights, and the smell of snow in the air. Lingering scents of firewood and burning herbs washed over me, the muted sounds of townspeople mulling about the main square just a block away from the apothecary still audible through the window.

Autumn was normally my favorite time of year. When the darkened leaves flowed like crimson and orange waves beneath my feet, the brightness of the moon stirring the Alchemist magic in my blood, the smiles of strangers and whispers of spirits and crisp scent of spice and smoke...it awoke something in me.

But not this year. Not with the cloud of the Decemvirate hanging over our heads, and the fact that soon, my entire family would be packing for the month-long visit to Veridia City.

I brushed a windswept strand of hair behind my ear, then paused.

The hair on my neck raised as my breath caught and my muscles tensed.

What felt like an invisible blanket fell over the room, momentarily sucking the air from my lungs—the telltale sign of a spell being cast. It brushed against my skin like a caress until it vanished.

Two hands grabbed my waist from behind.

"*Got you.*"

A strangled gasp left my lips as I jolted. "*Fates*, Aven, I'm going to *kill* you."

Aven's deep chuckle sounded in my ear. "Always so violent." He spun me around until I faced him, his deep brown skin glowing in the moonlight. Mischievous dark eyes twinkled down at me. "You can pray to the Fates all you want, but I'm the only one here."

I smacked him on the chest and untangled myself from his arms. "Was it you that opened my window?"

The smug look on his face answered my question. "And cast the silencing spell. Didn't want that little cousin of yours listening."

"I don't have time, Aven," I said, untying my apron and throwing it on top of my mother's Grimoire. "I have too much to do to get the shop ready for when we leave."

His hands found my shoulders and began kneading out the knots. "I don't see why you can't stay here while your family goes to the capital. Your aunt told you you didn't need to go. What am I supposed to do while you're gone?" he pouted.

Extracting myself from his touch, I scoffed. "What you do every time I'm busy. Find someone else."

"Don't be like this, Rose," he said exasperatedly, as if surprised I had the *nerve* to turn him away. "I'm going to miss you, that's all."

I pursed my lips at his wide eyes, his downturned mouth, the crease on his forehead. He was good.

I was better.

Stepping toward him, I raised my hand to cup his cheek, my nose grazing his. Our breaths mingled in the space between us. I felt his pulse quicken. "I know you will, Aven." My tongue came out to swipe along his lower lip, and he sucked in a breath. "Tell Amelia hello for me tonight, yes?"

I gave him a sweet smile and slipped away. Reaching into my pocket, I pinched a thistle leaf between my fingers then placed it on my tongue. "*Finiscere,*" I muttered, feeling the spell bubble and flow from my fingers, banishing Aven's silencing charm.

That's when I heard the shout.

My neck snapped up. *Beau.*

I crossed the room in three strides and threw the back door open, the amaranth stem from my pocket already halfway to my mouth before I stopped in my tracks.

Beth lay crumpled on the floor, her brown hair blossomed around her head like a cloud. Beau's entire body shook as he held a hand to his pale forehead.

"We were talking, and she—she just collapsed," he said, swallowing thickly. "It's the curse. It has to be."

I exchanged a look with Aven, whose face was grim. Walking to Beth's still form, I crouched down and gingerly lifted an eyelid, holding my breath against what I knew in my bones I would find.

Blood-red irises.

Heart sinking, I swallowed back panic, the truth plummeting like a weight in my chest.

"The Somnivae Curse," I whispered.

3

ROSE

It took Beau three days to get over the shock of watching Beth fall prey to the curse. He hadn't ever seen it happen up close before—perhaps from a distance, when we were at the market or a crowded area and someone was struck. But never right before his eyes. Never someone he knew.

I'd witnessed it four times now. Five, if I counted Beth. And I remembered each as vividly as if it happened yesterday.

Once when I was seven, a group of girls were playing a ways from me in the schoolyard, and one of their toys landed at my feet. When I picked it up and walked it over to the little girl, her limbs suddenly locked and she crashed to the ground, unable to be roused.

Again when I was ten—I was racing through the forest near our house and came upon our neighbor collecting various herbs for spells. He smiled and waved cordially, but before I could return the sentiment, he froze and collapsed. I remembered fleeing back to my uncle so he could retrieve the body.

Several years later, on my first date, the boy was escorting me home when he stumbled and fell face first into the snow. I had to scream for someone to come help carry his limp body to his family.

This was when the quiet whispers of the town turned to ferocious gossip. That made *three* times I'd been with someone when they were cursed. One or two they could overlook, but three was no longer a coincidence.

The fourth time was a year ago. An elderly gentleman and his wife had come to the Arcane looking for a pain remedy for his arthritis. I turned to grab a vial, and when I looked back, his wife was slumped over the counter, unresponsive.

That was the nail in my metaphorical coffin. Nobody wanted anything to do with the Arcane after that, if they could help it.

Each time someone fell to the curse, it was the same. They collapsed as if in a deep slumber, their blood-red eyes the only sign of the Somnivae Curse. Not dead. *Asleep.*

There was no warning. It could take any of us in an instant, in a single breath. There wasn't a day that went by when I didn't think I might be next. Or Beau, Morgana, Ragnar.

It started twenty-seven years ago, before I was born. This curse, this fear...it was all I'd ever known. I couldn't even imagine a time *before*, when the empire didn't have this heavy weight looming overhead.

According to those who had lived through it, the night the royal Aris twins had been born to the former Emperor Branock Aris and his wife, a curse had descended upon the entire land like a bright red plague. Some said it was because the royal family was cursed by the Fates, or the twins were an abomination, or Emperor Aris had sold his soul to amass his wealth and this was the punishment.

Our world was forever changed in that single night. Emperor Aris' empire crumbled and he was unable to face the growing insurrection, choosing instead to abdicate and hole himself and his family away, hoping his penance was enough to stop the curse from ravaging his people.

That had been over two decades ago. And still, the curse raged on.

In the beginning, it had started slowly, claiming a handful of victims across the provinces every few months. With time, however, it grew greedier. Hungrier. More and more cases popped up all over the empire. This past year alone, almost a hundred people from Feywood had fallen to it.

Not a soul had been able to figure out how to counteract it. Even here in Feywood, where curses and charms were in our Alchemist blood. The Somnivae curse didn't *kill*—it didn't seem to do any bodily harm, as far as we could tell. The victims simply fell into a deep sleep. Their bodies stayed preserved and healthy, even the ones who had been cursed decades ago. They didn't age, didn't need food or water or medicine. It was as if they were frozen in a moment in time.

Forever alive, forever asleep.

And now, it had claimed Beth. My closest friend—my *only* friend. Seeing her normal lively, excited features turn motionless and ashen had been like looking into the face of a complete stranger. I may only see her a handful of times a year, but she knew me better than anyone. I would never get to laugh with her again, to trade stories and gossip of our provinces, to hear her go on about her latest flame back in Celestria.

Another person taken from me.

More pain to hide beneath my layers.

Uncle Ragnar and I had argued over what to do with her—he insisted she would be better cared for at the local infirmary since we were about to be gone for an entire month, but I feared what the people of Feywood would do to her, an outsider in their midst. Plenty of locals wouldn't shop at the Arcane because of my reputation and because they knew we sourced many of our herbs from Celestria. How would they react to a Strider kept tucked away in the Feywood infirmary, vulnerable and unable to defend herself?

"There's nothing else that can be done, Rose," Uncle Ragnar had told me. "Until we can find a way to contact her family in Celestria, we're unable to cross the border. You have to let her go. She'll be safe with the healers—that's their job."

His words did little to quell my anxieties. But I'd done what he said and let her go, silently promising to visit her every day until we left.

And I did. I sat by her side for half an hour each afternoon, reading her bits and pieces of our favorite books and shouldering the gossip and bitter stares that followed my every move.

I was walking home from the infirmary a week after Beth had been cursed, the brisk wind nipping at my nose and cheeks as I pulled my cloak tighter over my hunter green dress, when I saw Uncle Ragnar's hulking frame coming toward me on the street. He was the spitting image of what I imagined Beau would look like in thirty years—the same light brown hair and silver eyes, with a clean-cut beard and wrinkles gracing his strong features.

He waved to passersby as he made his way to me, stopping every few feet to say hello to a familiar face or shake someone's hand as they undoubtedly offered their well wishes for his impending trip to the capital.

My uncle was a cornerstone of this province. He inspired respect and admiration among the citizens—it was why he'd been chosen as the Feywood challenger. One year before every Decemvirate, each province held an election for who would be the lucky pick. I'd heard stories of how the other provinces selected—in Drakorum, where they held the power of shifting, there were rumors that the nominees had to fight to the death in their animal forms. And in Tenebra, the province with the power to wield shadows, their competitors were forced to spend weeks in the isolated, cursed Shadowmere wastelands, where shadows and spirits of the dead roamed the twisted branches and howling mountains. Whoever emerged with their sanity still intact proceeded to the Decemvirate.

If all of that was true, it made me thankful my province wasn't full of masochists.

Here, the nominees had to attend a festival in central Feywood to present their talents. A series of tests, both in skill and knowledge, and a showcase among the governor of the province and his council.

It was a glorified *popularity* contest.

But popularity aside, Ragnar *was* powerful. And not someone I'd want to cross.

Eight years ago when divisions among provinces really started to get bad, a group of Illusionists from Iluze had broken across their border with us in the middle of the night. Their advances had quickly turned violent when they were caught by a couple of border guards.

I witnessed the attack firsthand. Our house wasn't too far from Lake Leznem, the sole border between Iluze and Feywood, and I'd been collecting herbs nearby for a new potion I wanted to try. I would never forget the way the border guards had been stopped dead in their tracks by the powerful Illusionist magic, frozen in fear by some invisible mirage conjured for them and them alone. All I could see from my hidden spot behind a thicket of trees was the guards falling to their knees before the Illusionists, their faces contorted in horror. Screams pierced the air and made me cover my ears to stem the onslaught of terror that coursed through my body.

I hadn't been able to move. I wanted to run for help, to do something to save those innocent men, but something about the Illusionists and their power had been so hauntingly familiar. They dredged up murky memories from the darkness of my past, leaving me useless and cowering in the grass and dirt.

Someone from the village had heard the attack and summoned Ragnar. I vividly remembered the image of my uncle charging to the lake side, his black cloak billowing behind him as his face lit with rage. A weight like a charging horse slammed into my chest, the very air sucked from the entire clearing, the taste of magic sweet and sticky on my tongue. I could taste it even now, eight years later.

In a heartbeat, all seven Illusionists laid sprawled on the ground, their arms and legs bent at horrific angles. The memory still spiked my pulse, the sound of their cracking bones just as sharp as it was almost a decade ago. Watching them writhe on the flattened grass with the shadow of my uncle looming over them, fury like ice across his hard features...

Perhaps this Decemvirate, Feywood stood a chance at winning.

When Ragnar met my stare a few yards down the street from where I strolled, he raised his eyebrows and tilted his head with an exasperated expression I knew far too well. I sighed. What had I done this time?

"Well, hello, Uncle," I said pleasantly, tucking a strand of hair behind my ear as I approached him.

He shot me a look that said he wasn't buying my act and turned on his heel to fall into step beside me. "I heard some interesting news from Madeline Bailey's father today."

"Oh?"

"Turns out, the poor girl has been sick all week. Headaches, can't eat, has a terrible rash. He said it began after she purchased a sleeping tonic from the Arcane." He glanced at me out of the corner of his eye. "Care to explain?"

"Sounds like she's come down with something," I said with a shrug.

"Rose."

I rolled my eyes. "Honestly, of all the things the two of us have done, this wouldn't even make the top five worst."

He grunted, and I pursed my lips to hide a smile. My uncle and I shared a similar sense of retribution, a fondness for bending rules and living in a gray area between proper and...well, poison, in my case.

"Be that as it may, I can't have you using mine and your aunt's business anytime someone crosses you—"

"Crosses *me*?" I scoffed. "You *do* remember what Madeline did to Beau, right?"

He furrowed his brow. "Well, I knew he was keen on the girl. He was upset when she got engaged to that Nathaniel fellow."

I sighed and gave my uncle a pat on the shoulder as we walked. Ragnar and Morgana loved their son, but more often than not, parents never truly saw into the lives of their teenage children.

"Beau and Madeline had been seeing each other for months. He found out she'd cheated on him with Nathaniel three nights before the two announced their engagement. Did Mr. Bailey happen to tell you *that* part of the story?"

Ragnar blinked at me, the wrinkles at the corners of his eyes deepening in thought. "No, he didn't. Nor did Beau. I—I had no idea." He rubbed at the scruff on his jaw. "Is that why he's been so...temperamental?"

"He's only a kid," I said softly. "He was embarrassed and heart-broken, and probably didn't want to run to his parents about his love life. He'll be okay. He's doing much better now, but right after it happened, he was a mess. When I saw Madeline in the shop last week, I just...well, you heard." I snuck a peek at Ragnar, wondering how upset he was going to be with me. He had a point—it wasn't my best move, using their shop as a means to get revenge.

Hindsight, and all.

His face was unreadable. We walked in silence for a minute as we turned the corner and the Arcane appeared up ahead.

"So, how much foxglove did you give her?" he finally asked.

"I never said it was foxglove."

"I know you, Rose. When you're being petty, you use foxglove."

I feigned offense, clutching my chest. Perhaps I was more predictable than I thought. "*Petty?* I was going for *vindictive.*"

He tapped his nose, eyes sparkling. "If you're vindictive, you go for the bones."

A grin broke across my face. The fact that we could now joke about that day in the clearing, the day he'd mutilated those Illu-sionists and broken almost every bone in their bodies, spoke volumes of our twisted humor. "Noted. And, for your information, I didn't give her *that* much—only a pinch in her tea leaves. It should be wearing off soon." As much as the words pained me to say, I added a quick, "I'm sorry, Uncle. I reacted rashly."

Reaching for the door to our apothecary, he said, "Nobody died. In my eyes, that's good enough. Just...don't tell your aunt."

"Oh, absolutely not," I said quickly, entering the shop and slipping my scarf and cloak onto a hook by the front door. "Are you sticking around, or do you need to get home?"

"Actually, I wanted to talk with you." The unease in his voice made my hand clench at my side as I crossed behind the counter. "About the Decemvirate," he added.

This couldn't be good.

He scratched his head. "I've spoken with Morgana about this, of course, but Beau...well, there are some things he might not be able to handle."

I hummed and rested my elbows on the counter. "He can handle more than you think."

"Perhaps this isn't a conversation *I* can handle, then." He rubbed a hand over his face. "You know how dangerous this tournament can be. We don't know what to expect, what trials the architects will design, who the other challengers will be. There's no way to ensure I'll be successful, or that I'll even make it out in one piece."

Fear rose inside of me, breaking through the layers I worked to squash it beneath. "You're going to be fine," I said curtly. "Nobody has died in a couple decades."

"Death isn't the only outcome. You've never met someone who's come back from the tournament, Rose. Not all of them are..." He trailed off, a shadow passing over his eyes before he blinked it away. "Anything is possible. I must be prepared for all probabilities. Which is why I wanted to talk to you about the Arcane."

My spine straightened. "What about it?"

He reached into his pocket and pulled out a sheet of parchment, folded into thirds. Holding it out to me, he said, "It's yours."

"What's mine?"

"The *shop*."

I froze. "*What*?" I asked with a strangled yelp.

That brought a small smile to his face. "We should have done this a long time ago. She's been yours for years—at least now, it can be official."

When I still didn't take the paper, he shook it in front of my face with an amused expression. I snapped my mouth shut and reached for it, unfolding the pages carefully, drinking in the words.

The deed to the Arcane Apothecary. In *my* name. *Rose Angelica Wolff.*

I drew my gaze back to my uncle's. "But...why?" I'd been saving to buy it from them one day—one day far, *far* from now, but still. I didn't understand why they'd decided to simply hand it over to me. Unless...

I shoved the deed into his hands. "If this is some sort of 'dying request,' you can take it back. You'll be *fine*," I repeated, colder than I intended.

While the rational part of my mind knew he was wise to make such preparations, another part, a *deeper* part, gnashed its teeth in protest. Ragnar may be my uncle, but he was like a second father to me, and the idea that even *he* had doubts about the upcoming tournament...

I didn't know what I would do if I lost him. Or Morgana, or Beau. The number of people I had left in my life were few.

I *needed* my uncle to be safe. I needed Aunt Morgana and Beau to be safe. If they weren't...if something happened to them that I couldn't prevent, it would feel like my fault all over again. The way it had been when my mother died.

And my father.

Panic blossomed, and I quickly shoved that thought away. Gritting my teeth, I said, "I don't want the shop out of pity or as a last resort."

"It's neither of those, Rose," he said exasperatedly. "Don't you think you deserve it, after everything you've done to keep this place running? Morgana and I have discussed it at length. We agreed it's time. This is what your parents would want—it was their dream to begin with. We merely followed along."

Guilt, yearning, and stubbornness struggled inside of me, a tangled web of emotions. What he said may be true, but I knew it was more than that. I knew he was preparing for the worst, should he die in the coming month. Perhaps this was his way of keeping control over the situation—as I was wont to do, as well.

And...*Fates*, I wanted the Arcane. More than I'd ever wanted anything.

I swallowed. "Fine." An awkward tension sliced through the room as I lowered my hand, the deed clutched in my fingers. "I—thank you, Uncle Ragnar. I'll make a payment plan, set aside part of the profit from each month to pay you—"

He shook his head and cut me off. "That's not necessary. We have more than enough."

"I *will* pay you back," I repeated, louder, sturdier. "I'll force the money into your hands if I have to. And I expect to be able to annoy you about it for a very, very long time, you got it?" The last part was weaker—a question and a plea, wrapped into one.

His gaze softened. Placing his hand on my shoulder and squeezing, he said, "That's the plan. This doesn't mean I'm not going to fight, understand? I fully intend to show Veridia City what we can do here. That they should never discount Feywood again."

A smile crept up my lips. If anyone could do it, it was Ragnar Gregor. "Going for the bones?"

He swiped playfully at my nose. "Going for the bones."

4

ROSE

"Have we packed the healing charms yet, Rose?" my Aunt Morgana asked as she took a pouch from my hand and settled it in Ragnar's travel bag.

I checked my notes. "Yes, I think we've got everything," I said, tying a bow on an extra bag of protection herbs. Ash from a blackthorn tree and shredded mistletoe leaves—paired with the right spell, created a force field around your body that warded off any unfriendly advances. A few years ago, I'd experimented with protection charms and discovered that adding a stem of amaranth to this concoction made it not only a defensive spell, but *offensive*, as well.

I'd used it once walking home from the forest at night and noticed a shadow following me. When I started to run and the strange man grabbed my arm, he bounced right off me as if he'd struck a barrier, and the sickening *crunch* from his wrist told me all I needed to know.

I had some fun with that spell over the years. Probably another reason I wasn't a favorite among the town.

Wiping my hands on my apron, I straightened. "That's the last of it. We need to load up the horses and we'll be ready for the morning."

The morning. It was strange to think the day was finally here. Tomorrow, we'd be leaving for Veridia City—which was only about two days' travel, but given that I'd never stepped foot outside of Feywood, it might as well be a different world.

"About that...are you *positive* you want to join us, dear?" Morgana asked, glancing at me uneasily.

This conversation was getting old. It was the fourth time she'd tried to convince me not to go. I opened my mouth to respond, but my cousin jumped in instead.

"Give it a rest, Ma. Rosie's already said she's coming. Why are you hounding her about it?"

I shot him a grateful smile. Morgana bristled but held her hands up in surrender, sharing a strange look with Ragnar.

I didn't understand why she was so adamant on changing my mind. She knew how eager I was to see more of the empire, despite the growing danger. I'd glimpsed Celestria through the Feywood Forest and could see the outskirts of Iluze to the north over Lake Leznem, but had never been allowed to cross. All I'd learned about the other provinces and the capital were from books and stories.

I was most familiar with Celestria through my friendship with Beth. We traded with them often, and I'd met several other Striders, as well. Although we shared a water border with Iluze, I had learned to stay away from the cunning Illusionists at a young age. Their magic had always reignited a fear rooted deep within me. Anyone with power such as that over the mind couldn't be trusted. The Illusionist challenger won the Decemvirate more often than any other province, so their magic was always much more potent than ours. I never wanted to face someone with that ability.

To the east of Iluze rested the province of Emberfell, the furthest from Feywood. It was home to the Lightbenders—people who could create light with a simple touch, bend it to their will and even form it into solid matter.

Emberfell shared a border to the south with Drakorum, the land of the Shifters. Being the loudest and most volatile magic wielders, I'd heard plenty of rumors about their people. Everyone born to a Shifter line could transform into some sort of animal—whether it was a partial or complete transformation depended on the strength of their bloodline. If I was being honest, I hoped I'd get a glimpse of a Shifter or two in the capital. The idea of being able to turn into something else, become an entirely new being, all within your control...it fascinated me.

The final province wasn't too far from us, separated on the east by a small strait of water. Tenebra was the most elusive of the lot, incredibly mysterious and unpredictable. They possessed a form of magic called Shadow Wielding: the power to turn incorporeal darkness into weapons of the night. To control shadows. Their land was brutal and harsh, with the iciest and most mountainous of landscapes, and I heard the people were just as cold. Ruthless and aggressive, most of the deaths in the history of the Decemvirate had come at a Shadow Wielder's hand.

The six provinces of the Veridian Empire formed a circle around the capital. Veridia City was an island surrounded by the Eldertide Ocean, which we would have to cross to reach the nearest port. I could tell Beau was nervous about that part of our voyage, even if he tried to shrug off my concern, so I made sure to tuck a few potions for nausea into his bags.

"Beau Beau," Morgana started, gesturing to my cousin. "Will you pass me the—umm, the purple crystal." She snapped her fingers, trying to remember the name. "Yes—that one," she said when Beau pointed to the crystal on the countertop.

"It's amethyst, Ma," Beau said with a laugh, tossing her the small, sharp rock. I was happy to see his mood had lightened considerably over the last few days, back to his endearingly scatter-brained and affable self. "If you don't know what it's called, maybe you shouldn't be using it," he joked.

"Do you hear that tone, Ragnar?" Morgana faked a gasp, red nails on her wide hips as she shook her head in mock disappointment.

"Yes, dear, and I have *no* idea where he gets it from," Ragnar responded, jumping from the counter and placing a kiss on his wife's cheek. He pulled a thistle leaf from his pocket—one of the few charms any wise Alchemist always kept on their person, since it could break almost all enchantments—and waved it in her face. "And this is a *leaf*, Ana, my love. In case you weren't sure."

I snorted, and Aunt Morgana lunged at him. "Ragnar Gregor, you better pray to the Fates I don't curse you in your sleep," she said as she chased him around the front of the store. He turned and grabbed her by the waist, slinging her over his shoulder as she squealed. Beau shook his head but chuckled along with his parents, his bright gray eyes crinkling in amusement.

I quickly turned to the glass cabinet behind the counter, hiding my sudden shortness of breath. It would hit me sometimes when I least expected it—the longing, the heartache.

I wanted to share in their joy. I wanted that sparkle in my eyes. I wanted the smile of a mother and the embrace of a father.

The Gregors loved me immensely—and I loved them, of course. They were the closest thing I had to parents. They took me in as their own daughter when their world fell apart with the death of my mother and father, long before Beau was born. But no matter how deep their love for me went, I knew I would always be a reminder of the family they'd lost, of the life they were forced into. Of the blood that stained their past.

I was a piece that would never fully fit in their puzzle. In *anyone's* puzzle. People wanted neat, clean edges to mold into their idea of normalcy. Predictable. Ordinary.

I was jagged cuts and sharp fringes. Nobody wanted to hold me for too long. And I was perfectly content with that.

But moments like this...sometimes, I wished for the soft spirit of my aunt, for the power of my uncle, for the innocence of my cousin. For tenderness and sweetness, instead of the bitter shadows that clung to me.

"Come on, Rose—let's go get dinner. We've done all we can for tonight," my aunt's voice, still tinged with laughter, sounded from the front of the shop. I turned to find her and Ragnar hand-in-hand, Ragnar's free arm draped across his son's thin shoulders.

I swallowed the lump in my throat. "Alright." I walked to the far window, where the shop's cat Spindley often perched, and gave her ears a good scratch. To my surprise, she leapt from my reach and strode across the floor to my aunt and uncle, her long tail swishing. She wound her lithe body between my uncle's legs, brushing against him with a loud purr.

Ragnar laughed and ran his fingers through her fur. "Think she'll miss me?"

My eyes snapped from the cat to his face. I forced a smile, but a sense of foreboding crept down my spine like icy fingers. Spindley never let anyone besides myself touch her.

I shook off the unease. It was ridiculous. Cats were fickle creatures—I was foolish for reading too much into her behavior.

But it felt like, for a moment, she was saying goodbye.

———

THE NEXT MORNING arrived with gray skies and biting winds. We hitched our two horses to the small carriage and loaded it with our baggage and supplies for the next month. The entire town had awoken with the dawn to gather in the main square to see us off, showering Ragnar with both words of encouragement and slander against the competing provinces.

"Finally, Feywood stands a chance at winning."

"This is an old family recipe for increased eyesight and hearing —works every time, I swear!"

"We're counting on you, Gregor."

"Don't forget—those Illusionists pricks can't trick you if they can't see you. If you get in a bind, go for the eyes, yeah?"

Interesting. I didn't know that last part.

Ragnar accepted their words and gifts with a grand smile— ever the portrait of power and humility. I stayed hidden in the carriage, tired of the pointed stares and whispered remarks directed toward me.

"She's not even his daughter."

"Nothing but a bane on that entire family. She'll ruin his chances, mark my words."

"Did you hear *two* people have now fallen under the curse at her shop within the last year? Wonder if there's something to it."

"She's been visiting that cursed Strider for the last two weeks. If she loves their kind so much, why doesn't she join them?"

It made me roll my eyes. Honestly, did these people have nothing better to talk about?

Still, their words pricked something in me. Stinging and sharp, like a needle under my skin.

Half an hour later, Ragnar bid the town farewell and led the horses to the main road leading northeast, where we'd travel for the day and stop in an inn on the coast. Tomorrow morning, we'd board a passenger ship to Veridia City, hopefully arriving on the main island before nightfall.

The bustle of the town square slowly faded as the sun rose higher, the cadence of wheels over rough gravel lulling me into a trance as I stared out the window of the carriage. Brick buildings and cobblestone paths gave way to pine trees and dark green shrubbery, the occasional fox or hare slinking into the shadows.

"Hey," Beau whispered from my right. Across from us sat Morgana and Ragnar, snippets of their conversation drifting to my ears as they pored over notes. "Don't listen to them. All that stuff they say...it's ridiculous. You're our family, Rosie."

I cast him a glance and a tight smile. "Thanks, Beau Beau."

He nudged my shoulder with his bony elbow. "I mean it," he insisted. "They're just jealous you're so talented."

I snorted and nudged him back. I never knew how to respond when he or my aunt tried to ease the negativity swarming me. They were my own personal rays of sunshine, whether I liked it or not.

A moment passed, then my aunt spoke from opposite us. "Are you two excited to see Veridia City? The new food, the colors, the people...there will be so many wonderful things to try."

I contemplated her question as I fiddled with the pouch of

herbs in my lap. On any normal day, I typically only carried thistle and amaranth in my pockets for protection, but I had a special container for when I wanted an abundance of charms on my person. Alchemists accessed our magic through items found in nature—herbs, seeds, stones, and the like—so I needed a way to carry many kinds all at once. This pouch had been my father's. A leather-worn, hexagonal shaped container about the size of my hand that opened on opposite ends to reveal five small compartments each, giving me space for ten charms. Feeling the leather between my fingers always seemed to settle my mind.

"I suppose," I finally answered. "Although probably not for the same reasons."

"Right, I forgot how you don't like anything *fun*," Beau quipped.

"No, not fun. Just people."

Ragnar snorted at our exchange. "Then what *are* you excited for, Rose?"

The ironic part was that I *was* most excited to see the different people. Not that I necessarily needed to interact with all of them... but how many opportunities would I have in my lifetime to be in the same place as citizens from all six provinces? To observe their magic and learn how it works, maybe even take a few tricks back home to Feywood.

"The magic," I said truthfully. "Alchemy's in my blood, but I've always wanted to see what else is out there."

"Well now, am I going to end up fending off some Shifter or Lightbender suitor who persuades you to move across the empire?" my uncle teased.

Beau barked out a laugh. "As if. I don't think anything could drag Rosie away from the Arcane."

I turned back to the window with a shallow smile as their lighthearted laughs and conversation about Veridia City became background noise to my thoughts.

He was right. I loved the Arcane, loved the connection to my parents and the sense of purpose in my bones. So why did his comment nag at me?

Perhaps that was all I was good for—experiments and concoctions, minding my own business and living a quiet life in my personal solace. Protecting what was mine at all costs. Ignoring the ignorant words of the town. Continuing the legacy my parents had left me.

There was nothing wrong with that.

That's what I told myself as I peered through the window, watching the only home I'd ever known become a speck in the distance as rays of sunlight tried to dispel the growing shadows.

5

ROSE

The rest of the journey through Feywood passed uneventfully. By the next morning, we'd paid to keep our carriage and horses at the port and boarded a ship to sail the short distance across the Eldertide Ocean.

It took all day to reach the port at Veridia City. Aunt Morgana and I leaned against the railing on the quarterdeck as the sun set behind us, highlighting the oncoming island in rays of orange, gold, and deep pink. The wind blew our hair back, the matching strands of black dancing and weaving in the air—the only trait I shared with her, seeing as my mother had the same dark locks. But while Morgana was pale and fair, I'd inherited my olive-toned skin from my father, along with a strong jawline and high cheekbones.

My aunt tapped her fingers on the wood, her eyes distant as she took in the land looming before us.

"How are you doing with all of this?" I asked.

She seemed surprised I had spoken. Clearing her throat, she dropped her hands with haste. "Oh, I'm fine. I trust Ragnar, and I trust the Fates. He's more than capable of keeping himself safe with their help."

The Fates. The mystical, omniscient *Fates* who had our futures wound around their fingers, playing them like strings on an instru-

44

ment. I'd never been much for the legends of the three beings who weaved the destiny of this world, choosing to place my trust in my *own* hands. The Fates were mostly myths at this point anyway, their existence a mere household expression instead of worshiped and revered as they once were.

But my aunt wished to keep them sacred. For her, clinging to the higher power of the Fates provided a refuge when her world ran out of control. I would never deny her the comfort they brought, even if I was more skeptical.

Who knew? Maybe they *were* listening.

"You know, you're allowed to tell me the truth every once in a while," I said, raising my eyebrow in jest. "I'm not a child anymore. You can tell me if you're worried."

Chuckling, she patted my hand. "I do sometimes forget how much you've grown. You're the age I was when we adopted you." She faced me fully, her hand coming up to cup my cheek. "You look so much like her," she whispered.

I didn't have to ask who she was referring to.

The emotion in her words overwhelmed me, and I looked away, back to the glistening navy blue waters lapping against the side of the boat. "What do you think she would've thought of this?" I waved my hand through the air. "Visiting the capital?"

"My, your mother would have eaten this up. I can't tell you the number of times she tried to cross through to Celestria or Iluze when we were kids. Granted, that was back when it wasn't against the law. She loved to make a ship out of blankets and pillows and pretend we were sailing off on adventures." Morgana laughed and shook her head. "And, oh, that girl could *talk*."

A smile tugged at my lips. I'd asked about my parents hundreds of times over the years, eager for any morsel of truth, any taste of their lives. I never got tired of hearing about them.

"She lit up any room when she walked in," my aunt continued. "Yes, I think she would've enjoyed this trip very much. If she were here, she'd make fast friends with every person we came across. Now, your father, on the other hand..."

My shoulders tightened, then slowly loosened. I remembered bits and pieces of my father—his quiet laugh, his dark blue-gray eyes peering at me over thin spectacles as he read by the fire, his strong hands lifting me in the air. But every time I imagined him, something snagged at the recesses of my mind, something that sent ice snaking down my spine. It was like a veil hanging in front of a portrait, and if I could reach out and pull it away, I'd see—

I swallowed as I quickly buried the ominous feeling deeper into that well inside me before my mind could tread any further. Morgana gave me a look, testing my features, and I nodded for her to keep going.

"He quite literally would have *begged* to stay home. I think that man could've lived in a cave and been happy. As long as he had his Ayla, of course. By the Fates, he loved your mother." Morgana tucked an arm around my waist, and I stiffened at the contact before relaxing into her.

"I'm sorry you never got to know them well, dear. Especially your mother. But she loved you from the moment she found out she was carrying you. So, so much. 'My little flower,' she'd call you." Her hold on me tightened, her voice cracking. "Oh, I'm sorry," she suddenly said, wiping at her eyes and pulling away. "I suppose this whole ordeal is setting me on edge."

"It's fine. I—I like it when you talk about them." I rubbed at the side of my neck, holding onto the brief image she'd given me. "It's going to be alright. With Uncle Ragnar, I mean. He's been preparing for months, and we've stocked him up on all the charms he could possibly need."

"I know, dear. You're right. We've done all we can do—it's in the hands of the Fates now." Morgana gave me a smile before trodding off to check on Ragnar and Beau.

I cast my gaze back to the water, the bright spot of land even closer than before. I could see trees dotting the edges of the coast, the unfamiliar buildings and docked ships of the port taking shape.

It's in the hands of the Fates now. My aunt, the devout one. The one to find safety behind platitudes, to smile and shrug when things didn't go her way. But I think my uncle and I both understood—we couldn't stand aside and wait for something else to intervene. We made our *own* fate.

And that made it all the more sweet when it bent to our will.

———

MY FIRST IMPRESSION of Veridia City was how *bright* it was.

Even though the sun was almost completely set, the docks were still busy welcoming guests into the capital. Lanterns hung every few feet, blinding me as I stepped off the gangway. Workers scampered about the deck to help secure incoming passenger and cargo ships, carrying crates of supplies to and from the storage units off the port. It smelled like fish and oranges, and the cool breeze coming from the water was so very different from the brisk, dry air in the forests of Feywood.

Our family was quickly ushered from the ship and to a small wooden outpost beyond the dock. The workers were orderly and efficient, having more than likely welcomed *thousands* of spectators coming for the Decemvirate. I barely had time to take in the multitudes of people before they'd found our assigned carriage and sent us on our way.

The driver greeted us kindly but swiftly, assisting Ragnar in loading our belongings.

"My name is Larson, and I will be your driver throughout your stay in Veridia City." Larson gave a bow, extending his head low enough for me to see the balding spot in the center of his gray hair. "I am at your service to take you and your family anywhere you desire, except during your trials, of course, sir," he added as he opened the door to the carriage. "It will be about an hour to the palace in the central sector, Master Gregor. With the influx in visitors, the main roads are busy, so we will be taking an alternate path."

"Central sector?" Beau asked. "What does that mean?"

Larson dipped his head to Beau before responding. "The capital is divided into five sectors: north, west, east, south, and central. You will more than likely be spending most of your time in the central sector, where the palace and busiest markets are."

"Sounds wonderful, Larson. Thank you," Ragnar said, shaking the elderly man's hand before helping Morgana and myself into the carriage.

"It's my pleasure, sir." Larson gave another bow and shut the door with a *snip*. A moment later, the carriage rustled as he situated himself in the box. I heard the sharp snap of reins and we were off, heading east through the bustling port.

As I'd done the previous day leaving Feywood, I now found myself gazing out the glass window, transfixed by the foreign, outside world. We passed through a village with the brightest colored buildings I'd ever seen—white and pink, orange and yellow, blue and purple. The rainbow of stucco shops and houses assaulted my senses, so different from the dark wood and brick structures in Feywood. Citizens still roamed the streets, finishing up their shopping or mingling as the last of the sunrays finally set beyond the horizon. Even their clothing was different from ours, with their cropped linen tops and flowing pants or skirts, showing far more skin than our colder province would ever allow. My thick sweater and leggings were already sticking to my skin with sweat despite the slight breeze of the autumn evening.

Slowly, the bright cobblestone path turned to rocky gravel road as we left the portside town behind and ventured deeper into the woods. These trees weren't the same tightly packed pines I was used to, with sharp needles and bristly branches. The leaves here were broader, their branches wider and higher, like a vast canopy opening up above our heads. I could hardly see the shrubbery surrounding us. The soft glow of the lanterns attached to the side of the carriage was the only light illuminating the ground.

Shadows crept along the path like snakes, crawling their way from the dense greenery. The sound of crickets and owls created a symphony through the brush of leaves. For a brief moment, I thought I saw a flash of a long, dark tail slithering through the grass, but when I trained my eyes on the spot, it had vanished.

I leaned my head against the leather interior and closed my eyes, longing for a warm bath and a bed.

Suddenly, the carriage lurched to a stop. I threw my hand out to stop my body from careening into my aunt.

Ragnar cursed under his breath, rapping his knuckles against the small sliding door between us and the driver's box. "Larson?"

A thud sounded on the other side.

Ragnar stiffened, and he and I both instantly reached for our respective pouches of herbs. In a breath, I had an amaranth stem mixed with mistletoe and blackthorn ash on my tongue, the sweet, nutty flavor bursting through my mouth, preparing to cast a spell.

"Stay here," my uncle commanded the three of us. Beau tried to protest, but the look on Ragnar's face silenced him. Soundlessly, Ragnar eased open the carriage door, and the curiosity and adrenaline pumping through my veins made me instinctively rise from my seat and follow on his heels, ignoring Morgana's pull on my cloak.

My heart pounded faster at the loud shout and the sound of boots scuffling along rocks. I turned to find Morgana clutching her son's arm, looks of alarm blaring across their faces. Before they could move, I took a pinch of blackthorn ash and blew it toward them, watching it coat their bodies with a gray shimmer.

"*Slentium.*" I felt the spell for silence stretch and snap into place, momentarily stealing my breath. "I'll be back," I whispered before they could argue, then slipped out the door.

Creeping around the side of the carriage, I saw our two horses pawing the ground anxiously. Rough voices mixed with my uncle's, making me pause to assess instead of jumping into view.

"Nice night for a ride, isn't it?" a low, gravelly male voice said.

"We don't want any trouble," Ragnar responded. Keeping my body hidden by the carriage, I peered around the corner to find my uncle standing off against three men in black cloaks. A glint of silver in the hand of the middle man caught my eye. A knife.

Not a friendly visit, then.

The amaranth still lingering on my tongue burned in anticipation, my fingers fluttering at my side.

"Fancy carriage like this, with a personal driver and everything. Who do we have here, Sawyer?" The man in the middle whistled and nudged the one to his right. "Think we found ourselves a challenger?"

Swallowing, I quietly reached up to the door of the box and cracked it open. "Larson?" I whispered.

Something heavy fell against the door, and it took all my restraint to hold in a scream.

Larson's head leaned into the wood, four brutal claw marks weeping blood down the front of his face. One had cut through his nose, flaying it in half, his cheeks a mangled mess of flesh and fat.

I shut the door and pressed my back into the side of the carriage, forcing down bile and letting out a shaky breath. It looked like an animal had ripped through his head. *Shifters*. These men must be Shifters, either from Drakorum or the capital—nobody else could leave marks like that.

My eyes caught on something at the edge of the trees—a tail. Similar to the one I'd seen crawling on the ground before. Was it a Shifter? Someone working with these men?

"Gentlemen," my uncle stated evenly, drawing my attention back to the scene. "Challengers are protected under Veridian law until midnight on the start of the Decemvirate, which is not for another twenty-seven hours. Should word get back to the architects of your interference, you could be held in contempt of—"

"*Of course*, we had to go and pick a talker," the one to the right said with a scratchy scoff. "Enough of this."

My jaw dropped as the man threw his cloak and lunged, transforming mid-air into a roaring snow leopard.

One hundred pounds of dense muscle, sharp claws, and white fur soared for my uncle, its knifelike teeth bared at his throat. I sucked in a breath and lurched out from the side of the carriage, an incantation on my lips, when suddenly—my uncle disappeared.

"I tried to handle this with diplomacy, yet here we are." Ragnar tutted from the treeline behind the remaining two men, rolling up the sleeves of his button down shirt.

"He's a filthy Strider," one of the men spat.

"Not a Strider, no." My uncle's lips curled upward. "An Alchemist."

In the blink of an eye, he flicked his wrist and a dark purple shimmer fell over their bodies. Ragnar's lips moved soundlessly. The two men howled in agony, collapsing to the ground as everywhere the wolfsbane powder touched burned their flesh to ash. One of them shifted, his hunched body elongating and thinning until yellow and black scales of a serpent shone under the moonlight. Dark spots dotted its skin from the burns as it hissed and raised its head, coiling to strike.

"I don't want to kill you, Shifter," Ragnar warned, pressing a finger to his tongue.

The snake struck.

"*Incendar.*"

Before it could sink its fangs into my uncle, the tail of the serpent caught fire, blazing a trail up its long body, consuming it inch by inch until it was nothing but ash and burnt scales falling to the forest floor.

My eyes were glued on the remaining man, and I almost didn't hear Ragnar's cry.

"Rose!"

A growl erupted behind me. I whirled to find myself face-to-face with the snow leopard, mouth ajar and teeth glinting.

I bit down on the amaranth still clinging to my tongue and threw up my hands, muttering, "*Aegesis nova!*"

The sensation of air being ripped from my lungs and pulled taut as a bowstring fell across my skin as the snow leopard leapt toward me. He instantly slammed into an invisible barrier, and I watched in both horror and morbid fascination as my spell took its effect.

Chunks of flesh tore themselves from his shoulder, as if caught in the snare of his own sharp jaws. He yowled and collapsed to the ground, blood oozing from the wound as he struggled to find his footing.

I panted from the exertion of such a strong spell. Turning back to my uncle, I searched for the third man, only to find the coward had disappeared—sprinting off into the darkness, not even sparing a look for his *companion*. Blood rushed in my ears as I scanned the darkness for Ragnar.

And then I saw him.

My stomach plunged to my feet.

"*Uncle*," I breathed, the energy in my body dissipating as I rushed to his side. He lay crumpled on the leaves and dirt, motionless but still breathing. My eyes roved his body for signs of injury— had the last man attacked when I was distracted?

But I could find no wound. His breaths were strong and even, his pulse thumping beneath my touch.

No. No, no, no, no, no.

A rustling in the grass made me whip my neck around, but all spells fled my mind as the injured snow leopard stalked toward me and my unconscious uncle. Before I could think, the air around me tightened. My lungs constricted—burning, aching, tugging. *A spell.*

But who was casting it?

The beast reared up on its strong back legs, preparing to lash at me, when suddenly, it let out a strangled cry. I heard the snap of its neck and it fell to my side, dirt scattering beneath its weight.

It was dead.

And in its place stood brown boots. Tight, black pants. A dark tunic and gray cloak. My eyes traveled the length of the stranger's body to meet a sharp jawline shadowed by the hood of a cloak, glittering onyx eyes the only thing visible in the darkness as he stared down at me.

"Watch your back," was all he said, his deep voice sending a shiver down my spine.

Warning bells rang in my head, but I didn't care. My uncle was—

I turned to Ragnar's still form. "Can you help me?" I asked the stranger, looking back with a plea on my lips.

He was gone.

My hand covered my mouth as I gently lifted my uncle's eyelids, already knowing what I would find.

Eyes as red as blood

My uncle was cursed.

6

LEO

The tournament had yet to start, and too many bodies were already piling up. Too many emboldened Veridians taking it upon themselves to solve the problems of this empire.

I should know. I was one of them.

I had no qualms with maiming or even killing rash Shifters and competitive highwaymen when they threatened innocent travelers. I just preferred to not have an audience while doing so.

As I hastily stepped into the stirrup and threw my leg over my black stallion, Nightshade, I reminded myself that the woman hadn't seen my face. Even if she had, she was a foreigner—an Alchemist, surely, by her display of power. But she wasn't from here; she wouldn't know who I was. *What* I was.

That man she was with...he had fallen prey to the Somnivae curse, surely. I would know the signs in my sleep. Guilt burrowed its way beneath my skin, making a home in the crevices of my mind, as it always did.

I grabbed the reins and squeezed Nightshade's sides. He took off through the night, the breeze knocking the hood of my cloak to my shoulders as we barreled down the familiar, darkened path. With so many hours left until sunrise, I couldn't stop yet. It was the eve before the tournament. There was plenty of bloodshed to be found in these woods.

Attacks always ran rampant this close to the Decemvirate. I remembered them from the last time, when I was seventeen. Thieves and robbers stranding carriages in the middle of roads, looting travelers from the surrounding provinces. Angry capital natives who despised outsiders—"provincers," as some called them—and used their intrusion as an excuse to send a message. People hoping to impede opposing challengers to give their province an edge in the competition. The motives for violence were endless.

Needless to say, tension was high, and morals were thrown out the window when magic came into play.

Clucking my tongue, I urged Nightshade faster. I'd already been seen once tonight, and I didn't need to get caught by the roaming Royal Guards this close to the palace.

The sound of hooves beating against rock reached my ears. I quickly turned Nightshade to the right and into the shadows of a copse of trees, holding my breath and clenching my hand around the hidden pocket of herbs lining my cloak.

The rider came into view, and the sight of the familiar sleek, brown mare and gray mane loosened the weight on my chest.

"Leo, it's me," Chaz hissed. "Get out here. I've got news from Rissa."

I tapped Nightshade with my heel and we sauntered out into the dark clearing. Chaz's gaze met mine as I pulled my hood back over my head. He scratched at the black beard on his chin, the wrinkles on his umber forehead deepening.

"Fun night?" he asked, his deep voice rumbling with humor. I gave him a blank stare, and when his eyes flicked down to my boots, mine followed. Bits of flesh and drying blood graced the tip of the brown leather, white fur sticking to the outside. I must have stepped too close to where the woman had incapacitated the snow leopard Shifter.

I *still* didn't know how she'd done that. I'd never seen a spell like it, and I wasn't easily surprised.

Scrubbing a hand over my face, I ignored Chaz's pointed question. "What's the news?"

"There's a band of highwaymen monitoring Westhaven, north of the river. They've already attacked two passenger carriages since this morning."

My jaw ticked. "Drakorum?"

Chaz lifted an eyebrow. "No, it's locals. Why? Have you had a problem with Shifters?"

"Not anymore." I looked down at my boot again. Everyone was out tonight, it seemed. Natives and foreigners alike, all targeting guests for the Decemvirate, whether they be challengers or not. If I had to guess, the attacks over in Westhaven were simply a way to anger Emperor Gayl. Their message was clear: stop letting everyone cross our borders.

It was a vicious cycle with no end. The provinces needed the Decemvirate to replenish their magic, and the emperor desired it for the economic boost it brought him and Veridia City, but many who lived here resented the influx of people it brought. They didn't want to compete for resources or dilute the power of the land. So the capital natives took to solving the problem the only way they knew how: attacking visiting entourages with fury. No matter their background, no matter their purpose for visiting. If they were intruders, if they were *unwelcome*, they had to be dealt with.

I may not be able to do much good here, but I could stop this. I could fight under the shadow of night. I could try to guard the peace of my home, however unstable it may be.

"Do you want me to handle it?" Chaz asked. "I can easily stride over there if needed. You look like you've had enough for one night." He wasn't wrong—being a Strider with ancestors from Celestria, Chaz *could* deal with the situation faster than me.

But I was restless. And so, it seemed, were the capital citizens.

"I'm fine," I responded curtly. "Tell Rissa I've got it." Tightening my hold on the reins, I swung Nightshade's head to the west, in the direction of the river.

"She's not particularly happy with you right now," Chaz called to my retreating backside.

The corner of my lip twitched. "Tell me something I don't know."

Nightshade and I tore through the night, racing along dirt paths and weaving in between unruly branches. The moon was bright tonight. Bright enough to light the way and leave shadows in our wake, and to make the Alchemist half of my blood writhe with anticipation.

Within twenty minutes, I could hear the rushing waters of the Scarre River, just south of Westhaven, where Chaz had reported the recent attacks. It was a common passing point for travelers coming in from the western provinces of Feywood, Iluze, and Celestria. By this time of night, I would think there would be no more passenger carriages until morning, but with the Decemvirate beginning in a mere twenty-four hours, stragglers were likely. People hoping to catch the festivals at the start of the legendary tournament before touring the capital and then heading back to their respective provinces.

Visitors came and went throughout the month of the Decemvirate. A rare few stayed for the entirety of the event. That was by design—a constant stream of new faces, new magic, and new coin, ready to empty their pockets on the goods of the capital.

I strained to hear hooves on gravel and wheels crunching leaves, but all that came to me was the soft hooting of a nearby owl and wind rustling through branches.

I needed more.

Letting out a sigh, I closed my eyes and concentrated on the other half of my magic, the half my mother possessed.

Slowly, my senses came awake. The once calm breeze now bit into my skin, and the scent of damp moss, sweet wood, even lingering meat and baked goods from the nearest town miles away flooded me. Opening my eyes, I took in the scene with bright clarity: the canopy of trees glowed in a golden haze, the darkened path now alight and focused. I could see each individual twig, each rock, each shadow of a branch.

And there—murmurings muffled by leather and closed doors. Wheels churning on a distant road. The snap of reins and snort of a horse.

"Let's go, boy," I whispered to Nightshade, nudging him with my knee and steering him toward the oncoming carriage.

Sure enough, less than half a mile from the unsuspecting passengers, I spotted a group of four figures lying in wait near a fork in the road.

Here in Veridia City, you could never be sure what magic one might possess. We were a conglomerate of magical blood; a rare few held mixed heritages like myself, while most inherited a single type from their parents. Since people from all across the empire had settled here over the centuries, we weren't bound by a sole brand of magic like the six outlying provinces.

But there was almost always a tell. If one knew what to look for, they could find it.

These four were no different. I swiftly took in the sight: two of them were crouched low to the ground, leaning forward on the balls of their feet, like predators waiting to strike. *Shifters.*

One was playing with the fringes of his cloak, his fingers twitching at every sound. Alchemist, probably. Preparing to retrieve his stash of charms.

The final one lurked in the shadows of a tree, head tucked low. The darkness seemed to breathe with them, moving and swaying as if it had a mind of its own. *Shadow Wielder.*

Reaching into the inner lining of my cloak, I placed a pinch of blackthorn ash on my tongue. "*Slentium,*" I muttered, feeling the silencing charm take form around me. Nightshade weaved through the trees until we were at their backs, and I dismounted smoothly, pulling my hood low over my face as I stalked toward them.

"A bit late for a stroll, boys," I said, letting the wind carry my words.

The four of them spun. The hood of the Shadow Wielder fell and revealed a tall woman with striking silver hair. Shadows collected at her feet as she sneered.

My eyebrow raised. "I stand corrected. My apologies."

Before they could attack, I slammed my hands together, vibrations shooting up my arm from the rings I wore on my middle fingers. The charm held in the special henbane and amaranth infused rings thickened the air, and I embraced the familiar tightening in my chest as the incantation flowed from my tongue and burst from my hands.

In an instant, all four were on their knees, clutching at their throats as the oxygen left their lungs.

With a gasping breath, the Alchemist reached for his pocket.

"No, you don't," I growled, my body reacting instinctively. A long, dark brown tail wrapped around his wrist, yanking it to the ground with a *snap*. He recoiled and gave a half scream, half choke as my tail retracted and slunk back into the darkness behind me.

"You're—one of them—" one of the Shifters said through pained breaths.

"So you've heard of me." I flashed a smile from beneath my hood. "Good."

7

ROSE

"The head architect will see you now," a middle-aged woman with hair pulled into a bun said as she peeked her head out the opening of the grand wooden door.

I kneaded my forehead with my knuckles then pinched my cheeks, hoping to prick some life into my deadened features.

I was exhausted. It took longer and longer for me to come back from using so much magic, and I still hadn't fully processed what had happened with the Shifter attack. I couldn't believe my uncle was another victim of the Somnivae curse. It didn't feel real.

After I found him, I vaguely remembered telling Morgana to come out of the carriage. My voice had been low and monotone, void of the emotions I'd managed to stifle and shove away in those precious seconds after the mysterious man had left. When my aunt saw Ragnar, she screamed for Beau, whose face went pale and gaunt. While they froze in their distress, I couldn't seem to stop moving. Acting. Going through the motions like a puppet on a string, handling things in the only way I knew how.

Emotionless. Controlled. Hollow.

I wouldn't have been able to function otherwise.

I used a levitation spell to lift Ragnar's body into the carriage, ignoring Morgana's sobs, then climbed into the driver's box with that mutilated corpse at my side and followed the path until we hit a brick road. The gilded spires of the palace had come into view as we approached the entrance gates, but I was far too distant to take in the sight. I demanded the guards summon a stablehand to take the horse and carriage, a healer to take the dead body and my uncle, and a servant to take me to the Decemvirate's head architect: Larken Everest. The one in charge of designing and implementing the tournament.

Action. Purpose. Movement.

Morgana wouldn't leave Ragnar's side, and Beau wouldn't leave his mother's. The two of them were so distraught, they didn't even notice when I failed to follow them to the healer's wing of the palace. As much as I didn't want to be separated, neither of them were in the headspace to deal with the aftermath. Someone had to figure out what to do next.

I'd been waiting to speak with the head architect for hours. And with the waiting came the despair I'd forced aside, the panic I'd strangled in the face of necessity. It was all creeping back in, like spiders crawling beneath my skin.

This was going wrong. So horribly wrong. Nobody had woken from the Somnivae curse in *twenty-seven years*—the empire had all but lost hope the victims would ever be revived.

My uncle...he was as good as gone.

My mind swirled with endless, unanswerable questions. How would Morgana and Beau get through this? What would happen now that Feywood's sole challenger could no longer compete? How could we go back home with the weight of our province's magic on the shoulders of a lifeless heap of flesh?

Flowing beneath each worry was a single thought, like an undercurrent of darkness that seemed to follow me with every step I took.

Once again, someone had been taken from me. And once again, I hadn't been able to stop it.

"Dear? Are you ready?" the woman asked again, breaking me from my spiral. I cleared my throat and nodded, rising from the wingback chair I'd been sitting in overnight and following her inside the chamber.

With everything going on, I hadn't been able to fully appreciate the splendor of the palace. The dark mahogany floor, rich emerald rugs, and sparkling candelabras in the open room before me felt muted by a blanket of gray. I just needed to get through this. Tell Larken Everest what had happened and figure out how we could get another challenger from Feywood to the capital as quickly as possible.

In the center wall of the large chamber stood a desk with two upholstered chairs sitting before it. A pair of bookshelves was on either side of the desk, filled with leather bound tomes, framed maps, and other trinkets. Seated behind the desk, to my surprise, was a woman—probably only ten years older than myself, if that. Her long, black hair was plaited down her broad shoulder as she hunched over an open ledger. Eyes so dark they were almost black met mine when she looked up, a tight but not unkind smile breaking out across her deep brown face.

"Ah, Miss Wolff. I'm sorry you had to wait for so long. Please, have a seat," she said, her voice strong as she motioned to the chairs in front of her desk.

This was Larken Everest? The head architect? She was...not what I expected.

My thoughts must have shown on my features, for she gave a small smirk. "Before you ask: yes, I'm the youngest architect in two centuries. Yes, I'm a woman. And yes, I do, in fact, know what I'm doing. Does that answer any questions you may have, Miss Wolff?"

Twisting my hands in my lap, I swallowed. "I was surprised, that's all." And a bit embarrassed, not knowing the head architect was a *woman*. All of the past emperors had selected men for this position—and aged men, at that. The vast majority of architects were old enough to have witnessed multiple Decemvirates in their lifetime. Larken Everest probably only remembered one, *maybe* two.

Humming, she reached for a tea tray a servant had placed in front of her. "Would you care for some tea?" She held the ceramic pot in the air, gesturing toward me.

"No thank you, Miss Everest."

"Please, call me Lark." She poured a cup for herself and stirred in a sugar cube. "The guards filled me in on your situation, and I'm very sorry to hear about what happened to your family." Her tone was genuine, remorseful. "I wish I could say attacks like that are abnormal, but unfortunately, we receive reports nonstop this close to the tournament. The emperor sends his guards to patrol, but it doesn't seem to do much good, does it?"

My eyes widened as she took a sip of tea, her gaze watching me closely over her cup. Such a small statement, but even that was as brazen as I'd imagine someone could get toward the emperor, especially under his very roof.

"The attack isn't what I'm here for, Miss—Lark. We got out of that unscathed." Except for poor Larson. I closed my eyes as guilt gripped me. I'd scarcely thought of our elderly driver, how he'd lost his life simply for doing his job.

I was lucky not to have met the same end. I owed my life to the hooded mystery man, who my thoughts had wandered to several times in the hours since. How had he known we were in trouble? He had to be an Alchemist, or at least part Alchemist, with the way he'd cast to kill that Shifter. But who *was* he? Why had he been there?

Shaking away my thoughts, I continued. "My uncle fell under the Somnivae curse last night after we were attacked. He is—*was* the Feywood challenger."

Lark nodded, slowly rubbing her finger along the cup's rim. "Yes, I'm aware of who your uncle is."

I waited for her to say more, to offer some trite condolence or solution, but she stayed quiet. I pressed on. "Then you know the difficult situation that puts us in. I came here to see what could be done about it. My entire province is relying on him to compete."

Lark leaned back in her seat. "They are relying on *someone* to compete."

I blinked, unable to get a good read on this woman. "Yes, and that *someone* is currently lying in this palace's infirmary, unable to wipe the drool from his chin. Is there time to bring in another challenger from Feywood?"

Faint wrinkle lines appeared on her dark features when she frowned. "I'm afraid that would take far too long, first to get word to them, then to arrange passage from Feywood to here. The Decemvirate begins in less than twenty-four hours."

"Then postpone the start. Can't you do that?"

"Unfortunately, that's out of my hands."

Irritation bubbled beneath my skin. It was like she didn't *want* Feywood to compete, didn't want to work to find a solution for my people. I couldn't think of a single instance in the history of the Decemvirate where a province failed to produce a challenger. What would happen to our magic if that happened? Even when people had died in past Decemvirates, their provinces still received a small amount of magic in honor of the challenger who had participated. But Feywood wouldn't get the chance now. What if our magic wouldn't be replenished because of this? What if it continued to weaken until it disappeared altogether?

"Alright, then we find someone from Feywood who's here for the *revelry*," I offered, a bit of a bite to my tone. "There have to be plenty of people already in the city who could be at the palace within a couple hours." And more than willing to wear the glory of the title.

"You're right, there probably are," Lark mused. She put her cup down and steepled her hands in front of her face. "What makes me curious is the fact that *you* have not yet volunteered."

My mind went blank. "I—volunteered for what?"

"To take your uncle's place."

Was she *joking*?

I let out an involuntary snort, and her eyebrows quirked upward. "You find this suggestion funny?"

This whole situation was the furthest thing from "funny" I could imagine. Stumbling over my own tongue, I said, "I—I can't do that. I can't compete. I'm not—" My mouth hung open, words escaping me.

"You're not what?" Lark leaned forward, her ample chest flush with the desk. "From what your uncle tells me, you're very much like him in many regards."

The hair on the back of my neck raised, my lips parting on a shocked exhale. "When have you spoken with my uncle?" *What was going on?*

She stayed silent. With a flick of her wrist, shadows billowed from the desk. I sucked in a breath at the unfamiliar display of power. Darkness tumbled over itself as some shadows solidified and sealed themselves in the cracks of the chamber door and others raced along the windows behind the desk, blocking the morning sun that peeked in through the curtains.

In an instant, the entire room was as dark as night, the only light coming from two flickering candles on Lark's desk.

A Shadow Wielder. I'd never met one before. The way her shadows moved...it was like they were breathing. A living extension of her. It was *incredible*.

I snapped from my daze and leapt out of the chair, reaching for my pouch of herbs. "What are you—"

"I'm not going to harm you, Miss Wolff," Lark said, standing and holding her arms up in a sign of peace. The movement cast shadows that danced eerily in the candlelight.

Eyeing the darkness creeping at her heels, I said dryly, "Consider me comforted."

"You may not know who I am, but I know *you*. Ragnar speaks very highly of you. An accomplished Alchemist from a young age, with a will and a bite as strong as his own." She chuckled at that, and my eyes widened in stunned silence. "I suppose I should take your shock as proof of his discretion."

My mind reeled. It felt like I had walked into a different world, one I didn't understand. How did Ragnar have connections in the palace? "What are you *talking* about?"

She crossed to the front of her desk and faced me, resting the heels of her palms on top of the sturdy wood. "What are you willing to do to save your uncle?"

I licked my lips. This woman obviously knew Ragnar—how, I wasn't sure. Was he working for the emperor? Did he help design something for the tournament? I couldn't believe he didn't tell us. Countless questions burst into my thoughts, vying for attention.

But he couldn't answer them. He was gone.

"We—we can't save him," I stammered. "There's no cure."

"That's not what I asked."

I bit down on the inside of my cheek to hold back a retort. "Anything," I grounded out. "I would do anything to save him."

A beam broke out across her lips. "I was hoping you'd say that. Because there may be a way, Miss Wolff. In fact, it was the very reason your uncle came here in the first place."

My eyes darted around the room, still wary of her shadows and being confined in this chamber, but I couldn't deny the fact that she'd piqued my interest. I kept my fingers hooked around the opening of my satchel as I nodded for her to continue.

"I've been in contact with your uncle for quite some time trying to find a way to break the Somnivae curse, among other things. He's been studying the nature of curses, and his insight has proven to be quite valuable. Tell me, Rose—what do you know of it? The Somnivae curse?"

Her question made me open and close my mouth in confusion. I wasn't sure what to make of the direction this had gone. What did the curse have to do with the tournament?

I bit my bottom lip, taking a moment to respond. "Well, I know it began twenty-seven years ago, when Emperor Aris' wife gave birth to twins. Theories say since Branock Aris was an Alchemist, he brought it upon the empire himself. That it was the price he paid for his wealth and success—"

"No," Lark interrupted with a shake of her head, her braid swinging behind her back and sending a burst of wind scattering over the candle flames. "I don't want to hear about the history. Tell me what you know about the curse itself."

My jaw ticked. "It makes its victims fall into a slumber, one they can't wake up from. Their bodies stay healthy and intact, and they don't age or show any passage of time at all. The only marker is their eyes—they turn a deep red, like blood."

As I spoke, Lark nodded. "And what of curses in general? You're an Alchemist, like your uncle. What can you tell me about that brand of magic?"

I had an inkling she already knew anything I could possibly say, and this little *test* was purely to humor her. Even so, my curiosity won out over my annoyance—I wanted to know where this was heading. "Curses can be cast with the proper potion or charm, but they can also be consequences of other spells. Someone could unintentionally create a curse if they tried to cross boundaries of natural magic or used too much of their power in one go. There are common curses that most Alchemists know, but they can also be created for a specific purpose."

That's how I'd discovered my dual protect and attack charm when experimenting with old spells and herbs—it was a protection spell combined with a curse that caused an assailant's intended actions to backfire on them the moment they tried to harm me. The snow leopard's mangled shoulder popped into my mind.

"Hmm." Lark tilted her head and crossed her arms. "And is it possible to reverse a curse?"

"Well, yes," I started, that same frustration rising again. Over the past twenty-seven years, a countless number of people had tried to reverse the Somnivae curse. Alchemists were *still* working on it. So far, it had been hopeless. "You have to know the original curse that was used—all incantations and ingredients. And it can only be reversed by the one who cast it."

A curse could also be dispelled if the original caster died, I supposed. But none of this mattered, because nobody knew for sure who cast the Somnivae curse. The vast majority once believed it to be Emperor Branock Aris, whether intentional or accidental, and he had died fifteen years ago. Yet the sleeping curse lived. So someone *else* must have cast it.

"I'm sorry, but what does any of this have to do with my uncle or the tournament?" I finally asked.

"I'm getting there." A slow smile unfurled on her face, one that spoke of mischief and resolve. "What if I told you I know who cast the curse?"

I clenched the back of the chair in front of me. That was impossible. "You're lying."

Her eyes shone with eager triumph. "I'm not. And your uncle knew, too. *That* is why he competed to become the Feywood challenger, so he could use it as a means to come to the capital and help put an end to it. The Decemvirate, the tournament"—she brandished a hand in the air as if batting something away—"none of that matters as much as *this*. What your uncle came here to do— uncover the person who cast it and reverse the curse."

If that was true, if Ragnar had hid his true motive for coming to Veridia City, if he was using the tournament as a cover...that meant the person behind it all was still *here*.

Trepidation trickled over me, clinging to my skin. "Why should I believe any of this?"

Lark didn't seem offended by my distrust. Instead, she actually grinned. "I thought you might ask." She swiftly moved behind her desk and, using the candle to illuminate her drawers, pulled out a stack of parchment tied with twine.

"Letters," she said, setting them on top of her desk. "From your uncle." When I made no move to grab them, she gestured toward me. "Please, read them. I have nothing to hide from you."

My eyes slowly fell from her to the papers as I stepped closer to see the fading ink by the glow of the firelight. The pile was large, indicating months and months of correspondence, if not years.

The slanted letters, the way the words bled into the next

sentence as if the writer's thoughts were moving quicker than his fingers...it was my uncle's handwriting. There was no doubt. I would recognize it anywhere.

I grabbed the bundle and flipped through the pages, seeing his scribbled signature at the bottom of each. They even smelled faintly of Feywood—crumpled leaves and spice. I paused to read a couple, my forehead creasing with each paragraph. One simply spoke of the weather and how Ragnar wished for the balmy seasons of the capital. Another talked about recipes for a new potion he was trying.

"Is this all some sort of code?" I asked, glancing back up at Lark.

She smirked. "We couldn't very well spill our secrets on paper for inquiring minds to read."

"But you're trying to get rid of the curse. That's a *good* thing. Why do you have to hide it?"

Her lips fell into a thin line. She took her time answering, thinking through her words. "There are very few people in this world I trust anymore, Miss Wolff."

"If that's true, then I don't understand why you're telling *me* any of this."

"Because in the years I've known him, your uncle has only ever inspired the highest confidence in you. Because *he* trusts you. And I trust him." Her voice softened, and she paused. It was strange, seeing how this person I'd never met in my life was so affected by my uncle's condition. I could tell she truly *had* known him. Truly had cared about him. It made my exasperation fade ever so slightly.

Lark cleared her throat. "And because Feywood is now in need of a challenger. Someone who can follow in his footsteps."

Someone who can take on this task, was what she didn't say.

"I understand Feywood needs someone to compete. But why do you need a *challenger* for this...this mission? Why was my uncle involved at all?" I held out a hand to her. "You seem more than capable all on your own."

Lark ran her tongue along her teeth. I could tell there were things she was trying to keep private, only certain parts of her plan she was ready to convey. But if she was expecting me to risk myself for this cause, I needed to understand.

"There are...liberties I am granted in this empire, yes," she said slowly. "To remain here in a position of power in order to help others, however, there are places I cannot go. People I cannot cross. I want to tell you more, I truly do—but you can still walk away from this. I haven't divulged enough yet to put you *or* myself in any danger. Once you cross that line, once you agree, there's no going back. So I'm giving you a choice, Rose." She let out a deep breath. "I know it's not fair after everything that's happened to you in the last hours. But we are running out of time."

I rubbed at my temple. This was ludicrous. So completely out of the realm of possibility. I couldn't compete. I couldn't stop this curse. I wasn't...

What? What *wasn't* I?

I wasn't *unskilled*, I supposed. Not nearly as powerful as Ragnar, but my bloodline was strong, even though it had been dampening over the past years with our weaker magic. I'd learned many useful lessons from my uncle and my parents' Grimoires. Strike where it hurts. Observe everything. Be merciless when you can, and merciful when it's hardest.

And...I wasn't *frightened*. Not of this tournament or what the other challengers could do to me, at least. I was used to defending myself. But Ragnar's true purpose was different. What would be required of me? Would I even be able to find the original caster and figure out how to reverse the curse? Because failure...*that* frightened me.

In the end, so much was at stake. Not just the magic of my people, but also the chance to save thousands of lives. To end this plight that had taken over my empire.

I was desperate. And perhaps a bit prideful. The image of me in the tournament, proving to the Drakorum scum and everyone else that Feywood was not to be overlooked, breaking the curse and bringing back everyone who had suffered...it steeled something within me.

My heart pounded in my chest, its beat ringing through my ears. Fates, I didn't know what I was doing, but I feared I was in too deep to stop now.

"I'll do it."

Those three little words hung heavy in the air, sealing my fate. I wasn't even sure they'd come from my lips. Was I really ready to do this?

Did I have a choice? This could change *everything*.

She smiled, and the shadows around us seemed to swirl in excitement. She took a step toward me. "Excellent. Because we have no time to waste. I need you to do something for me." The darkness tightened, and her tone gave me the foreboding sense that I had barely scratched the surface of this mission. "I need you to get close to the man who cast the Somnivae curse. Uncover *how* he cast it, and what we need to reverse it."

Unease gripped my insides. The only way I'd be able to do that was by finding the Grimoire of the Alchemist in question, and that was nearly impossible. Grimoires were the most valuable item an Alchemist possessed—I couldn't simply waltz into someone's house and take a quick peek. Most, like myself, had a plethora of defensive charms in place around theirs, only accessible by those they trusted.

"Who?" I asked curtly, trying to hide my worries.

Lark's eyes flashed as she backed away. "That's the main reason we needed Ragnar in the tournament. The reason we need *you*. As a challenger, you are afforded more freedoms both in the city and the palace. You'll have eyes upon you, yes, but not eyes of suspicion. They'll never suspect someone like you. It will be much easier for you to get closer this way."

Gritting my teeth, I leveled her with an irritated glare. "Get closer to *who*?"

"You haven't worked it out yet?" Her head cocked. "Branock Aris didn't cast the Somnivae curse, Miss Wolff. It was his right-hand man. The most powerful Alchemist in the empire, and someone the Aris family trusted with their lives."

Shadows caressed my ankles, leaning in closer as if they wanted to hear her words, too.

"I need you to steal the Grimoire of Emperor Theodore Gayl."

8

ROSE

"I'm sorry, you're *what*?"

"I'm taking Uncle Ragnar's place in the tournament."

Aunt Morgana clutched her hands to her chest. "Rose, dear, are you out of your *mind*?" she exclaimed as she crossed from Ragnar's bedside and met me at the curtain separating him from the rest of the patients in the infirmary.

I cringed. This was going about as well as expected. Grabbing Ragnar's bag of charms from the floor, I dropped it onto a nearby wooden chair and began hurriedly transferring the items to my own pack.

I'd come immediately from my meeting with Lark to the healer's wing of the palace, where Morgana had been sitting with Ragnar the entire morning. Beau had been here, as well, until he left to go find the three of us some food. Not that I imagined I'd be able to eat anytime soon.

The walk across the palace from Lark's office had felt like a fever dream. I barely remembered the path, barely remembered the guard who had shown me the way. It was as if I was watching the scene take place from outside my body, going through the motions in an exhausted daze, while my mind was back in that shadowed-tinted room.

Was I making a mistake? Had I jumped into this decision too rashly, too fueled by my own desperation and pride? Why would I ever think *I*, a simple Alchemist from Feywood, could go up against the *emperor*? Not to mention compete in this tournament with five other challengers who were far more prepared than I was.

Beyond that, there was still a chance I was being a fool for trusting Lark so quickly. My uncle *had* been working with her—the letters were proof enough of that. But she was asking me to spy on the *emperor*. How could she be positive that Emperor Gayl was even behind the curse? Maybe this was all some ploy to get him out of the way, and I was the naive woman from an unsuspecting province who Lark easily manipulated into doing her dirty work so she could make a bid for the crown. Or maybe it was a test, seeing who would be willing to commit treason of this level. Guards could be knocking down my door at any moment.

Stomach churning with unease, I focused on controlling my breaths, reminding myself that *Ragnar trusted her*. If I was certain of anything, it was him. And he was willing to risk his life in the tournament for this cause.

My hands shook as I took the labeled pouches of herbs and vials of potions that had been neatly tucked away in Ragnar's bag and crammed them into my small satchel. I could faintly hear the sounds of feet on wood floor, of cloth brushing against the other side of the gray curtains surrounding Ragnar's makeshift room. Palace healers tended to other patients, going about their daily routine while my world changed with each passing second.

"How did this even happen?" Morgana's trembling words came from behind my shoulder. "By the Fates, you're going to get yourself killed! Do you know how dangerous this is?" Her voice rose an octave, but I tried to ignore the despair in her tone, tried to curb the looming sense of dread inside of me.

"Rose. Rose! Stop moving for a second and talk to me!" my aunt cried.

"I don't have time to *talk*!" I barked back, whirling to face her. "I have an hour until I need to report to the great hall for a debriefing, and at midnight, the Decemvirate begins. I can't turn back now, not when the entire *province* is relying on this. Not when Ragnar—" I cut myself off with a sharp exhale and shoved a lock of hair out of my eyes. I wasn't sure how much she knew. Surely, Ragnar would have told her of his true intentions, wouldn't he?

My chest heaved from my outburst, and my aunt stared back at me. Her features were unreadable. She searched my eyes, her lips parting with every breath.

"They've asked you, haven't they?" she finally whispered, taking a step toward me. "To—to carry it out?"

Relief flooded me. So she *did* know. I wouldn't have to keep this from her, at least. When I nodded, a quiet sob escaped her.

"This burden should not fall to you, Rose." Her voice and hand shook as she brought it up to cup my cheek. "Please. You don't need to do this. Let them find someone else. *Anyone* else."

I covered my aunt's hand with my own and squeezed. "Uncle Ragnar made his choice. He must have believed it was possible. He must have believed the chance to free the cursed was worth fighting for. This is so much bigger than me, Aunt Morgana. I can *do* this."

Even if I only said it to comfort her, the admission gave me strength. Not just for the mission, but for the tournament, too. Challengers had to set aside the weights that kept them down in order to do what must be done. Fear, uncertainty, anxieties...those would always be there, waiting to take over my mind. I had to push past them if I wanted to stand a chance in what awaited me.

"I know you can. But you shouldn't have to."

I pulled her into a hug. "It's going to be alright, I promise," I said into her hair, her arms wrapping tightly around me. It felt strange being the one to comfort my aunt, when I'd spent so many years seeking *her* strength and stability. "I'm going to get through these trials and break the curse. We're going to get him back."

She broke away, tears glistening behind her forced composure, and held my stare for a heartbeat. Two. Then finally nodded with a sigh. "I learned long ago not to argue with a Wolff when they had their mind set on something. Your father was the same way."

A smile worked its way onto my lips—probably the first one since this whole ordeal began. When I reached for Ragnar's bag, she suddenly stopped me with a hand on my arm.

"I want you to know, I *do* think you can do this. Break the curse *and* win the Decemvirate, that is." My eyes snapped up to meet hers. "Oh, don't look at me like that," she said with a tired chuckle. "You're good, Rose. Just like your parents. If I could bet on anyone, it would be Hamilton and Ayla's daughter."

I smiled faintly at her assured words. I knew what she meant, but I doubted anyone in the tournament was considered *good*. Skilled, cunning, and competent, sure. But one didn't compete out of *goodness*. They fought because they had to. They fought for glory and dominance. They fought to keep their power, no matter what it took.

"I don't know about that," I responded. "But I'll try to be better than the others."

9

ROSE

A heavily built guard with a sleek silver uniform and a bushy blonde beard braided to his waist was waiting outside the infirmary with instructions to take me to the great hall for the debriefing with the other challengers. While I'd been in the palace for several hours already, I hadn't been able to take in the grandeur around me until now. It was like stepping into a new world, its opulence so very different from our modest structures back in Feywood.

Vibrant tapestries with golden accents against multi-colored backgrounds were displayed along the length of the long corridor, brightening the gray marble walls. Gold candelabras hung from the ceiling, with matching sconces lining the marble and gleaming trim running across the baseboards and ceiling. The dark wood floor echoed with the sound of our footsteps. As we turned down several hallways, I saw servants bustling in and out of chambers, finely dressed men and women with an air of importance around them striding through the halls, and guards stationed at various chamber doors.

I'd never been somewhere so...extravagant. But its beauty was lost on me in the face of the tasks ahead.

"How far are we from the great hall?" I asked the guard, length-ening my steps to keep up with him. My father's small satchel of herbs hung from my leather belt next to my dagger and swung against my thighs as we walked. I'd never had a chance to change from the thick leggings and dark purple sweater I wore when we left Feywood, and sweat clung to every inch of me.

"Not far," he answered, his voice deep and gruff. His thick beard bobbed when he spoke.

"Where will I be staying? Can someone take me to my rooms afterward?"

He responded with a grunt.

A man of few words.

My eyes scanned the closed chamber doors as we passed, and curiosity got the better of me. "Will all of the challengers be staying in the same wing?"

"Knowing where the others are won't help you win, girl. Each room is warded against intruders."

Interesting. Not what I'd asked, but it felt like important information nonetheless. I wondered if all rooms in the palace were warded or if it was only the challengers'. I could banish a simple warding spell easily.

I needed to gain a better understanding of the layout of the palace. If I knew where Emperor Gayl spent most of his time, that would be a good place to start looking for his Grimoire.

We turned right at the end of a corridor, then another left, and suddenly, the hall opened up to a massive entryway. Rich emerald green drapes billowed from the tallest windows I'd ever seen, the bright noonday sun pooling on the wood floor before them. The chattering of voices reached my ears. Across the entryway stood double doors thrown wide open, revealing the grand hall and the mingling guests and challengers.

I straightened my spine and steeled my nerves. This was it. These were the people I would be competing against for the next month, the lords and ladies who would be observing us like animals, and the emperor behind it all. The emperor who, if Lark was correct, had condemned thousands of lives to his curse.

"Are you ready?" my guard asked, looking back at me.

Swallowing, I tucked my anxieties and fears away, covering them with that worn cloak of mettle. My lips twisted upward. "Are *they*?"

To my surprise, he met my smile with a slightly more grimacing version, his mouth splitting into a grin across his ruddy features. "Horace Banathery," he said.

I blinked. "Excuse me?"

"Name's Horace. Horace Banathery. Might as well get that out of the way, as you'll be living here for the next month."

"Oh. Well...it's nice to meet you, Horace. I'm Rose."

At that, he snorted and turned away, walking straight into the great hall.

I followed him inside and was greeted by the sight of two long banquet tables set up in the center of the enormous chamber, each holding a multitude of plates with pastries, cakes, slices of meat, cheese, bright fruits, and more foods I didn't recognize. Servants wandered among guests with trays of flutes balanced on their hands—some glasses were filled with a sparkling white liquid, others deep red, some green, and the occasional dark gray.

"Horace, what's in the glasses?" I asked before he could get too far away.

"White and red are wine. Green's a special drink the emperor requests—it relaxes the mind, a bit stronger than regular wine. Stay away from the gray."

My gaze locked on the nearest servant with a gray flute on his tray. "Why?"

"You'll be spilling your secrets to anyone who asks," he responded. I snapped my eyes back to him. "That's my free advice to you for the day, girl. Don't expect me to walk you through everything." He shot me a wink, almost imperceptible beneath his thick blonde eyebrows, before sauntering off to take his stance at the front of the great hall.

He was rather growing on me.

"My, my, Ragnar, you certainly have changed over the years," a smooth baritone voice said from behind me.

Ragnar?

I turned to find a handsome man in a tweed jacket several steps away: tall and built—surprisingly so, for someone who appeared to be in their late forties or fifties—with dark brown hair streaked with gray and a matching short-cropped beard. His light green eyes held mine with a kind humor, like he was exchanging a joke with an old friend. I merely raised an eyebrow, not wanting to speak too soon and give more of myself away than I wanted. That was something Ragnar had taught me—*silence is a powerful defense.*

The man chuckled at my lack of response and crossed his arms. "Where is the old fellow, anyway? I had it on good authority he was the Feywood challenger this year."

"Who told you that?" I asked sharply.

"Him." He winked. "Ragnar and I go way back. Used to pop by and see him for a spell when I traveled to Feywood on business. Before, well...before border laws became so messy. He got me out of a tricky situation with some Striders once, and I've owed him ever since." The man looked around me. "Is he with you?"

I narrowed my eyes. Fates, how many people did Ragnar keep in contact with outside our province? "I don't know who you're talking about."

He tapped his nose, his light eyes sparkling. "If you want to try and blend in here, perhaps lose the satchel"—he nodded to my pouch of herbs—"and the winter sweater. You're not in Feywood anymore. Also," he leaned in closer, and I fought the urge to reach for my pouch, "You look just like your mother."

I inhaled sharply. "How do you..." I couldn't finish my sentence. My shock was palpable, coiling through me and making me shiver.

"My mother is from Feywood," he explained. "I spent several years there in my youth, before our family moved to Tenebra to be with my father's side. That's how I met good ol' Ragnar."

Tenebra. He was certainly not as I imagined someone from the cold Shadow Wielder lands to be, based on stories I'd heard. A Shadow Wielder with an Alchemist mother—I wondered if he possessed both types of magic. It was a rarity to have multiple, and incredibly powerful.

"I'm a bit older than Ragnar, I admit, but I took a liking to him. He was always up for a challenge." He smiled fondly. "Let's see, I think the last time I saw him and Morgana was...well, I believe your mother was with child. I knew that must be you the moment you walked in—Ayla's spitting image. A bit of Hamilton, too."

His warm smile pricked something in me. I'd never met anyone outside of my aunt and uncle who talked about my parents. Who sounded like they truly *knew* them.

"How are they doing, by the way?" he added.

My heart stuttered. Images of blood and smoke erupted in my mind, the taste of sickly fear coating my tongue. Swallowing, I slammed my walls back up, forcing my face into one of neutrality. "They passed away when I was young."

His face fell immediately. Eyes lit with concern, lips turned down, shoulders softening. "Well, I'm very sorry to hear that. They were good people. What's your name, if I may ask?"

I hesitated before saying, "Rose. And you are?"

"Oh, how rude of me." He held out a calloused hand. "My name is Alaric."

My lips parted. "Alaric? As in...Alaric *Rinehart*?" I asked, too surprised to even take his hand.

Alaric Rinehart was the runner-up in the last Decemvirate, and his story was well known across the provinces. He was the Tenebra challenger ten years ago and had been in the lead until the last trial, when the Iluze challenger had tricked him with a vision that left him momentarily blinded. Alaric still finished in second, but Tenebra and Iluze had been up in arms for *months* after the fact.

I wondered why he was back—perhaps to mentor the new Tenebra challenger. Previous competitors did that, sometimes. Ragnar had met with one of Feywood's prior challengers once or twice to gather as much information from her as he could.

Alaric's grin was back, a hint of a dimple on his left cheek appearing among wrinkled skin. "I'm offended Ragnar never mentioned me. He knew I would be here."

My surprise soured, the reminder of my uncle slamming back into me. "Ragnar is...he's unable to compete." I bit the inside of my cheek before adding, "He fell under the Somnivae curse last night."

Alaric's hand flew to his mouth. "*Last night?*"

"And...I'm taking his place," I said, scratching awkwardly below my ear.

His eyes widened. "Well, this day is getting more and more interesting." He bore an expression I couldn't read as he said, "I hope there are no hard feelings, Rose."

"What do you mean?" I asked, tilting my head.

"Attention challengers, guests. Please make your way to the south end of the hall," a loud voice called out above the mingling crowd.

Alaric looked toward the south end as people headed in that direction, then back to me. "I'll be seeing you more, I suppose." He gave me a grim smile. "I'm the Tenebra challenger."

He bowed to me before striding off after the others, leaving me to collect my thoughts and my jaw, which had hinged itself open. He was the Tenebra challenger *again*? The same person competing twice...it was unheard of. Completely unprecedented.

I quickly ran through our conversation, wondering if I'd given any information he could use against me, cursing myself for getting caught up in his talk of my parents. Fates, I couldn't trust *anyone* here.

It didn't matter how kind they may seem, how harmless, how endearing. Every single one was a wolf in sheep's clothing.

Myself included.

Brushing off my shock and growing nerves, I passed the tables of food and stood behind the gathering crowd, taking in my surroundings. There were thirty or so people in the great hall, a handful of whom wore decorative cloaks and fine jewelry—various court members, I assumed. Several men and women sat directly in front of a raised podium, pencil and parchment in hand. More than likely reporters preparing to record the debriefing to disseminate to the public later on. My eyes glazed over other attendees, wishing I knew who the challengers were.

Out of the corner of my eye, I saw a flash of movement, and turned to meet the gaze of a tall, tan man with broad shoulders and dark blonde, wavy hair that swept a little past his ears. He peered back at me from across the hall, his expression unreadable, his hands folded behind his back. I held his stare with equal impassiveness until the corner of his lips twitched and he looked away.

"I'm grateful to you all for being here today as we begin the thirty-second Decemvirate of the Veridian Empire." The familiar voice of Lark Everest drew my attention to the front of the hall, where she stood on a raised podium, her black hair now in a bun at the top of her head. "My name is Larken Everest, and I'm this year's head architect." She paused for a smattering of applause.

"As you all know, the Decemvirate is a highly anticipated tournament among the six provinces, designed to test skill and power to determine how the limited magic of the empire will be divided. This year's Decemvirate will consist of three separate trials. The first two will begin seven days apart from one another, and then we will hold the traditional tournament masquerade ball two weeks later, followed by the third and final trial."

The scribes wrote furiously, jotting down every word she said.

"The first starts tomorrow morning. This trial will test your intellect; the second, your mettle; and the third, your courage. You will be given relevant information before the start of all three. You are free to go anywhere in the capital you desire—as long as you are back at the palace by the eve of the trials to receive instructions, and are in attendance at the debriefings after the conclusion of each. Failure to comply will result in your province's immediate disqualification.

"Rankings will be updated following the individual trials and will be determined based on how quickly and proficiently you pass each." Her voice turned sharp as she continued. "We do not allow any misconduct toward your fellow challengers in the interim between trials. Guards will be stationed around the palace day and night to prevent brutality and violence."

Ahead of me, a young man with black hair shaved close to his dark scalp called out, "What about *during* the trials?"

Lark leveled him with a stare. "There are no laws regarding your interactions with one another or the components of the trials while you are inside of them. Your goal is to get through them as swiftly and skillfully as possible."

In other words, anything was fair game.

The man who'd asked the question twisted his head to smirk at someone to his side. He was another challenger, I figured. And one who seemed particularly pleased by the idea of no restraints in the trials themselves.

Clearing her throat, Lark added, "That being said, if you are found to be behaving in a way that puts innocent civilians of this capital in any danger, whether it be threatening, harassing, or harming of any kind, you will be disqualified and punished to the fullest extent of Veridian law."

"What about cheating?" a woman asked from the side of the chamber, leaning on the wall with a knee bent, foot propped against the marble. I raised an eyebrow and held back a snort.

Lark gave the woman a sly smile. "You're welcome to try. I think you'll find my trials a bit harder to cheat your way through, Arowyn."

The woman shrugged and crossed her arms, a disinterested look on her features.

Arowyn. Another challenger? I took a moment to brand her into my memory, tucking away my observations. Long, light hair—almost white, hanging straight down to her mid-back. Heavy black kohl lined her eyes, and it was difficult to tell her age beneath the makeup. Perhaps a few years older than myself. I wondered what province she was from. There was nothing to give her identity away, no telltale colors, no crest, no weapons. She wore tight black pants that hugged her voluptuous curves, with brown boots and a loose, white tunic tucked into the front. Emberfell, maybe? The boots could fit in the swampy Lightbender province to the north. Or Celestria. I often saw Bethaly wearing similar loose blouses.

"Well, then," Lark finished, clapping her hands together. "That's everything you need to know for now. Remember to trust your instincts, and that the end goal may not always be what you think." Her eyes strayed to me at those words, lingering longer than necessary. I shuffled my feet and anxiously fingered the satchel of herbs at my waist.

"Before we part, I'd like to introduce His Majesty, Emperor Theodore Gayl."

At Lark's words, a large door opened to the side of the podium, revealing a cloaked man emerging from the shadows.

My eyes trained on his long, silver-flecked black hair extending to his shoulders in waves, his billowing dark green cloak, his powerful strides. When he roamed his gaze over the crowd, a shiver went down my spine at his piercing eyes: one a deep blue, and one so light it appeared white.

Theodore Gayl was the most powerful Alchemist this world had seen in recent history. Maybe *ever*. As much as I hated laws like the strict border mandates he'd put into place, and as furious as I was about his inaction toward the growing violence and separation, I'd also always had a twisted fascination with the man. Or more so, his magic.

I didn't know much about his life before he became the emperor twenty-four years ago, except that he'd lived in the capital and served the former Emperor Branock Aris in some advisory capacity. His bid for the throne came at a shock, considering his closeness with the Aris family. Now that Lark said he was behind the curse that ultimately led to Emperor Aris' downfall, it made sense.

It seemed that everything he did was to gain more power and control over the empire. Ragnar used to tell me how when he was younger, the citizens of each province were free to roam the empire, visiting neighboring lands without worrying about reper-cussions. Without ridiculous laws and vicious border guards. Exploration and travel and learning about each culture was once *encouraged*.

But Gayl had planted seeds of unease within his citizens across all provinces with his ideas that our power, our strength, was the only thing that mattered. Was what defined our worth. Not unity, not freedom. *Magic.* And above all, we needed to focus on culti-vating our individual powers. The Decemvirate had always been a competition, of course, but he had turned it into so much more than that.

Once upon a time, our magic had been a gift—a tool and resource to help in times of need, to aid us and make life easier where it could. Now, it was viewed as our *right.* Our value and status in the empire was measured by the magic that ran through our veins. The more powerful provinces like Iluze and Tenebra were raised on a platform, receiving wealth and resources from the capital because of their prestige. Their elevation led to enmity and a bolstered sense of entitlement—Beth had told me how there was even talk of these stronger provinces threatening to invade the weaker, to claim more land and magic as their own.

And if they truly wanted to, they could. There was nothing but an icy lake and a handful of border guards stopping Iluze from declaring war on either Feywood or Celestria, whose weakened magic and little support from the capital left us defenseless. If our territory was conquered, would our magic go to our captor? Would Alchemy cease to exist? Would we lose our power altogether? These were questions nobody had tested over the centuries, but now seemed to be more and more enticing.

The man before me had undeniably made the world darker, colder, more power-hungry. I wished for a better future, of course. A future where our worth as people didn't dwell in our magic, where we could live harmoniously as *Veridians* instead of defined by the power in our blood.

But as I watched Emperor Gayl command the entire chamber

with his mere presence, and as I felt that Alchemist power radiating from him and stirring something in my magic, it was difficult not to be impressed. *Envious*, even. That he could have this control in the palm of his hand, the ability to twist the world to his will and break it apart with a thought.

If Lark was right, *this* was the man who had started the Somnivae curse. *This* was the man I had to stand against.

My jaw tightened as my hands clenched at my sides. He was the reason Uncle Ragnar was lying in an infirmary. The reason I was forced into this position in the first place. The reason thousands of families were suffering and mourning, that hatred among provinces abounded, that children couldn't safely cross from one forest to another without fear of an attack.

I met Lark's gaze as she stepped to the side, and the edge of her lips curled ever so slightly. Resolve pounded in my bones. I'd already agreed to help her, but I think we both realized in that moment that each of us would do whatever it took to bring him down. We were on the same side.

And once this tournament began, there was no turning back.

IO

ROSE

"Thank you to Miss Everest for her work implementing the Decemvirate this year," Emperor Gayl began. All eyes instantly locked on him. His voice was the kind of low, quiet strength that demanded you hold your breath and will your heart to pause, if only to hear it linger in the air.

Lark dipped her head in acknowledgement, and he settled his attention over the crowd.

"Every ten years, this empire asks its citizens to prove themselves. To show themselves worthy of power, and to take that which is theirs." He extended a fist and clenched his hand, which was gloved in thick, black leather. "Six of you have answered the call, and for that, I commend you. But this is only the beginning. These trials are designed to show who among you is greatest, who among you deserves the magic from our land, and what you are willing to do in order to gain it." He paused, eyes sweeping over the crowd. "I have a feeling this will be a Decemvirate to remember," he finished softly.

The room was silent, save for the quiet echo of his words. The atmosphere grew thick with challenge. His gaze raked over us one more time before he turned away, his emerald cloak swishing at his heels as he exited the chamber. Two guards followed swiftly. Excited whispers began as soon as the door shut.

"Well, he is *exactly* as I thought he would be," a sultry voice said from a few steps behind me. My hand inched toward my satchel as I twisted to find the same man who'd caught my attention before Lark spoke, the one with wavy blonde hair and a matching beard.

I was immediately on my guard. Anyone that handsome knew *exactly* what they were doing.

His dark blue eyes flecked with silver gleamed as he caught my movement, and he *tsk*ed. "Such nimble fingers, darling. Save that for the tournament."

"Who are you?" I snapped.

"You can call me Nox."

"Well, Nox. Thanks for the advice." Stepping around him, I made my way to the nearest refreshment table, eyeing a cream pastry with melted chocolate drizzled on top.

A rough hand littered with glittering rings enveloped my upper arm and pulled me back. Instinctively, I reached for the dagger at my belt and whirled to press the blade against my assailant's wrist.

"Nimble fingers, remember?" I taunted darkly. The humor on Nox's face grated on me, making me push a little harder than necessary.

"You're a viper, aren't you?" he said with a chuckle. He held his hands in the air in a sign of peace. "I'm not going to hurt you."

I rolled my eyes and lowered my dagger. "Has anyone ever told you not to go around grabbing strangers?"

"Oh, some of them don't mind," he said, his gaze roving over a few of the nearby guests. The ones closest eyed us warily, but within seconds were back to mingling and drinking. I supposed it wasn't so unusual for two challengers to already be at each other's throats during the Decemvirate. At least, I *assumed* he was a challenger.

"What province are you?" I asked sharply, tipping my chin at him.

He reached to a table and grabbed a flute of gray liquid. "Drakorum. At your service."

Drakorum. *Shifters.* My eyes narrowed, a white hot flash of anger pulsing through me. Before he could take a sip of wine, my hand shot out to grip his arm.

"Did you send your people to attack my family last night?" I hissed.

The confusion was evident on his face—creased brow, parted lips. This close to him, I could tell he wasn't quite as young as I first thought. Small wrinkles graced the skin around his eyes and forehead. He couldn't be more than eight years older than me, although his spirit seemed much younger.

"I don't know what you're talking about," he responded. When I only squeezed harder, he lowered his voice, keeping our conversation from drawing more attention. "I swear to you, I know nothing of any attack."

I searched his face for another moment. The mischievous glint from earlier was replaced by genuine concern. I didn't know if he was telling the truth, but there wasn't much I could do about it in this crowded hall. Releasing his arm, I pushed away.

"What was that you said about grabbing strangers?" he grumbled, flexing his hand then taking a sip of his drink.

Gray wine. The one Horace said made people spill their secrets. Did Nox realize what he was drinking?

"Who attacked you?" he asked. "Tell me everything."

Glancing around, I kept my voice quiet as I answered. "Three Shifters. A snow leopard, a serpent, and a coward. The last one got away, but the first two are dead." I paused, waiting for some sort of indignation that his people had been killed, but his features remained smooth. "They stopped our carriage in the middle of the night on our way to the palace. They killed our driver and tried to kill my uncle, but we got to them first." My thoughts once again strayed to the cloaked man from last night, his dark eyes flashing at me when I blinked.

Nox took another drink. "I'm sorry that happened. But I promise, I had nothing to do with it."

"Why should I believe you? You're the Drakorum challenger, aren't you? How do I know you didn't find out the Feywood challenger was in that carriage and send them to take out the competition?"

"Because I don't care if I win this ridiculous tournament," he spat out, enunciating each word with heated blue eyes. For a split second, his pupils seemed to elongate.

I stepped backward and blinked my shock away. He didn't care about winning? That didn't make any sense. "Then why are you even *here*?"

Sighing, he inclined his head to a shadowed alcove beyond the rest of the guests. After a moment of deliberation, my curiosity won out over self-preservation. I nodded and followed him.

"You don't understand what it's like where I come from," he said in hushed tones. "In Drakorum...there's no higher honor than being selected as the challenger. No more important purpose. And if you fail or reject what you're told, their retribution is swift and without mercy."

He must be an incredibly powerful Shifter if they chose him. I could understand the significance each province placed on their challengers—we *all* took the Decemvirate seriously. But the haunted look in his eyes told me Drakorum was an entirely different breed altogether. One I should be thankful not to be involved in.

"I don't wish to be here, but I have no other choice. My people" —he cleared his throat—"have ways to ensure my obedience. But believe me, I despise everything this Decemvirate stands for, and have no desire to play into their twisted obsession with power."

My eyes shifted around us, shocked by his brashness. This man was toeing a dangerous line. "Why would you say any of this to me? I could report you for treason."

"Yes, you could," he said simply, bringing the flute to his lips again.

"And why are you drinking that?" I blurted. "Don't you know what it does?"

"Do *you*?" When I hesitated, he smirked. "Grimlock makes one incapable of lying. Very dangerous. I don't recommend it," he added as he drained the entire glass.

"Then why drink it?"

"Because, viper, the truth can be just as useful as a lie. Do you believe what I've told you? Do you believe I mean you and your family—or any other challenger—no harm?"

I ran my tongue along my teeth. Nox was a puzzle. Cocky and sly, yet genuine and open. My brain told me not to trust him, even with the supposed truth wine he'd ingested. We'd been conditioned to believe everyone was only looking out for themselves, and that the path to glory was paved by those you trampled beneath your feet.

But he seemed...different. Someone who had seen firsthand the ferocity and mercilessness this empire stoked and truly didn't want a part in it.

Plus, the Grimlock. He wouldn't have been able to say these things if they weren't at least partially true.

I let out a breath, hoping I wouldn't regret this.

"It's Rose, not viper," I finally said. "My name is Rose."

At that, he chuckled. "Rose. How fitting. I certainly don't want to be at the end of your thorns." He tipped his empty flute to me. "What do you think of the rest?" he asked, motioning with his head to the chamber full of preening guests.

"I haven't met many of them," I answered, still keeping my distance. Searching the room, I spotted a tall, brown and gray haired figure laughing with a group of the emperor's council by a table of drinks. "That's Alaric Rinehart, the Tenebra challenger."

Nox shot me a look of surprise. "I recognize that name. Didn't he compete last time?" When I nodded, he let out a snort. "Well, that either bodes very well for us, or very poorly." Using his glass, he pointed to the blonde woman who'd been leaning against the wall during Lark's speech, the one who had asked about cheating. Arowyn, I thought Lark had called her.

"She's the Strider," Nox explained. "We arrived at the same time last night, and I saw her use her magic. Seems rather… prickly."

As we watched Arowyn, she kicked from the wall and sauntered over to one of the finely-dressed ladies of the court, plucked a pastry from the woman's outstretched plate and a bottle of wine from a servant's tray, then crossed to the entrance doors and kicked them open with one foot before disappearing down the hall.

What an exit. I couldn't help but be slightly impressed.

"Alright, so that's Tenebra, Celestria, Drakorum, and Feywood," I recounted, pointing to Nox and myself as I said the last two provinces. "I wonder which one is Iluze."

Iluze had won the last Decemvirate, meaning the newest Illusionist challenger would have the most buzz surrounding them. They had difficult shoes to fill, as the reigning champion, but also wielded the most powerful magic.

I searched the crowd and saw a bright flash emanating from behind me. Jerking my head around, I let out a choked gasp as the flames from the decorative lantern at my back jumped to the sleeve of my thick sweater. I rapidly beat at my arm to smother the fire, glancing up to see Nox's bewildered expression.

"What in the world are you doing?" he asked.

My jaw dropped as I pulled on the end of my sleeve, getting ready to rip the entire thing off. The flames wouldn't go out, and the heat was beginning to sear my skin. "What am I *doing*? Seriously? I'm trying to put out this fire!"

A snicker sounded from the left. "He can't see it, but please, don't stop taking off your clothes on my account," the new voice said.

In the blink of an eye, the flames disappeared from my sleeve, the fabric not even scorched or smoking.

It wasn't real.

Fates. I hated Illusionists.

Closing my eyes, I clenched my jaw and slowly turned on my heel. When I opened them, I was staring into the face of the young man I'd seen earlier in the crowd, the one with close-cropped black hair who'd seemed amused by the idea of brutality among the challengers. His square jaw flexed, his full lips pulling up in a smug smirk. A circular ring piercing his bottom lip glittered in the fire-light from the perfectly intact lantern. Anger licked at my skin like the false flames I'd felt moments ago. Looking around, I expected to see a guard or someone coming to confront him for attacking me, but we were too far to the side for anyone to notice.

"You two are getting cozy awfully fast, aren't you?" he asked, motioning between Nox and myself. His voice was low, with a hint of haughtiness that set my teeth on edge. "Is spreading your legs for fellow challengers a new tactic?"

Illusionists were so arrogant. I schooled my features into a look of apathy, picking a loose thread from the opening in my satchel of herbs. "Are you offering?"

His dark eyes flashed. "For you, Feywood, I'd consider it. If only to save you from having to ride that piece of Drakorum—"

Before he could finish his sentence, my fingers closed around crushed henbane petals in my pouch. I quickly placed one on my tongue and muttered, "*Phyxie.*"

The man clutched his throat at my curse, his eyes bulging as the breath lifted from his lungs.

"I'm sorry, I don't think I caught your name," I said sweetly as I took a step toward him. I counted the seconds in my head, making sure I had enough time to banish the curse. His nostrils flared and his forehead creased in panic, one hand still around his throat while the other reached for me angrily.

I *tsk*ed. "Do they teach you manners in Iluze? Ask *nicely*."

His knees dipped and he grabbed at the wall, his fingers digging into the marble for purchase. A few more seconds...

"*Finiscere,*" I said, feeling the spell banish from the air. The Illusionist fell to the ground, taking deep, gasping breaths.

Now, *that* got people's attention. From the right came two guards, glaring at me with their hands on the hilts of their swords.

"I don't need a new tactic, *Illusionist,*" I spat down at him. "I'm doing just fine on my own."

I turned my back on him and faced the converging guards. "I can see my way out," I said with a mock bow, then marched out the entrance doors.

II

LEO

The bartender slammed three glasses on the table, sending liquid sloshing over the sides and pooling onto the wood. Horace, Chaz, and Lark all grabbed one.

"Drinking on the job?" I asked the latter as I leaned back in my chair, hood lowered over my head.

"It's my last night of freedom," Lark reminded me. Spirals of dark curls came loose from her tight bun. "You know how it will get when the Decemvirate starts tomorrow."

"Yeah, Leo, let her have her fun," Horace said, stroking his beard with interest, his beady eyes roaming over her rounded curves as she took a sip.

Setting the glass down, she pursed her lips at him. "My eyes are up here, Blondie."

I hid a smirk. "Horace, I thought you said the guards had extra rounds now because of the tournament. Shouldn't you be at the palace?"

"Not till tomorrow, technically." He chuckled and took a sip, then held his glass out to Lark. "And the one you told me to keep an eye on? She's feisty. You picked well."

Chaz glanced at me in confusion, and I narrowed my eyes at

Lark and Horace. "What are you talking about? Picked who for what?"

Twisting her lips, Lark said, "I think we should wait until Rissa gets here."

My muscles tightened in frustration. What was going on? And why had Rissa not told me about it?

The leader of our cloaked group was late for the meeting. Clarissa had asked the four of us—her "trusted advisors," she jokingly deemed us—to meet at the normal tavern in the south sector one final time before the tournament began. We'd claimed a table in a secluded corner of the Drakin's Lair, where nothing but the cockroaches gracing the wood floor and the birds perching outside the cracked glass window could hear us.

"I think I see her," Chaz commented from across the table, peering to his right at the front door of the tavern. It was blown open, letting in a balmy breeze and a glimpse of the night sky beyond. Between the numerous bodies of townspeople drinking and chattering further down the bar, I saw a familiar lithe figure slip among them, a burgundy hood concealing her features. Except...

"Is she *limping*?" Lark hissed. I'd noticed her strange movements, too, and my blood heated, momentarily forgetting my irritation with all of them.

Clarissa approached silently and took a seat at the table, lowering her hood to reveal blonde curls, a fair, freckled face, and eyes that gazed back at me with a warning.

Beneath one of her onyx eyes, the twin to my own, was a darkened circle of sickly green and yellow. A mark that had certainly not been there this morning. I gritted my teeth and gripped the corner of the table.

"Before you go off and kill someone, little brother, let me explain," Rissa said to me, raising her hands.

"There's nothing to *explain*, Rissa. Who hurt you?" I snarled, straining to keep my voice low.

"One of the guards saw me shifting as I snuck off palace

grounds earlier. He must've thought I was from Drakorum and trying to mess with the tournament. Don't worry—you know I heal fast. The bruise is already almost gone. And besides, he looks worse than I do," she said with a smirk.

Next to me, Horace's body stiffened. I knew how uncomfortable he was with being part of the emperor's Royal Guard, with their elitist attitude and violent reputation hanging over him everywhere he went. But he was a good man. He'd joined the Guard many years ago, when he was too young to see how corrupt the emperor's hold had grown. Over time, however, his eyes had been opened.

He told us how he'd witnessed countless beatings of innocent civilians, how the Royal Guard would often accept coin in exchange for letting crimes slip through the cracks. How they intentionally turned a blind eye to the seedier areas of Veridia City, such as the south sector the Drakin's Lair resided in, because it was heavily populated with provincers. Many residents here were forced to sleep with blunt knives beneath their pillows or tucked into their waistbands when wandering the streets. They, like myself, had learned long ago to never expect safety from our dear emperor.

It hadn't always been this way. But most of us were too young to remember a time before.

Horace had experienced this injustice firsthand when he'd been foolish enough to try and approach Emperor Gayl with his concerns. He had been threatened with removal from the Guard's ranks should he continue questioning their methods. Though he'd never spoken of it, every once in a while I'd catch a glimpse of lacerations peeking beneath his clothing, crawling up his neck and down his shoulders.

Whip marks. All because he had the courage to speak his mind.

That was when he found us.

The Sentinels, a group of Veridians who sought peace and justice and weren't afraid to use an occasional blade to accomplish it. Adding a member of the Royal Guard to our numbers had been a stroke of luck; it gave us inside access to some of the most important people and resources in the empire, as well as eyes on any suspicious activity within the palace walls.

Horace looked like someone you wouldn't want to cross, with his towering frame, his unruly blonde hair, and eyes that gleamed with savagery. Yet beneath the hard exterior was a man of few words who wanted to do right by his people, who would gladly give his life for those he called a friend.

While I was hard pressed to bestow much honor to the Fates after what they'd done in my life—in *all* our lives—bringing Horace to us was one thing I would always be thankful for.

"Told you it wasn't wise to go sneaking around there this close to the tournament," Horace commented gruffly. At the same time, Lark stood from her chair and rounded on Rissa, her frustration and concern both evident as she examined the injury.

"He's right—everyone is on high alert right now," Lark agreed.

"I'm fine, Lark, honestly." Rissa waved her away. "More upset that he messed up my pretty face than anything else. You might actually be the better looking twin tonight," my sister said, shooting me a wink. I put an elbow on the table and squeezed the bridge of my nose. Only she could find humor in physical assault.

"It's not funny, Rissa. You need to be careful. If they find out what you're doing..." I trailed off, the air suddenly heavy with tension.

When my sister decided to create the Sentinels over five years ago, we never imagined what it would grow to. A network of at least two hundred spies scattered through the capital, plus many in each province, all connected through one purpose: ending Gayl's rule and bringing harmony to the empire, regardless of magic or background.

If Gayl caught Rissa *or* myself where we didn't belong, he'd find some reason for execution simply because of who we were. Who our *parents* were. But the fact that Rissa was also actively leading a group of people in committing treason against him...

He would have her head mounted on his wall in a heartbeat.

My sister and I had gone our entire lives looking out for one another in the midst of a cruel world that hated us for what we were born into. The number of times I'd seen Rissa come home battered and bruised still made my hackles rise. One look at the mark on her eye and the wince on her face as she crossed her leg under the table made the Shifter half of my blood stir while a growl built in the back of my throat.

Without knowing what I was doing, something long slipped from beneath my cloak and flicked angrily in the air.

"Hey," Rissa said softly, putting a hand on my knee. "I'm okay. Trust me, alright? I've had worse—it will heal." When she gave me her beautiful crooked smile, my chest constricted. She looked so much like our mother.

The closest people left to me in this world, and one was lying in a sickbed while the other was trying to save the empire. Two of the strongest women I'd ever known, both fighting for their lives in very different ways.

Rissa asked me to trust her. And I did. But that didn't make it any easier. It didn't make her pain any less hard to watch.

"Leo, put that away before someone sees," Lark scolded from across the table, motioning to the tail still twitching in anticipation. I hastily tucked it under my cloak as my anger began to cool, and the memory of why we were here came rushing back.

"So, what is it you three have been hiding?" I asked Horace, Lark, and Rissa in an even tone, rapping my fingers on the tabletop.

My sister sighed. "We're not *hiding* anything. There's a…sensitive mission Lark has been working on. But it's finally been set into motion."

"A mission? Why wasn't I made aware of this?" My sister may be the unspoken leader, but she had always confided in me. Always looked to me for support. It had been her and me for so long, ever since our father died and our mother took ill.

With a wince at the betrayal in my tone, Rissa said, "Well…you *do* know about it. Just not everything." She motioned toward Lark, as if to say, "your turn."

Lark straightened in her seat, looking to the side to be sure no one was close enough to eavesdrop. We weren't too concerned about the kind of patrons that frequented the Drakin's Lair overhearing our conversation; for the most part, everyone minded their own business here in the underbelly of the capital. If anyone *did* hear, they were more than likely already connected to the Sentinels or would have no qualms with a rebellion against the emperor. It was why we met at this location so often. Still, one could never be too safe.

"It's about Gayl," Lark started, and my jaw ticked involuntarily. "We've had definitive proof for some time now that his spell created the Somnivae curse all those years ago, as you know."

I nodded. For a while, the entire empire was convinced Branock Aris had cast the curse—some *still* were. But when he died fifteen years ago, questions arose. We had tracked down a healer who had been there the night the curse began and got her firsthand account of what happened. How Gayl had saved Evadine Aris' life with what the healer believed was dark magic. That's what finally solidified our theories that Theodore Gayl was the one behind it all.

Lark continued. "Locating his Grimoire has been our biggest obstacle, not to mention somehow getting him to reverse the spell."

I interrupted her with a growl. "I've told you, let *me* try. I'm the only Alchemist here, I can—"

"*Half* Alchemist, Leo, and as I've told *you*, that's out of the question," Rissa interjected.

I bristled. "You can't sneak around without telling anyone and get yourself caught by palace guards, then force me to stay in the dark."

"I can, and I will. Unless you'd like to challenge me?" Rissa's voice hardened, her black pupils elongating slightly as her eyes took on a golden tinge—a sign of her imminent shift. A powerful leader ready to stake her claim.

Sometimes, I forgot exactly who my sister was. What she was born to be.

I held her gaze, grinding my teeth. She knew full well I wasn't going to challenge her for leadership; I respected her too much. But that didn't mean I had to approve of her running headfirst into danger any chance she got, nor that I was pleased with being excluded from plans while my constant request to *do something* was once again ignored.

"If you two are finished, can I continue?" Lark's sharp voice broke our stare. She cleared her throat. "I had already found someone for the job. An acclaimed Alchemist from Feywood. We've been in contact for the past eighteen months, working to get him here for the Decemvirate so he could get close enough to find the emperor's Grimoire. From there, we had a plan to figure out what we needed to do to reverse his curse."

"*Had?*" Chaz asked, crossing his arms over his broad chest.

Lark's dark features twisted into a grimace. "We hit an...obstacle. But I think I've found a solution."

"It involves someone in the tournament. That's all you need to know," Rissa jumped in. "Horace knows because he'll be inside the palace and can watch over them and relay messages if needed. But the less people who are aware of the details, the more likely we'll be able to keep this task out of prying minds."

Frustration roared back in full force. Lark and my sister had been planning this for *eighteen months* without me? Was Rissa truly this intent on keeping me from it? On refusing my petition to sneak into the palace and steal Gayl's Grimoire myself? Or perhaps it was because she had so little faith in my ability to be successful. *Half* Alchemist, as she had thrown at me.

Her fair features softened as she took in my reaction. "Leo, I promise this isn't about you. You know I trust you more than anyone. This is about keeping the mission and all involved safe. The more people who know, the higher chance something slips."

I ran my thumb along my lower lip, willing myself to hold my resolve against that *face* she always made. The one that would have me handing over my piece of cake when we were kids because she begged for it. The one with the big, sad eyes, the slight pout of the lip, the batting eyelashes.

"You're impossible," I grunted, and she beamed. Fates, I could never stay mad at her for long. "But how do you know you can trust this person, whoever it is?" I pressed. "How do you know they're capable of doing the job?"

Sneaking around the palace for any reason, much less to locate Gayl's personal Grimoire under his very nose, wasn't a feat most people could take on. It was why we hadn't succeeded thus far. A few Sentinels had volunteered a couple years ago, and they had ended up either victims of Gayl's guards or dead by their own hands, unwilling to risk betraying the rest of the rebellion if subjected to torture and questioning.

Too many lives had been lost for this cause. Each time, I urged Rissa to let me try. And each time, I was denied. Was this mysterious spy simply going to be another tally added to the list? Or who was to say they wouldn't betray us for favor with the emperor, or lose their nerve?

Lark's lips thinned. "Let's just say they have a vested interest in things going our way. As for being capable, only time will tell. But they've been highly vouched for by someone I know and trust. Horace and I will do our best to keep them as safe as we can inside the palace."

I knew by the look on her and Rissa's faces that there was no point in arguing. While the two of them may believe this was a good plan, the idea of placing this responsibility into the hands of a stranger made me uneasy. Outing Theodore Gayl as the Alchemist behind the Somnivae curse and finding the spell he'd used to cast it was essential to ending his reign. We had to remind the people how much *better* this empire could be when out from under his thumb. How it had once been. That Veridians should be united again, without fear of crossing borders or suffering attacks for being *different* or staying silent because you knew no one would care. It was perhaps the most important task we'd ever have, and we were handing it over to someone most of us had never met.

The small, selfish, prideful side of me couldn't help but think it should be *me* risking my life to bring Gayl down. It was a vow I'd made to myself all those years ago when our father died: vengeance on the man who had ripped the legacy from my father's name and the crown from his head.

Rissa turned to me, seeming to read my thoughts no matter how hard I tried to cover them. She tilted her head, a mass of blonde curls trailing down her side. The bruise on her eye was nothing more than a shadow now, the healing powers of her Shifter blood working quickly.

"Come on, little brother," she said, a sly grin pulling at her lips. "Look at the bright side. After all these years, don't you think it's about time we avenged our parents?"

Chaz lifted his glass, and the others followed. "To Branock and Evadine Aris."

His murmured toast echoed from the lips of our friends, and I met my sister's gaze. The firstborn to Emperor Branock Aris. Her black eyes tinged with gold held such power, such cunning determination, that it caused resolve to thicken inside of me.

Yes, it was about time.

And when the person Lark had selected to infiltrate the emperor failed, I would be ready.

It was time for Theodore Gayl to burn.

12

LEO

" I bet you ten silver coins you can't knock the apple from that man's hands," Chaz said to Horace, nodding at the shiny dart in the latter's hand. Horace leaned back in his chair and eyed the man with the apple laughing across the bar.

"Don't you even think about it," Lark snapped. "You'll take his eye out."

"Nah, Horace is a great shot, aren't you, big guy?" Chaz smacked him on the shoulder.

I snorted. "Have you *seen* him shoot?"

"Just for that, I'll take your bet." Horace put his hands on his knees and braced himself to stand. Lark's exasperated sigh made me chuckle.

"Are you not going to stop these idiots?" she directed to Rissa, who lounged in her seat with an arm draped lazily over the back of her chair.

"You're right. This is ridiculous. Horace"—Rissa lifted a finger to get his attention—"make it twenty coins."

"You don't even *have* twenty coins," Chaz shot back.

My sister winked at him. "And he can't make that shot. So I think I'll be fine."

Lark gave a disgruntled scoff. "I'm surrounded by children."

The sound of laughter and clinking glasses and feet pounding on wood mingled with my friends' voices as they discussed Horace's dart-aiming prowess, which soon devolved into his aiming prowess with *other* things, and the challenge with the apple became long forgotten.

I shook my head and grinned along with them, soaking in the moment of normalcy. Too often, especially as the Decemvirate drew nearer, our nights were spent tracking down potential victims and putting a stop to random attacks on the capital streets. More and more fugitives from the six provinces were seeking the safety of Veridia City as their own borders became too dangerous to live near, only to find capital-dwellers even *less* welcoming.

I supposed one had to be truly desperate to exchange one hell for another. Either that, or the provincers didn't know what they were walking into when entering the capital. Didn't know that true refuge no longer existed in this empire.

Despite the dangers, there were still pockets of happiness to be found. I looked forward to nights like this, where the smiling faces of those closest to me broke through the constant sense of vigilance I carried. Perhaps not family by blood, but family by duty. By choice. I was stuck with Rissa, as she so often liked to say, but I knew I would have chosen her as my sister in any life. There was nobody else I could walk through this dark world with. Nobody else with whom I would have wanted to grieve the loss of our father, care for our sick mother, endure the spite and shame this legacy placed on our shoulders.

Lark came into our lives during one of our lowest points, only three years after our father died and our mother fell ill. Rissa and I were two teenagers trying to take care of ourselves in a city that still believed the curse was Branock Aris' fault and refused to give our family so much as the scraps from their tables. Lark, in her early twenties at the time, caught my sister stealing food from her bakery in the south sector, and instead of reporting her, offered her a job. The first person to have seen us as something more than our surname, to truly give us a fighting chance at becoming our own people.

It was a gift I could never repay. I didn't know if Larken Everest quite understood what she did for us that day. What she meant to my sister and me.

Chaz and Horace were later additions to the Sentinels, and while our history may not run as deep with the two of them, I trusted them with my life. Chaz was the son of one of the elderly lord's on Emperor Gayl's council, while Horace was a member of the Royal Guard. Two men with everything to lose, who were willing to sacrifice their reputations, their jobs, even their lives for the vision my sister and I had of what this empire could be.

I took another sip of my drink and snuck a glance at Rissa. She seemed to feel my gaze on her and looked over with that crooked smile, a silent moment of thankfulness passing between us.

The door to the tavern flew open with a bang.

Four huge men in the silver Royal Guard uniform sauntered in, swords clanging in sheaths against their legs. They swaggered toward the bar, gleams in their eyes as they took in the crowd. The din went from raucous and uninhibited to hushed whispers and strained near-silence in a matter of seconds, eyes shifting and spines straightening.

"What are *they* doing here?" Rissa muttered. Horace and Lark immediately turned so their backs were to the guards, their normally composed features now tight with alarm. If the newcomers were to see them, a fellow member of the Guard and the head architect of the Decemvirate, meeting with a group of strangers in this part of town...

If the hidden marks on Horace's body were any indication, the Guard didn't wait to ask questions before doling out punishment.

"How can I help you?" the bartender asked, his voice tense, eyebrows drawn together.

"Oh, why the long face?" one of the guards jeered, planting his hands on the top of the wooden bar. The patrons nearest him leaned away, their discomfort evident even from my seat all the way across the tavern. "My boys and I are just here for a night out."

"Welcome to the Drakin's Lair. It's an honor to serve members of His Majesty's Guard," the bartender bit out. I winced at the hint of derision in his tone. With men like this, it was best to hold your breath and lie low. To not draw attention to yourself. That was how you inevitably ended up in a back alley with your face plastered to a brick wall.

"You hear that, Kipper?" The guard turned to the man on his left. "An *honor*. Is this how you treat those with honor here in the south sector?" He flourished a hand toward the silent bar, the looks of wariness and repulsion staring back at him.

"I would say not, Pax."

Their dramatic exchange set me on edge. My eyes flitted briefly to Lark and Horace, who attempted to look casual, keeping their heads facing away from the front.

"Although, wouldn't have expected much more from the filth down here," the one called Kipper added with a smirk. "Bunch of province scum."

A man sitting at a table near them gripped the side of his chair, a movement I wouldn't have noticed if it weren't for my sharpened Shifter senses. The guards honed in on it instantly. Rissa's quick inhale next to me showed she saw it, too.

"You got a problem with that?" Pax said to the man, tilting his neck. The other three slowly drifted to the table.

The man shook his head. All eyes were on the scene, no longer pretending to keep to themselves.

"He asked you a question," a third guard said with a sneer, kicking the back of the man's chair. The action had my legs clenching as I fought the urge to stand. Rissa put a hand on my back, subtly shaking her head.

"No, *sir*," the man said through gritted teeth.

Pax hummed and nodded at the guards to back off, then roved his gaze over the rest of the tavern. People lowered their eyes to their drinks or plates of food. It felt as if the entire building held its collective breath, pressure mounting so quickly I could feel it strain against my skin.

"What are you all looking at?" he barked. "I got something on my face, Kipper?" He turned to his friend, who snickered. Pax continued roaming the tables, taking in the rotted wooden ceiling and the flies buzzing around rusted sconces. Some conversations began to pick up again as people tried to put the guards out of mind, but the voices were stilted. Forced.

Finally, Pax, Kipper, and the two nameless guards made their way back to the bar. "Four of your finest ales," Pax said to the bartender, who nodded and busied himself with their tankards.

A bit of tension released, and chatter grew again. I turned my head to hear the guards better, seeing my sister brush hair behind her ear to do the same. Leaving now would only make them suspicious, so all we could do was wait it out.

"Say, barkeep, where are you from, anyway?" Kipper asked.

"Here," he replied briskly.

The fourth guard snorted. "Quite an establishment you have. Been in your family long?"

The bartender slammed four glasses in front of them. "I was born here in the capital, if that's what you're getting at. *Sir,*" he added, the word practically a hiss.

Pax raised his hands in mock defense. "Hey now, we're just making conversation. You've got nothing to hide, do you, friend?"

"Of course not."

"Good, good," Pax said, stroking his dark beard. "Wouldn't want that, would we?"

Kipper flicked a silver coin onto the bar and grabbed his tankard. When he took a sip, he grimaced. "Tastes like piss."

"What did you expect down here?" the third guard said with a chuckle that made my teeth grind. "Provincers who don't have enough magic or coin to wipe their—"

"I think you should leave." A chair scraped against wood as the man from before stood, his chest puffed out in false bravado as he faced the four guards.

I closed my eyes and stifled a groan.

Pax's face broke into a wolfish grin. "Boys, what do we have here?" He strolled to the man, crossing his arms over his muscular chest. "Someone with a pair of balls on them?"

"We're just trying to enjoy our evening," the man said, his confidence slipping by the second. "Y-you're making everyone uncomfortable."

Pax raised an eyebrow. "Oh, I'm sorry. I had no idea." Quick as lightning, he grabbed the chair of a woman in the table next to them, twisting her so she faced him. Her companions gave a gasp of shock at the movement.

"Am I making you uncomfortable?" Pax leered at her. Eyes wide and frightened, she shook her head.

"And what about you?" The guard clapped his hand down on the shoulder of someone at a nearby booth. They cringed and stuttered a half-hearted "No, sir," eyeing Pax's hand as if it were a venomous snake.

"You see?" He turned his attention back to the man still standing. "I think *you're* the one making people uncomfortable. Now, we can't have that, can we?" He nodded to Kipper, who gave him a vile smile. In a single breath, shadows billowed from Kipper's hands, wrapping around the man and pulling his hands behind his back. He let out a yelp before more shadows stuffed themselves down his throat. His pleas turned into strangled muffles. Two of the guards grabbed him by the elbow and dragged him out the front door, the other pair following close behind. Their victim eyed his friends at his table as he thrashed against his magical bindings, but everyone stayed silent, eyes pinned to the ground.

That was how it was here. You lowered your eyes to escape your shame, praying you never caught the attention of those in power who reveled in the weakness of others.

But not all of us.

Before Rissa could stop me, I slid from my seat and prowled toward the front door, pulling my hood low over my head. My henbane rings seemed to buzz with pent-up energy, as if they knew a fight was brewing.

Slipping out the front door, I followed the sounds of boots and the man's dull cries until I saw their shadows sneak into an alley down the street from the tavern. A moment later, I heard flesh pound against flesh, and a crack rang through the night.

A growl ripped from me as I swiftly turned down the alleyway. Pax and Kipper were chuckling as one of the other guards lunged, aiming another punch to the man's sagging face. His mouth and hands were still gagged and bound by shadows, tears and blood falling down his bruised cheek.

Taking a pinch of hellebore root and placing it on my tongue, I quickly brought the henbane and amaranth rings on my middle fingers together and whispered, "*Vellus.*"

The invisibility charm worked immediately. The spell pressed on my chest as my body disappeared from sight.

A whimper left the man's shadowed lips, snapping the last of my restraint. Before the guard could slam his fist into the man's face again, I darted forward and grabbed his wrist, yanking it back until his shoulder was wrenched out of its socket with a sickening pop.

He staggered backward. The other three guards unsheathed their swords as their eyes scanned the darkness for their invisible foe. Shadows retreated from the man at the wall as Kipper, the Shadow Wielder, redirected his focus.

"Get out of here," I whispered in the man's ear. He jumped and let out a cry of surprise, but had the sense not to question his rescue. Pushing off the wall, he stumbled out of the alley, eager to get away from the bloodshed.

"Show yourself, little trickster," Pax crooned. "Your games are fun, but you're no match for four of us."

"Want to bet?" a sweet voice said from behind me. Two small daggers whizzed from the darkness and embedded themselves in Kipper's thigh and the shoulder of another.

I whirled to find a figure cloaked in burgundy flashing me a crooked smile from beneath her hood.

Shouts rang from Kipper and his companions as the three injured guards struggled to stand, swords abandoned on the ground in an attempt to stem the flow of blood from their wounds. One cradled his dislocated arm against his chest. Pax, the only one left unharmed, snarled in Rissa's direction.

Fates, my sister was dramatic. Rolling my eyes, I released my invisibility spell and materialized before them. Pax's gaze flitted back and forth between our hidden features as his fellow guards moaned at his back.

Rissa slowly pulled a third dagger from her cloak and whirled it between her fingers. Lowering her voice into an icy semblance of the woman I knew, she said, "I will give you five seconds to leave this alley before I bury this blade in your skull."

His jaw twitched, arm flexing as if ready to attack. "The emperor will hear about this," he said through gritted teeth.

Rissa cocked her head. "Will he also hear how you terrorized a tavern full of people? How you tortured a defenseless man?" She flicked her wrist and Pax flinched as her dagger soared past him, skimming his cheek and leaving a thin scratch. A warning.

"Better get your story straight," she said. "Our great emperor will never believe you were bested by some low-life, province-loving scum."

Hatred dripped from Pax's red features as he stared her down, nostrils flaring. A beat later, he glanced at the other three and stiffly nodded, hauling the guard with the knife in his leg to his feet.

The four of them limped toward us. We backed further into the shadows as they neared the entrance to the alleyway, careful to stay concealed. Pax turned to face us before they disappeared from sight and muttered, "You better watch your back."

Rissa's white teeth shone from beneath her hood. "Shouldn't be a problem. It's a rather nice back, from what I'm told."

As they ambled off into the darkened street, I mumbled, "I had that covered."

She laughed. "Sure, you did."

"Always such a show-off."

We waited several minutes before making our way back to the tavern, which had returned to its normal liveliness.

Nights such as this were common. Especially in the south sector, which was known for its acceptance of provincers. People who "didn't belong" in the capital.

And every night, I had to remind myself what we were working toward. What this was all *for*. A better future. A different world. The hope was in our hands—we just had to take it.

13

ROSE

I splashed cold water on my face then gripped the edge of the granite countertop in my personal washroom, watching the water drip, drip, drip from my skin and onto the porcelain bowl. Gazing at my reflection in the gold-lined mirror, it was hard not to notice the shadows under my green eyes, the pale sheen to my skin.

My attention snagged on the locket hanging around my neck, the one my aunt and uncle had given me when I turned thirteen. The gilded oval face had a single rose delicately etched into it, and it opened to reveal two small charcoal portraits of my parents, Hamilton and Ayla Wolff. I fingered the locket, wedging my nail between the divide and cracking it open to stare at their miniscule likeness.

I briefly wondered how they would feel about this turn of events, with me taking Ragnar's place as the Feywood challenger to uncover secrets of the emperor. Would they be proud that I was working toward something I believed in? For something larger than myself? Would they be worried for my safety, insistent like Morgana that this wasn't my burden to bear?

I closed the necklace with a quiet *snap* and kissed the back of it, the metal cold against my lips, before tucking it into my shirt.

Quickly running my fingers through my hair, I braided it down my back and secured it with a leather strap.

A knock sounded at the door to my bedchamber. I paused, peering around at the door. I figured it was Aunt Morgana and Beau coming to say goodnight. After the briefing, I'd been shown to my private chambers on the third floor—accompanied by a stern talking-to from Horace on attacking fellow challengers in the palace. I'd immediately sent word to learn where my family would be staying. They were in a separate wing, closer to the infirmary, and had wanted to see me one last time before the first trial began in the morning.

I crossed the room and pulled the door open, expecting to see the familiar dark hair of my aunt and lanky form of my cousin.

Neither one stood in the doorway.

Instead, Nox leaned against the frame, his arms crossed over his chest, silver rings shining in the firelight. "Well, you sure made an impression today."

"Why am I not surprised you're here?" I asked with a sigh.

He grinned, his dark blue eyes flaring with mischief. "Are you going to let me inside?"

"Wasn't planning on it, no."

Shrugging, he said, "Probably wise. Don't let anyone in without first knowing who it is and what they want. That breaks the wards."

I pursed my lips, mirroring his stance and crossing my arms. "What do you mean?"

"All of our chambers are warded against intruders, but if you give someone permission to enter, the wards are disabled against them for the rest of your stay."

Raising an eyebrow, I hummed in response. Horace had mentioned the rooms being warded, but not whether other areas of the palace were, as well.

Nox continued to stare at me, and I shook my head. "I'm still not letting you in, Nox. Not after finding out you'll be able to enter whenever you please. I don't need to wake up one morning with a knife pressed to my throat."

He lifted a hand to his chest in feigned offense. "After all we've been through, this is how I'm treated?"

I rolled my eyes but couldn't help the snort that escaped me. "What do you want?"

"Just to make sure you're still alive. Callum is pissed, as you can imagine. He's practically calling for your head on a platter."

"Who?"

"The Iluze prick you tried to kill."

Oh, *him*. I scoffed. "I didn't try to *kill* him. He had plenty of time before that happened."

"Ah, so this is a common enough occurrence for you, viper?" Nox asked, a smirk crossing his tan features. "You almost took out the competition before this tournament even began. That was, if I recall, breaking one of the only rules we were given."

"First of all, that's a bit dramatic," I said. "Second of all, he deserved it."

"Be that as it may, you're putting a target on your back. You need to be careful."

I knew he was right—I'd been too reactive. Too volatile. I often let my anger get the best of me, the simmering rage that sat so close to the surface easily goaded when pushed just a *bit* over the edge. And that Illusionist—Callum, Nox called him—had practically shoved me off the cliff with his mind tricks and hateful words.

There was something about Illusionists that got to me.

"I can handle being a target," I said, my pride peeking its head out and sniffing the air.

"I don't doubt it. But tell me, Rose, did you come to the capital alone?" I froze, the blood draining from my face. He must have noticed my reaction, for he added, "Can you handle *them* being one?"

I hadn't even thought of Ragnar, Morgana, or Beau when I'd retaliated against Callum, of how each of my actions could lead directly back to them. Even though putting innocent civilians in harm's way had been expressly forbidden, I wouldn't put it past someone to disobey if I made them mad enough.

Fates, I was an *idiot*. If anything happened to my family because of *me*...

I had to pull myself together. I couldn't let my emotions control me, those hot surges of anger that consumed and made me lash out irrationally. I had a mission to accomplish and people to keep safe.

"You're right," I conceded quietly. "I won't let it happen again." I made a mental note to find Beau and Morgana before the night was over and ensure they kept plenty of protection charms on them.

Nox nodded. "Oh, by the way, I met the last challenger after you stormed out of the great hall. *Callista*," he said, dragging out the word. "The Lightbender from Emberfell. She's a crowd favorite, I can already tell. Knows how to put on a good show. She had the entire court entranced with her fancy light magic, like some performing monkey." He chuckled darkly. "I could have shown them a few tricks myself, but I doubt they would have applauded me."

"What do you shift into, anyway?" I blurted, unable to stifle my curiosity.

"That's a rather personal question, darling."

I rolled my eyes. "Well, you've seen my magic at work."

"So this is an 'I'll show you mine if you show me yours' type of request?" he asked, wagging his eyebrows. I put a finger to my temple. Keeping up with this man was exhausting.

Laughing at the annoyance on my face, he said, "If I ever have to shift, you'll know. I plan to lay as low as possible until absolutely necessary." He pushed off from the door frame. "I'm glad we had this talk. Good luck with the first trial tomorrow, viper," he said, then turned on his heels and disappeared down the empty corridor.

THE
FIRST
TRIAL

14

ROSE

I dreamt of butterflies.

Delicate blue wings laced with black and yellow fluttered onto the tip of my finger, a faint tickle making me shiver when it brushed against my skin.

In my dream, I smiled.

Until blood began to drip from the wings and down my hand.

Ruby red glistened over my skin, coating it in the thick, hot liquid. I jerked my hand back with a scream and the butterfly flitted away, but still, the blood came.

On both my hands now. The ground, my feet, my legs. I couldn't run from it.

Knock. Knock. Knock.

I woke from my nightmare with a jolt. The sound of something scratching against the wood floor drew my attention to the door. My fingers instantly closed around the handle of my dagger beneath the pillow.

Squinting, I scanned the room by the faint light of the rising sun coming from the window. The knocking had stopped, and the air was silent once more, save for the sound of my heart pounding in my ears. I released the hold on my dagger and scrubbed a hand over my face with a groan. *It's too early for this.*

Untangling my legs from the sheets, I climbed out of bed, stretching as I padded across the floor to the door. On the ground rested a folded envelope with the official seal of the Veridian Empire staring back at me. I cracked the door open to stick my head out and see if anyone was there, but the corridor was empty, except for Horace. His back was to me as he paced down at the end of the hall. Had he been there all night?

When he turned and caught my eye, he gave a grunt, then continued to ignore me.

Not a morning person either, I took it. I had a feeling we would get along splendidly.

A flutter of nerves erupted in my stomach as I shut the door with a soft *snick* and crouched to pick up the envelope, finding my name on the back in bold letters and the title *Feywood Challenger* written below it.

Today was the first trial.

I hadn't had much time to think about what this challenge might be. The past couple of days had been such a whirlwind, but in hindsight, it was probably best that I wasn't able to dwell on it for long. It would've only added to the unease and anxiety building in my mind.

Now that it was here, however, my thoughts raced, apprehension creeping in tenfold.

We had record books of the past Decemvirates; whether the tales told within them were entirely fact or fiction, I'd never know. One that stuck out in my mind was that two centuries ago, the head architect at the time had experimented on a reptilian Shifter and found a way to transform him into a mythical dragon, twenty times the size of any human, with claws that could shred skin and lungs that breathed fire. The challengers were tasked with escaping this beast before it burnt them to a crisp.

Another story was that the challengers were transported to the Shadowmere Wastelands of Tenebra, which were cursed by ancient spirits and corrupted shadow magic. Challengers slowly lost their minds, and if rumors were true, they had to cut the tournament short, as no one was fit to continue competing after that.

I didn't necessarily believe everything I'd heard or read. People wove intricate stories over the years, turning the truth into larger-than-life tales of impossible quests.

Some of the more *common* trials that had been used often over the centuries included hidden magical objects the challengers had to find, dalliances with poisons, or being forced to escape from somewhere in an allotted period of time. Once, I'd read the challengers were all dropped in the middle of an enchanted forest without access to their magic and had to track their way out.

I had no idea what to expect of this Decemvirate. Lark had said the theme of the first trial would be to test our intellect. That could mean any number of things, and unfortunately, I doubted it would have anything to do with Alchemy—the only area I considered myself intelligent.

These other five challengers have had months, if not years, to train and prepare. To study past tournaments and develop strategies, to practice their magic and defensive skills.

I'd had twenty-four hours. And very little sleep.

I licked my lips as my fingers danced across the edge of the wax seal, my heart beating like wings in my chest. Hurriedly ripping the envelope open, I unfolded the letter.

And let out an annoyed exhale.

It was blank.

"What—" I flipped the paper over, examining every inch of it and the envelope it came in. Nothing.

"Is this supposed to be funny?" I muttered to myself.

What I didn't expect was for the paper to answer me.

Ink blossomed on the cream surface, cursive letters forming as if an invisible hand were penning them before my eyes.

Hello, Rose Wolff.

I yelped and dropped the paper. It fluttered to the floor, the words disappearing as quickly as they'd appeared. Blinking, I rubbed at my eye with the heel of my hand and peered down at it again.

Enchanted parchment. Hadn't seen that before. Curiosity got the best of me and I knelt to retrieve it, running my fingers along the creases. This brand of magic was intriguing. How did it work? What kind of enchantment was used?

"Incredible," I marveled in a whisper.

More words materialized in response.

Thank you. I am courtesy of Larken Everest, Head Architect of the Veridian Empire.

My eyes widened and I let out a small laugh. Magical *and* polite.

"Are you...here to help me?" I asked tentatively. This was a piece of paper. I was talking to a *piece of paper*.

And it was talking back.

I am here to instruct you on your first trial, a challenge of intellect, cunning, and intuition.

I waited for more, but it went silent. Pursing my lips, I said, "Great. So where exactly do I start?"

A moment passed, and then script materialized like magic to form long lines of poetry.

Your first trial begins when the clock strikes nine.
An artifact of blood you then must find.
Hidden in truth across the eye
Six paths to victory each do lie.

Well you will stride if you fear not the flight,
Follow the imprint where paths unite.
One with the beasts of wild and wise

A shift in heart will help you to rise.
Reality is not always the truth—
Deception prevails where words do soothe.
The dawn of faith comes with new light
And glory often favors grace over might.
But navigate shadows with precision and care,
For one cannot seek that which is not there.
Find me with charm where bones and echoes reside;
It is cloaked in the day, and revealed in the night.

Only one shall reward you that which you seek,
And be wary of enemies alone you may meet.
By the midnight toll, you must claim your fate—
Welcome, Rose Wolff, to the thirty-second Decemvirate.

It stopped, the black words gleaming like fresh ink.

A riddle.

I twisted my lips and gripped the parchment in my fist. I should've expected as much for a trial about *intellect*. A fight, I could prepare for. Or some sort of magical entrapment, perhaps. I was in my element when forced to think on my feet and react quickly. But riddles? Those required a patience I didn't have. My fingers itched to act, to *do* something, to feel the familiar crunch of dried herbs and nettles, the smooth curves of vials and potions and stones.

Quickly rereading the lines, two things immediately stood out: one was that this was some sort of hunt for an artifact. The second was the last part—*by the midnight toll, you must claim your fate.* I only had until midnight tonight to find whatever it was I was supposed to search for.

Rolling my shoulders, I grabbed my travel bag and changed into a pair of thick leggings, a tight-fitting black shirt, and my dark green vest inlaid with numerous pockets. I slipped my dagger into one of the side pockets and rummaged through my pouches of herbs for what I needed to replace in my father's little satchel.

Instinctively, I went for my normal charms—thistle for banishing spells and curses, a vial of cedarwood oil for healing, and my special amaranth stems for protection, along with several other basics. All the while, I let my mind wander through the words on the paper.

Your first trial begins when the clock strikes nine. I glanced at the clock on my wall—it was a half hour till. *An artifact of blood you then must find.* That didn't sound particularly pleasant. Blood made me think of violence, but surely the trial wouldn't be asking us to harm someone?

I had no idea what "hidden in truth across the eye" meant. But six paths to victory...there were six challengers, of course. Six different kinds of magic. Six provinces. That couldn't be a coincidence.

Looking back at the riddle, I read it through again, taking time to focus on the longer middle section. It still read like a bunch of nonsense, but slowly, I began to pick up on certain words. Shadows and light, beasts, charms. There were references to all six of the magic types embedded in the poem. Clues for each of us, perhaps?

Only one shall reward you that which you seek. Only one what? Artifact? Clue? Impatience already burned under my skin, and it had only been a few minutes. I needed to *act*, not sit here rereading words on a paper. I hastily laced up my boots, grabbed the parchment, and hooked my herb pouch to my vest, comforted by its weight swinging against my hips as I strode to the door and twisted the handle.

It wouldn't budge.

Forehead scrunching, I gripped the knob harder, pulling with more force. Still, the door refused to move.

I tugged as hard as I could, jiggling the handle and throwing my weight into it, then let out a frustrated sigh. Was this some sort of joke? Had someone locked me in? The locking mechanism on my side of the door was untouched—I turned it back and forth to be safe, but it stayed sealed shut.

Grumbling, I unlatched my pouch and took a pinch of crushed dandelion leaf and whispered the spell for opening. "*Vata lai.*"

Nothing.

"Am I going to have to break down this door?" I muttered, flicking the end of my braid over my shoulder in irritation.

Movement on the parchment in my other hand caught my eye. The riddle faded away, replaced by something new.

Patience is a virtue of wisdom.

My lips thinned. I was being lectured by a piece of paper.

The clock read three minutes until nine. I flexed my hand, forcing myself not to reach for the door and try again. It was obvious this little condescending riddle master was keeping me prisoner in my own room until the clock struck nine.

Where was I going to go, anyway? The part of the clues that hinted at Alchemy spoke of "bones and echoes." The only thing I could think of was some sort of graveyard—plenty of bones lived there. But I knew nothing about the capital. I would need a map, at the very least.

Maybe that's where I would start. Find a record hall or library that would let me see maps of Veridia City.

My gaze flicked up to the clock, following the big hand as it ticked, ticked, ticked closer to nine o'clock. I looked down at the parchment one final time to catch new words scrolling across.

Let the Decemvirate begin.

The handle gave way beneath my touch, and I bolted out the door.

———

I BARELY MADE it down two hallways before I knew something was off.

The corridor was silent, the air heavy and strained. Every hair on the back of my neck rose as I turned another corner and reached into my satchel to place an amaranth stem of protection on my tongue.

Where was Horace? He'd been there this morning when I peeked my head out the door, but now he was nowhere to be found. I quickly retraced my steps back to my room, thinking I'd gone the wrong direction to get to the main stairwell, when I saw—

Was that *blood*?

Small beads of red were splattered across the dark floor mere feet from my door, creating a crimson path leading down the hall and to a small alcove on the left. With alarm singing in my veins, I followed the blood with my dagger in hand until...

I saw him.

Black boots peeked out from the shadowed nook of the corridor. My hand trembled as I crept forward. Inch by inch, my eyes trailed over the length of the body, over the familiar silver guard's uniform and long blonde beard smothered in blood. A pool of it rested by his head.

Red leaked from his slit throat.

The edges of Horace's body seemed to flicker as my stomach fell to my feet, a memory resurfacing. His form was replaced with another, more familiar one—

I backed away quickly, bile rushing up my throat. Who would have done this? And right outside my room—it must have been *seconds* after I left. What if they'd been targeting me?

My breaths came out ragged as I turned to race down the hallway, only to find myself face to face with a haughty smirk. Smooth hands grasped my elbows while a cruel chuckle echoed off the walls.

"Where are you heading so quickly, Feywood?"

I glared into the dark eyes of Callum, the Iluze challenger I'd almost suffocated the day before. Rage burned in my core.

"Did you do this?" I snarled, yanking out of his grasp. "Did you kill that guard?" Without realizing it, my blade was already aimed at his chest, the sweet amaranth charm on my tongue itching to be put into action.

"What are you talking about, girl?" a gruff voice said.

The air left my lungs. I spun around to find Horace standing behind me, not a speck of blood on him, his face twisted in confusion as his beady eyes flashed between Callum and me.

My pulse pounded in every inch of me. The shock of seeing his throat slit and bleeding to him appearing as good as new in the span of a heartbeat was making my head spin, unable to keep up with reality.

It was an illusion.

Horace must have seen something in my features, for he swiftly side-stepped me and put himself between my body and Callum's. I couldn't turn around to watch, couldn't make my limbs move, couldn't hear past the ringing in my ears. It was like I was frozen in place, burrowing in on myself as my thoughts tunneled down the pit I worked so hard to keep covered. The pit I never let myself remember.

I was five years old, playing with my favorite stuffed doll in our front yard. Papa had told me to come back inside as soon as the sun started to go down, but I still had a few minutes left. I twirled around with her small hand in mine, the wind rustling through the skirt of my dress.

Suddenly, a blue butterfly appeared on my arm. I giggled as its wings tickled my skin, then gasped in delight. It started to change color, going from blue to pink to yellow every time I blinked.

Three more just like it flew from beneath my hair, and, gaping at them in wonder, I shook my head to see if more would come out.

They were so pretty. Papa would love to see these. I reached out a hand to try and catch one, but they flew away too fast. Letting out a giggle, I chased them around the yard, clapping as they shifted from one bright color to the next.

The butterflies led me to the big tree a little ways from the house. I stopped when they flew straight toward two strange men. The biggest one held his finger out and let the pretty butterflies rest on top before they all disappeared in the blink of an eye.

He looked at me and smiled.

I clutched my dolly to my chest, turning my head back to the house. Papa was going to be mad at me. I ran too far away.

"Hi there, Rose," the one who'd had the butterflies said. "Is your father home? We're good friends of his, and we wanted to come by to surprise him."

I smiled shyly and swayed on my feet. He knew my name—Papa probably told him, if they were friends. Twisting a strand of hair around my finger, I said, "He's home. I'm s'posed to get back before the sun goes down, so I have to hurry!"

"Well then, let's go!" the other man said cheerfully, his grin wide and playful. "We wouldn't want you to get in trouble."

I nodded enthusiastically and turned on my heel, dashing back to the house. I hoped Papa wouldn't be too mad that I was late.

When I burst through the front door, my papa looked up at me from his chair by the fire.

"Papa! Some friends of yours came by to see you!" I said, setting my dolly on the table in the entry.

He scrunched his forehead. "Rose, sweetheart, what are you talking—"

The door behind me swung open, and Papa jumped to his feet. A big hand grabbed me by the waist and covered my mouth before I could scream.

Papa's face was like an angry cloud when he shouted my name. I kicked against the man holding me as my chest suddenly felt too tight, like someone was squeezing the breath out of me. In a second, it was over, and I felt a huge blast of magic fill the room, knocking the scary men to their feet. I fell to the ground and Papa scooped me up. He wiped the tears from my cheeks as I cried against him.

"I need you to listen to me very carefully," he said, hurrying through the house with me clinging to his neck. We passed the kitchen and my bedroom, then turned toward Papa's office. "Until I come get you, I want you to stay hidden in here. Alright, sweetheart?"

He set me down on my feet, cupping my cheeks in his hands. "I'll come get you in a few minutes, I promise. Can you be a big girl for me? Be my brave Rose?"

I sniffled and nodded, and he swiped another tear away. Down the hall, the sound of scuffling and footsteps grew closer. The bad men were coming.

When my father stood, I wrapped my arms around his leg, unable to stop the tears dripping off my nose. "Papa, no! Don't go!" I cried. I wanted to be brave like he said, but I was so scared. Why were those people here? Were they going to hurt us?

"It's going to be okay, sweetheart." He unwound my hands from his leg and pulled me into a tight hug, kissing my forehead. "I love you, Rose. Stay here."

Before I could argue, he strode out the door and shut it behind him. I felt that same pressure and burst of magic, like what happened when he did a spell.

I hurried backward and ran beneath Papa's desk, huddling close to the wall. Every shout, every clatter, every thump made me squeeze my eyes tighter. The men shouted and something banged against the door, and I heard it creak open.

Peeking out from under the desk, I squinted through puffy eyes to see if anyone was there, but the loud noises had stopped. I rubbed at my face and slowly crawled out.

"Papa?" I whispered once I reached the door. When nobody answered, I slipped through the small opening, then looked down the hallway.

There were black marks like smoke all along the floor. The air smelled like it did when Papa would light a fire in the backyard, and I'd fall asleep listening to him and Aunt Ana and Uncle Ragnar talking. Some of the pictures that used to hang on the walls were smashed on the ground.

My hands shook as I walked closer to the living room. Something smelled funny. Like copper that stung my nose. Where was Papa? He said it would only be a few minutes.

Right as I made it to the corner, I heard a choking sound.

My feet stopped.

There was a shadow of someone tall on the ground in front of me. Leaning forward to peer around the corner, I saw the man with the butterflies standing in front of the fireplace, pushing my papa against the mantle.

I almost stepped out of my hiding spot to run for him when Papa saw me. His eyes widened and he whispered something I couldn't hear, but then the air felt too heavy on my chest. It was hard to breathe. He must have cast a spell.

"Branock Aris sends his love," the man holding Papa said in a scary voice, before pulling out a knife and—

"Papa!" I shrieked, my hands reaching out to him as I tried to run forward. But I couldn't. My skin hit something solid, an invisible wall blocking my path. I kept crying for him, hot tears burning my cheeks, my throat already sore and my body aching from the effort of trying to push past his spell.

I watched, unable to move, as my papa slumped to the ground. Blood poured from his neck where the man had cut. I could barely see through my thick tears, but I swore the man looked back in my direction, his eyes brushing over where I stood as if he had no idea I was there. Then, he and the second man turned and ran out the front door, leaving me alone.

Papa choked, a horrible, gurgling sound, and then the invisible wall went away. I dashed to his side and saw the gash on his neck, the thick, red blood streaming from it like a river, covering the floor in front of the fireplace.

I fell to my knees with a scream.

"Wolff? Wolff?" A hand shook my shoulder, turning me. "Was this man hurting you?" Horace asked, gesturing to Callum.

"What would it matter if I was?" Callum sneered. "The first trial has begun. There are no rules."

I gasped as their exchange ripped me from the memory, forcing my breaths to even out as I met Callum's smirk.

"What's wrong, Feywood?" he asked. "Can't handle a little trick?"

A sinking weight settled on my chest, adrenaline pumping through me as the image of my father's murder burned on the backs of my lids. Wiping any hint of emotion from my features, I held Callum's gaze, unwilling to give the reaction he sought.

"He's right," I said, voice steely. "There are no rules. I'm fine, Horace."

I couldn't deal with this right now, the mind games and retaliation. With the small hint of amaranth still on my tongue, I whispered a spell for protection and strode past Callum, getting away as swiftly as I could while promising to make him regret this once I could *think* again. Once I could breathe.

Once I wasn't falling apart.

"I'll be seeing you," he called after my back, and I thought I heard Horace say something in response, but I was too far down the hall to care.

The pounding in my ears grew louder, my vision graying around the edges as I twisted the knob of the closest door I could find. *Locked.* The next one was, too. My thoughts spiraled as I tried to find a private place to collect myself.

I stumbled to the end of the corridor, spotting a narrow staircase spiraling to the floor above. Without thinking, I forced myself up the steps, my hands seeking out the grooves in the stone as I climbed. The cold, rough edges on my fingers kept the dizziness at bay and helped me stay grounded until I reached the next landing.

Before I could catch my breath, I collided with a hard body.

"Careful, there," a deep voice said, and I looked up to find a pair of eyes.

A pair of strikingly familiar onyx eyes.

I stiffened. It was him.

The man from the forest.

15

LEO

I t was her. The Alchemist from that night. The girl with the spell that leveled a *fully grown* snow leopard Shifter.

I wracked my thoughts for why she would be *here*, of all places, when I remembered—she'd been traveling in one of the palace's carriages that night. That meant she was either a highly regarded spectator, a challenger herself, or family to someone involved.

Her skin was warm beneath her black clothing as I reached out to steady her. Dark hair was pulled back into a braid, small tendrils breaking free and framing her sharp cheekbones. What gave me pause was the sheen of sweat on her olive features, the dilated pupils, the shaking hands.

I knew I didn't have time for this. I wasn't even supposed to *be* here, especially after the conversation at the Drakin's Lair last night. Rissa could tell how irritated I was that they'd chosen someone else for the task, and she more than likely expected me to do something rash. If my sister caught word I'd disobeyed her and snuck in to search for evidence of Gayl's Grimoire, she'd wring my neck.

But something was obviously wrong.

"Are you alright?" I asked, turning her body so we were out of sight from anyone coming up the stairs.

Her eyes snapped to mine, recognition dawning before she closed them and slumped against the stone wall. The sight was so at odds with the fearsome Alchemist from the other night, whose green pools had blazed with dark, cold fire when facing those Shifters.

"I'm fine. I just...need a minute," she said, her voice softer than I remembered.

I didn't have a minute. I could hear voices coming from the other end of the hall, far too close for comfort. If the emperor discovered I was here, it could jeopardize our entire plan *and* put my sister and myself in grave danger.

A frustrated noise built in the back of my throat. I glanced to my left before taking her by the elbow and leading her to a nearby alcove, hidden by a large woven tapestry.

"Here," I said. "Nobody will bother you."

"Why did you help me?" she asked suspiciously, her face slowly regaining color.

My brow furrowed. "You look like you need help."

She shook her head. "I mean the other night. In the forest. That was you, wasn't it? What were you doing there?"

So, she *did* recognize me. I carefully considered my words. "I suppose you looked like you needed help then, as well."

Footsteps sounded from the other side of the tapestry, and we both instinctively took a step further into the wall, her chest brushing against mine as she held her breath. This close, I could feel the anxious heat coming from her in waves, the scent of florals and something earthy reaching my nose when she turned her neck to look at me.

The air was heavy, neither of us willing to breathe as the voices lingered mere feet from where we hid. Her pupils had finally gone back to normal, but slight tremors still flowed through her body. When she swallowed, I involuntarily tracked the movement before flicking my attention to the tapestry. I could no longer see outlines of boots beneath, nor hear voices of guests passing by.

To be sure they had truly left, I opened up the Shifter half of my blood like one would open a door, listening to them retreat further down the stone stairwell.

I instantly realized my mistake.

With my Shifter senses, her sweet scent of lavender and sage mixed with earthy undertones of amaranth—the same herb I smelled that night in the forest—was infinitely stronger, drawing me in and slowly wrapping around me like smoke. The erratic beat of her heart was heightened in my ears, the pulse at her neck thrumming with life as she took a shallow breath, her eyes shifting back to me.

"I think they're gone," she whispered. Her words fanned across my cheeks, breath hot against my skin.

I hesitated before nodding, quickly slamming a wall up on my Shifter instincts. Still, neither of us moved.

"What were you running from?" I asked.

"What were *you* hiding from?" she countered.

The corner of my mouth twitched. "I've helped you twice now. You first."

Her lips pursed as she leaned further away from me. I fought the urge to curve my body toward her in response. "I didn't ask for your help either time, you know."

My eyes widened slightly. *Stubborn, this one.* "Most people say 'thank you' when someone saves their life."

"Yes, most do," she said, brushing a loose strand of hair behind her ear before turning and pushing back the tapestry.

"I hope you can get away from it," I murmured before she was out of sight. She looked back at me, a question in her gaze. "Whatever it is you're running from."

She blinked twice, her eyes flitting between mine like she wasn't sure what to make of me. "Thank you for helping us that night," she finally said. "I—I wouldn't be here if it weren't for you."

"I don't know if I believe that. You were holding your own there, if I remember correctly."

The woman faced me fully, features lit with suspicious curiosity as her arms crossed over her chest. The motion drew my attention to her curves, to the way her black shirt hugged her body where it met the top of her tight leggings, before I forced my stare upward.

Get a grip, Leo. Fates, I didn't even know this woman's name. I needed to get back to Rissa and the others.

"Why were you in those woods, anyway?" she repeated her earlier question.

I glanced down the hallway, expecting more passersby to appear at any moment. "It's the Decemvirate," I answered, my tone low and hurried. "You weren't the only one who needed help that night."

To my surprise, she snorted. "Some sort of vigilante, then? Trying to be everyone's hero?"

Something clicked against the hard floor nearby, and I stepped closer to her. "I never said I was a hero."

Her eyes narrowed. "What are you—"

I pressed my hand to her lips, silencing her. "Someone's coming," I murmured, close enough that my nose brushed the top of her head. She went stiff beneath my touch, her breaths shaking in an attempt to stay quiet. Slowly, I felt them even out, matching with mine as her body began to relax. Her nearness sent warmth coursing through me. I couldn't seem to remove my gaze from hers, even as the tapping of heels on stone faded away.

I saw so much in those emerald eyes. Ferocity, caution, pain, loneliness. The guarded expression of someone forced to build a wall, suddenly stripped bare by a stranger in a dimly lit corridor.

Removing my hand from her skin, I swallowed, silently chiding myself for getting in this position. I'd almost been spotted not once, but *twice*. I should be out of the palace and halfway back to my family's cottage by now.

"Why do I get the feeling you're not supposed to be here?" she asked, a bit breathlessly.

"And here I was, thinking I was being subtle."

She cocked her head, unamused. "What's your name, anyway?"

"Wolff!" a familiar voice shouted, coming from the stairs. She jerked her head toward it, her eyes widening.

I cursed under my breath. That sounded like Horace, and if he knew I was here, he would tell my sister in a heartbeat. Pulling the hood of my cloak over my head, I quickly backed away and disappeared down the hall before she could say anything else.

16

ROSE

"What happened back there, Wolff?" Horace asked as he guided me down the stairs and back to the third floor. "With that Illusionist?"

I'd managed to momentarily push Callum's cruel trick aside after the shock of finding the same stranger from the forest again, but as we entered the hallway where I'd seen Horace's dead body, everything slammed back into me.

The memory of my father's death was a wound that had never fully healed. I'd covered it for two decades with layers of flesh, bone, and pure nerve, pushing it down so far I'd convinced myself it hadn't happened. I hadn't thought of that day in *years*, beyond the ghost of a scar burning beneath my flesh.

Now, the scab had been ripped open, and I couldn't stitch the mangled skin back together, no matter how hard I tried.

It had been my fault. *I'd* led those Illusionists straight to my father. I'd been too trusting, too young and naive to see the danger they posed. And because of me, my father had been murdered.

I could still feel his blood, warm from the gaping cut in his neck, pouring onto my little hands as I knelt over his body and screamed.

I could still see his dark blue-gray eyes fixed on the ceiling, glassy and unmoving despite my pleas for him to *wake up*.

I could still smell the lingering herbs from his charms, weighing down on my senses and making me dizzy.

Aunt Morgana and Uncle Ragnar had found me hours later, lying next to him with my arms flung around his chest and my body covered in blood. I didn't remember much of the following months. Or years, if I was being honest. People didn't know how to act around me, how to talk to me—the orphan Alchemist, whose mother had died giving birth to her and whose father was murdered before her very eyes. They kept their distance, afraid of getting too close to the strange, quiet, cursed little girl.

Rumors *still* circulated. What had Hamilton Wolff gotten himself into? How had two mysterious men from Iluze crossed the border undetected and snuck onto the property? What did they want from the Wolff family?

I never found out the answers. Any time Morgana and Ragnar had tried to talk to me about it, I'd shut down like I did moments ago. I couldn't do it. I couldn't remember. I didn't *want* to remember. But the dam had broken, the suppressed memory pushing and surging forward, and suddenly, it was *all* I could remember.

And one phrase stood out among the rest. Like a slow-burning flame, a festering poison that slithered on the fringes of my mind, fueling my rage, my pain.

"Branock Aris sends his love."

I'd forgotten that snarled confession, but twenty years of repressed wrath and blame rested on that single sentence. *Somehow* Branock Aris was responsible for my father's death.

My jaw clenched. It was a shame he was already dead.

Horace grunted and pulled me to a stop, crossing his arms in front of his large chest. "What did that boy make you see?" he asked, his normally gruff voice surprisingly gentle.

I understood now why I had such a fear around people like Callum. *Illusionists.* Why he had ignited something colder, something deeper than mere anger when he'd used his powers on me in the Decemvirate meeting. I *hated* that he could incite such dread, that he now held this power over me. The mere thought of him made me tighten my fingers around the pouch of herbs dangling from my vest.

I gritted my teeth. "I don't want to talk about it."

"Well, that's too bad."

"I was under the impression they paid you to guard the palace, not talk to me."

Horace scrubbed his face with exasperation, and I thought I heard a grumbled "*Emperor's tits,*" before he leveled me with a stare. "Fine. But whatever he did to you back there, you can bet your little bag of charms he'll do it again. Would be a shame if you ended up dead because you couldn't set your pride aside and figure it out."

I held his gaze, a silent battle of wills taking place between us. He was right, of course—if this happened in the middle of a trial and someone like Horace wasn't there to help, it was possible I'd end up far worse than at the bottom of the rankings.

Dropping my eyes, I said, "He showed me a vision of you. Dead. Outside my room."

This took Horace by surprise. He leaned back on his heels, one bushy eyebrow raised slightly. "Didn't know you cared about me so much, Wolff."

I stifled my sudden smile, the tension clearing as his eyes twinkled. That light vanished a second later, replaced by his somber expression. "Is that all you saw?"

I opened my mouth, but a cold wave of panic filled me like an icy river, making every inch of my skin tingle. I'd never talked about this with anyone. The words clawed up my throat and stopped, as if an invisible force had weaved around my neck, my lips dry and raw. I was back on that living room floor, screaming. *I can't I can't I can't—*

"Hey, hey—it's okay," Horace said, patting my shoulder awkwardly. "Sorry I pushed. But you need to be careful." He looked around us, then lowered his voice. "Has anyone ever told you how to stop an Illusionist from using their magic?"

I blinked and cleared my throat, the panic once again subsiding. "Go—go for the eyes," I breathed out, recalling the townsperson who shouted the advice at my uncle on our way out of Feywood.

Horace tapped his nose, then backed away and held out an arm, motioning me forward.

"You know, I don't think you're supposed to be telling me how to fight the other challengers," I said.

"There're a lot of things I'm not supposed to do. I won't tell if you won't."

My lips raised into a grudging half-smile before a realization struck with a groan. "I have to go," I said, cursing. This was still the middle of a trial. Fates, I'd wasted so much time. The others were probably figuring out their clues and trying to find their artifacts.

Maps. I needed a map.

"Horace, does this palace have a library?" I asked hurriedly, looking around for a clock to check the time. We'd left the corridor with my room and descended a floor, surrounded now by a high stone ceiling with beautiful portraits of the landscapes of Veridia City lining the wall, and a thick, forest green rug beneath our feet. Sounds of palace life waking surrounded us. Servants rushed by with fresh towels and trays of food; sharp heels and heavy boots clicked against wood floors; the creaking of doors and chattering of guests and chirping of birds came in from a nearby open courtyard.

Ten o'clock, an ornate clock down the hall read. An entire hour had already passed.

Horace raised an eyebrow but didn't ask questions. He led me down several more hallways, each as lush and opulent as the last, eventually stopping in front of dark oak double doors, nearly twice my height and inlaid with carvings of delicate swirls and loops. The bronze handle gleamed in the light from the sconces framing either side of the door. Horace pulled on one and threw it open, welcoming me inside with a jerk of his head.

It was the most magnificent room I'd ever seen.

No, calling it a *room* didn't do it justice. The entire chamber was the shape of an enormous circle, with three stories of floor-to-ceiling wooden shelves full of books. A grand staircase with a gold railing sat to the left, leading to the upper levels. I spotted a handful of men and women meandering through shelves or drifting up the stairs with stacks of books and parchment, the quiet ease with which everyone flowed through the library settling my mind.

My gaze wandered over the thousands and *thousands* of leather spines and sturdy bindings, noting the occasional potted plant in between shelves or hanging portrait dotting the cream walls. If I wasn't in such a rush, I could have spent hours exploring this place.

A cough sounded in front of me, coming from an elderly man standing behind a desk at the entrance, almost unnoticeable amidst piles of books scattered around him. One pencil was tucked in his ear and another held in his hand.

"May I help you?" he asked in a frail voice, peering at us over thin spectacles.

I glanced at Horace, but he was already halfway out the door. "Thank you," I called out, to which he threw his hand up in a half-hearted wave.

Turning my attention to the man behind the desk, I said, "I'm looking for maps of the city. Anything that might tell me where the major sites in the capital are."

"Taking a tour?" he asked with a kind smile.

"Something like that."

He tapped his wrinkled nose. "I'll be right back."

I fiddled with my herb pouch as I waited for him to return, my lips twisting back and forth as nerves and restlessness rose. The urge to *act,* to do something, to take off running itched under my skin, my competitive nature bursting forth.

What felt like hours later, the librarian finally returned with a wide, thin book in hand. "Here you are," he said. "This should have several maps of the city and the sectors. Each location is labeled in the index." I opened my mouth to thank him, but he licked his thumb and began flipping through pages of the atlas. "Ah, yes, this is one of my favorite spots. I always recommend it to our guests." He inclined the book toward me and pointed to the west side. "See here? There are beautiful gardens by the—"

"Yes, thank you, I'll make sure to visit those," I rushed out, reaching to grasp the book. "Is it alright if I take this with me?"

He adjusted his spectacles. "Why, of course, but I must get some information first. You know, procedures and all," he said with a huff of a laugh as he patted down his sides. "If I can find that pencil..."

I pinched my lips together to hold back a scream. "I actually don't have much time, if I could just return it tomorrow?" My feet inched backward, my internal clock ticking the minutes away.

The librarian gave me a stern look. "Well, now, palace property must be recorded, and I—wait, where are you going? Young lady, I cannot simply let you—"

"I promise I'll bring it back! Thank you!" I called over my shoulder, pivoting and sprinting out the door. His disgruntled cough followed me down the hall.

A dry chuckle left me as I found the nearest staircase and made my way to the north palace entrance. Fates, this tournament was already turning me into a thief. I'd have to find some way to make it up to the kind man.

I eased the atlas open as I walked, taking in the weathered paper and black ink, looking up occasionally to avoid slamming into a column or passing servant. Each page outlined different parts of the city—the five sectors, as our carriage driver had explained on the way to the palace. Rivers, forests, and mountains were labeled; the ports along the coasts; major trading posts and important landmarks.

Fourteen hours left to search an island I'd never seen in my life. I closed my eyes and let out a breath, stress mounting.

When I opened them, I realized I hadn't been paying attention to where I was going with my nose stuck in the book. I found myself facing a quiet hallway with guards stationed in intervals down its length, their features expressionless and their hands fixed on the pommels of their swords, as if any sudden movement would raise an alarm. I slowly backed away into the adjacent hall, the silence and tension in the air telling me I was somewhere I probably shouldn't be.

And then a familiar voice caught my attention. I peered around the corner, holding my breath.

Out of one of the guarded rooms walked Emperor Gayl.

17

ROSE

All thoughts of the trial fled my mind. I knew I was on a time limit, but how many opportunities would I get to see where the emperor went in his spare time? Lark had stressed to me the importance of this task, of using my freedom and protection in the palace to do what others couldn't. I *had* to find his Grimoire.

Plus, I was curious.

Tucking the atlas under one arm, I reached into my satchel, grabbed a small amaranth stem and a pinch of hellebore root, and placed them both on the tip of my tongue.

"*Vellus,*" I muttered.

There was the normal tightening sensation in my lungs as the invisibility spell snapped into place—the same spell my father had used all those years ago to cloak me from his murderers. Slamming my eyes shut against the oncoming tide of memories, I bit down on the amaranth and hellebore and let the potent magic on my tongue ground me.

Slowly opening my eyes, I crept down the hall. Neither the emperor nor the guards so much as looked in my direction as I swept closer. Gayl was accompanied by a short, balding man in black robes. The two of them strode toward the opposite end of the corridor from me, but I could still hear part of their conversation drifting back.

"Of course, Your Majesty," the robed man said, his nasally voice grating against my ears. "We will send them out immediately."

"And have we received word on the Sentinels?" Gayl asked, the quiet power of his tone once again jolting me, like a rolling wave at the height of its crest, readying to crash. I felt myself inching toward them, not wanting to miss a word.

"Not anything more than last time, I'm afraid," the other man answered. "My sources tell me they've spotted them in various locations throughout the city over the past week, but there have been no attempts to mobilize, that we can see."

Gayl nodded as the two of them reached the end of the hallway. "Good," he replied, moving his arm in a pattern I couldn't make out and throwing open a heavy door.

Was that door there a moment ago? I could've sworn there had only been a portrait occupying space on the wall.

Hoping the thick rug masked my footsteps, I picked up speed and slipped through the door right before it shut with a *click*. It took my eyes a second to adjust to the dim lighting. Hardly any sconces lined the walls, and the hallway was much darker and colder than the previous one.

I tried to keep up with the two men. My eyes took in the numerous doors dotting the hall. Gayl stopped in front of one in the center, his gray cloak swishing as he turned. "Keep an eye on them, Daye. I want to know the *instant* they make a move."

"As you wish, Your Majesty," Daye said, then scurried back down the way we entered. I barely had time to push myself against the wall to avoid him brushing me as he passed. I held my breath, adrenaline coursing through my veins.

Gayl reached for the handle of the door, then paused. Slowly, his head twisted in my direction, his mismatched eyes of blue and white trailing across the floor. They swept up the length of the corridor, my skin tingling with anticipation when suddenly—they stopped.

His eyes met mine.

He hummed softly, letting his gaze fall back to the door as he opened it. A shiver erupted along my spine.

"You are clever, young Alchemist," he said, so faintly I had to crane my neck to hear him. "But did you think you could hide from me?"

Stomach plummeting, my hand shook against my dagger, lungs bursting with how long I had gone without taking a breath.

"I will let you walk away this once," he murmured as he glided through the open door into a darkened chamber beyond. It shut behind him, but the whisper of his voice carried on the wind in his wake.

"Remember my mercy, for you will find no more of it within these walls."

18

ROSE

My feet carried me back through the mysterious door, down corridor after corridor, not pausing until I burst through the nearest exit and into the balmy early afternoon air. I rested my hands on my knees and breathed deeply, letting the autumn breeze sweeping through fallen leaves calm my racing heart.

Why had Gayl let me go? If he knew I was there, knew I'd been *spying* on him, why had he not taken me in for questioning—or worse?

The fact that he'd allowed me to walk away made me even more anxious than the alternative.

A single day, and I'd already made him suspicious of me. What was I *thinking*? I'd been overzealous and arrogant for believing a simple invisibility spell would fool someone like him.

I rubbed at my father's herb satchel, calmed by the familiar leather against the pads of my fingers. Taking a deep breath, I pulled my attention away from that cold hallway. *That* was a problem for future Rose. There was nothing I could do now that wouldn't draw his attention even more. I needed to shift my focus back to the trial—something I could act on.

Taking the folded piece of enchanted parchment from my

pocket, I looked around to make sure nobody was nearby and whispered, "Can you show me the riddle again?"

I wasn't sure it would answer me, but a moment later, the same long lines of verse scrawled on the blank page. I read it through once more, using it as a distraction against my still-heightened nerves.

An artifact of blood you then must find. After seeing each clue directed at the six different types of magic and the line about "only one shall reward you," I was fairly confident it meant each of us had to find the single artifact related to our province—our blood. But then why were we given clues for all six?

You could try to stop the others, a voice in the back of my mind said. I had to admit, it was an intriguing thought. To be able to find Callum's before him and ensure he'd fail.

I took a deep breath and silenced my vengeful nature. Lark had said in the debriefing that rankings were determined by speed and proficiency—meddling with Callum, even if he deserved it, would only slow me down.

Find my artifact first, win the trial.

"Find me with charm where bones and echoes reside; it is cloaked in the day, and revealed in the night." I was positive this part of the riddle was for me. It was the only one that spoke of charms, while the others all had some hint to their own magic. Pulling the atlas from under my arm, I sat on a nearby bench bordering the elaborate palace gardens. The sweet scent of an array of flowers washed over me. Bright lilies, blooming azaleas, and delicate clusters of hydrangeas swayed in the breeze amidst green vines trailing up a large wooden canopy. Their steady, vibrant presence helped to clear my thoughts.

Somewhere bones and echoes lived. A graveyard was still the only thing that came to mind. I scoured the maps, focusing on the more detailed ones of the individual sectors. Little icons were scattered across the page, marking permanent structures and features of the city. Triangles for the small mountains in the north sector, wavy lines for rivers, a tall, domed spire for the palace in the center. There was a temple in the northwest corner of the central sector, trading posts along each compass point, and a handful of academies—most bordering the central sector, where the heaviest population likely lived. I also spotted a theater, multiple infirmaries, and a library.

While we always called the capital "Veridia City," it wasn't merely a single *city*. Perhaps it began that way, but now, small villages and communities dotted the entire island. There was so much to take in, and my eyes wanted to glaze over the little lines and emblems.

Finally, something useful caught my attention.

A black hexagon sat right next to the symbol for the palace, so small I almost missed it. The name "Silver Mausoleum" was written in tiny letters above it. A mausoleum—that would definitely have bones. And it was close by.

Another hexagonal icon labeled "Ridgemore Cemetery" rested in the far east sector. And one more in the north, near a small stretch of hills.

Three potential options. Would I be able to try all of them by midnight?

I shut the book and got to my feet. There was only one way to find out.

The Silver Mausoleum was by far the closest, located on palace grounds. I was currently at the north entrance, and the map had shown the mausoleum on the west side. Hurrying along the stone pathway lining the perimeter, I passed training fields with soldiers of the Royal Guard sparring, stone statues of majestic animals, and members of court promenading around the palace.

Their heads turned as I scurried by, whispers trailing in my wake.

I was used to that. Used to the muttered remarks of those in my province who didn't think I could hear them. But these...these were different. They looked at me with curiosity, not scorn. Intrigue and excitement.

"She's one of the challengers."

"I heard there had been a last-minute change. Think she's from Feywood?"

"She's young. Healthy. Might be worth keeping an eye on."

Word of my replacing Ragnar had spread quickly, it seemed. Back in the provinces, we were too far removed to know much about what occurred during the tournaments until after the fact. But here, the people had access to news much faster. They could witness the trials as they unfolded. We were nothing more than a spectacle to them, a brief burst of entertainment after ten years of normalcy.

Still, a spectacle was better than a pariah.

The sun rose steadily in the sky as I reached the mausoleum. A giant stone structure greeted me when I rounded the last curve, easily two stories tall with a deep gray marble staircase leading to the entrance. The rectangular crypt's towering figure rose from the ground and came to a point at the top, with two marble columns at the enormous front door. Thick vines snaked over the crumbling stone. Several crows rested on the tip of the roof, their caws echoing on the wind as leaves crunched beneath my feet.

Before the winding path in front of the entrance stood a stone tablet resting on top of a post. Etched onto it was a dedication to the deceased former monarchs and their kin, whose bones now lay inside the mausoleum.

Excitement mounted in me as I approached the staircase, the large wooden doors looming closer and closer with every step. Slowly, I reached out to grip the wrought iron handle.

Snap.

I whirled around, my hand halfway to my charms.

Nothing was there.

Letting out a long exhale, I turned back and pulled the door open, stepping into the dark, dusty crypt.

The atmosphere was dry and stale. The only light came from one large window at the front and a circular one on the ceiling, projecting a small beam of sunlight into the center. Its rays revealed trapped dust hanging in the air, a plume of it rising around the door when it shut behind me with a *creak*.

It wasn't a very large building—a single room with four walls, three of which had rows and rows of marble rectangles embedded into the stone. Glancing at the nearest one, I spotted faint inscriptions carved into each, marking the resting place of late emperors and family members. I spent the next few minutes quickly scouring the space. I ran my hand along the edges of the wall, in between cracks in the stone, examining loose rock in the floor. *Anything* that looked out of place. But all I found were cobwebs and dead spiders. There were no doors besides the entrance, no other hallways to explore. Just this single, massive, empty room.

I was about to head back outside to walk around the structure and see if anything stood out when I remembered the second line to the Alchemist clue. *It is cloaked in the day, and revealed in the night.*

Well, I certainly wasn't waiting till nightfall. If the artifact was hidden during the day, perhaps I just needed to make it dark. I rubbed at the back of my neck, wracking my mind for a charm or spell that could take away *light*. Where was a Shadow Wielder when I needed one?

If I could shove a tall pillar in front of the window to block the sun, or perhaps run back to the palace to find a cloak large enough to hang...but then, there was still the one on the ceiling. I could perform a levitation spell for that. Or—

My gaze landed out the window to the sturdy green vines trailing down the marble columns. Would it be possible to...

I opened my pouch of charms and took a pinch of dandelion leaf. By itself, it was used to open—doors, locks, anything bound. But mixed with wormwood, it could expel items or bring them closer.

A summoning charm.

I put the two herbs on my tongue, focused on the sprouting vines, and muttered, "*Voquer*."

Like thick snakes winding across stone, the vines began to

move. Slowly at first, then picking up speed as more followed, some crawling their way to the window and others carving a path up the side of the mausoleum until they were out of sight above my head.

The room began to darken. It was as if a blanket had been thrown over the sun, shrouding the once-lit space in eerie shadows. There was still a faint hint of light coming in from the cracks, enough for me to barely see my hand in front of my face or the window at my side. The vines pulsed and writhed, a living barrier between me and the outside world.

Looking around the room, my gaze landed on a glow emanating from one of the boxes inlaid in the stone wall.

I crossed to it and felt along the corners of the marble rectangle. My fingers found a groove on both sides, and I tugged. The piece of stone broke from the wall and sent small rocks tumbling to the floor, leaving behind a cavity large enough for a body to fit.

Instead of brittle bones and cloth coverings like I expected to see, a single purple crystal lay in the opening. An amethyst crystal, one many Alchemists wore as amulets of wisdom and prophecy.

This had to be it. My artifact from the riddle.

Heart thumping wildly, a triumphant grin pulled at my lips as I reached in to grab the crystal.

The moment I touched it, the amethyst disintegrated.

My stomach dropped. I frantically searched the small space, running my hand into each crevice, extending my arm as far as it could go into the wall.

When it was apparent the crystal had truly disappeared, I pulled my arm from the hole and let out a frustrated groan, slumping against the wall and dropping my head back until it hit the hard stone.

A warmth fluttered at my chest. Hardly noticeable at first, then increasing in heat until it practically seared through my shirt. Cursing, I fumbled with my vest pocket and pulled out the enchanted parchment. Two words blazed across the paper.

Try again.

Frustration and disappointment ripped through me, a growl building in the back of my throat as I put a thistle leaf on my tongue and said, *"Finiscere."* Instantly, my summoning spell for the vines fell, and they receded from the windows back to the columns.

Daylight filtered in. And standing outside the clear window was Alaric Rinehart, shadows bursting from his hands.

I jumped to my feet in alarm. In several strides, I crossed to the door and pushed.

It wouldn't budge.

"Alaric!" I thundered, throwing my weight against it. From the corner of my eye I watched shadows cover the window where the vines had been, once again encasing the mausoleum in darkness. "Let me out!"

Through the door came his muffled voice. "Like I said, Rose. No hard feelings."

19

ROSE

He must have followed me from the palace. That *scumbag.* Didn't he know he was wasting time not going after his own artifact?

Knowing his past, however, it shouldn't surprise me. He'd lost the last Decemvirate due to someone sabotaging him —if I were him, I'd probably be more ruthless than ever.

Still. I didn't have to like him.

How was I supposed to get out of this? It wasn't a spell I could simply banish. This was only the second time I'd even *seen* shadow magic.

Think, Rose. The door was the sole exit. I spun around in the dark, wondering why I could still partially see the room, when I remembered the window in the ceiling. Sunlight shone onto the ground, meaning Alaric's shadows hadn't extended to the roof.

Hope blossomed in my chest. I could get out of here.

Using wormwood and crushed henbane, I performed the same levitation spell I used to lift my uncle's cursed body from the ground and into our carriage less than two days before. I'd never used it on *myself,* but the magic worked the same. Steadily, I began to rise. It felt like all my weight bubbled to the surface of my skin like water evaporating from a kettle. The magic tugged at me,

155

pulling me higher and higher. Trying to guide myself the way I would guide a floating object while still keeping my balance made me teeter precariously in the air, but eventually, I reached the tall ceiling and the small circular window.

With my dandelion leaves, I muttered, "*Vata lai.*"

Click. The window latch opened. Pushing against it, I ascended through the hole and above the mausoleum. I squinted as my eyes adjusted to the brightness, taking in lungfuls of clean, fresh air and keeping my spell intact long enough to carry me over the roof. I bent my knees slightly as my feet slammed onto solid ground. The effort of using such magic winded me, leaving my energy depleted.

Glancing back at the building, I gritted my teeth at the sight of the solid pillar of shadows swaying in the breeze. How much time had this cost me? First the false artifact, then Alaric's trick. By the sun's position, I guessed it was well after noon. I wondered if anyone had reached their destination yet.

From my examination of the maps, I had two leads left: a cemetery in the east, and another to the north. Unless I found a carriage or a horse that would take me, I doubted I'd have time to try both locations on foot. I remembered the driver, Larson, saying he would be available to take Ragnar anywhere he wanted to go in the palace's carriage, *except* for during his trials. I was left to my own devices to find a ride from someone else in the city.

Straightening, I forced back my exhaustion and took off through the thin forest surrounding the palace and into the central sector beyond.

————

APPARENTLY WORD HAD NOT YET SPREAD to the rest of the capital that there had been a change in challenger from Feywood. Unlike the lords and ladies from the palace, nobody in the main market of the central sector recognized me.

Signs of the Decemvirate were everywhere. Parchment with hand drawn portraits of each of the challengers—including my uncle—with their affiliated province were affixed to almost every storefront, every alleyway, every wooden post. Vendors sold scarves and flags from their booths in various colors of the provinces: light blue for Emberfell, burgundy for Drakorum, shades of black and gray for Tenebra. The dark green of Feywood flashed before me, along with Celestria's familiar purple and the white and gold of Iluze. Everywhere I looked, people browsed past sporting their support for their favorite province. Whether they were visitors or capital natives who were simply rooting for someone of their own magic, I couldn't tell.

Even pastries were decorated in honor of the tournament. A woman outside of a bakery had set up a table with mouth-watering cakes bearing the words "Welcome to the Decemvirate" in colorful frosting. At the end of the cobblestone street, a group of musicians played on their stringed instruments, the upbeat sound carrying for several blocks.

My eyes snagged on a building at the corner, next to the source of the lively music. A storefront made of brick was painted a dark green, with pink and cream flowers budding on small vines that twined their way up the iron handrail. Potted plants lined the black steps in front of the door. I ventured closer and spotted circular tables full of chatting families sitting in the outdoor lounging area, with smells of floral teas and delicious baked goods wafting through the air. The sign on the front read "Gershwin Tea House." Something about it drew me in.

A bell above the door rang as I stepped inside. There was a neat counter and display bearing several scones and breads, with an entire wall behind full of clear tins of tea leaves. Lush greenery hung from the windows, foliage and flowers and herbs living in every nook and cranny. I took it all in with childlike wonder, feeling Alchemy magic pulse through me.

"Is there anything I can help you with?" a dark-skinned woman with deep gray tresses hanging over her apron asked from the counter.

"Yes, actually." I cleared my throat and approached, catching sight of several crystals around her neck and wrists. These shop owners *must* be Alchemists. "I was wondering if you knew where I could hire a horse or carriage for the day?"

She raised an eyebrow. "On the first day of the Decemvirate? You'll have a hard time finding one." Leaning her elbows on the counter, she said, "Can I ask where you're looking to go? I might be able to help."

Did I tell her I was a challenger on a quest for the first trial? It wasn't technically against the rules, and it wasn't as if I were asking her to help me solve the riddle or find the artifact. Still, keeping some semblance of anonymity until the world discovered I'd taken Ragnar's place seemed wiser. The less attention I drew, the less likely another challenger would find me—like Alaric.

"I want to visit these cemeteries," I answered vaguely, pulling the maps out and showing her the ones to the east and north. "They seem a bit far to get to on foot."

She hummed. "You're right, you'd need transportation if you want to see both of them today." With a kind smile, she asked, "Not from around here, I take it?"

I chuckled. "You could say that."

"If you know who you're trying to visit, you could look their name up in the city archives." She gestured to my maps when I furrowed my brow. "To see which cemetery they were buried in."

Realization dawned. She thought I was looking to visit someone's gravesite. "Actually, I'm not sure of the exact name of the person I'm looking for. It's an...old ancestor I wanted to find. That's why I was going to try both."

Her lips twitched. I couldn't tell if she was buying my story, but she didn't press the matter. "Well, depending on how old the ancestor is, there's another place you may want to try, too." Pulling the book of maps between us, she pointed to a small icon in the west sector. "The Battle of the Dead Lands memorial also has burial grounds for some who fought in the war."

I leaned forward, interest piquing. "The War of Beginnings?"

She nodded. "How much do you know about it?"

"As much as they're willing to teach us in Feywood," I responded dryly. The war occurred three hundred and fifty years ago between the Veridian Empire and the Kingdom of Mysthelm to the southwest. It was a brutal struggle over the ancient magic that lived in the capital, which, at the time, was unoccupied. Magic given by the Fates, free for the taking.

If you were willing to fight.

The two civilizations had coexisted peacefully until the three Fates sent a prophecy saying whoever could conquer the magic would be given power beyond comprehension. That sparked the beginning of the end.

The five-year war concluded with my people overpowering Mysthelm and laying claim to the magic. Mysthelm was left with nothing—a magicless society forced back to their continent.

We hadn't heard from Mysthelm in three centuries. At least, that us *common* people knew of. The idea of an entire kingdom existing beyond our borders fascinated me. It was a land I'd more than likely never get to see, and part of me longed to know what it was like. A world without magic and the obsession it created. How the people lived, how they ran their kingdom, if they were as divided and hostile as we were. I wondered if they resented us for stealing their chance at this ancient power, or if they would ever take up arms again and invade our land for what they'd lost.

But we were taught next to nothing about them, nor about the specifics of the war. I had never even heard of this Battle of the Dead Lands the woman spoke of.

"It was the deadliest, bloodiest battle fought during the war, and it happened right here on Veridia City soil," she began. "Veridians caught Mysthelm soldiers crossing the Eldertide Ocean to try and get to the island, and they raced to meet them." Her lips turned down. "Thousands of people died. They say it was one of the final battles before Veridians overpowered them. The memorial was erected in honor of those who suffered, and it's still over in the west sector today."

I examined the map and saw the icon she'd pointed out was

only several miles from the port my family and I had arrived at. Less than an hour's ride by carriage.

Now I had three options. Two cemeteries and the memorial. After learning the history behind the memorial, my instincts were leaning that direction—it was symbolic of the Decemvirate and all that had been sacrificed to put us in this position of power. It felt exactly like somewhere they'd lead me. But I couldn't afford to keep choosing incorrectly.

The bell above the door chimed behind me. "Thank you for your help," I said, not wanting to take up any more of her time.

I turned to head back to the entrance when the two women who had just walked in noticed me and stopped in their tracks.

"Are you Rose?" one of them asked excitedly. "The new Feywood challenger?"

I stifled a groan. They must have a connection to the palace. So much for anonymity. Nodding tightly, I tried to sneak away before others were drawn in, when the shop owner called my name.

"Rose, is it?" When I stayed still, she beckoned me with a crooked finger back to the counter. Her dark eyes gleamed, a smile forming on her lips. "*You're* the Feywood challenger? Why didn't you say anything?" She lowered her voice. "My parents moved us here from Feywood over five decades ago. I might have been a young girl, but I remember it fondly. I say it's high time they deserve a win, don't you think?"

I held my breath, refusing to believe my luck. Turning, she pulled a thin vial of amber liquid from one of her shelves, discreetly covering it with her hand as she passed it across the counter and into my fingers.

"Family recipe. I always have one handy in case any trouble-makers come along, if you know what I mean." She winked. "Show them what we're capable of, yes?"

I grinned, grasping the vial and clutching her hand between both of mine in thanks.

"And, Rose? If you need to get somewhere quickly, take my horse."

I started to shake my head. "I couldn't possibly—"

"I insist. Just promise to come back and buy plenty of charms once you win this trial."

"Of course, I will," I said with a laugh. "Thank you. You have no idea how much this means to me, Miss..."

"Rothy. Call me Rothy." I nodded my thanks as she led me out the back door and to a little paddock fence where two horses grazed. I checked my map and mounted the white and brown speckled mare, which Rothy called Colette, adjusting to her tall frame and grabbing the reins.

I took off through the opening of the fence, barely hearing Rothy call out behind me, "Oh, and don't get too close to that potion when you use it!"

Tucking the vial into one of my pockets, I snapped the reins and followed my gut to the west.

20

ROSE

I rode hard out of the central sector, passing lively villages and crowded streets until I entered the less populated, more forested west sector. Lush trees lined the path, the rushing sound of the nearby Scarre River reaching my ears. I looked back over my shoulder a handful of times to see the tips of the tall, circular palace spires shrinking in the distance. Slowing Colette so I could check the map and be sure I was still heading in the right direction to the memorial, we eventually crossed a wide bridge across the Scarre River, my destination and hope growing closer with every step.

After another five minutes, the smooth stone path became interrupted with large thickets, the leaping waters of the river now muffled by the grassy undergrowth and copse of trees surrounding me. If I didn't have the ticking clock of this trial hanging over my head, it would be peaceful. Quiet. Only the sound of wind whistling through leaves and Colette's hooves tromping through kept me company.

Until—

A few yards behind me, another pair of hooves clicked over stone.

My head snapped around, Colette veering slightly to the right at the motion.

And just like at the mausoleum, there was nothing there.

I sighed in frustration, turning Colette back to the main path. "Fates, Rose, get your—"

Colette reared up, causing my words to catch in my throat as she almost threw me off her back. In the middle of the road, mere feet from her nose, was an enormous dark gray stallion.

With a smirking Callum perched atop.

"Fancy meeting you here, Feywood."

I cursed. "What are you doing? Are you *following* me?"

"I don't need to follow you. I have eyes and ears everywhere," he said smugly. "Spend a year preparing for this tournament, and you make some friends. But you wouldn't know that, would you?"

Anger burned in my core. His ego was so large, I wasn't sure how his head didn't blow clean off his shoulders. People like him who got off on making others feel inferior made me want to lash out irrationally.

I acted as if I was tightening my hold on the reins as I reached for my pouch of herbs. "Be careful, Callum. If you get too distracted, you won't be able to hold onto Iluze's precious champion title." Nudging Colette with my thighs, we trotted forward. "Now get out of my way."

He drifted even closer, as I knew he would. Before he had time to respond, the henbane was on my tongue and I whispered a hurried, "*Phyxie.*"

But instead of gasping desperately for air as all the breath escaped his lungs, Callum's smirk widened. His form rippled like waves on water.

A wicked laugh came from behind me. "Neat trick," he said as I whirled to face him. "But I won't fall for that again."

I flashed him a smile, the faint licorice taste of the angelica I'd grabbed mixing with the acrid one of henbane still on my lips. "Didn't expect you to. *Incendar.*"

This time, he wasn't prepared.

Flames burst at his wrist, quickly encasing his arm. He cried out in alarm and leapt from his horse, crashing to the ground. I watched with a sneer as he rolled on the grass to try and quell the blaze.

My energy was waning again. I could feel it, like a cavity in my chest hollowing out. I'd used more magic today than normal, but glaring down at him at the feet of my horse, I couldn't find it in me to care.

It was like the fire was a part of me. It licked at his clothes, his skin, tasting him and spitting him out like ash. His cries and heaving breaths against the smoke were music to my ears, a sweet melody of retribution.

Dismounting, I stalked toward him, not entirely sure what I was doing. When I blinked, I saw another image of a different man lying before a fireplace covered in blood. Panic clawed up my throat before I shook the memory away.

Illusionists. Callum was the same as the people who murdered my father. I'd never see those two men again, but the one before me…he would do just fine.

"Feywood—please—" Callum choked, still thrashing at the flames that couldn't be quenched. It spread to his legs, burning away the fabric and revealing dark skin beneath.

He isn't your true enemy, a voice whispered in my head. *Remember what you're here for.*

The mission. The curse. Saving my uncle.

That's what mattered, even more than this tournament, more than the vicious threats of challengers. Callum wasn't worth the mud on my boots, but he didn't deserve to *die* for his tricks. This was my past breaking free, my grief and fear taking control.

I had to hold myself together.

"Finiscere," I mumbled, taking my thistle leaf charm, and the flames immediately died. Turning my back on him, I strode to Colette. "Learn your lesson this time, Callum, and leave me alone."

In my next breath, a slew of bats appeared from the forest

behind my mare, aiming straight at my head. Colette bucked and I screamed, barely keeping my feet from being trampled as I swatted at the bats.

My hands fell through them like they were smoke. *More illusions.* His magic was so incredibly powerful. I *swear* I could feel their leathery wings beating against my skin, their sharp claws digging into flesh.

The bats disappeared, only to be replaced by writhing snakes, twining themselves around Colette's legs, then mine, slithering up our bodies without me feeling a thing. My mare's frightened whinnies filled the air. One of the fake snakes hissed, its beady eyes locked on mine and forked tongue flicking wildly. A whimper tore from me.

It's not real, it's not real, it's not real.

"Scared, Feywood?" Callum rasped, still on the ground, his clothes in tatters and smoke rising from his body.

"Why are you doing this?" I asked, hating the way my voice panted with fear.

He chuckled then coughed, ash spread across his arms as he gingerly got to his feet. "Don't kid yourself. You're not special—you should see what I did to the Lightbender."

I shook my head. "You would save yourself a lot of time if you tried to find your own artifact instead of coming after the rest of us."

"Who says I haven't?" he asked sinisterly. But there wasn't just *one* of him. Suddenly, there were dozens of Callums closing in from all sides, that cocky laugh echoing tenfold. My eyes flitted to the left and right, unable to escape the multitude of raised eyebrows, glinting lip rings, dark eyes that spoke of hatred and victory and vengeance.

I inhaled sharply. *Go for the eyes.* That was how you weakened an Illusionist. But which one was the real him?

There was always a tell. I may not know his kind of power the way I knew my Alchemy, but all magic had a weak point, a way to determine reality from illusion. My eyes darted across each of his faces as they converged on me, scanning for anything off, any sign of—

There.

The one to the far left, several steps back from the other versions of him. He was the only one limping—from when he'd fallen from his horse, I imagined.

I felt through my satchel of herbs until my fingers found blackthorn ash—not a particularly offensive herb, mostly used for silencing or in combination with other charms. But it could still do damage. In a burst of adrenaline, I lurched past the false Callums and straight to the real one.

And shoved the ash into his eyes.

The illusions vanished and Callum staggered, howling and clutching at his face.

I sprinted to Colette. The sound of crunching leaves followed me. *Fates*, I couldn't get rid of him. When I glanced back, he brandished a dagger, all cockiness wiped from his gaze. Instead, he wore vicious retribution.

No more tricks.

I reached into my pocket for the vial Rothy had given me. *"Don't get too close to that potion when you use it,"* she'd said.

Sucking in a breath, I tossed it at Callum's feet as he barreled after me, then stuck my foot in Colette's stirrup and hoisted myself up.

Crunch. The vial broke.

"Feywood! What the—"

Success blazed through me as I gripped Colette's reins, turning to find Callum pounding his fists against thin air, as if there was an invisible barrier blocking him. He couldn't take a single step in any direction.

Rothy, you little genius.

"See you in the second trial, Callum," I said with a smirk.

I patted Colette's side and she took off, but not before I saw Callum raise his hands.

Everything happened so fast.

Colette let out a neigh as loud as a lion's roar. She reared up on her hind legs, frightened by something in front of us that I couldn't see. My hold on her reins wasn't tight enough.

I went flying.

My head slammed into the ground, and my vision went black.

21

ROSE

I woke to something nudging my forehead.

Something...*wet*. And cold.

Releasing a groan, I reached out a hand to shove the intruder aside, when my skin met warm fur. I pried my eyes open and gasped at the sight of a black nose, a whiskered, white muzzle surrounded by a red coat of fur, and bright golden eyes staring back at me.

A fox.

I sat straight up, and a soft blanket fell into my lap. Confusion and alarm swept in. Where was I? What happened to me?

The fight with Callum came back in fragmented pieces, along with a pounding in my skull. I'd been on a path in the forest heading to the memorial. I fell off Colette and passed out, then ended up...

Slowly, I glanced up at the fox before me. The moment I moved, it sprang to all four paws and padded across the room to a door. With almost human-like grace, it wrapped its two front paws around the knob, turned it, and slunk out the door.

I blinked rapidly. How badly had I hit my head?

I stood from the small couch I'd been sleeping on, rubbing the back of my neck. The motion made me catch my breath as a sharp pain reverberated through my right side all the way up to the back of my head. Carefully, I peeled my black shirt up to find a massive bruise along my ribs. My fingers traced over the deep purple blotches, wincing at even the slightest pressure. Digging into my pouch, I pulled out a small ginger root and bit down on the end, muttering the spell for pain relief my aunt had taught me long ago.

I took a step forward and pain shot up my entire right side, my head spinning and throbbing. My magic was severely weakened from so much use today—it was going to take much more than a piece of ginger to make this go away. How was I supposed to get out of here? And where was "here," anyway?

Turning gently in a wide arc, I took in the space around me. It looked like a modest-sized cottage. Wooden rafters lined the ceiling. Natural light came from three windows stationed around the single large room, which functioned as a living space and a kitchen. The couch faced a brick fireplace in the center of the wall, with a couple of blankets thrown over the back and an empty glass resting on an end table. Past the couch and to my right was a circular table and three chairs, a shelf with three plates, three bowls, and three mugs, and a counter holding a variety of imperishable foods—bread, apples, and dried meat.

Sitting on the counter was a basket with little glass vials and burlap pouches, twigs of what I recognized as lavender and thistle sticking out from some of them.

Did an Alchemist live here?

I limped over to the basket, keeping my arm wrapped around my side as pain echoed in me with each step. I needed to find something to heal me. The only remedies I'd brought with me were the ginger root and a vial of cedarwood oil, which worked best on topical injuries like a knife wound.

The familiar sweet and earthy scent of herbs and charms washed over me when I reached for the first bag in the basket.

I paused, my fingers hovering over rough burlap. The back of my neck tingled, the hair on my arms raising as a ringing formed low in my ears.

Before I could turn, a thick, warm rope wrapped around my neck like a noose.

I inhaled sharply and choked, pain shooting down my right side as I tried to move both hands to claw at my throat. A strangled cry left my lips.

"That," a low voice growled from somewhere above me, "does not belong to you."

"Let—go—of me," I panted, reaching for my satchel.

"And let you use your charms on me? Not a chance, little Alchemist."

I stilled. I recognized that voice. "Who are you?"

A rustle sounded from the ceiling. I shifted my gaze upward, the movement making the rope tighten around my throat, momentarily stealing the breath from my lungs.

On the wooden beams of the rafters, mere feet above my head, crouched a shadowed figure. One I'd met twice before.

This time, he wore no cloak, only black pants and a loose white tunic with the sleeves rolled up his arms, exposing tan skin corded with muscles and a tattoo of two fierce animal faces on his fore-arm. The veins around it flexed as he clenched his hand, his piercing black eyes practically glowing in the darkness.

"Of course, it's *you*," I grumbled.

"Believe me, you're the last person I expected to find breaking into my home." In one swift movement, he leapt off the beam and landed before me. The rope at my throat twitched and unwound itself, falling to the floor and slinking behind him.

That's when I realized...it wasn't a rope.

Swallowing, I rubbed my neck, instinctively moving backward. "Is that...do you have a *tail?*"

"Tell me," he started, taking a step toward me with a suspi-cious glint in his eye. I could feel the wariness and distrust radi-ating from him. The scent of sandalwood and vanilla—the same scent that lingered long after I'd left the shadowed alcove yesterday morning—engulfed me. "Who sent you?"

I scoffed. "What are you talking about? Nobody *sent* me."

He growled softly and moved again, and I backed away until my spine hit a wall. A low hiss escaped me as an ache spiked through my skull and side.

Instantly, he stopped moving. His eyes flashed at the sound. "You're hurt," he said, almost surprised.

"I'm fine."

His gaze fell to my right side, which my arm was protectively wrapped around. My jaw twitched from suppressing a grunt as his eyes slowly trailed back up my body to meet mine once more.

The front door banged open. He didn't so much as blink. I craned my neck to see around him and spotted a beautiful blonde-haired woman in a deep burgundy cloak standing in the doorway, her hands on her hips.

"Leo! What are you doing to her?" she asked, dulcet voice sharp with annoyance.

He sighed and ran a hand through his dark brown hair. Turning to face her, he said, "I should have known she was one of your strays."

"One of her—" I shook my head to clear my confusion, then winced at the motion. "Excuse me, I've never met this woman before."

To my surprise, she smirked. "Funny way of saying 'thank you for saving my life,' but I'll take it."

I stared at her. "What are you talking about?"

"Yes, Rissa, I'd like to know that, as well," the man—Leo—said, irritation lacing his words. "I thought Lark had you helping with the first trial."

Rissa unfastened her cloak and threw it onto the back of the couch as she approached us. Growing closer, I could see her mischievous, glittering onyx eyes, so very similar to the man at my side. But hers held a softness that his didn't, a playful gleam that had me wondering if she enjoyed toying with us like this.

"She did. You're looking at it," Rissa responded casually, gesturing at me. "I couldn't very well let our charge lie alone in those woods after a horse nearly trampled her, could I?"

"*You're* the one who brought me here?" I asked, trying to piece together the last few hours. Fates, I didn't even know how much time had passed. And had Leo mentioned Lark? How did they know who she was? Or *me*, for that matter?

"Yes, well, after chasing off that maniac Illusionist once he broke free from whatever spell you had over him. Turns out, he's afraid of a little bite." On the last word, Rissa's eyes took on a golden glow as her pupils elongated. Large canines burst from her mouth and she bit playfully in the air, her features returning to normal a split second later.

I gasped and gripped at the wall behind me. "You're a Shifter?" She smiled in answer, and something dawned on me. The fox who'd been at my side when I woke up...it had similar golden, glowing eyes. "Are you a...a fox? The one who was here when I came to?"

Her smile widened and she gave me a mock bow. "At your service. Now, we need to get you back in shape so you can finish your trial. Lark's going to kill *me* if she finds out I almost let *you* get killed on the first day."

Anxiety raced through me. "What time is it?" I asked, whirling around to find a clock and instantly regretting the sudden movement. Pain lanced up my side, the ginger root hardly dimming the intensity.

Rissa pulled a pocket watch from inside the burgundy cloak hanging over the couch. "Six o'clock."

"*Six?*" Over half my time was gone, and only a couple more hours were left with full sunlight. I had to get back to the trial.

Leo looked at me, his features pulled into a scowl while his eyes burned with displeasure. "*This* is her? The person Lark enlisted for the mission?"

I didn't know how he knew about that, but his condescension made me bristle. "I have a name, you know," I snapped.

He ignored me and turned on Rissa. "It's been a single day, and already Lark's precious chosen one has ended up on our doorstep. You failed to mention she was a *challenger*—one who wound up injured barely into her first trial, by the looks of it." When Rissa stayed silent, he scoffed. "And this is who we expect to infiltrate the most notorious Alchemist in history." He stepped closer to Rissa and lowered his voice, but I still caught his spiteful words. "I've told you a thousand times, *I* should be the one doing this. This is a joke, and you know it."

Anger blazed through me, hot and poisonous. As he spoke with his back to me, my eyes landed on a familiar vial of pale yellow liquid sticking out of the basket on the counter. An idea sparked in my heated, aggravated mind, and I swiftly dabbed a bit of the oil on my tongue, along with mistletoe leaves from my pouch. Whispering a quick incantation, I pushed off from the wall and made my way toward him, ignoring the spike of pain in my side.

"Oh, *I'm* a joke?" I said through my teeth. "You didn't seem to feel that way when I took down that Shifter in the forest. Or when I saw you yesterday morning. Tell me, *monkey boy*," I mocked his earlier words, stopping inches from his face. His icy stare met my own. "What makes you think you're so much better than me?"

His eyes narrowed and he opened his mouth to respond when suddenly, his face froze. He swallowed, licking his lips, then tried again to speak. Nothing but a grunt came out.

"Not so mouthy now, are we?" I asked coldly. Turning to Rissa, I said, "Is he always this way?"

The fox Shifter simply stared at us with her arms crossed over her chest, curiosity and amusement on her features.

Leo moved his arm to grab me, but the motion was jerky and stunted. I *tsk*ed. "Did I say you could move?" Fingering the vial of oil, I leaned in closer. "I may be a joke to you, but at least I'm not arrogant enough to let an Alchemist get near enough to cast on me." I shoved the glass vial into his outstretched, still frozen hand.

"Now, we're going to start over, and you two are going to tell me who you are and what's going on. Yes?" I hissed at him.

"Yes, ma'am." Rissa's voice came from beside me, that smirk back on her lips. I looked at Leo, whose fierce eyes defiantly held mine for a second. Two. And then he lowered them, his sharp jaw tightening.

"*Finiscere,*" I said, taking my thistle and releasing Leo from the spell. He immediately staggered forward, a snarl working itself up his throat.

"Oh, come on, Leo," Rissa said, laughing. "You have to admit, that was good. What did you use, anyway?" She grabbed the vial from his hand and opened it. Taking a sniff, she said in surprise, "Calamus oil?"

"Among other things," I said smoothly. Calamus oil mixed with mistletoe had been a potion I'd found in my father's Grimoire that, when inhaled by your target, placed them under your control for a brief period. Back when I'd first discovered it, my magic had been stronger, able to hold the spell for longer periods. I'd used it for the first time when I was seventeen and caught a boy hitting young Beau. Needless to say, his schoolmates thought twice about tormenting him after that, and I further solidified my reputation as the poisoned, headstrong outcast.

But Beau had been safe—that's what mattered.

"Clever. Perhaps Lark picked well after all, hmm?" Rissa said pointedly to Leo, who hadn't taken his gaze off of me. "On that note, I think it's time for a proper introduction. Leo, this is Rose Wolff—the new Feywood challenger and the person Lark has chosen to trust with our little *quest*. Although, I get the feeling you two already know each other."

"We've met," Leo said curtly.

"Well, then." Rissa clapped her hands together, seeming to enjoy this far too much. She extended a hand to me, a warm smile on her fair and freckled face. "I'm Clarissa, Rissa for short. And this is Zareleon."

My blood ran cold. I knew those names.

My heart pounded in my chest, working its way up my throat, a roar filling my ears. Along with five words.

Branock Aris sends his love.

"You're...you're the twins. The Aris twins," I said hollowly, barely registering the words coming out of my mouth.

For the first time, Clarissa looked nervous. She tucked a blonde curl behind her ear and nodded. "In the flesh."

Something venomous snaked its way through my veins, boiling over, drowning me.

I turned slowly to face Zareleon. "Your father is the reason mine is dead."

And I launched myself at him.

22

LEO

I caught Rose's outstretched wrist as she lunged at me with bared teeth. She quickly twisted her arm and yanked out of my hold, reaching for a hexagonal shaped pouch hanging from her green vest. I whipped my tail around to circle her right arm, but she grabbed a hidden dagger with the other and aimed it at the length of fur wrapped between us.

Gripping her left hand just in time, I withdrew my tail and spun her around so her back was to my chest, my arm restraining her. Her ragged breaths filled the cottage, her soft skin hot with anger beneath my touch. My fingers grazed her wrist, applying enough pressure that the dagger fell to the floor with a clatter.

When she let out a sharp cry of pain, I remembered her injuries and instantly released her. "I don't want to hurt you, but you need to calm down," I said sharply, more harsh than I intended with my chest heaving.

She folded an arm around her right side, wincing at the contact. "I don't have time for this," she said, her voice shaking. From pain or barely-controlled wrath, I wasn't sure. At the mention of our surname, it was as if she had lost control. "I have to finish the trial and get back to the palace."

"You can't go anywhere like that," I said, pointing at her side. I may be irritated by the whole situation, but I didn't want the woman dead. "We can help you."

"I've had enough of your help over the last few days," she spat.

Rissa cursed. "Fates, you two…alright, here's what's going to happen. Rose, you'll let Leo mend whatever injuries your fall caused. Then, you're both going to tell me how you know one another. Lark and I have worked too hard to make sure the pieces of this mission fall into place, and this is our *best* shot. I won't have you two screwing it up because of your ridiculous pride." Her eyes burned into mine at that last comment.

To her credit, Rose straightened, her cheek flinching faintly before she smoothed her features. "I have no idea who you people are. Tell me why I should trust you, much less *obey* you."

My eyebrow hitched upward. This time, it was my turn to smirk at my sister, who was unused to having her authority questioned among the ranks of the Sentinels. As the proper heir to the Veridian Empire, she had naturally stepped into the role of a leader, and I would gladly admit she led our covert group of rebels beautifully. It had been quite a while since she'd come across someone who didn't immediately fall at her feet. I should have guessed Rose Wolff wouldn't be one of them.

"You should *trust* me because we're on the same side," Rissa explained, calmly but firmly. "While Lark may be the head architect for this Decemvirate, *I* am the one she answers to. Not Gayl. We couldn't care less if you win this tournament, but we're all counting on you to find the emperor's Grimoire, and we're willing to do what it takes to help. And I don't expect you to *obey* me like some mindless servant, Rose." Rissa took a step toward her. "I expect you to recognize the gravity of this situation and respect the fact that it's larger than you and whatever personal vendetta you may have against our father, and therefore, us.

"You're here because your uncle saw something in you, and Lark must have seen it, too. You're here because you want *change*. You want to see justice. That means you have to work *with* us, Rose, not against us. It's not a matter of obedience. It's a matter of choosing where your loyalties lie and committing to this cause. Do you think you can do that?"

My sister truly was a force to be reckoned with, when she wanted to be. But I had a feeling this Rose was not without her own thorns. I shifted my gaze between the two women, feeling the tension crackling and snapping in the air. Rose's breaths became louder, more labored, as if the pain from her injuries was becoming too difficult to bear.

"I think I've proven my commitment to you," Rose said, gesturing to her side. "You're right—we want the same thing. I'll do what you need me to do, but it's going to take more than a pretty speech to get me to trust you."

Rissa considered her silently for a moment. Finally, her face relaxed, her lips almost curving into a smile. "Well, then, I suppose we'll work on earning it. Let's start by fixing those broken ribs, hmm?"

Rose wet her lips and eyed us hesitantly, that same suspicion and anger lingering. Her pain and desire to get back into the tournament must have outweighed her reservations, for she gave a swift nod and limped toward the couch. Rissa raised an eyebrow at me and I took that as my cue to begin preparing a healing tonic—one our father had passed on to me before he died.

While I worked at the kitchen counter, I listened to Rose and Rissa talk.

"How do you two know Lark?" Rose asked.

"Lark has been a close friend for more than a decade. She's been working with us on our plan to use the Decemvirate as a way to get closer to Gayl," Rissa explained. "When she made a bid for the head architect position several years ago and was appointed, we knew it was fate. It was her idea to involve a challenger in the first place. She's the one who found your uncle."

"So, it's just you three? The masterminds behind this grand plan?"

I smirked as I chopped a bay leaf, and Rissa chuckled before answering. "It may have started with my brother and me, but it's become something beyond our wildest dreams. We created a group called the Sentinels over five years ago after seeing the growing problems here at the capital, and could only assume it was happening across the entire empire, too. We have two hundred faithful recruits spread over the city, as well as a handful in each of the six provinces, all part of a network that leads back to here."

Rose released a slow breath. "And what's the purpose of this group?"

"To remove Gayl from power, end the Somnivae curse, and bring this empire back to a semblance of what it used to be," Rissa answered succinctly. *And finally avenge our father*, I thought to myself.

Rose scoffed. "Just like that?"

Her question made me falter, my fingers stiffening as I added elderberry oil to my potion. "What do you mean?" I called out, glancing behind me to the couch.

With a shrug, she said, "You make it sound so...easy. Take him down and end the curse—and then it's over. What about his supporters? His court, the Royal Guard, those who practically worship him across the provinces, especially the stronger ones. Not everyone is like me, you know," she added. "Plenty of people think he *saved* us from your father's rule. And if you succeed, who would replace him? Would it be someone just as power-hungry, just as cruel? Would they actually *care* about the provinces?"

"Of course, we've thought about all these things, Rose," my sister answered. "And we have a plan. We're not ignorant to what's been going on outside of Veridia City. Trust me, that's not how we want it to be, either." She shook her head, blonde curls bouncing, and I went back to mixing the tonic. "This is something we've been building toward for *years*. I promise you, if we play our cards right over the next month, we have hope for a better future for *everyone*. This isn't some dimwitted plan of a bunch of amateurs."

"I—I never said it was," Rose said, her voice more unsure than usual. "These last couple days have been a lot to take in. I don't know who I can trust or who's out to get me."

I turned at her words, unable to resist seeing her in this moment of vulnerability. Uncertainty crept onto her features, so at odds with the thorns and sharp tongue.

"Well, you can trust *us*, for one," Rissa said. "And Lark, of course. There's a guard at the palace who's also part of our ranks. You've met him—his name is Horace."

Rose's mouth gaped open. "*Horace*? I should've known. But... you seemed surprised by all of this, too," she said, nodding to me as I made my way to the couch with a glass of the lavender tonic. I noticed her eyes were colder when she gazed at me as opposed to my sister, her olive features holding a hint of resentment.

I knew the feeling.

"When you saw me this morning, did you know who I was?" Rose tilted her head inquisitively at me. Dark waves of hair cascaded down one shoulder. My sister turned to face me, and I cursed, running a hand through my hair. She still didn't know I'd snuck into the palace against her wishes.

"What happened this morning?" Rissa asked with thinly veiled irritation.

At this interaction, Rose's face went from curious to sly understanding, her lips twitching as her green eyes flashed at me. The little wolf knew *exactly* what she'd done.

"I ran into Rose by accident," I said stiffly.

Rose quirked an eyebrow. "Why don't you tell her *where* you ran into me?"

I glared at her. Rissa, however, beamed. "Oh, I like this one," she purred.

This new development between the two of them did not bode well for me. "I was at the palace. Is that what you wanted to hear, Rissa?"

Her playfulness swiftly fell. "No, *brother*, it's not. What were you doing there? You know I *explicitly* told you to stay out of this. If either of us are seen—"

"I know, I know," I said through my teeth, cutting her off. "Can we have this conversation later?"

She glowered. "Fine. We'll talk when I get back. I'm going to get a message to Lark, tell her we have Rose safe here. You," she pointed to me, her finger like a vicious dagger at my chest, "take care of this." She gestured to Rose's broken ribs. When I nodded tightly, she grabbed her cloak off the couch, leaving us alone once more.

———

THE SECONDS DRAGGED in awkward silence. I took a seat on the short table across from Rose, wanting to get this over with.

She eyed the glass of lavender tonic warily when I held it out. "It's bay leaf, elderberry oil, and crushed lavender with bergamot to strengthen it," I explained. "After what Rissa said, you should know we're not trying to kill you."

She twisted her lips but relented, taking the vial and throwing the contents back in one go. When she straightened, a lock of raven hair swept across her cheek. My eyes followed her fingers as she pushed it behind her ear. "How long will it take to start working?" she asked, already getting to her feet. "I need to finish the trial before I become even more of a *joke*, as you've so kindly pointed out."

I rubbed my chin in exasperation. I was never going to live that down. She was perhaps more impatient and stubborn than even myself. "That's not what I meant, Rose." When she didn't respond, I sighed. "It will take all night to heal completely, but you'll be able to move with minimal pain after the next couple of hours. I can apply a topical potion as well, see if that helps speed it along."

"Fine."

Another moment of uncomfortable tension swelled. She peered down at me. "Well? Where's the topical one?"

I cleared my throat. "I need to see the injury first to know what tincture to use. If that's alright with you."

She pursed her lips but nodded, turning so her wounded side faced me.

"May I?" I asked, looking up at her. When she nodded again, I slipped my fingers beneath her black shirt, slowly pulling the fabric up, exposing smooth skin inch by inch. She sucked in a breath when my thumb brushed against her waist, and I paused.

"Is this alright?"

She swallowed. "Yes. It's just—your hands are cold." A flush crept up her cheeks.

I was unable to stop the myriad of ways I could keep my hands warm from flashing through my mind. But the sight that greeted me as I continued pushing her shirt above her ribcage cleared away any stray thought.

The patch of skin on her side was deeply bruised, with blotches of dark purple and red curving down to her waist and the underside of her breast. Small pockets of even darker red, almost black, dotted her olive skin where blood vessels had broken beneath the surface.

"Fates, what happened to you?" I asked on an exhale.

"Fell from my horse. Or rather, she threw me off. Probably stepped on my side too, if this is any indication." She lowered her shirt. "I was fighting the Illusionist challenger and tried to get away when he did something to spook her. That's the last thing I remember."

"I'm sorry," I said, cringing slightly at the image of a horse trampling her. "That sounds painful."

"There are worse kinds of pain."

A different image came to the surface, one of her from earlier this morning when she stumbled into my path. The terror, exhaustion, and panic I'd seen.

Needing a reprieve from the heaviness that had set over us, I rose from the small table and paced to the kitchen, gathering ingredients for the topical charm. I supposed her conviction was admirable—I don't know how many would be willing to return to the trial after what she'd already endured. No matter what vitriol had spewed from my mouth earlier, I *wanted* to believe she'd be able to find Gayl's Grimoire. But my sister knew me and my prideful distrust well; it was difficult to relinquish the part of me that knew I could do this, that was so convinced I was our best chance at ending things.

"Where did you learn how to make all these tonics?" she asked from the couch, breaking my thoughts.

The side of my mouth lifted as I worked. "My sister and I weren't particularly careful as children. Especially after Rissa learned how to shift."

"And what about you? You're half Shifter, so can't you shift, as well?"

I glanced over my shoulder. "What makes you think I'm half anything?

She snorted. "For one, you have a *tail.*" Her eyes darted to the floor, where my dark tail coiled at my ankles. "And I heard you cast a spell that night in the forest. Plus, you know your herbs and charms too well to be anything but an Alchemist."

"Yes, I'm half Shifter." I grounded the fleawort leaves with a pestle and mixed them with cedarwood oil until it formed a thin paste. "No, I can't fully shift."

"Why not?"

I knew she was merely inquisitive, and understandably so, considering she'd lived her entire life in a province surrounded by only Alchemy. She didn't know how other types of magic worked, had probably never even had a conversation with someone from a different province before this week. But still, my biting paranoia and defensiveness crept in, making my walls flare up the way they often did when my childhood was brought to the forefront. With it came memories I didn't want to relive, the deep well of guilt I didn't want to drown in again.

Growing up as pariahs, as exiles in this empire, watching the world turn on our father and crush my mother's spirit, had forced Rissa and me to lean heavily on one another. We were compelled to do things no child should have to do. Things I couldn't take back.

Things that had changed me forever.

I turned back to the couch, where Rose stared at me expectantly. I cleared my throat. "Magic doesn't always work the way you think it will," was all I said in response.

She opened her mouth as if she wanted to press the issue, but thought better of it. I set my mortar on the counter, taking a seat once again and gesturing to her midsection. She stood, gingerly lifting her shirt for me.

Remembering how my touch had been cold before, I'd cast a heating spell on the cedarwood and fleawort mixture. I dipped a finger into the warm oil and slowly spread it across the massive bruise at her ribs. Her answering sigh as she rolled her head onto her neck made my stomach tighten.

"My father taught me how to make this," I said carefully. A question burned in the back of my throat as I massaged her skin, one that had bothered me since she spoke the words. "What did you mean earlier when you said he's the reason yours is dead?" I asked.

Her neck snapped back to attention and her entire demeanor shifted, cold and guarded once more. She assessed me with those keen emerald eyes, and I could see her thoughts churning. Could see her deciding if she trusted me enough to share whatever had made her lash out.

She ran her tongue along her teeth. "My father was killed by men who worked for Branock Aris," she finally said, her words cutting and sharp.

My fingers stopped moving. "That's impossible."

"Why?" she challenged.

"When did your father die?"

She grinded her teeth together so loudly I could hear it. "Twenty years ago."

Twenty years. So my father had still been alive. But there was no way he would have had some Alchemist from Feywood killed. He'd already abdicated his throne at that point—what reason or resources would he have even had to send someone to do such a thing? Branock Aris had been a brash man with faults of his own, but he wasn't savage, and certainly not a murderer. She didn't know a thing about him *or* what the past years carried.

My father had more blame placed on his shoulders than any man should. He'd had his name—*our* name—drug through the mud for decades now. And it was all a lie.

He didn't deserve one more added to it. I wouldn't stand for his memory to continue being desecrated.

"Trust me, you don't know what you're talking about," I snapped, pulling her shirt down with more force than was necessary. I picked up my mortar and rose from the table the same moment she pivoted to face me. We were inches apart, her eyes blazing up at me, cheeks heated and pink.

"I don't know what I'm talking about?" she spat. Her indignation washed over my skin. "I watched as the man who slit my father's throat said, 'Branock Aris sends his love,' then left him to drown in his own blood." She shoved a finger at my chest, the tip seeming to burn through my thin shirt. "Who are you to tell me I'm wrong? That I don't know what I'm talking about? You have no *idea* what I've been through, and it's because of him. Your father."

She slid away from me and rounded the couch, grabbing a thin, wide book from the table and reaching for her dagger on the floor as she strode toward the door. Her staggered steps were already stronger.

Her eyes flashed at me once more, the moment of tentative peace we'd created earlier now shattered. "I'll work with you and your Sentinels, Aris. I'll break the curse. But *don't* ask me to trust you."

23

ROSE

I wasted no time heading back to the memorial site. The fox, or...Rissa, I supposed, had brought me miles southeast of the path I'd been on, which I'd discovered after leaving their little cottage and traveling a few minutes north toward a busy street in the south sector.

I *may* have stolen Leo's horse. Rissa's exact words had been "we're willing to do what it takes to help." Surely, letting me borrow a ride fell under that purview.

Disbelief clung to me at what this day had brought. Logically, I knew Lark couldn't have been working alone in her plan. But to find out there was an entire *network* of rebels, both here in the capital and in the provinces, eager to stop the curse and end Gayl's rule? That the very man I'd run into not once, but twice now, was part of this mission? That he and his sister were none other than Branock Aris' children?

It was too much to handle. I was ashamed of my outburst earlier, when I'd tried to attack Leo with my bare hands and broken ribs. But something had snapped. Branock Aris' *children*. The man who, somehow or another, was behind the murder of my father. And while I understood deep down that Clarissa and Zareleon didn't inherit the sins of their parents, I couldn't seem to separate their voices from the one of that Illusionist twenty years ago. Couldn't stop seeing the blood that coated my hands whenever Leo touched me. Couldn't wipe away the sudden surge of vengeance that rippled through me when I laid eyes on them.

How was I supposed to trust them when I could hardly look at them? When their words made that vicious snake inside of me rear its head before I forced it back?

The constant jostling of my skull and midsection as I rode Leo's beautiful black horse northwest and back to the Battle of the Dead Lands memorial became increasingly less sore as time passed. I had to begrudgingly admit his Alchemy was good. Probably one of the best healing tonics I'd seen.

He said his father had taught him how to make it. The same mind that ordered my innocent father's execution had once sat down with a younger Leo and showed him how to make someone whole again.

Bitterness coated my tongue, and I shoved all thoughts of the twins, the mission, and my father aside to focus on what was still ahead of me—finishing the first trial.

I estimated it took me another hour to reach the familiar path. That, combined with the slow movement of the sun heading toward the horizon, put the time closer to eight o'clock in the evening. Only four hours were left. How many of the other challengers had already found their artifact?

This tournament wasn't the only thing that mattered—I understood that. But my competitive spirit was as fierce as ever. I didn't just want to complete my mission. I wanted to *win*. I wanted to bring strength back to Feywood. Knowing Callum may have cost me a victory in this first trial made me see red. Gripping the reins so tightly my nails dug crescent moons into my palms, I urged the stallion through the line of trees and into the open clearing beyond where my map told me the memorial site rested.

The grounds were on an enormous, secluded plot of land surrounded by a forest. It looked like citizens barely frequented the area—there were no paths for carriages, no signs of life or civilization besides a stone plaque embedded in the forest floor with the name of the battle and what I assumed was an account of its history. A large statue of a man in armor with a traveling cloak around his shoulders holding a long sword stood in the center of hundreds of small gravestones. The sun had set behind the tree-line, making it difficult to read any of the engravings along the statue.

The encroaching darkness made anticipation coil in my stomach. *It is cloaked in the day, and revealed in the night.* Perhaps my artifact would illuminate itself in the absence of light, as the false one had in the mausoleum.

But as the stars began to wink into existence against a navy and orange sky, nothing seemed to change. I explored the clearing, trailing down each line of gravestones, examining the length of the statue, even going so far as to climb on top of it to search every nook. Out of breath and clutching at my sore ribs, I gingerly jumped back to the ground, leaves crunching underfoot. A twinge went through my skull, but it wasn't as painful as before.

Leo's horse was growing restless. I sighed and made my way back to him as he pawed at the ground and shook out his mane. When I passed the raised stone plaque that read "Battle of the Dead Lands," something tugged at my core.

Something that felt like *magic.*

Halting in my tracks, I slowly turned to face it, my eyes scouring over the inscription. Only, there was nothing beneath the title. No history or description of the battle that took place so long ago. It was an empty space about the size of three large Grimoires, fresh for carving.

I stepped closer, reaching out a hand, and that same heavy presence of magic circled around my throat and chest.

There was an enchantment here.

I took a thistle leaf from my pouch and placed it on my tongue, uttering the incantation to banish a spell. *"Finiscere."*

The enchantment snapped in the air like a bowstring. Where the plaque had been blank, piles of tiny purple crystals now dotted the edges. Amethyst, by the looks of it. The same crystal that had appeared in the mausoleum.

Could this finally be my artifact? What was I supposed to do with it?

I wracked my brain for every piece of knowledge related to amethyst, dredging up the texts I'd read and the spells it was used for. It was a spiritual stone, one that increased wisdom and intuition and gave some Alchemists ability to perceive beyond the physical world. They claimed to see spirits and understand words of prophecy, although I'd never had that experience.

As I thought, I grabbed a handful of broken crystals and let them fall through my fingers to see if they landed in any particular order on the plaque. Nothing. Was I supposed to cast a spell with them? Try to see the future, however impossible that was?

I looked down again, noticing my disruption of the crystals had cleared a space at the bottom of the plaque. In small letters, the words "by stars or by fate" were etched in the stone.

By stars or by fate.

Instinctively, I glanced up at the night sky above me, which barely held a hint of light. Deep navy blue swam across the heavens, a patchwork of stars dotting the expanse. Moonlight spilled like silver over the darkening forest around me. I closed my eyes and breathed in the night air, letting it soothe me, smoothing the rough fringes.

For a moment, I could forget. For a moment, I could just *be.* There was no Decemvirate, no curse, no mission. No memories of blood on my hands and lifeless blue-gray eyes. No delusions of grandeur and glory, no sense of inadequacy. No fear, no burning hatred, no spike of vengeance tainting my peace.

Opening my eyes, the constellations shone down on me. I tracked the twinkling stars, ones I knew by heart, even away from Feywood. There was the Surge constellation to the left, a network of stars that made the shape of a lightning bolt. Legend says the Fates put that one in the sky to remind us they could strike us down at any moment. The Dracos Ara, or the decorated dragon, which my father had first shown me when I was a little girl. And the Oracle on the far right—an image of a standing figure with a snake around its legs. Morgana had once told me a story of the Alchemist three hundred years ago who had supposedly summoned the Fates through an Oracle using his blood and—

Amethyst.

I gasped and grabbed the pieces of broken stone. I wasn't sure this would work, but it was the only idea I had.

One by one, I placed them on the empty plaque in the shape of the Oracle constellation, talking myself through it as I went. "The head is here, looking down at the snake, while the snake"—I glanced at the sky to make sure I had it right—"the snake is twisted at its feet."

I moved as fast as I could, feeling the time limit bearing down on me. Finally, the last stone took its place.

The air was silent.

My stomach crashed to my feet, disappointment knocking the breath out of me.

Then the crystals began to glow. A vibration shook the plaque, softly at first, then intense enough for the crystals to quake. Slowly, they moved toward one another, jagged edges finding their home and forging a single large, beautiful amethyst.

Eyes wide, breath trembling, I reached out to grab it. My finger landed on a sharp point at the top, pricking the skin. I winced as a bead of blood coated the tip of the stone, deep red on bright purple.

The grass at my feet vanished, replaced by swirling, white fog, so thick I could barely see my feet. Trepidation crept up my spine, spreading down my arms and making the hair over pebbled flesh rise.

"Beautiful night, Rose Wolff, is it not?" a voice called from behind me.

No, not *a* voice—dozens of voices all at once, woven together like a tapestry on the wind. I whirled to find a figure shrouded in white floating above the fog. Smoke billowed from beneath their ivory veil, and what looked like streaks of lightning pulsed at their feet.

"Who are you?" I asked hesitantly, my hand angling toward my pouch of herbs.

"You fail to ask the question you ought." The words encompassed me, setting my teeth on edge and pulling me closer at the same time. I couldn't tell if this being was young or old, male or female, *human* or other. But their presence captivated me. My feet stumbled forward of their own accord.

When they didn't continue, I rubbed my fingers along the opening of my pouch, nervous energy bubbling in my gut. "Well, what question should I ask, then?"

A chill whipped through the clearing, bringing with it whispers that brushed against my skin.

"We are the great Oracle of right, conjured amidst this knowledge plight." I hadn't realized I'd been inching closer until the lightning at their feet stung my ankles. I leapt back with a grunt. "We shall grant you one clue as to what lies ahead of you."

"One clue? As in, for the second trial?" That nervous energy turned to intrigue. Help for the next trial?

The figure nodded, a pale, gray hand sneaking from beneath the white veil and crooking their finger at me. Wordlessly, I floated toward them, pulse pounding.

"A reward, dear Rose, for you have well played your part. The next trial will test the depth of your heart." The voices rose and swelled in tandem, sending a shiver through me. "There is much for you to learn, and this is all we can tell: when the time comes, believe the gray bells."

I stared at them, blinking. "What?"

"Believe the gray bells," they repeated.

"Is—is that all?"

Silence.

Believe the gray bells? All of this for some cryptic clue? My shoulders sagged, my body breaking from their hypnotic hold over me.

"Believe the gray bells. Got it. Thank you, oh great Oracle," I said sarcastically, turning on my heel to head to Leo's agitated horse. Fates, what a waste of—

A strong, wrinkled hand grasped my wrist. I gasped and spun around, trying to yank from their hold, but their grip was as strong as steel. The light smoke curling around them deepened to black. When they spoke again, it wasn't the honeyed blending of voices, but a low rasp that scratched my ears.

"When you look in the mirror, what do you find?" They cocked their head. "A rose in full bloom, with thorns on the vine?" Something like a chuckle slithered through the air, echoing around me. "We see dark, hidden secrets, a deceitful tongue. For in the wake of the wicked, your poison will come." Their voice dropped even further. "We know how this ends, daughter of the moon—only you will decide who meets their doom."

They retracted their hand, the smoke once again clearing to white. I stared at them slack-jawed, my hand cold where their fingers had clasped.

"Wh-what was that?" I asked shakily. "What does that mean?"

More silence.

"Is that all you can tell me? Was that last part about the second trial, too?" I tried again, desperate for an explanation.

Again, I was only met with the sound of wind whistling through the trees, making my hair lift and swirl around my shoulders. I took a deep breath and closed my eyes, and when I looked once more, the Oracle was gone.

Heat radiated from a pocket in my vest, the same way it had in the mausoleum when the enchanted parchment had something to say. I quickly pulled it out, reading the words as they appeared.

Time is almost up. The palace doors lock in two hours.

Fates, I still had to get back to the palace. Grabbing my artifact from the plaque, I sprinted to Leo's horse and we bolted through the forest.

24

ROSE

It took an hour to reach the central sector. The moon hung high, and creatures of the night slithered and hooted and pawed along the path as I rode. My legs and backside ached from all the hard riding today, my muscles unused to sitting atop a horse and clenching for so long.

When we finally reached the treeline that opened to the enormous palace grounds, some of the tension I'd been holding in my shoulders fell away. It was over. I'd done it. And now all I wanted was blessed *sleep*.

A small shadow darted in front of me, coming from the south side of the trees.

Another challenger racing back? Snapping the reins, I chased after the figure, which grew larger and larger as I crossed the grounds. Just as I was preparing to cast to slow them down, the figure stopped and turned, hearing my approach.

Wavy blonde hair, tall, broad shoulders, and a hint of a smirk peeked out as I drew closer. *Nox.*

"Nice night for a stroll?" he asked casually, sticking his hands in his pockets.

I shook my head in disbelief. "You've *got* to be kidding me."

"What? Not happy to see me?"

Dismounting, I tied the reins to an iron bench bordering the nearby gardens. I'd figure out what to do with Leo's horse after midnight. Glaring at Nox, I held an arm toward the palace. "Why aren't you going in?"

He shrugged. "Ladies first."

My eyes narrowed. I couldn't figure this man out. He seemed genuine, but I couldn't help thinking there was something I wasn't seeing. "Why?"

"Because, my very distrusting viper, I've already told you—I don't care if I win this tournament. And I've taken a liking to you." He nodded at the entrance to the north, the ends of his ear-length hair swaying in the breeze. "Call this a sign of good will. I'd rather get through this month with someone tolerable at my side than fight with you every step of the way." He raised an eyebrow, that familiar yet unsettling glimmer of mischief and honesty in his blue gaze. "So, have I earned your trust yet?"

I chewed my bottom lip, fighting the urge to reject his olive branch and push him to the side. My instincts screamed that this was somehow a trick, that he would abandon or turn on me once I got too close. Trusting Nox...that could potentially be the biggest mistake I'd make this entire tournament. He was *powerful*, I could tell. And already knew far too much about me. If he betrayed me, if he got beneath my defenses...he'd be my most formidable opponent.

But everything he'd done so far had been in favor of earning my trust. Drinking the Grimlock wine and confessing his thoughts about the Decemvirate. Confiding in me about his own province hanging his participation over his head. Telling me about the other challengers and warning me against poking Callum too strongly.

Perhaps he truly didn't care about winning. Perhaps he truly hated the purpose behind this tournament—as did I. And I had to admit, it would be nice knowing I had at least *one* person who wasn't trying to sabotage me at every turn.

I let out a sigh as I met his gaze. "*Fine*," I said. "But if I so much as *sense* you're about to betray me, I'll curse you so fast you'll wish you had stayed in Drakorum."

His cheek twitched. "If you were from my province, that wouldn't be the threat you think it is." Before I could respond to those cryptic words, he bowed low and swept an arm out ahead of him. "After you."

———

PALACE GUARDS OPENED the grand entrance doors as we approached. Nox stayed a few steps behind me, letting me go first as promised. When I crossed the threshold, the familiar bushy blonde beard of Horace appeared, taking me abruptly by the arm and leading me down the darkened entryway. Flames flickered from the sconces along the wall, the only light in the entire palace.

"Took your time, didn't you," he said with a grunt.

I gaped up at him. "Do you even know what happened today?"

"I heard."

"Oh, right," I said with a scoff. "I forgot, your good friends Ris—"

His large hand came up to press firmly against my mouth. "Quiet, girl," he grumbled. "What are you trying to do, get us killed?" He released me, looking back at Nox and the other guards behind us. His voice lowered. "Save this conversation for when there are less nosey minds around."

I muttered an apology, then added quietly, "I took their horse, by the way. Can you get it back to them?"

This earned me an actual chuckle. "Emperor's tits," he said. "You really *are* trying to get yourself killed."

"I'd like to see him try," I said under my breath. We continued down what I recognized as the corridor leading to the great hall, where whispers and rustling cloth reached my ears. "Where are we going?"

"Another debriefing. It's required after every trial. They'll go through rankings and scribes will record it all to be turned into news pamphlets for the capital and provinces."

"We're doing this at *midnight*?" I asked, pressing a finger to my temple. Exhaustion set heavily into my bones, making my feet drag.

Horace simply shrugged. "They love the drama of it. And it gives time to get the news out by morning. Your face and ranking will be plastered on every market square in town tomorrow."

"Wonderful."

We entered the great hall, and the mood from the meeting yesterday afternoon had drastically shifted. Whereas then it was mingling and laughter and pastries and wine, tonight was dark cloaks and murmurs. Beady eyes and competitive glances. Torches were scattered across the vast room, firelight crackling and casting eerie shadows along the dark stone floor.

All of the other challengers were here. My chest deflated at the sight, humiliation twisting in my gut. I was the last one.

Well, *second* to last. But only because Nox let me go ahead of him. I clenched my jaw, feeling my neck and cheeks heat as heads of various lords, ladies, and guests of the capital turned their attention to me.

In the open streets of the central sector earlier today, I'd felt comfortable in my anonymity. Protected. Even the people who might have recognized me were simply curious, wanting to get their peek at the mysterious, last-minute replacement. Now...they knew who I was. And by the disappointed looks of pity, they knew *what* I was.

A failure. A joke, as Leo had called me.

Was this worse than the disdain, the snide remarks, the lingering looks of contempt from my own province? I wasn't sure, but it filled me with equal parts shame and resentment.

My eyes scanned the crowd of dozens of guests for faces I recognized. Leaning on the far left wall was Arowyn, the Strider from Celestria with the long, almost white hair whose aloof, disinterested attitude the day before had been refreshing. Tonight, however, her icy blue eyes were narrowed on every conversation, fingers tapping at her thighs.

There was another woman near her that I'd never seen before. Her left arm was in a sling and she was the only one in the entire room smiling. A few finely dressed ladies from court stood around her, and when she whispered something to them, they all burst into quiet laughter. She tossed her auburn hair back, her tawny cheeks crinkling into a smile.

I had a guess who she might be. Callum's words from earlier came back to me—"you should see what I did to the Lightbender." Based on her injury, this must be Callista, the Emberfell challenger. Nox had said she was a crowd favorite, and I could see why. People flocked to her like bees to honey, vying for a sliver of her attention. Watching her with them, I had to admit I was a bit jealous of how naturally it came to her, how well she commanded the group of women. A genuine smile here, a well-timed laugh there, a confidence in the way she carried herself that inspired respect. She knew how to play the game. That kind of recognition and favor in the eyes of the powerful often held more weight than the magic that ran through one's veins.

I spotted Alaric's dark brown and gray hair in the back corner, talking quietly with a member of the Royal Guard. My jaw ticked as I took a step in his direction.

A hand clamped down on my shoulder. "Be smart, girl," Horace whispered in my ear.

From several feet to the right, someone *tsk*ed. "She's got a nasty temper, doesn't she?"

At the sound of his voice, my blood ran cold, then strikingly hot. I glared at Callum, finding his black eyes just as full of vengeance as mine surely were. Gone were the days of cocky pretension, of snide remarks hidden behind sharp smirks.

Callum's expression was clear. I was no longer a plaything for him to toy with on a string. I was his enemy. A *threat*.

For some reason, that realization made satisfaction hum in my chest. I cocked my head and let a small smile play on my lips. I didn't want him to see how much he affected me. How easily he got under my skin. Despite Horace's low growl of warning at my back, I sauntered over to Callum, straightening my spine and taking my time as I sized him up like a predator hunting their prey.

"Looking forward to the rankings, Feywood? I can't wait to see you where you belong," he sneered. "Always knew you'd look good beneath me."

"Careful, Callum," I hummed, drawing out his name. "Those are strong words for someone I had begging on their knees mere hours ago."

His fingers came out to wrap around my wrist, digging into my skin. "You think you're so clever with your little plants and potions." His voice was low and menacing in my ear as his fingers tightened their hold. "But you're nothing without them, are you, Feywood? That's why people like you will never win. Will never be strong enough. Your magic is *useless*."

He pulled back and glanced behind my shoulder as heavy footsteps approached, but I kept my stare focused on Callum. He released me, dusting off his shoulder and adjusting his jacket.

"Keep your charms, because that's all you have," he hissed. "When it comes down to it, we all know your province is the weakest link. I wonder what will happen to your people when you fail." With one last feral grin, he smoothly stepped aside and into the crowd, leaving me still as stone.

That same tide of humiliation and bitterness rose and swelled, but for a different reason. He was right, in a way—Alchemists were the only ones who needed an outside element to perform our given magic. All five of the other provinces could conjure their own power without aid. It was innately *part* of them. Being isolated in Feywood, I'd never had that fact wielded against me. Never understood what an advantage the others had, not being dependent on what resources lined their pockets or what herbs and potions were at their disposal. Never realized we were viewed as *less than* because of it.

I swallowed hard and contained the doubts swirling within me, not letting it break my impassive features.

The deep toll of a bell echoed through the hall. Midnight. From the front came Lark's voice, signifying the end of the trial and gathering us all to the center. A hand pressed into my back and guided me forward. Rotating my neck, I saw Nox at my side.

"Don't listen to him," he murmured as we followed everyone else. "He's an elitist prick who had his balls handed to him and is trying to get a rise out of you. He's wrong; you're—"

I arched away from his touch. "I don't need you to tell me how strong I am, Nox," I said coldly.

His hand fell to his side, and I didn't miss the look of hurt that passed over his face before he smoothed it back out and smiled. "Just as well, then. Don't want it going to your head."

I turned my attention to the south end of the hall where the same podium from the briefing was stationed. As last time, Lark Everest took her place behind it, clearing her throat to silence the whisperings of the crowd. Motion made my eyes flicker to the wall behind her, and my heart stuttered.

Emperor Gayl was here.

His blue and white mismatched eyes sliced into mine across the hall. Tonight, he wore a midnight blue cloak, his long black and silver streaked hair gathered in a strip of leather at the nape of his neck. His gloved hands were steepled at his chest as he silently observed in the background.

I held his stare. He didn't look angry, even though he knew I'd been spying on him. He looked *curious*. His head tilted to the side ever so slightly, his lips twitching as neither of us broke our gaze. I wouldn't let myself cower. Wouldn't allow myself to show the fear he so easily amassed from his people.

As if he could read my thoughts, he suddenly smiled. Chills cascaded across my skin.

There was something so...*familiar* in that smile.

"Congratulations to our six challengers for successfully completing the first trial." Applause went around the hall at Lark's words. Horace nudged my shoulder, and I finally ripped my eyes away from Gayl, bringing my hands together in a lackluster attempt at celebration.

"In a moment, we will reveal the current standings of the tournament. After today our challengers will have six days of rest before the second trial begins." Lark brushed a mass of black curls away from her face. Her loose hair sprung around her face in tight coils, free of its thick plaits. "The evening before the second trial, Emperor Gayl and I would like to invite all of the challengers to a feast in honor of finishing the first task. You will receive more information later. And yes, Arowyn"—Lark shot a knowing look to the white-haired figure with her arms crossed—"it *is* mandatory."

Lark clapped her hands. "And now, for the rankings." Shadows appeared in her palms, tendrils of darkness rising and twisting through the air. The candlelight in the hall flared brightly as her power formed above our heads. Positioned directly in front of Lark were two women and one man, each with their heads buried in pieces of parchment. Their fingers flew as they scribed every word the head architect said, readying to deliver the news of the first trial far and wide.

"Each challenger was tasked with locating and retrieving an artifact related to their magic. They were required to solve a riddle leading them to a position in Veridia City, where they faced obstacles along the way. The first person to find their artifact and return to the palace before the stroke of midnight was Arowyn Garrolas of Celestria." Shadows formed Arowyn's name in thin letters, hanging in midair. "Arowyn located the golden key, a symbol of knowledge and success in her province of Celestria, in the mountains of the north sector. Congratulations to Arowyn for her excellent use of magic and intellect in the face of fear." A round of applause sounded at the sight.

For some reason, this surprised me. I'd anticipated Callum being in first, given how confident he acted when we fought. I snuck a glance at Arowyn, who appeared as bored as ever. The only indication she was paying attention was the way her shrewd eyes scanned over the crowd.

"In second place, who expertly uncovered the Cloak of Shadows in the ancient ruins where our capital's jewel mines once stood, is Alaric Rinehart of Tenebra." New shadows appeared below Arowyn's name, spelling out the Shadow Wielder's. The spectators clapped, some of the members of the Royal Guard patting Alaric on the shoulder. He raised his hand in a polite wave and nodded in thanks. I took a deep breath and let it out slowly, my exhale transforming into a growl at the end. Alaric caught my eyes and smiled feebly.

At least he had the sense to look ashamed for what he did to me.

"Next, the third challenger to complete his task was Callum Orlox of Iluze. The Illusionist found the gilded mirror, which appears on the crest of Iluze, hidden in the great Veridia Theater."

I rolled my eyes at the smug expression on Callum's face as his name appeared in shadows. Hatred surged inside of me when he raised his eyebrow at me in challenge, flicking the metal piercing at his bottom lip with his tongue.

"Callista Greyhound of Emberfell claimed fourth place." Lark's shadows forged Callista's name in the air beneath the other three. "With grace and power, she found the crystal pearl, an object representing a myth of her people. She traversed the High Temple in the central sector to retrieve it."

The cheering was exponentially heightened for her, even though she was in fourth place, and she beamed at her admirers. A blush graced her cheeks. The perfect picture of a humble, thankful challenger. But her eyes gave her away. At the last second, I saw her turn a piercing glare toward Callum, the venom in that single look making me smirk.

It seemed I wasn't the only one out for blood.

"Rose Wolff of Feywood."

I jerked at the sound of my name, watching slithering shadows form the letters.

"In fifth place, but not for lack of strength. She solved a puzzle in a battlefield memorial, leading her to a crystal of great spiritual magic."

I knew I'd be toward the bottom, but the sight of those four names before mine was a kick to my pride. I nodded tightly at the polite applause that followed, pointedly avoiding Callum's haughty face and Alaric's uncomfortable expression. If it weren't for them, I would've reached the memorial faster. Who knows how high of a rank I could've had? Climbing back from the bottom would be almost impossible.

"Remember what you're here for," Horace muttered, too quiet for anyone else to hear. I twisted my neck to see his dark, beady eyes trained on mine, one bushy eyebrow slightly raised.

"I know," I whispered back. He was right. This wasn't about winning the tournament. Not in the end.

"Finally, Nox Duma of Drakorum."

Murmurs swept across the hall. Drakorum had *never* fallen to last place—not in recent history, at least. By all accounts, Nox should be leading the pack. Shifters and Illusionists were notoriously the strongest. Seeing a Strider at the top of the rankings was shocking, to say the least.

"Nox braved the wild forests of the south, retrieving a replica of the talisman of the dragon, an artifact Drakorum holds dear," Lark finished, waving a hand at the six names written in shadow. They pulsed and writhed in the air, but didn't dissipate.

"Well, there you have it. The end of the first trial." She clapped her hands once. "This is shaping up to be quite the interesting Decemvirate."

25

LEO

My mother's hand felt so small in mine. It had been over a decade, and I still hadn't gotten used to seeing her like this. The hands that were once larger than life, that once tucked me into bed at night or tenderly held me through my nightmares, now frail and fragile in my own.

I took in her graying hair from the light of the moon coming in the window, a bit of her vibrant blonde peeking through the strands. The same blonde as my sister. The wrinkles on her gaunt face were slightly less defined when she slept. Her thin chest moved up and down slowly with her breaths, the only indication she was still alive.

It was late, and with my rare night off from Sentinel duties, I should be sleeping. But I often came to her room when I couldn't get my mind to quiet. I would sit here in silence and hold her hand, or, in the times she was actually awake, I would read to her. Rissa and I kept a collection of her favorite books on her bedside table. Sometimes, I would simply talk. Ten years ago, she was still responsive enough to respond. I would sit and tell her of mine and Rissa's recent escapades while she slowly knitted or wrote in her journal, stinted conversation taking place until she became too tired.

Over time, those kinds of visits were few and far between. Her hands shook too violently to hold her needles, so we'd sit by the fire in the living room instead. When sitting straight for long periods of time became too difficult, we held her hand in her bed. Our stories earned us smiles and nods, an occasional whisper of encouragement.

But eventually, she stopped responding at all.

It began shortly after my father died. The healers said his sudden death, combined with the stress and change of the last years of our lives, pushed her over the edge. She succumbed to the weight and it fractured her mind, which in turn made her body break down. She took in just enough food and water to stay alive, some part of her still cognizant of her bodily needs, but not aware enough to so much as know who Rissa and I were anymore.

Watching her fade away like this...it was the hardest thing I'd ever had to do.

The window at my back was cracked an inch, letting in the midnight air. I could hear the crackle of the leaves in the wind, the rustling of twigs and grass as small animals crept along the ground outside the windowsill. The crisp scent of pine and spruce filtered through. It reminded me of nights spent laying under the stars with my sister and our parents. Of simpler times. Not easier, necessarily, for we'd always faced hardships, but at least we'd been *together*.

Memories speared through me like a knife, making me grip my mother's fingers tighter. Her and Father dancing in the kitchen of our cottage, her apron and rosy cheeks streaked with flour, my father sweeping her into his dirt-smudged arms. Rissa's fingers twisted in her blonde curls as she sat in our mother's lap, her bright eyes entranced in the fairytale our father read by the fire. The first time Rissa fully shifted, when my father and I watched her little red tail trailing my mother's large, wolven body through the trees by the house, pure joy in their high-pitched barks.

My lips curved upward.

Then, the images changed.

Rissa sneaking into the house with large black and purple splotches covering her arms. The feel of rough leather beneath my fingers as I scoured my father's Grimoire. Deep red blood drip, drip, dripping onto dried herbs, salt and copper blending with sweet earth.

Pain. So much pain. It was everywhere—my back, my bones, my skin.

Magic has a price.

My father, collapsed on the—

"You're up late, little brother."

My neck snapped to the doorway, where Rissa stood with her arms crossed over her chest. "Couldn't sleep," I said with a grunt.

"Me either." She padded to the chair on the other side of Mother's bed and sat. "How is she?"

We asked each other the same question every time, and the answer never changed. "Same as usual," I responded dully.

"Do you want to go get some fresh air?" she asked after a moment.

I nodded. I knew what that meant; she wanted to visit the clearing a little ways from our cottage. One we would often go to as a family because of how secluded and peaceful it was. For a family of Shifters and Alchemists, we felt most at home and connected to our magic out in the wild freedom of nature. When the worries of our world became too large, my sister and I found solace under those stars in the middle of the forest.

We made our way to the familiar clearing. Rissa laid down a blanket she'd grabbed on the way out and sat, leaning back to gaze up at the night sky. Her long hair brushed the top of the grass as she closed her eyes and breathed in.

I settled in next to her. The cool breeze raked against my skin, whistling through the trees. "Did she make it through the trial?" I asked.

"Yes. Fifth place, Lark said. We knew her detour here would set her back."

"I'm sure she was thrilled about that." Rose seemed like the kind of person who didn't take defeat well.

"Well, we don't need her to *win*. Just get close to Gayl." She twisted to look at me. "You sure made an impression on her earlier. Although, probably not the first woman to try and attack you on sight."

"Hilarious."

"What happened with her, anyway? Things felt...heated."

I scowled. "That's what happens when you keep mission critical information from me and I find out by someone breaking into my cottage in the middle of the day."

She shot me a look. "Yes, and I wonder why I didn't tell you everything, considering you took it so well."

"Why *did* you keep it from me? All of it?" I asked, then sped ahead when it looked as if she was about to interrupt. "And none of that about fewer people needing to know the details. I'm your brother, Rissa. You always tell me everything."

She sighed and faced the sky again. "I guess I wanted to protect you. To keep you as far away from this mission as possible. I *know* what being around Gayl does to you—you've always held onto that anger and vengeance. Not that I haven't, but it's just...different." She shrugged. "I thought the more you knew and the closer you were to the details, the more likely you'd jump in and try to play the hero."

"Why do people keep calling me that?" I muttered under my breath.

With a scoff, she said, "Please, Leo. You can't help but come to the rescue. It's practically in your blood. How many people did you beat up as a teenager because they so much as *looked* at me weirdly? And all those fugitives you save on your patrols. You're a protector, brother. That's not a bad thing."

"We *all* help people," I said.

"We do," she agreed. "In different ways. But some of us focus on the bigger picture. The *why* behind it all. I'm not saying you don't," she rushed out when I opened my mouth. "But you take every individual person, every family, every night one by one, and you make it your personal responsibility to save them. It's beautiful, Leo, how much you care for each and every one. It can make you forget to watch out for yourself, though. And as much as I love you, you're just like our father in that regard—you make rash, stupid decisions."

My exhale came out as a huff. "Tell me how you really feel."

But she wasn't wrong. And she didn't even know of all the rash decisions I'd made for the sake of safety. *Her* safety.

"Look, I'm sorry I didn't involve you in the details from the beginning. I promise to keep you updated from now on, though," she said.

I nodded. "We're a team. You should use us, Rissa. We all bring something to the table that could help. If you called a meeting where we *all* knew the relevant information, we could make this work. We could help Rose."

My sister eyed me. "I'm surprised you want to be in the same room as her again after how today went. What *is* it with you two?"

"I don't know what you're talking about." When she continued to stare at me, I said the first thing that came to my mind. "She stole my horse," I grumbled.

"Emperor's tits, Leo," Rissa said with a laugh. "How many times have you met, anyway?"

I sighed. "The night before the Decemvirate started, her carriage was attacked by a couple of Shifters. I was patrolling the west sector that night."

"Oh, so you were there when her uncle was cursed?"

Her uncle. That must have been the man fighting with her. "I assume he was the original Alchemist Lark had found to work with?" I asked, and Rissa nodded. "I saw her again in the palace this morning, as you heard. She was running from something and we hid together in a hallway. I had no idea who she was."

She gave me a sharp look. "Yes, *about* that—"

"Trust me, I know. You don't approve of my palace visits." I scrubbed a hand down my face.

"Then why do you keep doing it?"

"Why do *you*?" I shot back, recalling her bruised eye and hurt leg from the other night.

Her mouth snapped shut. "Fine. We're both reckless idiots."

"At least I didn't get caught."

This earned me a laugh, albeit an annoyed one. She fell back onto the blanket and stared up at the stars. "We have to be careful, Leo," she said softly. "There's no telling what Gayl will do if he catches us sneaking around. That's why we have Rose. We have to trust her."

I rested my head near hers. "What if Lark was wrong about her? What if we're making a mistake?"

"She's done nothing to make us think she's not capable. So what if she got stumped at the first trial? She's going up against five other challengers who have had much more time to get ready, plus many with far stronger magic than hers." Rissa propped herself up on her side and faced me. "You have to give her a chance. You're so quick to expect the worst in others, little brother. Sometimes you have to look harder to find their best."

I swallowed hard. "It's not as if I want her to fail."

"Then don't act like you expect her to. Don't act like you don't *believe* in her."

Her perceptiveness always surprised me, no matter how often she showed it. "When did you get so wise?"

She patted me on the arm. "You'll get there one day."

We laid there for a few minutes, listening to the sound of the forest buzz around us. "I'll try to do better. I understand she's our best shot, and I'll do what I can to make this mission successful." *Even if she's the most stubborn woman I've ever met*, I thought with a sigh.

"I know you will," Rissa said. "You always do." She grabbed my hand sitting between us and gave it a quick squeeze. "I couldn't do any of this without you, Leo."

"Yes, you could," I insisted. "But if there's one thing I *can* promise, it's that you'll never have to."

We stayed there until the first rays of golden light began to peek through the trees, the way we used to as teenagers. When it was the two of us against the world, with the sun chasing our shadows away beam by beam.

If only they could truly disappear that easily.

26

ROSE

The next morning hit me like a brick to the head. I woke to a metaphorical pounding in my temple and a literal pounding on my door—far too early after the events of yesterday.

"Go away," I groaned, turning over and yanking my pillow over my head.

"Rosie! It's us!"

I grimaced. It was Beau, probably the only person capable of getting me out of bed right now.

With great strain, I lifted myself into a sitting position and carefully pulled my shirt up, checking on my bruised ribs. The skin was a light brown color, almost yellow, with a sickly green indicating its rapid healing. It was truly incredible how well that tonic had worked. I hardly felt any pain when I pushed two fingers onto the tender area.

Another frantic knock sounded at the door. Brushing a hand through my disheveled hair, I padded across the room and opened the door. Beau's extended fist fell forward and he tripped over the doorway. Instead of stumbling into my room, however, it was as if he hit an invisible barrier. His head and fist bounced off a solid shield of air, causing him to fall back into my aunt.

"Fates, I'm sorry, Beau Beau—that must be the wards." I'd completely forgotten. Nox had said once I gave permission for someone to enter, the wards would be disabled for them for the rest of my stay. I quickly allowed them inside the room, and they both walked through tentatively, Beau's face bright red with embarrassment.

Once inside, my aunt gave a sigh of relief. "How are you feeling, Rose? Are you alright?" She gripped my forearm, her concerned eyes searching my body for signs of injury.

"I'm fine, Aunt Morgana, I promise. A little banged up, but nothing I can't handle."

"How was the first trial?" Beau asked excitedly. "They wouldn't tell us anything yesterday, and Ma wouldn't let us go see the rankings." He shot his mother an accusatory look.

"That's probably for the best," I said, shuddering as I imagined my little cousin and aunt surrounded by people like Callum, who wouldn't be above using them against me.

"What was it like?" he pressed. "Did you have to fight anyone? Were there *dragons*?"

I laughed and tousled the top of his head, making him duck and shove my arm away. "No, *Beau Beau*." This earned me a glare. "You know dragons aren't real. But I did see a lot of the capital." I continued to tell them a shortened version of the trial and the riddle I had to solve. When I recounted how the mausoleum had been a diversion and that Alaric had followed me to trap me inside, Morgana gasped.

"Alaric Rinehart!" she scolded. "The next time I see that man, I'm going to—to—"

Beau snickered at his flustered mother. "What, Ma, curse him so his feet are cold forever? Put itching powder in his collar?"

Morgana smacked his neck playfully. "If you're not careful, I'll put itching powder in *your* collar, young man."

"Oh, I'll find a way to get him back," I said with a chuckle, my anger from yesterday slipping ever so slightly as I watched my aunt and cousin bicker. Hearing her reprimand the great Alaric

Rinehart like he was some schoolboy, despite the fact that he was older than her, made me smile.

I continued to tell them about Rothy and her tea house in the central sector, and how she helped me find the memorial site. I left out the part about fighting Callum; I still didn't want to face what I'd almost done. That the idea of killing him had briefly crossed my mind, paired with the murky memories of my father's death and the blistering wrath that had consumed me. I could already see my aunt's face if I were to confess how I'd nearly burned him alive. How I'd *wanted* him to die, if only for a moment.

A moment was all it took.

Beau was infinitely impressed by how I solved the constellations puzzle and the creepy Oracle who'd been summoned by it. At the end, they were both beaming with pride, even after learning I'd come in fifth place.

"I knew you could do it, my dear girl. Your uncle would be proud of you," she said, cupping my face between her hands.

Another knock came from the door. Morgana turned toward it, startled. "You're quite popular this morning, aren't you?"

I crossed the room and opened it to find Horace standing in the frame, wearing his normal gruff expression. I introduced him to my aunt and cousin, and he nodded politely before saying, "Sorry to take you away, but Lark wants to meet with you." He gave me a pointed look, and I knew this wasn't about the tournament.

Glancing back at Morgana, I could tell she understood, as well. Her lips moved into a grim line as she swallowed and took Beau's hand. "We should let Rosie attend her meetings, Beau Beau. Maybe we can catch up with her later."

"I'll find you as soon as I can," I promised, giving Beau a one-armed hug before pulling Morgana in tightly.

"Be safe," was all she whispered. The two of them left, and Horace shut my door behind them.

"It's not just Lark," he said. *Straight to business.* "There's several more who will be there. C'mon, get dressed."

Disgruntled, I moved to my bags to pull out a fresh set of clothes. "Several more *what*? And where are we going?"

"Those Rissa trusts most." He opened the door and stepped outside to give me privacy. "Hurry up. I've gotta take you to the Aris cottage."

———

THE ARIS COTTAGE was only a twenty minute ride south from the palace. Horace rode his own horse while I took Leo's black stallion, dreading the confrontation that was sure to happen when I brought him back after stealing—*borrowing* him.

Horace told me there was nothing to worry about, that Lark and Rissa simply wanted to meet with the Sentinels' inner circle and myself while there was a break between trials, since almost all of them knew about me now anyway. There were six days, including today, before the next one began, and I agreed this would be a good time to discuss my *other* mission.

Still, I wasn't necessarily looking forward to seeing Leo again, especially after my abysmal ranking from last night. Just another reason for him not to believe I could accomplish what they needed. Not to mention the idea of being in that house, one Branock Aris himself may have once lived in, made my anxiety rise like the tide.

We arrived at the cottage, and I took it in for the first time. I'd left too abruptly the evening before to give it a backward glance. The white wood stuck out in the middle of the green forest, even though it was stained and faded by the elements. The dark roof was patched with a chimney sticking out the right side where I knew the mantle and fireplace rested. Two windows were positioned by the front door. Several pots of plants rested on the windowsills, their leaves reaching toward the morning sun.

Horace told me to go inside while he tied our horses to a post and did a quick check of the perimeter. When I opened the door, the scents of savory meat and freshly baked bread hit my senses.

Rissa stood in the kitchen, putting slices of a red apple into a bowl next to a plate of thinly sliced ham and a loaf of bread. "Good morning," she said, looking up at me. Her blonde waves fell down one shoulder as she smiled. "Sleep well?"

I snorted. "Not even a little." Peering around the kitchen and living room, I hesitantly asked, "Is your brother here?"

"Not yet. He had an early morning patrol shift, but he'll be back soon. Everyone's on their way." She gestured to a seat at the small kitchen table with her knife. "Go ahead and sit down. Are you hungry?"

"Starving," I said. I wasn't even sure I'd eaten yesterday, save for an orange Horace had stuffed in my hand after taking me back to my room following the ranking.

She busied herself with setting a glass of water and a plate of apples, bread, and ham in front of me. "How are your ribs?"

I could tell she was trying to keep the atmosphere light, but an awkwardness had settled in the air. She knew I'd been on edge here yesterday, and my feelings toward her and her family hadn't gone away overnight. I briefly wondered if Leo had told her what I'd confessed about my father and theirs.

But she was attempting nonchalance, so I'd go along with it. "Much better," I said, taking a bite of bread. "That healing potion worked wonders."

We sat in silence for a moment, her cleaning the kitchen while I ate. Finally, I said, "I never really thanked you yesterday. For chasing off Callum and bringing me here to heal. I—I don't think I would've completed the trial without your help."

"Oh, I think you would've found a way. But you're welcome, Rose."

I couldn't meet her eyes as she smiled at me, those piercing gems so very similar to Leo's. A small voice inside wondered...did they get those eyes from their father?

Branock Aris sends his love.

My grip on the glass of water tightened as I took a sip, washing the acrid taste of the memory from my mouth.

Rissa must have seen the shift in my demeanor, for she walked to the table and stretched an arm out as if to rest it on my shoulder. "Rose, listen—"

I shifted out of her reach and cleared my throat. "So, who all is meeting us here?"

She sighed and dropped her hand. "My brother and Horace, of course. Lark is coming up from the palace. And another Sentinel member named Chaz. While I initially wanted to keep your involvement just between those who absolutely needed to know, Leo helped me realize these are the people I trust the most. I want them here to discuss a plan of action for your time in the palace hunting down Gayl's Grimoire."

I swallowed. I knew this conversation was coming, and that I'd eventually have to tell her about the utter disaster with Gayl the previous day. Fidgeting with the hem of my shirt, I nodded tightly, embarrassment seeping in and mixing with my discomfort. As much as the knowledge of her being Branock Aris' daughter still ate at me, I didn't want her—or the others—to think I had failed. That I wasn't up for the challenge.

But part of me wondered if someone else would be better suited for this task—someone like Leo, as loath as I was to admit it. It was obvious he wanted the job in the first place. He'd nearly turned green with envy when he found out I was the one Lark had chosen after Ragnar.

I'd been discovered within *minutes* of following Gayl. I'd been bested by both Alaric *and* Callum during the trial, putting me almost in last place. The only reason I'd even completed it was because Rissa had saved me in time. What if I *wasn't* a wise choice for this task? What if my skills consisted of sharp remarks and the occasional well-timed enchantment? The future of this empire wavered above my shoulders, and perhaps it was the exhaustion talking, but I feared I wouldn't be able to bear it.

Rissa continued, unaware of my internal struggle. "Having someone like you in the palace for an entire month is the biggest break we've had in years. Just be sure you're staying safe and out of sight." Nerves coiled inside me at her words. "As a challenger, you'll have more freedom and leniency than any of us could ever dream of. A protection that allows you to get away with more, as the empire has a very compelling reason to keep you and the other five challengers alive. But Rose"—she reached out to grip my arm, and I fought the urge to flinch—"you still need to be careful. Your position and our power can only go so far. That's what we're going to talk about today. How to keep you safe and—"

I pulled my arm away, the little food I'd eaten now climbing up my throat. "Rissa, I don't know if I can do this." The words were out of my mouth before I could stop them, but the moment I spoke, fear and uncertainty spilled from me like water.

I'd been foolish and arrogant to think I could do this—*any* of this. The Decemvirate, the mission, the spying. Who was I to walk into this city and think I could change things with a little bit of quick spellcasting and a chip on my shoulder? That I could take on not only five challengers with far more experience and preparation than myself, but the great and powerful emperor of the Veridian Empire?

My breaths came fast and sharp. I wasn't used to not being able to squash these intense feelings away. I raked shaking fingers through my hair as I tried to shove at the rising panic. This was a mistake. There was still time for them to find someone else.

"Rose—Rose, hold on. What are you talking about?" Rissa asked, crouching and grasping my shoulders, forcing me to face her. "Did something happen?"

I bit down on my tongue, tasting blood, and swallowed hard. "I messed up," I said in a flat voice.

Instead of the anger I expected, Rissa looked at me calmly, her features softening. "Take a deep breath. We can work through this. Tell me everything."

I recounted how I'd accidentally found a hidden wing of the palace and overheard Gayl speaking with one of his advisors, and how I'd followed them into the secret corridor. When I admitted that Gayl had seen through my invisibility charm and the threat he'd made in response, Rissa's face tightened. She twisted her lips back and forth, thoughts spiraling behind those eyes faster than I could keep up.

"First of all, thank you for telling me," she started. "I know that must've been difficult, but we've got to be open with each other—that's the only way any of this will work. And second, I don't blame you, Rose. If anything, I'm glad Lark found someone as bold as you. Someone willing to take a risk. Perhaps we need to work on subtlety"—she let out a snort—"but if I'm being honest, this is partially my fault."

My brow furrowed. "How so?"

"Because I should have found a way to meet with you as soon as Lark told me she'd convinced you to volunteer. We left you on your own, with no instructions, no plan, no way forward. Emperor's tits, I would've done the exact same thing you did. And probably gotten myself killed."

I blinked at her. "So...you're not upset with me?"

She studied me carefully, and even though she was only a couple of years older than me, I felt like a child beneath her examination. Clarissa Aris seemed wise beyond her years, someone who'd been to hell and back and seen things I'd never imagined in my wildest dreams. I hated how in just these two meetings with her, I'd begun to crave her approval—this woman whose father I despised. It was impossible not to admire her.

Over time, I'd learned how to disregard what others thought of me, to stop caring about seeking favor. When I'd lived my entire life under the scrutiny of a province full of people who'd made their judgments long ago, there wasn't much left to lose. But Rissa and Lark...they saw potential in me. And that was something I didn't know I needed until this moment. People who could look past the cold, jagged edges and see the fire that burned within.

"No, I'm not upset with you," she said, and my trepidation eased. "We'll need to adjust our approach going forward since you've been compromised, but it's not the end of the world. We'll find another way. I'll talk with Lark and the others, make sure we're all on the same page."

I let out a breath, a small weight lifting from my chest. Rissa smiled and squeezed my arm, and this time, I let it comfort me. "You don't have to do this alone, you know," she said. "Nobody is expecting you to have all the answers or be perfect every step of the way. We're going to help you as best we can, alright?" When I nodded, she winked. "And maybe next time, run your plan by one of us first. Gives us an excuse to abandon ship and charge the palace if you wind up missing."

I knew she was exaggerating, but her joke made me wonder... "Why don't you? Just unite your rebels and make a move on the emperor? If you have as many loyal people as you say, I imagine you'd stand a chance at taking him down."

Eyeing me, she said, "If by taking him down, you mean assassinating him, that's not how we work. Expecting people to follow a new regime built on the blood and bones of the one who came before is exactly what got us into this position." Her eyes flashed, and I knew she was thinking of her father, of how Gayl had betrayed him and cast him aside.

I didn't believe I'd *ever* feel sympathy for Branock Aris, but I hadn't stopped to think about what it might have done to the rest of his family. How such a deep betrayal had affected the two young children I now knew.

Before I could respond, the sound of footsteps and muffled voices came from outside the door. Rissa gave me that mischievous smirk I'd come to recognize and rubbed her hands together.

"Chin up, Rose. We've got a mission to plan."

27

LEO

My morning patrol shift had immediately followed mine and Rissa's late night excursion, so I hadn't gotten any sleep. While our conversation put me in a better headspace, that had quickly soured with my exhaustion and the fact that I'd had to borrow Rissa's mare to complete my rounds. I *still* didn't have Nightshade back.

Perhaps that was why I'd been rougher than necessary with the man I'd caught breaking into a supply house for province fugitives in the south sector. He didn't need those teeth, as far as I was concerned. He had been armed to the brim with explosives, ready to destroy the resources we'd so painstakingly gathered for those in need. Anyone who held such malice for provincers simply seeking refuge in our capital didn't deserve to walk away with their limbs intact.

Other than him, it was a fairly uneventful rotation. Chaz and I were in charge of assigning willing Sentinel members to patrol duty—a pseudo Royal Guard, in a sense. We kept watch over the five sectors, ensuring the less fortunate and needy, such as those crossing over from their provinces, still received protection they were owed. Protection Gayl didn't seem to hold in high regard. We changed out the rotations often so that the Royal Guard and those loyal to His Majesty wouldn't become suspicious. Heavier care was given to the evening and early morning shifts, especially around the Decemvirate. Chaz and I often took on more rotations than the others. Since he was a Strider, he could move more conveniently from place to place. As for me...well, I grew tense when I knew there was work to be done, people to help, and I sat back doing nothing.

I'd put an end to many robberies, attacks, and brawls in the past few months. Had come away with my fair share of bruises and broken bones, as well, but it was worth it to know the people had some semblance of protection in this city.

That resolution did nothing to quell my foul temper this morning, though. After being up all night, now covered in sweat and splatters of blood from the would-be arsonist, and the fact that the woman we were entrusting our mission to had run off with my horse, I was in no mood to meet with her and the others. Even if it was my idea.

I sighed as Goldie, my sister's pale yellow mare, trotted along the dirt path toward our cottage. When it came into view, I let out a scoff.

There was Nightshade, tied up to our post, grazing on a patch of grass.

"Unbelievable," I muttered, dismounting and taking care of Goldie before heading into the house.

I was the last one to arrive. Chaz and Lark stood at the counter, conversing with cups of steaming liquid and half eaten plates at their sides. Rissa chatted animatedly with Horace, who sat at the table with his thick legs spread wide, his fingers twisting in his beard as he listened. And there was Rose, sitting across from him with that guarded expression she wore so well. That long, dark hair was pulled into a braid, small tendrils framing her olive features. Her arms were folded across her chest, her fingers playing absently with the edge of her pouch of herbs. Subconsciously or not, she never seemed to be far from her charms.

When those green eyes turned and landed on me, something

stirred in my chest. There was a flash of apprehension hidden there, a hint of the wariness I saw during those close moments in the alcove. But then, as quick as it appeared, it was gone. Her eyes narrowed, steely distrust aiming back at me. Distrust that grated on my nerves, for it wasn't something *I* had earned.

"Kind of you to return my horse," I said with a grunt as a way of greeting, shutting the door a bit harder than I intended.

"He was the perfect gentleman," she responded. She leaned back in her chair with that same taunting air about her as when she put me under the compulsion spell the day before.

"Sounds like Leo could learn a thing or two from him," Chaz said with a chuckle.

Lark glanced at me. "Do I even want to ask why there's blood all over you?"

I shrugged off my cloak and hung it on a nail by the door. Rissa clucked her tongue at me and rushed to grab it, muttering about it needing to be washed. "Ran into a problem at one of the supply houses in the south," I said. "Someone tried to break in and destroy the place, but I took care of him."

Rissa shot me a look. "And by 'take care of,' you mean…"

"Made sure he would think twice before attempting something like that again." When she raised an eyebrow, I scowled. "I left him in an alley with some broken bones and fewer teeth."

Horace grunted, which was his version of a laugh. "Better than dead."

Rose's eyes caught mine, a curious gleam lighting them. "Does this type of thing happen often?" she asked.

My sister gave a grim nod. "More than we'd like. The Decemvirate makes it worse. People's emotions are heightened, adrenaline is running, and they think they have a right to take matters into their own hands. Some capital natives are unhappy with how many…*guests* the city receives during this time. It allows people from the provinces to sneak in and stay without anyone noticing."

Rose's brow furrowed. "Are a lot of people moving to the capital?"

"*Trying* to," Chaz answered. "The majority right now are from Emberfell. Their border with Drakorum has become way too hostile for some of them to keep living over there. But there's quite a bit from the others, too."

Rose let out a soft hum. "I had no idea. I mean, I knew things were getting bad in the provinces. We see that even in Feywood. Our border with Iluze has gotten worse these last few years." A small shiver went through her, but she shook it off. "I didn't realize people were trying to come here to get away from it all."

"Unfortunately, our emperor hasn't been the most welcoming host," Rissa said, leaning against the counter. "But that's why we're here, isn't it? To hopefully bring some change, to both the provinces and the capital. And we believe that starts with the Somnivae curse. It's the one thing uniting *everyone*. We all despise it. We all want it to end. If we can prove Gayl started the curse, it's the perfect opening to bring everyone together against him. Provincer or capital native, rich or poor, weak or strong. We can force him to end the curse and take him off his throne. And that's where *you* come in." Rissa gave Rose a sly smile.

Lark picked it up from there, a seamless transition between the two women. "Over the next few weeks, we need you to gain access to Emperor Gayl's Grimoire. We have maps of the palace, places we know he frequents and wings that are typically closed off to the outside, things like that. But nobody has gotten close enough to him or his private chambers to locate his Grimoire. That's the first challenge.

"The second is to learn as much about the curse as you can. Once you have found his Grimoire, we assume information regarding *how* he cast it will be inside. We will then have proof that *he* was the original caster and, with the support of the entire empire, can force his hand in reversing it."

We all sat in silence for a moment until Rose scratched her nose and said, "Right. So, nothing too difficult."

Horace, to my surprise, chuckled.

"We'll take it one step at a time," Rissa said encouragingly. "Let's start with the maps. Horace?"

At her summons, Horace stood and pulled several folded pieces of parchment from his back pocket. Laying them out on the table, he leaned over and began pointing at the various floors.

"These are the guest wings. The servants' quarters, the ballrooms, the dining hall. These areas in the center will be the busiest during your stay." His finger moved north. "The northern wings are quieter. You'll need to be more careful here. The armory and treasury are kept there, so they're more heavily guarded than others."

"I highly doubt he's hiding anything there, anyway," Lark offered. "It's far too high profile."

Horace swept his hand to the west side of the map, but Rose held up a finger. "What about here?" She pointed to a small corridor in the northern wing that dead-ended into the edge of the palace. "Is anything there?"

Bending to look closer, Horace said, "Not that I know of. Just storage rooms."

Rose pursed her lips together, her eyes roaming across the area. "And you're sure these maps are accurate?" When Horace quirked an eyebrow at her, she waved a hand in the air apologetically. "Sorry, I just...I thought I saw another hall connected to this one yesterday."

"What were you doing over there?" I blurted.

Giving me a sharp look, she said, "I might have seen Gayl on my way to the first trial and...followed him." She and my sister exchanged a passing glance.

Surprise swept through me. The girl was fearless. I'm not sure even I would be brave enough to track him so quickly.

Chaz laughed. "You sure do have a pair on you."

"Did you find anything?" Lark asked eagerly.

Suddenly more reserved, Rose fell back into her seat. "No. I mean, he walked down another corridor, and then I left. I could have *sworn* there was a hall right there, though."

"You must be wrong about the wing," I said, which earned me another glare.

Lark's shoulders sagged slightly. "Well, perhaps you can find the correct one and see where he may have been heading."

Rose nodded in agreement, her fingers once again playing with the edge of her pouch.

"Good. Keep going, Horace. We've got a lot of ground to cover," Rissa instructed, gesturing to the map.

We spent the next couple of hours reviewing the wings, theorizing what sections would be most likely to contain anything of importance, and charting a plan for Rose to follow that would keep her safe and away from prying eyes.

As time went on, Rose became a bit more relaxed in our presence, even grinning once at a ridiculous joke Chaz tossed out. But there was still an apprehension around her. The constant picking at her shirt or pouch, the tight features, the withdrawn eyes. Something that seemed...reserved. She was a puzzle I couldn't quite figure out. First, the blazing, powerful, brutal Alchemist from the forest. One who wasn't afraid to use her magic to its full extent. Then the frightened, timid woman who needed shielding from some unseen threat. A woman bold enough to follow the most powerful man in the empire on a *whim* down an unknown corridor, unafraid to curse me in my own home and attack me with broken ribs. She was capable, there was no denying that. But I couldn't reconcile that with the woman who looked as if she felt uncomfortable in her own skin.

The task that faced her was daunting. I couldn't blame her for any hesitations or fear. But part of me knew there was more to it than that. After what she'd said to me yesterday, about blaming my father for what happened in her past, I understood her distrust. I knew my father would never order an innocent man's death, but hers was still killed. She was still fatherless. And my claiming her ignorance on the matter wouldn't change that.

I scrubbed a hand over the rough stubble on my chin, replaying that conversation from when I'd healed her ribs. I grudgingly realized my sister had been right about the way I treated her, and my defensive words had been a mistake.

No wonder she stole my horse.

The clock on our mantle struck eleven, and Rissa decided we had enough of a plan going forward to get us through the second trial and hopefully yield results from Rose's search. When Rissa asked if Rose would stay for lunch, she shook her head and said she wanted to spend time with her family.

"Well then," my sister said, turning to give me a look that spoke of trouble. "I'm sure my brother would be happy to take you home."

Rose grimaced, that crease at her forehead deepening with dislike. "I think I can manage."

I gritted my teeth. How did this girl manage to get so under my skin with a single look? My guilt and understanding from a moment ago seemed so fragile in the face of her disdain. "Horace can give her a ride to the palace just fine," I countered.

"Can't," Horace said. "Rissa asked me to stay behind for something."

"Of course she did," I said under my breath.

"It's not safe for you to travel alone, Rose," Rissa pointed out. "Plus, if I recall correctly, *you* don't have a horse here."

"*Fates*," Rose grumbled, cursing. "Fine. Let's go, monkey boy."

Chaz spat out his water, spraying Lark across the face. "*Monkey boy?*"

Whirling to the door, I pulled it open, muttering, "I hate all of you," as I walked outside.

As she strode past me and to Nightshade, Rose flicked her braid over her shoulder and said, "Better stay on my good side, or I'm tossing you off his back."

28

ROSE

Just when I was beginning to think I liked Rissa, she went and pulled something like this.

One horse.

I supposed this was what I deserved for taking him on a little *detour* without permission.

My back was straight as a rod as we trotted north to the palace, my legs clenched tightly around Nightshade to keep me from moving back into Leo's chest. I was still sore from yesterday, and my muscles screamed at me to release my ironclad hold, but something about this man put me on edge. He had a sort of broody arrogance—different from Nox's confidence or Callum's cockiness. Even only being with him a few times, I could see he believed he was *always* right. *He* thought he should be the one to carry out this mission, not me. He brushed off my memory of my father's death, simply because he didn't think I was right. He instantly assumed I had the wrong hall when pointing it out on the map.

His lack of faith in me itched at my skin. It made me want to prove him wrong.

A strong hand came to rest on my thigh, the stubble at his chin brushing the top of my ear as he leaned forward and said, "You need to relax. You're spooking Nightshade."

His breath so close to me sent goosebumps along my neck and down my arm. I swallowed, willing my legs to relax around the stallion. The tight coils unwound slowly, and my back pressed into Leo's solid chest as Nightshade stepped into a dip in the road.

That same hand moved from my leg to my stomach, keeping me from being jostled. The warmth of his skin seeped through the thin fabric of my shirt. How had it felt so cold on my ribs yesterday? Now, it was like a searing ember, indicative of our mutual animosity. I saw the way he looked at me when his sister told him to take me to the palace. He didn't want to be in this position any more than I did.

"So," he said gruffly, "you know why I was hiding when we ran into each other at the palace yesterday morning. But I still don't know what you were running from."

"Is that a question?"

His fingers curled slightly at my stomach, the friction grating across my skin. I could practically see his teeth grinding. My lips curved into a faint smile—as much as he frustrated me, I rather enjoyed frustrating *him*, too.

"Yes, it's a question."

I rolled my lips together. "The Illusionist challenger decided to have a little fun once the trial started. He found me outside my room and...made me see something I wish I could forget." That's all I would give him. That's all I *could* give him. Even the memory of Horace's body blurring into my father's on that bloody floor made my throat tighten.

"The Illusionist? Isn't that who Rissa said you were fighting when she helped you during the trial?"

"The one and the same."

A rumble went through his chest, sending a buzz along my back. "I hope he got what he deserved."

Shrugging, I said, "He got a taste. I'm not done with him yet."

"Good."

Surprised by his agreement, I turned my head to the side to see him better. "What, no snide remark? No comment about him getting the best of me?"

He sighed, a scowl back on his features. "Contrary to what you seem to believe, I don't think you're incapable."

"Could have fooled me."

"Are you this stubborn with everyone?"

"Yes, actually." I gave him a saccharine smile before facing forward again. "It's why everyone back home finds me so charming." When I moved, his hand left my stomach and wrapped around the reins, leaving my skin cold.

"That's not the word I would use."

A snort left me. "Yes, well, neither would they. Maybe peculiar. Improper. Poisonous. Take your pick, honestly."

"Your people say these things about you?"

"When you've grown up as a social outcast with a tendency to go a little too far with your magic, people don't have the nicest opinion of you," I said, toying with a small string hanging from the pommel of the saddle. What had begun as self-deprecating humor now felt more real. More raw. I wasn't sure why I was sharing this with him. It was different, not being able to see his face or that scowl that said he was waiting for me to fail.

He hummed, and the motion fluttered across my back again. Nightshade stepped over a log in the path, forcing me further into the saddle. Leo's thighs were now flush with the backs of mine as his hand came to my stomach once more to hold me in place. The gesture was like second nature to him. I was beginning to see how deeply his protective instincts ran, what with the Sentinel patrols and how he'd saved me that night in the forest. How he'd pulled me aside to give me solitude during my panic attack. Even in the care he showed in healing my injuries.

It soothed my annoyance, blanketing it with a softness I didn't expect.

"If they saw how you took down a fully shifted snow leopard, they wouldn't call your magic 'too far,'" he said.

"Careful now, Aris, or I might think you're complimenting me."

"Well, I *was* the one who killed him in the end."

"There it is," I said, my lips twitching upward.

We were almost to the palace. I could see the tops of the spires peeking out over the trees as the forest thinned. After a minute of silence, Leo said, "I'm sorry about yesterday." The words were so low and quiet, I wasn't sure I'd heard him correctly. "I shouldn't have said you didn't know what you were talking about when you spoke of your father's death. It was an impulsive thing to say."

I twisted my lips. "And do you believe me now?"

He didn't respond immediately. Nightshade slowed, even though we hadn't reached the palace grounds yet, and came to a stop near a large tree shadowed by the thick canopy. Removing his arm from around my midsection, Leo dismounted smoothly.

When he offered his hand to me, I ignored it and grabbed the pommel of the saddle, swinging my leg over and jumping to the ground.

"I believe *you* believe something more happened. But no, I don't believe my father had anything to do with it."

My jaw shifted, the banter we'd fallen into now slipping back to frustration. "So the fact that *your father's* name came out of the murderer's mouth means nothing to you? That I've been hearing those words echoing in my head since the moment I met you and your sister?"

He threw his hands in the air. "I don't know what you want me to say. Perhaps they were lying. Or you misheard them. You said it was twenty years ago, yes? You were young. I can't imagine what that was like, watching what happened to your father. But memories can be deceiving. I *know* my father. I know the kind of man he was. He cared for his people and was a firm, just ruler. What reason could he possibly have for ordering yours to be killed?" He shook his head, his tense shoulders deflating. "There's something you're not seeing, Rose. Something else behind this."

"It's a shame we'll never get to ask either of them, isn't it?" I said roughly, my chest constricting and burning all at once.

His words made sense. I'd been a bundle of anger and

repressed grief and nerves for the past day, and my mind needed something to latch onto. Something to blame and take all this funneled energy. Branock Aris was an easy target, and part of me didn't *want* to think rationally. I wanted to rage and scream and cry and do everything I'd been forced to lock away in the face of the first trial and what followed.

I needed to grieve. But I didn't think I could handle that. Not on top of everything else.

Leo took a step toward me, and I moved back on instinct. "I don't want this to affect our alliance in this mission or your loyalty to the Sentinels," he said. "My sister and I are *not* our father. If you can't separate your beliefs from that truth, I don't know how to get you to trust us fully."

I closed my eyes and rubbed at my temples, trying to fight back my pride and some unhelpful sharp reply. That was how I handled emotions I didn't want to deal with: a snarky comment intended to take the weight off my shoulders.

But he was right. Whatever happened in the past, I needed to separate it from my purpose. From what stood right in front of me.

More than that, I needed to be alone. To have a moment of rest without the fate of this tournament and the mission occupying my mind. Too much had happened in the last twenty-four hours for me to make sense of it all.

"I have to go," I said finally, weariness evident in my tone. I couldn't give him what he wanted to hear right now. Not when the memory of my father's death was constantly mere *seconds* away from emerging and pulling me under, and the next time it happened, I wasn't sure I'd be able to stop it.

"Rose, if you would just—"

"Thanks for the ride, Aris," I said. Before I turned to face the palace, I added, "At least you can tell your sister we didn't kill each other."

It wasn't trust. But it was something.

29

ROSE

I took a valerian root sleeping draught and slept through the rest of the day and night. My body needed it, and the Fates only knew my mind did, as well. When I woke the next morning, I felt more clear-headed than I had since the attack on our carriage.

But that clarity brought what I'd put off for so long. What I'd feared to let take over.

The raw weight of grief and anguish was no longer cloaked by the urgency of a trial or spying or meetings. These were the first moments since I'd remembered everything that I had to myself. The first moment to *think* without distraction.

And it was like a flood.

Memories of my father crashed through me, as far back as I could recall. Roaring campfires under the stars while he taught me about crystals and spirit magic. Rolling down soft hills of grass and shouting the names of root herbs in between squeals of laughter. He made magic come alive. It was so ingrained in me from the very first spell I watched him perform.

I'd forgotten so much of this. Had replaced these vivid moments with shaded versions of a near-stranger, instead of the father I'd loved so deeply as a little girl.

I'd only been five when he died. A lifetime of memories with him had been taken from me. I wondered what magic he could have taught me as I grew, what advice he would have given me, how differently my future might have looked. Would we have run the Arcane together? Would we have had weekly dinners with Ragnar, Morgana, and Beau? Would *he* have entered the Decemvirate instead of Ragnar?

My morning and afternoon were spent in the only thing that brought me comfort—my magic. It started with the need to take some sort of action instead of drowning in my thoughts, so I began assessing what herbs I had left in my father's pouch. Every new charm, leaf, and petal drug up memories of him explaining what each herb did or the feel of his Grimoire beneath my fingers as I came across spell after spell penned in his hand.

It was strange to be feeling these kinds of strong emotions decades after it had passed. I thought I'd come to terms with it. I thought I'd patched this heartache. But it had never healed—it had simply been cloaked. As I went through all my bags and pulled out charm after charm, potion after potion, magic and memories and sorrow swelled to the surface, with nothing left to tether them down.

And I let them come.

I let them wash over me, cracking me down the center. I let the tide pull me under until it felt as if I couldn't breathe, sobs breaking through the waves like a storm cresting the shore. Tears for that five year old girl who watched her father, the strongest man in her world, crumble and fall. Tears for the little orphan who didn't understand the hand this life had dealt her. Tears for the growing child whose heart was hardened and whose tongue was sharpened by the cutting glares of people who wouldn't see the truth. Tears for the young woman who never had the chance to live freely, out from the scrutiny and judgment of the world. Who had never had the chance to find herself outside of the labels she was given.

At some point, my aunt's muffled voice came from outside my

door, and when she realized it was unlocked, she came in to check on me. She found me sitting on the floor with vials and petals and leaves spread around me, tears streaking my face and my locket clutched in my grasp.

"Oh, my dear girl," was all she said before falling to her knees and wrapping her arms around my shoulders.

We cried together for what felt like a lifetime, until no more tears were left. And then she held me. No questions, no words, no pressure. Giving me the space I needed to process what I'd spent years avoiding.

"This was the very first herb he showed me," I said after we'd sat soaking in the silence. My voice was hoarse and my fingers shaky as I held up a brittle amaranth stem. "I could barely say the word."

Morgana chuckled and smoothed down my hair with one hand. "Of course, he did. Your father and his protection spells."

"Can you tell me more about him?" I whispered, my head still on her shoulder.

She kissed my temple. "I didn't know him well before Ayla brought him around, but it was clear from the moment she introduced us that he was simply infatuated with your mother. Fiercely protective and loyal, but in his own quiet way. Like the ocean. I used to say your mother was fire, and he was water—steady and strong. Set in his ways. A bit stubborn sometimes, like someone else I know," she said with a laugh in her voice.

She told me stories of him and my mother, their whirlwind romance and quick marriage. Some memories were funny, like when my mother charmed his pencil to spell every word he wrote incorrectly. Some were joyful and full of pride, such as starting the Arcane together and finding out they were pregnant with me.

"Rose," she said, moving her shoulder so she could look into my eyes. "You may not be ready yet to talk about what happened to him, but just know that I'm here when you are. You have *never* had to face this on your own. Ragnar and I just...didn't know how to navigate it. You were so young." Her voice cracked, eyes shining with tears once more.

Her words reminded me of what Rissa had said the day before. It was easy to feel alone when all you had for so long was your own anger and repressed trauma, always knowing *something* was wrong but never being able to put your finger on it.

That anger was still there. I wasn't sure it would ever truly leave me. I knew it would rear its head again, my stubborn nature refusing to back down and show vulnerability. Anger was such a comfortable substitution for me, and now I had a better understanding of why.

But knowing I wasn't alone...it made it all a little easier to bear.

I gave myself a single day to sift through those emotions and recover from the resurgence of memories. In a way, I was thankful to have so many other things vying for my attention, forcing me to get up and move.

Morgana, Beau, and I had a quiet dinner that night in the infirmary at Ragnar's bedside. Beau and I played cards while Morgana read softly to my uncle, the three of us finding pockets of calm in the storm of these past days.

When the next morning came, I woke with a sense of purpose and determination. I had four full days until the second trial. Four full days to search the palace, to learn every nook and cranny and find a way to slip past Gayl's defenses.

I threw on a pair of leggings and a dark tunic, brushing quickly through my hair before swinging the door open and searching the corridor for the familiar guard. There he stood, at the intersection of another hall, steadfast and surly as ever. Like my personal grumpy guard dog. When I caught his eye and beckoned him closer, I could see a thick blonde eyebrow hitch even from this distance.

"Didn't see you much yesterday, girl," Horace said, eyeing me as he drew nearer. "Everything alright?"

My purge of emotions the day before must have lingered, because I felt a surge of compassion for this man. He not only upheld his responsibility to be there when I needed, but also seemed to truly care about me. His indignation at Callum, his gentleness when dealing with the aftermath, his short words of wisdom to keep me from spiraling or attacking.

My first real friend from the capital.

"I'm fine, Horace," I said. "I just needed some time. But I'm ready to start making progress." Opening the door wider for him to come in, I glanced down the hall to check for listening ears. "Do you still have those maps?"

He grunted. "Yes, but can't keep them much longer. I borrowed them from our commanding officer when I told him I wanted to tighten up security for the challengers. He expects them back soon."

"That's fine. I'll make a copy to keep with me." I found spare parchment in my bags and got to work tracing the lines of the palace layout, adding a few labels at Horace's direction to remember where important halls and chambers were.

I folded my fresh map and tucked it in a pocket, then stuffed new supplies into my pouch of herbs. When the two of us marched out the door, Horace cleared his throat. "Be careful. I've got orders from the Guard saying I have to stick to a certain area, so I can't follow you everywhere. Just...don't get yourself killed." Patting me awkwardly on the shoulder, he added gruffly, "It's good to have you back, girl."

A genuine grin split across my face. "I'm just getting started."

30

ROSE

My first course of action was to find that hallway at the northern end of the palace that I'd followed Gayl down. I'd been so positive during the meeting with the Sentinels that I knew which corridor it was, but in reality, I hadn't been paying much attention. It was entirely possible I'd misre-membered, as Leo had pointed out. I just didn't want to admit that to *him*.

My thoughts had swayed to him more than once since I left him on the outskirts of the palace grounds. The time to myself had allowed me a fresh perspective on things. Maybe I'd been harsh on him, using my fury at his father for a shield against what rested beneath, and then letting that twist every word he said, every scowl he made. I could still see his onyx eyes narrowed in disap-proval, the dark stubble shadowing a clenched, strong jaw, veined hands running through his hair in irritation.

I tried to push him from my head. Tried not to contrast that version of him with the fleeting stranger in the alcove, whose brows had furrowed in concern as warm hands steadied me. How ironic it was that *he'd* been the one who calmed my panic. With his body shoved into mine, the friction of my spine against the rough stone wall, the weighted anticipation of someone finding us...it had been the distraction I needed.

But now I needed to focus. And trying to unweave these contradicting ideas of the prideful, protective, handsome rebel wasn't helping.

The north end where I'd found Gayl was down two flights of stairs and through a maze of hallways. I took my time retracing my steps, paying attention to the hand drawn maps and noting anything of interest. I quickly discovered the palace was *full* of passageways and entries cloaked in shadow, secret staircases and servant's shortcuts hardly visible to the untrained eye. If one passed by too quickly or wasn't intentionally looking for things out of the ordinary, they were easily missed. My mind turned it into a game, seeing how many secrets I could uncover, how many puzzles I could solve.

I marked them all on my map, promising to come investigate later. My goal now was to find that dark hallway Gayl had disappeared in three days ago. But as I turned down corridor after corridor, nothing sparked my memory. They all looked the same: long, stone hallways with arched wooden doors and guards stationed at the entrances. The same gilded portraits with some landscape or another, the same green rugs beneath my feet, the same decorative clocks and mirrors and chandeliers.

I spent the entire day hunting for that ominous door at the end of every corridor, but each time I thought I'd found the right one, it was a dead end. There were no hidden doors leading to that cold, darkened hall. No sign of Gayl anywhere in this wing, in fact.

Maybe I was in the wrong area. Maybe it had been the west side I'd mistakenly traveled down, too lost in the maps of the city to notice.

The next day was much the same. Staying away from suspicious glances as I pretended to tour the massive palace, scrawling my notes and even being bold enough to follow a few guards under an invisibility spell to see where they went. There were a handful of times I had to shield myself or scurry into a shadowed alcove when I heard the familiar voices of other challengers passing by. Dealing with Callum or Alaric while my ego was still bruised wasn't going to help matters.

By the end of the third day, my patience was wearing thin. Not that it was my strong suit to begin with. I'd been searching for that hallway for three days and had nothing to show for it besides some semi-legible notes and a list of questionable hiding places.

With frustration mounting, I decided to head back to the north entrance and get some fresh air out in the gardens. I hadn't been outside since leaving Leo and Nightshade, spending all of my time combing the palace or eating meals with my aunt and cousin in the infirmary or one of our rooms. I figured the night sky and open grounds would do wonders for my anxiety.

As I wound my way through the halls to the north entrance, something snagged the back of my mind. Something that felt familiar, like I'd followed this exact path before.

I circled back, my senses on high alert. I'd examined all these halls in the last few days, but maybe I'd missed something.

My feet stopped at a particularly quiet archway, my body somehow sure in its resolve even when my mind told me I'd already ruled this one out. There were a handful of guards positioned as they were last time, the same tension and intensity making my heart pound and my stomach flutter.

Moving out of sight, I shoved an amaranth stem and a heaping pinch of hellebore root in my mouth before casting the invisibility spell, strengthening it with several drops of bergamot—an oil that doubled the power of a charm. I wasn't taking any chances of being discovered again.

Anticipation grew as I glided silently down the hall, the guards not so much as blinking in my direction. But when I approached the end, my exhilaration was cut short.

A solid wall stared back at me.

No heavy wooden door leading to the cold, dark passageway.

Not even the outline of an entrance or a tapestry to hide its where-abouts. It was completely gone, as if it had never been there. The only thing gracing the wall were two sconces on either end and a decorative painting of a fountain.

I reached out a hand to the stone and moved the portrait to see if something was behind it, feeling along the hard plane for a break in the wall, a hidden button, *anything*.

Disappointment rose. How was this possible? I *knew* this was the right hall. It had to be. How could an entire wing of the palace have disappeared?

I held in a groan, leaning against the wall as I contemplated my next course of action.

Suddenly, I smelled smoke.

Looking up, a fluttering piece of torn parchment appeared in the air, its edges burning with soft orange and yellow embers. I blinked several times as it landed on the ground before me. The guards lining the hall didn't seem to notice; they stayed still, eyes straight ahead, hands either fixed on their weapons or hanging at their sides.

I swallowed and knelt to the floor. When I saw my name at the top of the paper in unfamiliar cursive, I held my breath. A message about the second trial, perhaps?

> *Rose Wolff,*
> *Such a clever, curious young Alchemist. I'm unsurprised it did not take long for you to wander back to these halls. Your father was the same. If my threats cannot keep you away, then perhaps the truth will. Meet me in the west tower at ten o'clock tonight.*
> *-T.G*

T.G.

Theodore Gayl.

"You're out of your mind if you think you're going to that tower," a low voice said in my ear. Before I could cry out, a hand pressed into my mouth, pulling me flush against a hard body. The familiar scent of sandalwood and vanilla surrounded me.

"We've got to stop meeting like this," Leo murmured while I struggled to rein in my thrashing heart. "If I let you go, will you be quiet?"

I nodded, but right as he removed his hand, I bit down hard on his finger. Whirling around, I mimicked his actions and shoved my hand against his lips to stifle his grunt, pulling out my dagger and holding the tip to his neck.

"What do you think you're doing, Aris?" I hissed. "You're going to get us caught."

He turned his head to free his mouth, and my hand fell back to my side, curling into a fist. "And here I thought we were becoming friends." When I rolled my eyes, he nodded to a nearby guard and added, "Don't worry, they can't see us. I noticed your spell fading, so I cast another over both you and me."

I bristled. "It wasn't *fading*. I was...distracted."

He eyed the blade still at his throat. "If you're going to stab me, you might want to do it when my spell isn't what's keeping you safe."

"I wasn't going to stab you," I grumbled, putting the dagger away. "Just thinking about it."

Truthfully, I hadn't meant to react so rashly, but after everything that had happened with the Shifters in the forest and then Callum, I was constantly on high alert.

Not to mention the memory of that tail wrapped around my neck.

For some reason, heat raced to my cheeks. I shoved the thought away and sprinkled blackthorn ash across our hiding space, whispering the spell for silence. "How did you know I was here, anyway? Are you following me?" I asked.

"Horace seems to think you're going to get yourself in trouble, and since he has obligations with the Guard and can't always keep an eye out, he asked me to check on you tonight."

I let out an irritated scoff. "I don't need the two of you trailing me like mother hens. I can do this. Besides, isn't it dangerous for you to be here? I seem to remember your sister being fairly unhappy with you for sneaking around the other day."

When he crossed his arms over his chest, his cloak fell back and my traitorous eyes were instantly drawn to the flexed forearms and faint outline of that beautiful tattoo beneath thin, white sleeves. I tilted my head up as I shifted my feet.

"Rissa may not know how I've chosen to spend my evening," he said simply, as if daring me to press him.

My eyebrow lifted. "I'm surprised Horace asked you to disobey her."

"Yes, well, I think he's taken his responsibility over you a bit personally." That admission made my fondness for the guard grow. "He knows this is important and that you need to be protected. As do I. Which is why this"—his stare flicked to the parchment still on the ground at our side—"is a bad idea."

I crossed my arms, mocking his stance. "Afraid of taking chances, Aris?"

"Ones that could wind up with members of this mission dead, yes," he growled, letting his arms fall to his side and stepping closer. My eyes traveled up his collar, his neck, his jaw, until I met his gaze. Those black pools glittered back at me like angry jewels. "You need to get back to your chambers, Rose."

"But it would be so rude of me to decline an invitation from our dear emperor," I said, giving him a sweet smile. I flushed when he narrowed his eyes at me.

"Is this a game to you?" He was dangerously close now, the slightest inhale making his chest brush against mine.

"That depends. Am I winning?"

His jaw fluttered, our breaths mingling and warming the space between us. This was a challenge, and I refused to be the first to back down.

Several heartbeats passed. His gaze flitted to my lips before returning to my eyes.

I smiled.

"Go back to your chambers, Rose," he repeated as he swallowed. "There's nothing to gain from meeting him tonight. He's either going to torture you for information, trick you into betraying us, or kill you—"

"Well, none of those sound good, do they?"

"—and we can't afford another mistake."

I recoiled, my cheekiness fading with my next exhale. He always had to go and say something like that, ruining the tentative peace we seemed to be edging toward. "Not everything I do is a *mistake*, Aris. You obviously read the note; how can you not be curious?" I picked the paper up and thrust it in his face. "I could try and get something helpful out of him. He may slip up, especially if he thinks I'm—"

He grabbed my outstretched wrist. "It's not worth the risk. The plan was for you to stay out of sight and away from suspicion until you can find the Grimoire. He's already caught you once, what do you think—"

"Of course, Rissa told you about that," I said, cheeks flaming. Another reason for him to think I was incapable. "No wonder you and Horace want to follow me around like I'm a child."

"I don't think you're a child." He let go of my wrist as his voice lowered. "I think you're brave and quick on your feet. But you're also *reckless*. I think you can do this, but you're going to get yourself killed if you're not careful."

I blinked at him, wetting my lips. I wasn't expecting that.

"I'm on your side, Rose. When are you going to realize that?"

I sighed. "Look, this opportunity is too good to pass up. If we're all on the same side, you can't stand here and tell me your sister wouldn't want me to take it."

"I'll go with you, then. I'll stay hidden under the invisibility spell and make sure he doesn't—"

"That's a *terrible* idea, and you know it. Invisibility charms don't fool him; you'd be caught in an instant. What would happen to you or your sister if he found you? Rissa was adamant that you can't be seen in the palace."

"Fine, I won't go, but my original statement stands. Neither are you."

I groaned, thankful the guards couldn't hear our argument. "You're *unbelievable*. Why can't you see this is a good idea?"

"Because this could ruin everything, Rose!" he exploded, his hands coming out to clutch my upper arms. His eyes blazed as his nostrils flared. This wasn't just anger. There was something more. Some innate fear in him that I couldn't put my finger on, but that paralyzed me all the same. "You can't go running straight into the arms of the most powerful, most dangerous man in our empire. He could get into your mind and force you to spill our secrets. He can kill you in a single *breath*." His grip tightened, automatically pulling me closer. "If he hurts you—"

I ripped myself from his hold, only for his hands to land on my waist instead. "Then I'm sure you'll be ready and waiting to take my spot."

He went silent for a moment, his features annoyingly unreadable. I was suddenly very aware of his rough hands on my waist, the material of my shirt doing little to keep out his touch.

He was trying to keep this mission safe. I understood that. And perhaps I was being impulsive. Reckless, as he called me.

But Theodore Gayl had said the *one* thing that took precedence for me. The one thing that would ensure I moved mountains to meet with him.

Your father was the same.

The emperor knew exactly how to force my hand. That thought should have scared me, should have made me heed Leo's warnings. Instead, it only solidified my resolve. I *had* to know what he meant about my father.

"I could make you stay, you know." Leo's dark eyes bore into mine, commanding me to listen. A man who wasn't used to being defied. His thumb dragged across the fabric, and I let out a small breath when his skin met mine.

"You could try," I said, holding his stare.

He kept me there, challenge and resentment and tension

rolling and swelling thickly. My fingers edged toward my pouch, wondering if I'd have to curse him in order to get away, when his arms fell to his side. He didn't speak, but he took another step back, his silent way of letting me go.

I crushed Gayl's note in my fist and wrenched my gaze from his as I darted down the corridor.

31

ROSE

I flew through the palace, following my map to the west wing and hunting for the entrance to the tower. When I turned left down another hallway, I was met with the sight of a winding wooden stairway, the steps becoming increasingly narrow as they extended into the upper levels and out of sight. I took a deep breath and gingerly eased myself onto the first step.

The wood creaked as I ascended the spiral staircase, the air growing colder and mustier the higher I climbed. I could tell I was nearing the top when a draft whistled across the steps and made the ends of my hair flutter. When I finally reached the highest point of the tower, the steps opened to a mostly empty room, save for a bench, a large, cracked mirror, and several dusty sconces lining the dark stone wall.

And a man standing in a high, open archway overlooking the palace grounds.

His gloved hands were held behind his back, which faced me, and his dark hair was tied and hanging at the nape of his neck. The cool night wind had his navy cloak billowing at his heels, casting a shadow that skulked along the wooden floor. He didn't turn, even when the top step squeaked as I entered the tower, nor when I joined him at the archway.

We gazed down at the world spread at our feet, the trees mere flecks against the ground, streams flowing and branching like the veins in my palm. The buildings in the nearby village were as small as ants scattered across the terrain. My breath caught at how close the moon and the stars appeared—almost as if I could reach out and capture them in my hand.

"Many are afraid of such great heights," Gayl said quietly, breaking the silence and making my muscles tighten in surprise. "But I've never understood this fear."

He paused, as if expecting me to respond. I didn't know what he wanted from me, so I said the first thing that came to my mind. "I'm not afraid of them, either. Just not particularly keen on the falling part."

"Yes, that's understandable," he said with a chuckle, a low rumble that seemed to make the very air waver. "What I fear is the idea that inevitably, there will one day be nothing greater. No higher climb. Nowhere else to go. Eventually, you reach the end—a point where you will have no choice but to look down on what you have left behind."

A chill swept through me. "Well, you have a lot of that, don't you, Your Majesty?"

My eyes widened at my own brazen words, preparing for his wrath. But it didn't come. Instead, he hummed.

"I know of your ire toward me, Miss Wolff, and it's not unwarranted. However, I imagine you are angry for the wrong reasons." He turned to me, and I matched his motions, seeing him for the first time in such close proximity.

His blue eye was as dark as an endless ocean, while his white was a sharp glacier, piercing me to the wooden floor. Deep wrinkles adorned the weathered skin at his forehead, beneath his eyes, and around his mouth. Shadows of a beard formed on his normally clean-shaven face. A tendril of black and silver hair had escaped its leather strap and fluttered against his neck. There was something in his features, in the cleft chin and straight nose, that sent a wave of familiarity cascading over me. Perhaps it was my Alchemy blood sensing his own great power.

"Do you fear me, young Alchemist?" he asked softly, tilting his head with his hands still clasped behind his back.

My heart pounded in my chest. "Yes."

"Then why did you come?"

I considered my words, unable to read the expression on his face. "Because I want the truth."

He nodded. "The question is, which truth? I have many to offer."

"I...I don't understand, Your Majesty."

"I imagine you want the truth about the Somnivae curse, no?" My lips parted in surprise as he brought his hands up to a steeple in front of his face. "Or perhaps you'd like to hear what I know about those Sentinels you have become so fond of."

Ice crawled across my skin. I took a step back, my spine hitting the brick of the archway. *He knew about the Sentinels.* And then I remembered—this wasn't the first time he'd said that. When I'd eavesdropped on him and his advisor, they'd been talking about the group of rebels.

How much did he know?

But he wasn't done. "Or you might be curious about your father and the truths of his past."

The floor seemed to shake beneath my feet as his words knocked me off balance. "What are you—"

"Which will it be, Miss Wolff?" His voice was soft, unassertive, as if asking what I wanted for dinner.

It wasn't a question I had to consider for even a heartbeat.

"My father," I responded. "What do you know about my father?"

Gayl's lips split into a sad smile. "Oh, I knew your father well. We grew up together."

I blinked, my jaw falling open. "*What*? You lived in Feywood?" He nodded. "How—how did I not know this?"

Theodore Gayl was an Alchemist, of course, but all manners of magic lived in Veridia City. I'd always assumed he'd been born here in the capital, perhaps even in this very palace, and that was how he'd gotten so close to the former emperor.

If he grew up with my father...how had my aunt and uncle never told me? It seemed like the kind of information one might be intrigued by, that the emperor of our realm used to climb the same trees as me, run through the forests of my childhood, practice magic on the very soil I was raised on.

"Not many people know of my origins," Gayl explained, turning away and walking deeper into the tower. "I changed my name and moved to Veridia City well into my second decade of life, and as far as history is concerned, this was where my story began. But yes, I was born in Feywood. I knew who you were the moment I laid eyes on you in the Decemvirate briefing, Miss Wolff."

I swallowed the lump in my throat. "Did you know my mother, too?"

He shook his head. "No, sadly, I left before Hamilton met her. But you look so much like him—perhaps not in your features, but in your mannerisms. The way you hold yourself, that cunning glint in your eye, the rare smile I caught a glimpse of in the great hall. It's as if I'm seeing him again."

As he spoke, a writhing sensation began in the pit of my stomach. A small, sharp thought pecked at my mind, whispering words I didn't want to hear. Piecing together fragmented edges I'd rather leave broken on the floor.

"Your Majesty," I whispered, closing my eyes as if that would blind me to his answer. To the truth. But I had to ask again—I had to *know*. "How did you know my father?"

Thick silence permeated the air, aside from Gayl's strong, steady breaths. I, on the other hand, couldn't seem to force air into my lungs.

"I think you already know the answer to that," he said quietly.

My head shook as I turned away, back to the open air of the archway, letting the cool breeze ground me.

"Rose, look at me." His voice was right behind me,

commanding yet gentle at the same time, urging me to turn around and face the truth.

Staring back at me was the same dark blue-gray eye that haunted my visions these last few days. The same eye I saw gazing up at me from a pool of blood. The same eye that once admired me adoringly while reading in front of the fireplace, that tightened in concern when I skinned my little knees, that glowed with pride when I cast my first spell.

How had I not seen it?

How had I not *known*?

Gayl took a deep breath before uttering the words that irrevocably shattered my world.

"Hamilton Wolff was my brother."

32

ROSE

The tower spun.

His *brother*.

My *uncle*.

I took a step back. Dozens of thoughts flew through my mind, cresting and falling and overlapping so quickly I couldn't think straight. The emperor of the Veridian Empire was my uncle. The same man who had allegedly cast the Somnivae curse, who had doomed a whole host of people to its clutches and took the power of the empire for himself. The same man I had made a vow to tear down from his throne, piece by piece.

Shock, denial, and bitter betrayal warred within me. Morgana and Ragnar had never told me. I'd grown up believing everyone on my father's side was dead, fallen ill to a pandemic that swept Feywood decades ago.

What else had they lied about?

I had *family* outside of them. Someone else who shared my blood, hundreds of miles from my home. Someone who knew my father, who remembered him as he was—not the lifeless, gray-skinned, bleeding hunk of flesh I saw every time I closed my eyes. Gayl had memories of him I'd never imagined until this moment, but now, I desperately wanted to learn. What was he like as a child? When did he learn his magic? Who was his first love? His favorite food? Was he like *me*, with a hard exterior simply begging to be cracked, our deepest desires and fears simmering beneath a surface of quick-witted remarks and a proud mask?

I wanted to know all of the things I never got to ask my parents, the pieces of myself I'd forged from nothing when I should have had hands guiding my way. Morgana had given me so much of my mother, had told me stories from their childhood and made sure I could see the joy that filled my mother's short life. She gave me what she could of my father, but she hadn't known him the same way.

This man before me...he did.

I thought what I'd had of my father had been enough to bridge that gap. But now...now it seemed like a gaping hole, pleading to be filled.

Gayl beckoned me closer. "Come, step away from the ledge. Explaining the demise of a Decemvirate challenger will be quite the headache."

"Why tell me any of this?" I asked, refusing to move. My voice sounded distant and muffled, like I was wading through water.

He sighed. "Believe me, I was as surprised as you when you walked through the doors of the great hall that first afternoon. I did not intend for any of this to happen. But I haven't seen my kin in so long, and when I saw you, I..." He trailed off, looking to the side at the cracked mirror leaning against the tower wall. His eyes carried a heaviness I didn't want to try and decipher. "Forgive me. I am a sentimental man."

His words had the opposite effect of what I imagined he expected. My resentment soared, shoving aside any twinge of sympathy I may have begun to feel for this man. *How dare* he try to appeal to my emotions, to think because I shared his blood that I would overlook the casualties he'd caused, his unjust reign over the last two decades. When he moved to reach out to me, I recoiled.

"I know your mother has died," Gayl said, taking a slow step to me. "Your father, too. I tried to prevent that. I tried to protect him from Aris' wrath—"

I jolted forward. "Wait, you *knew* Aris was going to murder him?"

He nodded grimly. "I had my suspicions. Aris and his family had gone into hiding, of course, but I kept eyes on his whereabouts. When I heard he was lashing out at those nearest to me in an attempt to seek revenge, I worried for Hamilton's safety. I sent men to warn him, but it was too late."

Branock Aris sends his love. My blood heated. The former emperor had been searching for those connected to Gayl and killing them one by one, just to send a message. My father was caught in the middle of a battle between these two rulers, an innocent bystander in a war far beyond his control.

"This was all your fault to begin with," I said, so softly the words barely reached my ears. But he heard them. Regret lined his eyes, dejection showing in the downturn of his lips. "Branock Aris may have killed him, but *you're* the reason he's dead, aren't you?" I asked, stronger this time, with a cold edge I used to cut through him like a sword. "If you hadn't cast the curse, if you hadn't stolen Aris' throne, none of this would have happened. *Your brother* would still be alive."

He met my stare. "Perhaps you are right, but you don't know the full story."

My hands shook. "Then tell me the truth."

"The *truth*," he mused, the word rolling from his tongue like honey as he paced across the wooden floor. "A fickle thing. For the truth to myself is not the same as it is to Branock Aris, or even, I daresay, to you. You have your own perception of what happened all those years ago, your own ideas buried beneath fear and whispers. Sometimes a lie is far prettier than the truth, Miss Wolff. The truth can sting worse than any poisonous fang." He stopped moving and cocked his head at me. "Are you sure you can handle it, niece?"

I blanched at the title and the way he said it, as if he held some new power over me. "Why start caring now, *uncle*? You haven't for the past twenty-five years."

He flinched, but didn't deny it. "Twenty-seven years ago, Evadine Aris went into labor with her firstborn. A daughter by the name of Clarissa. She was born swiftly in the middle of the night, a great answer to the many prayers uttered to the Fates. But what they did not know was that Evadine had been blessed with twins. A rare occurrence, especially for two people of different magic lines.

"Their son, Zareleon, was unexpected and caused complications within Evadine. The baby was in distress, and his mother was losing too much blood. The midwife made the decision to cut into her to remove the baby by force. She told Branock the chances of both his wife and his son surviving the procedure were slim. And so, he summoned me." Gayl paused, looking down at his gloved hands.

"I had gained the favor of Emperor Aris in the short time I'd been here in Veridia City. I'd arrived only three years prior with nothing but the clothes on my back and the charms in my pocket. I spent what little money I had on seeds to grow my own herbs, then sold various potions and remedies in the markets. Not six months into my time on the streets, the emperor paraded through the sectors, as he often did to check on his people and see how they fared.

"There was an accident. His horse was spooked and threw Branock from its back, leaving him with several broken bones and a critical injury to the head. I happened to be nearby and was able to heal him with charms on hand. He said he had never seen a healing spell work so well and so quickly, even being from a family of Alchemists himself. He insisted I accompany him back to the palace and serve in his court.

"We became as close as brothers." Gayl cleared his throat and turned away from me at the word. "Together, we honed our magic. We grew strong. We solved the problems of the empire—eradicating illnesses, ending food shortages, creating more resources.

He trusted me above any other. Which was why he turned to me when his world was falling apart. He called me that night from my slumber to save his wife and son. To do the impossible. What Branock did not know was that the babe's life left him upon birth. The Fates had been ready to take him.

"But I stopped it. I saved him. *I brought him back.*" His words pulsed around me, the very air between us thickening and sweetening with the taste of power. "And magic that strong has a price. It demands payment. The Somnivae curse is more than a *curse*, Miss Wolff. It's a *reckoning*. A consequence for what I took from the Fates—for what Branock made me take."

Was he saying that he'd *brought someone back to life?*

That was impossible. Leo should be dead, according to Gayl. If the Fates were truly out there, there was no way they'd allow something like this to go unchecked. Someone with the power to overthrow their precious plan for destiny, who could bend laws of nature and rewrite the stars at will. I couldn't fathom the boundaries he'd crossed, the amount of magic he'd used, all to save the baby's life.

"H-he was dead?" I stammered. "You brought him back from the dead?"

"I did what I had to do."

"*How?*" I blurted, then shook my head furiously. "No, no, I don't want to know. That's dark magic, Your Majesty. Unnatural." *So why was I so intrigued?* "How come you haven't gotten rid of the curse?"

He scoffed. "You think I haven't tried? After we understood what the curse was doing, I spent months attempting to reverse the spell I had cast to bring Zareleon back. Branock and I enlisted the help of every trained Alchemist we trusted, but nobody could figure out what had gone wrong. Over time, however, the truth became clear to me.

"There was one component to the spell we had not touched. One variable I had not been as forthcoming about with His Majesty. Not an ingredient, not a spell."

I froze, my sudden inhale sharp and icy in my lungs. "The baby. Zareleon," I whispered.

Gayl nodded. "I had never told Branock how his son's life had been forfeit, nor the depths of power I'd had to draw from in order to bring him back. It was too dangerous. All Branock thought was that I'd healed his wife. But it was the missing piece. In order to reverse the curse that had been cast as payment for saving Zareleon—"

"He would have to die," I finished for him, horror snaking through my veins. Gayl merely stared at me, unmoving, confirmation shining back at me through his white and blue eyes.

It explained everything. Why the curse was connected to the birth of the twins, why nobody had been able to banish it after so many years. I couldn't believe Leo was still alive, if he was the key to ending the suffering and loss of so many people.

"Have—have you ever tried to kill him in order to break it?" I asked warily.

He grimaced. "I have considered it many times. Watching this nightmare unfold and knowing I had the power to stop it...I warred within myself for a long time. Once, Branock caught me in the nursery standing over his son's crib with a pillow in my grip." When Gayl saw the horrified expression on my face, he shook his head somberly. "I wouldn't have done it, of course. But the *thought*..." His jaw tightened. "You look at me with revulsion, but you cannot begin to understand the way this burden weighed on me. The way it still weighs on me. Branock had me imprisoned and forced me to explain what was happening. I think, in the end, the *truth* was what began his downward spiral. He turned utterly paranoid, thinking I had told others and we were plotting against his family, preparing to kill his child at any moment. He was rash and suspicious, a terrifying combination for the man ruling an entire empire. The people blamed him for the curse and in a way, they were right. I had warned him the night the twins were born how the price would be too much for him, and he didn't care. The guilt ate at him, but he was unwilling to give up the life of his son to save thousands. Eventually, it became too much for him. He abdicated his throne and fled the palace with his family."

"And how convenient it was that you were more than willing to wear his crown," I said, but my words lacked bite. I felt both hollow and overflowing with information at the same time, his story and my own doubts weaving a spider web in my mind.

"Make no mistake, Miss Wolff—I am not a saint. But perhaps"—he took a step toward me, and I didn't back away—"I am not the monster you have been so eager to believe."

I don't know what to believe anymore.

Apparently I'd said the words aloud, for Gayl smiled, a resigned upturn of his thin lips. "I don't expect you to readily trust me. But there is so much more I wish to tell you, Rose, if you will allow me. So much your father would want you to know."

I met his stare at those last words, sensing the growing urge within me to feel connected to my father, the yearning for the life with both him and my mother that had been ripped from me.

What if Gayl was telling the truth? What if Rissa and the Sentinels had it wrong? Branock had obviously never told his children how the curse had really come about, since they still believed they could find the secret for banishing it in the pages of Gayl's Grimoire.

It was pointless. His Grimoire would solve nothing. Their entire focus of the last five years was for naught.

I closed my eyes. *The mission.* I was still expected to find the book and help them counteract the curse, removing Gayl from power in the process.

I still wanted that, didn't I? Only...to break it, Leo would have to—

This wasn't something I was ready to deal with tonight.

We know how this ends, daughter of the moon—only you will decide who meets their doom. The parting words of the Oracle splintered through my mind. Had they known? Was this what they had been referring to? This knowledge Gayl and now I possessed that could decide the fate of so many people...it was like a bucket of ice water had been thrown over me.

Too much. This was all *too much*.

"I—I need time, Your Majesty," I choked out, opening my eyes to his pale features, the moonlight making his eyes glow.

Gayl bowed his head. "Of course," he murmured. "I understand. All I ask is that you do not speak to anyone about what we've discussed tonight. I've kept this knowledge hidden from the world for over two decades in order to protect Branock Aris and his family, even in his death." His gaze bore into me. "I'm afraid your new friend will wind up dead within hours if others were to learn the truth. It's one of the reasons I made sure Zareleon and his sister stayed far away from this place. Living as a recluse in this city is the best way to ensure he is not hunted and sacrificed."

I pursed my lips and nodded. He was right—people would line up at Leo's cottage demanding his head on a spear if they knew the real story. But that meant Gayl had been *protecting* them this whole time. Some sort of savior in the shadows. Did I really believe that? That his actions were completely selfless, that the idea of Clarissa rising up to claim her rightful title as the Aris heir had never influenced him to keep her far from the throne?

Nobody was that altruistic. He'd said so himself—he wasn't a saint.

But perhaps he wasn't the villain, either.

I had never been the naive girl who believed every word fed to me. I wasn't like Morgana and Beau, desperate to see the goodness and sincerity in the darkest of lives. There was always both. A balance. We all lived in shades of gray—some lighter than others, some so bleak you had to search for the smallest glimmer, the faintest spark. And as difficult as it was to question *everything* I'd accepted about our emperor over my life...he'd planted a seed of doubt tonight. Maybe there was truth to his words, some goodness to his actions over the years.

Gayl stepped to the side and swept an arm to let me pass, his cloak swishing at the wooden floor as he moved. I took a step toward the stairs, but before I could go far, his hand fell to my shoulder.

"While I have pardoned you, my own blood, for wandering these halls in search of my secrets, that forgiveness only extends so far. I protect the Aris heirs from the mistakes of their father and from certain violence that would come if anyone discovered the truth, but if I find them and their little group of rebels continuing to lurk where they don't belong, I cannot promise the same forgiveness." He released his grip. "I hope to see you again soon, niece."

I held his stare and nodded once. *There* was the threat I'd been waiting for. *There* was the all-powerful Emperor Gayl, the one who incited both fear and awe in his subjects.

And I felt both.

His words hung over my head the entire way down the tower and through the palace, an uneasy sense of foreboding slithering across my skin, lingering even as I entered my chambers and slammed my door shut.

Only the sound of tapping on my window snapped me from my spiral.

33

ROSE

I rushed across the room to the windowsill, brow furrowing at the shadow on the narrow ledge outside. An amaranth stem was already beneath my tongue and waiting as I slowly turned the bronze handle. A cold wind swept through the small space, the midnight air bleeding into my dark room, making my skin prickle.

A hand grasped the edge of the window pane, and I gasped.

"Sorry to frighten you," a familiar voice said.

I let out a huff, my heart racing. "*Aris.* What are you doing?"

"What does it look like I'm doing? Making sure you're not dead."

Everything I'd learned in the last hour lingered fresh in my mind, Gayl's final threat still ringing in my ears. If he caught Leo sneaking around the palace with all of his grand ideas of treason and dethroning...it wouldn't take much to give the emperor a reason to strike.

"You shouldn't be here," I hissed, keeping the window cracked. Leo gazed back at me with mild irritation, his usual cloak pulled low over his forehead. My attention flicked down to where he crouched on the ledge, mere inches from falling three stories to the hard ground below. One corded arm rested casually on his knee while the other held the window open.

"How did you even get up here?" I asked.

He smirked. "You *do* remember I'm half Shifter, right?" As if summoned, his brown tail twitched beneath his cloak, coming up to swipe at the wrist I had firmly pushed against the window pane. "Let me in, Rose."

I refused to budge, worry working its way through my system. As usual, my lips moved quicker than my brain, tossing out the first thing that came to mind. "But what will people say? The two of us alone at this hour. How *scandalous*."

"Funny. Would you rather I throw rocks at your window all night?"

"Well, now, *that* sounds romanti—"

"Alright, I tried being polite." He flexed his arm and pushed against the pane, causing me to rear back as it banged open. But when he attempted to slide through the window, he slammed into something solid, as if an invisible barrier had appeared in the air. He let out a curse and a grunt of pain.

It was my turn to smirk. "Did I not mention my room is warded against trespassers?"

He growled something that sounded like "*Horace,*" and glared at me expectantly. "Are you going to let me in?"

I tapped my finger on my chin. These games with him were becoming more fun as time went on. He was so easily riled, and I welcomed the diversion after the conversation with Gayl. "What's the magic word?"

"*Rose.*" His face was practically apoplectic. When I simply raised an eyebrow, he rolled his eyes and said, "*Please,* will you let me in?"

"That wasn't so hard. Fine, you may enter."

Gracefully, he pulled himself through the open window and unfolded into a standing position, towering over me. "Did he hurt you?" Leo asked, all annoyance and banter forgotten as his eyes raked over my form. It sent a wave of heat under my skin.

"No," I said quickly. At his suspicious look, I added, "So sweet of you to care, though. Really, I'm touched. But you can leave now."

He scrubbed a frustrated hand over his chin. "Do you ever take anything seriously?"

The smile wiped from my face. "I'm sorry, Aris, I guess volunteering for a tournament that could kill me while agreeing to spy on the emperor for your *little rebel group* wasn't serious enough for you."

Regret leaked onto his features. "That wasn't what I—Rose, I'm sorry. I was...worried." His jaw ticked at the admission. "I watched the west tower from the forest, waiting any moment for your body to go flying off the edge."

I swallowed and turned away. I could see how genuine he was, and the idea that he'd cared enough to watch for me made something squirm in my chest. No matter what cheeky or defensive words I continued to throw at him, he still waited.

Grabbing my robe off the bed and striding to the bathing chamber, I quietly said, "I'm fine. I promise."

I wasn't fine. But I wasn't ready to have that conversation with anyone.

The chamber was so silent for a few moments that I thought he'd actually left, but then the wooden chair by my bed creaked. *He still waited.*

I ignored him and the confusing emotions bubbling inside me, continuing to strip out of my clothes in the bathing chamber. I felt Gayl's presence, my *uncle's* presence, lingering like smoke over every inch of fabric. I wanted to be rid of it until I could figure out what the last couple of hours meant to me.

"You couldn't bother to shut the door?" Leo asked, voice strained.

That made my lips twitch, momentarily knocking the meeting with Gayl aside. "Not exactly used to having guests," I said, keeping my body out of his eyesight but making a show of tossing my worn clothes and undergarments onto the bed. I splashed cool water on my face and pulled on my robe, pinning my long hair back with a clip. When I entered the room again, I found him sitting in the chair, one leg propped atop the other knee, eyes trailing me.

"What do you want, Aris?" I asked, not unkindly.

He uncrossed his legs. "What do I *want*? You just had a private meeting with *Theodore Gayl*."

I tightened my robe around me. "Official business, then."

He paused. "And to make sure you're alright."

There it was again. That flicker of concern. "Thank you," I said softly. "I'm safe, though. He didn't touch me."

Leo nodded, but his lips were twisted, as if he didn't quite believe me. "What did he want to meet with you for?"

I busied myself with going through my pack of herbs, if only to give my hands something to do. What could I tell him? That Gayl was my uncle? Absolutely not. I wasn't prepared to *touch* that revelation yet. The idea of revealing that I was related to this man we were actively working against made me feel...shame, for some reason. As if there must be something wrong with *me*. I'd already had my entire province view me in a negative light, and I didn't want to ruin what I'd potentially found with these strangers. I still wanted to work with them, and I needed time to sort through my feelings.

Could I tell him the real story of the night he and Rissa were born and how the Somnivae curse was cast? Could I fling those truths at him now? How Leo had to—

No, I needed to sort through *that*, too. If Gayl had been lying, I didn't want to send Leo hurtling toward some self-sacrificing suicide mission. Even though I hadn't known the man before me for long, I knew that was something he'd do without a second thought.

But if Gayl *wasn't* lying...if Leo *did* need to die to end the curse...

I shut down that line of thinking. What was I going to do, stab him in my bedroom and see if thousands of people all over the empire woke up?

My fingers twitched, imagining for just a moment what might

happen. Freezing him with a compulsion spell, watching those dark eyes widen in shock. Holding my dagger to his throat, so close my chest would brush against his, feeling the strength of his heart beating to mine. The tip of my blade scraping that rough stubble. His strong jaw flexing, hands fighting the magic, veins in his neck straining.

One second. That's all I'd need to end this curse. A dagger across his throat, warm blood coating my fingers, rivers of red flowing and coalescing down my arm.

My father's face appeared in my vision, causing the edges to go gray. I rubbed at my temple and took a deep breath. There had to be another way. A way that *didn't* involve another innocent man dying.

I just needed *time*.

Leo was still waiting for me to respond. I poked and prodded through Gayl's tale to see what little information I could offer. Some shrapnel of the truth, if only to keep the Sentinels off my back while I figured things out.

"Gayl is originally from Feywood," I said, picking nervously at a small burlap pouch. "Did you know that?"

"No, we didn't." He went silent, giving me space to continue.

"He grew up there. And he—he knew my father." I swallowed hard, fighting to tell the entire story. "They were friends, I think. He said he recognized me when he saw me the day before the first trial, and he wanted to meet me. See if I was really who he thought I was."

Leo's eyes narrowed. "That's all he wanted? To chat about *old times?*"

"He didn't give me the secret password to his hidden lair of Grimoires, if that's what you're asking."

"You're deflecting again."

I threw my hands in the air. "I don't know what he wanted, alright? Maybe he missed an old friend. I don't know what else to tell you, Aris."

Perhaps I am not the monster you have been so eager to believe.

We both went quiet. Tension filled the air, but not the same kind I'd felt with him before, with a spark of warmth that pushed at my chest. This tension was cold and empty. A chasm widening between us, any hint of our growing rapport siphoned from the space.

I shifted uncomfortably on my heels as Leo ran his fingers through his dark hair, causing a strand to fall and curl against his forehead. "Rose, I—" He let out a sigh. "Can we start over?"

I stared at him, lips parting in surprise.

He rose from his seat. "I don't know what I did to make you dislike me so much—"

My eyes widened in disbelief as I let out a soft snort.

"Alright, fine, I said some things I shouldn't have. Things I didn't mean. Rissa is always telling me..." Shaking his head, he took a step forward. "I'm sorry. It's easy for me to get caught up in what's at stake and what I could lose. My entire life has been focused on protecting those close to me, and it's made me..." He trailed off, his eyes roving the air as if searching for a word.

"Obstinate?" I offered dryly.

"*Determined.* I know we didn't get off on the right foot."

I crossed my arms. "Are you referring to when you tried to choke me, or when you called me a joke?"

"You're not so innocent in all of this, either." He took a step closer. "Might I remind you how you cast a compulsion spell on me, then tried to attack me, then outed me to my sister for sneaking around the palace?"

My lips twitched, the cold strain from the room beginning to soften. "That last one might have been too far."

"Not everything has been bad," he said, quieter this time as he stopped right before me. "I *did* save your life in the forest. And healed your injury." His eyes fell to my side, his stare burning a hole through my thin robe.

"I suppose that's true," I murmured back.

"I want us to work together. Not only out of necessity, but because we *want* to. I may have been bitter at first about Lark and my sister giving this task to you, but that's only because it's something I've been working toward for so long. Bringing Gayl down... it's personal to me. After everything he did to my father, everything he took from us, this isn't just another mission.

"But I know now that it's personal for you, too. Your uncle is under the curse. I see how resolved you are, and I think Lark chose well." His voice was intent, focused, as he gazed down at me. He was always so *intense*. So powerful. It pulled me to him, like I was caught in his orbit. "Forget what you heard me say before. I was an idiot. You're the furthest thing from a joke, Rose Wolff, and you'll never catch me saying it again."

I opened my mouth and then closed it, pressing my lips together. This man kept surprising me. "I'm sorry, too," I finally said. "I haven't made it easy for you, attacking you every time you tried to talk to me. Defensiveness is second nature to me at this point."

"Because of the people back home?" he asked, that crease at his forehead deepening. "And the things they say about you?"

He remembered. I'd forgotten about that part of the conversation on his horse. Nodding, my eyes fell from his and onto a spot on the wall behind him.

"I'm not like them, Rose."

I gave him a half-hearted smile. "I used to think you were. But maybe I was wrong, too."

"So what do you say?" he asked, so close his breath warmed my cheeks. "Can we start over? Be friends?"

I met his penetrating stare, remembering all too well the sense of anger and retribution I'd had toward him after discovering Branock Aris was his father. The frustration at his enormous ego, at the way he seemed to have so little faith in me, at those backhanded comments that masked his own pride. It's not like I didn't have pride of my own. To an unhealthy degree. I knew he hadn't meant those words, just as I knew the man before me was *not* his father.

This grudge I'd held, this vengeance for a man who was long

dead, was a bitter excuse to keep Rissa and Leo at arm's length. To do what I always did and drive people away. To protect myself from giving *too much* to someone, only to lose them in the end. My mother, my father, Beth, Ragnar, even Aven—perhaps not *him* personally, but every boy who'd seen me through the eyes of our town. A wicked little secret, a social outcast they could use and discard when better options came along. When they found someone they could build a life with, once they had their fun with me.

I didn't have *this*. I didn't have...friends, outside of my family and Beth, whom I only saw several times a year. The fact that Leo wanted that with me sent an unfamiliar light through my chest, stretching my walls.

Searching those deep pools before me, I tried to let that misplaced, molten well of revenge against him go.

He wanted to start over. I did, too. If I could only turn that part of me off and release this vendetta.

But I couldn't tell him everything. I couldn't tell him his life was the key to ending the Somnivae curse. I couldn't tell him I was related to Theodore Gayl. What if he no longer trusted me? What if he thought I was on *Gayl's* side the whole time and was going to betray them?

And I couldn't tell him that maybe, just maybe, I'd started to believe Gayl wasn't who we thought he was.

What was one more secret? One more lie?

We see dark, hidden secrets, a deceitful tongue. For in the wake of the wicked, your poison will come.

Let it come. I'd deal with that later—right now, I wanted to take something for myself.

"Yes," I said. "I think I'd like that, Leo."

His answering smile tore through me, stealing the breath from my lungs. I don't think I'd ever seen him smile—not like this, not like the sun breaking through the clouds, those dazzling eyes sparking like a jewel in a flame.

"That's the first time you've said my name."

I bit my lip, holding back my own smile. "That's the first time you've earned it."

He huffed out a soft laugh, right as his hand came up to brush an escaped tendril from my face. I froze, the rough pads of his fingers like a searing trail of heat against the sensitive skin at my cheek.

His arm fell away. "I'm glad he didn't hurt you."

The words triggered something in me, and my spine stiffened even further. The idea of Gayl hurting someone...

"There's one more thing," I rushed out. "He knows about the Sentinels. When I followed him the first time, he and his advisor mentioned it, but I forgot about it with all the chaos of the first trial. He asked if they'd received any word about the Sentinels and to keep an eye on them. He wants to know when you make a move. But it didn't sound like they had any more information."

The fabric of his shirt strained across his chest as he flexed his shoulders, slowly taking in my report. Then he sighed heavily, backing away with a curse. "We've been afraid of that. And you're sure he didn't say anything else? About who his informants are, maybe?"

I shook my head. I genuinely wished I had more for him. The last thing I wanted was for any of the rebels to be hurt.

He gave me a grim nod. "I have to go and tell Rissa, make sure we let the rest know they could be tracking us."

"Just—be careful," I blurted. "He knows you're up to something. He told me as much tonight, and that he won't hesitate to punish any one of you if he catches you."

His lips gave a small tick. "So sweet of you to care," he said, mimicking my earlier words. His gaze lingered on me a moment longer before he made his way to the window, his tail caressing my ankle for a split second as it collected itself under his cloak.

"Thank you," I said quickly, my cheeks heating. "For checking on me."

His eyes flicked down to the top of my parting robe, then back up my face. "You don't have to thank me, Rose. It's what friends do."

Without waiting for a response, he pulled the window open and slipped into the night. I ran to the sill to catch a glimpse of him crouching at the ledge before he lunged and landed soundlessly on the one right below. He repeated the action down one more floor, and then to the ground. The flickering candlelight from the outer courtyards of the palace illuminated his face enough for me to see him look back up at me with a wink. He turned on his heel and disappeared into the darkness.

I couldn't stop the smile that pulled at my lips. Monkey boy, indeed.

34

ROSE

I had to take another sleeping potion to get any rest. My mind kept replaying the conversation with Gayl over and over, trying to reconcile the tyrant I'd seen him as with the image of him and my father growing up together. Little boys, unruly teenagers, brothers and confidants and *friends*.

I wondered what had forced Gayl to leave Feywood. Why he'd left his family behind, changed his name, and never bothered to visit—even after knowing his brother had died. He'd never even *met* my mother. There was more to the story, and the longer I stewed in my own thoughts, the stronger the urge to uncover our family secrets grew.

His story about coming to Veridia City and growing closer to Branock Aris pricked at me, too. I knew Gayl had been a trusted advisor—it was why the empire was in shock after he seemingly overthrew Aris and took his position on the throne. That was the ultimate act of betrayal. But from how Gayl told the tale, Branock had made the decision to leave on his own, and for a good reason. His son's life was the answer to breaking the curse—what man could live with that hanging over his head?

The next morning dawned far too brightly, and I knew before I could focus on any of this, I had to get through the challenger's feast that night and the second trial starting tomorrow. *And* breakfast with my aunt and cousin. We'd made plans for one last meal before the trial, choosing to visit the Gershwin Tea House—the one I'd met Rothy at the week before. I didn't imagine this would be the cozy get-together Morgana expected, though. I had some choice questions for her after everything I'd learned.

The short carriage ride was...uncomfortable. Morgana and Beau kept asking me about the other challengers, if I'd made any friends, if I was ready for the second trial, whether or not I thought I'd have to fight a lion or tiger or some other wild beast. That last one came from Beau—his obsession with the dangers of the trials was endearing, I had to admit. I could only give short answers, too distracted and, if I was being honest, too upset that Morgana and Ragnar had kept such secrets from me.

We arrived at the familiar green brick shop. The flowers bloomed as vibrant as ever under the bright morning sun. Smells of floral teas and delicious baked goods wafted through the air as we ascended the short black steps and made our way inside.

Behind the counter, Rothy's eyes lit when they landed on me, the smile lines on her dark skin creasing with pleasant surprise. "Rose! I wondered when I might see you again."

I gave her a sheepish grin. "Had to make good on my promise of buying all your teas and charms. Did Colette make it back to you safely?" I felt terrible for not checking back with her sooner. The past week had been such a blur, and all the things I held guilt for were beginning to blend together.

"She did. My girl always comes back home. I'm glad you're alright," Rothy said, her lips turning down slightly into a look of pity. "I saw the rankings. You'll get them next time, I'm sure of it."

I forgot how publicized the rankings were here, having been tucked away at the palace. I couldn't stop my grimace. "Thanks, Rothy," I said. "Oh, and this is my aunt and cousin—Morgana and Beau Gregor of Feywood."

The three of them shook hands and chatted politely while we placed our orders for tea and pastries. Morgana and Rothy hit it off immediately, discussing various herbal blends and what kinds grew here as opposed to Feywood. By the end of their conversation, a line had formed behind us and Morgana had promised she'd come back later to try a couple of Rothy's charms.

We took our seats at a table in the back of the outdoor seating area, a secluded little spot up against a small garden. "You've been rather quiet this morning, dear," Morgana said, covering my hand with hers on the table. "Is everything alright?"

My stomach churned. It was now or never, I supposed. "Actually, there's something I wanted to talk to you about." I licked my lips, swallowing my nerves. When I took out my pouch and sprinkled a bit of blackthorn ash for a silencing spell, her brow creased with worry.

"I received a message from His Majesty last night," I started, and Morgana instantly went still. "He said he wanted to speak with me, so I met with him in the west tower."

I didn't think my aunt was breathing. Her face paled as she pressed her lips together. Beau glanced awkwardly between the two of us over his chocolate muffin.

"And what did His Majesty have to say?" Morgana finally asked, her voice tight, eyes focused on her steaming tea.

"He said he grew up in Feywood." When Morgana hummed, I pressed on. "And that he knew my father." Nothing but a raised eyebrow as she took a sip. I crossed my arms, my temper and stubbornness flaring. I wanted to give her the chance to confess, but she was making it difficult. "I'm surprised you never bothered to tell me you were friends with the emperor, that's all."

"We were no friends of his," Morgana hissed, slamming her porcelain cup down.

"But you knew him!" I cried out. "You knew what he was—what he *is*. To me." My voice broke on the last word. I gripped my tea cup tightly. "Why didn't you tell me?"

Her eyes pleaded with me. "Rose—"

"Tell her *what*, Ma?" Beau asked.

I licked my lips. "That Emperor Gayl was my father's brother."

Beau's cup clattered to the saucer, a bit of chocolate falling out of his open mouth. "*What?*" he barked.

"This is not the place for this conversation," Morgana said in hushed tones, glancing around at the nearby tables.

"If not here, then where?" I countered. "I cast a silencing spell. Nobody can hear us. I want to know why you and Ragnar never told me about this." Realization struck me as I spoke, and I leaned forward. "Wait, was *this* why you didn't want me to come here? Why you tried to convince me to stay home?" She didn't respond, which only bolstered my anger, a venomous heat burrowing under my skin. "This whole time, I believed you were my last living relatives, and that everyone on my father's side died in the pandemic. What else have you kept from me? What else have you *lied* about?"

"Nothing!" she said in a barely-controlled whisper. "Your grandparents—Hamilton's parents—*did* perish from illness. We didn't lie to you about that." She closed her eyes and took a deep breath. "Your father made us promise not to tell you about Theodore. He didn't want you to know the sins of his past, dear. The mistakes that stained him and his brother's youth."

Confusion swirled within me. "What are you talking about? What *sins?*"

"Your father was a good man, Rose. You must know that," she began. "But Theodore...he was never like the other children, from the stories we heard. Ragnar and I didn't know him personally. He was a bit older than us, and left Feywood when we were still young. But...people talked.

"He was dark. Troubled. He mostly kept to himself, constantly sequestered in his room researching and creating unnatural spells. He liked to experiment on others—wild creatures from the forest, even children of the village. The things we heard..." She shuddered. "He hid bones of small animals under his bed, kept vials of hair and nails and skin in his dresser, and was often seen with cuts along his hands and fingers. It was all rumors at the time, of course. I actually pitied him when I was younger, although I'd never spoken a word to him. He seemed...lost. But then your father told us the truth. Theodore had been practicing *blood magic*"—Morgana lowered her voice and snuck a glance at Beau, as if scared for him to hear the words—"for years, ever since he discovered it as a teenager."

The air seemed to chill several degrees. Blood magic was strictly forbidden in Feywood, though I would be foolish to believe there weren't some who practiced it anyway. It was incredibly powerful magic, so potent it could increase the effects of a normal incantation by tenfold. But its consequences were just as devastating and frighteningly unpredictable.

Twelve years ago, a man not too far from our home had used blood magic to raise his wife from the dead. It had worked, to an extent—her corpse had indeed risen, but not her spirit. She'd become a lifeless, soulless husk who slaughtered her husband in front of their child with the very knife he'd used to shed his own blood. I remembered Ragnar and several other leaders of the village being summoned as the animated corpse rampaged the street, stopping her only after she'd killed three other innocent people.

They burned both her and her husband's bodies. I'd smelled the lingering scent of burnt flesh and sickly sweet, decaying magic for weeks.

It was dangerous. I *knew* it was dangerous—but my thirteen-year-old self had still been somewhat...curious. A morbid fascination with this family and how it had gone so terribly wrong.

"And...he taught Hamilton how to wield it, as well," Morgana continued.

I recoiled at her words, pulled back from the memory. "My father practiced *blood magic*?"

Morgana worried at her lip, her fingers tapping anxiously against her cup. "This was why he asked us not to tell you. He was so ashamed of this part of his life. Hamilton was barely into adulthood when their parents died, and was susceptible to his older brother's machinations. He couldn't bear for you to know the dark things he did." Her voice dropped even lower. "And we didn't want you to remember him that way. He changed long before you were born. He and Theodore had a terrible falling out, right before Theodore fled Feywood and moved to Veridia City."

My mind couldn't keep up with all I'd learned over the past twenty-four hours. What had my father *done*? What sort of magic had he and Gayl performed? I was intrigued and horrified at the same time. The memories I held of my father seemed to merge with a version of him I'd never known, making me question everything.

"What was their falling out over?" I asked.

"Hamilton didn't want to walk that path any longer. He tried to convince Theodore to stop practicing such magic, and Theodore refused. Things became heated. Your father never told us the specifics, except that they fought and Hamilton decided he wanted nothing to do with his brother if he continued in that lifestyle. Theodore left the next day and was never seen in Feywood again."

The timeline lined up with what Gayl had told me. He left for Veridia City, changed his surname—which made sense now, given what he was running from. Made his life in the capital and never looked back, not even when his brother got married or had a child or *died*.

My stomach roiled at the sympathy I'd begun to feel for the man. He'd pulled my father into his dark magic, convincing a grieving, impressionable mind to participate in who knew what kinds of wicked deeds. It was safe to assume he hadn't stopped practicing, given the fact that he brought Leo Aris back from the *dead*. I should've realized it when he told me last night—blood magic was the only thing powerful enough. And he had to be *significantly* powerful for it to work, as opposed to turning Leo into a breathing corpse the way the man from Feywood had.

My aunt gripped my hands. "Rose, dear, I'm so sorry you had to find out this way. We were honoring your father's wishes, but I hate that it might have caused you any pain. Ragnar and I, we—we love you so much." Silver lined her eyes, her hands trembling around mine. "I would never want you to think you can't trust us.

We just...didn't know what else to do. Didn't know how you would react even if we *did* tell you, considering how difficult your father's death has been for you."

"I understand," I whispered. "I still wished you'd told me."

She dabbed at her eyes. "I know. We should have. Fates, I never expected to have to have this conversation without him."

Beau and I glanced at each other. We both knew the "him" she was referring to. With a look of sympathy, Beau scooted his chair closer to his mother. "Hey—Ma, he's going to be okay," he said, throwing a gangly arm around her. "We'll get him back."

"Oh, I know, sweet boy." Morgana sniffed and leaned on his shoulder, turning her gaze toward me. "We will, won't we?"

I swallowed. I read past her words and into the question she was really asking. Had this revelation changed anything about my mission? Was I still committed to reversing the curse?

"Yes," I said quietly. "Somehow."

"And are you going to tell *them* about this?" she asked, straightening. Beau shot her a confused look.

I blinked. "Tell them about—about Gayl and my father?"

"Don't make the same mistake we did, Rose," she said. "We stayed silent out of respect for Hamilton, yes, but also out of fear. We didn't want to make life more difficult for you, or for anything to change between us. But we should have been *honest*. And... things are so much bigger now. You have a responsibility to consider."

Fates, I hated it when she pulled honor and logic into her arguments.

"This doesn't have to change anything," I said, although I wasn't sure I believed my own words. "I can still be loyal to them. Just because he's my uncle doesn't mean he means anything to me."

She gave me a look only a mother could give. It made my heart clench. "Even if that's what you believe, dear, don't they deserve to know? Trust me, openness and honesty is the only way you will be able to work effectively with them. We all want the same thing.

Don't let your pride and fear get in the way of that. You need to tell them the truth."

The truth. Gayl's words rang through my head. There were so many truths, more than even my aunt knew.

"What if the truth could hurt someone?" I murmured, no longer thinking about Gayl, but of Leo's connection to the curse.

Her lips turned down into a frown. "Who could this information possibly hurt, Rose?" she asked, oblivious to the thoughts churning in my mind. "The only thing at stake here are those under the curse. You're doing this to *help* them. Like you said, this changes nothing except further strengthening the Sentinels' trust in you."

I closed my eyes. She was right—about telling them Gayl was my uncle, at least. Truthfully, it was selfish of me to want to keep that to myself. I didn't want them to see me any differently. But they had a right to know all the facts.

Unless it might hurt them. They didn't need to know *every-thing*. Not yet, anyway.

A heavy sigh left my lips. "Alright," I said. "I'll tell them."

She smiled. "I'm proud of you, Rosie."

"Okay," Beau said with a huff, slapping a hand on the table. "*What* are you two talking about?"

I snorted, almost forgetting he'd been listening. "Oh, Beau Beau," I teased, reaching across the table to ruffle his hair. "I'll tell you when you're older."

THE SECOND TRIAL

35

LEO

"You want Westhaven or Ridgemore tonight?" Chaz asked, the high-pitched sound of his knife sliding against whetstone grating my ears as he sharpened his blade.

"Doesn't matter to me," I said with a grunt. He rolled his eyes at my tone. I'd been in a mood all afternoon. My sister and I had a heated discussion that morning over me disappearing to the palace again last night. Even the news about Rose securing a one-on-one meeting with Gayl didn't deter her from her tirade for long. Once we both calmed down, I'd debriefed her on what Rose had told me, including confirmation that Gayl knew about the Sentinels. She'd been gone ever since then to track down a few of her contacts in the capital and get the word out about our compromised situation.

It was now mid-afternoon, and Chaz and I were at the cottage preparing for our nightly patrol. I scrubbed a hand over my face; the maps and notes on the table in front of me were beginning to bleed together.

"If you don't care, you can have Ridgemore," Chaz said. "I don't want to deal with that tonight. Not since we found out those Emberfell fugitives are arriving in less than a week. Attacks are running *wild* over there—people trying to get the port shut down."

"Mhm," I mumbled, eyes glazing at the words before me. I flipped over the page of notes, but instead of the cool, stiff parchment, I felt warm skin and soft hair. Instead of lines on a map, I saw green eyes staring back at me. I blinked and pinched the bridge of my nose, shaking myself out of memories from the previous night.

"Are you even listening to me?"

Something hard smacked into the back of my head and I jolted, looking down to find the leather strap for a knife at my feet. "What was that for?" I asked, whirling to face Chaz.

"You're distracted," he said.

"I'm not *distracted*."

"Really?" He raised an eyebrow. "Rissa told us how it was with Rose that day of the first trial. That the tension was so thick, she—"

I threw the leather strap back at his face to cut him off. "You should know better than to listen to my sister," I growled.

He looked wholly unconvinced. Shrugging, he picked up his knife and continued sharpening it on the stone. "She wasn't wrong. I saw it with my own eyes when Rose was here the other day." He chuckled and wagged his eyebrows at me. "You know what else I saw with my own eyes?"

"Don't finish that thought."

"I'm just saying, the girl's easy to look at. Been a while since someone new has come along. If you're not interested, maybe I'll try and—"

Slamming my hands on the table, I stood and crossed into the kitchen. That smug grin on Chaz's dark face told how easily he could read me, how easily he could rile me up.

I rummaged through the basket of charms we kept on the counter, deciding what I wanted to bring on patrol with me tonight. My fingers landed on the vial of calamus oil Rose had used to cast the compulsion spell on me, and her face popped back up in my mind.

Chaz was right—she *was* easy to look at. The fact that she was beautiful wasn't a secret. Anyone with eyes could see that; the way her dark hair shone like black velvet, how her full lips smirked when holding back a quick retort, those endless eyes that cut right through you. It didn't help that I knew how her skin felt beneath my fingertips, how her body felt held against mine in a darkened corridor.

Maybe I was attracted to her. Maybe her stubbornness had given way to something else. But I wasn't *distracted*. We had a mission, and I knew my priorities. Keeping her safe and making sure she was able to do what we needed her to do was part of that. So was earning her trust.

I knew deep down, though, I wanted that trust as more than allies. Even as a young boy, when I saw someone hurting, I had this urge to pick up the pieces. To heal them and make things right. Every time my sister walked through the door of our home with more bruises, I wished I could be the one to bear that pain. Every day our mother drifted further and further from us, I wished I could bridge the gap and take her illness away.

And Rose...she was hurting. The way she spoke of her father's death and how the people in her province treated her drug up the same desire in me to be what she needed. Last night, it was a friend.

I wanted her to feel safe and comfortable with me. I wasn't sure when the shift had taken place, but now I wanted to break down her walls, to see what demons she held beneath that tough exterior, what haunted her past and caused the helplessness and insecurity that tried to crack through her carefully curated shell.

That has nothing to do with the mission, Leo, a voice whispered in the back of my mind.

"Ridgemore," I said curtly, getting us back on track. "What's the latest report?"

Chaz cleared his throat. "The Emberfell fugitives will be here within the week. Things are as bad as ever up there at the border between them and Drakorum, and more families are on the run. Word got out, and there have been attempts the last few days to get the northern *and* eastern ports shut down so they can't enter. Mostly the work of a handful of angry locals, but we've been keeping an eye on it." He looked up at me from his knife. "Just be careful. Wouldn't want to mess up that pretty face for Rose," he finished, his eyes flashing humorously.

I shot him a glare, but it held no true anger. As much as he and the others enjoyed irritating me, I didn't know what I would do without them. They were my only family.

It was easy to withstand a few jokes to have them by my side.

We spent the next quarter of an hour going through the reports from the last week of the various sectors across the capital, lost in talk of strategy and placement when there was a knock on the door.

Chaz eyed it. "You expecting someone?"

"Anyone we know wouldn't bother knocking." I flipped a knife in my hand and stood, stalking to the door.

I pulled it open, surprise licking at me like flames. "I didn't think I'd see you again so soon."

Rose tucked a strand of hair behind her ear and gave me a soft smile. One free of sarcasm, of derision or distaste or distrust. The beams from the afternoon sun shimmered around her, making her olive skin glow and her green eyes sparkle.

She was...stunning.

Fates, I was in trouble.

"Can we talk?" she asked, biting her bottom lip.

"I—sure, of course. Come in." I held an arm out, wondering what had come up that made her travel here the day before the second trial began.

"Well, hello there," Chaz crooned from the table. I ran my tongue over the top of my teeth, holding back a retort.

"It's Chaz, right?" Rose said, tilting her head at my friend as if she hadn't spent hours with him just four days previously. A hint of a smirk pulled at her lips.

Chaz held a hand to his heart. "You wound me."

I pointed to him and motioned for him to stand. "You. Up. We've run through enough reports for today."

Giving me a dramatic bow, he said, "As you wish, sir." He straightened and winked. "Don't do anything I wouldn't do."

I moved to smack him on the back of the head, but in the blink of an eye, he disappeared in thin air. We heard his muffled chuckle on the other side of the door growing more and more distant.

"He seems like a handful," Rose said with a snort.

"He is," I agreed. "He's also my best friend, strange as it may seem."

She nodded. "No, I can see it. I mean, you're so...you," she said, holding a hand out as if that explained everything.

I took a step toward her. "And what am I, exactly?"

"Serious. Brooding. A chronic scowler." She grinned, but it didn't reach her eyes. Even in the short time I'd known her, I could see how swift she was to use jokes and sarcasm to cover up her vulnerability.

I wanted to reach out and comfort her, but instead I clenched my hands at my sides. "What's wrong, Rose? Why did you come here?"

"Is—is Rissa here?"

"Not right now, but she should be home soon if you want to wait for her."

"No, it's alright. It might be better this way." Her cheeks flushed. "I need to tell you something. Something I should have told you last night."

My guard was instantly on alert, apprehension sliding over me. "What are you talking about?"

She sighed heavily and closed her eyes. "Look, I may not have been completely honest with you." Opening one eye and peeking out at me, she winced. "About my meeting with Gayl."

I gritted my teeth, but reined in any emerging anger. *You're so quick to expect the worst in others, little brother. Sometimes you have to look harder to find their best.* My sister's words from the other night came roaring back, urging me to stop anticipating the worst. To not close my mind down in the face of suspicion and betrayal. To listen and trust and *look*.

"Come sit," I said, turning and leading her to the couch. "What happened?"

Rose balanced on the edge of the cushion, refusing to meet my eyes. Her fingers rubbed furious circles into the leather of her herb pouch. There were so many of her layers left to uncover. So many sides beneath the bold, reckless, sharp woman I was used to seeing. This side of her...it reminded me of that morning in the alcove. Pained, scared, and running.

She took a deep breath. "I should have told you last night, but I was just so—so overwhelmed. Gayl talked about my father, about living in Feywood and it—it was a lot to take in. I didn't know what to think. I wasn't sure if I even believed him."

Reflexively, I extended a hand and rested it on hers, pausing her nervous habit. "Slow down, Rose. Start over. What did he say?"

She met my eyes, wariness shining in those emerald pools, and licked her bottom lip before saying, "Theod—Gayl is my father's brother. He's my *uncle*, Leo."

We sat there in stunned silence for a moment as I tried to wrap my mind around what she'd said. "Your...uncle? How is that possible?"

"Everything I told you was true—he *is* from Feywood. And he *did* know my father. It's just a little more complicated than that. They had a big falling out years ago, and Gayl changed his name and moved to Veridia City long before I was born." She took her hand out from beneath mine and ran it through her hair, those long strands dripping like ink down her chest. "I'm sorry, Leo. I was in shock. I was angry with Morgana and Ragnar for never telling me, and I needed time to—to let it sink in. You surprised me at my window while I was still processing it all."

Theodore Gayl was her uncle. The man I'd spent my entire life despising, who had ripped our lives out from under us, shared her blood.

How had this happened? How was it that the person we'd

found to carry out this duty ended up being related to the very man we wanted to overthrow?

Was this how she had felt when learning I was Branock Aris' son, who she believed killed her father? The irony of the situation wasn't lost on me. But she was *not* her uncle. Shared blood didn't determine the choices one would make or who they would become.

And yet...a small part of me wondered if it was all a coincidence. If she and Gayl had somehow conspired to trick us, getting close enough to us to turn this whole operation around and expose us as the rebellion.

But did I believe that? Or was that me expecting the worst in others, denying them the grace my sister was so adept at?

What would Rissa say?

My sister would remind me that Rose's entire existence up to this point hadn't been devoted to our cause, as mine had. That I couldn't expect her loyalty to us to be so unwavering after a mere *week* that she would set aside her own needs, her own turmoil and shock, in a single moment. She'd tell me to swallow my pride and pessimism and remember all Rose has been through and what she'd put on the line for us.

Letting out an exhale, I stood abruptly and paced in front of the couch, needing to release this frustration before it grew. It would do me no good to aim it at her—not when she had come here for the right reasons.

"I wish you had said something last night, but I suppose I can't blame you," I said slowly, glancing at her. "You've been through a lot the last few days."

Her eyes narrowed. "You're taking this...well."

"I'm thinking."

A timid, relieved smile played on her lips. "Better than yelling," she said. I grunted, and her smile widened slightly. "There's that scowl."

I stopped in front of her, and her face fell. "I *am* sorry, Leo," she said. "But I'm here now."

"How can I be sure this doesn't change your commitment to us? Your loyalty?"

"Because I wouldn't have come to you if it did. I still want the same thing I did yesterday before finding all of this out. I still want the Somnivae curse broken and this empire set free from his rule." She stood and gazed up at me, the top of her head reaching my lips. She looked so fierce, so resilient, even in the face of her obvious distress. A beautiful storm ready to wipe out those in her path.

"And even though I kept this from you, I still meant what I said last night," she added. "I *do* want to be friends. But as you can see, there's a reason not many people want to get close to me." She spoke the words as a challenge, not a plea for pity. Not an excuse.

"Perhaps they're scared," I murmured.

"What do they have to be scared of?"

Fates, this woman. I couldn't seem to stop myself from responding. "Themselves, maybe. The way you might make them feel. How bold you are with your magic, how unapologetic you are with your words. You challenge them. You challenge *me*." My fingers itched to graze hers, the hitch of her breath chipping away at the tightness around my chest. "That's enough to make anyone feel a bit of fear."

She held my stare, surprise glistening in her eyes. She wasn't expecting that. Maybe I had layers, too. Sides she was beginning to uncover bit by bit.

That thought used to frighten me. But for some reason, knowing she was letting her walls down too, that we were both toeing that line, scared of the precipice yet walking it all the same... it made it less daunting.

"Thank you, Leo." Her voice was so quiet, it was like a breath. "Thank you for listening. For not getting angry and turning me away."

This time, I couldn't stop my hand from raising to rest on the back of her neck, my thumb skimming her jaw. "I told you last night, you don't have to thank me."

"Because we're friends," she said, drawing out the words.

My lips twitched. That title felt searing with my skin against hers. "Yes. Because we're friends."

She swallowed, and I tracked the motion, the air crackling and snapping around us. I could feel her pulse at her neck, could see it thrumming the way it had in that alcove last week. I brushed my thumb along it and sensed it jump beneath my touch.

The door flew open with a bang.

Rose inhaled sharply, turning to move away from me.

"Leo, can you please tell Chaz to—oh, I'm sorry, am I interrupting something?" my sister asked, her voice hitching up at the end as she stared at me with her head cocked. A sly grin peeked on the edges of her lips. Any hint of our confrontation that morning seemed forgotten.

I glanced at Rose, a silent conversation taking place between us. We needed to tell Rissa about her newfound relationship with Gayl, but I wanted to make sure she was ready.

Rose bit down on her lip, then nodded at me. I turned back to my sister. "Rissa, there's been a…development."

When I paused, she unclasped her cloak and threw it onto the couch, giving me an expectant look. "Well, am I supposed to guess?"

Rose jumped in. "I came here to talk to you both because I found out that Gayl is my father's brother." Her voice was stronger this time as she talked to Rissa, not stopping to wait for a reaction. "He grew up in Feywood until his mid-twenties, when he and my father got into a massive fight and he left the province. I confirmed everything with my aunt Morgana this morning. It— it's true." She cleared her throat, her nerve seeming to falter. "He's my uncle."

Rissa stared at her, her eyes roaming over Rose's features for a moment, and then strolled into the kitchen, grabbed an apple from a small basket, and leaned against the counter. The only sound in the house was the crunch of her first bite as she examined both of us across the living space.

"Did you know or have any suspicion about this before last night, Rose?" she finally asked.

"No."

"And did you give the emperor information regarding us or your mission?"

"No," Rose answered firmly.

"Do you want to pursue any sort of relationship with him that would create a conflict of interest?"

"No. I don't want anything to do with him."

Rissa took another bite. The apple's sweet, tart scent filled the air. "Do you still want to work with us? To carry out the plan?"

"I want to figure out how to end the curse," Rose said. "And I want him gone."

Another bite, followed by more silence.

"Alright," Rissa said.

I blinked. Next to me, Rose said, "Is that all?"

"If you're being honest, yes," Rissa said with a shrug, pushing off the counter. "And if my dear brother here hasn't chewed your head off already, then that's a good sign. I have to ask, though, why didn't you tell him this last night when he had his little *tryst* at the palace?" She shot me a sharp look, and I scowled.

"Like I told Leo, I was just...scared. Shocked and a little ashamed to be related to this man who's caused so much harm. Angry that I didn't know sooner. I should have said something, but I wasn't thinking clearly."

Rissa nodded in understanding. "I'm glad you told us now. Because I think this is the perfect opportunity."

"You do?" I asked, wondering what my sister was up to. She had that cunning look about her, one that spoke of plans taking shape and lines being crossed.

"Do you think you could meet with him again?" Rissa asked Rose.

Rose looked at me out of the corner of her eye, almost as if she needed reassurance. Then her gaze flitted back to Rissa. "He said he wants to see me again. To—to tell me more about my father."

"That's good," Rissa said, her excitement mounting. "He trusts you—or at least, wants to get to know you. To keep you close. If you're willing, Rose, this could be our opening. Your way in without having to sneak around the palace. If he's keeping a closer eye on the Sentinels, we can't take as many chances, but *you* have already gained a footing. Meet with him, get to know him, make him trust you. Who knows what information he'll willingly hand over?"

She had a point. This was a kind of advantage we would have never seen coming.

Rose didn't answer immediately. She seemed to be warring with herself, her brows knit tightly together, her eyes searching Rissa's face as if she might find something there. Was this too much to ask of her? To exploit this brand new part of her heritage and put herself into a different kind of danger?

I didn't know if I'd be able to bear seeing her body added to the list of ones we'd lost for the sake of this empire. Seeing *anyone's* body added to it.

But Rose's features hastily fell into determination, and she gave my sister a curt nod. "Yes," she said, eyes shining with resolve. "I'll do whatever you need."

36

ROSE

I finished braiding my hair for the challenger's feast and wrapped it around the crown of my head, securing it with a couple of pins. The reflection in the mirror showed a woman ready for combat, of sorts. A tight, sleek black dress as armor; rose-tinted cheeks and darkly lined eyes as a shield; deep red lips and sharp tongue as a sword. This dinner would be a battle, just not in the same way the trials were.

The reflection didn't show everything, though. It didn't show my guilt. It didn't show my unease. It didn't show my fear.

I'd lied again. I'd kept more from Leo than he could imagine. *And* I had agreed to keep helping them, to use my relationship with Gayl to our advantage, all under the premise of finding some Grimoire I knew would do us no good.

Despite everything, they still trusted me.

When you look in the mirror, what do you find? A rose in full bloom, with thorns on the vine?

I was beginning to see those thorns now.

And it didn't help that Leo had been so *understanding*. I'd expected anger—anger, I could handle. I was used to that. But it was like he was a different person from the man who'd been so quick to write me off. Even when I'd given him every reason to

289

walk away, when I'd warned him against getting too close, he didn't back down. He said I *challenged* him. He didn't see my brashness as a flaw, but a strength.

I closed my eyes. His acceptance made me feel a kind of safety I'd hardly ever experienced. And here I was, keeping perhaps the most important revelation of his life from him. But it was *because* of his life that I was holding back the truth. Because I couldn't bear to see him lose it.

A knock on the door made me open my eyes, meeting the gaze of the woman staring back at me in the mirror. She looked like a challenger. A spy. A warrior.

I felt like a fraud.

Moving to the door, I opened it to find a servant with an envelope resting on a tray, my name written on top in what I recognized as Gayl's handwriting. Being careful not to rip the contents, I tore the envelope open and pulled out two pieces of parchment. One was a handwritten letter, and the other was...a portrait.

Of my father and Gayl.

They appeared to be in their early twenties. The charcoal drawing showed my father with his arm slung around his older brother, his dark hair cropped and clean-cut while Gayl's was wild and unruly, almost touching his shoulders. They were both smiling, their youthful happiness so contagious it made my lips twitch up in response. My shaking fingers traced the outline of my father's strong jaw, his laughing eyes, his kind smile. It had been so long since I'd seen him, besides the tiny picture kept in my locket. It was easy to forget he'd once looked like this, so carefree and young.

A tear fell and landed on the edge of the portrait. I hastily wiped it away, the backs of my eyes stinging with the effort to keep my emotions at bay.

I reluctantly set it aside and turned my attention to the note.

> *Rose,*
>
> *I apologize for last night and the way I forced such news upon*

your shoulders. I didn't intend to cause you alarm, but I fear my story may have pushed you further away.

My brother was first and foremost a scholar. A man who loved the written word and the wealth that knowledge provided him. It's a shame that the world will never know of the epiphanic discoveries he made, but I believe he would have wanted to share them with you. To pass along the hidden depths of our magic to his daughter, whom I know he treasured beyond all else, even if I never spoke with him of you. That was who Hamilton was. A man of few words, but a heart and mind as wide and endless as the sea.

I found this drawing in what little possessions I took with me from Feywood. Whenever you would like to know more about the Hamilton I knew, pen your response on the back of this parchment. I will receive it.

I look forward to meeting with you once again.

-T.G

I crumpled the bottom half in my grip as I finished, then cursed and quickly spread it out on my bed, smoothing away the wrinkles as best I could.

The hidden depths of our magic.

What would my father have been able to teach me, had he lived long enough? Aunt Morgana had made it sound like Gayl had coerced him into some dark life of blood magic, but Gayl's words told of how passionate my father was, how he made these profound discoveries. It pricked at my curiosity, dusting off some bone-deep desire.

I let myself dwell on the note for one more moment before tucking it away. I would deal with it later—first, I had to get through this dinner and the second trial that began in the morning.

After carefully folding the drawing so my father's face stared up at me when I placed it on my bedside table, I made my way out the door, unsurprised to find Horace waiting for me.

He scanned me head-to-toe appraisingly, taking in my dress and heels. "You look...different."

I snorted. "Be careful, Horace. Keep talking to me like that and we won't make it to dinner."

He frowned at me, and I couldn't help but laugh. "It's a *joke*. Always the big, grumpy guard," I teased, flexing my muscles and slouching, forcing my features into a sullen glare.

"I don't look like that," he grumbled as we descended a staircase, heading to the dining hall. I smiled when he shifted his shoulders back to stand straighter.

"You're right, Horace. You're very handsome," I said, nudging his shoulder. "Do you have someone back home? A wife or anything?"

He shook his head with a grunt. "Hard to have much of a personal life with the Guard on one shoulder and Sentinels on another." He lowered his voice at the last part, even though we were the only two in sight.

My playful mood dimmed. "I hadn't thought of it that way. It must be hard, living a double life. What made you want to do it?"

"I was tired of seeing nothing be done to fix things," he said with a shrug. "Too many people who should be keeping the capital safe are happy to turn a blind eye. Our emperor included. I got sick of it. You can only watch so many hypocrites walk away from a crime or so many starving kids in the streets before realizing something's not right."

I nodded. "Did Rissa find you? Or did you find them?"

"I found them. Caught Chaz skulking around the perimeter on my night watch and told him I could either turn him in or he could tell me what he was doing and I'd let him go. He told me about the Sentinels, and I knew I had to meet them."

I considered his story, wanting to ask even more questions but knowing people might be within earshot at any moment. I couldn't imagine the courage it took to cross his employers, cross the *emperor*, right under their very noses in order to take a stand on what he believed in. And to continue doing it for years, with the threat of discovery waiting around every corner...

"You're a brave man, Horace," I said quietly.

He looked at me out of the corner of his eye and grunted.

I huffed out a laugh. Some things never changed.

We reached the dining hall, which was smaller than I'd anticipated. More intimate. A long table stood in the middle, tall candles and strands of greenery as the centerpieces. The low ceiling was painted a light cream with ornamental gold candelabras hanging from it, casting the space in a warm haze. The walls were dark blue and adorned with large landscape paintings—a beautiful cliffside, a snow-capped mountain range, a sunset over a beach. It was all very...relaxing. Cozy.

I was instantly suspicious.

A servant greeted us at the entrance and showed me to my seat, while Horace took his place with his fellow guards at the walls. I glanced down the rectangular table to find each of the challengers' names written in swirling black ink. Mine was the very last seat on the left side, while what I assumed was Gayl's seat of honor was at the opposite head. Peering at the name next to mine, I rolled my eyes.

Alaric Rinehart.

"Not my biggest fan, I take it?" Alaric asked from behind, then took his seat beside me.

I didn't respond. I wouldn't let these people rile me up tonight. I'd chosen my outfit and appearance carefully; the tight, thigh-length black dress with long sleeves extending to my wrists, little silver loops hooking around my middle fingers that glistened when I silently reached for my glass. The black liner beneath my eyelids, sharp enough to wound. The dark red lips that spoke of sin and blood and roses.

I was in control. I'd had enough of letting others think they could say whatever they wanted or walk over me and leave me in their tracks. I may be an Alchemist, one of the least powerful provinces, but I wanted them to know I didn't belong *beneath* anyone.

Nox strode in soon after and, to my relief, sat right across from me. He took one look at my steely expression and smirked.

As everyone else filtered in, I noted the seating arrangement. Callista and Callum were next to Alaric on our side of the table. There had been an obvious tactic to the placement—the four people who held such animosity toward one another, forced in tight quarters. Callista's arm was still in a sling from whatever had happened between her and Callum in the first trial, and while she laughed and spoke cheerfully with Lark and the two architects across from her, I saw the way her eyes narrowed when the Illusionist sat down. The way her hand inched ever so slightly toward her dinner knife, a small beam of light twirling between her fingers.

I knew putting Alaric and me next to each other wasn't a coincidence, either. I caught Lark's eye at the opposite end of the table and raised an eyebrow, tipping my head subtly in Alaric's direction. She gave me a sheepish grin and a shrug. What was more entertaining than sticking a group of hot-headed challengers in a single room with a bunch of forks and knives at our disposal?

Not that we needed sharp objects to hurt one another.

Next to Nox sat Arowyn, who immediately plopped down in her seat, grabbed the bottle of wine from the servant pouring the glasses, and propped her boots up on top of the table.

I shared a look with Nox. Fates, I wanted to be her.

"No hard feelings there, Emberfell?" I heard Alaric say, and turned to see him holding out a hand to Callista.

Tawny skin crinkled at her eyes as she smiled sweetly. "Of course not, Alaric. We all know how these trials go." She took his outstretched hand, and I could've sworn a bolt of static like lightning zipped through the air. Alaric grimaced and flinched when she pulled away.

"Hmm," I said, "I take it I'm not the only one you graced with your presence in the trial, Alaric?"

"Our paths may have crossed on my way out of the central sector. She looked a little too confident, and I couldn't have that, now could I?" he said, tapping his nose and offering a light chuckle. "But I didn't harm the girl. She must have run into the Iluze boy later. Ah, Nox!" Alaric raised his hand across the table in greeting. "Haven't seen you around the palace much. Been off licking your wounds?" He laughed at his own joke, and I rolled my eyes.

"I've never been better, Rinehart," Nox said smoothly as he tipped his glass.

"You know, I don't think I caught you during the trial at all. Tell me, what is your form, anyway?" Alaric asked.

I raised my eyebrows over my glass. I'd posed the same question days ago, but still, it was a very intrusive thing to ask someone. I *was* curious, though. The fact that he hadn't revealed his Shifter form yet made him an enormous threat.

"Probably some sort of rodent," Arowyn said, shooting Nox a lazy smile from her slumped position. "Like a squirrel. Or a naked mole-rat."

I coughed. My drink burned as I choked it down.

"Something like that." Nox's eyes flashed in amusement. "If you want to see me naked, Strider, you only have to ask."

"Pass. You're not my type."

"Darling, I'm *everyone's* type."

Arowyn smirked. "Trust me." Taking a swig of the bottle, she planted her feet on the ground and looked up at the head of the table. "Where's our gracious host, anyway?"

On cue, the entrance doors to the dining hall opened once more, and in strode Emperor Gayl. Lark immediately rose to her feet, and the rest of us followed suit. He wore no cloak this time, opting for a coattail dinner jacket of such a dark green that it appeared black. His gloved hands rested at his sides as he swiftly and silently paced to his seat, flanked by the same short man I'd seen with him the evening I got caught. Daye, I think he was called.

"Be seated," Gayl said, taking his own seat at the head of the table. Daye sat in the only open spot next to him, across from Lark and the other architects. At once, servants filed in, each carrying a silver platter with a domed lid. The scent of savory spices hit me as they took their spot behind each seated guest.

Gayl flicked his wrist, and the servants set the platters down before us, removing the lids in synchronization.

"Please," Gayl said, motioning to the food, "Enjoy the evening. It's for you, after all. Completing the first trial in the Decemvirate is quite a feat. Celebrate it while you can." His eyes met mine, and I immediately looked down, my stomach churning.

I wanted to forget about our meeting, forget about his past and his note and his offer. I wanted to put aside the guilt I bore for lying to Leo and the promise I'd made to continue searching for answers. But they were like a dozen weeds poking through the soil in my mind, refusing to die, refusing to lay dormant.

The first course was a delicious roasted garlic soup with potatoes, followed by herb-crusted chicken on a bed of wild rice. It was all far more elegant than any food we had back in Feywood, with the fancy garnishes and drizzled sauces. The meat practically melted on my tongue and kept my mouth occupied while I listened in on the conversations around me.

"So, Alaric," Callista began, twirling her fork in the air at the man. "How did you find yourself here for a second time?"

"Are you the best they had to offer?" Arowyn added, and I grinned around a bite of chicken.

Alaric laughed along with the others. I had to admit, he was surprisingly good-natured despite being on the receiving end of many snide remarks. Most of which had to do with his age or the fact that he lost the last Decemvirate.

"Suffice it to say, I have a personal score to settle," he answered with a smile, but I didn't miss the shadows that pooled at our feet before dissipating.

Callum leaned back in his chair. "Speaking of which, Geoffrey said to tell you hello for him, old man." He smirked, and I had the sudden urge to plunge my fork into his eye. Or somewhere lower.

Alaric stiffened, his grin faltering for a split second. Geoffrey

Bardelou, the Iluze challenger whom Alaric had lost to ten years ago, was a common household name, given the dramatic nature of their feud and how it had continued between Tenebra and Iluze for so many months after the fact.

My resentment toward Alaric eased a fraction. He carried himself confidently, and he was no doubt one of the most powerful beings here, but I hadn't considered how this past decade might have been for him. Tenebra was notoriously one of the most aggressive and unstable of the provinces, and I can't imagine they were very *forgiving* when Alaric failed to secure the title of champion last time.

This Decemvirate meant more to him than a mere win. It was a redemption. I couldn't fault him for doing what it took to best me.

I stabbed my fork into the chicken. Perhaps I could still be a *little* mad.

"I may be old, boy, but I still managed to surpass you, if I recall correctly." Alaric bore his jovial smile, although it looked more like bared teeth.

"My, the masculinity in this room smells like sweaty balls and mediocrity," Arowyn said as she took a bite of her dinner roll, her wine glass in the other hand. "I bet you boys wouldn't last five minutes against the three of us." She motioned to Callista and myself. Her tone was casual, indifferent, but her eyes sparked with challenge.

Scoffing, Callum said, "What, the Strider, Lightbender, and Alchemist? You do realize you're the three weakest provinces, right?"

I bit my tongue, fighting the urge to make some snappy retort, but Nox beat me to it. "A Strider who's currently at the top of the rankings and an Alchemist who incapacitated you in front of the entire hall," he said into his glass. "Might want to be careful there."

Callista propped her elbow on the table and rested her chin on her fist. "Hmm, *interesting*," she purred. "I wouldn't mind putting such confidence to the test."

"This feels like an apt time to remind you that there are no inter-challenger duels between trials," Lark called dryly from her seat next to Gayl.

My eyes shifted from Lark to Gayl while the others continued talking, and I found his expression to be as bored as if we were talking about the weather. He saw me staring and his lips fell into a thin line. Holding my gaze, he tipped his glass toward the rest of the challengers and quirked an eyebrow. I could practically hear him say, "This *is the cream of the crop?*"

I pursed my lips together and looked down at my food, but I knew he caught my little smirk.

Conversation began to break off into smaller sections of the table; the architects on one end were fascinated by Callista and Callum's stories of their provinces, and it seemed they were attempting to outdo one another in their wild tales of magic. Nox was trying desperately to get Arowyn to laugh at his ridiculous jokes, but she merely rolled her eyes and shot him down each time.

To my annoyance, Alaric twisted to face me. "Look, Rose, I really am sorry for how things turned out there at the mausoleum. It's the way of the tournament; you know how it goes."

I sighed. His words might be nonchalant, bordering on arrogant, but his eyes told of his regret. I knew he'd do it again, if put in that situation, but I also could tell he wished he didn't have to. I supposed we were all in the same position.

"I imagine you would've done the same thing to Uncle Ragnar, if he'd been in my place," I conceded.

"Ah, Ragnar," he said, his light green eyes growing distant with nostalgia. "That old fellow would have hunted me down if I'd done that to him. I'd have a few more broken bones added to the list."

"Don't give me any ideas," I muttered.

"If you're anything like the rest of your family, I wouldn't put it past you," Alaric said, chortling. "Like I said, I knew your parents, too. Your mother was a natural with her charms. And Hamilton... Hamilton was something else entirely. Don't tell Ragnar this, but if your father was still alive, it would be *him* in the Decemvirate this year." He shook his head. "Never seen someone perform magic the way he could. Aside from our emperor, of course."

As he finished talking, his brow furrowed slightly, and he twisted his neck to look over at Gayl. But before he could start putting any pieces together, Lark stood to get everyone's attention.

"I wanted to thank you all for joining us on the eve of the second trial. Before we retire for the night, His Majesty would like to give a toast." She gestured to the servants lining the wall. They began passing out slender flutes of sparkling wine to the guests.

The dining hall went silent as Gayl stood, shadows flickering on the walls behind him. He raised his flute in the air. "Well done, challengers. You have proven your knowledge with a trial of puzzles and riddles. Tomorrow, we discover the truth of who you are at the heart of the matter." His mismatched blue and white eyes landed on me. "To your mettle and your spirit. I pray you will not be disappointed by either."

At that, he lifted his glass higher, then tilted it back and drained it.

And the rest of us drank with him.

37

ROSE

I woke with a bittersweet taste in my mouth and my tongue glued to the roof so thickly I had to work to pry it down. Stretching, I rolled over in bed, groaning against the bright sunlight turning the back of my eyelids red.

An abrupt realization chased away all grogginess.

The second trial was supposed to start today. I wondered if I'd receive a note like last time, or if there was some other method the architects had devised to tell us what to do.

I hurriedly bathed and dressed, opting for a pair of comfortable black pants that fit snugly inside my boots and a fitted shirt that wouldn't get in the way if I had to move quickly. I grabbed my dagger and took stock of my charms, distributing them between my pockets and my small pouch, then hooked it to my belt loop.

Surprised nobody had called for me yet, I crossed to the door and opened it, peering down the hall to find it...empty. Horace was gone, and there were no maids scuttling about like normal, bringing towels or breakfast or dusting the decor lining the walls. I made my way to the closest adjoining hall, expecting to see lords with their fancy cloaks, messengers delivering mail, or guards stationed at various intervals.

But it was empty, too.

The palace was eerily silent.

A pit formed in my stomach. Where *was* everybody?

Suddenly, shattering glass and a scream broke through the quietness. Following the sound, I raced down the corridor and turned a corner to find a window had been smashed. A young maid cowered on the ground before it with her hands over her head.

I rushed to her and helped her back to her feet. "What happened?" I asked.

She hiccuped through her sobs. "Ev-everyone i-is—" But she couldn't finish her sentence, instead nodding out the window to the palace grounds beyond.

Slowly, I stepped across the glass littering the floor and leaned over the stone sill of the window, heart faltering at what unfolded before me.

Shouts and clashing steel met my ears. Plumes of dark gray smoke and flickers of red and orange flames rose from the village barely visible over the surrounding forest. Figures in the Royal Guard uniform of silver mixed with those in civilian clothing dashed from the palace and through the trees, making their way toward a thunderous boom coming from beyond the woods. Even from three stories up, I could hear the desperate cries of the wounded citizens under attack in the central sector.

"When did this start?" I asked the maid, shaking her shoulders urgently when she did nothing but cry into her hands. "What's happening?"

"M-Mysthelm, my lady," she wailed. "A-attacked just an hour ago. Everybody l-left to fight."

My jaw fell open. *Mysthelm?* I thought we hadn't heard from the non-magic kingdom in *centuries*. What in the world was happening? Why would they be attacking us? Had the emperor been keeping some conflict with them a secret from the rest of the provinces?

I released the maid and turned away, but she grabbed my arm. "Th-they're in the palace, my lady," she whispered, terror etched on every inch of her face.

My stomach plummeted to my feet. *Beau and Morgana.*

Bolting to the nearest stairwell, I descended to the bottom level, commotion growing louder the closer I got to the main hall. Men in armor I didn't recognize were fighting with Veridian soldiers, the corridors littered with broken wood, glass, ripped tapestries, and pools of blood. Several bodies lay mangled on the floor, and I jerked my gaze away when it landed on a severed hand detached from a fallen guard. Dodging flailing limbs, I reached into my satchel to cast an invisibility spell over myself.

I knew something was wrong before I even reached the infirmary.

Bloody footprints led away from the entrance. Sobs haunted the corridor, making the edges of my vision gray with panic. I almost slipped on slick blood as I entered the healer's wing, stifling a scream at the sight.

The curtains that had hung as partitions between patients were shredded, shelves full of supplies knocked over, beds tipped and cast aside, broken vials and bandages and potions scattered across the ground.

And every single patient...

Every patient was dead.

I covered my mouth as a horrified cry worked its way up my throat. I recognized the men and women from the times I'd come to visit Ragnar, now slumped lifelessly in their beds, blood bubbling from their slit throats.

Blindly, I tore through the wing, past bodies of nurses and broken furniture.

I stopped before a familiar bed.

My knees hit the hard floor, sending a shockwave up my legs and spine.

Ragnar.

His right arm hung off the side of the bed, his head bent at an unnatural angle on the pillow. Blood dripped from his neck and pooled on the stark white sheets.

I screamed.

I screamed until my throat was raw and my head pounded from exertion. Until the sound became a strangled whisper.

I screamed, but there was no one there to hear.

I was spiraling, caught between the past and present, between my father's glassy eyes and my uncle's closed lids, between my little hands soaked in blood and the fingers now clawing at my tear-soaked eyes. I felt my invisibility spell drop, but didn't care. I couldn't breathe, I couldn't think, I couldn't move—

Where were Morgana and Beau?

That single, penetrating thought was the only thing that pulled me from the darkness. The image of my aunt's raven hair and cousin's gangly arms gave me strength to rise from my knees and follow the path out of the infirmary. The hope of finding them safe and secure in their room kept me floating across the hall as if in a daze until I reached their door and twisted the handle.

It was unlocked.

I threw myself into the room, tearing and scrabbling and stumbling through every nook and cranny, calling their names until I didn't recognize the sound.

Nobody was there.

They were gone.

"My lady!" a voice sounded behind me, and I rounded on them like a feral cat, slamming my hand against the stranger's throat and shoving him into the wall by the door.

"Where are they?" I snarled.

The man sputtered beneath my hold, and I loosened my grip. "Civilians were—were taken hostage," he finally got out. I released his neck and staggered backward, the backs of my knees hitting the bed.

"*Hostage*? Where did they take them?"

"W-we don't know, my lady." He rubbed at his throat. "Our guards saw a black carriage carrying some toward the central sector. We think that's where the attack originated."

Hostage.

Central sector.

Black carriage.

I stormed from the room and retraced my steps to the main hall, my normal charm of amaranth stem mixed with mistletoe and blackthorn ash already on my tongue. When I grabbed my dagger from my waist, the weight of it settled something in me. Alchemists didn't rely much on weapons of steel, but Ragnar had taught Beau and me from a young age how to wield basic swords and daggers. *"Never be so confident in magic that you fail to use all tools at your disposal,"* he would say.

I would not fail.

As I rushed toward the palace entrance, a band of four soldiers in unfamiliar uniforms rounded on me, their swords raised high and glistening red. Mysthelm, I presumed.

I didn't even have a chance to feel fear. Not for *myself*. Not when all my dread was consumed in thoughts of what could be happening to my innocent aunt and cousin at that very moment.

I slipped an angelica leaf into my mouth, its sweet licorice taste mingling with the amaranth protection spell.

"Incendar," I muttered, and my open palm filled with fire, mildly warm against my skin but deadly to my foes.

The men exchanged wary glances. I cocked my head. "What, never seen an Alchemist before?" Flicking my finger, I sent a stream of fire blazing at the one on the far left, watching with cold eyes as the flames enveloped his body. His companion next to him yelped, leaping to help put it out. The two remaining faced me with renewed vigor.

"Get out of my way, or I'll be the last one you ever see," I growled.

They merely smirked.

"Fine." I beckoned them closer, and they charged. *"Aegesis nova."*

The instant the first soldier tried to thrust his sword at my chest, there was a squelch and a choked cry. A hole appeared in his breastplate, showing the gash beneath caused by an invisible blade. My retaliation charm had worked better than I thought.

Blood squirted from the wound as he dropped to his knees, confusion and anguish written on his features.

Within seconds, he was dead.

The other one glanced between him and me, then decided to take his chances and lunged. He was smarter than his friend, aiming for non-fatal blows: my ankles, my shoulders, my elbows. Each time, he cried out as thin lines of ruby red welled from his skin, while mine remained untouched. After the fourth try, he clutched at his wrist, dropping his sword. I strode toward him and kicked him in the stomach. He sprawled backward and tripped over his dead companion. Scrambling to the nearest column, he tried to stand, but I shoved my forearm against his neck and pinned him to the wall, pressing my dagger into his cheek.

"The civilians who were taken hostage. Where did they go?" I demanded. When he failed to respond, I dug the tip of the blade in deeper, his cheek dimpling as blood bloomed on the surface and dripped to the ground. "*Tell me.*"

"You'll never catch them," he said through gritted teeth.

"What are your people going to do with them?"

"What do you think?" He spat to the side, lips curving into a sadistic smile. "They'll get what all you magic freaks deserve."

My insides froze. I began to back away, when I caught the scent of...of peppermint and rubbing alcohol.

Like the ointments in the infirmary. Coming from the man under my hold.

With a sharp, distant voice I barely recognized as my own, I asked, "Were you the one who killed them?"

"You'll have to be more specific than that," he spat.

My grip on my dagger tightened. "The patients in the healer's wing."

His sick grin broadened.

Fury blinded me. Before he could move, I pulled my forearm off and dragged my blade across his throat.

He died with that smile still on his face.

Disgusted, I pushed away from him and watched as he

slumped to his knees, then landed face first onto the ground. I swallowed down rising bile and clenched the handle. Whirling on my heels, I forced any thought beyond getting to the central sector from my mind.

The fighting and the fallen blurred together as I sprinted past them and burst into the morning air, following the sounds of explosions and shouting to the north. The pillar of smoke rising behind the treeline guided my way.

Everything except my heaving breaths and pounding of my feet on the forest floor faded. I would find Morgana and Beau, whatever it took. They *had* to be safe. I couldn't lose them, too.

I sped north through the small forest, forcing air into my lungs and pushing past the stitch in my side. Soon, the trees and undergrowth thinned and leveled out, opening to the village of the central sector.

Shop windows were blown in, thatched rooftops had been set ablaze, and civilians and soldiers alike swarmed the open streets. Men in what I recognized now as the black armor of Mysthelm barged forward, bringing as many Veridians to their knees as they could. Magic also filled the air—bright beams of sun rays shot from Lightbenders, wisping shadows of the Shadow Wielders engulfed enemies whole, giant creatures of all kinds prowled underfoot, ripping limbs and heads from Mysthelm guards.

And there was blood. So much blood.

It was chaos. It was carnage.

But there were no black carriages in sight.

For a split second, the light and shadows and fire seemed to shimmer, but when I rubbed my eyes, the effect waned. In my peripheral vision, I saw several hooded figures crouching low to the ground with children burrowed in their arms. At first I thought they were the enemy carrying off innocent young ones, but then I realized they were using *shadows* to cloak them from sight.

Veridians, not Mysthelm soldiers. And they were heading toward a building secluded from the rest that hadn't yet been touched. They were taking them to *safety*.

I darted into the nearest house, searching for signs of inhabitants. A woman and a little girl were tucked away in a closet, the mother rocking her daughter close to her chest as tears streamed down her cheeks.

"Come on, you need to get out," I said hurriedly, offering my hand. I pulled them both up and we rushed out the door, keeping low to the ground and the shadows of the street.

"Do you see them? Heading toward that building?" I pointed, and the woman nodded. "Follow them. They'll keep you safe."

I watched as they scurried off, then made my way from house to house, rounding up any straggler I could find and sending them off as swiftly and inconspicuously as possible.

Exiting one of the houses, I was almost trampled by an oncoming horse and carriage making its way west.

A black carriage.

The back of it contained rows of steel bars, with men, women, and children crammed inside, hands flailing out the space between rods as if trying to get free.

A face stared back at me from behind the cage. A face I knew as well as my own.

"*Beau!*" I shrieked, throwing myself into the street and racing after the carriage. For a moment, it flickered, and I blinked against the mirage, holding my hand out as if I could catch him.

A female Veridian guard flew into view. She grabbed onto my outstretched arm, blocking Beau and the carriage from sight. I screamed at her and pulled out of her grip so I could get to my cousin, but her next words made me stop.

"Were you helping those people get to the shelter?"

I slid my focus to her as she gestured to the building behind us. "Y-yes," I gasped, my mind spinning. "They're—"

She shook my shoulders. "They're going to blow it up! I heard a Mysthelm soldier say they're planning to drop an explosive on it. We have to get them out!" she insisted, dragging me with her back toward the building.

Away from Beau.

I ripped my arm away. "I c-can't," I pleaded. "My family—"

"Didn't you see how many people were being led there?" Her voice was frantic. "We can't leave them to be slaughtered!"

My neck snapped to the direction the carriage had gone in, pulse pounding so hard I felt it in my palms, my ears, my gut.

I closed my eyes against the destruction around me.

I knew I should save the mass of innocent lives holed away in that building—many of which *I'd* put there under the promise of safety.

But my heart...

My heart was stuck behind the bars of a cage, barreling toward an unknown fate.

"I'm sorry," I whispered weakly, and took off after my cousin.

38

ROSE

The scent of blood, copper, and sweat spun around me as I ran through a village blanketed in red and steel, cries of the slaughtered and helpless ringing in my ears, fading away with each breath. Each blink. Each heartbeat.

For a moment, all sound ceased entirely.

I watched the violence unfold but was unable to hear it, like there was some sort of veil between myself and my surroundings. In the next second, it all rushed back, and I shook the strange sensation off.

The carriage was heading west. There was no way I'd ever be able to keep up on foot. Spotting a saddled, dapple-gray horse tied to its post off the side of a stable, I sped to it and pocketed my dagger, hastily untying the reins and trying in vain to calm the frightened creature. He pawed at the ground, his muscles shaking as he snorted at me with flared nostrils.

"I know, boy—I know it's scary," I murmured, my voice a tremor, my trembling hand reaching out to stroke his nose. Wide, brown eyes locked on mine. "But I need you to help me save my family, okay?"

When I was certain he wouldn't buck me off the second I tried to mount, I stuck my foot in the stirrup and swung my leg over his back. Steering him in the direction of the carriage, we fled past torn bodies and shrieking children, past growling Shifters and blood-thirsty men.

Wind whistled through my hair, and soon, the sound of rushing water grew increasingly louder over the cacophony behind us. The Scarre River, I remembered from my trek here during the first trial. I urged the horse faster until the dark wood and metal of the back of a carriage came into view.

Beau.

"I'm coming," I whispered, clenching my thighs and snapping the reins. Within minutes, the rocky path gave way to a grassy riverbank, and roaring water filled the air with a crisp dampness. Glancing behind me, I could still see the tips of the tallest buildings of the central sector, the top of a bell tower and spires of the palace like a beacon against the rising smoke and haze.

The carriage suddenly stopped. Five Mysthelm soldiers jumped from the box and strode to the back, unlocking the bars of the prison. With a cruelty that had my blood boiling, a man yanked them out, each stumbling as they tried to land on their feet while their hands were cuffed with some sort of black metal. Beau collapsed to his knees, his lanky legs sprawled behind him. One of the soldiers kicked his side with a shout to "Get up!"

That was it. He would die first.

I slid from the horse and reached into my pocket for hellebore and amaranth.

A blade appeared at my throat.

"Not so fast," came a hiss from behind me, a hand snaking around to grab my wrist. With the knife digging into the flesh at my neck, my captor shoved me forward with the rest of them. My mind raced, trying to devise a plan, a way out of here. The protection charm had worn off by now—I needed to get to my herbs. Or back to the horse. Maybe I could gather reinforcements and return to save—

I glanced at the brown horse behind me. Brown? Wasn't the one I rode here gray and dappled?

"Caught another one," the man behind me drawled. "Might be one of the witches. Saw her reaching for her pockets." His fingers strayed low on my waist, and I stiffened.

"Rosie?" Beau croaked, staring at me in slack-jawed horror from the ground.

My heart jolted. "It'll be okay, Beau. We're going to be fine," I assured him, fighting the urge to whip away from my captor and run for my cousin. But I didn't know what these soldiers would do. I couldn't risk them attacking.

Even from a distance, I could see the pain in Beau's eyes. The terror and heartbreak reflecting in his silver pools made my blood turn to ice. "Rosie...my ma...they—" He choked on his words, and that ice within me shattered.

Morgana.

She couldn't be...

"Take her weapons," one of the men instructed.

This time, I did fight. The man behind me jerked the satchel from my belt loop and with his slackened hold on my throat, I pivoted and slammed the heel of my palm into his nose. It snapped with a satisfying *crack*, and he wheeled backward, clutching his face and shouting obscenities.

Two more soldiers converged. Before I could reach for my charms, they had my arms behind my back. Cool, metallic cuffs clamped over my wrists, and it was like something clenched deep inside of me at the same time. I struggled against its hold but couldn't move an inch. My shoulders and neck strained wildly as they tugged me to the water's edge with the rest of the hostages. If I couldn't get to my charms, if I couldn't cast, I—

"Line them up. Kill them. Go get the next group," the soldier in charge barked to his subordinates.

Wails of protest and pleas for mercy rose at the command. My gaze met that of my cousin, his wide, frantic eyes staring back at me. Looking to me for answers. For safety.

Numbness blanketed me. I didn't know how to get out of this one. I didn't know how to protect him, how to get either of us away from danger.

"Don't touch him," I snarled as one of the men pulled Beau roughly toward the river. He turned and laughed at me.

"She's feisty," he said, licking his lower lip. "I call that one."

"Why don't you come and get me now, then?" I glared at him and he tilted his head, assessing me. Examining me.

To my relief, he released Beau. Sauntering forward, ignoring the hysterical hands from the Veridians reaching out to him for pity, he pointed his sword at me. "And mouthy, too. I think *you* want to go first."

"Why are you doing any of this?" I hurled at him. "What have we ever done to you?"

"We've been biding our time for decades, little witch. Your magic is a *curse*," he spat. "Your people are a poison. This entire empire is unnatural—it should have never gotten such power in the first place. So we're cleansing it."

"You're just going to kill *thousands* of people?" a hostage cried out.

"Silence!" the Mysthelm soldier roared. "This isn't a negotiation. We have our orders. Get them in a line," he said to his companions, who rushed to obey.

How was any of this happening? How had we been so ignorant to their attack? To their blatant hatred of us?

None of this even made any sense.

"Why isn't anyone fighting back?" I hissed to the woman next to me as we were both shoved forward.

"The sh-shackles." She motioned down to the black cuffs. "They take away our magic. We can't fight."

They could take away *magic*? That must have been the strange effect I felt when the cuffs circled my wrist. Was that what Mysthelm had been doing all these years? Developing ways to stifle our powers so they could make a move?

The sight of a dozen men, women, and children being led to

the water's edge with knives at their backs had panic flooding me. Blood roared through my ears, my vision growing cloudy as I tried to *think*—

I glanced up, squinting at the sun hanging over the bell tower in the central sector, and I swear the sky turned...*pink*. When I blinked, it was back to a clear blue, but my thoughts began churning...

A rough hand clamped down on my shoulder, forcing me to my knees. Distantly, I heard my cousin scream for me, but above that, I heard...

Ding. Dong. Ding. Dong.

I froze.

My eyes searched the treeline and landed on the bell tower, three gray bells swinging at its tip.

Believe the gray bells.

The Oracle.

This was it. This was what the Oracle had warned me about. The gray bells had been my clue for the second trial. But did that mean—?

The strange mirages I'd seen in the village, where everything seemed to sway and flicker. The gray horse changing to brown. The sky just now, appearing pink instead of blue. A ridiculous, inexplicable attack from a silent kingdom.

This...this *was* the second trial.

Believe the gray bells.

"None of this is real," I whispered to myself, realization barreling into me. Slowly, I twisted my neck to face my cousin, his face red and eyes swollen. Was I willing to risk his life on it? On a wild, half-hatched theory?

Before me, the Mysthelm soldier smirked and raised his sword. "Any last words, freak?"

I swallowed hard. There was no more time to think, to deliberate, to fight back. This *had* to be the trial—to test my heart and see what choices I'd make under duress. To see if I could figure it out and beat their little challenge.

I *had* to be right.

And if I wasn't...I prayed death would come swiftly.

"Tell the emperor," I rasped, knees digging into the grass and soil, "I'll see him soon."

Then he plunged his blade into my heart.

39

ROSE

I woke up screaming and drenched in sweat. My head spun as I bolted upright, blinking away the visions of massacre and fire and smoke staining the backs of my eyelids.

I was...I was in my bed. In the palace. Still in the leggings and oversized tunic I had gone to sleep in after the dinner—no dagger or charms in sight.

Had it truly not been real? Had it all been a—a *dream*?

Scrambling out of bed, I barely made it to the bathing chamber before I emptied the contents of my stomach into the wash basin, the cool porcelain a welcome reprieve against my hot cheeks.

Morgana and Ragnar had been—I couldn't even *think* the words, couldn't stop picturing blood spurting from Ragnar's neck. Images of dead bodies in the infirmary swirled around me. The cloying scent of death and decay suffocated me as I retched again.

After a few minutes had passed and my stomach seemed to settle, I rinsed out my mouth and washed my face. I tried not to stare at the yellow pallor of my skin and the way my hair hung limp down my chest. Throwing my boots on, I grabbed my charms and dagger then barged out the door, stumbling my way down the hall.

I forced breath through my mouth and into my lungs, fighting against a flurry of panic. What if the second trial wasn't over? What if I still hadn't passed?

I couldn't trust anything. Not even what was right in front of me. Not even my own *mind.*

"Rose, you're awake! Where are you going?"

I twisted at the sound of Horace's voice, holding my blade in front of me. I didn't know what to believe. If this wasn't real, if he was part of the trial...

He held his hands in the air. "C'mon, girl, I'm supposed to get you to Lark—"

"Stay away from me!" I snarled, backing up to the nearest stairwell. A sudden shout came from down the hall and I flinched, picturing enemy soldiers barreling through the narrow path—but it was simply laughter from passing guests. When Horace saw my fear, he turned around to search for a potential threat.

I took my chance. Bounding down the stairs, I ignored Horace's shout and the bewildered looks of guests as I sprinted to the first floor. The corridor seemed to darken and lengthen, and I couldn't tell if it was a figment of my imagination or some magic from the second trial. It felt like every shadow was stretching toward me, whispers and glares shooting at me like daggers from the Mysthelm army. My chest tightened; it was hard to draw breath, hard to see past the haze clouding my thoughts. I had to get to them, to my family...

Bursting through the infirmary door, I collided with a nurse, her tray of bandages and glass vials flying into the air.

She was alive, at least. That was a good sign.

I stammered an apology and kept moving past bedsides with warm, smiling faces—but then I blinked, and I saw slit throats and swaying limbs. Rubbing at my eyes, I felt something wet.

Blood or tears?

I didn't know. It was all the same.

Ragnar, Morgana, Beau...Ragnar, Morgana, Beau...

I skidded to a stop. Familiar wide hips and dark tresses leaned over a bed, with a tall, skinny figure on the other side.

"Beau," I whimpered, fumbling across the floor, almost falling when I saw Ragnar's body beneath the sheets.

Whole and unharmed. Still motionless and under the grip of the curse, but no wound marred his flesh. No red stained the bed sheets or pillow. He was alive.

"Rose! You're awake!" Morgana exclaimed, her features alight with relief. She rushed to me, clutching my shoulders tightly. "It's been almost three days, sweetheart. We were so worried. They said you would be fine, but—"

Three days?

I ripped myself from her grasp. "Are you alright, Rose? What's wrong?" she asked, taking a cautious step toward me as if I was an animal that would spook at the slightest sound.

Now that I knew they were alright, it felt like the walls of this forsaken palace were closing in on me, claws readying to sink into me and shred me to pieces.

I needed to feel safe. I needed to *get away.*

"I can't—I have to go," I gasped. "I can't be here."

Tearing back in the direction I'd come from, my mind replayed the same motions from the dream, how I'd stepped over broken furniture and lifeless bodies, moans and screams echoing around me. I squeezed my eyes shut for a split second to try and banish the memory, but it wouldn't leave.

I had to get out of here.

40

LEO

"It's been over *two days*, Rissa. Shouldn't someone check on her?"

My sister gave me an exasperated look. "You know what Lark said a couple hours ago. Only one of the challengers has even woken up—the Shifter, I think. You have to give her time. Lark mentioned it wouldn't be unusual for this trial to take days, with the way they designed it."

My stomach roiled. When Lark had told us what this trial entailed, I'd been shocked she had agreed to such a thing, much less *developed* it. Although I knew she was simply following Gayl's instructions.

At the dinner three nights previous, all the challengers had ingested a potion with their final toast that induced a dream-like state for them to complete the second trial. A dreamscape, Lark had called it. Even she seemed hesitant to tell us of what they would each be experiencing, as if she felt ashamed at what she had subjected them to. Or, what Gayl made her subject them to.

In their dreamscape, the challengers would be faced with the same initial scenario, but how each progressed depended entirely on the challenger. The premise was the same: the magicless kingdom of Mysthelm to our south had invaded Veridia City, placing the central sector and the palace under their control.

"It might take a while for the challengers to discover their inciting incident—the situation that drives them to the crux of the trial," Lark had explained to Rissa, Horace, and myself. "They've been put under great duress, whatever that looks like to each of them, and are facing a crucial decision of character. The emp—*we* want to test where their heart lies. Once they work through the demands of the dreamscape and decipher reality from fantasy, they'll wake up."

"And...if they don't wake up?" Rissa had asked.

Lark hadn't answered.

For nearly three days, Rose had been trapped inside her own mind. The Fates only knew what she was enduring.

I had volunteered to patrol the forest surrounding the palace tonight. My sister hadn't asked questions when I convinced her to accompany me for the second night in a row, although I knew she suspected the reason behind my insistence.

I wanted to be nearby in case Rose woke up. Or, *didn't* wake up. The idea of her in this unknown dreamscape, alone and confused and scared, had nagged me incessantly over the last two days. Especially knowing the terrors she'd been through in her life and how weighed down her mind already was.

"Leo, she's going to be fine," my sister said softly next to me. "She can't be hurt. It's only a dream."

"They may not be able to harm her physically, but there are far worse ways to cause pain, Rissa. We both know that."

If this dreamscape was by and large a product of her own subconscious, I feared it was more of a nightmare than a dream. I couldn't stop thinking of how I'd found her in the hallway over a week ago, signs of a panic attack evident on her features. That girl held everything inside; what would happen when there was nowhere else to go besides the inner workings of her mind? When the demons that haunted her were brought into the light?

"I can't believe Lark would agree to this," I muttered as we made our rounds of the palace perimeter.

"You know she doesn't always have a choice. If Gayl proposes an idea for the tournament, she has to go with it."

"Yes, but why would he push for this? Something so..."

"Intrusive? Twisted? Wicked?" my sister offered.

I let out a humorless laugh. "Always such a way with words, sister."

She nudged my arm with her elbow. "When was the last time you smiled? You've been an anxious wreck lately."

The north palace entrance was in view, with the large gardens and their regal archways leading to the front doors. There was barely enough light from the setting sun to illuminate the path, but I could still make out smatterings of guests and members of court on nightly strolls beneath the dusk sky.

"I don't know what you're talking about," I mumbled, pushing a branch to the side.

Rissa snorted. "Emperor's tits, Leo, you never were a good liar."

Suddenly, the palace doors burst open, and a figure stumbled across the grounds. My muscles coiled tightly as a pit formed in my stomach. Something about that figure looked so familiar.

It raced toward the forest, a courtyard's distance away from where Rissa and I patrolled. Long, raven hair whipped in the breeze.

Without thinking, I moved. My sister hissed at me, but I ignored her, my feet carrying me along the treeline, scarcely managing to stay within the shadows.

She grew closer. I could tell the moment she noticed me; her neck turned and she froze, like a deer caught in the sights of a predator. And then, she was running.

To me.

"Leo!" she gasped, her face sallow, eyes wild, before she slammed into me.

I instantly brought a hand to cup the nape of her neck, my other holding her steady at her back. Her breaths were uneven and shaking against me, her nose nuzzling into my shoulder as I gripped her tighter.

"I've got you. You're safe now," I murmured into her hair. Her choked sobs wrapped around my heart the way my fingers wrapped around the strands of her dark locks.

I caught my sister out of the corner of my eye within the shadows of the trees, her knowing gaze searing into the two of us as she gestured for us to get out of sight.

"Rose, we need to get into the forest," I whispered. She nodded, her hair brushing my neck, and let me lead her further into the treeline. I stopped once we were safely out of view and guided her back against a thick tree trunk. Her body still trembled, like there was some terror she couldn't shake.

She finally met my eyes, a mere shadow of the vibrant green they normally were, and swallowed. "How do I know this is real?" she asked, so quiet I had to strain to hear her.

Anger flared in me at this cursed trial and what it had done to make her ask such a question. To not be able to discern reality from the nightmares. But I shoved the rage aside and carefully grabbed one of her hands, placing it on my chest, above my racing heart. I took her other one and rested it atop her own.

"Close your eyes," I said, and she obeyed. "Take a deep breath. Focus on what's right in front of you. Can you feel this?"

My chest pounded against her palm, my pulse racing from a combination of her touch and my own worries. Slowly, her hand ceased its shivering as she took several deep, steadying breaths. Finally, she nodded.

"This is real, Rose." I moved her hand from my chest to my cheek, twining her fingers between mine. "Whatever happened, whatever you saw, it's gone. It's over."

She didn't respond but kept her eyes closed, her thumb warily tracing a path across my cheek, then my jaw, then the bridge of my nose and down to my lips. My eyes fluttered shut, a chill sweeping over my shoulders while heat built low in my stomach as her fingers explored my skin. I stepped closer into her, and she opened her eyes. I could have fallen to my knees in relief at her clear gaze, dispelled of the terror that had taken her captive.

There she is.

Her fingers still skimmed my mouth, as if in a trance. My lips parted on an exhale and my tongue involuntarily flicked against the rough pad of her thumb. She sucked in an almost imperceptible breath and pressed harder into my bottom lip.

Rissa cleared her throat behind me. My control snapped back into place, and I closed my fingers around Rose's wrist. Lowering her hand, I stepped away to give her space.

But it didn't matter how much space I put between us.

The damage was done—I couldn't get her out of my head, and I realized I no longer wanted to.

41

ROSE

"When did you wake up?" Rissa asked, her eyes full of concern.

"Just a little while ago. I—I had to check on my family, to make sure—" I stammered over my words, unable to finish the sentence. Although there was more distance between us, Leo's tail came out to skim against the back of my leg. His way of bringing comfort when I was on the verge of breaking again.

I swallowed. "My aunt said it's been over two days. Is—is that true?" I directed the question to Leo, hoping I'd see reassurance in his eyes. Instead, I found grim resignation. He nodded. I gritted my teeth, pinching the bridge of my nose to hold back a fresh wave of distress. I *hated* this panic and dread. This weakness.

"I'm sorry, Rose. We had no idea what was happening until Lark filled us in at the start of the trial." Rissa moved toward me, holding out a hand. "Do you want to talk about it?"

I shook my head, taking a step closer to Leo without meaning to. His tail flicked against my ankle, covered by the darkness of the night and thick underbrush at our feet. It wasn't that I didn't appreciate Rissa—I could tell how sincere she was, how worried they'd been for me. And the fact that they'd been here, waiting for me to wake up, pulled tight at the strings of my heart. I'd never had anyone besides my aunt, uncle, and Beau care enough.

But I was still far too on edge. Logically, I knew this was real and that the second trial was over. But logic and fear didn't always agree. I was like a wounded animal, expecting a new threat around every corner, another trap about to snap me in its jaws.

For some reason, Leo made me feel safe. His intense, protective, surprisingly tender way of caring for those around him made me believe nothing could reach us.

"We need to let Lark know you're awake," he said gently. "The healers are supposed to examine each of you—"

"I—I can't go back there. Not right now," I cut him off, blinking away the burning in my eyes. I was wholly aware that my brave veneer from the last week lay crumbled at my feet, but it wasn't as if he hadn't seen that before. "Please, don't make me go back."

"Leo—" Rissa began, but Leo shot her a look. A silent conversation took place between the twins. I didn't care what "protocol" was—Horace had seen me, he could tell Lark and the others I'd finished the trial. There was no way I was walking back into that palace until I'd had time to process everything.

"It's alright, Rose, you don't have to go back right now," he finally said. "We'll take you to our cottage. You're safe," he reminded me. His deep voice seemed to calm the feral, anxious beast in me.

The three of us traveled south along the treeline until we came to two horses tied to a tree. Rissa mounted hers, while Leo approached Nightshade and held his hand out to me. My heart picked up speed as I took it, and I forced away the memory of the dapple-gray horse I'd chased after the carriage on.

That wasn't real.

Leo situated himself behind me, his arms coming around my waist to grip the reins and steer our horse to follow Rissa's. This was different from last time, when I'd tried so hard to keep my body away from his, each of us clinging to that shared bitterness. I let my heartbeats fall into step with the rhythmic cadence of

Nightshade's trot, finding comfort instead of irritation in Leo's corded arms resting on my hips as the movement pushed me deeper into the saddle.

I'd spent my entire life keeping people at arm's length where it mattered, allowing them access to the most shallow parts of me but never the hidden well of doubts and insecurities. Never to the heart. Physical contact was either a nuisance or a tool—even with my own family, I only tolerated their hugs and signs of compassion because I knew it mattered more to them than it did me. I wielded beauty and charm like a weapon, giving subtle touches and soft whispers to those who craved it in order to get what I wanted. Which was usually an escape, or simply blessed silence.

But with Leo...it wasn't the same. I found myself seeking what I once thought was juvenile—a warm embrace, soothing words, a graze of a finger against my anxious pulse. Even now, on the back of this horse, our bodies forced together in a way that would have once made discomfort blare through me...I felt calm. As calm as I could be, anyway.

When the horse jolted and his hand shifted to my thigh, that calmness morphed into something more.

I wondered if his Shifter half made him able to sense the change in my heartbeats, the way my breath caught and then quickened, the pulse now fluttering at my neck. If he could tell that my muscles were still stretched as taut as a bowstring from those moments in the forest, when the feel of his skin beneath my fingertips banished the darkness and lit something new.

His chest straightened at my back, his single-handed grip on the reins making his knuckles turn white. The tip of his nose grazed my ear and, without thinking, I tilted my head to the left, an open challenge to see what he would do.

I didn't even know what I *wanted* him to do. I'd once thought of him as a distraction—someone who just so happened to be around when my world was caving in, an easy way to distance myself from memories too unbearable to face. Maybe that's what I needed again.

But he knew it, too. He let out a long breath and pressed his forehead into the back of my head before pulling away. "I won't be a way for you to ignore your problems, Rose," he whispered. Not accusatory, but tenderly. With a hint of strain, as if he were refraining from doing exactly that. "You need to rest. I promise, we can talk later."

Instead of the sting of rejection, his words left me surprisingly...at peace. Full instead of hollow. I settled against him, and as his hand splayed protectively across my stomach, I felt like something cherished. Something precious worth holding as opposed to wielding.

And just for this moment, I pretended it was true.

———

WHEN WE REACHED THE COTTAGE, I'd calmed enough for exhaustion to creep in. Every inch of me was tired. My eyelids were barely able to stay open as Leo helped me dismount. I slumped against him, nearly falling over my own feet while he guided me through the doors.

"What's wrong with her?" I heard him ask, but it sounded distant and muffled, my brain already halfway asleep.

"It's that potion," Rissa answered. "Lark said it had side effects. That's why she wanted her to see a healer when she woke up, but..."

My neck rolled onto my shoulder. Leo put a hand behind my knees and easily swept me off the floor. I inhaled the scent of sandalwood and vanilla mixed with the night's wind and leaves.

"You saw how she reacted," he said, charged and defensive. "I wasn't about to force her back to the palace. Lark will get over it."

Rissa gave an exasperated sigh, one I recognized all too well as the sound of an older sibling resisting the urge to throttle their little brother. "You don't have to snap at me, Leo. I'm not arguing with you. Just take care of her, alright?"

"I can still hear you, you know," I mumbled into Leo's chest.

Big hands cradled me closer as he carried me across the living room. I peeked out from my fortress to see us entering a narrow hallway, one I hadn't noticed the last times I'd been here. Three doors lined the path, and when he carefully kicked one of them open, it revealed a small, neat bedroom.

A large bed rested against the center of the back wall, black sheets and a slate gray blanket folded on top. In the corner beneath a window stood a desk and wooden chair, and next to it, a waist-high bookshelf with a handful of books stacked on the shelves. I would bet anything they were in alphabetical order—unlike my own collection at home, which was organized by whatever mood I'd been in at the time. There were hardly any personal items or pieces of decor, besides a framed photo of Leo, Rissa, and what I assumed were his parents atop the desk.

The sight of Branock Aris sent a pang through me—he looked so much like Leo, with their strong jaws, sharp eyes, and dark hair. I turned away, too weary to give that man any more of my attention.

"Room could use a bit of color, Aris," I taunted weakly, covering my yawn with the back of my hand as he set me on the edge of his bed.

"I'll keep that in mind." He lowered to his knees before me, and suddenly, my exhaustion slipped away.

"What are you doing?"

He glanced up with a smirk that sent a horde of butterflies loose in my stomach. Silently, he reached for my right ankle, gripping my calf as he slowly pulled my boot off. Even through my leggings, the heat of his touch was searing. He moved to my other boot and repeated the process without taking his eyes off me, his fingers lingering on the inside of my leg.

I bit my bottom lip. He was toying with me, as I'd often done to him. Helping take my mind off the terrors pressing against me.

It was working.

He stood and made his way to the head of the bed. Pulling the sheets back, he beckoned me to climb under them. The soft fabric beneath my fingers was a welcoming embrace, making my eyelids grow heavy as he positioned the blanket around me. The bed shifted when he eased himself off, and I threw out my arm to grab his hand.

"Wait—where are you going?" I asked sleepily.

"To talk with my sister. Go to sleep, little wolf. It's late."

My limbs felt like lead and I couldn't pry my eyes open, but I held onto his fingers for a moment longer. "Will you come back?"

He paused, then asked, "Do you want me to?"

The effects of the potion, my own sleep-deprived mind, and the security of finally being somewhere safe seemed to have completely erased my filter for the night. "Yes," I slurred, my arm falling and tucking beneath me as I curled under the blanket. "I want you to come back."

The only response was something soft skimming my cheek as sleep dragged me below the surface.

42

ROSE

I was in the middle of a bloody battlefield.

Soldiers and civilians warred on either side of me, clanging swords and crying children and severed body parts littering the hard ground.

This time I knew it was a dream, but I still couldn't wake from it.

Ragnar, Morgana, and Beau lay before me in a pool of red, a dagger the size of my forearm held in my hand above them. Their blood slid from the blade and down my fingers until my entire hand was covered in it.

Sunlight caught the steel, making my reflection shine back at me. My eyes were ablaze, cheeks flushed, dark hair whipping around my face.

And I was smiling. A deep, sinister smile that made my insides shrivel and my spine tingle.

"*No!*" I shouted, hurling the dagger away, and as it embedded itself in the dirt, I sprung forward.

My eyes flew open. I found myself sitting upright, tangled in unfamiliar sheets. A warm hand steadied my back.

"It's only a dream," a voice said, rough with tiredness. "You're safe, Rose."

Leo. It took me a moment to reorient myself with visions of the second trial and my nightmare clogging my senses, but I slowly started to remember. He and Rissa had brought me back to their cottage, where I'd passed out in his bed.

The confusion subsided, replaced with a nervous energy. I knew none of it was real, but it *felt* real. And with it came memories of my father—memories that were so true and potent, I could still feel his blood on my skin.

Leo propped up on one arm to my left, the other still at my back. His dark hair was mussed from sleep, his eyes hooded and tired. It was still dark out, and the only light came from the moon shining through the window above his desk, landing on the foot of the bed and creeping up the black sheets.

Seeing him like this, loose and unguarded and lying next to me, made something press against my chest, diverting attention away from my unease. *Fates,* nobody had the right to look that good, especially in the middle of the night.

I settled back onto my pillow, turning to face him and pulling my knees up into a curled position. Resting my head on my arm, I studied his features as he mirrored me, surprised by how much I'd missed in the light that was now revealed under the moon.

His hair always seemed perfectly placed, but now there were small curls at his ears and neck, stray tendrils hanging low on his forehead. Those eyes drew me in, soft and searching, as if in the dark he could finally let his guard down, could finally stop caring about keeping up his intense, moody bravado. I knew it came from a place of protection, a constant need to be on the alert, but I liked this side of him. My gaze traveled further down to a small scar on the edge of his jaw. He didn't so much as flinch when I reached out to trace the length of it, feeling its smoothness against rough stubble.

The image of my back digging into a tree trunk while my thumb ran along his lip came back to me, and I dropped my hand, swallowing hard.

"Do you want to talk about it?" he asked quietly. "The trial?"

I closed my eyes. Did I want to? No, not necessarily. I'd never been one to talk through things or share my troubles with others. Everyone had their own burdens to carry; I figured they either didn't need to add mine to them, or they didn't truly care. Either way, I was used to shoving things beneath that heavy cloak in my mind, stifling them of their power over me.

I wanted to do that now. To reject him, turn my back, and pretend to sleep. Then we'd wake up in the morning in an awkward silence, right back to how things were a week ago when we left this very cottage with forced trust and heightened vexation. I'd been so frustrated with him and his pride, how he'd quickly brushed me off as a mistake, as someone not worthy. Beneath that, though, was my burning desire for revenge against his father transferred over to Leo's unwitting head.

That wasn't an excuse anymore. I don't think I was ever really angry with *Leo*, anyway. He didn't have anything to do with the actions of his father. And I couldn't fault him for his pride. Those offhanded comments he'd made that had struck so deeply in the heat of the moment were more easily understood now that I'd gotten to know him. Now that I could clearly see the singular focus for most of his life had been protecting him and his sister and finding a way to usurp Gayl. Looking at it from his perspective, I wouldn't trust myself, either. It must be nearly impossible to hand this task over to an outsider with no remarkable ability, who had a knack for getting herself into unfortunate situations.

I couldn't help but remember how he looked at me—not with the wariness of the people back home, but with intrigue. Admiration, even. The things he said about me...that I was bold, brave, unapologetic. That I challenged people.

It made me feel good. It made me feel *seen*.

So where did that leave us? I had no reason for retribution, no anger holding me back, no sharp chip on my shoulder.

Instead, I was in awe of the way he loved his family so unabashedly. I was curious about his background, how his

Alchemist and Shifter blood worked together. I had an acute desire to know what that scar on his jaw felt like against my lips.

And I had secrets.

The truth behind the Somnivae curse gnawed at my mind, unwilling to release its hold. I couldn't tell him. Not until I knew I could trust Gayl's confession, or until we found another way. I refused to believe Leo's death was the sole solution to saving *countless* lives.

A lock of hair came loose from behind my ear and he reached out to brush it back, the movement so natural it was like second nature to him.

"It was a test," I started in a whisper, clearing my throat. "The second trial. It was a test to see what choices we would make when thrown into this...battlefield." He didn't look surprised, but lowered his hand to the space between our chests on the bed, leaving it near my arm.

"I woke up and the palace was empty. I could see signs of an invasion out the window into the central sector...buildings burning, people fighting and running. And it was in the palace, too. Mysthelm soldiers had made a surprise attack, some sort of crusade to rid the world of our magic. They'd taken over and were—were killing Veridians on sight. The servants, the guards, the patients in the infirmary —" I choked on the words, and Leo shifted closer to me.

"Your uncle," he acknowledged simply.

I nodded. "They were all dead. I tried to find my aunt and cousin, but they'd been kidnapped. Taken as hostages to the central sector. I fled the palace. I—I killed a soldier." I sucked in a breath. "I killed *two* soldiers." The first had been inadvertent; he'd tried to stab me, and my protection charm made his actions rebound onto himself. The second...the second had been my choice.

"Rose, anything that happened in that dreamscape wasn't real. You didn't kill anybody."

"I might as well have. I made the decision—*that* wasn't fake." I closed my eyes, fighting the urge to pull away. "But he—he had killed all those innocent patients. I didn't have a choice. He smelled like them. He *enjoyed* it, he—" I cut myself off, realizing I wasn't making any sense. Again, Leo stayed silent, letting me figure out how to tell my story.

"I followed the chaos to the central sector, trying to find Morgana and Beau. It was…a nightmare." I shuddered, and his fingers came up to skim my arm, the touch featherlight but grounding all the same. "Bodies fell left and right, and there was so much smoke it was hard to see through the haze. Magic against metal. Houses were set on fire, children were—were screaming through the streets, and you couldn't step anywhere without the scent of blood and copper and burning wood—"

I stopped again, taking a deep breath to expel the smoke clinging to me. "I helped get some people to safety. There was a shelter we were trying to get as many civilians to as we could. But then…I saw Beau. In the back of a prisoner's carriage. And I think…I think that was the point of the whole trial."

"What do you mean?" Leo asked.

I shifted onto my back and stared at the ceiling, forcing his arm to fall away. "The carriage was taking off in another direction, toward the Scarre River. At the same time, I found out a group of Mysthelm soldiers were planning to drop an explosive on the shelter." My voice dropped to a whisper. "I had a choice."

Save Beau, or save an entire building of frightened, innocent people.

"Rose, none of it was—"

"Don't tell me it wasn't real, Leo," I snapped. "You weren't there. It was the *only* real thing. The fighting, the death, the terror. It's still here, buried in my skin, in every breath I take. I made the choice to sacrifice all those people for the sake of my cousin. Nobody may have died, but that doesn't change the fact that *I still did it*. I would do it again, real or not." I paused, twisting my fingers in the edges of the sheets. "A 'test of the heart'…well, they know mine now, don't they?" A bitter scoff left my lips. "Selfish and cold."

"You can't honestly believe that," Leo said. "You were given an impossible choice in an impossible situation. This trial was out of line. They should have *never* put you through such cruelty, Rose. I don't fault you for a moment for choosing to save your cousin."

I rolled my eyes and twisted my neck to face him. "Oh, really? The noble Zareleon Aris would have left those innocent people to die?"

"For my sister? Or my mother?" His features turned icy. "Without a second thought."

"Then perhaps we're *both* selfish and cold," I whispered.

Leo's hand found mine on top of the sheets at my waist. "You risked your life to take the place of your uncle so your entire province could have hope. You agreed to help a rebellion full of strangers in order to see the wrongs of this empire righted. You are the furthest thing from selfish, Rose." His fingers drifted across my knuckles. "As for the other..." He turned my hand over and brushed his thumb along the sensitive skin at my palm, sending lightning through my arm. "What does this feel like?" His warmth seeped into me. It covered the icy shame I'd been edging toward. It felt...burning. Consuming. "Is that cold to you?"

I met his gaze. "What are we doing, Leo?" My voice was barely a breath as it flowed over the moonlight.

His lips quirked up the smallest amount. "Talking. Isn't that what friends do?"

Just like that, he slipped back into our easy rapport, but this time, I didn't think it was to hide or run away. I think he recognized how close to some sort of metaphorical cliff I was, how deeply this second trial had messed with my mind. In the small amount of time we'd known each other, he'd learned my masks put me at ease. That I needed a semblance of control when everything inside me felt like spiraling. And here he was, sharing that control with me.

I raised an eyebrow. "This doesn't look like you want to be my *friend*."

"I asked if we *could* be friends. Not that that's what I wanted."

My lips parted. I was used to this—banter filled with insinuations, lingering looks, meaningless words. Where anything bordering on significant was drowned beneath the reminder that nobody truly *saw* me, that nobody truly wanted the strange, doomed orphan Alchemist.

But this...this didn't feel meaningless. Nothing with him ever did.

"Then what *do* you want?" I asked.

His hand drifted higher, a finger coming up to twirl around a lock of my hair. It was as if our embrace in the forest earlier had unlocked some part of him that couldn't stop touching me. "I want you to be open with me. I want you to trust me. I want to get to know the *real* you, not a shadow version." He released my hair and traveled to my jaw, lightly running his finger up to my cheek. His eyes tracked the movement, like he was reveling in the freedom our solitude provided. Even the barest of touches from him was much more intimate than I was used to.

"I want that too," I whispered.

We lay in the silence, each testing the waters, finding our own comfort in this admission. His arm fell between us again, and I caught sight of the tattoo I'd seen the first time we were in this cottage together.

I brushed my fingers against the black ink on his forearm, noting the way goosebumps rose in response. It was a beautiful drawing of an animal face: half of it was a fox, and the other half looked to be a wolf. Delicate vines swirled around it and down his arm all the way to the top of his hand. Leaves and henbane flowers sprouted from the stem.

"What does it mean?" I asked softly.

His eyes were on my fingers as they moved across the design, his features contemplative. "It's my family. It was a way of keeping them with me. The fox is Rissa, the wolf is our mother. The henbane petals represent my father. It was his favorite charm, and I inherited these rings from him." He twisted a dark gray ring on his middle finger. "He taught me how to infuse them with his favorite combination of henbane and amaranth."

I hummed, tracing the pattern of the flowers with the tip of my finger. "You haven't said much about your mother. She was a wolf Shifter?" I asked, diverting the conversation away from his father.

"She still is."

Pausing as I reached the image of the wolf, I glanced up at him. "Oh, I'm sorry. I assumed it was just you and Rissa."

His teeth scraped against his bottom lip. He took his time before responding. "Our mother is still alive, but she's...sick. Lost. She fell ill shortly after our father died and has only worsened since."

"I'm so sorry," I said, my heart aching for him, for the distance in his gaze. "Where is she?"

"Here. In the room right next to us. Rissa and I have taken care of her for the past decade. It started as fatigue, her body and mind unable to handle the grief. It slowly morphed into...well, the healers aren't exactly sure. It's as if she gave up." When he paused, I slipped my hand into his and squeezed. This type of openness was something I hadn't had before, and I found myself wanting to melt into him, to give him my strength when words failed him.

"Her body is stable, for the most part. But her mind...we lost hope that she would recover long ago. She sits in silence, never moving, never speaking. We're lucky if she so much as looks at us when we go read to her or sit with her in the mornings. Watching her become a—a shell of what she used to be..." He closed his eyes and paused again as he collected himself. "I can't even remember the last time she spoke to me. It's not something I talk about often."

I tucked my arm beneath my head. "That must be so hard. I'm sorry, Leo. I had no idea."

"Neither of us are strangers to hardships."

Fates, wasn't that the truth.

"What about your parents?" he asked gently. It wasn't pressing, simply curious. He'd said he wanted to get to know me, that he wanted us to be open. The fact that he was lowering his own walls made the coil in my chest that furled so tightly around the memory of my parents loosen. I could do this. I could talk about them. I could let someone share my grief.

I took a deep breath. "I think the reason this trial affected me so much is because my entire life has been filled with loss. My mother...she died during childbirth. I was born into blood, and sometimes it feels like I'm still trying to crawl my way out. And this trial...it showed me more bodies piled high, more people I couldn't save.

"The day my father died..." I chewed on my bottom lip, exhaling slowly. The familiar panic—the weight on my chest, the dry lips, the tightening around my neck—appeared, but it was muffled. Distant. Easier to work through. "The day he died, I was five years old. A few Illusionists found me outside our house and tricked me into bringing them to my papa."

I told Leo the story, speaking the words aloud for the first time. I recounted how my father had forced me to hide, how he'd protected me against the men, how I'd come out of my spot and saw the Illusionist slit his throat. Leo's features remained focused; the only reactions he showed were when he threaded his fingers through mine, occasionally rubbing his thumb against the side of my hand.

"The morning of the first trial, Callum—the Illusionist challenger—tricked me. He created an image of Horace dead in the hallway outside my room. He was lying in his own blood with his throat cut, the same way I found my father. It triggered the memory, something I'd been repressing for decades." I swallowed and grasped Leo's hand tighter. "It all came rushing back. It was like...I'd had a crack inside of me ever since then that had slowly been leaking, but I could always patch it easily enough. Then after *this*, it was a flood. A tidal wave I couldn't run from. Everything that's happened since has just opened more gates to let water rush in and drown me."

I squeezed my eyes shut before any tears could form and fall. I felt Leo raise my hand, felt the soft press of his lips into my knuckles. I wasn't used to such an outward display of affection, especially from someone like him—someone who had seemed so impassive in the beginning, all hard lines and ruthless stoicism.

I liked him this way. Gentle and soft. Lending strength instead of merely possessing it.

"It feels like something is wrong with me," I finally said. "Nobody wants to get too close. Bad things always seem to happen to those around me. My parents, Ragnar, countless people I know who have fallen to the Somnivae curse. And now I find out the emperor is my *uncle*? The things he's done..." *The things my father has probably done*, I thought with a shudder. "Maybe there's something in my blood that's cursed. Doomed to spread destruction."

The bed shifted and Leo rested a hand on my waist. "Come here," he murmured. One of his arms slid under me while the other wrapped around my back, and I rested my head on his chest as he pulled me in. My top leg instantly tangled between his, his warmth and solidness cocooning me in a way that felt both familiar and completely new at the same time.

"Growing up, part of me believed the Somnivae curse was my fault," Leo began, his voice hushed with my ear against his chest. My pulse beat a little faster at the mention of him and the curse. The truth pressed into my tongue, sharp and bitter, and I swallowed it down. "Many thought Rissa and myself were some sort of plague on the empire. Being born into that legacy...it meant we were never accepted. Not for who we truly were. Never seen as anything other than a curse, we were forced to live as outsiders in our own home, scared of what others may do to us out of a twisted sense of balance or retribution."

His thumb tapped at my lower back, a tick I found endearing. When he continued speaking, I heard the hesitancy in his words, like he didn't often let others bear this burden, either.

"It doesn't take long to wonder...if they're right. If Rissa and I *are* cursed, and we're the reason so many suffer."

I leaned away to meet his eyes, heart sinking at the thought of the twins so lost and alone, carrying this guilt for something they had no control over. I didn't know how to navigate this. I wasn't one others came to for relief or empathy. But even if he was connected to the curse...it *wasn't* his fault. He didn't deserve the hand the Fates had dealt him. One would have to be blind not to see how devoted he was to this empire, even when he'd been treated with such malice.

"It's not your fault, Leo," I said, pushing on his chest to see his face clearly. His muscles flexed and tensed beneath my touch. "You've done *nothing* wrong. Those people...they're scared of something they don't understand."

"I know." His breath fanned across my skin. "Knowing something and believing it aren't always the same. And you're no more cursed than I am. You've also done nothing wrong, Rose. Do *you* believe that?" His eyes searched mine, turning my words back around on me.

I let out a huff of laughter, lowering my gaze. "You're not playing fair."

"I never said I was playing." The hand at my spine pressed further into me, and I burrowed back into his hold, tucking my chin and letting our heartbeats lull my racing thoughts.

"I'm sorry about your father," he said after a moment. "Nobody should have to go through what you did. Nobody should have to see violence like that."

My stomach twisted. We'd found some sort of...peace, or whatever this *thing* between us was, and I didn't want to ruin it. But we'd also never had a conversation about Branock's involvement that didn't end in anger or denial, and the urge to find closure pressed against me. I sat up, looking down at him and the distance I'd created.

"There was something else Gayl told me about my father when we met. He said he knew that—that Branock Aris was going to go after him. It was after your father went into hiding. He was tracking down those closest to Gayl to get revenge on him for stealing his throne, and that my father was high on the list."

Leo stiffened. "Why are you bringing him up again, Rose? We've already talked about this."

"I don't know," I said, my voice strained. Not at him, but at *myself*. That I couldn't seem to let this go. "I guess I—I just want to understand. I don't know what to believe anymore—Gayl's story or your conviction. And part of me feels like I'll never be able to get over this without some sort of explanation."

"And you're searching for an explanation, for the *truth*, in Gayl's words?" Leo sat up straighter. "This is what he does. He's a manipulator. You can't believe anything he says, *especially* about someone like my father, who he betrayed without a backward glance."

I let out a groan and ran my fingers through my hair. "I know you're right. But his words are all I have. That and my memories. I —I don't know how to let this go."

"If you can't learn how to do that, then how is any of this supposed to work, Rose?"

The room grew cold and silent, something sour tarnishing our space of solace.

I was an idiot. Why did I do this to myself? Did I feel him sinking beneath my skin and get scared? I was so accustomed to people rejecting me that I'd begun to force them into it. It was like I subconsciously tested how far they were willing to go before I said something to push them back. To make them walk away.

I didn't want to be the one to watch him walk away, though.

I untangled my legs from the sheets and threw them over the side of the bed, hunting around in the dark for my boots.

"Where are you going?"

Stumbling, I narrowly avoided banging my leg on his desk in the dark. "This was a mistake. I'm sorry. I shouldn't have said anything. I—I'll sleep on the couch until I can go back to the palace in the morning."

He followed me out of bed, placing a hand on the door frame to block me from opening it. "I didn't say I wanted you to leave, Rose."

"But you're angry," I insisted.

He gave me an incredulous look. "You *assume* I'm angry. I just... I don't know how to navigate this. I'm confused and tired, not angry. Even if I was, that doesn't mean I want you to leave. Is that what people have done to you your whole life?" I glanced away, but he caressed my cheek, urging me to look up at him. "Made you think your only option was to retreat?"

"I—I don't know," I stammered. "I guess...it's easier." Swallowing, I toyed with the ends of my shirt. "Easier than facing their anger or judgment."

His thumb brushed along my skin. "I'm not upset with you. I want to understand, like you. While I don't believe my father was behind this, that doesn't invalidate what you went through. It doesn't make it any less hard. We can talk about this. We can help each other learn how to let go. You don't have to leave, unless you want to." He stepped closer. "But *I* don't want you to."

His words settled into me, and the compulsion I'd felt to run slowly dimmed. I was so used to avoiding conflict, so used to *assuming* people wanted nothing to do with me, that the idea of him trying to talk through things and come to an understanding *together...*

It was more intimate than any touch.

I didn't have to run. I didn't have to hide myself behind masks of indifference or sharp edges. I could be *free.*

And for the first time, I realized that's all I'd wanted all along.

Something in my chest broke open. A tear tracked down my cheek, and Leo's eyes widened in concern. "What's wrong? Was it something I said?"

I shook my head and sniffed. "Nothing's wrong." I leaned forward and stood on my toes until my forehead met his. We stood there for a moment, our breaths mingling as my tears subsided. I knew our conversation about my father's murder wasn't over, but I didn't think I could take much more tonight. I was still reeling from my nightmare, still struggling to accept these new emotions toward Leo, still exhausted yet exhilarated all at once.

My heart pounded in my ears, a tingle spreading over me at our nearness. Without thinking, without knowing what I was doing, I lifted my face slightly so my nose brushed his. A test. A question.

But not a game. Not anymore.

His hand splayed on my lower back, drawing me in. He kissed the tear lingering on my cheek, then moved his lips down and along my jaw.

My breath caught. "What are we doing, Leo?" I repeated my earlier question, voice shaking.

This time, his response held no humor. "I don't know."

We stayed like that, his lips a whisper from mine, neither of us moving besides our chests rising and falling in time to heavy breaths.

"You should sleep," he said softly, his lips skimming my jaw. "It's been a long day."

He was right. I was too emotional, too on edge, and I didn't want this—*him*—to be a distraction. A decision made on a whim. No matter what doubts were creeping around my mind, I knew for certain I wouldn't let Zareleon Aris be a *mistake*.

I nodded slowly in agreement and licked my lips, the motion causing my tongue to graze against the side of his mouth. He let out a small groan, and I smiled.

"Back to sleep, monkey boy," I said, breaking away. His smoldering glare made my stomach flip.

Perhaps we could still play some games, after all.

43

ROSE

I woke to the sound of birds chirping outside the window, the scent of coffee and baked bread wafting through the bedroom door, and the feel of a calloused hand on my stomach.

Leo's body curved around mine, my head resting on his forearm. Nightmares and visions of blood and steel had tapped at the edges of my unconscious mind, but they'd managed to stay away for the rest of the night.

I stretched my legs, wrinkling my nose at an unfamiliar sensation rubbing against them. Lifting the sheets, I grinned when I saw a long, dark brown tail wrapped around my calf.

Leo stirred at my back, the hand at my stomach clenching as he nuzzled his nose into my neck, mumbling incoherently.

"Good morning, sleepyhead," I teased, turning to face him. His hair was even more disheveled, and a little annoyed crease appeared on his brow as he stubbornly kept his eyes closed. It was surprisingly adorable.

"I was comfortable," he grumbled, burying his face into the pillow and tucking me closer to him.

I laughed. Morning Leo was so *grumpy*. And affectionate. I couldn't resist—I brushed my hand through his hair, relishing the

343

last few moments in this strange but peaceful bubble we'd created before real life burst through.

"We should get up," I said half-heartedly. "Before your sister wonders what happened to us."

"Too late!" a melodic voice called from somewhere far outside the door.

I jumped and sat straight up, accidentally jerking my leg and yanking Leo's tail. He cursed and gripped my thigh in alarm.

"Sorry!" I whispered, clamping a hand over my mouth.

"Shifter, remember?" he said with a grunt. "My sister can hear everything."

"*Everything?*"

He chuckled, unfurling his tail and easing out of the bed. "Don't worry, she doesn't listen in all the time. Only when she's worried something might be wrong. Or wants to annoy me."

"So, all the time," Rissa's voice called again.

Leo rolled his eyes and walked to his desk, pulling out a pouch of herbs and pinching some between his fingers. He mumbled a spell I couldn't hear, and I felt the normal sensation of a charm snapping into place, tight and constricting on my chest.

"There. Now she won't bother us."

I laughed and stepped out of bed. Seeing them like this, their loving yet antagonizing brother and sister act, made me think of Beau.

"I need to get back to the palace," I said with a sigh. "I've got to check in on Morgana and Beau. I ran out on them last night and I'm sure they're worried. I've ignored my problems long enough."

He nodded, and I could already see his walls coming back up as he prepared for the day, the tenderness slipping away. We hadn't discussed much about his past, but I remembered how he said his family had been forced to live as outsiders. That others only saw them as a curse. I realized how similar we were, in some respects. Always feeling the need to wear a mask, to anticipate what others might think of us before we gave them a chance.

I didn't want the magic of the night to fade. What had

happened between us…it didn't *feel* fleeting. It didn't feel like something that could be covered and thrust beneath the surface, like everything else in my life.

Rubbing my shirt between my fingers, I asked, "When will I see you again?"

"Do you *want* to see me again?"

I looked up to meet his eyes across the room. "Don't friends spend time together?"

His answering smile made my heart squeeze. "I'll take you back to the palace so you can talk with your family and finally see a healer. Lark's probably not happy with us." I scowled at the mention of the head architect, tasting bitterness when I thought about how she'd put me through the dreamscape. He stepped toward me. "Try and play nice. It doesn't excuse how horrible this trial was, but she was only doing her job."

I let out a long sigh. "I know, I know. It's Gayl I'm pissed at anyway, not her. All of this was his idea, wasn't it?" Leo nodded. "I knew it—it had him written all over it." The thought of the emperor made me curse. "Fates, I forgot about his letter."

"Another one?"

"Yes. He had a note delivered to me the evening of the dinner, right before the second trial started. It told me how to get word back to him when I was ready to meet. I suppose I have to now, since I promised Rissa I'd use this to get closer to him…" My words faded as Leo pulled off the shirt he'd slept in and grabbed a new one, arms flexing when he shrugged it on and began buttoning it. The broad plane of his chest stared back at me, a dusting of dark hair spreading down past my line of sight. I remembered pressing my hand against it during the night, and knew exactly how hard those corded muscles felt beneath my skin. Like steel and—

"Eyes up here, little wolf."

My gaze snapped back to his face, which bore an enormous smirk as he finished the last button. Cheeks heating, I cleared my throat. "Anyway, I'll probably try to meet with him soon."

"Are you sure you're comfortable with this?" he asked. "My

sister shouldn't have pushed that on you. She can be a bit... ambitious."

I gave him a quizzical look. "I thought you were willing to do anything to bring him down."

"I was. I...am." He ran his fingers through his hair, something I noticed he did when anxious. "I saw how upset you were after you met with him. I don't want you to feel forced into meeting with your—with the emperor. Not if it's too much for you."

"I can handle it," I said.

"Just because you *can* doesn't mean you should *have* to."

I grabbed his hand and squeezed. "I know. But I promise, I *want* to do this. I want to help you." It wasn't a lie, but what I didn't want to admit...what I *couldn't* admit, was that a small, dark part of me had stirred at what Gayl had promised. To learn magic my father had discovered, magic he might have one day passed along to *me*.

He nodded. "I won't ask again. But you'll tell me if—"

"*Yes*," I said in fake exasperation. "You know, you're worse than my aunt."

"Well, what are friends for?" he said with a wolfish smile, stepping closer to me.

A knock sounded on the door. "Emperor's tits, what are you two doing in there?" Rissa called. "Never mind, don't answer that. I have breakfast ready if you're hungry." She paused, then banged on the door again. "For *food*."

Leo's jaw flexed, and I stifled a laugh. "I think I like your sister."

"Fates save us all," he muttered. "Do you have time to stay for breakfast?"

I glanced down at the leggings and shirt I'd worn to bed *four* nights ago now. My stringy hair was unkempt and greasy. I hadn't bothered to wash it or change after waking up from the second trial. I didn't dare smell myself—horror gripped me at the realization that I'd slept next to him all night like this. I'd *cuddled* with him. My cheeks heated again. Breakfast with Leo and Rissa was the last thing I—

"Hey," he said softly, nudging my head up with his finger. "It's just breakfast."

He was looking at me like he had last night—walls down, sincerity and compassion and a hint of desire shining through. My resolve crumbled bit by bit.

"Okay. Just breakfast."

44

ROSE

Checking in on Morgana and Beau wasn't as difficult as I thought it would be. They were relieved to see I was alright, especially after my dramatic exit the previous evening. I didn't go into much detail on the second trial. Keeping our reunion short and sweet was the only way to ensure I didn't start envisioning their bodies lying dead at my feet.

When I finally made it back to my room in the palace, my sole focus was taking a bath. I soaked in the hot water for over an hour, till I couldn't tell where the water ended and I began. I couldn't seem to get *clean* enough. The feel of dirt, grime, smoke, and blood clung to my skin and hair no matter how many times I washed.

I wondered if I would always feel this way, if I would always carry the trials of this Decemvirate with me. Distantly, I recalled one of my last conversations with Ragnar and how he said death wasn't the only outcome of this tournament. I was beginning to understand what he meant.

As I dried my hair with a towel and pulled my robe on, I let out a groan. I still needed to report in with Lark and the other architects. I wondered who else had completed the second trial. I'd been so isolated from the palace and tournament over the last night, it was easy to forget what was going on around me. When would the second trial debriefing and ranking be? What if someone hadn't woken up?

A pounding sounded on my door. "Rose? Rose, are you in there?"

Nox. Relief flooded me at the sound of his voice. I was glad he'd made it out. I hadn't realized how worried I'd been for him, so caught up in my own trauma.

"Yes, I'm here and I'm fine," I called back. "Give me a second to change."

"Always here to lend a hand if you need help, darling," he quipped.

Laughter escaped me as I pulled on a pair of pants and a light sweater, then tugged open the door to find him standing with his arms crossed. "Same old Nox, then," I said.

"A little dream won't keep me down for long." His words were casual, but his eyes were haunted. Guarded. Carrying a despair I hadn't ever seen in him.

Before I could stop myself, I wrapped my arms around his waist. He hesitated before returning the embrace.

"I didn't take you for a hugger," he said with a tired chuckle.

"I'm not. You just looked like you needed one."

Nox patted me on the back before releasing me. "So, that bad for you too, I take it?"

I let out a long breath and led him into my room. "This tournament is vile."

"Can't say I disagree with you." He lounged in the chair by my bed. "When did you wake up?"

"Yesterday evening. You?"

"Two nights ago."

I whistled. "Were you the first one out?"

"Yes. And I think you might be the second. Callum and Arowyn woke up this morning. I haven't heard about Callista or Alaric."

A thrill shot through me, followed by disgust. I threw myself onto the bed with a groan. "I hate that I'm *excited* about something as ridiculous as rankings after all this. It feels wrong."

"Yes, well, they're turning us into what they want us to be," he said, pulling out a dagger and a small piece of wood. "Competitive savages who care only about winning and power." He put the edge of the blade against the block and began carving it.

"I didn't know you were an artist," I remarked, marveling at how skillfully his hands moved to slice away small shards of wood.

"I can make any creature you'd like. It takes my mind off things I'd rather not dwell on." A sliver fell to the floor. "I've had plenty of time to practice."

The off-handed comment made me wince and wonder what his life back in Drakorum was like. What the terrible things he'd "rather not dwell on" were.

"What happened?" I asked quietly. "In your dream."

His lip twitched, deft fingers pausing before continuing shaping his new project. "I woke up to people screaming." He spoke slowly, as if recounting the trial took all of his focus. "When I entered the hallway, chaos had broken loose. Mysthelm soldiers had invaded the palace and were going door to door, dragging out guests and setting rooms on fire. They killed the men, took some of the children hostage, and the women..." Nox closed his eyes and swallowed hard. Bile crept up my throat. "After taking what they wanted, they bound them all and forced them into carriages.

"At one point, some generals nearby were talking of their plans. They were preparing to transport hostages to their ships on the west coast to take them down to Mysthelm. They wanted the children for experiments, and the women...they wanted them for breeding stock," he spat. "To bring magic to their kingdom permanently." My nostrils flared at the thought, but I let him continue.

"I knocked out a soldier and stole his uniform so I could masquerade as one of them. I overheard them discussing how they needed to find a person of each magic to acquire all six. Like we were some sort of collectibles to possess." His tone filled with anger. He dug into the wood a little too sharply, causing him to knick his thumb. I watched in fascination as blood welled and dripped down his hand, only for the wound to sew itself together almost instantly. *Shifter blood.*

"But they were looking for particularly powerful Veridians. And only among the children, so they could do experiments from an early age. Learn how to replicate their magic without the risk of them fighting back. Young ones are so much more impressionable, after all." He accidentally stabbed the palm of his hand this time, cold rage taking over his features.

I almost didn't want him to keep going. The idea of soldiers taking these innocent children captive to torture and use them and mold their minds against their will...it was unimaginable. But I knew he needed to talk about this. Knew he needed someone to listen, someone who could understand, because I felt the same.

"I followed the soldiers to the central sector under my disguise as they went from home to home, searching for targets. I learned Mysthelm had some sort of detector where they could test someone's blood and see the strength of their magic. That was how they chose who to keep and who to...discard." His cheek twitched at the term. "They struggled to find someone of Drakorum lineage they deemed 'acceptable.' Until the group I was with reached the final house."

There was a shift in the air, tension ballooning around Nox as he spoke. I didn't breathe, terrified of what happened next.

"There was a mother and her two children. I sensed they were Shifters, like me. A soldier pricked all three of them with his sensor, and one of the children..." He paused, his throat moving as he swallowed. "The youngest boy was incredibly powerful. I volunteered to take the family to the carriages as a ruse to help them escape, but the soldier wanted to hand-deliver this child. Said his blood was the strongest they had seen yet.

"I attempted to argue, and things escalated. He became suspicious of me and tried to restrain me, ordering the other soldiers to kill the mother and spare child and be done with the whole ordeal."

Nox dropped his carving into his lap and met my gaze, his navy eyes burning. "I realized I had a choice. My magic was ten times stronger than any of those people. If they only knew what power lived in my blood, they would release dozens of hostages to take me instead."

The room was silent, save for the sound of our breaths.

"I knew what they would do to these children. To *me*, if I let them. I've seen the kind of experiments those who live in fear conduct on people they don't understand. I've heard their cries, I've felt their pain, I've *lived*—" He cut himself off. "For a moment, I considered staying quiet. Sparing myself."

His eyes fell to the wooden armrest of the chair, and he slowly dragged a long nail across it. "I seized one of their sensors and pricked myself, and when the soldiers saw my level of power, I negotiated. All of the children's lives for mine. They accepted."

Nox went silent again, deep in thought. "How did you get out of the dream?" I whispered.

"Did you receive a clue for the second trial after finding your artifact in the first?" When I nodded, he continued. "That's how I got out. When we left the house and they forced me into a prisoner's carriage, something felt...off. There had been small moments that seemed strange throughout it, but this tugged at my mind. A strong gust of wind blew through the central sector, but it wasn't normal wind. It blew *upward*. Coming from the ground. My clue was 'wait for the wind.'" He chuckled, but there was no humor in it. "A bit blunt, if you ask me. I realized then it was the second trial. They locked me behind bars, and the next thing I knew, I was waking up in my bed."

I didn't know what to say. Question after question ran through my mind, more and more reasons to hate Gayl and this Decemvirate cropping up with every passing second, but I was frozen. What does someone say to those who saw what we saw? Who were forced to make decisions that would impact us for life, whether or not they were real? The way Nox spoke of these *experiments* as if he'd lived them made my skin crawl. This trial seemed to have pulled on our deepest fears and traumas, forcing us to face them head-on.

I had no words to offer. Instead, I leaned over and rested my hand on top of his clenched knuckles. "Some trial," I said.

"Some trial," he echoed sadly. We sat there for a minute, letting his story settle around us. He didn't pressure me to speak, but I found I wanted to share my tale with him, anyway. He was one of only a few who could possibly understand.

"My dream started similarly," I began. I told him of the Mysthelm soldiers, the infirmary and dead patients, the men I'd killed, and how my family had been taken. I relived the destruction of the central sector and my attempts to get people to safety, of the plan to obliterate the shelter and the choice I had to make. Shame once again swept in that I'd chosen to save my cousin over an entire building of people, whereas Nox had willingly sacrificed himself for the sake of dozens. But his eyes never once judged, never questioned.

I recounted how I followed Beau and his captors to the river and was caught, and how my clue from the first trial was also what helped me come to the conclusion that it was all fake, right as I was stabbed through the heart.

"Stabbed? Well, now, that was a bit dramatic," Nox said.

I tried to smile, but it fell flat. "What are we supposed to do now?" I finally asked. "The idea of facing everyone and having this trial paraded around as a success story, then competing in a *third* in just a few weeks..." I shook my head. "I don't know if I can do it."

"Are you kidding me?" He stood. "Don't let them make you believe you're not strong enough for this. You're a viper, darling. *They* are the ones who should fear *you*."

I scoffed. "That's easy for you to say, the fearsome Shifter from Drakorum."

"And *you*," he said, offering me a hand, "Are the fearsome Alchemist from Feywood. Don't doubt yourself. Do you know why I called you a viper that first day?"

I shook my head, taking his hand and meeting his glittering eyes.

"Because I've seen what you're capable of when provoked. You *strike*."

———

Nox and I talked for another half hour before Horace banged on my door, telling me Lark requested my presence *immediately*. I supposed I'd put off meeting with her long enough.

"There you are!" she exclaimed when I arrived at her office, throwing her hands into the air. Shadows instantly billowed from them, sealing any space beneath the door so we could speak freely. "Do you know how foolish it was of you to go running off like that?"

"Don't start," I snapped, plopping myself in the chair across from her desk. "Let's get this over with."

Lark looked taken aback by my tone and shared a look with Horace. Leo had confirmed she and the other architects had no control over what occurred in the second trial and that the idea had been Gayl's to begin with, so I wasn't truly upset with *her*. But my distress from the last twenty-four hours was morphing into anger—an emotion I was comfortable with. One I knew how to wield.

She crossed to stand behind her desk, and when she met my eyes, the pity I found only increased my agitation. Did she have access to what I'd seen in the dreamscape? To what choices I'd made, what I'd had to endure?

Suddenly, it was difficult to meet her gaze.

"Please state your full name," she said, sitting and pulling out a pencil.

"Rose Angelica Wolff."

"What province do you reside in?"

"Feywood."

"And where are you currently?"

"In Veridia City." She looked up and raised an eyebrow, as if to say, "go on." I sighed and crossed my arms. "In the emperor's palace, being asked annoying questions in his head architect's office."

Lark scratched at her brow with the end of her pencil. "Rose, I know you've been through an ordeal, but—"

"*Been through an ordeal?*" I snorted. "You make it sound like my carriage lost a wheel or my cat got sick. What you did to us was *traumatizing*, Lark. I can't believe you can sit there and act like you didn't force us to live through our worst nightmares, all for the sake of appeasing the mighty Emperor Gayl. I thought we were on the same side."

Alright, maybe I was a *little* upset with her.

For a moment, her face crumpled. Horace grunted behind us. "Hey now, don't take it out on her. She was doing her—"

I whirled around in my seat. "Doing her job? Yes, I know. And I suppose you were, too, taking me down to that dinner, acting like nothing was wrong. Did you know what I was walking into? Did you know they were going to drug me?" My voice broke, the strength of my anger fading quickly. "Did you know what they were going to make me do?"

Guilt filled his ruddy features. I don't think I'd realized how fully the depths of this betrayal had gone until facing him now, someone I'd trusted and had even called a friend—such a rare word in this world of mine.

"Rose, please," Lark began. "I hate that we put you through this. I hate that I couldn't warn you or fight against it. But that's why our mission is so important—to change the way this empire is ruled. To be rid of this struggle for power and not live under the fear Gayl has created. You can see that, can't you? This is what we're fighting for. What *you're* fighting for."

I blinked back the burning in my eyes and cleared my throat. "Why would Gayl even do this? Why did he push for this trial?"

Lark swallowed. "Our emperor may not be a good man, but he is a brilliant one. He takes pleasure from pain and turns it into a weapon. I don't know what his exact motivations were, but he's not a fool. He knows there's unrest in the empire, and spreading fear through the strongest of each province? Fostering such a deeply embedded hatred for any opposing kingdom, for anyone who doesn't believe what we believe, and reminding you that *he* holds the power?" She leaned back in her seat, looking wearier than I'd ever seen her. "You and I are simply pieces in his chess match, Miss Wolff."

"It's time to wipe out the entire board," Horace grunted from the door.

Lark nodded. "Rissa has informed me that Gayl has sought you out as a sort of apprentice, given your shared Alchemy magic." Gratefulness flared through me. It seemed Rissa hadn't openly told them about my heritage. "I understand you'll be meeting with him more often. There are two weeks until the masquerade ball, and then the third trial will commence soon after. We still have plenty of time." Lark planted her hands on her desk and stood, summoning conviction into her voice as she locked onto my stare. "You want someone to be angry with? Turn that fire to *him*, Rose."

A series of frantic knocks beat at the door, and Lark jerked to attention, reining in her shadows before motioning for Horace to answer it. A woman with a slight frame and dark hair burst in. I thought I recognized her from the challenger's feast—another one of the architects, maybe?

"Lark, it's the trial," she rushed out, not seeming to care that I was present. "Alaric woke up, so we tried using the restoration potion on Callista, since she was last. But it—it won't work."

Lark strode around her desk, alarm instantly on her dark features. "What? What do you mean, it won't work?"

"She won't wake up." The woman's throat bobbed as she swallowed. "She's dead, Lark. Callista is dead."

45

ROSE

The great hall was eerily silent as Nox and I made our way through the doors. Nobody spoke a word, not even the lords and ladies who'd joked and conversed during the first debriefing like it was some sort of party.

Instead of refreshment tables full of food and drink, chairs were lined up facing the raised platform on the south end. Challengers, guards, palace staff, and guests alike took their seats, all dressed in the Emberfell colors of light blue. On the platform rested a glass box, and even from across the hall I knew what it held.

Callista's body.

She had never woken from the challenge. When the healers tried to give her the potion that was supposed to wake you after all the other challengers had passed the trial, nothing had happened. She'd already been dead.

They didn't know exactly how long ago her heart had stopped. The head healer estimated only a couple of hours.

The architects spent the rest of the day yesterday consoling Callista's family and planning her memorial ceremony paired with the second trial's rankings. The five remaining challengers were ordered not to leave palace grounds until after the news had been spread. I passed the time with Morgana and Beau, trying not to think about how easily it could have been me.

Nox and I sat together toward the back of the hall, watching as a few remaining guests filed in. While the space appeared light and cheery with all of the pale blue rushing like a summer's wave, the mood was anything but. The only sounds that echoed off the stone walls were that of the scribes, once again stationed at the front with their pencils scratching against paper, and awkward shuffles and coughs from those in attendance.

Once the hall was full, Lark stood and walked to the podium. Her dark hair was wrapped around her head, with pearls dotting the braid. She wore a light blue pantsuit that hugged her thick curves. Her tone was somber, showing genuine regret for losing a challenger on her watch.

"We are here today to remember the life of Callista Greyhound. A Lightbender from Emberfell, but more importantly, a Veridian. One of our own, who so bravely represented her people and fought for the chance to bring glory back to them. She was an example to us all, a light in a time of competition who didn't let the prospect of danger dim her spirit."

She went on to talk of Callista's skill during the first trial and other accomplishments of her time back in Emberfell. As she spoke, three women at the front cried in silence, their shoulders hunched over and a handkerchief passing between them. Her family, if I had to guess. The ones who had come with her. I wondered how many people she left behind in her home province. People she would never see again.

This tournament had delivered blow after blow, but this one... this one felt different. More permanent. More threatening.

When Lark stepped down, the three women took her place. Looking at their faces, I could definitely tell they were related to Callista. The oldest one had the same dimples on her tawny cheeks, evident even as her features were crumpled with grief. The other two were younger, similar in age to Callista—sisters, perhaps. All three of them spoke a few words, telling stories of love from Callista's youth. Sniffles rang out in the hall from guests of the city as they spoke.

I, however, felt only frustration. That they would use this time in honor of her memory as a spectacle for the tournament. Did these guests, these outsiders, think of us as real people? Or were we simply entertainment for them, beings to cheer for or against in this power play of the empire? Even this memorial served a double purpose. Heightened drama for the following rankings. Higher stakes for the remaining challengers. This entire evening would be on display for others to read by morning.

Callista didn't deserve that. She didn't deserve for her *sacrifice* to be turned into a performance.

Gayl wasn't even in attendance. I'd searched for him when we first entered, but he was nowhere to be found. Indignation burned within me. He couldn't be bothered to show honor to a citizen who died under his very roof.

The memorial portion of the service ended, and Lark took her place behind the podium again.

"Now, we will reveal the rankings for the second trial and overall standings for the entire tournament."

There was no fanfare this time, no flourishing speech about the trials or summary of each challengers' courageous acts. Lark simply raised her hand and conjured her shadows, speaking each name in a carefully controlled tone.

"The first challenger to pass the second trial was Nox Duma of Drakorum." His name appeared in black wisps like ink, but there was no applause. The hall stayed silent, still wrapped in the heaviness of the evening. "Next was Rose Wolff of Feywood."

I felt nothing at the sound of my name. No spark of pride or excitement. I just wanted it to be over.

In quick succession, shadows formed Callum's name, then Arowyn's, and finally, Alaric's. There was a poignant pause when Callista's name should have appeared last.

"After the completion of both trials, the rankings have been combined and averaged as follows." Slowly, the names written in shadow rearranged themselves, forming a new list.

Arowyn was still in first, her lead after the first trial enough to give her an edge even when coming in fourth this time. Callum was next. And then Nox, Alaric, and I all tied for third.

Whispers of interest swept the hall. Three of us in the same position.

I glanced at Nox, who gave me a grim smile. There was no such thing as a tie in the Decemvirate. The third and final trial always broke them, and it usually wasn't a pleasant break.

It was a good thing we still had over two weeks to prepare. Two weeks for me to put the tournament out of my mind and focus on my other purpose: getting close to Gayl. I wasn't sure which I was more frightened of.

As we stood to exit, voices picked back up, the solemnity of the memorial cracking. I turned toward the entrance doors and stopped.

Swishing at the floor was a familiar long, emerald cloak, the end of it barely visible as the figure strode out of the hall, his dark, shoulder-length hair fluttering when he disappeared from sight.

46

ROSE

I'm ready.

My hand shook as I wrote the two little words on the back of the parchment Gayl had sent the evening of the challenger's feast.

Conflicting emotions warred within me. Wrath at him for what he'd put me through, yearning for more of my father's past, curiosity about the magic he'd learned. And in the mix of it all, guilt. Both for the secrets I was harboring, even if it was to keep Leo safe, and for my own desires. No matter how much I ignored it, part of me *wanted* these meetings with Gayl. As much as I despised the man, he represented a piece I'd been missing for twenty years. He possessed a magic that drew me in, that sang to the darkest parts of my soul. A magic that said "you're not alone."

Within seconds of setting the paper on my bed, it burst into flames and vanished. I gasped and jolted backward, barely having time to recover before a second note appeared in thin air, the ends smoking. I caught it and winced at the slight heat. Gayl's response was penned in black, the ink still wet.

Meet me where you once found me in half an hour. Our blood reveals the entrance.

-T.G.

Nervous anticipation wound around my gut as I waited a few minutes, then collected my dagger, pouch of herbs, and hand drawn map of the palace. Horace was instantly at my side when I stepped out the door, but I held up a hand to stop him from following me.

"I need to do this alone, Horace."

I could tell it went against his very nature to acquiesce and watch me head off toward uncertain danger, but he knew this was Rissa's request. It was for the Sentinels.

That's what I told myself, anyway.

The journey down two flights and to the northern end was quick and quiet. Hardly anyone loitered in the corridors, as most people were likely eating dinner or in bed at this hour.

I came upon the familiar hallway, and to my surprise, the usual slew of guards was nowhere to be found. Striding to the end and standing before the same wall as before, I examined my surroundings, first feeling along the edges of the two lit sconces, then kneeling and swiping a hand at the bottom of the stone wall. Nothing was out of the ordinary. No mechanism that triggered the opening of a door, no hole or button or switch. The only thing left was the painting of the fountain in the center.

I crossed my arms and stared at it, willing it to show me the answer. With a sigh, I ran a finger along the golden frame and the outline of the garden surrounding the fountain, gliding my thumb across the pool of crystalline, blue water.

A sharp sting sliced through the pad of my thumb. Jerking my hand back, I saw a bead of blood blooming at the tip and stuck it in my mouth to soothe the ache. When I looked back up at the portrait, my eyes widened.

From the center, dark red oozed over the blue, turning the

water in the fountain the color of my blood. The ripples and whorls deepened, trickling over the side of the fountain. I watched in half amazement, half disgust as the blood bubbled down the painting and began to shimmer. Not just the blood—the entire portrait was flickering, like some sort of mirage.

When I blinked, a door stood in its place.

It opened soundlessly when I pulled on the handle. Before me stood the same narrow, cold corridor I'd encountered the first time. The hallway seemed to extend forever, with closed doors lining the sides and only a handful of dimly lit sconces gracing the stone walls. Slowly, I made my way to the door in the center, the one I'd seen Gayl stop at the day he caught me spying.

The moment I stepped before the door, it swung open with a creak, leading to a dark room with shadows of furniture slinking across the floor. Silhouettes elongated and reached out to nip at my feet. Shivers raced down my spine, a chill settling in my bones.

He certainly had a flair for the dramatic.

"Come in, Rose," Gayl's soft voice said, coming from deep inside the room. I hesitated before shutting the door, willing my anger from earlier to reemerge. Anything was better than this unease.

The chamber was much larger than I'd originally thought. Lining the wall to my left was a long row of bookshelves, full of pristine, leather-bound books and stacks of disheveled pieces of parchment. Quills and inkwells, marble pestles and mortars, crystal glasses in various shapes and sizes, and dried herbs hanging from twine littered every free space. A large desk stood in the center of the room, with several tapered candles resting in brass holders, shedding light on the man sitting in the burgundy wingback chair.

Gayl appeared more casual than I'd ever seen him, with brown suspenders and a white tunic tucked into gray pants, the same gloves he always wore still tight around his hands. His long, silver and black hair was unbound and hung to his shoulders, a matching beard growing in fuller than last time. He leaned over the desk, scribbling something in a notebook, not bothering to look up as I approached.

My wariness waned as I took in his Alchemist's den. I could feel his magic coating the room, and as the scent of familiar herbs and the sound of his quill scratching against paper washed over me, my magic stirred.

"Congratulations are in order," he said, still looking at his notes. He set the quill down and peered up at me, my father's blue-gray eye catching me off guard again. "You completed the second trial swiftly. You should be proud of yourself."

My curiosity vanished, replaced with indignation. "*Proud?*"

He didn't react to the venom in my tone. "Yes, proud. It's quite an accomplishment. You did better than I would have expected."

I gaped at him. "It's not an *accomplishment!*" I gritted out, my voice raising. "I barely got out of there with my mind intact. I can't even look at my family without imagining them dead. I killed people in that dreamscape, and one of us died in there. You have the nerve to tell me I should be proud?" My fingers clenched at my side. "Forgive me, *Your Majesty*, if I don't find your cruel tricks particularly gratifying."

He sighed. "Rose, you must know I had no control over what you would see during the trial. My architects and I designed the potion, of course, but only the initial scenario. *Your* mind conjured the rest. *Your* subconscious filled in the gaps, bringing life and your own unique journey to the simulation." He rounded the corner of his desk to step closer to me, and I backed away. "The potion was created to seek out the inner turmoil of your heart and find what would best test you. What would show your strengths and weaknesses. How you reacted to that test was the true trial."

I waved my hand angrily in the air. "You still knew what you were doing! How does magic like that even *work*? You can't control it." My brow furrowed as I tried to imagine ways such power could be used. "It—it's chaotic. *Dangerous*. What if all of us never woke up, like Callista? What if we lost our minds in there? Do you even *care*?"

"Of course I care. That's why we had protocols in place once each challenger awoke to ensure their safety and recovery. Miss Greyhound was an unfortunate accident." He took another step toward me. "Simply because you do not understand this magic does not mean it's *dangerous*, Rose. That's what I wanted to show you. What your father—"

"I know you tricked him into practicing blood magic," I snapped. "My aunt told me all about your past together, how you took advantage of him after your parents died until he came to his senses and wanted nothing to do with you."

To my surprise, Gayl chuckled dryly. "Did she, now? Your aunt is a foolish woman."

Rage enveloped me. I opened my mouth to defend her, but he cut me off, a sliver of his power breaking through that calm demeanor. "She doesn't know anything of our past. Hamilton was the one who approached *me* about my magic. *He* desired to know the full extent of our abilities. There was no manipulation, no compulsion. We worked *together* to both overcome the grief of our parents and learn the inner workings of what was rightfully ours." Gayl didn't move, but he seemed to grow taller and tower over me, his presence all-consuming. "Are you so eager to paint me as the villain in this story that you would blindly believe any empty-headed lie without attempting to seek the truth? I expected better of you, Rose."

I don't know why his words pierced me when moments ago I didn't even want to believe anything that came from his mouth. My voice was smaller, reluctant, showing my lack of confidence when I said, "Morgana wouldn't lie to me."

He turned back to his desk. "She may not have done so knowingly, but biased ignorance is just as harmful." Sitting in his chair, he refused to meet my eyes. "You may go."

My stomach sank. "What? Why?"

"Because you seem to be following the same path as her, and

so many like her. Dismissing what you don't understand. Believing that which you desire most to be true instead of searching for real answers. *That* is not the daughter of Hamilton Wolff I intended to speak with tonight."

I flinched. Was he right? Had I been convinced for so long that Theodore Gayl was the enemy that I willingly accepted any slander against him, with no thought of if it were *true*? Without hearing his side? I didn't have proof that he spoke the truth, but I didn't have any proof that Morgana knew what she was talking about, either. Gayl had done some terrible things in his time as emperor, things I didn't agree with, but how much of that was because it was cast in a negative light?

He could be called a curse bringer, since the Somnivae curse was born of his magic. Or...a savior. He *saved* lives that night. He'd created division among the provinces, yes, but he also strengthened them. Even I would be naive not to admit how powerful some of the provinces had grown. It was why he still had supporters in the empire, why some still praised his name. Perhaps, with time, he might see the damage he'd inflicted and work to change it for the better.

I would never know if I didn't give him the chance.

I took a deep breath. "Maybe you're right. I won't pretend I understand everything. *Or* that I'll always agree with you. But...I know what it's like to be judged before someone gets to know you. To have people only see the worst in you." Gayl continued scribbling in his journal as I spoke, and I rubbed at the fringes of my sweater, sudden desperation setting in. I could feel the last hope of recovering those pieces of my father sliding away.

"Please, Your Majesty. I—I want to learn about my father. I want to learn about what the two of you discovered, about our magic and the things we can do. I just—I just want to *know* him." *Please, don't give up on me. Please don't let me lose this.*

He finally looked up, one dark and one light eye staring back at me. Searching. Weighing. My breaths were shallow as I waited for his response, my chest and the backs of my eyes burning.

He set his quill down. "I think that's enough with the formal titles, don't you agree? You may call me Theodore."

I let out a breath. "Does that mean you'll let me stay? You'll teach me?"

"Yes, Rose." The wrinkled lines around his mouth deepened as he gave me a faint smile. "I will teach you."

47

ROSE

My fingers trailed along the collection of glass vials on a bookshelf. Some were clear and empty, others tall and full of a dark liquid, and several more were rose or sage-tinted with crushed flower petals layering the bottom. All were marked with cream labels bearing Ga—*Theodore's* hurried, cramped cursive. Bay laurel sprigs, eye of rowan, vervain, wishbone powder, snake skin shavings.

"Your note said my father had made some incredible discoveries with Alchemy," I began after we'd spent several minutes in silence while he finished what he'd been working on. "Did any of that have to do with...blood magic?"

I tried to keep the unease out of my tone, but he caught it anyway. "Tell me, Rose. What has you so convinced that blood magic is such an atrocity?"

I craned my neck to peek at him, still seated in his chair with notes spread on the desk before him. "It's dangerous," I said. "Unnatural. People who use it end up ruining their lives. It's too unpredictable and powerful."

He stopped writing and leaned back, twisting his quill between gloved fingers. "And yet, it intrigues you, does it not?"

I pressed my lips together, refusing to give voice to that part of my mind.

With a knowing look, he continued. "Unpredictable and powerful, yes. But only when not controlled properly. Many people have used it incorrectly and ruined their lives, as you say. But have lives not been ruined even when using magic in an orthodox manner?" He raised an eyebrow. "The type of magic doesn't necessarily matter. It can *all* be dangerous. It depends on the wielder, you see."

"But Alchemy is based in the earth around us," I argued, repeating what I'd heard others say in Feywood. "We defile that by taking blood or—or bones or skin"—I gestured to some of the glass vials beside me—"against something's will instead of working *with* nature to give us its power."

Theodore steepled his hands in front of him. "I don't disagree with you. Forcefully taking anything and bending it to your whims is dangerous. But that is not the foundation of blood magic." He stood and began pacing. "Blood magic is, in its base meaning, the use of power found within that which bears *life*. How is that unnatural? How is the blood that runs through our veins unnatural? It's innately the most natural power we possess.

"The other five provinces use magic that flows within them. They don't require a conduit or outside force to conjure shadows or light or illusions or whatever it may be." His hands moved animatedly as he spoke. "This fact was what sparked your father's curiosity so many years ago. Why is *our* magic type the only one expected to source power outside of ourselves? Why should we be any different, Hamilton wondered?"

I stared at him, transfixed by his passion and conviction, remembering the same thoughts that had captured my mind days ago when Callum confronted me in the great hall. His spiteful words echoed all around me, lighting a fire beneath my skin.

"You think you're so clever with your little plants and potions. But you're nothing without them, are you, Feywood?"

"People get carried away and lose themselves, taking their

magic too far or stealing power that is not theirs to wield," Theodore explained. "*That* is where the danger lies. Harming others, using force or violence, destroying nature. But"—he pulled the glove from his left hand finger by finger, then grabbed a letter opener from his desk—"when given *willingly*...it is magic unlike anything you have seen." My eyes widened at his exposed hand, which was riddled with dozens of thin, white scars.

In his next breath, he pricked the tip of his forefinger and muttered, *"Vellus."*

Instantly, he disappeared.

But it wasn't just *him*.

Every single item in the chamber vanished into nothingness. Every book, every charm, the desk, the chair, bookshelves, *all of it*, save for the lit sconces on the walls.

Gone.

It wasn't a mere invisibility spell like I'd cast hundreds of times. This was...unbelievable. Unthinkable.

Lips parting, I breathed, "How did you—"

His voice materialized behind me. "It is as natural as drawing breath. It is our *birthright*."

In the blink of an eye, the chamber went dark, the sconces snuffed out. "You can do it, too, Rose," he whispered in my ear.

Suddenly, my dagger appeared in my open hand, the feel of cold steel burning my palm.

Was it truly possible? To practice Alchemy with nothing but our blood? No more bags and pouches, no more relying on what herbs were in my pocket or if I would have enough time to arm myself before it was too late. No more sickly taste of dried leaves on my tongue or fear of running out of charms.

No more *tricks*. No more *weaker magic*.

What was wrong with that? Theodore was right—as long as one didn't go too far, as long as they didn't mess with the balance of nature, this was no different than what Rissa did when she shifted, or Lark when she wielded her shadows.

I raised the dagger, my hand trembling so hard in the dark that

I couldn't see where I was aiming. Invisible, wrinkled fingers clasped around my wrist, guiding me.

My breath caught as the blade inched closer to my skin, the air around us stretched tight with expectation. It was like my blood knew what was happening; my pulse pounded in every part of me, drawing the dagger nearer. Calling for it. Pleading.

The sharp tip bit into the pad of my thumb, and I gasped at the sting. Without thinking, without waiting, I whispered, "*Incendar.*"

Half of me believed it wouldn't work. That Theodore was playing an elaborate prank, and I would look like a fool, chanting spells into nothingness.

But in my heart, I knew it was real.

My body erupted and flooded with power. While casting normally felt like a tightening in my chest, this felt like *liberation.* I was weightless yet full of strength at the same time, my magic vibrating and flowing within me, blending into my essence until I couldn't separate it from my very being. It was as if I had never truly breathed until this moment.

I'd cast the fire spell intending to create a small flame at my fingertip to light the dark space before me. But the moment the word left my lips, the entire room lit with a golden glow.

My mouth dropped open. Theodore must have banished his invisibility spell, for all the items were back in their place, and each candle in the chamber had ignited. Dozens of tapers lining the shelves and floor, every sconce on the stone walls, the candelabras above our heads. They flared to life with fervor, flickering in time to the thumping of my heart.

I met Theodore's gaze, his eyes mirroring the wonder and energy likely gleaming in my own.

"I did it," I breathed.

"And how do you feel?" he asked, bringing a handkerchief from his pants pocket and wiping the small trickle of blood from my thumb.

I glanced around the chamber again, taking in the light,

reveling in the power still racing through me. With a deep breath, I closed my eyes, and a smile curved the ends of my lips.

This was what it was supposed to be. Nothing separating me from my magic, nothing holding me back from what I was meant for. Alchemy in its purest, most natural form.

"Free," I finally said, locking eyes with him once more. "I feel free."

Theodore smiled, and a spear shot through my chest. He looked so much like the father I remembered from my childhood. The father I'd lost.

But maybe...maybe I hadn't lost him completely. Maybe I could find him here, in a dark, invisible chamber, with the man I'd spent my life despising.

"Can I show you something?" he asked. I nodded, and he led me to a tall book stand in the corner of the room. It was made of dark wood, with beautiful etchings of vines spiraling up its length. Atop sat an old leather book, the pages weathered and frayed on the edges.

Theodore carefully set his hand on the open page. "This was your father's Grimoire, Rose."

I blinked in surprise. "But I already have his Grimoire back home. My aunt and uncle gave it to me when I turned sixteen."

"That must be one he created after he and I parted ways. *This*" —he gestured to the book—"was his first. It contains his notes on blood magic and the spells and potions we crafted. And it's exceptionally detailed," he added with a hint of a smile. "Hamilton was a thorough researcher, whereas I was a bit impatient. Always wanting to act. He would often have a theory and wanted to take time to investigate it, but I grew restless, eager to put it to the test.

"Once, we were attempting to spell our house cat to be able to speak to us. I was a tad ambitious and ended up casting on every animal in a half mile radius from our home." He chuckled lightly, a sound I'd never heard from him. "You should have seen the two of us. Me, desperately running from a horde of wild creatures, and Hamilton racing through his notes to fix my mistake."

I grinned at his story, trying to picture the two young men and their adventures. My eyes lingered on the Grimoire, my fingers itching to explore its pages. To feel this new connection to my father.

Theodore's gaze flickered from me to the book. "Go on," he encouraged.

I swallowed and took a step toward the stand, reaching out a hand to brush against the old pages. "Can I read it?"

His hand covered mine. "Rose, you can *have* it. It's yours by right."

My attention snapped to him. "What?"

When he closed the Grimoire, a small cloud of dust puffed in the air. He clasped the book shut with a leather strap, his fingers skating across the etchings of the moon and series of constellations on the front.

"Treat it well," he said, placing it in my open arms.

A rush of emotion flooded me as I stared at the cover. The heaviness of the leather tome sat in my heart like a weight, but it wasn't uncomfortable. It wasn't burdensome. It *filled* me. My chest expanded as I drew a deep breath, something settling inside.

Another missing piece finding its way home.

48

LEO

I leaned against a tree trunk and crossed one ankle over the other, my tail twitching anxiously against the forest floor. Staring up at the third story window of the palace, I chided myself for the fifth time. I was being ridiculous waiting out here so late at night. Chaz had called me a stalker.

But when Horace sent word that Rose had left to meet with Gayl again, I couldn't wait idly in the cottage.

The other night when she'd woken from her nightmare in my bed, I'd wanted to do everything in my power to take it all away. It brought me back to those days growing up, how my sister would walk home with bruises on her body before her Shifter blood could heal her quickly. How I'd catch my mother crying in the closet or watch my father's paranoia consume him from the inside. So much pain, and all I'd desired was to remove it.

Rose said she felt as if something was wrong with her. That nobody wanted to get close. Ever since then, I'd imagined her alone up there in her empty room, facing the aftermath of the second trial and all that had happened to her thus far with nobody by her side.

She didn't have to be alone, though. Not anymore.

A light flickered inside the room, illuminating the curtains in a pale glow. Pushing off from the tree, I made my way through the shadows of the palace grounds, pausing several stories beneath her window. I summoned my Shifter half, and my senses were immediately overwhelmed by the increased scents and sounds as I adjusted to the environment. I could smell her, even down here. The way the lavender and sage wrapped around me and beckoned me to her should have frightened me. It should have made me turn away and retreat to my cottage, never to look back again.

This life I lived...it wasn't conducive to whatever might be happening between us. Constant secrecy and violence, looking over our shoulders at every turn, Sentinel meetings and patrols and missions and scheming. I didn't need something else to focus on, not when change was coming. Not when danger lurked around the corner. If things went poorly, we could be on the verge of a civil war.

But none of that seemed to matter when it came to her.

Crouching low, strength reverberated in my bones as I lunged to the first ledge, then the second, then the third. Before I muted my Shifter instincts, I caught a glimpse of her through the thin fabric of the curtains, my sharpened eyesight making me acutely aware of every inch of her. She sat on her bed, legs crossed, her thick, dark hair cascading down one shoulder as she bent over a book. Her hand came up to brush it behind her ear, and I could see those beautiful high cheekbones, long lashes that brushed the tops of them when she blinked, bright eyes intently focused as they flitted across the pages.

Chaz was right. I was a stalker.

I tapped on her window and reined in my Shifter half. Her neck turned toward me, a myriad of reactions racing across her face. She thought she hid her emotions well beneath those layers of hers, but I could read them. Her brow pinched in confusion, then widened when she saw my silhouette, her lips curving upward. But her grin fell as she scrambled to close the mysterious book and tuck it away.

My apprehension grew. Was she still hiding things from me?

She walked to the window and pulled it open, leaning against the frame and crossing her arms. A coy smile played on her lips. "And what might you be doing here at this hour?"

"Horace told me about your meeting with Gayl. I wanted to see how you were doing," I answered honestly.

"I'm fine," she said, shrugging one shoulder.

I narrowed my eyes. *Stubborn girl.*

With a sigh, she dropped her arms and opened the window wider, letting me step over the ledge and into her room.

"Maybe not *completely* fine. These last few days have been...a lot to wrap my head around."

"I heard about the challenger who died in the trial," I said. "I'm sorry that happened."

"I didn't really know her. I feel bad for her family, though. They held a memorial for her today, but it was just for show." She shook her head. "The rankings came right after. Reporters were there to record the entire thing. It was disgusting."

"That sounds like Gayl. Exploiting the suffering of others for the sake of the tournament. I know Lark has had her hands full since the trial ended—we've barely heard a word from her."

Rose gave me a sheepish look. "I *might* have yelled at her and Horace earlier," she said, rubbing a hand at the back of her neck. "I just got so angry after the second trial. They knew what I was walking into, and after these last couple weeks, I thought we were...I guess *friends* is too strong of a word, but still."

She was hurt. Understandably so. And Rose's first and foremost reaction to anything that hurt was anger—something I knew all too well, myself.

"I know this is difficult," I began, taking a step toward her. She averted her gaze and stared at the floor. "The lines between ally and friend are always blurred for people like us. I even struggle with Rissa and knowing when to separate the mission from the fact that she's also my sister."

She eyed me. "People like us?"

"You know, charming. Outgoing. People pleasers."

She snorted. "Yes, that sounds just like us."

Sliding a finger under her chin, I let my teasing grin fall and gently angled her to face me again. "But I promise, you can always talk to me if you need someone. I know how hard it is to make friends when you're constantly on guard, when there's *always* an agenda."

"Always waiting for the other shoe to fall," she added, eyes wavering to my lips. "Worried people only want you for what you can give them. Or that anything good will eventually come to an end."

"Something like that," I murmured. I was unable to look away, unable to pull myself out of this hold she had on me. My pulse raced when she bit her lip, dragging her eyes back to mine.

"I'm glad you came," she admitted. "Maybe I did need someone to talk to."

"Did anything else happen?" I asked.

Swallowing and giving a small nod, she backed away to sit on the edge of her bed. "When I met with my—with Gayl, I might have yelled at him, too."

I ran a hand over the scruff of my chin, letting out an exasperated laugh. "Fates, little wolf, are you trying to get yourself thrown in the dungeon?"

"He deserved it," she retorted, that defiant spark back in her gaze. "It went well, all things considered. I mean, I'm still alive."

"Setting the bar high, I see."

She snorted. "We talked about the trial. And...my father." Her voice became hesitant as she looked down and played with the edge of the bedsheet. "It sounds like they were close. It was strange to hear him tell stories about the two of them. But...kind of nice. My father loved experimenting with magic, like me." She shot a quick glance at the bundle hidden beneath a blanket.

"I saw you reading whatever that is through the curtain," I confessed, motioning to the concealed book. She straightened, and I hastily added, "I'm sorry, I wasn't trying to pry. I caught a glimpse right before I knocked. You don't have to tell me anything if you don't want to."

I craved her trust, but it wasn't something I could force her to give me. So when I saw her shoulders loosen and that guarded expression fall, it was like a brick had been lifted from my chest.

She nodded. "It's my father's Grimoire from when he and Th— Gayl were young. He gave it to me tonight." Her hands traveled beneath the blanket and pulled out the thick leather tome. As her fingers traced the outline of the moon on the cover, I noticed a small bandage around her thumb.

"What happened there?" I asked, pointing to her hand.

She shifted her arm so her hand was hidden beneath the sheets. "Nothing. Just a cut."

I stifled a frustrated growl. It felt like I had taken two steps forward and one step back with her. Something had changed between us the other night, and I believed she was finally opening up to me. Finally trusting me. If she would simply let me in, she would see that she didn't have to bear all of this alone. She didn't have to hide anytime she felt threatened or someone tried to get close.

I *hated* that this was the way she'd come to see life. It must be exhausting, holding everyone at arm's length. I was thankful to have had my sister through our darkest days, but Rose...had she ever had anyone truly at her side? An equal, a partner, a confidant.

Even if I hadn't completely broken through her walls, maybe I'd removed a piece of them. If I had to tear them down brick by brick, I would. Everyone deserved to have someone see them, to fight for them the way Lark had for my sister and me. Rose should *know* she was worth it.

"I experimented with magic when I was young, too," I offered, breaking the silence. "I still do, but am a bit more careful than I used to be."

She chuckled softly. "I can't imagine you being anything but meticulously careful," she said with a taunting edge.

"Are you calling me *boring*, Miss Wolff?" I stalked to the bed, hiding my smirk behind a pretend scowl.

"Oh, I would never. You just seem like someone who doesn't stray far from convention. A *proper* Alchemist," she said, putting air quotes around the term.

"For Fates sake, I have a *tail*, Rose," I said with a laugh. "What about that screams 'proper' to you?"

Looking down to the edge of my cloak, she suddenly bore a bashful expression. My smirk widened. "Whatever you want to say, say it. Trust me, I've heard it all."

A blush crept up her cheeks. "Can—can I touch it?"

A rare grin split my face. She was adorable. Slipping it from beneath my cloak, I unfurled my tail on her bed, the blanket soft and supple beneath its weight.

She reached out a hand and felt along its length. I shivered involuntarily, unused to the feel of someone else's skin against it. Flinching, she snatched her fingers back, glancing at me warily.

"It's fine, it's just...sensitive," I said.

A wicked gleam entered her eyes. "What else can you do with it?"

"What do you mean?"

"Well, you obviously like to choke people," she said, and I rolled my eyes. I would never live that down. "What else do you use it for?"

Nobody had ever asked me that. "I suppose it's like a third hand. It has more reach, which is convenient." I demonstrated by uncurling it and letting it slink along the bed.

"Very," she hummed as I drew closer to where she sat.

"Makes it easy to restrain people."

She cocked her head, raising an eyebrow. "Excuse me?"

"When I'm on patrol, of course," I said, smothering a laugh. "There have been many times when having the ability to wrap this"—I flicked the end of my tail against her neck—"around someone's arm or leg has saved my life in a fight."

"I never thought about that," she mused. "You haven't told me how it works." She brandished her free arm at my body. "You said you're half Shifter, but can't fully shift."

My chest tightened. It wasn't a question. The last time she'd asked, I'd given her a cryptic response. She was leaving me a way out if I didn't want to answer her.

I'd never told anyone the full story, not even Rissa. My twin knew my unconventional anatomy had left scars on me, both figuratively and literally. She knew I'd suffered and had been too ashamed to ever speak of it. It was the moment in my life I regretted more than any other. But she didn't know *why*.

Indecision warred within me. I wanted to leave it buried, to brush off Rose's interest and placate her with some muddled, humorous version of the story. But how could I expect her to want to lean on me, to confide in me, if I couldn't do the same?

This was the first time I'd felt even remotely safe sharing the truth with someone. The fear of judgment or condemnation didn't exist with her. I knew she would accept me no matter what skeletons lay in my closet, and that in and of itself was a form of freedom.

She must have been able to read me as easily as I could her, for she shifted to the other side of the bed and laid down, patting the now empty spot. "Come here," she said softly.

Shrugging off my cloak and draping it over the back of the chair, I lowered myself onto the warm sheets.

"You don't have to talk about it," she said.

"I know." I faced the ceiling and rested my hands on my chest, taking a deep breath. "I've told you some of how my sister and I were treated as children. We were pariahs, living in constant anxiety because of who our father was and what had happened the night we were born. Rissa inherited our mother's shifting abilities and struggled to control her magic at such a young age." I tapped my thumb against my wrist, memories coming back to light. "With shifting comes increased senses, both physical and emotional. She was easily angered and would break down into tantrums at a moment's notice, then dissolve into tears the next. She couldn't stop herself from partially shifting when that happened…sometimes it would be her tail, others her ears, occasionally a paw.

"Being in public is hard for an early Shifter. Crowds overwhelmed her, and when they saw who she was and how uncontrollable her magic was, they assumed the worst. Assumed the cursed twins were only going to bring destruction to the capital. They were scared of her, thinking she'd erupt and hurt someone. We tried to make sure she was never alone when she went out, but some days…" I trailed off, remembering how difficult it had been to watch our parents work themselves into the ground and still barely have enough food on the table. How my sister and I often scavenged the surrounding village, looking for extras to bring home or stealing the occasional spare coin. My father flew into a rage if my sister, mother, or I left the house unprotected, but we couldn't sit by and do nothing.

"One winter when we were twelve, she came home crying. I begged her to tell me what was wrong, but she was so shaken she couldn't speak. She took her coat off…and that's when I saw the bruises." Rose sucked in a breath. "All across her arms and neck, like she'd been hit repeatedly and—and choked. They had started to heal already, but I could tell they were fresh."

I gritted my teeth, anger clawing at me. I hadn't been there to protect her. That image had been branded on my mind for fifteen years. Sometimes, when I closed my eyes, I saw the blue and purple marks on the back of my lids. Her swollen red eyes, her disheveled blonde hair.

"I snapped. I didn't know what to do or how to help her. All I wanted was for her not to be alone. She was my twin—we'd gone through everything together, but I was an Alchemist. I'd never shown signs of having Shifter blood. This was a path I couldn't follow her down, and it killed me."

Swallowing hard, I braced myself for what came next. The same hopelessness that had gripped me back then roared to life. "I took my father's Grimoire and searched for something—*anything* —that could help. I didn't even know what I was looking for when

I found a transformation spell, one that could turn simple objects into another. Water to wine and wood to steel, or more complex matter, depending on the power behind the spell. I thought...if I could *make* myself like her, a Shifter, then she wouldn't be alone."

Rose's breath hitched. She placed a hand on my forearm and squeezed. "Leo, you didn't..."

"I didn't know what else to *do*," I repeated hoarsely, turning to face her. It was easier like this, when it was only the two of us. I didn't have to pretend. "I got the ingredients and waited until the next full moon, when our magic is strongest. There was no part of me that thought this would work. I was young and desperate and careless. But I'd heard rumors. Rumors about ways to make spells even more powerful."

"Blood magic," she whispered. When I didn't respond, she moved her hand to cover mine, ceasing my anxious tapping. She threaded her fingers through my own and slid closer to me. As I spoke, I rubbed my thumb against hers.

"The spell called for pieces of what you wanted to transform and what you wanted it to become. So I used my own blood and some animal fur I'd found in the forest. It was...the most excruciating thing I've ever felt." I paused, words trapped in my throat, still able to feel the phantom ache burning in my spine, my bones, my head. Every cell in my body had been set ablaze, ripping my organs to shreds. Even the memory of it had me twisting my free hand in the sheets as my muscles locked.

Her warm hand cupped my face, those sharp, beautiful eyes grounding me back in the moment.

"The spell worked," she said quietly, her tone laced with awe. "You *made* yourself a Shifter."

"Not fully. The tail is permanent—I can't shift that at will. I've always thought of it as a consequence for trying to defy the laws of magic. Over time, I learned how to hone my other animalistic senses, how to turn them off and on. I suppose it hasn't been the worst ability to have."

She let out a disbelieving laugh. "I can't believe you actually did it. That it's even possible. For a spell to be able to do something like that...it's *extraordinary*."

I pulled myself into a sitting position to face her. "It's *dangerous*, Rose. We shouldn't have power like that. It's not natural, and something that strong...it always has consequences. A price to be paid. I thought mine was merely pain or this ridiculous tail, but it—it was more than that."

Her brow furrowed. "What are you talking about?"

I threw my legs over the side of the bed and stood, pacing back and forth along the length of the room. "We've always known this. The basic principles of Alchemy are that any curse, any magic too powerful, has a price. I should have known. I should have seen it coming, that my trying to alter the very *nature* of who I was would take something in return." I was rambling, but couldn't seem to stop. The moment I said the words aloud, they became true. I needed Rose to understand. And I couldn't bear to have her look at me when—

"Leo." She stepped in front of me, one hand coming to my shoulder to cease my striding and the other landing on the side of my neck. Her gaze was steady. Controlled. Comforting. "What happened?"

I was sure she could feel my pulse fluttering frantically beneath her touch as the confession rolled up my chest and onto my lips.

"I killed him."

Rose blinked, her lips parting. "Who?"

"My father." My fist clenched at my side. "I killed my father."

49

ROSE

"Leo..." I started slowly, pausing to lick my lips. He'd only been *twelve*. Surely, he was mistaken. "What do you mean, you killed your father?"

"He must have heard me screaming in the woods outside the cottage." The slight tremor in his voice made my heart constrict; I didn't know how to help him, other than listening. "He came out and tried to stop me, but it was too late. The spell had taken effect. The magic burst from me, ten times more powerful than anything I'd expected. And the *second* it stopped, my father...he collapsed." His throat bobbed. "He wasn't breathing. I couldn't find a pulse. It was as if the magic it took to transform me stole his life in exchange. The healer we summoned said it was a—a heart attack. But I know the truth. It was the price I paid to become *this*." His eyes swept down his body.

"It could have been a coincidence," I offered, although I knew it was in vain. Anything I could possibly say he'd undoubtedly told himself hundreds of times already. This wasn't the kind of burden that sat close to the surface, easily swayed by emotions or logic. This...this was ingrained in his soul, intertwined in the very fabric of his past. The roots of this conviction, that he'd killed his father, ran so deep that nothing anyone said would convince him otherwise.

If anyone could understand that, it was me.

He shook his head. "It wasn't a coincidence, Rose. You know how strong magic like that works. If I hadn't performed that spell, he'd still be alive."

"You don't know that for sure. Even if it was a consequence of the spell, you didn't do it on purpose, Leo. It wasn't your—"

He pulled away from me. "Accidental or not, it doesn't change the fact that it happened because of me. If a stray arrow kills a man, is it not the shooter's fault? Whether or not they *intended* to do so? How is this any different?"

My arms hung at my side. I didn't know what to say. A better person may have been able to come up with some sage advice or words of comfort, but that wasn't me. I knew if I were the one telling this story, I wouldn't want someone to mollify me. I'd just want to be *heard*. So I stayed quiet and let him speak.

"I ran inside to get my mother once I could move through the pain. I hid Father's Grimoire and any signs of what I'd been doing. I was so scared, so worried she would be angry. She and Rissa found out about the spell eventually, of course, but I never—I never told them it was the reason Father died. I never told them the details." He scrubbed a hand over his jaw, speaking more to himself than me at this point.

"Rissa still doesn't know?" I asked.

Leo shook his head.

I sat down on the edge of the bed, my mind reeling from the turn this night had taken. "Well, we're both pieces of work, aren't we?" I muttered. He let out a tired chuckle. His shoulders dropped, some of the tension leaving his body. He stopped pacing and stood before me, more timid than I'd ever seen the strong, assured Zareleon Aris.

Reaching out, I grabbed his hand and pulled him close, until his knees touched mine and I had to crane my neck to see his face.

"I know how that kind of guilt changes you," I said. "I don't think it was your fault, but *you* do, and that's shaped your entire life." I suddenly realized how similar this conversation was to the same one we'd had about Branock and my father. "Just...don't let it convince you that you're not an incredible man. We all make mistakes, and what you did, the love you had for your sister to be willing to go to the ends of the earth for her..." I shook my head. "I would give anything to have someone care for me that much. She's lucky to have you."

He tried to smile, but it didn't reach his eyes. I tugged on his arm to make him sit on the bed beside me. Wrapping my arms around his waist, I leaned my head on his shoulder. Perhaps I was turning into a hugger, after all.

A moment later, he rested his chin on top of my head. His hand found mine in my lap and he twisted our fingers together. I stared at the sight in silence, wondering when this had happened. When we'd begun to find comfort in each other's presence, where even a simple touch could calm our thoughts.

I hadn't thought about the second trial or the nightmares that awaited me when I fell asleep the entire time he'd been here. It was getting late, and it was dangerous for him to be in the palace, but the idea of him leaving made my stomach sink.

"Do you have to go?" I whispered, staring at the window.

He shifted at my side, bringing my attention back to him. His thumb drew a circle on my hand. "Not if you don't want me to."

"You're a rebel sneaking into the palace illegally, remember?" I said, biting my bottom lip. His eyes flicked down before meeting mine again. "You could get in trouble if you're caught."

"Then I won't get caught. If you want me to stay, I'll stay."

I stared back at him, inches from his face, those dark eyes drowning me whole. "I want you to stay."

His forehead fell to mine as his hand gripped my waist. "What are you doing to me?" he murmured.

We were both emotional. We'd both been through so much trauma, reliving these moments from our past that left us damaged. Was that what this was? Two people trying to deal with their brokenness? Because I'd never felt this before. I'd never had someone be this raw with me, someone I could share my demons with. This *pull* that tugged at me every time he was near...it was different.

With others, *I* pulled the strings. I hid behind a curtain and watched everything unfold. But Leo...he yanked that curtain away, forcing me into the light. Forcing me to face what I'd normally tuck away.

Like what I was feeling for him. And how much I wanted him to kiss me.

His nose trailed mine, so close his lashes grazed me when he blinked. Slowly, painfully slowly, his lips brushed against my cheek, the lightest of kisses sending a shiver down my spine and making my breath hitch. He dragged his mouth across my skin until it met the corner of my lips. Without realizing it, I squeezed the hand still intertwined with mine, my heart beating so loudly I was sure he could hear it. I felt his lips curve into a smile.

Knock knock.

"Everything alright in there?" Horace's voice rang through the air.

Leo pulled away. Irritation burned through me. In my mind, I twisted Horace's long, blonde beard around his own neck and choked him.

Rolling my neck on my shoulders, I let out a sigh. "Yes, I'm fine," I called back.

"Just checking." His knuckles rapped once on the door. "Thought I heard loud voices earlier."

"I want a new guard," I mumbled under my breath. Leo chuckled and eased himself onto his back, putting his arms behind his head.

I pushed onto my feet and made my way into the bathing chamber to wash my face and change for bed. Over the sound of running water, I heard Leo tease, "So, you think I'm incredible?"

Snorting, I pressed a towel to my face and stuck my head out the door. Seeing him lying in my bed so casually made my stomach flip. "*That's* the part you picked up on?"

He grinned. I walked around the room and blew out the candles, coating us in darkness save for the moonlight coming from the window. Sauntering to the bed, I sat on the edge across from him until he leaned over and pulled me closer.

"What, exactly, is so incredible about me?" he continued.

I shoved his side. "You're incredibly full of yourself, for one. And incredibly *moody*." He laid back and gazed at me, that lazy, happy smile so at odds with his hard lines and piercing eyes. "And thoughtful," I conceded, lowering on my side to face him. "Loyal. Handsome. Dedicated and compassionate."

He hummed, and the sound vibrated down my spine. "What was that?"

"Dedicated? Compassionate?"

"Before those." His fingers played with my hair on the pillow.

I rolled my eyes. "I guess one might find you handsome."

"Really, now?"

With a smirk, I batted his hand away. "I take it back. This is all going to your head."

He laughed then propped himself on his elbow to look down at me. His smile faded, replaced by an earnestness that made me swallow and fight not to look away.

"You're the incredible one, Rose," he said softly. "I've never told anyone about that night. About what the blood magic caused. Thank you for letting me."

"Of course," I responded, a little hoarsely. "You can tell me anything."

As I spoke the words, bitterness slithered up my throat, a reminder of what I was still keeping from him. The list kept growing. The cut on my thumb seared beneath the bandage, physical proof of my latest secret.

Blood magic. The very thing he believed killed his father.

But it didn't *have* to be that way, did it? It could be controlled. He was young; he hadn't known how to use it correctly.

Nothing that felt so right could possibly cause that much harm.

He leaned down and kissed my forehead. "Goodnight, Rose."

With a deep breath, I whispered back, "Goodnight."

50

ROSE

For the first time in forever, I was happy. Which didn't make any sense.

I was a challenger in a dangerous, deadly tournament meant to pit the provinces against one another. I was away from home in a city I barely knew, surrounded by strangers. My uncle was cursed. My *other* uncle was the ruler of the Veridian Empire. Nightmares of my past, of blood and loss and darkness, crept on the edges of my mind whenever I bothered to look close enough. And I was keeping secrets from the only man I'd ever let into my heart.

Past me would have laughed. I had no reason to be this happy. No *right*.

But...while I hated what the Decemvirate stood for, it had brought some unexpected friendships into my life. The twins, of course, and Lark and Horace—who I'd reconciled with after my outburst from the second trial. I knew they were simply doing their jobs and that they'd had no idea what the dreamscape would entail. Nobody had. And it's not as if I could stay angry with Horace for long. He was like a big, grumpy teddy bear, trailing me throughout the palace, always watching over me and making me laugh.

390

I'd spent more time with Nox and, surprisingly, Arowyn over the last few days—or rather, Nox and I had forced her into our company, and she seemed to think we were tolerable. Two days after the memorial, Nox and I had been heading to the library when Arowyn stormed through the palace in a tirade, her pale cheeks flushed with anger. Nox had tried to stop her and find out what was wrong, but she used her Strider abilities to disappear from his grip.

Fifteen minutes later, she'd magicked right to our table in the library. I almost had a heart attack. She'd put her finger to her lips in warning, grabbed a book, and acted as if she'd been there the whole time. Mere seconds after that, we heard a very angry Callum marching past the library doors with a small battalion of guards on his heels.

Arowyn picked at her nails with a shrug. "He must be having a bad day."

Ever since then, she, Nox, and I had formed a tentative friendship.

They weren't the only ones I spent my time with over the next few days. I had breakfast with Beau and Morgana every morning at Ragnar's bedside, followed by a walk through the palace gardens. It was getting...not *easier*, but more bearable to see my uncle lying lifeless in his bed. Because for once, I had hope.

After I'd seen what blood magic could do, I had hope. I was going to find a way to end the Somnivae curse *without* sacrificing anyone.

I spent any spare moment I had poring over the pages of my father's Grimoire or hunting in the palace library for more information on curses and blood magic. All my fear, all my guilt, all my bitterness had melted into resolve. If Leo could change the very *makeup* of his body, then surely I could find a way to undo what Theodore's spell had caused all those years ago.

Having a purpose, a *goal*, lit a fire in me. It bled into everything I did.

And I was happy. As happy as I could be, at least. My days were spent with friends or with magic, and my nights were spent with Leo.

He'd made a habit of sneaking up to my rooms almost every evening when he didn't have patrol duty. We had a routine now of casting defensive charms around the space to protect him from discovery. I think he knew without me having to say anything that I was afraid of the night after what had happened in the second trial. The idea of going to sleep, unsure where I'd be when I woke up, haunted me. But the nightmares weren't as bad when he was by my side. Any time they grabbed me, he was there, holding me through it and bringing me back.

I think he needed me, too. We were so much more alike than I would have ever imagined. Growing up, we'd both been surrounded by people who thought we were *other*, who didn't understand us or feared getting too close. He loved his sister and his friends, that much was obvious, but there were some things he couldn't talk to them about. Knowing he trusted me, that he wanted to let me in on the darkest parts of him, that *I* was the one he turned to when he needed comfort...it was a desire I never knew I had. Every time I settled into his side and he stroked my hair, our whispered stories and confessions filling the space between us, I felt more at home than I ever had in Feywood.

It pushed my determination to find an answer for the curse to a whole new level. The idea of losing him wasn't an option.

I just needed to be strong enough. I needed my *magic* to be strong enough.

So I practiced.

When Leo left before dawn in the mornings, I studied my father's Grimoire. I relearned my old spells without the aid of herbs and charms, relishing the release and thrill of practicing magic based in my very blood. They were simple spells, ones that didn't require much, but even that was enough to unlock a new part of me. Power soared and coated my veins, unchaining me. I'd been living my life with one hand tied behind my back.

But now, I was free.

One way or another, I would find a way to end this curse *and* keep Leo safe.

Five days had passed since the last time I'd seen Theodore. I was becoming restless, wondering if he'd forgotten about his promise to teach me. Only nine days remained till the masquerade ball and soon after, the third trial would follow. And then...I would have to go back to Feywood. A desperate longing gripped me when I thought about it. I couldn't believe half my time here in the capital had already gone by; it felt as if I'd only just arrived, and yet I could hardly imagine what my life was like even a month ago.

As I grabbed a fourth book from the shelf and carried my growing pile to the table Nox, Arowyn, and I had claimed at the library, I shoved thoughts of masquerade balls and trials and *good-byes* from my mind. There was still time—I didn't need to worry about that yet.

"You know, if you'd told me we'd be spending all our time in the library, I never would've agreed to hang out with you two," Arowyn drawled, twisting her near-white hair around her finger and throwing her legs onto the top of the table.

"Yes, you would have. You can't resist our charm," Nox countered, smacking her feet with a book. "Feet off the table."

She stuck her tongue out at him and moved her feet to his lap instead. "Remind me again why we're here?"

"Because I don't have access to this many books on magic in Feywood and I want to take advantage of it while I can," I responded, flipping through *Alchemy Index Volume III: Blood Rites*. I'd been feeding them half-truths; there *weren't* this many books back home. But my search was focused on a bit more than general magic. "And Nox thinks he looks good in reading glasses," I added and nodded to Nox, who readjusted said glasses.

"It's true; I do."

"Well, *I'm* bored." Arowyn kicked her legs off Nox and stood. "I'm going to go sneak some wine from the cellars. Maybe see if I can find Callum and make him piss his pants again."

"Did you notice she always seems to have alcohol in her hands?" Nox whispered loudly to me.

Arowyn rolled her eyes. "And did *you* notice you have an incredibly small—"

"Fates, am I going to have to separate the two of you?" I asked with an exasperated laugh. "Let me read in peace."

Sighing, Nox said, "You don't have to be so rude ab—"

Before he finished his sentence, a flaming sheet of parchment appeared midair, floating down onto the table in front of me.

Arowyn promptly sat back down. "What's that?"

I knew exactly what it was. Theodore was the only one who'd delivered a message to me this way.

Snatching it from the table and blowing out the smoldering edges, I scanned the familiar cursive, hurriedly tucked it into my pocket, then glanced at the clock on the library wall.

"Secrets are for the bedroom or the grave, darling," Nox said, clicking his tongue and eyeing me curiously.

"It's from my aunt. She and Beau want to have dinner tonight." The lie slipped from me like honey. "Speaking of which, I should probably get ready." As I spoke, I stacked my books and collected my various notes, anticipation coursing inside me at the thought of another magic lesson.

"I thought we were going to meet in my room tonight," Nox reminded me. "I found that stash of Luxe Arowyn and I wanted to try, and *you* agreed to be our sober caretaker."

"Oh—right. I don't know what time we'll be done with dinner. How about tomorrow?" I asked, grabbing my bag.

I felt a slice of guilt at the disappointed expression on his features. I'd forgotten we'd made plans for the night. Nox was especially excited to try the palace's favorite drink, the green one Horace had told me about my first day here. But Theodore's message said he wanted to meet in less than an hour, and I had no idea how long our lesson would last.

Arowyn shrugged. "Fine with me. Wouldn't want to get in the way of whatever shady deal you've got going on tonight."

I blinked at her, my lips parting. Before I could respond, she grinned at me lazily. "Kidding. Have fun with your family. We'll try to save some for you."

My heartbeat slowed and I threw them a quick wave, then checked my books out at the librarian's desk and headed back to my room.

I was weaving so many webs of lies. Part of me wondered how much longer I'd be able to control it, or if I'd soon become ensnared myself.

———

"You've been practicing," Thedore said, nodding his head approvingly at the apple I'd frozen midair. He plucked it from the empty space and took a bite out of it.

As he crunched on the sweet red fruit, I rubbed the drop of blood still blooming at the cut on my finger and muttered, "*Voquer.*" The apple flew from his lips mid-bite and into my outstretched hand. I tossed it and caught it again, crossing my arms and smirking at the look on his face. "These are spells I've known since I was eight, Theodore. I thought you were going to teach me something *new*?"

He smiled, tapping his nose with a wrinkled finger then pulling his long hair back, securing it with a leather strap at the nape of his neck. "Very well. I assume you are familiar with common healing spells and tinctures?"

Nodding, I recounted the various herbs and oils I usually used for healing, most of which I'd seen on the shelves of his den we were currently practicing in. "Cedarwood for wounds, ginger for pain relief, carnations to restore strength." I ticked names off on my fingers. "Fleawort, elderberry, a bit of lavender mixed with—"

He cut me off with a chuckle. "You've made your point. Quite the studious Alchemist. You may understand the basic principles behind these charms, yes, but what about how it *feels*?" He crossed the room to me, that intense passion kindled in his mismatched eyes. "If you no longer rely on the nature around you to aid in the healing process, you must call on the power within *yourself*. It's more than these simple spells you've been practicing. Performing magic on another living being instead of inanimate objects is profoundly more difficult."

Theodore held out his hand and sliced a thin mark into his scar-littered palm, letting the blood well as he murmured a spell. Out of nowhere, a small crow appeared in his hand. I jumped backward, surprised by the shrill caw as it flapped its wings but stayed in place, looking around at its surroundings with beady eyes. Theodore stroked its head and tittered to calm its anxious fidgeting.

"Wh—*how* did you—"

I didn't get the chance to finish my question. Before I could blink, he took one of the bird's wings between his other forefinger and thumb and snapped it.

I let out a sharp gasp and covered my mouth. Its shriek echoed in my ears, making my stomach roll with disgust.

"Come here, Rose," Theodore said quietly. "You can heal it. Take its pain away."

I shook my head, still processing what he'd done. "I—I can't. It doesn't work that quickly. Healing takes time. That bird will suffer for—"

"That is how your magic *used* to work." He came closer and I sucked in a breath, my body going tense. "Trust me, niece. You can do so much more than you have ever dreamed."

Swallowing hard, I cautiously stepped forward, my brow furrowed in concern. I'd healed minor injuries on myself and others countless times in my life, but it always took time. Nothing worked instantly; even the miraculous healing potion Leo gave me after the first trial took hours to work. Being able to fix a wound like this *instantly*? It was life changing.

I picked up the knife from the nearby desk and held it to my finger. The sharp sting had become second nature at this point.

"Feel the injury," he instructed, cupping the bird in both hands and holding it out to me. "Imagine being able to see the shattered bones, the torn muscles. Look beneath the flesh and picture your magic, *your* blood, coursing through it. Replacing weakness with strength. Pain with comfort. Broken with whole."

I placed my trembling, bloody finger on the bent curve of the wing, flinching when the bird squawked at my touch. I could feel the unnatural angle of its matted feathers, the fragmented bone beneath soft plumes.

I took a deep breath.

"*Revie scurae.*"

The healing spell flowed out of me like a shadow, into the trickle of blood, and over the little creature. I did what Theodore commanded; I envisioned the bone snapping back into place, pictured its wing restored and strengthened with my magic pulsing through it. As the tip of my finger throbbed with heat, I felt that same addictive, tantalizing sensation of every pore, every vein, every cell flooding with power, like a window being thrown open to let in the sun.

There was a small crack.

The bird flexed its wings and let out a caw as its feathers ruffled. It pushed out of Theodore's hands and took flight, soaring around the room.

I tracked its movements with my mouth hanging open. It was perfectly healthy, as if nothing had even happened. In a heartbeat, in a single breath, I had taken away its pain. I had healed it completely.

"Impossible," I whispered. What *else* could I do? What else could this amazing magic I'd once thought of as forbidden accomplish?

Theodore shook his head. "Nothing is impossible, Rose. Not anymore."

51
LEO

"You have *got* to be kidding me. You expect me to wear this?"

Rose laughed next to me on the settee. "It's a *masquerade*, Lark. What did you think you were going to wear?"

"I look ridiculous."

"Rose is right—you have to wear the mask. And you look amazing," Rissa said, standing next to Lark and the full length mirror. Snapping at Horace, Chaz, and me with her fingers, my twin said, "Doesn't she look amazing, boys?"

I eyed Lark in her pale pink gown and silver mask with light blue stones framing the eyes, a matching pink feather extending from the left side. To be quite honest, I didn't care what any of them wore to the Decemvirate ball in a week and a half. The whole thing felt ridiculous, another way to turn the tournament into a pageant. But my sister thought we could all use a reprieve from the intensity of the past weeks, so here we were. Picking out ball gowns and masks for an evening only three of us would be able to attend.

Perhaps she was right, though. This afternoon was one of the first ones in recent memory where we were all together with no mission or emergency to discuss. I'd almost forgotten what it was like.

Chaz, who was slumped in the velvet chair opposite me, cleared his throat. "You look—"

"Like a flamingo," Lark finished. "I look like a *bird*."

Rissa pinched her lips together to keep from giggling. "But a very *pretty* bird." At the glare Lark shot her, my sister lifted her hands in the air. "Alright, fine. Let's try the next one."

The two of them shuffled off into the back of the shop. Horace and Chaz struck up a conversation, and I looked over at Rose, who was smiling softly into her glass of sparkling wine.

"What's that look for?" I murmured.

Trailing a finger along the rim of the glass, she shrugged and said, "This is...nice. Being with you all." She met my eyes and smiled. "Being with friends."

I would give the world for that smile. It got a little brighter, a little more genuine, with every night we spent together.

A small crease appeared on her brow. "Are you sure it's safe for us to be here? Don't you and Rissa try to stay out of public as much as possible?"

"In most areas of the capital, yes. But here in the south sector, we can roam a bit more freely." I motioned to the front of the dress salon, where the owner moved about organizing her displays. "Mali is a close friend. We trust her. She's a Sentinel, as are many of the shop-keepers and merchants around here. They've all been victims at some point or another and want to see change. Almost anyone who may walk through that door is someone who knows us and wouldn't dare report us. And if we get worried, that's what Horace is for."

"Why, because he's a member of the Guard?" Rose asked.

"That, and he's an Illusionist. He's used to disguising our appearances if we get in a tight spot."

The color drained from Rose's face. Her lips parted and she clenched the stem of her flute. "He's a *what*?"

Sensing a shift in the mood, Horace and Chaz paused their

conversation and glanced back at the two of us. Fixing Horace with an expectant stare, Rose asked, "Why didn't I know you're an Illusionist?"

"You never asked," he said simply.

I squeezed Rose's knee, confused by her reaction, until I saw fear flash behind the outrage.

Her father. He'd been murdered by an Illusionist.

Still staring at Horace, she asked, "After what Callum did to me, you didn't think that was something I'd want to know?"

"Don't compare me to him, girl," Horace said, a warning in his voice. "There are bad seeds in every province. Just because we share the same magic doesn't mean we're anything alike."

Rose's jaw shifted as she swallowed, her eyes searching Horace as if looking for some hidden secret. Nobody spoke, the tension thick and heady, until Rissa strode out from the back of the shop.

"Are you ready to see the next one?" she asked.

"I need some air." Rose abruptly stood and made her way to the front, the bell above the door chiming as she exited.

Rissa crossed her arms. "Leo, what did you do?"

"What makes you think I did something?"

"Just a guess."

I ignored her and rose from the settee. "Let me go talk to her."

Following Rose's path, I left the shop and spotted her pacing in front of an alley adjacent to the building. I gathered her hands in mine and led her into the alleyway, away from wandering shoppers. Several rough bandages on the tips of her fingers scratched my skin.

"Talk to me, Rose," I said gently.

She took a deep breath. "I can't believe I didn't know he was one of *them*," she said, a bite to her tone. "How do we know he hasn't been lying to us this whole time? He can hide anything. *Be* anything. Make us think one thing and do another."

"I know you've had bad experiences with Illusionists," I said, tucking a strand of hair behind her ear and keeping my hand cupped at her neck. "But they're not all the same. You know Horace is a good man, Rose. His magic doesn't change that. He would give his life for any one of us."

She closed her eyes. "You're right. I just wish I had known. With what Callum has done to me, and the men who killed my father..." When she opened her eyes, they flashed at me fiercely. "They're still out there. Illusionists are *dangerous*."

I squeezed her neck one more time and let go. "Their magic can be dangerous, but just because some have abused that power doesn't mean they all have. Take Gayl, for example. One of the most dangerous Alchemists in the world, but you and I aren't like him." Rose shifted on her feet. "And Callum may use his magic to torment, but Horace uses it to *help*. You have to be able to see beyond the power and into the person. We're more than our magic."

She met my gaze. "Are we, though?"

A prickle crept down my spine. "What do—"

"I need to go apologize to Horace, alright?" Placing her hand on my cheek, she softly ran her thumb across my skin. I nodded and kissed the inside of her palm before she took it away. We walked out of the alleyway and reentered the shop to find Lark and Rissa both in ball gowns. Lark wore a stunning black velvet dress that hugged her large curves, with gold beads dotting the waist and neckline. Her mask was solid gold with black lace and had what appeared to be antlers rising from the sides, beyond her mass of black curls.

"Is that *bone*?" Rose asked with intrigue, stepping toward Lark. In answer, Lark gave a smirk and ran her gloved fingers along one of the ivory antlers. "That's incredible. You have to get this one."

"Rissa, why are you trying anything on? You know we can't go to the ball," I said, taking in her red gown and brown fur wrap. Chaz, my sister, and I were here solely for moral support.

Rissa smiled slyly and pulled a mask from behind her back, holding it up to her eyes. Chaz and Horace let out barks of laughter. Swirls of red, gold, and orange raced across the mask, extending down to the tip of a long nose and up to a pair of pointed ears.

"A bit on the nose there, sister," I said, grinning at her fox mask.

She winked. "I couldn't resist."

As Rissa straightened out Lark's dress, Rose approached Horace and sat across from him on the settee.

"I'm sorry, Horace," she said. "I wasn't trying to compare you to Callum. I was surprised and reacted poorly."

He grunted in response, rubbing a hand over his beard. "Don't be sorry. I should've said something before. That boy's messed with your head enough. I guess I didn't want you to be scared of me, too."

Her lips quirked up at him. "I could never be scared of you."

With a glower, he crossed his arms. "Well, *now* I'm offended."

Chaz kicked him with the tip of his boot. "She's right, big guy. You wouldn't hurt a fly."

Rolling his eyes to the ceiling, Horace mumbled incoherently under his breath, his beard twitching with the movement as he got to his feet and lumbered away. Something that sounded like "more wine" drifted back to us, and the tension from before dissipated into laughter.

"Rose, come on!" Rissa said, waving a hand at her. "We need to find you something to wear."

Rose pretended to look disgruntled as she heaved herself from the cushions, but I saw a smile flash on the corners of her lips. She looked back at me and the grin widened, her nose scrunching with hidden excitement, when Rissa took her hand and hauled her away.

"You're beaming like a fool," Chaz's deep voice said from beside me.

Was I?

"She's got to you," he continued smugly. "I knew it."

"Knew what?" Horace asked, rejoining us with a large, murky glass bottle in his hand.

I eyed the bottle. "*That* is not wine."

Chaz ignored me and answered Horace. "Knew Leo was a goner for Rose."

"Obviously." Horace took a swig of the dark amber liquid. "Why do you think I asked you to keep an eye on her when I couldn't?"

"You little matchmaker," Chaz said with a chuckle.

I scowled. "You two are ridiculous."

"That may be true." Horace shrugged, handing me the bottle. "But are we wrong?"

Without responding, I took the drink and raised it to my lips, swallowing the bitter liquid. I choked as it slithered down my throat like thick acid. My face screwed in disgust. "Fates, Horace, that's horrible."

He took it back. "I know. Can only find this stuff here in the south sector."

"What, is it too offensive for their *delicate sensibilities* up in the palace?" Chaz teased, swiping the bottle from Horace and taking a drink.

"You'd be surprised by the drinks they have up there," Horace countered. "That stuff is a little more dangerous than strong liquor."

Chaz scratched his beard. "There's the green wine for a good time, and then the gray one, right? The wine that makes it impossible to lie."

"Grimlock," I confirmed, nodding. "It makes you more susceptible to telling the truth."

"They've been trying to slip it to me the past few days," Horace said absently.

Chaz and I both straightened, jokes forgotten. "What?" I snapped. "*Grimlock?*"

Horace closed his eyes and leaned back. "Caught the head of the Guard pouring some into my cup three nights ago. I created an Illusion to make him think I drank it, but threw it out the first chance I had."

"Why would they do that?" Chaz asked. "Are they trying to interrogate you?"

"The Sentinels are making waves, even among the Guard. I think they're suspicious of me. Heard talk of meetings being called in secret, but myself and a couple others haven't been invited to most of them." Horace took another drink, his monotone voice hiding any emotion behind his report. "Was relieved of some of my duties yesterday and today. No reason, no notice. It might all be coincidence, but I wonder if they're planning something." His jaw clenched ever so slightly beneath his full beard. He was trying to conceal any worries he had about this latest development, but I could tell it bothered him.

"As in, planning something against us?" I asked.

"I don't know." Horace paused and practically drained the bottle on his next gulp. He was acting strange. More distant and aloof, even for him. "I'm trying to find out what I can, but there's only so much I can do if they're starting not to trust me."

Grabbing the bottle from him, I set it onto the table in front of us. "Horace, we know you're doing everything you can. But we want you to be smart. Stay safe. If you need to lie low for a little while and cut ties with us until they trust you again, we understand."

He nodded curtly, his shoulders dropping a fraction. "Figured you'd say that."

Something snapped into place. Had he been hesitant to tell us this news because he knew we'd warn him to stay away? I'd never stopped to consider how Horace felt about his precarious position, how much weight the Sentinels had thrusted onto his shoulders. Living a double life, carrying the expectations of both sides of his duties, unable to fully let himself rest or be at peace...and yet he did it without complaint. We were more than a mission to him. More than a job or side project.

We were his only family, and here I was, telling him to keep his distance. Acting as if he meant nothing to us besides another asset to the rebellion.

Scrubbing a hand down my face, I said, "You're important to us, Horace, but not only for the work you do undercover." I clapped a hand on his shoulder. "There's nobody else I'd rather have by my side. You know that."

"Yeah, and if they get too nosey, just say screw 'em and come back down here with us lowly folk," Chaz chimed in.

Horace huffed out a laugh. "It won't come to that. Wouldn't want to leave you high and dry without a man on the inside."

"Rissa would pull you from the palace in a second if she thought you were threatened," I said. "You're not a disposable pawn, brother. We need you because of who you *are*, not what you can do for us."

Chaz nodded. "Leo's right. Don't let yourself get caught trying to be a hero. Or worse, a martyr. Take care of yourself in there."

With a nod, Horace cleared his throat and swiped at his nose. "Thanks, boys," he said brusquely. I raised an eyebrow at Chaz. This was the most emotion we'd ever seen from the rough, burly guard.

"Oh, come on, who made Horace cry again?" Rissa said from the back of the shop as she and the other two women emerged.

When I saw Rose, my lips parted on an exhale.

Chaz guffawed. "Like I said. Goner."

52

ROSE

I met his gaze across the dress salon, and everything around us faded. I didn't know how I felt about the *look* he was giving me.

It was too much but not enough at the same time. His eyes were dark, hot coals, and I was the flame they craved. Even in the middle of the shop with others surrounding us, he made me feel like I was the only person in the room. The only person that *mattered*.

I decided I liked it.

My lips curved into a sinful smirk. I held the lace burgundy mask to my face, batting my eyelashes at the boys. The slit in the matching gown opened to my thigh, and Leo's eyes drifted across my skin before anchoring back to my eyes.

"Do you like this one?" I asked innocently, turning in a circle to give him a view of the glittering silver buttons that were only done halfway up my back.

"I do," Chaz called out appreciatively. Leo glared at him.

"I need some help buttoning this," I said to Leo, motioning toward the back of my dress. Rissa and Lark said something to the other two about finding a mask for Horace, but I was too focused on Leo and the black shirt straining at his chest as he put his hands on his knees and slowly rose from the couch. While the others talked, he stalked toward me, the heat in his eyes burning through the layers of this burgundy gown.

"Turn around," he commanded, and I obeyed.

I set the mask down and faced the full length mirror, watching as his hand carefully brushed my mass of hair over one shoulder, knuckles kissing the nape of my neck. His fingers trailed down the bare skin at my back, eliciting a shiver through my entire body. He met my stare in the mirror as he found the first button.

"Look at you," he said, lowering his lips to brush the tip of my ear. "So beautiful."

The entire world could have been drowning and I wouldn't have cared. I was set ablaze, every part of me honed in on his fingers, his chest at my back, his lips grazing my skin.

He took his time with the buttons. I couldn't tear my gaze away from our reflection—his sharp jawline shadowed in deep brown scruff, those black eyes that glittered back at me. They swept over the exposed skin at my leg, the fabric clinging to my waist and hips, the dip of the neckline and wine-colored sleeves that hung off my shoulders. His stare made my cheeks blush and my breath catch.

I'd never thought much beyond my appearance besides what it could do for me. Beauty was either a weapon or a shield. Something you were hated or desired for in equal measure. But the way he looked at me, the way *he* called me beautiful…it felt like devotion. A plea for me to see what he saw, to see past the layers of armor I wore like a second skin.

He thought I was beautiful. Even after seeing my bitterness, my anger and fear and everything in between.

It was…liberating, to be wanted so deeply, despite all of the reasons nobody had wanted me before. *Because* of those reasons. But more than that was the way he made me believe it could be true. The way he helped me see myself through his eyes. A woman who didn't have to hide. A woman who could challenge others instead of push them back.

"Is this the one you'll be wearing to the ball?" he asked, fingering the sheer fabric of the sleeves.

I spun to face him and patted his chest. "Maybe. Such a shame you can't go. I'll have to find someone else to wear the matching suit."

He gripped my wrist, narrowing his eyes. "Careful, little wolf," he rumbled, the sound shooting to my core.

Rissa slinked up beside me and grabbed my other hand. "There are a couple more gowns that caught my eye for you."

Leo glowered at his sister as I pulled away. "She's the boss," I said, winking.

The two of us walked back to the dressing room, which was a chaotic mess of tulle, heels, feathers, and satin. Rissa pulled me to the clothing rack and held up another dress.

"You know, for someone who leads an entire rebellion, you sure are messy," I pointed out with a laugh as she tossed the gown to the ground.

She waved her hand in the air. "People are easy, if you can find what keeps them motivated. *Fashion*, on the other hand..." Smiling, she brandished a sleeveless black gown that billowed like a dark cloud at the waist. Intricate silver flowers trailed down the skirt, sparkling when they caught the light from the high window.

"Black?" I questioned. "That doesn't seem like your style."

"Haven't you heard? Black is this year's pink." She winked and hung the dress separately from the others. "Besides, it's not for me. I happen to know it's Leo's favorite color."

I snorted. "Why am I not surprised?"

She helped me undo the buttons on the burgundy gown. I'd enjoyed spending more time with her today. There were so many things about the bright-eyed, exuberant yet level-headed leader that intrigued me. She was an enigma; calm and easy going, full of jokes and laughter. But I'd seen the other side—the calculated Sentinel, the woman who could take charge and bend others to her will with a single sentence. How had she become this fearless figurehead who commanded such respect?

Stepping out of the first dress, my curiosity took control. "So, Leo told me a little about your childhoods," I said slowly. "I had no idea how difficult it was for Shifters when your magic comes in so young."

Rissa handed me the black gown. "It feels like a lifetime ago, honestly. I remember the first time I shifted—partially, anyway. I was nine. My mother had scolded me for not cleaning my room. She said I wasn't allowed to go outside and play with Leo until I made the bed. I was so angry that when I tried grabbing the pillows, my hand shifted into a paw." She chuckled, her blonde curls waving. "Shredded right through the fabric. But Mother was so excited, she didn't even care."

I let out a soft laugh, then cleared my throat. "He said the beginning was challenging. I could tell it was hard for him to watch you go through that."

Her features tightened slightly. "Yes, well, adolescence wasn't easy. For either of us."

"No, it wasn't," I murmured in agreement. "But look at you now. You're..." I waved my hand at her and she smiled.

"Quite impossible to describe? I get that a lot." She smirked playfully, but her face fell a moment later. "Sometimes I wonder if things would have turned out differently had Leo and I not been forced to grow up so fast. Our father died suddenly when we were twelve, and Mother got sick not long after. We didn't have anyone to help us hone our magic. I had to learn how to control my emotions, to keep a cool head and work through the hard days without losing myself to my Shifter half. Most people have years— *decades*—to master that, but I..." Her eyes drifted to the side while I finished pulling on the gown. "Suffice it to say, tolerance and acceptance didn't always extend to people like me."

"I suppose that's what makes you such a successful leader," I mused.

Rissa fussed over the fabric of the front of my skirt, smoothing it down and fluffing the bottom. "What makes you say that?"

"Because *you* had to learn tolerance through that. You had to figure out how to put what was important over your own emotions, all while dealing with your grief and being shunned by society." I shook my head and let out a long breath. Rissa had made the most of her trauma, wearing it like a battle scar and sharpening it as a tool. I, on the other hand, had let mine pierce me through. "It might have been for survival at first, but I can see it in everything you do now. Even if I've only known you a couple weeks."

She flushed. "Here I was thinking you were trying to get my brother to fall in love with you, not *me*."

My heart stuttered, then picked up speed as my body jerked reflexively. "What? I don't—"

"Oh, please," she said with a smirk. "I can hear your pulse from a mile away." When I moved again, she winced and looked down at her hand, where a small dot of blood had bloomed from a pin snagging her skin.

"Sorry," I said with a cringe, reaching for a handkerchief next to my bag and helping her wipe the blood away. The cut healed within seconds. "How far *can* you hear, anyway?"

She shrugged. "It depends what form I'm in. Fully shifting gives me the most powerful instincts. But even partial increases my senses a bit." In the blink of an eye, her dark irises took on a golden tinge and her human ears lengthened until I was staring at two fox ears on the side of her normal human face. She wiggled them at me.

"How efficient," I said with a laugh. Motioning toward the doors leading to where the others gathered, I asked, "What are they talking about back there?"

She paused and listened, her lips pulling up. "Lark is pestering Horace, Chaz is laughing at the beak mask Lark made Horace try on, and Leo's staying quiet. Probably brooding since I took you away from him."

My cheeks heated again and she laughed, turning me so she could lace up the gown. "I haven't seen him this happy in...I don't know how long. I think you're good for him, you know."

The blush spread to my neck. "We're not—we haven't really talked about…" I trailed off, unsure what I was even trying to say. Whatever was between us was fleeting. How could it be anything else, when I was leaving in less than two weeks?

Rissa raised an eyebrow. "You think I don't notice him sneaking back home at the crack of dawn every morning?" She fixed my hair so it flowed down the side of my neck. "You light a fire in him, Rose. One I haven't seen in ages. I think my little brother is so used to being the protector that he sometimes forgets how to live his life outside of that role. He's become jaded and cynical, with a one-track mind. But lately, he's been like his younger self. More present. He gets along better with everyone and even makes jokes. A little irritable, sure"—we both laughed at that—"but he's finally passionate about something other than the mission." She spun me to face her, dark eyes sparkling. "And my gut tells me *you* might feel the same, yes?"

I pinched my lips together. "We barely know each other."

"On the contrary, I think you know each other better than most of the people you let into your lives do."

Fates, she was annoyingly accurate.

"I'm leaving in two weeks," I said in another feeble attempt to brush off the turn in this conversation.

"I know." Her keen gaze pierced me. "But think about this. If none of this existed, no rebellion, no tournament, no divisive provinces and hundreds of miles between you…would you want to be with him?"

My jaw shifted. What was I supposed to say? That Leo was the first man to see beneath my armor? That he made me feel valued and cherished and desirable and protected, all at the same time? I'd spent my entire life hiding from emotions like this, and yet in mere weeks, he'd uncovered my angry, smothered heart and showed me how to make it feel joy.

I'd never thought much about my future beyond running the Arcane. It was mostly blurry images of passing time, with the shop and my magic as the only constants. Often, I didn't even picture *myself*—my future was more of an abstract idea. A predetermined route. An endless void ahead of me.

Imagining anything but Feywood and the shop felt futile. Except sometimes...

Sometimes I wanted more. In those brief moments of solitude, those stolen breaths between the expected and ordinary.

I wanted freedom. Freedom from the past that weighed me down like an anchor. Freedom from the shadowed reputation I couldn't seem to run from.

I wanted purpose. I wanted my work, my magic, my voice, to mean something, even if it was just to myself.

And perhaps...I wanted him, too.

"Yes," I whispered, before my senses got the better of me and I retreated to my shell.

The moment I admitted it, my hands became clammy. I wiped them along the soft fabric of the black gown, tearing my stare from Rissa's. I hadn't allowed myself to go there, to picture anything outside of the confines of the tournament. I took it one day, one night, one flirtatious smile at a time. Nothing more. Because in the end, I was still keeping secrets from him. From *everyone*.

I was the rose with thorns on the vine. *I* was the one with hidden secrets, the deceitful tongue, the poison the Oracle had spoken of. Anything in my path was likely to be struck. How could I expect Leo to want me once he found out the truth? That despite his vulnerability and trust in me, I'd still lied to him?

I glanced back up at Rissa, who gave me a knowing look. "Then I guess you have a choice to make, don't you?"

An incredulous laugh bubbled out of me, breaking through my anxiety. "A *choice*? Rissa, you can't expect me to walk away from my life for a man I met not even three weeks ago."

"That's not what I meant." She backed up to the dress rack, picking up gowns along the way. "You have to decide if your happiness is worth the risk, or if you're going to let fear of the unknown get in the way."

I ran my finger along my lip, letting her words sink in. "Has Leo ever complained about how irritatingly perceptive you are?"

"It's one of my many amazing qualities. So"—she clapped her hands together—"do you like the dress? Is this the one?"

I faced the mirror, twisting my hair into a bun and assessing my reflection. It *was* a beautiful dress. The silver vines and flowers on the black fabric made it look like something out of a dark fairytale.

But in the mirror, another dress caught my eye. It was cast aside from the others, as if an afterthought. Discarded. Unwanted.

My lips curved upward. I nodded my head to the shadowed corner where it lay tossed over a stack of boxes. A matching mask rested on the ground beside it.

"*That's* the one."

She followed my gaze, then looked back at me with a feral grin. "Perfect."

A second later, Chaz came bursting through the door, causing Rissa and me to jump in alarm.

"There's been an attack," he said swiftly, his chest heaving. "We need to go."

53

ROSE

We rode hard through the small villages and forests of the south sector. Leo's viselike grip on the reins held me in place between his arms as we followed Chaz's lead northeast. Adrenaline raced in my veins and branches scraped against my skin, wind and sunlight beating down on my cheeks.

Leo quickly explained as we dashed out of the dress shop that a group of fugitives from Emberfell had recently arrived from the northern province. There were several families seeking to escape from the violence on their border with Drakorum, hoping to find a better life waiting for them in Veridia City.

But they quickly learned there were monsters in every corner of our empire.

Enraged Veridians had ambushed the families in their little shack in Ridgemore, a community in the east sector. A neighboring Strider who happened to know of the Sentinels had magicked to Rissa as quickly as possible with the news, but it had taken him some time to find us, even with his powers. Dread gripped me at what those precious minutes could have cost the victims.

We slowed as we reached a more populated area. When Chaz turned right at the end of the busy street, the change in atmosphere was almost immediate. The tidy, shining brick structures gave way to rotted wooden buildings. Moss and overgrown vines hung between windows and across entry ways. Rodents and people alike scurried over the gravel, the latter not pausing for casual conversation or to exchange pleasantries.

We traveled until signs of life and civilization became background noise to the rustle of wind through trees and birds crying in the distance. I spotted an occasional dingy house or field of crops, but it was mostly an isolated part of the east sector.

Chaz halted just short of a broken fencepost, and that's when I saw it.

A small cottage, no larger than two or three rooms, with boarded windows and patched holes in the roof. Two small children—a toddler and one perhaps five years older—huddled in the dirt, little eyes tired and frightened.

And blood smeared on the front door.

A warning.

Rissa and Leo dismounted and handed their reins to Chaz, who secured them to the fencepost. Lark swiftly but calmly made her way to the children while the twins and Horace drew their weapons, being careful not to alarm the young ones. The four of them worked seamlessly together, each knowing their role and carrying it out without question.

My chest tightened at the thought that they'd had to do this many times before.

Commotion and distressed voices reached my ears as we approached the blood splattered door. It banged open and a middle-aged woman came flying outside, her face streaked with tears, her hands the color of dried blood.

Her eyes widened as she took in the sight of our weapons.

"We're not here to hurt you," Rissa said smoothly. "We've heard there's been an attack and came to help."

The hesitancy on the woman's face was evident, but based on the cries coming from the cottage, we were the least of her worries.

"They struck so fast," she whispered hoarsely, turning to the side to allow us entry into the house. "We didn't know what to do."

The sight that greeted us made a chill creep down my spine.

Broken glass littered the wooden floorboards. Sections of the walls were splintered with holes, like someone had thrown heavy objects at them. Clothes and fabric and curtains were ripped to shreds and red dripped across the floor, glistening in spots of sunlight shining from torn pockets in the roof.

There were so many *people*. At least a dozen, if not more, crammed into this small, dilapidated space. Feet shuffled frantically across the room, cries and moans filled the air, and there were devastated faces and voices and tears everywhere my eyes landed. Several bodies lay on the ground with pools of blood drying where they rested.

"Who are you?" a burly man in a torn white shirt barked at us. A blunt knife was clutched in his outstretched, bloody hand and swirls of light were poised in the other. Magic bloomed in the air as two others joined him, Emberfell Lightbenders preparing to strike.

"My name is Clarissa," Rissa said, unfazed by their defensive stances. "We mean you no harm. We're part of a group here in the capital dedicated to helping people like you find safety. I know we're strangers to you, but please, let us help." She brandished an arm to Leo and me. "We have Alchemists who can heal your wounded and others who can provide protection while you get back on your feet. Just tell us what you need."

The three leaders of the families exchanged wary looks, but seemed to realize how dire their situation was.

"Him," the man said gruffly, nodding to a body lying feet from him. "And three others in the back." His voice lost its edge, turning into a strangled plea. "Please, save them. I—I couldn't protect them."

Beneath the copper, salty tang of blood and musty scent of dirt and old wood was the sweet hint of herbs. Cedarwood. Lavender. Ginger. My eyes found a cloaked woman kneeling on the ground next to the body of the young man their leader had pointed to, her hands stretched over him with herbal rings lining her fingers. An Alchemist healer, surely. She mumbled under her breath, but I knew by the pale blue tinge of the man's face, the deep lacerations in his side, and the almost imperceptible movement of his chest that it was no use. He was almost gone.

"There's nothing more I can do," the healer said to the man in charge, whose face immediately fell.

A wail ripped through the air.

Staggering across the room and flinging herself at the boy's body, a woman cried out in anguish, burying her face in his neck. The house went silent save for the sound of her ragged sobs.

The hush of death stretched and settled over us like a blanket.

A moan from the back of the room broke the spell and time sped up, everyone rushing to their duties.

"Back here," said one of the men, ushering the healer to her feet and toward the remaining injured people. Leo followed, already reaching into his pouch of herbs, but something kept my feet planted. I stared down at the young man. He was no older than sixteen or seventeen. Beau's age.

I took in the deep, jagged claw marks in his side, the torn tunic, the flesh stripped and hanging from bone. The way his fingers twitched and his eyelids fluttered, his chest barely moving with the last few breaths his body clung to.

He was too young for this.

He wasn't dead—not yet. But herbs and potions wouldn't save him.

Moving to crouch by the weeping woman, I gently placed my hands on hers. "I can help him," I said quietly, making sure the others were out of earshot.

She looked up at me, eyes swollen. "How?"

I didn't answer.

Her breaths slowed as she blinked at me and nodded. Face paling, her eyes went round and filled with tentative hope. "Do what you must," she whispered, backing away.

I took my dagger and sliced it across my palm, then pressed it to the boy's cooling skin. Theodore's words floated through my mind.

"Feel the injury. Imagine being able to see the shattered bones, the torn muscles. Look beneath the flesh and picture your magic, your blood, coursing through it. Replacing weakness with strength. Pain with comfort. Broken with whole."

This was so much more than a broken wing. This was willing flesh to mend and organs to renew. This was coaxing the soul back from the precipice of freedom and into a mangled, torn body. This was magic beyond anything I'd dared to perform.

My head and heart pounded in time with the blood pumping from my hand and mixing with his. The healing spell dripped from my lips like a prayer.

"Revie scurae."

Nothing happened.

No familiar power zipped through me, no lightning bolt of magic poured into his wound like it had with the bird.

Disappointment crashed into me and my shoulders sagged, a heavy exhale leaving my parted lips. Why did I think I would be able to do this? How could I *possibly* believe that a few days of practicing blood magic meant I'd be able to bring someone back from the brink of death? It was ridiculous. Impossible.

"Nothing is impossible, Rose. Not anymore."

I bit down on my lip. What would Theodore say if he were here with me now? If this was simply another lesson in his study?

He would tell me to stop thinking of my limits, to stop living by the rules of magic that once bound me. To remember that *this* was my birthright. What I was born to do. He would say my power was more than I could possibly dream.

I took a deep breath. I calmed my heart and focused on the sound of it thumping resolutely in my ears.

I am unlimited.

Magic sparked in my blood, lighting my veins on fire.

It happened in an instant.

It felt like my very being was ripping apart and molding into something new. Something stronger. Something that transcended the magic I once knew, that broke the barriers my own mind had placed on me for all these years. It was as if a cage had not only been opened, but completely shattered. Power like a sweet siren's song flooded me, drowning me, filling me.

I let out a gasp as the boy's heart picked up speed beneath my touch, his skin warming as blood rushed through his body. The gashes in his side pulled back together, sewn by an invisible hand. His cheeks pinkened and his chest rose as he took a full breath.

He was alive. He was *healed*.

"By the Fates..." his mother murmured, awestruck.

I pulled my hand away, leaving a bloody print where his wound once was. Hastily, I moved his ripped shirt so it would cover the spot, elation at what I'd done quickly falling to panic that the others would find out. They wouldn't understand. They'd think it was an abomination, like I once did. But they didn't know the *good* blood magic could do.

His mother gripped my hand, keeping her voice low. "You saved him. When he couldn't be healed, you saved him. Whatever you want, I will give it to you. I—I can never repay—"

"Tell no one," I said, cutting her off. "That's all I ask."

She met my eyes, understanding passing between us. "You saved him," she whispered again, more to herself than to me.

But will there be a cost, an obtrusive voice slithered through my mind.

Leo approached. "Rose, can you—" He stopped short, eyes on the boy as he stirred. His brow furrowed. "What happened? How is he alive?"

I scrambled to my feet, imagining the look on his face if he figured out what I'd done. The same magic that tormented his past, that he thought killed his father...

"The healer must not have used the right herbs or given it enough time." I balled my cut hand into a fist and slid it behind my back, forcing myself not to wince at the ache. "I used a different combination. Tried a new spell. He's going to be fine, that's all that matters."

Leo caught my movement. He stepped toward me, concern in his dark gaze. "What did you do to your hand?"

I shrugged and gestured to the dirty floor. "Cut it on a piece of stray glass."

The crease on his forehead deepened. He looked down at the boy, who managed to sit up with the help of his mother. His shirt shifted to reveal the edges of the wound that once marred his side but was now only a bright pink scar crusted with dried blood.

Leo's stare returned to mine. His hand came out to trace a path down my injured arm, leaving goosebumps in its wake. I reluctantly let him grip my wrist and pull my hand from behind my back. The jagged cut in my palm practically glowed with a crimson confession.

"A new spell," he said, repeating my words slowly.

"Yes."

He tilted his head. "Must be some powerful herbs."

Tension snaked around us, thick with unspoken accusations. The way he was looking at me, full of mistrust and uncertainty where unwavering adoration once lived, sliced through my chest.

I didn't respond. I *couldn't*—if I so much as opened my mouth, I feared the truth would spill free. *Every* truth.

His jaw hardened and he stepped back. "You should clean that," he said in a low voice, motioning to my hand. "Wouldn't want it to get infected."

Then he walked away. A shaky breath escaped me as if it were trying to follow after him, trying to tug my body forward and drag him back to me. That inescapable hold he had on me tightened until it felt like I couldn't breathe, and then it snapped, my stomach sinking to my feet at the realization.

He didn't trust me.

He *shouldn't* trust me.

I deserved to be held at arm's length. Lying had always been as easy as breathing for me, yet now it felt like suffocation.

I glanced at the boy in his mother's arms, her joy and relief evident in every line of her face. I had done that. I had saved him.

But magic that strong had a price.

What if losing Leo was mine?

54

ROSE

The ride back to the twin's cottage was uncomfortable, the silence interrupted only by occasional murmurings from Horace and Chaz as they discussed the attack.

We'd spent hours helping the families from Emberfell tend to their wounded and restore what they could of the damaged house. Leo kept his distance from me, throwing himself into his work, his features tightened with intensity as he patched broken holes and cleared away debris.

When the sun began to set and we left the Lightbender refuge, he had mounted his horse and taken the lead, leaving me to Rissa and her pale yellow mare.

It was better this way. I didn't know what I would do if I had to feel his chest at my back, his arms caging me in, the unease rolling off him in waves that had once been heated tension.

As we traveled back to the south sector, my regret gave way to a different emotion. Something icy and familiar that molded so perfectly back into my mind, it was like it had never left to begin with.

Anger festered inside me the more I thought about those innocent Lightbender families. They were seeking a reprieve from the dangers of their home province, hoping for safety these borders were *supposed* to provide, and they'd been met with brutality. Misplaced prejudice harbored by people who didn't want so-called "outsiders" brought into their fold.

I had no idea how common of an occurrence this had become until I asked the others about it a couple weeks ago, but it was different seeing it with my own eyes. And I knew exactly who was responsible. Who was charged with taking care of his people, yet turned a blind eye to their suffering. Who let destruction and bloodshed run rampant in his streets as long as he kept their power in check.

How many times would I let Theodore make excuses? How many times would I accept his words because they sounded pretty and magical and full of promise? It was like I'd created a separation in my mind. Theodore, my father's brother, the brilliant, isolated man who'd taught me in mere *days* how to accept my magic in its full glory and surrender to what it was meant to be. And Emperor Gayl, the quiet but lethal ruler pulling the strings of the empire, callously playing provinces like pieces on a chessboard and not caring who was hurt in the process. Two separate men, both powerful in their own right.

And both were dangerous. Both hiding their true motives and desires. Both capable of so much more than I knew.

If it weren't for Theodore, I wouldn't be keeping these secrets from Leo. I would still be living in ignorant bliss, set on spying and uncovering the truth behind the Somnivae curse, none the wiser to what truly happened twenty-seven years ago.

But...I also would've never known the freedom of my magic. The wild, restless part of me that beat vibrantly with every pound of my heart, every throb of my pulse.

For better or worse, this time with the emperor had changed me. Irrevocably. I didn't think I could go back to the woman I used to be. I didn't *want* to. How was I supposed to reconcile that with the man who not only welcomed ruthlessness and dissonance, but seemed to revel in it?

And how was I supposed to get Leo to understand any of this?

To see how conflicted my thoughts had become, and how I desperately wanted to give him *all* of me.

But I was scared.

Fates, I was scared. Rissa had been right—I was letting fear of the unknown stand in my way. Fear of telling him the truth, fear of *not* telling him, fear of what would happen when this month was over, of whether or not I could find a way to stop the Somnivae curse, of the power I now held in my hands. Both literal and figurative. Because Theodore Gayl and I were the only two people who knew how to bring an end to this curse, and I didn't know what I would do if I had to make that choice.

"Only you will decide who meets their doom."

Rissa pulled on the reins, jolting me out of my thoughts as we approached the familiar wooden cottage in the forest. We all dismounted and shuffled in stilted silence to get our packs off the horses, exhaustion swirling around us. Rissa, Lark, Horace, and Chaz all made their way inside. Horace mumbled something about needing a stiff drink. I lingered by Rissa's horse, gently running my hand along her mane and trying to quell my anxiety. I felt Leo's presence hanging over me like a cloud, watching me from his own stallion.

The strip of cloth I'd wrapped around the cut on my hand was stained red. I picked at the fringes of it, the skin still tender and raw where I'd sliced it. The sound of crunching leaves met my ear and I turned to find Leo walking inside the cottage, leaving me in the soft moonlight of the clearing.

My heart sank. Of course he was angry with me. Of course he didn't want to be alone with me. In one moment, I'd ruined everything between us, reminding him he couldn't trust me and—

The door creaked open again and Leo walked back out, a small glass vial and a roll of gauze in his hand.

"You never took care of that," he said gruffly, looking at my haphazard attempt at bandaging.

I swallowed. "It will heal."

"Always so stubborn." His voice was tired, the usual cross

between humor and exasperation now absent. "Come here," he said as he turned over a bucket on the front porch and gestured for me to sit.

He knelt before me, placing the potion and gauze on the ground before taking my hand in his. His fingers were calloused but his touch was gentle as he unwound the cloth, careful not to let it brush against the open wound. When he unbottled the vial, the woody scent of cedarwood overwhelmed my senses. I flinched slightly at the sting as he poured it over my cut. He whispered a healing spell and rubbed the oil in soothing circles, his thumb dragging across my palm.

"Are you going to tell me what really happened today?" he finally asked, his tone quiet and even. No hint of malice or accusation. It sounded like he was resigned, which was worse than the anger I expected.

I bit the inside of my cheek. "I saved that boy's life. Nobody had to die. Isn't that what matters?"

"I suppose so." He placed a pad of gauze on the cut and laid a fresh bandage on it, winding it inside my thumb and then back around the other side.

He made to stand from his crouch, but I held onto his hand. "Leo, please. Let me—"

"Let you what, lie to me again?" The bitter edge was a welcome reprieve from the emotionless way he'd spoken before. A spark lit in his eyes as he met mine. "I've stood there and watched you keep things from me and lie to me as if it was your natural instinct. How can I believe anything you've said, Rose?"

I wanted to tell him that this was the first time, that it wouldn't happen again, but the false words fell to ash on my tongue.

After these weeks of growing closer to him, of finally finding someone I wanted to let in, I had broken it in a single breath. We'd built something based on mutual respect and trust. We'd spent time learning how to take our walls down and not hide from each other. And I'd thrown that all away.

Had it even existed to begin with? Could a foundation made on omissions and lies ever hope to stand firm?

Fear gripped me when he stood, but this time, I knew exactly what I was afraid of—and it wasn't the unknown. It wasn't the future or the curse or the tournament.

It was him walking away.

"Blood magic," I said steadily, keeping my eyes on him, letting him see I wasn't hiding anymore. "There were no herbs, no new spells. I—I used blood magic to heal him."

Leo clutched the glass vial in his hand, shaking his head in frustration as he looked away. "I didn't want to believe it, Rose. How could you be so *reckless*? Don't you know what blood magic does? The consequences it has?"

I rose to my feet, thankful to have an outlet for my anxiety. "You just don't understand it. I didn't, either. We've been taught our whole lives that it's some terrible form of dark magic, but that's because we've never taken the time to *understand* it. To learn how to control it. You saw what I did today, how it can—"

"I saw you bend laws of nature. That boy should have *died*." His voice grew harder. "You're not the Fates, Rose—you don't get to decide who lives and who dies."

"Screw the Fates! Those families wouldn't have been attacked if the Fates cared at all about what was happening!"

"What if it had gone wrong? What if you had hurt the boy? That kind of magic is unpredictable and dangerous. And it *always* has a price."

"All magic can be dangerous!" I shouted, raising my arm in the air. This conversation was eerily similar to the one I'd had with Theodore weeks ago. If only I could make Leo see it the way I eventually had...

"Why are Alchemists the only ones expected to use some sort of aid to do magic?" I pressed. "Why are we the only ones who can't use *what we've been given*, our natural birthright and power?"

Leo clenched his jaw, turning from me and pacing further into the forest. "You sound like *him*, Rose."

I bit my tongue, fighting the urge to defend Theodore. "No, Leo, I sound like *me*. For once, I feel like I have a purpose. Like I can *do* something. I saved that boy's life today!" I followed after him, desperate for him to grasp what I was saying. To stop looking at me like he didn't know me. "It *can* be harmful, but it can also be controlled. Just like learning any new magic, it takes practice."

He whirled on me. "And how long have you been practicing? Years? Months? Do you even know what you're doing?"

"Since—since I started meeting with Gayl," I confessed, wincing at the anger in his eyes.

He let out a disbelieving breath. "So while we thought you were working for us, trying to find out more about him so we could stop the curse and bring him down, he's been teaching you dark magic?" He stepped closer, towering over me, the moonlight and shadows making his onyx eyes gleam.

"Rissa asked me to get close to him!" I protested. "What do you think I'm doing? I'm *trying* to find a way to end it. Have you ever considered that blood magic may be the solution?"

A vein in his neck throbbed. "Blood magic killed my father, Rose!"

"And it *saved your life*!" I exploded, realizing the moment the words left my mouth what I had done.

The air hummed around us as his brow slowly furrowed. I clenched my uninjured hand at my side.

"What are you talking about?" he asked, chest heaving.

I closed my eyes. The fight had drained from us both, leaving a cold emptiness.

The truth was all I had left to offer.

"I found out the full story about the night you were born," I began. "The night the curse started."

Leo's jaw tightened. "What full story? Gayl protected my mother's life as a ruse for cursing my father's rule."

"No, Leo, that—that's not all of it." I took a deep breath. "He didn't just help your mother. He saved *you*. You *died* that night."

His head shook, his tail brushing against the leaves and dirt. "That doesn't make any sense."

"Gayl told me how there were complications with your birth and your father summoned him to help. Branock commanded him to do whatever it took to save you both. When your mother gave birth, you...you were born without life. But he used blood magic to bring you back."

He looked at me, and I prepared for dismissal. For disbelief and rage. What I found was even worse.

He looked scared.

I stepped forward and took his hand, surprised when he didn't pull away. "Gayl brought you back from the dead. But magic as great as that, it—"

"Has a price," Leo finished on an exhale.

I steeled myself and nodded.

"The curse," he said, realization dawning on him. "The curse is —is because of me." His words were low and drawn out as he put the pieces together.

"It was the cost Gayl warned your father about," I whispered. "He tried to reverse it. He and your father tried for years, and almost every Alchemist since. The truth is what eventually drove your father from the throne. He wanted to keep you safe."

"The truth," he said slowly, his eyes locking onto our clutched fingers. Then he dropped my hand. "Because I'm the answer to reversing the spell he cast. It's *me*. My death, as it should have happened."

I held my breath, pulse pounding relentlessly in my ears. He turned away and closed his eyes. As he rubbed a hand across his face, my chest caved at the despondency on his features, every inch of me yearning to comfort him, to reach out and—

Before I could stop him, he twisted and slammed his fist into a tree.

55

LEO

My roar echoed through the forest. The skin on my knuckles split, but the sting was a light affliction to the thoughts racing in my mind.

It would heal quickly. It didn't matter. Nothing else mattered.

Rose gasped. "Leo—"

"This whole time," I panted, pressing my forehead into the trunk. "We've had the answer this whole time. We could have saved *thousands*—"

"But you would have died!"

"I wasn't supposed to live to begin with!" Pushing off from the tree, I faced her again, watching her beautiful features solidify into resolve.

Part of me wanted to deny everything. To rage against her words, toss them aside as more lies fed to her by the emperor. But deep down, I knew.

My father had always been paranoid. A man constantly being chased by his past, never willing to put us in danger. I remembered how outraged he was when Rissa, Mother, or I would leave the house, how terrified he was of something happening. Of someone finding us. He'd established wards to protect the cottage, made us

429

swear we would never speak to a soul if we didn't have to, and panicked at the slightest sign of sickness or injury.

And the guilt. His guilt had rested on his shoulders every day of his life. It made sense now—the price to keep his family had meant the downfall of his empire.

My mother...she must know, too. The truth was slowly eating her alive, the way it had eaten my father. But instead of the paranoia and aggravation his guilt had manifested as, hers was burrowing into her, a poison she couldn't escape from. Ever since Father died, she'd been losing pieces of herself, unable to bear the weight of it alone.

How was one supposed to live with the knowledge that their mere existence was the reason for an entire empire's pain? For thousands of peoples lives being stolen, frozen in a single moment in time?

How was *I* supposed to live with it?

"How long have you known?" I asked.

She didn't answer immediately. Her teeth pulled at her lower lip, and I cursed my body for still wanting her. For still hoping to find comfort in her as I had these past weeks.

"Since the first night I met with Gayl."

I replayed that night again in my mind. Finding her in that dark hallway, begging her not to go see him. Then climbing up to her window just to make sure she was safe.

The night I asked her if we could start over.

I scoffed, channeling my hurt into anger. "I don't know why I'm surprised. Nothing else about that night was the truth, was it?"

Her green eyes sparked with challenge. "I'm sorry, Leo, but I thought I was doing what was best. I didn't know how to tell you the truth. I knew this would crush you, and I thought I could figure out a way around it. I thought I could find another solution that didn't involve you."

"Over two decades and countless highly trained Alchemists, and you thought you could solve everything in a handful of weeks? On your own?"

Her cheeks flushed, and my blood heated. Good—I wanted a fight. I needed to feel something besides this empty pit opening wider and wider, threatening to pull me under.

"I was trying to *save* you," she said in a raised voice, stepping closer to me. "If I'd told you, what would you have done? Gone off and sacrificed yourself like some noble martyr?"

"That would be *my* choice to make, Rose!" I argued. "*You* hiding this from me has taken that choice away."

Her jaw twitched, but she didn't back down. "I'm right, though. You would have chosen to die," she pushed. "I shouldn't have taken your choice away. You have the right to know the truth, and for that, I'm sorry." She threw her hands in the air. "I'm sorry for *so many* things. Look, I know you don't approve of me learning blood magic. I should have told you about all of it, but...Fates, can't you see I'm doing this *for* you?" Her brow knitted together, her words turning into a plea. "Getting close to him, learning about his past and his magic, figuring out how to become strong enough... it's for *you*. It's been killing me to keep this a secret, but you know what?" Eyes blazing, she tilted her head to look up at me, wild and emboldened. "I would do it again, Leo. Because I'm *not* going to lose you."

She was so close now, I could reach out and grab her. I was stunned. In all our nights together, she was so controlled, so careful not to let her true feelings for me slip. Despite her refusal to speak them aloud, I felt it in the way she tucked her body into mine. The way her hand sought my fingers when the nightmares overtook her. The way she smiled at me when nobody else was looking, as if to say her joy was only for me.

But there was power in words. And Rose hid behind her fear of that, of giving voice to what had grown between us. I understood now why she'd kept that part of herself closed off.

Rose didn't know how to give herself fully to someone. Not when there was something blocking the path. These secrets she'd been holding onto, the lies she'd been weaving...even when I thought I was seeing all of her, there had been a wall in my face.

Now, it was shattered. Every brick tumbled around us, and I was finally looking at her for the first time. Nothing separating us. Nothing keeping us from sinking into the depths.

I was *furious*. She'd betrayed my trust and forced me into the dark. She'd lied to me even when I gave her the space to be open. She was dangerous and sharp and willing to do whatever it took to make things play out the way she wanted.

But somehow, I was still falling. I had been since the moment I found her in that dark alcove.

I swallowed hard, taking in her words and the truth behind what she said. "You would condemn the world for the sake of one man?"

"I know. I *know* it's wrong," she murmured, drawing nearer. Her breath was warm on my neck, the scent of lavender and sage enveloping me. The forest faded around us as she reached out to brush aside the lock of hair that had fallen over my eye. I caught her wrist, and her fierce gaze snapped up. "But I don't care."

She grabbed the back of my neck and pulled me to her, crashing her lips into mine.

This kiss wasn't timid. It wasn't hesitant, like two beings scared to learn one another for the first time, afraid to lose themselves or push too far.

This kiss was my annihilation. The tearing down of everything I'd known before. The second I held her in my arms, the second I tasted her, the damage was done. My anger, betrayal, desire, dread, and passion collided and fractured as my fingers wound in her hair, a groan of relief vibrating between our bodies.

This kiss was my destruction. My downfall. But if this was falling, I never wanted to stop.

Her nails dug into my skin, pressing me closer, desperate to apologize in a way words alone couldn't. She let out a sigh, sending a scorching trail of heat to my core. Gripping the backs of her thighs, I lifted until she wrapped her legs around my waist. My body buzzed everywhere we touched. I pushed her against the nearest tree, bracing her head with my hand. She gasped at the contact as I broke away. Her pupils were blown out, cheeks flushed and lips swollen.

I lowered my head to her neck, trailing my mouth along her pulse and grounding out, "Is there anything else you'd like to confess?"

She squirmed and ran her nails up my back, which sent a distracting shiver through me. I raised my tail and wound it around her wrists, yanking them away from me and holding them above her head, pressed into the tree trunk.

She blinked, her chest heaving. "I—I don't—"

I silenced her with another kiss. My Shifter half emerged against my will, summoned by my adrenaline, and I was flooded with so much of *her* that it almost brought me to my knees.

Lightly nipping at her bottom lip, I grazed my nose along her cheek and over to the space below her ear. "It's a simple question," I murmured, savoring the way her eyes fluttered. I released her wrists and backed away to cup her face. I couldn't do this if she was still hiding things. I was already on the brink of no return, but I couldn't lose myself if there was any chance that would happen again.

My thumb brushed across her cheek, and I sensed her breaths slowing. "I've been nothing but honest with you since the night we agreed to start over, Rose. I've shown you the broken pieces of my past, the parts I hide from everyone else. Because I want to. I want *you*. But I won't let you make me a fool. If this isn't—"

"No, no, it's—this is what I want, too, Leo," she rushed out, fisting my shirt in her hands. "You know everything now, I promise. I'm done hiding. I—I'm done keeping things from you. I've always been afraid people won't like what they see if they get too close, but I'm not scared anymore." She brought her forehead to mine and my grip on her waist tightened, keeping her in place. "I want to earn your trust back. I want you to see all of me, the good *and* the wicked." Leaning her head back, she met my gaze. "No more lies. No more secrets. Only us."

"Only us," I agreed softly. "You don't have to be scared with me, Rose. I want all of you." I placed a kiss on her jaw. "Every piece you keep tucked away"—my lips skimmed her neck—"every part you think is too dark"—I kissed the edge of her lips—"I want it all."

I pulled back to scan her face, shadowed by the thick canopy of trees. Moonlight broke through the space between leaves, illuminating her olive skin and bright eyes.

"You are so beautiful," I said, voice gravelly as I tucked a strand of dark hair behind her ear.

She caught my hand and held it to her face. "Kiss me, Leo."

Leaning forward, I captured her lips with mine, wrapping my hand around her neck to pull her closer.

If the first kiss was my destruction, this was my creation. My entire being centered on this single moment, forging what was broken into something whole.

I craved her like the night craved the dawn. The languid strokes of her tongue against mine settled into me like warm rays of the sun, melting me, molding me, marking me.

I was hers. Completely, utterly, wholly hers.

I squeezed the nape of her neck and broke apart. "Rose, I—"

The loud bang of a door slammed into my heightened senses, followed by my sister's scream. "Rose! Leo!"

We both turned to the sound. I set Rose on her feet, my heart pounding for an entirely different reason. My sister...she never sounded that terrified.

"Rissa?" I called. Rose stayed at my side as I strode across the forest floor and toward our cottage.

My sister came into view, running to me with her blonde curls flying wildly around her face. "It—it's Chaz," she said shakily. "It got him."

I gripped her shoulder. "*What* got him, Rissa?"

She took a deep breath. "The curse."

56

ROSE

My fault.
    My fault.
    My fault.

I'd been foolish, not thinking of the consequences of using such strong magic, not thinking of the *price*...and Chaz had paid it.

Leo stormed past Rissa and into the cottage, leaving his twin and me outside in the silvery glow of night. She shot me a worried look and then reached down to grab my hand, squeezing it before leading me after Leo. Warmth spread in my chest, followed by a bitter sting—if Rissa knew I'd done this, that my actions had caused one of her best friends to be cursed, would she still want to be near me?

The cottage was silent as death. Chaz's sleeping body lay on the couch, with Horace slumped in the chair next to him and Lark leaning against the wall in the kitchen. Sorrow was written on her dark features. Leo knelt at Chaz's side, pulling his eyelid open to expose the blood-red iris.

He didn't speak, his face unreadable. Swiftly, he rose from his crouch as his tail snapped against the legs of the end table.

"Let's get you back to the palace," he said, crossing the room and placing a hand on my waist. I wanted to argue, wanted to insist that I stay to help or at least sit with them, *be* there for them, but the tired look in Leo's eyes had me nodding in silent agreement.

Rissa pulled me aside and gave me a tight hug. "We'll see you soon, alright?" Leaning back, she offered a small smile that didn't reach her eyes. "Stay safe, Rose."

"You too," I murmured. "Will I see you before the third trial?"

Lark answered from across the room, her voice flat and distant. "That won't start for a couple days after the ball. We should have plenty of time to debrief before then."

I nodded again, letting Leo turn me away and to the front door. At the last second, I twisted my neck to take in the view of the four of them. "I'll fix this," I promised. "We'll find a way to end the curse."

Lark met my gaze. "I know you will."

Leo's strong hand around my upper arm urged me out of the cottage. He helped me mount Nightshade and we took off into the forest toward the palace.

Tension shifted like smoke in the air between us, but I couldn't place where it came from. Was it from our fight? The kiss? The news about Chaz?

I closed my eyes. I wondered if Leo blamed me, too. If he realized Chaz being cursed was because of my magic.

"You were right," I whispered, feeling his arms clench around me as we rode. "I was careless. I didn't think about what might happen, and now..."

One of his hands came to rest on my stomach, pulling my back closer into his chest. "You think this is your fault?" he asked.

"Isn't it?" I craned my neck to glance at him. "Magic that strong has a price. You said it yourself—I bent laws of nature. I saved that boy when it shouldn't have been possible, and the price was Chaz."

Sighing, Leo's muscles relaxed slightly. "I don't know, Rose. Blood magic is complicated. I shouldn't have gotten so angry with you about helping the Lightbender boy. You did an amazing thing

—truly. You changed that family's life." He pressed a kiss to my temple. "But there's still so much we don't know about this kind of magic. We've seen multiple times what that power can bring. My father, and now Chaz, and Gayl with the curse…" He trailed off, clearing his voice and tightening his grip on me.

"Are you going to tell the others? Your sister?"

He didn't respond at first, then said, "Not yet. It will only make her worry, and she has enough to deal with. She would divert her attention to keeping me away from the mission instead of focusing on what's important. I'll tell her when the time is right."

We rode in silence for a few minutes, giving me time to think. I bore no regret for finally telling him the truth, for finally being honest and bringing down that last barrier between us. But I would never forget the way he slammed his fist into that tree. The truth had broken a part of him, like I knew it would.

I was afraid his grief and shock would catch up to him and make him realize this night was a mistake. That what he'd admitted to me was a product of heightened emotions. That he didn't know what he was doing when he kissed me or said he wanted me. *All* of me. Maybe now he realized what that meant, and—

"I can feel you spiraling," he said into my ear, breaking me from my thoughts. His lips lingered there, and I fought back a shiver.

"No, you can't," I mumbled. "Do you want to talk about any of it? The curse?"

He released a breath that came out like a hum. The sound rumbled through my body and into my core, igniting new heat. "I want to talk about it, yes. Eventually. But right now," he said in a low voice, his thumb rubbing slowly across my stomach, "I'm having a hard time thinking about anything else."

Holding the reins with one hand and reaching the other to turn my face, he brought his lips to the corner of my mouth, dragging them down to my jaw and back up. The motion traced a path of fire on my skin. I held my breath as he hovered over my lips, his nose skimming mine.

"What about the horse?" I murmured, the movement making my bottom lip brush against his.

"He knows the way." His warm breath washed over me, and my eyes fluttered shut as his lips met mine.

He moved slowly at first, drawing the kiss out, tasting me. The hand at my cheek shifted to the nape of my neck, leaving goose-bumps as his fingers trailed upward, the calloused pads pressing into my skin. They wound through my hair and gave a tug that made me gasp. The kiss became more urgent. Feverish. Like he was no longer simply relishing it, but *needing* it.

I broke away panting and rested my forehead against his. His entire world had been turned upside down tonight. Maybe this was going too fast.

"Am I just a distraction?" I asked. "Is this even real?"

He pulled back to meet my stare, his eyes darkened with both desire and pain. I knew that expression. Not knowing what to think, what to say, what to feel. Wanting a way to cover it up and shove it aside, to cling to something that made you feel alive.

"Why can't it be both?" he responded.

Nightshade's gait slowed as we neared the palace. He stopped a ways from the treeline at the hidden spot Leo always kept him to avoid detection.

I swallowed and scooted forward to Nightshade's neck, lifting my body so I was balancing on the horse's back.

"Rose, what are you—"

I turned around to face him, lowering myself back down into the saddle. He sucked in a breath and let the reins fall. The horse remained in place, his tail swishing against a low-hanging branch.

"I'll be your distraction, if that's what you need. But I also want to be your *peace*. I want to be the thing that tethers you when you feel your world crumbling." I rested my hand on his heart, feeling its wild beats. "Take what you need tonight, but I'm not going anywhere. I promise."

His eyes softened as he tucked away a lock of hair that whipped across my face in the wind. "All I need is you."

I covered his hand with mine and kissed his palm, mapping the lines on it with the tip of my finger. His skin was smooth yet rough at the same time. Soft and calloused. Strong and gentle. Much like him. I pressed my palm flush to his, marveling at how we fit so well together, his hard edges to my soft curves. At the fact that this man wanted *me*.

He intertwined our fingers and used his other hand to guide my chin forward, his lips meeting mine in a tender kiss that stripped away all fear, all hesitancy, all pain.

I sucked in a breath through my nose and pressed further into him, winding my arms around his neck, meeting him stroke for stroke, touch for touch.

I was melting. I was flying. I was *falling*.

I may not have done many good things in this life. I may not have been the perfect niece or the perfect Alchemist, the kind, doting girl who forgave easily and loved freely. But if there was *one* thing I would do right, it was protect him.

There was another way out of this curse. There *had* to be. And I would burn the world down to find it.

———

We entered the palace under an invisibility spell and made our way up to my room. I was too tired to deal with guards questioning my whereabouts so late in the evening, even though challengers were allowed to roam freely.

Fatigue swept over me. The heat from my time with Leo was so at odds with the guilt over Chaz's predicament that my mind was left reeling, unsure how to cope.

I wanted to take a bath, eat, and sleep. Maybe kiss Leo some more. Not necessarily in that order.

But when we slipped inside my room, I knew none of those things would be happening tonight.

A sealed envelope rested on my bed with my name in

Theodore's familiar handwriting. Groaning, I grabbed it and took out my dagger, carefully slitting open the top.

"Is that from—" Leo hissed as he reached to see what the envelope said and the tip of my blade sliced his finger.

"Sorry—here," I said absently, handing him an extra strip of cloth from my bag to wrap around his finger, then answered, "It's from the emperor." I quickly scanned the contents, relaying them as I read. "He wants to meet again tonight. Another lesson. He expected me"—I glanced at the clock on the wall—"half an hour ago."

"Can you send him a message? Push it off to tomorrow?"

"Yes, I—" My brow furrowed. Something tugged at the back of my mind. Something that wouldn't let me put this off.

I wet my lips. "I—I think I should go. I don't want him to get suspicious of anything. He already knows I'm close with the Sentinels, and has assured your protection only so long as he doesn't think you're up to something."

Leo ran a hand through his hair. "I know we don't see eye to eye on this and you're more than capable of taking care of yourself. But I don't like what he's teaching you. He's not telling you the full truth about this magic. What does he want from you? Why does he insist on these meetings?"

"I understand how temperamental blood magic can be—trust me, Leo. I don't want what happened today to ever happen again." I swallowed. The truth of my statement was at odds with the idea of letting this power go. Of having this taste of ecstasy and freedom, only to have it ripped from me. "But I have a part to play, remember? I'm getting close to him. I think I could even try to read his Grimoire, see if there are any notes or spells in his research that hint at a way to get around this curse. He told me he'd never found another solution, but I don't know if I believe him anymore. I have to at least try."

He put his forehead to mine and breathed out. "I don't like this," he said.

I laughed softly. "Is the big, bad *half* Shifter worried about me?"

He kissed my cheek, stealing the humor and replacing it with a heavy warmth deep in my chest. "You have no idea. I become a useless wreck every time I know you're with him. Every time I know I can't help you if something goes wrong." A dry chuckle left his throat. "Chaz called me a stalker last time."

His face fell at the mention of his friend, and I cupped his cheek. "I'll be fine. Theodore won't hurt me."

My use of the emperor's first name made Leo's forehead crinkle. "You seem to put a lot of faith in him." His tone wasn't accusatory, only concerned, and for once, my defenses didn't raise. I needed to be open with him, to stop seeing every word as a threat or reproach.

I sighed and closed my eyes. "I know. And I know he's done terrible things. I'm not trying to deny that. But I—I'm just confused." I hadn't talked much about my time with Theodore for fear of letting something slip, but now that Leo knew the whole truth, it was a relief to finally share everything with him.

Slumping onto the end of the bed, I leaned back on my hands and faced the ceiling. "I used to hate him. I hated this shadowed figurehead that ran the empire, who let all these terrible things happen to the provinces and seemed to love feeding into people's darker sides. Then...then I found out who he was." My brow furrowed, my words slowing as I thought through them. "The fact that he's my uncle didn't negate any of that, but...I started seeing him differently. He wasn't who I expected him to be. He was sentimental, regretful, even. I think he truly misses my father and what they used to have."

I snuck a glance at Leo, surprised to find him attentive, no judgment or disapproval on his features. It gave me courage to continue. "He represented something I didn't think I'd ever have again. He could tell me about my father, about his life before me, his dreams and passions and talents. And when I found out about the blood magic...it gave me a sense of purpose. Power. I'd always been told it was this monstrous, evil magic that corrupted you and broke every law of nature." I pressed my lips together. "Maybe it is, in some ways. But he made me think about it differently. And maybe...maybe not everything is so black and white. Good or evil. I think all magic can have a bit of both in it. Fates, *people* can have a bit of both."

Standing abruptly, I paced in front of my bed. "He has this passion that's so *contagious*. And a way of forcing you to see things in a new light. But you're right. It's dangerous. Because even when I *know* I'm right, even when I confront him, I leave questioning... everything. It's like he has this hold over me, and I—I can't see past that when I'm with him."

Leo put both hands on my shoulders, stopping me from my movements. "You're not the only one, sweetheart. That's why he's so powerful. Having strong magic is one thing, but the power to convince people? To influence them so completely that they question their own beliefs? That's *true* control. And that's the danger, Rose. Not his magic." He pulled me into an embrace, his hand slipping beneath my shirt and pressing into my lower back. I sank into his hold and closed my eyes.

"Be careful," he whispered in my ear, his lips soft against my skin. "He can't control you unless you let him. Remember how you feel right now, and don't let his words twist inside your head."

I nodded, pulling back to look at him. "Will you be here when I get back?"

A gentleness settled in his eyes. He played with a strand of my hair, winding it around his finger. "I'm not going anywhere, Rose."

57

ROSE

I barged into Theodore's private study, barely feeling the sting from where I'd cut my hand on the magical portrait.

"I was beginning to think you would not show," Theodore said, his back to me as he reached for a book on a shelf behind his desk.

Seeing him standing there so casually, so unaffected, when I'd spent my whole day with hands covered in the blood of victims of *his* empire, made fresh rage surge to the surface.

My jaw ticked. "Well, I'm here."

He turned toward me and raised an eyebrow. "Are you angry with me?"

Ignoring him, I said, "Why did you ask me to come here so late?"

"I apologize," he said, shutting the book with a thump. "I know it's been nearly a week since our last meeting. I've been caught up in urgent matters."

I hummed in response, refusing to look at him, instead running my hand along the spines on a nearby bookshelf. My finger caught a small glass vial, and I watched as it tipped over and fell, rolling to the edge of the shelf and crashing to the hard floor. The sound of

443

shattering glass echoed in the quiet study, but neither of us reacted.

"What kind of urgent matters?" I asked stiffly, eyes still on the shelf as I plucked a leatherbound book from its spot.

"A new king has been crowned in Mysthelm."

My gaze snapped to him. "Why is that urgent?"

He sighed. "The former king passed unexpectedly and his son has taken the throne under...less than ideal circumstances. Incidents over there have reached a critical point, enough for them to make contact after so many centuries."

I swallowed, my previous bitterness now at war with my curiosity. "I'm surprised you're telling me this."

"Is there a reason I shouldn't trust you?" he asked, cocking his head.

I felt as if I was being examined under a magnifying glass. Every move, every word was a test. Did he trust me? Did we trust *each other*? It was all a mind game—a minefield of hidden traps, each step more precarious than the last.

"What do they want from you?" I asked slowly.

"Well, first and foremost, they wanted assurance that I didn't have their king assassinated."

"*Did* you?"

His cold gaze pierced me. "You believe I would do such a thing?" His voice was quiet, controlled, but his words slithered across my skin like oil. "Who exactly do you think I am, dear niece?"

"Someone who takes what they think is theirs." I shoved the book back in its place. "At least, that's what you told the challengers, isn't it? That we should be willing to do whatever it takes to gain what we want?"

His eyes narrowed as he crossed to his desk, letting my words hang in the dust and shadows of the room. Only when he pulled his chair out and took a seat did he respond, his attention now on the ink and parchment before him. "I have no interest in gaining anything beyond our borders, Miss Wolff, and I don't appreciate your insinuation. Now, if that's the only reason you came here tonight, then—"

"Fine," I said, cutting him off and striding to his desk. I gripped the edge of the wood, and it bit into my fresh cut. "What about *within* our borders? Do you still care about what happens there?"

He met my gaze, something lethal lying in wait behind his mismatched blue and white eyes. "Speak candidly, niece. I grow tired of this game."

My anger split open. "Your people are being attacked in the streets and you do *nothing* to stop it. Do you even know what's going on in the provinces? In your own capital?"

The air chilled several degrees, but Theodore stayed silent, baiting me.

I scoffed. "Allow me to enlighten you." A warning in the back of my mind told me to stop, to beg forgiveness before I crossed a line, but the words flowed from my mouth unbidden. "The provinces are *crumbling*. Those with stronger magic think they have the right to invade the weaker ones to the point where people living on the borders uproot their entire lives to find safety in Veridia City. Because that's what they should find here—protection. A better life. Justice. Isn't that what you want to give your people, *uncle*?" His eyes tightened, and that voice inside my head grew louder, a pounding rising in my bones. "Instead, they're met with violence. Anyone considered an outsider, anyone deemed 'less than,' is tossed aside. Are you telling me you haven't heard of the attacks happening beneath your very nose?"

A muscle in his jaw twitched. "I am aware of certain extremists taking matters into their own hands, yes."

"Then why aren't you *doing* anything about it? Is it because they're too weak to deserve your attention?"

He held my stare. "Choose your next words very carefully."

Taking a breath, I tried to calm my boiling blood, but it was like trying to rein in a tempest. "None of this would be happening if people didn't think they could get away with it. If they don't think our own emperor cares, why would anyone else?"

"Survival thrives on competition," he said, his voice slow and imbued with power. "I have spent my reign ensuring this empire is mightier than ever before. My people have the strength to fight for what they need. To rise above what they used to be. You may not know what this land once looked like, what weaknesses the Veridians once had to endure, but I made a vow to cut that away." He enunciated every word, his lips curling as if fighting a snarl. "Poverty is down. Hunger and disease are almost eradicated. People feel *empowered.* They know how to fend for themselves and pursue their desires, how to openly embrace their magic instead of shy away from it. *That* is the world I have created, Miss Wolff. *That* is what I have been doing for the people."

I felt that same inkling I always felt in his presence, urging me to stop and consider his view, to take a step back and understand his point. But my cold fire chased it away, the memory of the ransacked house burning across my eyes.

"Have you ever thought we might be becoming *too* reliant on that magic?" I pressed. "What you've created is a society based on conflict and superiority. Sure, some people may be better off, but only if their magic deems them worthy enough. And even *that* comes from this ridiculous tournament." I gritted my teeth, years of bitterness pouring out as my voice rose. My hair rustled against my chest, but I ignored it, my focus solely on the man before me. "What about the provinces whose magic is dying? Your own *home*? Who will fight for them? I've seen attacks at our borders. I've seen families beaten for nothing less than the type of magic running through their blood. Do *we* not deserve the same empowerment?"

I broke off, chest heaving, only to find Theodore's eyes trained on something behind me. Spinning around, the sight before me made me stagger back against his desk. My hand grappled for purchase on the slick wood. I looked down to find blood from my cut smeared across the surface.

"Wonderful," he murmured. I swallowed thickly, taking in the scene.

Books and loose pages had floated from their stacks and were suspended in midair. Inkwells, glass vials, packets of herbs, dried plants, every item lying around his study was floating of their own accord, hovering as if on an invisible cloud. Even the liquid from the vials was frozen, like miniature waterfalls free flowing from nothing.

Wind swirled again at my hair, and I glanced over at Theodore to find his long locks swaying at his neck.

"What are you doing?" I whispered.

"Nothing." He took a step around his desk. "This is *you*, Rose."

"But I—I didn't even cast a spell. I wasn't trying to do anything."

He bore the same look of pride on his face that he had the day I used blood magic for the first time, but this expression was laced with something more. Something that made my feet shuffle backward.

Something like triumph.

"I once told you this is magic unlike anything you have seen. Unshackled. Natural. *Free*." He drew closer, brandishing an arm. "Look what you can do with a mere *thought*, niece. Imagine what you could accomplish when taught how to hone it." Gripping my shoulders, he met my gaze. "How does it feel?"

I bit down on my tongue hard enough to draw blood, forcing myself to stay silent. To stay in that room with Leo. To not let Theodore's words get inside my head.

Because I was afraid of admitting how it felt.

"Deny it all you want, but I see it in your eyes." His voice dropped to a whisper, but that didn't make it any less potent. Any less searing. "I see the *pride*. The *strength*. I want all of my people to know that feeling. To have such confidence in their magic, no matter their province, no matter their bloodline, for that was something I didn't have until your father and I found it together. I want to help you, Rose. The way he helped me."

My breaths were ragged as I wet my lips and looked back at what I'd done. I hadn't thought such a thing was possible with Alchemy—to be able to perform magic without a *spell*. What else didn't I know? What else was there to learn about this power I'd had my entire life?

I closed my eyes and shook my head. He was doing it again. Getting in my mind, twisting my thoughts, making me forget my purpose.

"I—I can't do this," I stammered, pulling from his grasp and stumbling toward the door. "I don't know what you want from me, but I'm not my father, Theodore. This isn't—"

"Rose," he thundered, that single word turning into a command and making my footsteps falter. Blindly, I reached for the door handle and tugged it open, but it slammed shut once more. Pressure mounted inside of me, a cascading well of confusion and power and anger and yearning.

"Rose, there is so much you don't understand. So much I can teach you, if you will—"

"Let me go!" I screamed, throat hoarse and hands shaking as I spun to face him. Suddenly every book, every vial, every object that had been hanging came crashing to the ground, the sound of shattering glass and deafening boom of tomes hitting the floor splitting my ears.

"I have to go," I whispered frantically, and to my surprise, the door opened when I turned the handle.

The last things I saw before it banged closed were his white and blue eyes staring after me, and his fingers dipped in red.

58

ROSE

The days passed in a haze.

Any note from Theodore, I promptly burned. I spent my time either with Leo or buried in the pages of my father's Grimoire, pleading and praying for something to bring me closer to an answer. To figuring out how to end the Somnivae curse.

Perhaps refusing to face the emperor even though he was the empire's best chance at freedom from the curse made me a selfish coward, but I couldn't go back to that study. Not yet. Every time I got near him, he burrowed deeper into my head, erasing my convictions until I didn't know what to believe.

And a small part of me still thought...what if he was right? What if he was doing what was best for the empire as a whole by making us stronger, giving us courage and pride and power? I couldn't deny the way my magic made me feel or the newfound assurance I had in myself. All thanks to Theodore.

But when those confusions slipped in, when those emotions began to wedge themselves between my desire for justice and a better empire for *everyone*...that's when I was the most frightened. That a single man in a matter of weeks could so easily twist my own beliefs.

I didn't have to figure it out alone, though.

Leo stood by me through it all. Day after day leading up to the ball, he listened to my muddled thoughts, helping me decipher truth from lies. When I strayed too close to the edge, he walked me back to the line. When the ache to feel that electrifying magic hit its peak, he replaced it with a different yearning.

We'd grown close in those weeks before the attack on the Lightbenders, but it was nothing compared to the days since. I'd always thought my freedom relied on keeping myself untethered, on fading touches and distant words that meant nothing. But I'd never known such freedom and peace as I did when I finally let someone *in*.

It was as if all my pain, all my guilt and confusion and the shadows that were bottled inside of me no longer weighed as much as they once did. *Leo* was there to share it with me. When the dark thoughts pushed at my mind, when memories of my father or moments of self-loathing and anger threatened to pull me under, I didn't shove them beneath the surface as I so often did in the past. There was someone who cared, someone who wanted to know every last part of me.

I wanted to know him, too. More than I'd ever wanted anything. I wanted to cut through the fabric of his heart and mind to carve out a spot for myself so he would always know he had someone who saw him, who desperately craved his light and his dark. His good and bad.

It was all beautiful to me.

A week had passed since my last encounter with Theodore, and I'd ignored four of his attempts to reach me. I knew if he truly wanted to see me—or throw me in the dungeons—he could have done so with the snap of his finger. The fact that he was giving me this choice, giving me a way to deny him, only succeeded in gnarling my thoughts even further.

I'd steered clear of Nox and Arowyn besides the occasional meal, throwing out excuses so I could study my father's Grimoire. In reality, though, a part of me was already preparing to have to say goodbye to them. The ball was tomorrow night, and Lark had said the third trial would occur a couple of days after, and then...it was over. If we made it out unscathed, at least. We would all go back to our provinces, presumably never to speak again.

I couldn't rip Leo from my heart even if I tried, but my friends... it would be wise to create distance. I should make the end easier to bear, do us all a favor and back away while I still could. Before it would hurt too much.

They, on the other hand, had other plans.

"Rose, open the door," Nox called from outside my room, his loud knock making me jump from my bed.

I closed my eyes. "Now isn't a good time, Nox."

A rustle of wind brushed against my skin. "We weren't asking."

My heart leapt up my throat as Arowyn appeared beside me, arms crossed over her full chest.

I let out a flustered exhale and grumbled, "What did I say about doing that?"

She shrugged, then crossed to the door to let Nox in. His ear-length, wavy hair was perfectly mussed, the rings on his fingers glittering as he brandished a green bottle at me.

"You're not getting out of this one, darling," he said. "We've only a few nights left to thoroughly corrupt one another, and you've been avoiding us all week."

"I've been busy."

Arowyn sank into the chair by my bed. "You've been a coward."

I shot her a look, and she raised an eyebrow. "What? Scared one of us will beat you in the third trial?" she taunted.

"You know I don't care about that," I said, rolling my eyes and pulling a blanket over my legs to cover my father's Grimoire.

"I know. Just trying to get you to admit it," she said.

"Admit what?"

Nox threw himself onto the bed next to me. "That you *love* us," he said dramatically, drawing out the words. "That you're so heartbroken to never see us again that you've locked yourself away."

I nestled further into the raised pillow at my back. "You two think you're so smart."

"We are," Arowyn responded. "I guess we also wanted to make sure you were still alive."

Nox cut in. "And catch you up on the latest news. You've missed a lot in this cage of yours."

I stared him down, tapping my finger against my side, neither of us willing to break, until...

I sighed. "Fine, what's the latest news?"

He smirked. "Arowyn saw one of the architects sneaking out of Callum's room two nights ago."

"*What*? Why?"

Arowyn snorted. "Why do you think? I saw him heading to the training room yesterday, so she obviously wasn't killing him."

"I wish someone would," I mumbled.

Nox handed me the green bottle of Luxe with a mischievous glint in his eye. "Drink up, darling. There's a lot more where that came from."

Arowyn leaned forward and snatched the bottle. "To our last night of normalcy," she toasted, then took a swig. I laughed along with Nox, the sound unfamiliar to my ears after being tucked away for so many days.

Perhaps moments like this would be worth having to say goodbye.

———

SEVERAL HOURS LATER, Nox and Arowyn had their fill of Luxe and were experiencing the after effects of its exhilarating relaxation. I'd only had a few sips, finding the idea of my mind being ripe for the plucking uncomfortable. Arowyn lounged on the ground against my window, where she threw her sharp little daggers at a spot on the wall across the room, striding to retrieve them every time she ran out. At first I'd protested, then realized...it was the palace's room. Why did I care if she mutilated it?

Nox lay next to me on the bed, humming a hauntingly melodic tune I didn't recognize. Every once in a while I'd catch his fingers shifting to sharp claws and back again. I couldn't make out what kind of animal they belonged to. As much as I itched to ask, I didn't want to take advantage of his alcohol-induced state if it wasn't information he was willing to share.

"You're awfully somber, viper," he drawled. "What's on your mind?"

I ran my tongue along my teeth, considering my words. My mind had been preoccupied with thoughts about the curse and magic. I'd gone through my father's Grimoire and more books in the library than I could count, but nothing stuck out to me. I needed to see things in a new way, to approach it from a different direction.

"Have either of you ever discovered something new about your magic? Something you hadn't known before?" I asked.

"What do you mean?" Nox replied.

"I don't know, just...something you didn't think you could do before."

He shrugged. "All Shifters learn as we grow. We don't always take the same form as our parents, or anyone in our bloodline for that matter, so everyone has to figure it out as they go."

Arowyn's next dagger whizzed past my feet. "Striders are kind of the same. We have different levels of power, at least. It took me a while to realize I could do things others couldn't."

Nox glanced at her. "Very ominous. Do tell?"

"Everyone from Celstria can stride, but distances and how often you can do it vary. What no one's really taught is how we leave a bit of our...essence, I guess, whenever we stride."

"Your essence?" I asked, brow furrowing.

"Yeah. An imprint of our power. The stronger you are, the more you leave behind, and the more often you stride to a certain spot—say, your home—it's like a nexus for your individual magic. And if you're powerful enough..." Arowyn trailed off with a smirk, raising her hand in the air with her palm facing up.

A faint shimmer appeared before a small box materialized in her open hand.

I sucked in a breath. "Where did that come from?"

"My house."

"In *Celestria*?" Nox asked, mouth agape. She gave him a bland look, not bothering to confirm the obvious. Nox shook his head in disbelief. "How did you do that?"

"My essence is the strongest around my home since that's where I use my magic the most. I can summon objects from there at will, if they have enough of my power in it."

I blinked at her. "I've never heard of Striders having an ability like that." Bethaly hadn't mentioned it before, and none of the limited books I'd read on the other provinces even hinted at the possibility.

She smiled smugly. "Why do you think I was chosen as the challenger?"

"Well, aren't you full of surprises," Nox said with a chuckle.

"How did you end up figuring out you could do that?" I asked. "Did your parents teach you?"

"My mother said she did it once. She was walking home late one night near the Feywood Forest and someone jumped out of the trees and attacked her. She swears she wasn't carrying a weapon, but she somehow ended up with our kitchen knife in her hand. She hasn't been able to do it again since."

"You must have been surprised the first time it happened," Nox mused.

"Eh, I was, but I went along with it. Learned how to use it to my advantage. I think a lot of us look at our magic as something stagnant, but really, it's always changing. I'm sure Shadow Wielders like Lark had to learn how to make their shadows take different shapes, and Illusionists find new ways to make the mind see what they want." She gestured lazily to my bag of charms sitting on the dresser. "Even your spells. You've probably done the same ones all your life and one day you wake up and realize hey, maybe this spell can also do something else." Her words were slightly slurred from the Luxe, but still, they resonated with me.

She made an interesting point. What if there was a spell I'd been using for years, but only for one certain purpose? I experimented with new enchantments often—that was how I'd discovered my dual protect and attack charm, and my compulsion one, and all the ways dandelion leaves could modify a spell. I'd been searching for *new* spells, *new* charms, thinking something as powerful as what Theodore did had to call for a type of Alchemy I'd never heard of. But maybe that wasn't true. Maybe there was a way to change the concept of a spell I'd seen before and make it work in a new way.

"Why all the questions?" Nox asked me.

"I'm trying to learn more about you so I can beat you in the third trial, obviously," I quipped.

"I knew this was a bad idea," Arowyn said, picking up the empty bottles. "She's plying us with Luxe."

I snorted. "Pretty sure tonight was *your* idea. I'm an innocent bystander."

"I don't think the three of us have ever been innocent in our lives," Nox said, laying his head back on the pillow beside me. "We wouldn't be here if we were."

Arowyn and I exchanged a glance. "That was awfully...dark," she said.

Nox drummed his fingers on his chest, those sharp claws coming out once more and pricking through the material every time they landed on it. Four small beads of blood bloomed at the surface. "When you've seen what I've seen, been through what I have, you realize this tournament"—he brandished his hand, talons retracting—"must be some sort of punishment from the Fates. A penance for who we are."

My eyebrows knit together. I'd never heard him talk like that. He was always so charming, so carefree, except for the rare times he'd brought up his past. Did he really believe the words he was saying? That he was here for a cosmic punishment?

I swallowed hard. "I think that's enough Luxe for one night."

"I'll help him get back to his room," Arowyn offered, standing and lugging him from the bed. "I thought this stuff was supposed to make you relaxed. What a downer."

The three of us said goodbye, Nox's eyelids already drooping as the pair left my room and made their way to their own chambers. The night had certainly ended more drearily than I'd expected. But I was reinvigorated to explore my father's Grimoire after the conversation about magic, eager to brainstorm new functions for spells I'd used before.

A tap on the window made me jump from the bed and hurry over to unlatch it. Leo crouched at the sill, his eyebrow raised.

"I see I wasn't the only guest here tonight," he said.

I laughed. "Were you spying on me?"

Stepping through the window, he tugged me to him and glowered at the door. "I got here a few minutes ago and have been waiting for them to leave."

I wound my arms around his neck. "Do I sense a bit of jealousy?"

His body felt stiff and strained pressed against mine, and a slight scowl was still on his face. Fates, he really *was* jealous. The thought made me smirk as I rose onto my toes and brought my lips to his neck, lightly kissing along the sensitive skin. I breathed him in and let out a hum. I always loved how good he smelled, like sandalwood and vanilla.

His limbs slowly began to relax. "Still jealous?" I murmured, trailing my nose on his jaw.

"That's not the word I'd use."

"Good." I placed another kiss on his neck and leaned back. "That was Arowyn and Nox. You have nothing to worry about."

Recognition lit in his eyes at the names. "I didn't realize Nox was so...pretty," he said grudgingly.

"Not my type," I said with a wink. "I prefer my men tortured and brooding. And with tails," I added, then tapped my lip. "Which Nox might have, actually."

With his hands at my waist, Leo pulled me closer. "You're incorrigible."

"And I have a feeling that's *your* type."

His lips met mine in a sweet kiss that had me melting into him. "Wait," I groaned between kisses. "I want to tell you something."

"I will kill him," Leo growled.

I laughed. "Possessive is a good look on you. Don't worry, it's not about Nox. You know I've been trying to find some new spell or magic to break the curse, and so far there's been nothing. But what if there's something we missed?"

"And hundreds of Alchemists before us? I highly doubt it."

"No, not something *new*. Something we already know, but that can be applied differently."

"So, modifying a spell?" he asked, dropping his arms as I pulled away to grab my father's Grimoire.

I nodded. "Kind of like how you changed the transformation spell when you were younger. That was a spell for transforming objects, but you went beyond that—you figured out how to transform living beings."

He pressed his lips together. "I wouldn't exactly recommend doing that again."

"I know, but that's just the basic idea. It's how I created the spell that attacked the snow leopard Shifter that night. I combined multiple protection charms that ward off unwanted presences into something that will *literally* backfire on your attacker. There are so many ways to use our magic. We're only limited by our own minds." Excitement built as I fingered the Grimoire, the urge to create and experiment flowing through me.

For a split second, I saw my father with me. The father from the portrait Theodore gave me that still sat on my nightstand. Theodore said he was studious and passionate, eager to explore his magic and revel in new theories. I felt him here, in the echoes of these worn pages. Saw him pushing his thin glasses up the bridge of his nose. His kind smile and curious eyes.

He would be here, if he could. Guiding me and searching with me. Celebrating discoveries. Practicing our magic.

I squeezed my eyes shut, my fingers gripping the leather binding. Fates, I wanted that. I missed him, even this nonexistent *idea* of him, so viscerally it felt like a knife through the chest.

Leo's lips pressed into my temple as his arm wrapped around my back. "I wish I'd known him," he said, nodding to the book. "The man who raised such a brave, resilient woman."

I smiled lightly. "I don't know about that."

"I do." His hand played with the bottom of my shirt, fingers grazing my skin as he spoke. "Look at you. Refusing to accept the way we've known Alchemy to work for centuries just to find a way to keep me from my fate. Your determination inspires me, Rose. It *humbles* me. To think that you believe I'm worth all of this..." He let out a soft breath that washed over my cheeks and made my heart constrict.

"Zareleon Aris," I said firmly, setting the book down and turning to face him. "You're wrong. This is not your fate. We make our *own* fate. There are no laws of magic I won't push, no boundaries I won't cross to prove it. I think there's a reason Gayl has wanted you to stay hidden. I don't understand why he's known the truth this whole time and has let you live. I was so blinded by my connection to him and the world he showed me that I believed his motives were altruistic, but now..." I exhaled loudly, my forehead scrunching as I tried to put my jumbled thoughts to words.

It had been nagging at the back of my mind, but my yearning to prove myself worthy of my father's past had made me ignore the warnings. Made me far too trusting of the emperor's words.

"I think there's more we don't know," I finished. "More he's hiding from us. And protecting you, not allowing Gayl to keep ruling this empire with his secrets...*that's* worth *everything*." I put both hands on the sides of Leo's face. "*You're* worth everything."

His gaze burned into me, swallowing me. Slowly, he lowered his forehead to mine, his shoulders releasing tension as we stood there.

"Thank you," he finally murmured.

My lips quirked up. "You don't have to thank me," I said, repeating the sentiment he'd shared with me multiple times now. "That's what friends do."

He laughed and took a breath. "So these ideas of yours. Where do we start?"

"Well, are you up for some light reading?"

"The night is young. Put me to work, little wolf."

We grabbed my packs of charms and climbed onto the bed with the Grimoire resting between us. "Back to the basics," I started. "Curses. What do we know about them?" I thought about my first conversation with Lark and how she'd interrogated me over this. Maybe she'd been on the right path after all.

"They're spells that cause harm," Leo said. "Or are accidental consequences of powerful magic. Either way, the results are damaging."

"What are some you can think of?" I asked, flipping through the pages.

"The sleeping curse, of course. There are many others that inflict physical pain. Blindness, skin afflictions like boils, breaking bones, suffocating."

I eyed him. "You seemed to think of those pretty quickly."

"I have to use what's at my disposal when stopping attacks in the capital," he said, his lips set in a grim line.

I contemplated the examples he gave. "Some of them are temporary and will go away after a while, but some of them have to be stopped by the person who cast it," I mused. "Such as when I cast the spell to steal the breath from Callum's lungs. Technically, that was a curse. And if I hadn't banished it, he would have died."

"We know Gayl isn't going to banish it," Leo said. "Either because he can't or doesn't want to."

"No, but there are other ways to stop a curse."

"Are you suggesting we kill him?"

The thought had crossed my mind, but I remembered what Rissa had said when I brought it up in their cottage. That was no way to start a new dynasty focused on peace. It was an option, though.

Then, Leo said something that made the wheels in my head start to turn faster.

"What if it's not the *caster* who has to die, but the magic?"

My eyes snapped to his. "The magic?"

He nodded. "That's what's holding the curse in place, not his physical body. If we can stop his magic, either pause it somehow or —or take it away, its hold would break, wouldn't it?"

That was *genius*. I leaned forward over the Grimoire and grabbed the back of his neck, hauling his lips to mine. "You're not just a handsome face, are you, Leo Aris?"

His hands gripped my waist and I toppled on top of him, his back hitting the bed. "Do you want to find out?" he murmured against me.

"I'd love to, but you know what I'd rather do more?" I kissed him again. "Figure out how to keep you alive and break this curse."

He sighed, his breath sending heat to my core. "And here I thought *I* was the responsible one."

I dragged myself off of him, trying and failing to ignore the way his shirt had ridden up, exposing tan, toned skin pulled tight across his lower abdomen. I exhaled slowly and forced myself to focus, even as he smirked up at me with those sparkling onyx eyes.

"I'm about to make you leave," I said.

Sitting up straight, he held his hands out in feigned innocence. I cleared my throat and asked, "Alright, so how do we get rid of someone's magic?"

"I've never heard of a person having their magic taken away, short of them leaving the borders of the empire."

I chewed on my thumbnail. The magic of the Veridian Empire only extended to our coasts. Once you left, magic didn't exist in other areas of the world—that we knew of—and therefore, *our* magic couldn't exist. It was why not many people ever left. There were a few accounts I'd read about some explorers who traveled too far out to sea and temporarily lost their ability to perform magic until they crossed back into the boundary of the empire.

"I wonder if there's a way to get Gayl across the borders," I said, then an idea hit me. "Can Striders carry other people?"

"I don't think so. Chaz never mentioned anything about it. You can't transfer powers over to others like that."

"But what if you *could*? That's the whole point of this—to think about things in a new way." I hastily pulled my father's book into my lap and flipped through the pages. There were a few spells that came to mind. It was a stretch, but it was *something*. "What if there was a spell or combination of spells that let you transfer magic into something else? Even if only temporarily?"

His eyes lit with intrigue and he moved to sit next to me, peering over my shoulder. His chin grazed my neck as he used my waist to balance himself. His fingers pressed into me, the rough pad of his thumb slipping beneath my shirt. When he caught me pausing, he chuckled low in my ear. "I'll be good, I promise."

Wetting my lips, I turned back to the Grimoire. There was a powerful replenishing enchantment I'd found in here days ago. It was for refilling herbs or other physical objects, but who was to say we couldn't strengthen it and use it on more intangible things? Not exactly what I needed, but maybe combined with something, we could reverse the effects and make it a depletion spell, instead.

"What about this?" Leo asked, pointing at a page as I was about to pass it. "A siphoning spell. Used for siphoning water and other materials away, or"—he leaned closer to read my father's faded scribbles—"he says he tried it for healing purposes. Siphoning away fluid from the lungs and infections from the body."

He looked at me as he finished speaking, and I could tell we were both thinking the same thing. "What if we could siphon *magic*?" I asked breathlessly.

Grinning at me, he said, "There's only one way to find out."

59

ROSE

"Do I have to go to the ball?" my cousin whined from his slumped position in the chair by my bed. His floppy brown hair swayed to the side as he looked behind me at Morgana.

A swift tug at my head had me rearing backward. With my hair still in my aunt's hands, she twisted to face her son. "For the fifth time, *yes*. Now stop complaining and let me finish Rose's hair."

She caught my eyes in the large mirror before us and smiled sheepishly at the wince on my face. "Sorry, Rosie," she said, loosening her grip. "What do you think, up or down?"

If it were up to me, I would've gone to this ball with my hair still wet from my bath, but Morgana had glowed at the chance to help me get ready. As little as I cared about this ridiculous masquerade in the midst of everything else, seeing her so excited after these weeks of torment by Ragnar's side was something I couldn't take away from her.

My features softened when I smiled at her in the mirror. "Whatever you think would look best."

Beaming, she turned to rummage through her bag, pulling out a comb and several pins. As she worked, and as she and Beau talked about palace life and shops in the village and all the new people they'd met, I felt my anxiety and looming sense of dread fade away. These moments of peace and *normalcy* with my family were so rare, I didn't want to forget a moment of it. No matter how fleeting it was.

"Once I'm done with Rose, it'll be your turn," Aunt Morgana said, pointing her comb at Beau.

He gaped at her. "What for?"

"I'm going to finally cut that mop of yours." She waved her hand in the air. "I've let it go on far too long—no, no arguing, it's got to go! Rose, don't you think his hair needs a good trim?"

They both stared at me expectantly. "Oh, I'm not getting in the middle of this," I said with a laugh. "But—you *do* kind of look like a mangy dog, Beau Beau."

Aunt Morgana cackled while Beau threw his hands up. "Women," he huffed, which made me break out into another fit of laughter. He crossed his arms and looked out the window. "Pa would be on my side."

The moment he said it, the air in the room seemed to still, and his eyes widened. "Sorry, I—"

"Your father would certainly want you looking sharp," Morgana interrupted, turning her attention back to my hair as she twisted the ends into an elegant knot. "Especially if he knew you'd been eyeing that girl from the palace for weeks." When she gave Beau a smile, the tension lifted.

"What's this about a *girl*?" I sang, winking at my cousin.

His cheeks reddened. "Aww, Ma, come on..." he grumbled, but the hint of a smile formed.

Mumbling around a pin in her mouth, Aunt Morgana plucked at my hair and said, "The daughter of one of the lords, I think. We've seen her walking in the gardens with her little dog, and Beau can never take his eyes off her."

"It's *true love*," I said dramatically, bringing my hands to my heart. "Does this girl have a name?"

My aunt shook her head. "I don't know—"

"Eliza," Beau muttered, embarrassed. "I heard her father calling for her the other day."

Morgana and I exchanged a glance. For the next ten minutes, we pestered him about Eliza until he was red in the face and looked ready to jump out the window. A warmth in my chest spread as Morgana finished my hair and moved to sit in front of me, her pouch of cosmetics in hand.

"I'm glad you're here," I said, grabbing her free hand.

She squeezed mine. "I am too, Rosie. I'm so proud of you. The courage it took to volunteer in Ragnar's place is something not many have. And sticking with it, especially after Emperor Gayl ambushed you like that, with all the talk about your father..." She shook her head, irritation lining her features as she swiped rouge across my cheeks. "I'm glad that group of boys walked away from Theodore while they still could."

I straightened. "What group of boys?"

"The ones who were always with Hamilton and Theodore all those years ago. I thought I told you about them?"

"No, you only mentioned my father and Theodore. There were more?"

Nodding grimly, she motioned for me to shut my eyes and brushed powder onto the lids. "Unfortunately, Theodore amassed quite the following among the young men in town. There were three or four I'd see regularly gathering around him. I kept my distance, you know, but the rumors..." I felt her hand stop moving, and I opened my eyes. "The Sanguivex, they called themselves. Purveyors of blood magic."

A beat passed, the name lingering in the air, until I heard Beau breathe out, "*Cool.*"

Morgana shot him a cross look as chills swept down my spine. "What happened to the rest of them?" I asked. "Are they still in Feywood?"

Morgana's jaw tightened. "No. They're dead."

"*All* of them?"

Nodding, she said, "Died within a couple years of your father."

We both went quiet as she applied kohl to my eyes and a cream to my lips. Gayl had said Branock Aris was responsible for my father's death, that he'd sent men out to kill those closest to Theodore as revenge for Gayl causing the curse. Did that mean he'd had those other men, the Sanguivex, assassinated too? Leo mentioned his father was brash, especially in the later days of his life, but the longer I got to know Leo and hear about his family, the harder it was to believe the former emperor would have done such a thing.

"Enough of that," Morgana said with a sigh, backing away and pasting a smile on her face as she admired her handiwork. "You look beautiful, Rose." She placed a finger under my chin and tilted my head up to meet her eyes. "So much like your mother."

I swallowed the lump in my throat. "I know I...I never knew her. And I've spent every day wishing I did. But I couldn't have asked for anyone better to be put in my life instead." I bit my lip, unfamiliar tears threatening to be set loose. "I love you and Ragnar so much. All three of you," I added, casting a glance at Beau. "I think I get too caught up in feeling sorry for myself that I forget how lucky I am. How thankful I should be, that fate gave me to you."

Morgana sniffed and took my hand. "Who are you, and what have you done with our Rose?" she asked teasingly as a tear tracked down her cheek. Motioning for Beau to join, she enveloped the two of us in a tight embrace. "My sweet children," she said softly. "How I love you both more than words can say."

I smiled at Beau and ruffled his hair as Morgana pulled away with another sniff. "Now, let's get *you* into your dress"—she pointed at me—"and *you* into the chair." She gripped Beau by the neck and plopped him in the seat I'd just vacated, then grabbed a pair of small scissors. "It's time."

———

"WELL, darling, I had no idea you'd take my nickname to heart," Nox drawled as he leaned against the doorframe to my room, taking in my ball gown.

Sheer dark green fabric hung from my shoulders, cascading down my arms until it cinched at my wrists. Gold designs in the shape of serpents were threaded delicately along the sleeves. The solid deep green bodice fastened at the chest with gold laces, then opened at my waist to flow like a cape down my legs, which were encased in matching tights with decorative snakes slithering up the sides.

I pointed my toe out with a sly grin, showing off my gold sandals. "I figured it was time I embraced it."

Beau and Morgana had already left for the ball, seeing as the challengers were supposed to arrive after everyone else to make our grand entrance. Arowyn peered out from over Nox's shoulder and raised an eyebrow at me. "Green looks good on you."

I reached for my gold mask, slipping the dagger next to it in a small sheath at my thigh. "Are you two ready?"

Nox held out his arms to Arowyn and me, and I slid mine through. "Don't get any ideas, Nox," I joked, glancing between the three of us. Arowyn's long, pale blonde hair hung down to her waist, brushing against the beautiful navy cloak she wore over a silver bodysuit. The sheen material flowed over her large curves like moonlight and ended in her normal pair of combat boots.

"Where's your mask?" I asked her.

"I'm wearing it." She pointed to her face, the black kohl beneath her eyes more prominent than normal against a pale blue shimmer on her cheeks. Black paint lined her lips, and when she smiled, it was a kind of lethal beauty that would have her enemies tucking their tails between their legs. "It's called feminine rage," she said dryly.

Nox chuckled. "You look the same as always."

"Exactly."

I eyed Nox as we began our walk down the hall. He looked like sin and mystery wrapped in one with his all-black ensemble, down to the glittering rings on his fingers. He wore a sleek black button down beneath his velvet jacket, the top buttons undone and showing a glimpse of his chest. Tied around his head was a black and white fox mask with ears that came up above his forehead.

I couldn't hold back my smile. Rissa would approve.

As we descended a floor and approached the second-floor entrance to the ballroom, the sounds of tapping heels and ringing laughter grew louder. Sweet scents of wine and pastries mixed with fresh flowers and perfume caressed us as the hired musicians played a beautiful melody that echoed through the halls.

"Now," Nox started, clearing his throat. "We're all in agreement that after tonight, we go back to being enemies?"

"Obviously," Arowyn said. "How else am I going to beat the two of you in the third trial?"

I turned to straighten Nox's lapel. "Of course. I can't stand you anyway."

He scowled and gripped both my hand and Arowyn's, forcing us into twirls in front of him. "At least the pair of you keep me humble."

"I don't think that word's in your vocabulary. Come on," Arowyn said, leading him to the entrance. "I'm thirsty."

"When are you *not*," he grumbled.

"I'll catch up with you," I called after them. "I need to get my mask on."

Their steps blended into the rest of the noise as they entered the ballroom. I fumbled at my head with the thin strand of ribbon on my gold, serpentine mask.

"Allow me," a deep, familiar voice said at my back, before warm hands covered mine. My heart jolted.

"Leo," I breathed out as he tied the mask in place. "What are you doing here?"

He ran his fingers along the exposed skin at the back of my neck, then replaced them with his lips. "I wanted to surprise you."

I twirled to face him and found myself staring into dark eyes surrounded by a simple but elegant black mask, complementing his black jacket and white dress shirt. "What if you're caught?"

"It's a masquerade," he said with a smirk, motioning to his mask. "And Horace said he would hold an illusion over me. That's the only way I could convince Rissa it was safe to come. Nobody will know who I am."

I licked my lips hesitantly, still worried someone may recognize him, but my happiness at seeing him won out.

"I'm glad you're here," I confessed.

"How could I miss seeing you in this?" he said, his eyes roving hungrily over my gown and tights. His hand fell to my wrist, then trailed up the fabric until moving to my waist. "How could I miss being able to dance with you in front of all these people?" Drawing me closer and lowering his head, his nose skimmed against mine as the edges of our masks touched. "I love our nights tucked away together, but I want just *one* where we don't have to keep it a secret. You're not meant to be hidden in the dark, little wolf, but adored in the light."

My breath caught in my throat. His dark eyes glittered with the depth of his feelings for me. It was a look I wished I could freeze on his features for eternity.

"Then what are you waiting for?" I reached to place a kiss on his lips, then backed away with a wink. "Come adore me."

60

LEO

The capital spared no expense for their precious ball. Lush, deep emerald and gold drapes hung from the ceiling of the three-story grand ballroom, cascading in waves down the six marble columns that lined the perimeter. A myriad of gilded lanterns, some as tall as my waist, bordered the entire room. Greenery dotted with red roses filled the space in between, making it feel as if we were stepping onto a bed of flowers.

Circular tables dotted the floor. Some held glasses of sparkling wine while others contained platters of pastries with gold frosting, savory meats, and fine cheeses. The vibrant colors, loud laughter, and mingled scents of florals, sugary spices, and smoked delicacies overwhelmed my senses, forcing me to cut off my Shifter half completely in order to dull the onslaught.

As Rose slipped away to where the challengers were supposed to meet and I faded into the shadows, I watched the masked couples dressed in their finest gowns and suits gliding across the dance floor to the music coming from the back of the hall, their inhibitions lowered under the mystery of the night.

Lark strode across the ballroom and onto the raised platform in her black gown and mask made of antlers. She held out an arm and shadows formed at her fingertips, swirling around the lit sconces and chandeliers until the lighting dimmed. A hush swept over the crowd.

"Ladies and gentlemen, welcome to the thirty-second Decemvirate ball." Applause rang out in the hall. "I hope you enjoy this night of revelry and indulgence on all the empire has to offer as we honor the challengers of our great provinces. They have competed well in their trials, and now only one more remains. One more to determine their strength and courage, their power and fortitude."

I glimpsed several reporters near the stage. Their pencils moved quickly across paper, soaking in the display. No doubt painting a perfect picture of intrigue and magic and beauty to release to the public the following day, romanticizing this tournament and what it stood for. I couldn't help but think of that Lightbender family we'd helped a week ago and all the other victims my path had crossed over the years. They didn't want a fancy ball with decadent meats and glasses dripping in gold.

They wanted safety and security. They wanted enough food to feed their families. They wanted to live without fear.

I saw a hint of the same disgust on Lark's dark features as her eyes scanned the crowd, her upper lip twitching as if holding back a sneer. She'd been forced to become so adept at restraining her emotions in this role. It was something I didn't give her enough credit for, having to live in the middle of what we all despised.

"Would you like to meet your challengers?" Lark asked, and the guests erupted into cheers, feet pounding and glasses clinking. "Currently in first place is the Strider from Celestria, Arowyn Garrolas."

The Strider stepped from the shadows behind the platform. She was a curvy woman wearing a silver bodysuit and navy cloak, with light blonde hair that flowed to her waist. I recognized her—she'd been in the bedroom with Rose and Nox the previous night. Rose had spoken of her some, mentioning how the three of them had formed a friendship over the weeks in the palace.

In second place was Callum, the Illusionist who'd attacked

Rose multiple times at the beginning of the tournament. The sight of his smug features as the guests cheered and clapped for him had me tightening my grip on my flute.

"And finally," Lark called out, "our three remaining challengers all hold the third position. Alaric Rinehart, Shadow Wielder of Tenebra"—the older man stepped out, waving jovially and nodding at his supporters—"Rose Wolff of Feywood"—she took her place next to Alaric, her face impassive and fierce—"and the Shifter, Nox Duma."

The same man from Rose's bedroom sauntered across the platform in his fine black apparel. Nox's gaze landed briefly on mine when he looked out over the ballroom, and a prickle of awareness rose on the back of my neck. I shrugged it off as nothing more than jealousy, as Rose had accused me of.

The applause ended and the music began again. Rose made her way through the crowd and back to me, stopped every few feet by guests wanting to shake her hand and congratulate her. Her eyes brightened when they found mine. I glanced over at Horace, who stood near the entrance in his silver Royal Guard uniform, and he gave me a subtle nod, confirming his illusion was in place over me.

I stalked out of the shadows, drawn to her as if there was a string tying us together. There were so many threats looming in on us—the trial, the curse, Gayl—that had my protective instincts always on alert, always wanting to feel her soft and steady and safe at my side. I didn't want to think about her competing in the third trial so soon, of her being out of reach, surrounded by people she couldn't trust, facing magic she hadn't been prepared for...it made a fear I'd only reserved for Rissa and my mother grip me.

Fear for her safety, and fear for what these emotions meant.

For how much I wanted her.

A month ago, nothing could have deterred me from this mission. From bringing down Gayl and finally making things right. My sister dreamt of a better future for the empire where justice and safety weren't afterthoughts for our people. Of course, I wanted that as well. But I'd learned over the years that while she was driven by her integrity, I was driven by revenge. It made me cold and hardened, more calloused toward the feelings of others than I wished to be.

Rose made me see past that solitary motivation. Made me realize that perhaps there was more to live for than this fixation, this resentment. For the first time, there was something blooming inside of me instead of festering. And I wanted to hold on to that, to *her*, for as long as I could.

But how long would that be?

A cold weight sunk in my chest.

The curse.

My life...it wasn't mine anymore. It was tied to the people of this empire, to the victims who had been suffering for over two decades. Entire lives, frozen. Gone. And I had the ability to end it. The *responsibility*. To save Rose's uncle, Chaz, and countless others lost to the curse. If Rose's plan didn't work, if we couldn't—

Suddenly, Rose's hand was at my cheek. "What's the matter? You look worried."

I wrapped one arm around her waist and covered her hand. I didn't want to think about that. Not on one of the final nights I'd get to spend with her before everything changed. "It's nothing." I kissed her palm. "Will you dance with me?"

She gave me a light smirk, the one that made my skin heat. "Thought you'd never ask."

My hand roamed to the small of her back and I pulled her flush to my body. It made me think of the first time we'd been this close and of all the excuses I'd made since then to touch her.

"Do you remember," I said as we swept across the dance floor, "that morning in the alcove?"

She nodded, her eyes never leaving mine.

"I recognized you the moment I saw you. The Alchemist from the forest. I remember wondering what could have made that same fierce goddess appear so..."

"Weak?" she interjected when I paused.

"No, Rose. I don't think you've ever been weak." I twirled her in time to the music, and she spun back into me. "I was going to say *lost*. And afraid. All I wanted was to take that fear from you. To see you light up the way you do now. To hold you like this"—I pressed my forehead to hers as we moved—"and tell you that you weren't alone. That I was lost, too. I didn't even know your name, but still, I wanted you then." Her breath hitched when I tightened my grip around her hand. "And when you broke into my house—"

She scoffed softly. "I didn't *break in*."

A chuckle rumbled through my chest. "So stubborn." When I saw her red lips twist into a smile and her green eyes sparkle, all thoughts left my mind. "So beautiful," I said, the words leaving my mouth unbidden as my thumb brushed her jaw.

"I *was* lost," she whispered, turning her head to gaze at the moving couples around us. We had slowly made our way to glass-paned double doors leading to a balcony. The evening breeze rustled against Rose's flowing tunic. "Sometimes I think I still am. But I'm not scared anymore. Not with you, anyway."

We drifted away from the dancers, through the doors and out onto the balcony. Vines twisted around the marble railing over-looking the palace gardens, our bodies sheathed in moonlight as the sounds of the ball faded.

"Well, that makes one of us," I said with a quiet laugh.

Her forehead moved, and I could practically see her eyebrows raising beneath the mask. "What are you scared of?"

I took a deep breath. "I used to be scared of my past. Of people discovering what I had done, how my actions led to my father's death...it's haunted me my entire life. But you didn't walk away, even after knowing the truth." We swayed under the stars, fears I'd never voiced falling from my lips.

"I'm scared of failing him, of never freeing his legacy and clearing our name. I'm scared of letting my sister down after every-thing she's worked for. I'm scared of...the truth." I swallowed hard, letting her clear gaze seep into me, strengthening me. "That the curse truly rests on me and that it's only a matter of time until—"

"Stop," she commanded, her throat bobbing. "I'm not going to let anything happen to you. There are ways out of this, remember?"

I smiled and dragged a finger along the edge of her mask, skimming her cheek. "Not even you can stop fate, little wolf."

Her features tightened. "Watch me."

My eyes stayed trained on her lips, captivated by them. By *her*. That ferocity inside I loved so much.

"And I'm scared of *you*," I confessed.

Eyes wide, she said, "Of *me*?"

My brow furrowed as I took her in. "All my life, I've been driven by a singular purpose. Steady, unyielding resolve. But you...you have *consumed* me, Rose. My every thought, my every breath." I brought her hand up to gently kiss her palm, then her wrist. "I've placed all of myself into your hands, and that's a beautiful, terrifying thing."

"Why is that?" she breathed out.

"Because you can either crush me," I said, closing her hand into a fist, "or love me." I brushed my lips over her knuckles.

Her arm trembled beneath my hold. "You could do the same to me, you know."

Slowly, I shook my head and put her hand on my chest. "I've already chosen to love you, Rose Wolff. Beyond sense, beyond reason. There is no part of you I do not *choose*."

Her lips parted on an exhale as her fingers curled around the fabric of my black jacket. "Leo, I—"

"Ah, there you are, Rose. Arowyn and I—" A voice stopped as soon as it started, followed by the sound of someone's throat clearing. I turned to face Nox. The moment I laid eyes on him, something vicious pounded in my sternum.

I straightened, inhaling sharply. Shifters had a certain instinct, a primal force inside that could sense the Shifter magic in others, if it was strong enough. While I'd never been to Drakorum, I was told that was often how roles of power and leadership were decided in their province; instinct helped decipher the strongest of the bloodline. It was an internal reaction to their magic.

I'd sensed it before when coming across other Shifters in the capital, but it always felt like a small prick. A nudge against my Shifter half. Sometimes it was so small, I barely noticed it at all.

But this man, this Shifter...

I had never felt something more powerful.

It was like a blow to the chest. Every muscle in my body seized for that split second his eyes were on mine, as if begging to submit. To bow down as an animal would to their alpha.

I gritted my teeth, a growl building in the back of my throat.

Rose trusted him. She'd once told me he didn't want to be here, didn't want anything to do with the power-hungry ways of the capital and all it stood for. And while that may be true, I couldn't help but wonder if there was more.

How had the Sentinels not heard of him before? We had eyes and ears in every province, spies among all the leadership, files on any person of interest across the empire. I wracked my memory, certain I'd never seen or heard the name Nox Duma in any report or document.

And yet here he was. A Shifter so powerful he made that half of my blood rise to the surface. A secret Drakorum had hidden from the empire.

"I apologize. I didn't mean to...interrupt." He cocked his head. "Who do we have here, Rose? Seems you've been keeping some secrets from us," he teased.

She met my eyes, and I gave an almost imperceptible shake of my head. Glancing back at Nox, she said, "He's a...friend. Can you give me a minute?"

"As you wish," he said with a shrug. His gaze lingered on me as he walked off. Not threateningly, but thoughtful. Curious.

Before Rose could speak, I moved us toward the edge of the balcony so the noise from the ball inside would drown out the sounds of our voices, should Nox choose to listen in.

"Are you sure you can trust him?" I asked hurriedly.

She paused, startled. "Who, Nox?"

"Yes. There's something off about him."

"I told you how he feels about all of this. He doesn't even want to be here, but his province forced him. And he's done nothing but help me."

"What exactly did he say about his province?"

A small crease appeared on her forehead above her mask. "He said that—that there was no higher honor than being the Drakorum challenger, and implied he would've been punished had he not come. He didn't have a choice."

"Or so he told you."

Her voice became impatient. "He was drinking Grimlock when we talked, Leo. He couldn't have lied."

"Grimlock doesn't always work. Not on someone strong enough to fight it. And Nox..." I ran a finger along my lower lip. "Shifters have this instinct when it comes to those who share our magic. I can *feel* his power. He is by far the strongest Shifter I've ever come across."

"Just because someone is powerful doesn't mean they're hiding something. Aren't *you* the one who told me we're more than our magic?" she countered.

I let out a breath. "You're right. Maybe he's telling the truth. But you said it yourself, he didn't have a choice. Drakorum has been hiding him this entire time. We would have heard about someone like him, unless they were intentionally keeping him out of sight. What if it's *them* we can't trust?"

Rose faced the gardens beyond the balcony and scratched her neck. Leaning my head back, I sighed, frustrated at myself for turning this night around. I knew she struggled with trusting others, and here I was, causing her to doubt one of the only friendships she'd formed here simply because of my paranoia.

I stood behind her and planted my hands on the balcony rail, pressing a kiss to her temple. "I'm sorry, Rose. It's probably nothing. Let's forget I said anything and go enjoy the ball, alright?"

Craning her neck to look up at me, she searched my eyes for a moment before nodding, then twisted out of my grip and led me back into the ballroom. I pulled her in for another dance, trying to let go of my apprehension.

Her eyes fixed on something behind me and her features hardened instantly.

Someone tapped on my shoulder.

"May I cut in?"

61

ROSE

Leo stiffened. I could barely breathe, hoping and praying that both his mask and Horace's illusion were enough to keep the emperor's attention away from his identity.

"Of course, Your Majesty," Leo said, clenching my hand briefly before releasing it. He kept his eyes to the ground when he bowed to Theodore, then swiftly slunk into the shadows. His gaze caught mine for a split second, revealing onyx pits of wariness and anger. I gave him a small smile as I tried to silence the fear screaming in my head. I hadn't seen Theodore since I ran out on him in his chambers. Would he be angry with me? Did he know Leo was here? Had he discovered what the Sentinels had been planning?

I swallowed and schooled my features, taking my uncle's gloved hand.

"You look lovely, niece," Theodore said. He kept me at arm's length as we danced alongside the other guests.

"Thank you. The ball is beautiful. You must be proud." My voice was stilted and cordial. He tilted his head, his hair pouring over one shoulder at the motion. Those mismatched blue and white eyes sliced into me, so much brighter surrounded by a deep emerald mask. He wore a black tailcoat inlaid with fine green and gold threading, but otherwise, he appeared like any ordinary guest. I wondered how many people flying past us even knew the emperor stood in their presence.

"I know what it is to be proud, Miss Wolff, and this pageantry"—his gaze roamed over the ballroom—"is not it." Each word was crisp, each syllable enunciated.

I kept my mouth shut for once, even though I wanted to snap and ask why he continued to hold such an event if that's the way he felt. I fixed my eyes on some point behind him, focusing on controlling my breaths.

"I saw such potential in you, you know," he said after a moment, almost inaudible over the sound of the music. "Daughter of the great Hamilton Wolff. As fierce and cunning and curious as he was. But I pushed you too far." My eyes shot to his. "I wanted my brother back, and it was unfair to place those expectations on your shoulders."

I stayed silent, blinking back my surprise.

His grip tightened. "Make no mistake, Rose. We could do many great and wonderful things together. Things your father and I only dreamed of. But it has to be your *choice*." The word came out in a hiss.

"Theo—Emperor Gayl," I stuttered. "I'm grateful for what you've taught me. And getting to learn more about my father...it's something I never thought would be possible. You've given me a piece of my past. But this—I can't be what you want me to be. I've made my choice."

The song ended, and the side of his lips shifted into a half-grimace, half-smile. He took my hand, placing a chaste kiss on my knuckles.

"As have I," he said. "I'm sorry, Rose."

My mouth went dry. "For what?"

He met my stare again. "Everything."

The sharp sound of metal clinking against glass made me jump and tear myself from his gaze to look toward the raised platform. Lark stood there in the black and gold velvet dress she'd tried on at the dress shop, the antler mask made of bone casting shadows on the wall behind her.

When I glanced back at the emperor, he was gone.

"I trust you have all had a magical evening celebrating the looming end of the Decemvirate. I am privileged to announce that our great Emperor Gayl is in attendance tonight and wishes to say a few words."

The audience clapped. A pressure built at the base of my spine, crawling its way up my back. Something was wrong.

Gayl strode silently along the platform, the tails of his black coat fluttering behind him. He stopped in the center and surveyed the ballroom before him.

"Thank you all for being here," he began, and the crowd went still. "It brings me great joy to see the people of this empire bonding. Royal"—he nodded toward a group of lords in the corner—"challenger"—his eyes crossed to me—"and guest alike. It's my wish that despite the storms that may come our way, we are able to stand strong together. Through the magic and might of this land, anything is possible."

A ringing formed low in my ears as I twisted my neck, searching for Leo. I needed to find him. Slowly, I began to inch my way to the back.

"That is why we have always held the Decemvirate in such high regards. It pushes each province to be at their best, to work toward a common goal. To strive for glory. And this year, we have been gifted with a particularly vigorous group of challengers."

I brushed against a black jacket and glanced up to see Nox. When he looked at me, I gasped. The pupils of his eyes were long slits encased in silver. His nostrils flared as he blinked and his eyes returned to normal.

"We need to get out of here, Rose," he whispered. A command laced with fear.

Confusion flew through me. What was he talking about? I opened my mouth to respond, half of my attention still focused on finding Leo, when Gayl spoke once again.

"They have shown competence and skill with their minds, passing our little riddles and tests. They mastered their hearts—or at the very least, discovered what lies at their core. But courage"—he paused, taking a moment to think as he paced the platform, all eyes trained on him—"testing courage is a difficult thing. For how does one assess the bravery of the strongest in the empire?"

"Now, Rose. We have to go *now*," Nox said again, the crowd beginning to rustle with restlessness. I searched the columns as panic bubbled to the surface. *Where is he?*

Something flashed in the shadows behind the green drapes.

I lurched toward it.

"Real courage displays itself in the face of the unexpected. The unprepared. I think you will find, dear guests, who will rise to the challenge"—Gayl's voice rang out as Leo's face came into view—"and who will fall."

I stretched out my hand to meet Leo's, my heart flying into my throat. But before our fingers could touch, the air between us rippled. My vision went in and out of focus. I blinked hard to wipe away the haze. Leo's fingers...they were fading. Fragmenting. Floating.

A heaviness swept over my skin. Looking down at my own hands, I sucked in a breath.

Somewhere nearby, glass shattered as Gayl's words echoed through the night.

"Let the third trial begin."

And the ballroom disappeared.

THE
THIRD
TRIAL

62

ROSE

I opened my eyes to stifling darkness. The world was black, like someone had draped a curtain over my face. I struggled to breathe in the suffocating space, the musty scent of earth and wood clogging my senses.

Something rough pressed into my back. When I turned to feel for it, my arms hit solid wood. I frantically pushed and thrashed against it, trying to free my limbs, but I barely had room to move.

I was trapped. Encased in some sort of box, probably underground if the scent and heaviness in the air was any indication.

My breaths came out in short spurts. A surge of panic rose from my feet all the way to my throat, threatening to burst through my skin. I couldn't stop the whimper that escaped me.

Where *was* I?

"Let the third trial begin."

This was the final trial. It had started early, catching all of us unaware. A test of bravery, of our courage and ability to act in the face of fear.

Off to a great start.

I swallowed down the dread, forcing aside the dizziness and clearing the sparks of racing adrenaline from my vision. I could do this. I could get out of here if I kept a cool head.

Taking a few deep, calming breaths, I steadied my mind. Slowly, I began to push against all four sides of the enclosure, testing the wood and feeling for gaps as best I could with the limited space. There was a small crack on the right side, as if it were the opening for a door. Pressing harder with my knees and palms, I tried to force the top open, only to be met with the sound of something clanging on the outside.

A lock.

I knew spells to open doors and break into locks, but hadn't brought any herbs with me to the ball. I'd let my guard down for *one night* and look at what had happened. I squeezed my eyes shut, letting out a groan of frustration.

Until I remembered...

I may not have brought my herbs with me, but I *did* have my dagger.

For a moment, I paused. I didn't want to keep using blood magic if I could help it. But how else was I supposed to get out? How was I supposed to survive this trial if I didn't use all the tools at my disposal?

I didn't have a choice.

Wiggling my arm down my side, I grunted at the awkward angle as I clawed through the outer fabric of my gown and to the thigh strap over my tights. I gripped the small handle and slid it upward until it was at my stomach. Carefully, I brought my other hand to my midsection, feeling for the blade. When my skin met cold metal, I pressed the pad of my thumb against it, waiting for the familiar sting.

"*Vata lai,*" I whispered, expecting to hear the click of a lock opening.

Instead, the entire top of the box blew open with a thunderous crash.

I gasped as chunks of wood sprayed around me, cutting across my cheeks and arms. Splinters embedded themselves in my exposed skin. I laid there in shock, the deafening sound still ringing in my ears as I tried to catch my breath.

"Well, that's one way to do it," I mumbled. Wincing, I gripped the sides of the box and hauled myself out, muscles and joints groaning from stiffness.

I ripped the mask from my face and took in my surroundings. Firelight flickered off dirt walls from torches lit every dozen feet. The narrow tunnel extended down as far as I could see, with nothing but scuttling insects and shards of wood from my would-be coffin in the path.

Buried alive. Fates, this trial.

I stepped out of the box and grabbed the nearest torch, then began to make my way down the tunnel.

What were we supposed to do, escape this underground pit? Find the other challengers and fight each other? Face our greatest fears? The unknown was worse than the actual trial itself. Silence rang through my ears, the stillness of the tunnels grating at my nerves, making me twitch every time I heard a small creature or the crackle of flames.

After several minutes of walking, I came across a fork in the path. The tunnel split into two identical sides of seemingly neverending dirt and faint firelight.

To the right, I noticed several torches at the far end waver, then snuff out. One by one, the light disappeared, the darkness making its way closer to the fork where I stood.

"Alright, then," I said, pivoting and plunging down the opposite path at a sprint.

This section was rockier than the last, with winding turns and dirt falling from the ceiling every few feet. My breathing was fast and heavy, and I had to cover my mouth to avoid choking on dust. Both the smoke from my torch and the crumbling dirt made it hard to see. I cursed these ridiculous sandals as blisters started to rub at my heels.

Suddenly, my toe snagged on a rock. I went sprawling, rough dirt scraping my skin as the torch flew from my hand and rolled across the ground.

Thick vines emerged from the dirt and surrounding walls,

encircling my ankles and holding me in place. I let out a muffled scream and pulled at them. They thickened in response, pushing my legs painfully into the ground. Kicking and flailing, I sawed at the stems with my dagger, trying to think past my shock and find a spell that could help.

But before I could use the blood still oozing from my thumb, another vine snatched my right wrist and sent my dagger flying. I swallowed a scream and latched onto the stalk with my free hand, pulling with all my strength to wrench it from the ground.

Nothing worked. My feet and hand went numb, pain radiating up my legs as the vine cut deeper, threatening to pull me down and bury me beneath the surface.

Another one appeared at my left side, snaking its way toward my stomach. Right before it reached me, a cloud of darkness enveloped my waist, so thick the vine couldn't penetrate its walls.

"What the—" I whipped my head around.

Behind me stood Lark, swathed in angry shadows. My dagger was in her hand as she bent forward and hacked viciously at the vine grasping my right wrist.

"Lark! What are you *doing* here?"

"Saving your life." The vine released me and I yanked my arm back, flinching at the red marks sunken into my skin.

Rubbing the last remnants of my blood between my fingers, I opened my mouth to cast a fire spell on the vines, then remembered how powerful my opening charm had been. An image of my legs being burnt to a crisp flashed through my mind.

"Grab a torch," I said to Lark instead. "Set them on fire."

She did as I suggested, and soon the vines shrank from my legs and into the ground, bits of it tattered and charred. I scrambled backward and rested my head against the wall, closing my eyes to catch my breath.

"Are you alright?" Lark asked.

I opened my eyes and glared at her. "What do *you* think? What's going on, Lark? Why did the trial start early?"

She slumped against the opposite wall as her shadows receded, then tossed my dagger across the floor at my feet. "I don't know. The emperor...he took all of us by surprise. The trial wasn't supposed to start for two more days. I had no idea he was planning this, nor how he did it without my knowledge." She paused, and I took a moment to study her.

Her long, black hair had been pulled into braids and bundled at the top of her head during the ball, but several sections were now dislodged and wild, framing her ashen features. She looked truly frightened—an emotion I hadn't seen on the head architect, who was always so poised and put together. Rips covered her beautiful black gown, her mask already foregone and the heels of her shoes broken off. In one hand she held the antlers from her mask, the sharp end coated in blood.

My eyes widened. "Do I want to know?"

She glanced down at the antlers. "It's not human, if that's what you're wondering."

"That doesn't make me feel better."

"I ran into a wild animal. The emperor wanted us to include some...obstacles for the challengers." She winced at the glower I gave her. "I'm sorry, Rose, but saying no to Emperor Gayl is a death wish. You must realize that."

I averted her gaze. "How did you even end up here?"

"I don't know." Her throat moved as she swallowed. "This wasn't the plan. But that doesn't matter right now. We need to get out."

She helped me to my feet and I collected my dagger, letting her guide me as we ventured further down the tunnel. "Where is 'here,' exactly?" I asked, grabbing another torch from the wall.

"In the underground tunnels of an uninhabited island a little ways off the coast of Mysthelm. I'm not even sure they know of its existence, honestly. Emperor Gayl has had us working over the past few years to turn it into the landscape for this final trial."

An uninhabited island. I wondered how many more areas of the world were out there that we weren't aware of. "So what, we're supposed to figure out how to get out of the tunnels?"

She gave me a look. "You're supposed to figure out how to get off the *island*."

"Great. And how do we do that, exactly?"

She opened her mouth to reply when a pale hand shot out from behind her, covering her mouth and hauling her backward. I whirled and caught a glimpse of long, blonde hair before shadows surrounded me.

"Lark!" I yelped, trying to step through the darkness. Shadows lashed at my skin in response.

"This wasn't how I wanted it to go, Rose," a familiar voice said. A figure parted the shadows, and I found myself face to face with Alaric Rinehart.

"Oh, we are *not* doing this again," I muttered and, without thinking, tossed my torch in his face. Using his momentary distraction to my advantage, I sliced the still-stinging cut on my thumb back open and said, "*Praetum firma.*"

A solid, shimmering shield shot from my hands, the force of it sending Alaric sailing through the air. His body slammed into the tunnel wall and his shadows instantly dissipated. He fell to the floor in a heap, blood glistening on the wall where he'd hit.

A sinking weight crashed to my feet. Had I *killed* him?

I scrambled to his still form, fingers shaking when I pressed them against his pulse.

I let out a breath. His heartbeat was there, however faint. He was alive.

This blood magic...it made everything so much stronger. I could have killed him when all I wanted was a way to defend myself. My skin prickled with unease and I glanced at the wound on my thumb, sucking it between my teeth to lessen the sting.

"Efficient. I like it." Arowyn's voice materialized beside me. I jumped back, only narrowly containing a scream as she said, "Thanks for getting him off my back. He was annoying."

"Were you *working* with him?" I shouted, betrayal blazing through me.

"I just want to get out of here, Rose. If teaming up with the competition is what it takes, then I'll do it."

I clenched my jaw. "Where is Lark?"

"She's down the tunnel." Arowyn motioned to our left. "We only wanted to split you two up so you couldn't fight together. I didn't hurt her. But imagine my surprise when we found you cozying up with the head architect." She cocked her head, her hair flowing down her side. Gone was the friend I'd made in those days at the capital. In her place stood a bloodthirsty, suspicious challenger, a Strider with everything to lose. "Seems our little Rose may not be playing fair."

"She doesn't know how she got here, Arowyn," I insisted. "Gayl turned on her. She had no idea the trial was starting tonight."

"She's telling the truth." Lark came into view, panting as she made her way toward us. "I show no favoritism, Miss Garrolas. I want to escape and figure out what's happening, the same as both of you. Perhaps we can work together."

Arowyn looked between the two of us with distrust in her eyes.

"Please, Arowyn," I said. "We can find Nox and get out of here."

She pinched her lips together and backed away slowly. "I—I can't work with friends."

My forehead creased. "Why not? We want to help you."

"Because I don't want to *hurt* you, Rose," she snapped, her nostrils flaring. "And there can only be one winner."

In the blink of an eye, she vanished.

63

ROSE

I stared at the spot Arowyn disappeared from. I understood why she did it—making friends in this tournament was a risk, knowing you'd have to face them in the end. But it didn't make it hurt any less.

Lark hunched over Alaric, checking his pulse and repositioning him so he was flat on the ground.

"Come on," I said. "We have to keep going."

She looked up at me. "And leave him like this? I'm still the head architect. The challengers are *my* responsibility."

"This whole *thing* is your responsibility, Lark!" I threw out a hand in frustration. "And look where that's gotten us. If you want to stay down here with him, then fine. But I have a trial to beat. One I'm only in because you put me here."

Lark kneaded her forehead with her knuckles. "Fine. When we get back to the capital, I can always have someone check on him."

I stayed quiet. I didn't want to say it, but I had a feeling if Lark was in here with us, her days of commanding others were over.

We walked deeper into the tunnels and came across another fork. "Do you know how to get out of here?" I asked.

"I oversaw the creation of the trial, but didn't work as closely

on this section. It's a labyrinth." She cleared her throat. "I have a...
basic idea of its structure."

I hummed. Her hesitancy didn't exactly inspire confidence, but
it was better than what I could offer.

We heard a shout in the distance. Lark and I glanced at each
other, equal looks of trepidation on our features. I scratched my
ear. "So, we should probably—"

"Let's go," she said, picking up the pace as we headed toward
the sounds of distress.

"Right," I mumbled to myself. "Let's go *after* the strange
shouts."

As we grew closer, shadows appeared on the ground ahead of
us from around the corner—what looked like two figures darting
at one another, their muffled words becoming clearer.

That's when I heard it. *Him.*

"I don't want to hurt you, Illusionist."

That low voice, one that soothed me to sleep, that sent shivers
down my spine when brushed against my ear...

"Leo," I whispered, pressing a hand to my lips.

"What?" Lark barked. "How could he possibly be here?"

I shook my head. "I don't know. But he said 'Illusionist'...
Callum must be with him." Blood roared in my ears. I broke into a
sprint with Lark on my heels. Turning the corner, I saw them—Leo
in his black pants with his white dress shirt rolled up his sleeves,
formal jacket torn on the floor behind him; and Callum in a
midnight blue suit, one of his sleeves ripped off at the shoulder
and wrapped around his thigh. Dark liquid seeped from beneath
the fabric, as if he'd been wounded. His eyes narrowed in a look of
furious concentration. Leo's henbane rings glowed with signs of a
recent spell. The air was thick with his magic and the scent of
smoke and herbs.

They both turned when Lark and I burst onto the scene.

"Leo, watch out!" I cried as Callum shifted his hands to create
some invisible illusion that made Leo dive to the side. I charged

toward Callum, anger simmering under my skin. He took one look at his three opponents, shot me a smirk, and took off in the other direction toward a three-way split in the tunnel. An enormous brick wall appeared in his wake, causing me to skid to a halt.

Groaning in frustration, I swiped my hand through the air, finding the wall to be an illusion—*of course*—but he'd already gotten away. I couldn't tell which of the three paths he'd taken.

"Coward!" I called, my voice echoing down the tunnel.

"Rose," Leo murmured behind me. I turned back to him, crossing the distance and throwing myself into his arms.

"How are you here?" I cried out. He wasn't supposed to be anywhere near the third trial. First Lark, now Leo.

Something was very wrong.

"I don't know," he said. "After we disappeared from the ballroom, I woke up down here. I thought it was Gayl finally making his move against me until I found Callum."

"We're in the middle of the third trial," Lark said. "The emperor has taken control. I don't know why you *or* I are down here, but it can't mean anything good. The magic for the challengers to be transported requires their blood, which we have, and the emperor had easy access to mine, as well. But how could he have magicked *you*, Leo?"

"Your guess is as good as mine. Perhaps there are medical records from my birth at the palace." He took my hand and faced Lark. "How do we get out of this?"

Lark's features were grim. "This is merely the first part. There's more to come." With that ominous warning, she turned on her heel and went in the same direction Callum had disappeared. "I can't be certain the emperor didn't change the trial, but follow me and I'll try to get us out alive."

———

We walked for what felt like hours but what I imagined was no more than thirty minutes. Signs of other challengers appeared as we passed—the carcass of a large wolf, probably one of the obstacles Lark spoke of, lay on its side when we entered one tunnel. Scraps of fabric from a navy cloak littered another. Crushed vines, a shredded tie, chunks of fur, and puddles of blood graced various parts of the path.

I wondered where Nox was, if he had gotten out yet or was still trapped here. Or worse. I flinched at the thought, and Leo squeezed my hand, pausing for a moment and pulling me aside.

I instantly burrowed into him. It was second nature at this point, the way my body craved his nearness. I wanted to stay there forever, locked against his hard chest, the feel of his arms comforting me even in the face of such uncertainty.

"It's going to be alright," he said softly, kissing the top of my head. "I won't let anything happen to you, Rose."

I squeezed him harder. "Right back at you."

He backed away and tipped my chin with his thumb and forefinger. Reaching up, I placed a gentle kiss on his lips, only to have Lark's impatient cough bring us back to the present. Leo winked at me and laced his fingers through mine as we followed after her.

The moment of peace was short-lived, however, when Lark's soft cry of *"No,"* floated back to us.

"What is it?" I asked, watching as Lark sank to her knees.

And then I saw it.

A body.

Hurrying to Lark, I felt a spark of recognition at the woman at our feet, but couldn't place where I'd seen her. Lark obviously knew who it was. Silent tears tracked down her dark cheeks. I crouched beside her and put a hand on her back.

"Who is she?" I asked quietly.

Lark wiped a hand over her face. "One of my architects. Salome." She stretched a shaking arm out and closed the lids of the female's eyes. "A friend."

I took in the sight of Salome's still body and the large gash in the center of her chest. It looked like a knife wound. Her slight frame and dark hair seemed more and more familiar the longer I stared, and then it hit me—she'd been in attendance at the challenger's feast, and she'd been the one to come tell Lark about Callista's death.

"I'm so sorry, Lark," I said.

"I tried to stop him," a brusque voice said from a few steps in front of us. I tensed as the air seemed to bend and fracture, and suddenly, Horace stepped into our line of sight, still in his Royal Guard uniform.

"*Horace?*" Leo exclaimed.

"Fates, is anyone *not* down here?" I asked.

Lark sucked in a breath. "You tried to stop *who*?"

"Vincent."

Lark cursed and stormed to her feet.

"I'm sorry, but—who is Vincent?" I asked. "And where did you come from, Horace?" So many questions circled in my mind, I wasn't sure what to focus on. How was any of this happening? I felt like any time I managed to get my head above water, another surprise dragged me back under.

"Vincent is the other architect. He, Salome, and I have worked closely on the Decemvirate for the last five years," Lark said, her tone icy as slivers of shadows began to twist around her body. "You're sure it was him?"

Horace nodded gravely. "Woke up in darkness. Had no idea what was going on and wandered around with an invisibility illusion until I heard fighting. Came across the two of them"—he gestured to the body—"arguing, and when I tried to stop them, he stabbed her, blinded me with his Lightbender magic, and ran."

"Why would he do this?" Lark hissed, and I could see her fury give way to heartache. I couldn't imagine working in such close quarters with someone for five years, only to learn they'd committed the most violent act of betrayal.

"I think he's been in Gayl's pocket the entire time," Horace said. "Heard him say something about needing to do what he'd instructed."

"That miserable piece of scum," Lark spat, her shadows licking at the ground.

"I'm sorry, Lark," Leo echoed my earlier sentiments, gripping her by the shoulder. "We'll find him and make him pay, if that's what you want. Both Vincent *and* Gayl."

She nodded tightly, her jaw flexing as she fixed her features into their normal composure. With a sniff, she straightened her shoulders, looking at me and gesturing down to Salome's body. "You should see if she has anything useful."

I bent low and rummaged carefully through Salome's personal belongings, finding a small metal tin in the pocket of her thick skirt. When I opened it, the scent of dried flowers hit me. An Alchemist. I'd have to take inventory of what was in here later, but it had to be better than relying on blood magic.

"I found her herbs," I said, tucking it into the lining of my tights. "No other weapons."

In silence, Lark led us through the tunnels, her steps taking on new vigor as she marched. Despite my aggravation toward her and the part she played in these trials, my heart hurt for her. For the calm detachment she felt the need to carry, for this role she'd been proudly given and now wore as a battle scar. Her entire purpose over the last half decade was now stripped away and left her just as confused, just as scared as the rest of us.

Leo and I fell behind. His hand brushed against the tears and rips in my long sleeves. "What happened?" he asked quietly, fingering the cuts on my skin, trailing upward to the small lacerations on my neck and cheeks.

"I woke up locked in a wooden box. I had to blast my way out."

He snorted. "Of course you did."

"The box sort of...exploded," I said sheepishly. "Cut up my neck and arms. I'm okay, though. It doesn't hurt too bad. I was going for an unlocking spell, but...well, I didn't bring my charms with me to the ball."

I glanced up at him and found him searching my hands. He spotted the gash on my thumb. As we walked, he took my hand in his and lifted it to his lips, softly kissing the wound. That simple action opened up the well of guilt inside of me.

Taking a deep breath, I said, "I know you don't like it when I use blood magic—"

"You did what you had to do, Rose."

"—but I didn't know what else to do. And again, when Alaric attacked me—" I paused, registering his words. "Wait, you're not upset?"

A growl vibrated from deep in Leo's chest, his eyes sharpening as he stopped mid-walk. "Alaric did *what*? Where is he?"

His anger sent a thrill through me. "Unconscious."

Those black eyes darkened in satisfaction, swallowing me, making my blood heat. "Good." His stare lingered over my various cuts and bruises. "You don't have to worry about my reaction to your magic. I trust you, Rose. I know if you use it, there must be a good reason. I only want you to be careful. Remember the consequences." He brushed a thumb against my bottom lip. "I'm not going anywhere just because we have a disagreement. Do you believe me?"

I mulled over his admission, letting it collect my residual guilt and squash it beneath his tenderness. It felt...good, learning how to release these defenses I'd had all my life. Learning how to let someone choose me. I'd never had anyone to call my own before.

"I've already chosen to love you, Rose Wolff. Beyond sense, beyond reason. There is no part of you I do not choose."

He wasn't going anywhere.

He was mine.

"I believe you," I whispered. "And, Leo, about what you said at the ball. I—"

"Rose! Leo! We're here." Lark's voice echoed down the tunnel. She and Horace had disappeared around a corner as Leo and I talked. He gave me a small smile and led me after them, my words forgotten as we rounded the bend.

The narrow tunnels opened to a circular cavern the size of a small house, with rocky formations jutting from the ceiling and

floor. Torches were fastened to the walls every few feet, illuminating the space. More strips of the same navy garment I'd seen
earlier were caught on the sharp edges. Clumps of dirt were strewn
about on the far side of the wall, as if the area had been disturbed
by movement.

"Is this the exit?" I asked.

Lark nodded grimly. "Somewhere in here. We have to find it.
This labyrinth was Salome's project." Her voice broke on the name.
"I signed off on the plan, but she was the expert with the details."

I sighed. "I suppose it was too much to hope for there to be an
arrow pointing to the door."

Horace slowly circled the cave. There were two tunnel
entrances leading to it—the one we had come from, and one
directly across from it on the opposite side. I crept closer to the
second one, squinting to see in the dark. There were no torches or
sconces lining this path. Shadows seemed to stretch and broaden
as I neared the entrance, summoning me with tendrils like fingers.
I thought I heard something moving deep inside...

"You know," Horace said with a grunt. "This looks like an
arena."

"For what?" Leo asked.

"A fight."

"That wasn't part of the plan," Lark countered.

I huffed out a bitter laugh as my feet guided me closer to the
second tunnel. "I don't think much of anything is going to *plan*,
Lark."

Lark growled angrily in response. I turned to shoot her a look
when the growling sounded from behind me again.

It wasn't Lark.

Everything happened in slow motion.

Lark's eyes widened as she reached for me, her shadows lashing. Horace unsheathed the sword at his side as Leo's lips parted
and took the shape of my name, but I couldn't hear him.

Hot air tore at my back.

Something furry circled my wrist, yanking me away from the

tunnel. Leo was at my side in an instant. He shoved me against the wall, using his body to shield me.

Out of the second tunnel came a raging, roaring beast. A cross between a lion and a bear, its paws were twice the size of my face, its canines as large as a sword. It shook its enormous mane and rose up on its back legs with a growl. Rounded ears skimmed the ceiling. It landed with a boom, shaking the entire cave.

"What are we supposed to do?" I asked Leo frantically.

"*You* need to get out. Go back the way we came."

"I'm not leaving all of you down here."

His jaw twitched. "So stubborn," he said, then crashed his lips to mine.

He kissed me for strength. For courage. And I took the same, my heart pounding faster, my body filling with resolve. He released me and pushed off the wall. The usual small, dark lock of hair fell across his forehead as he brought his palms together with a crash, his henbane and amaranth rings crackling with magic.

A smirk crossed my lips. "Show off."

"Want to join me?"

I glanced at Horace and Lark, who were already wielding their magic against the beast, and then eyed the cave walls. "One of us needs to figure out how to get out of here." The creature roared again, wiping the smirk from my face. I imagined those teeth ripping through Leo, shredding him, claws sinking into his skin.

Before I could stop him, he nodded, gave me a quick, "Be careful," and took off after the beast to join Horace and Lark in the fight.

They were a sight to behold. I'd never seen the Sentinels in action, but I could tell they'd been about more than espionage and secret meetings over the years. The three of them moved in synchrony. Horace distracted the enemy with illusions and slashes of his sword while Lark manipulated her shadows into weapons, dangerous spears of darkness that pierced through the thick, golden hide, then disappeared to reform. Even from the wall, I could see Leo's lips moving with silent spells. Force fields emerged before his companions right as the creature pounced.

The air was saturated with shadows and firelight, the cloying scent of magic and the sting of its power pressing into my chest.

I shook away the mixture of dread and awe, sharpening my focus on finding an exit. Working my way down the edges of the cave as fast as I could, I ran my fingers along the bottom and then up, tracing every dip and crevice I saw. Hoping for any sign of a hidden doorway or hollow wall. Some sort of enchantment or magical trap that would trigger an opening.

Anything.

Lark cried out, and I swung my head around to see the beast's jaws clenched around the long antler in her hand, almost tearing her arm off. She let go and the creature jerked the weapon with so much force that it went flying at the wall to its left side.

I expected the antler to clatter against rock.

Instead, it disappeared.

The other three were too distracted to notice, but something tugged at my mind. The creature wasn't moving. It stayed in place, fighting Lark, Horace, and Leo while keeping within a few paces of its position, right beside the spot the antler flew through. Almost as if it was guarding something.

I had to get closer.

Reaching into the lining of my tights for Salome's tin of herbs, I hastily flipped open the lid and dug around the familiar petals and roots and leaves. A shaky exhale left my lips when I spotted what I needed. Hellebore and amaranth. An invisibility charm.

I pinched the two together and placed them on my tongue. "*Vellus*," I whispered. My chest tightened with the spell. When the pressure released, I crept forward into the fray.

At first, it was alarmingly easy. Neither the creature nor my friends were aware of my presence, which allowed me to move across the cave quickly and quietly. I stayed low to the ground and out of sight behind the beast's back.

Until it took a blow to the neck and reared upward, its tail swiping through the air.

It hit me with the strength of a wooden rod, knocking the breath from my lungs as I soared into the wall behind me. My spine hit the rock first, then my head, and my spell broke.

White spots danced in my vision. I couldn't breathe, couldn't see with the pain shooting down every nerve in my body. I slumped to the ground and gripped my head in my hands, trying to stop the hammering in my temples.

The beast must have felt me, for he suddenly turned and sniffed the air. Its round, black eyes locked on me. I cursed, wincing as I got back to my feet.

I caught Leo's eye and shouted his name. "Draw it away from the wall!" I cried, gesturing at the wall to the creature's left. My head was still foggy and pounding, but I could heal myself later. I *had* to get us out of here.

Leo instantly obeyed. Working as one, he, Lark, and Horace got the beast's attention. Lark's shadow whips latched onto its snout and pulled. With an angry snarl, it faced them again, leaving me a clear path to the wall.

I struggled toward it and staggered as I knelt to pick up a large stone. Drawing near, I threw the rock at the same wall, holding my breath when it sailed through the air...

And vanished.

A smile broke across my tired face.

"It's this way!" I shouted to the others. "Through the wall! You need to keep it away long enough to get over here."

"Through the *wall?*" Leo asked, his hands raised, prepared to cast another spell.

"I'll hold it off," Horace grunted. "You two—*go.*"

He didn't leave Leo or Lark any time to protest. Faster than I thought possible for the burly guard, he sprinted away from the others, the creature's eyes following him and whatever illusion he was no doubt creating. It let out a thunderous howl, its paws clawing at something I couldn't see.

Leo rushed to my side. "What did you find?"

"Look," I said, tossing another rock and watching as it faded behind the dirt.

I stepped forward, only for Leo to put an arm around my waist. "Wait, Rose. Let me go first to make sure it's safe."

Pulling out of his grip, I turned to face him. "This trial isn't about safety, monkey boy. Just trust me."

Then I spread my arms wide and fell backward into the void.

64

LEO

I leapt to the wall as Rose vanished from sight, Lark close on my heels.

"Horace! Get over here, now!" she shouted at our friend, who had successfully lured the beast far enough away for us to make our escape. But I could tell his illusions weren't going to last much longer. The half lion, half bear was agitated, its ears pinned back to its head as it stalked toward Horace, apparently done with his tricks. Saliva dripped from its sharp, dagger-like teeth, and a low growl resounded in its chest.

"Go, Lark," I said quickly. "Find Rose. I'll get Horace."

"Are you sure?"

"*Go*. Make sure she's safe."

She gave me a skeptical look, then sighed. "Fine. Be careful. I don't want to have to answer to your sister if I bring your body back in pieces."

"Better you than me," I replied as she gathered the skirts of her black gown and stepped through the portal.

I turned my attention back to Horace. "Alright, we've established you're the bravest of us, now come on!" I yelled, angelica leaves already poised on my fingertips. Placing the sweet plant on my tongue, I focused on the beast's swishing tail and murmured, "*Incendar.*"

It instantly caught fire, distracting it long enough for Horace to sprint toward me. The creature gnashed its teeth and lashed its tail back and forth to put out the flames.

"Through the wall," I commanded as Horace neared. He barely gave me a second look before bursting headfirst into the rocky barrier, his body fading into thin air as the others had.

The beast let out an ear splitting roar and pounded across the cave. My last glimpse of it before I barreled through the portal was its furious eyes, spittle dripping from its maw, and a large paw lunging at the wall.

Blinding pain shot through my back.

The world went dark as I fell into nothingness.

It was like stepping beneath a freezing waterfall. Ice skittered across my skin, so intense it took my breath away, before the pit of darkness opened and I was spat onto soft grass.

"Leo!" Rose shrieked as my face landed on the ground. The coolness of the grass beneath me counteracted the burning coming from my back. I tried to rise to my knees but crumpled, my muscles giving way to throbbing ache.

"It got you," Rose said, gasping.

"I just...need a minute." I groaned, then flexed my arms and lifted my chest off the ground high enough for me to check my surroundings. "Where are we?"

"Above the tunnels on a small island near one of Mysthelm's coasts," Lark said.

"You mean that wasn't the end of the trial?" I rasped out. We were gathered in the middle of a large clearing with the night's sky above us. I could make out a forest to the right, but it was too dark to see beyond it.

"Not nearly," Lark answered.

"We'll worry about that later. I need to heal his back," Rose said. I turned my neck as she fell to her knees by my side, wincing when her delicate hands reached across my back. Even the barest of touches set my skin on fire. I couldn't see the damage, but I knew the beast's claws had sunk in deep.

"I have to move your shirt so I can clean it," she said. I nodded stiffly, sucking in a breath and clenching my jaw as her fingers grabbed pieces of shredded fabric and carefully pulled them away. Each movement sent pain slicing down every nerve. I let out a rough exhale when she peeled one strip away that had gotten embedded in the gash, and she stopped.

"Keep going," I said through gritted teeth. "I'm fine."

"It's almost clear." Another piece grazed the open wound. A moment later, her hands stopped moving. "It's done. Fates, that's..." She trailed off, but the horror in her tone left little room to question the state of my injury.

"Won't you heal on your own?" Lark asked.

"Not quickly enough," I said, craning my neck to look at them and ignoring the pulsing heat of warm liquid oozing down my side. "I have—some herbs," I forced out. "In my pocket." Bending my arm, I tried to prop myself up on one elbow and reach down for my pouch of charms, but Rose placed a hand on my shoulder to stop me.

"You know I can heal you quicker without those," she said, too quiet for the others to hear. Her green eyes were troubled, a small crease in her brow showing how worried she was for me.

"It's not worth the risk. Use what I have. It'll be enough to allow me to walk, at least."

Fire lit in her gaze, the urge to argue brimming to her surface. But I wouldn't let her win this one. Using blood magic to save herself was one thing, but this? I wouldn't be the reason she or anyone else paid a price.

She held my stare, a challenge hanging in the air and pulling taut between us. That burning, throbbing pain in the center of my back mixed with her heat, and her stubbornness drove me wild.

Finally, she nodded. She moved her hand from my shoulder

and down to the pocket of my pants, feeling for the healing herbs. I sucked in a breath as she pulled the pouch out.

"Tell us about the rest of the trial, Lark," I grounded out, needing a distraction from both the wound and having Rose so close to me as she guided her hands across my back, using a combination of charms to slowly work on mending the skin.

I couldn't see Lark or Horace from my position, but I heard the former's footsteps fall against the grass as she moved into my line of sight. She collected her full skirt and twisted it into a knot between her legs so it was fashioned more like pants, then planted herself on a boulder.

"We're on a remote island to the east of Mysthelm. Emperor Gayl's spies discovered it over a decade ago when they got lost on a reconnaissance mission, and he felt it was a perfect spot for a future trial. We've been working ever since we were elected as architects to prepare it. Since magic doesn't work outside of our empire, it took years to figure out how to set up the proper enchantments. Much of which was the emperor's doing, seeing as his Alchemy is one of the only one's strong enough to pull off a feat like this."

"So the tunnels weren't the end of it? There's more?" Horace asked, crossing his arms.

She nodded. "The trial has four main stages."

"*Four?*" Rose gaped.

"Yes, each one based on an element of nature. The objective is for the challengers to use their courage to face unknown foes and obstacles, all devised by the very nature surrounding them. The tunnels were the earth portion of the trial. Somewhere on the island"—she brandished a hand behind her—"they will face fire, water, and air." Pressing her lips together, she amended, "*We* will face them."

"You must know where these parts of the trial are, then," Horace said. "We go hunt them down, beat them, and get home."

"I will have *some* advantage," she conceded, shifting her feet. "Knowing what charms and traps were used will help us. But the island is *alive*. The emperor enchanted it to work of its own accord, catching the challengers unaware and throwing them into a new part of the trial when they least expect it. Even I don't know when or where we'll face each portion. The test is of constant vigilance, of courage when you don't know what's coming."

"Have I mentioned how much I hate this tournament?" Rose mumbled before placing several stems on her tongue and uttering a string of healing spells. The pain slowly lessened to a dull ache, and I was able to push off the ground into a sitting position for her to continue working.

"We need to find shelter and provisions," Lark said as she stood. "There's no time limit on this trial—it could take hours or days. But we don't want to be left out in the open in the middle of the night."

"How do you feel?" Rose asked me. "Do you think you can walk?"

The skin at my back was already beginning to stitch itself together, partially due to her magic, but I could also sense my Shifter half taking over. While it didn't respond as quickly as a full Shifter's magic would, I was grateful for the increased ability to heal.

"It's better," I said, taking the hand she offered me and rising to my feet, breathing through the twinge at my back. "Thank you."

I opened up my Shifter half to speed the healing process along, and the familiar sensation of heightened senses slammed into me. Darkness faded as I focused on the vivid colors of the nearby forest, the rustling of leaves on the wind, and the heat coming from Rose at my side.

"I'm sorry you got dragged into all of this," she said as Horace and Lark launched into a discussion on where to move next. "It doesn't make any sense. Why are all of you here? Unless it's some power move on Gayl's part. But Lark said your blood is needed to transport you here." Shaking her head, she bit her lip. "I don't understand how he could have gotten *your* blood. You've stayed hidden, you haven't had any interaction with him or the Guard..." She trailed off and let out a tired sigh.

"We'll figure it out, sweetheart." I brushed back a lock of her hair. "But it's not your fault. You don't need to—"

A breeze cut through the clearing, carrying with it a scent that made me jerk my head mid-sentence toward the forest.

I sucked in a breath, my hand frozen at Rose's temple. "*No.*"

And then I was running. Ignoring the pain from the still healing gash, blocking out the surprised cries of my companions, I tore across the field and into the dense trees. Instinct took over, my Shifter speed allowing me to race past fallen branches and over-grown roots.

Her scent practically blinded me.

I paused, nostrils flaring as I whipped my head to the side toward a small oak tree. A clump of reddish orange fur was twisted in the leaves at the base of the trunk.

A growl ripped through my throat as I followed the scent, growing stronger with each step I took. Drops of blood trailed the forest floor like a beacon leading me to her. A storm raged inside of me, primal anger and dread mingling together and battering against my skin, begging to be unleashed.

If she was hurt...

A soft whine reached my ears.

I moved through the thicket like lightning, zeroing in on the sound.

Wedged beside an overturned log was a bundle of branches, red fur visible beneath the leaves and twigs. I threw them all aside and nearly fell to my knees at the sight of her.

Rissa.

Still in her fox form, blood seeped from a tear in her leg. She had tucked herself into a tight ball and was carefully licking at the wound, her yellow eyes trained on me.

In the blink of an eye, she shifted. Her body expanded as she staggered out of the hole. Leaves and dirt were tangled in her blonde hair, which was pulled back with a strap of leather. Her face was pale, eyes bloodshot and tired. She wore tight-fitting, dark clothing, as if she'd been transported in the middle of a patrolling shift. Her pants were torn at the left thigh and I saw punctured skin beneath. A dagger wound. It must have happened recently, if her healing abilities hadn't yet taken effect.

"Leo, where are—"

"What happened to—"

We talked over one another as I reached down to help her stand, my back nearly giving out under the movement.

"This is the third trial," I answered, supporting her while she got her bearings. My legs trembled, but I ignored it. "Gayl's up to something. He gave a speech at the ball and announced that the trial was starting now, instead of in a couple days as was the original plan. The palace disappeared and we were transported here. The challengers, Lark, Horace...we're all here."

My sister's surprise quickly gave way to her analytical nature. I could practically see the theories and strategies running through her mind.

"He must know about Lark and Horace. We've been fools to think we could stay hidden while under his nose for this long. If he can wipe all four of us out in one fell swoop, he knows the Sentinels would descend into chaos. Unravel from the inside. We've got to make our move—"

I stood in front of her, placing my hands on her shoulders. "Rissa, we need to go back to the others and focus on getting out of here. We can't do anything for the Sentinels if we're trapped in this trial." I put her arm around my shoulder to help her walk, relieved to see the cut at her leg starting to clot. "What happened to you?"

She let out a huff, blowing a tendril of hair back from her face. "It was that Illusionist challenger. I woke up in a tunnel and didn't know what was going on. There were these animals..." She shivered, her arm going rigid across my neck. "I found him running away from something and decided to follow him. He was the first person I'd seen. He didn't know I was there until we got to the big cave and this huge *thing* came out of the tunnels. Emperor's tits, it was the biggest—"

"Trust me, I'm aware," I cut her off with an unamused laugh. Stopping, I pivoted so she could see the evidence. "We became well acquainted."

She inhaled. "He got you good, didn't he? Are you alright?"

"I should be asking *you* that question," I said, raising an eye at her leg. "I take it the beast wasn't what stabbed you?"

"No, that pleasure went to the Illusionist."

"Another reason for me to kill him." This prick's ledger was getting as long as Gayl's himself.

"We made it past the lion thing and somehow the Illusionist figured out how to escape. I followed him through the wall and he was waiting for me on the other side with a dagger—how he got it, I'll never know. He stabbed me in the leg before I could shift and get away, but I eventually lost him. I'd only been hiding in the woods for a few minutes before you found me."

She was already steadier on her feet, hardly needing my assistance as we neared the others. I snuck a peek at her leg to find the area now a bright pink instead of red and bloody. Stiffness had set into my back, a consequence of my venture through the forest, but the burning sensation had all but disappeared.

"I'm glad you got away. Callum is dangerous—I don't think he would hesitate to kill any one of us, if only to gain an edge in the tournament."

"You said this was the third trial. How in the *world* did we get here, Leo? Did Gayl catch you at the ball? I *knew* I shouldn't have agreed to let you go."

"What good would that have done, since you weren't there and you ended up in the same predicament?" I pointed out. "Lark said the only way we could be transported here is if Gayl had our blood. My guess is there are samples somewhere in the palace records, and he's been biding his time to use them until now." I clenched my jaw, thinking of all the terrible things someone with his power could do with our blood. One could have total control of another if they were willing to use dark magic such as his. The simple compulsion spell Rose used on me after the first trial that lasted only a few seconds was child's play compared to what Gayl was capable of.

"We'll get answers when we're back in Veridia City," I continued, pushing away a vine in our path. "For now, we need to survive the night."

65

LEO

The others were shocked to find me returning with my sister at my side and demanded to know what had happened. After Rissa quickly recounted her story, Horace took inventory of the supplies and weapons between the five of us. Rose's dagger, his own sword, Lark's broken antler mask, and mine and Salome's collections of herbs. Without knowing how long we would be on the island, our primary focus was to find shelter away from the open clearing. Lark knew the basic layout of the area and advised we head north in the direction of the lone mountaintop I could barely make out against the midnight sky, as there were a series of caves she said we could rest in for the night.

Before we left, Rose and I gathered a handful of thick leaves and sticks and fashioned them into small containers, then bound them with a patching spell I'd created as a teenager when the roof on our cottage wouldn't stop leaking. The containers held together firmly so that when we came across a water supply, we'd have the ability to carry it with us.

Horace and I took the lead as we journeyed through the dark forest and toward the small mountain. He cut down vines and branches with his sword while I lit several long boughs with a fire spell to use as torches. With my Shifter half still open, sounds of scampering creatures rang loudly in my ears, scents and sights of the island taking over.

I could smell a salty breeze coming from the east, carrying with it the distant sound of waves crashing against a shore. The tip of the mountain loomed ahead like a shadowed beacon marking our path. Wind whistled through the canopy above us, skimming my skin, keeping me alert.

It was impossible not to notice the serenity of this place, even amidst the danger.

As much as I loved my sister and the small family we'd made among the Sentinels, I'd grown to abhor life in the capital. The constant people, the busyness, the way nobody seemed to stop to breathe. There was always an agenda. Always something to do, somewhere to be. I enjoyed the solitude of our little cottage and the nightly patrols through the various sectors, if only because it allowed me to sit in the silence and hear myself think.

There was a sort of peace on this island, one I could rarely find in the capital. One I could rarely find in *myself*.

The wind shifted, bringing with it the sweet scent of lavender and sage and the image of olive skin and green eyes. My breaths evened out, my nerves settling.

She was my peace.

I'd spent the entirety of my adulthood seeking vengeance. It took one woman appearing in my life to make me see the beauty in contentment. The relief in quiet. And while I still desired retribution for my father, it was no longer the single driving force in my mind.

"What's going through your head?" Horace asked as we made our way through the forest.

Instinctively, I twisted my neck to catch a glimpse of Rose, Lark, and my sister trailing behind us. With deft fingers, Rose tore off a piece of thick fabric from Lark's gown, tying the corners together into a pouch and using thin vines to strap them around each of their necks.

"To carry food," she said with a shrug when she saw my bemused expression.

I couldn't help but smile as I turned my head back to Horace and the path before us.

He grunted. "Should've known."

"What about you?" I asked. "Do you think Gayl forced you into this because he and the Guard are still suspicious of you?" I remembered his agitation from a week ago when he first told us how strangely the Royal Guard had been acting toward him, going so far as to try and trick him into drinking Grimlock. We hadn't seen or heard from Horace much in the following days.

He scratched his scraggly beard. "I thought they'd stopped doubting me when I pretended to play along and answered their questions. They never outright asked about the Sentinels, but hinted they'd heard of restless citizens. They're not idiots—they know there's been more violence. They can feel a storm coming, and Gayl's trying to stamp it out. Suppose that's what all this is for." He motioned to the island around us. "Just yesterday after my annual medical check, they offered me an officer position." A snort left him. "Guess that was for show."

"They must have used your blood from that to transport you here," I mused.

"It's all mind games with them. Getting you to let your guard down, then pulling the rug out from under you."

That certainly sounded like Gayl. "And you hadn't heard anything about this? No rumors about Gayl's big plan?"

Horace shook his head. "Things were getting better with the Guard. Going back to normal. No more secret meetings, no more dodging me in training. Only rumors I'd heard for the last week were which of the whores at the Gold Jay they were going to screw next."

I could make out the hurt in his voice, though he tried to sound unbothered. This job was a cover for him, but it had still been his life over the past years. I couldn't blame him for wanting to be in good standing or even wanting some sort of relationship with his fellow Guard members; the line between duty and emotions was easily blurred.

"Well," I started, clapping him on the shoulder. "I think it's safe to say once this is over, you should quit."

He barked out a laugh. "You know, I just might."

"Are you two having fun up there without me?" my sister asked seconds before she wedged herself between us and threw an arm over both of our shoulders. I flinched at the sudden movement.

Rissa smiled apologetically. "Sorry, little brother. I forgot about your back."

"Yes, not all of us heal as quickly as you." I raised an eyebrow and glanced down at the hole in her pants, where the bloody gash was now only a few jagged scrapes.

"Yours looks loads better, I promise. It's too bad you ruined a perfectly good shirt," she joked and reached back to finger the cut edges of the fabric Rose had peeled away, leaving my back exposed.

"I'm not complaining," Rose called from behind us. I turned and she shot me a wink. Lark let out a sigh.

"What?" Rose said. "I'll take any entertainment I can get out here."

Horace grunted. "How about you save the entertainment for when we find the caves?"

"Don't get them started," Lark said with a groan as Rissa snickered, and a wicked grin broke out across Rose's face.

Before I could respond, my nostrils flared with a new scent, and both Rissa and I raised our heads higher. Curiosity gleamed back at me from her dark eyes.

"You smell it, too?" I asked. Musty, sweet, and strong. The wind picked up speed as clouds covered the moon and stars.

She nodded with a smile. "Smells like a good time to go hunting."

"Catch us something good." My twin loved to hunt in a storm. The rain softened the underbrush, making it easier to stalk through the night, and it drew out small creatures for her to find.

Within seconds, her pupils elongated, her eyes turning yellow and her canines sharpening before she lunged into the forest, shifting midair.

"Where is she going?" Lark asked.

"Hunting. We'll want food eventually, and she's an excellent hunter in a storm—"

"Wait, a storm?" Lark stopped in her tracks, her face ashen. "As in, rain?"

"Typically there's rain, yes. What's wrong, Lark?"

"We have to get Rissa back and head to the mountain. *Now.*" Lark looked up at the sky and the dark clouds moving overhead.

"What's the matter with a little rain?" Rose asked. "Isn't that a good thing? We need to find water soon anyway."

"You don't understand. This—this isn't *normal* rain." Lark strode in front of us, gripping Horace's arm and dragging him along. Her voice was frantic, pleading. "It's part of the trial. I didn't think it would happen so soon."

Thunder rumbled overhead, softly at first, then growing into a powerful *boom*. The birds and insects of the forest quieted their chirping and buzzing.

The hair on my arms raised.

"Calm down and tell us what's so special about this rain," Horace commanded, putting a hand on Lark's shoulder.

She took a deep breath. "The rain, it—it's poison. It takes your magic away."

Lightning flashed, and the first drop of water landed on my skin.

The shrill whine of a fox rang through the air.

66

ROSE

The instant the rain hit my forehead, a dullness swept from my head to my toes, like a blanket had been draped over my bones and pushed down tight. Pressure built along my spine, growing heavier and heavier until suddenly, it released, and a hollowness filled every cell of my body.

I was empty. Numb.

I'd never felt such hopelessness, such a loss of something so *vital*. As if my very essence had been snuffed out and ripped from me.

Leo staggered against a nearby tree as the rain descended faster. Rissa's yowls filled the air, and he rasped out her name.

"We have to get under cover," Lark insisted, shuddering against the rain pelting us.

"No, we have to find Rissa," Leo countered. "I can't smell her. I can't—I can't tell where she is."

"She's smart. She'll know something is wrong and head toward the mountain to meet us."

"Unless she's wounded! If our magic is gone, she can't heal. I'm not going to leave her out here."

The rain came down harder and the wind howled through the trees. My tights and bodice clung to my skin, suffocating me as the water continued to seep into my blood. We didn't have time to argue—but Leo was right. How could we leave Rissa unprotected?

I raised my voice to drown out the sound of the storm. "Horace, Lark—you two get to the caves. Find a spot we'll be safe in. Leo, you and I can go get Rissa." Horace opened his mouth to protest, his beard soaked and dripping, but I held up a hand. "We'll be fine. If we're not to the caves in an hour, then come find us, alright?"

He glowered at me but relented. "You have your dagger?" he asked. I flashed it at him and he grunted. "Here, take this, too." He handed Leo the broken piece of the antler mask.

"What am I supposed to do with this?"

Horace and Lark retreated into the shadows of the mountain. "You come across an enemy, stick the pointy end in them," he said.

Leo cursed under his breath. I wanted to laugh, but the numbness inside of me had spread, muffling any other emotion besides the dread and exhaustion that filled the void where my magic used to be.

"Come on," I said, taking his free hand.

We sprinted through the deluge in a mad dash. Fallen branches, waterlogged bushes, sinkholes, and exposed roots reached from the earth to trip us. The rain was coming down so hard now that I could barely see five steps ahead of me, but still, we ran, looking for any sign of the red fox.

Wind rushed through the trees and made the rain fall sideways. I gasped and spluttered against the wall of water. My foot caught on something hard, and my sandal straps snapped as my body flew toward the ground.

Strong hands caught me before I landed on the muddy forest floor. Leo wiped my sodden hair from my face and helped me back to my feet. His thumb grazed along the inside of my wrist before he bolted back into the tempest with grim determination. Tearing off my broken shoes, I followed on his heels.

Another whine pierced the night.

She was close.

Veering to the left, we followed the sound as best we could, redirecting when we heard her again.

Something splashed ahead of us.

I glanced at Leo and we both rushed forward, practically running into a dark red, drenched, severely pissed ball of fur. Her tail swung wildly back and forth in alarm.

"Rissa!" Leo exclaimed, falling to his knees before her.

She opened her mouth and dropped a dead, wet pheasant at his feet.

"You just *had* to bring something back, didn't you?" he said, shaking his head as he rubbed her ears, checking for signs of injury. She nuzzled her nose against his forearm.

"Why isn't she shifting back?" I asked.

"She needs magic to shift. She can't do it if the water took her magic away." Rissa whined softly in confirmation.

I wiped more rain from my eyes. We had to get back to Lark. Had to find out if this was permanent. What if Rissa was stuck like this forever? What if our magic never returned?

The idea of living without my magic, of being unable to ever use it again, rocked me to my core. It was unthinkable. Like a blow to the gut, it sucked the air out of me.

"Let's go," I gasped out, trying to ignore the tightening of my chest.

We ran through the rain. The trail inclined steeply as we neared the side of the mountain. The slope was slippery, with rocks crumbling and sliding on the mud at our feet, but we slowly ascended until we reached level ground that overlooked the forest and the tops of the trees we'd been beneath just a short time ago.

Rissa bounded ahead of us, the bird still in her maw. Her red tail disappeared around a corner. When Leo and I rounded the bend, we saw the opening of a small cave, almost indiscernible in the night and rain.

I reached for my borrowed tin of herbs as we entered the darkness, placing a crushed angelica leaf on my tongue and murmuring, "*Incendar.*"

My stomach sank when I realized my mistake.

My magic was gone.

The truth, the finality of it, hit me.

"We'll have to follow her," Leo said. "She can see better than us."

I swallowed and nodded. When I held my hand in front of me, I could barely make out its outline, but a soft brush of Rissa's tail against my leg helped me trail her through the cave.

Musty, wet earth and rock assaulted my senses. The ground at my bare feet was flat and even, unlike the rocky terrain of the underground tunnels. As we strayed deeper, the sound of the vicious storm outside melted into the background.

The path ahead of us became clearer as my eyes adjusted. Shadows of our figures formed on the dark brown and stone walls, almost as if—

"Is that light?" Leo asked, squinting. Rissa shot forward before we could stop her.

"Rissa?" Lark's voice called out from further in the cave. "Rose, Leo, are you there?" Her words echoed around us. Within moments, the tunnels opened up to a cavern the size of several rooms, with our two friends huddled around a circle of twigs, leaves, and a small but vibrant fire. At the far side of the space were three more tunnels, their paths visible by the light of the flames. Rissa set the pheasant down at Horace's feet and nearly stuck her nose into the flames to seek warmth.

"Are you alright?" Lark asked, her eyes sweeping over us. I nodded, slumping to the ground before the crackling fire.

"How did you two manage this?" Leo motioned to the fire pit.

"Some of us know how to start a fire without magic," Horace responded.

Leo ignored him. "Lark, please tell me this enchantment is temporary. That my sister won't be stuck as her fox half forever."

"I promise, it will wear off," she assured him. "It was meant to last less than twelve hours. As long as our clothes are dry and we pass any water we may have ingested, our magic will come back by then."

I could practically feel the relief in the cave as her words washed over us. *Temporary*. My magic wasn't gone for good.

But a lot could happen in twelve hours.

Looking out of the corner of his eye at the dead bird on the ground, Horace *hmph*ed. "Guess that's our dinner." Rissa curled into a ball beside the fire and licked her paw. "Can I borrow your dagger, Rose?" Horace asked. "I'll get this on the fire soon."

I handed over the weapon, and he and Leo sauntered off to the side to defeather and prepare the bird. Silence filled our little pocket of the cave.

Even though I knew our magic would come back, I couldn't help but feel some resentment toward the whole situation. Glaring at Lark, I hissed, "What kind of a trial is this? Whose idea was *magic-stealing rain*?"

She winced. "Well, technically, the initial idea was mine—but I had no idea how far Gayl would take it."

"Yes, who would have guessed?" I said with a sarcastic laugh, ringing out the water from my clothes. "Because our emperor has always shown such *mercy* and *consideration*. Why would he ever take a trial too far?"

I knew my ire wasn't helping, but the pit in my chest where my magic once resided made it difficult to feel much else. Except anger. Anger, I could feel. Anger was safe.

"I'm sorry, Rose. I know it doesn't mean anything given the circumstances, but I was simply doing my job. The emperor—he wanted something that had never been done before. Something radical." Lark sighed and leaned back on her hands. There was a weariness in her dark eyes, the faint wrinkles on her face more prominent in the firelight. My irritation eased a fraction seeing how much this affected her.

"You don't understand what it's like, being not only the youngest head architect, but the first *female* one," she said. "The weight of centuries of tournaments was on my shoulders. And while it had been the Sentinels' hope from the beginning to get me elected, it still felt like *mine*. Something I could take pride in, even if I hated working for Emperor Gayl. Even if I knew I wasn't in it for the glory, but to make change.

"I had everything to prove and everything to lose. And I—I might have gotten caught up in the intrigue of it all," Lark admitted, moving forward to rub her hands together over the fire. "The might of the trials, the ability to create from the ground up, the experiments with magic I'd never thought possible. I didn't want my work to hurt anyone, but it was ignorant to believe these trials wouldn't have consequences. And I'm sorry you're suffering through them, Rose. I'm sorry for the hand I played, and that it's my fault for forcing you to compete in the first place."

The fire crackled between us, casting shadows on the cave wall that twisted and twined with one another. I wouldn't want to be in her position, having to balance what's expected of you and what you feel is right, knowing the eyes of the most powerful man in the empire were on you every step of the way.

"It wasn't your fault," I finally said. "I could have refused. But... I guess I understand the idea of pride and glory. I wanted a bit of that for myself, if I'm being honest. To prove what I could do." Pausing, I pressed my lips together, mulling over my next words. "I know we're on the same side, Lark. I don't *want* to be mad at you. It's just...it's difficult to separate you from the trials. You from *him*." I looked away and tugged at the pins in my hair to let my dark locks fall around me, needing to give my hands something to do.

"I understand," she said softly. "I would be angry with me too, trust me."

I gave her a half smile. "I *am* trying. I promise. I know how much the Sentinels mean to you, and how much you love these three especially." My gaze fell on Rissa and Leo and Horace across the cave, then down to my fingers as they fidgeted with the ends of my sheer dress. "As easy as it is to be angry with you, I know who I should really be directing it toward. And I think you're incredibly brave for facing him day after day and not letting him...get in your head. Not letting him distract you from what truly matters."

I know how easy it is to give in, was what I wanted to say, but she seemed to understand my unspoken words.

"Power such as his can get to even the best of us, Rose," Lark said, her tone heavy. "I don't know what you've been through or what your meetings under the guise of spying for the Sentinels entailed, but if you ever want to talk...I'm here."

I nodded swiftly, still unused to the idea of these genuine friendships I'd made with the people in this cave. Rissa unfurled herself and padded over to me, laying back down on the ground and resting her head on my knee. My nerves settled, and for the first time since we landed in this nightmare, I felt the unease lifting.

———

BY THE TIME we'd eaten a dinner of cooked pheasant, our clothes had mostly dried and our eyelids were heavy with fatigue. We'd been awake for most of the night and the stress on our bodies had finally caught up to us. I watched Rissa's yellow eyes glaze over as she lay next to Lark, her lids falling shut every few seconds until the fire would crackle loudly and her sharp ears would shoot up, her eyes flying open.

I leaned against Leo, the hypnotizing flames lulling me to sleep as I ran my fingers gently over the exposed skin at his back. It was amazing how my healing charms and his Shifter magic had almost entirely closed the wounds. He still moved stiffly, but compared to what it had looked like mere hours ago, it was nothing short of a miracle.

"You should get some rest," he whispered before kissing my temple. I never thought I'd be the kind of woman to crave these simple touches, but I'd found over the past weeks that I loved how casually he showed his affection. How difficult it was for him to keep his hands away from me, even if it was a quick brush of his thumb against mine.

"Well, it turns out *someone* has gotten me in the bad habit of being unable to sleep without you at my side, so I guess you're joining me," I teased in a quiet voice.

"You know we can hear you," Horace said from across the fire.

"Then don't listen," I retorted.

The guard looked over at Lark. "If we're choosing sleeping partners for the night..."

She scoffed. "I'll take my chances with the fox."

Shrugging, he stoked the fire with a large stick and said, "Suit yourself. There's a fifty percent chance I smell better, though." He set down the stick and lumbered to his feet. "I'll take first watch."

The four of us spread out over the cave floor, the fire hot enough that its warmth covered the entirety of the space. Lark offered a goodnight and, true to her word, led Rissa over to the furthest corner and did her best to turn her gown into a padding to lay on. Within moments, I heard her soft snores bouncing off the walls.

Leo and I claimed a shadowed section near one of the other tunnel entrances. He motioned for me to rest on his arm, using him as a pillow while he stretched out on his side across the hard, stone floor, and tried to keep his back from touching the surface.

"Such a gentleman," I said with a yawn, curling toward him and draping my arm over his chest. He pulled me closer to him with his free hand, his fingers digging into my waist through the fabric of my dress. I could feel how tight and rigid his muscles were.

"What's wrong?" I whispered as I moved my head back to see his face. His eyes were tired and bloodshot, his jaw tensed beneath the dark scruff that had begun to grow thicker.

He met my questioning stare and softened. "Nothing. You should sleep, Rose."

I used his chest to push up, looking down at him with a raised eyebrow. "Try that again."

"So stubborn," he said, tracing circles on the back of my hand. "This night has put me on edge, that's all. Waking up and not knowing where we were, watching that creature in the tunnels throw you against the wall, finding my sister huddled in the dirt..." He shuddered and closed his eyes. "I know you're both alright, but in those moments, I felt like I'd failed you. I didn't know how to help either of you."

My shoulders dipped. I laid back down next to him, intertwining our fingers and squeezing. "You didn't fail us, Leo. We're here now, together."

"The worst part is that I can't see what's around the next corner. I don't know what's waiting for us when we open our eyes. This isn't a trial of the Decemvirate anymore. It means so much more than that, and I hate not knowing what Gayl's plan is." His grip on my hand was so tight, his knuckles were turning white. "There's a reason the only people besides challengers here are the Sentinels. He wants us gone. And if that's my fate, so be it. But my sister is meant for more in this world. Horace and Lark don't deserve to be punished for fighting for what they believe in. This all needs to *end*."

I extricated myself from his grasp to rest my palm on his cheek. "It will, Leo. We're going to get out of this—*all* of us—and we'll make sure the empire knows what he's done. We'll take the crown from him and put someone in his place who will do what it takes to bring peace back. And"—I angled his head so he was forced to look at me—"your family...your *father's* name, will be cleared. You should be proud of who you are, not hiding in the shadows for the rest of your life."

He gave me a half smile. "You seem very sure of all of this."

I shrugged. "If I'm wrong, then we can run away together."

His lip quirked up. "Run away together? That's your solution?"

"Why not? Somewhere nice and warm, but not *too* warm. Maybe near water." I twisted my lips, pretending to think. "You know, this island wouldn't be too bad. If it wasn't trying to kill us."

To my surprise, he didn't laugh off my ridiculous offer. The corners of his eyes crinkled in contemplation as he brought his free arm up and lightly ran his thumb along my chin, my jaw, my lips. "I would run anywhere with you, Rose. Even if it means we run to our end, I would go with you."

The words he'd said only a handful of hours ago at the ball echoed around me again. *"I've already chosen to love you, Rose Wolff. Beyond sense, beyond reason. There is no part of you I do not choose."*

I'd never responded. Nox had interrupted, and even if he hadn't, I wasn't sure what I would have said. I didn't have a quick retort, no joke to mask the gravity of his confession, no cloak to hide behind.

Love was an emotion, one I had reserved for as little number of people as possible. But it was also a *choice,* one I had actively avoided making for as long as I could remember.

Perhaps it looked different to everyone. Sweet nothings whispered in an ear, gifts and laughter and promises and secrets. Grand declarations under the stars. Stolen touches and heated looks, the feel of skin beneath your fingertips and passion that burned the world down.

And those were all true, I imagined.

But to me...love was a dagger pressed to a throat in the middle of a hidden hallway. Sharp tongues and writhing glares that made you come alive and come undone. An offer of friendship, an olive branch in a tempestuous sea of dread, a second chance when you didn't deserve it.

I think I'd known the truth for a while. At the dress shop, Rissa told me I had a choice to make: if my happiness was worth the risk, or if I'd let my fear get in the way as I always had before.

Fates, I was afraid of so many things. So much so that I'd denied its very existence and tucked it away, claiming to be impervious, untouchable, unmarred. I was *tired* of it. Tired of letting it control me from the shadows like a ghost hanging over my shoulder.

I chose *him.* I chose happiness. However fleeting it may be.

"Let's do it," I said abruptly. "Run away. When this is all over, when Gayl is out of power and the curse is broken and all is right with the world, let's go somewhere. Anywhere."

This time, he did laugh. It was a quiet rumble I felt with a hand pressed into his chest, his eyes lighter than they'd been all night. "We can't *run away*, Rose—"

"Not for forever. Just...to get away from everything. To explore and be around people who don't know us or our pasts. To be *together*." I sat up and dragged him into a seated position with me, taking both of his hands in mine. The fire snapped low behind me, making Leo's eyes gleam like coal set ablaze. "You told me that you've placed all of yourself in my hands. That I could either crush you or love you." Slowly, I kissed his palms, a rush of emotion swelling in my chest. "And I choose to love you, Leo."

I leaned forward and pressed my lips to his, not caring that his sister and friend slept across the cave, not caring that we were on a mysterious island fighting for our lives. In this moment, it was just us. A promise and a choice.

He broke away and cupped my cheek. "You are the last thing I expected, Rose Wolff." His lips were a breath from mine, the words brushing against my skin like a prayer. "And I love you," he murmured as his hands moved to grip my waist.

I smiled. "Say it again."

He dipped his nose down to my neck, placing soft kisses that sent heat trailing through me. "I'll say it however many times I have to. I love you, little wolf. When we get out of this, I'll take you wherever you want."

"Oh, really?" I leaned back and gave him a wicked smirk, which he then captured with his mouth.

"You're going to be the death of me," he said with a smile.

"Not if I can help it," I whispered.

67

ROSE

Sleep brought with it dreams of being in Leo's arms. Of his warmth encircling me, embracing me, heating me to my core. The novelty of the step we'd taken was welded into my skin, like molten lava coursing through my veins, almost hot enough to actually burn—

Something scorching licked at my feet.

I inhaled and immediately coughed. Opening my eyes, I gasped and scrambled to my knees, choking on thick, black smoke.

The cave was on fire.

"Rose! Leo!" Lark cried from across the cavern. Rissa, still in her fox form, tugged at Lark's gown with her teeth, her red fur standing up straight.

Leo was already on his feet and pulling me with him. I coughed again, doing my best to cover my nose and mouth with the fabric of my sleeves. I could barely see through the smog that enveloped the stone cave, the occasional flash of flames catching my eye. How could this have happened? The fire had been almost extinguished when we fell asleep, and Horace had been on watch—

"Where's Horace?" I called in between sputters.

"He must be stuck outside," Leo said. "Go with Lark and Rissa —I'll get him."

"Wait—Leo!" I tried to protest, but he let go of my hand and disappeared into the gray haze. Seconds later, the fire roared, violent red and orange flames bursting to the ceiling. Leo cried out and emerged from the smoke with his arm smoldering.

"The fire is blocking the entrance. We have to go through one of these." He gestured to the other three tunnels leading from the cave.

"What about Horace?" I asked.

"If he's on the other side, he can get out the way we came. We'll find him later. Right now we need to *move*."

As if on cue, the fire at our backs swelled and crackled. With a *whoosh*, it shot out at our feet, making me yelp and jump backward. Still, it grew, pushing us further and further toward the tunnels.

I tried to cross over to Lark and Rissa, but the flames seemed to be alive, their blazing fingers unfurling and snapping at my arm. They quickly crawled across my path, blocking Leo and me from our friends.

The inferno flared up again, almost catching Rissa's tail on fire. Lark cast me one final look of terror, my name on her lips before a coughing fit overtook her and the two of them were forced down the closest path right as the fire consumed their side of the cave.

My heart raced with adrenaline and fear and confusion. Eyes watering, I let Leo grasp my hand and drag me into the nearest exit.

"My magic, it—it's still not working," I rasped out as we stumbled down the dark path. Shadows flickered ahead of us. I craned my neck to look behind me and found flames following us into our small tunnel.

"This must be the fire portion of the trial," Leo said, his voice scratchy as he tried to clear his throat. "Normal flames don't act like this. It's like it's leading us to something."

"Or just trying to kill us."

"Always the optimist."

I shot him a wry grin, his level-headedness giving me courage while the blaze at our backs bore down on us. My breaths were labored as we ran, both from the smog and the incline of the tunnel. We were gaining elevation inside the mountain. Leo was right. The fire *was* leading us somewhere. Leading us *up*.

But what was at the top?

The path curved sharply, causing me to ram into the sidewall. Dirt and rocks embedded themselves in my skin as Leo helped me regain my footing, but those precious seconds cost us. With another surge of power, the blaze nipped at our heels and elbows. Sweat dripped from my forehead, my dress clinging to my skin like paste.

A fork in the path appeared ahead. Leo yanked me away from the flames and toward the left side, but his grip on my hand slipped. I called out his name and fell forward in an attempt to grab onto him, our sweat-slicked skin making it impossible to get a good hold.

My knees hit the floor as another coughing fit overtook me. Smoke flowed around us, so thick I couldn't even see him anymore. Soot clogged my throat. My eyes were heavy, my hands blackened, and the roar of the fire drowned out any sound of Leo's voice.

Flames erupted from the spot he'd stood moments ago. I let out a scream that felt like nails clawing at my neck.

"Rose!" shouted his distant voice. "Get out of here, Rose," he said. "I'll find you!"

The fire ripped past me and down the left tunnel, the one he'd been aiming for before we got separated. In a haze, I pushed to my feet and staggered down the right side, away from the inferno.

I was alone. No magic, no friends, not even a weapon—Horace hadn't given me back my dagger from when he gutted the pheasant.

There was nowhere to go but up.

I climbed higher and higher, looking back every few seconds to see if the blaze was catching up to me, but it seemed to have stayed where it was. If it wasn't chasing me, it was probably chasing Leo. The thought made me sick to my stomach. My lungs were filled with smoke, my vision swimming and pounding.

He would be fine. We would *all* be fine. I just had to keep going.

My thighs burned from the exertion of moving uphill, but I couldn't slow down. I skimmed my hand against the tunnel wall, both to keep myself going straight and to prevent me from falling.

Right as I thought I couldn't possibly move another foot, that there couldn't possibly be more to the path, I caught sight of the end of the tunnel.

But it wasn't an opening. It didn't lead to fresh air or a way out.

It was a dead end.

"*No*," I called out weakly, slumping to the ground.

This was it. The only way back out of the mountain was down the path I'd come.

Why would the trial have led me here only to force me back? If it was going to kill me, it had its chance. Was there something I was missing? Or perhaps it was to mess with my head. The Fates only knew Gayl loved to do that.

A cool breeze brushed against my hot neck. I let out a sigh and leaned my head back, welcoming a reprieve from the sweltering heat.

My neck snapped forward.

How was that possible? Where was the wind coming from?

I scanned the ceiling for cracks, but there wasn't so much as a sliver for the wind to get through. All that stood before me was a solid wall.

Like in the arena with the creature.

That had been a solid wall, and yet we'd walked right through it. An invisible portal masked to look like stone and rock. Could it be that simple? Another portal?

I felt along the ground for a rock and pulled one free, taking a deep breath to calm my thundering pulse as I threw it against the wall.

It disappeared.

I smiled. "Found you."

Getting a running start, I launched myself through the portal.

And then, I was free falling.

The first rays of the sunrise were blinding after hours in the dark cave. I blinked against the light and the rush of wind, a silent scream choking me as I fell, and fell, and fell. The tip of the mountain grew more and more distant. Hair whipped around me, blocking my vision, strangling me. I flailed through the air and tried to twist to get my bearings, but all I could think about was the contents of my stomach lurching up my throat and the impending death that awaited me at the end of this.

A sound broke through the wind. Something almost rhythmic. Like a pounding or beating of drums, only slower, and growing louder...

I managed to move my hair out of my face enough to see a dark mass flying on the horizon.

Flying toward *me*.

I squinted as it drew closer. The sound...it was *wings*.

Midnight blue and silver scales shimmered in the light of the morning sun, almost as if they were drinking in the rays. When the creature beat its magnificent wings, I saw veins of silver running through the translucent underside. An enormous tail slashed from side to side. The tip of it was like a jagged spike, sharp enough to flay skin. Four legs, each five times as thick as my entire body, stretched toward me as my gaze reached its head. It loomed large, long and angular, with curved horns shining like molten silver framing its face.

It can't be...

A dragon.

It flew directly overhead, its vast body blocking the light. The ground raced up to meet me and I closed my eyes, preparing for the crash.

But it never came. Instead, sharp claws encased me.

I screamed and opened my eyes to stare at the underbelly of the beast. It craned its neck to look at me, nostrils of its long snout flaring and a gleam in its silver eyes that was wholly disarming and somehow...familiar.

With a powerful flap of its membranous wings, it lowered us to the ground and released me from its grasp. I reeled backward, barely noticing the sand beneath my feet and the beach we had landed on.

Dragons...they weren't real. They were a *myth*. And yet that was the only thing this massive beast before me could be. It looked like the paintings in fairytales, with its ferocious maw and serrated teeth, its glistening scales and wings that could level an entire house.

The dragon was the width of my apothecary and twice as tall, its elongated neck reaching up so high I had to crane my neck to see its head and sharp horns. It looked down at me as I backed away, trying to put as much distance between us as possible—although I supposed no distance was too great for this creature to travel. It could snatch me in its jaws before I had time to breathe. But it simply stared at me, and for a moment, it almost looked as if it...it *smirked*.

Could dragons smirk?

Fates, I was losing it. I had to get out of here. I had to find Leo and the others and—

In the blink of an eye, those navy and silver scales disappeared, the monstrous body shifting into a sleek black button down shirt and pants, with dark blonde, wavy locks blowing in the wind as he rolled his neck.

Nox winked at me.

"Hello, darling."

68

LEO

These tunnels felt neverending. It was all I could do to force myself forward with the burning, acrid scent of flames and closeness of the stone walls threatening to overwhelm me. Fire bit at my heels as I sprinted, and I prayed to whatever was listening that the others were safe. That I was taking the brunt of it in order for them to get away.

Heat flared at my back, sparks brushing against the raw flesh. This torn shirt was doing nothing to protect against the open flames. My breaths came out harsh and rasping, like a blade was being ripped across my throat. How much longer could I do this? How much longer till the smoke and flames overtook me, till I couldn't draw breath?

Maybe it's for the best.

The thought pushed on my mind, making me think of the thousands of people who would wake once I died. *Chaz* would wake. Rose's uncle. It would be so easy; twenty-seven years of loss, of pain, gone in an instant.

Rose and Rissa flashed across my hazy vision. Horace and Lark. The people I loved, trapped here in this trial. I had to make sure they were safe, no matter what waited for me at the end.

I stumbled along as the fire chased me, nearly tripping over my own feet when the tunnel veered sharply to the right and began sloping downward. I descended faster and faster, gravity pulling me along so quickly it was all I could do to stay upright. The flames raged on, fueled by whatever twisted enchantment powered the island. I craned my neck back to catch a glimpse of blazing tendrils reaching, stretching, almost at my ankle—

I fell to the ground, my knees hitting the rock with a crash. The fire swarmed.

A hand appeared in my face.

"C'mon," Horace grunted.

Shock filled me as I gripped his hand and he hauled me forward into a small side tunnel I hadn't been able to see through the smoke. The fire kept down its path, oblivious to our hiding spot, but we only took a moment to catch our breaths before Horace guided me through this subsection of the mountains with a torch in his hand.

"Never thought I'd be so happy to see you," I said in between coughs, expelling black soot from my lungs.

"You can kiss me later," he said dryly. "I got your sister and Lark, too."

I closed my eyes, relief flooding my chest.

"Where's Rose?" he added.

Distress crept back in. "I'm not sure. We got separated. I think she might be following a path to the top of the mountain."

He nodded as we ran. "We'll go back up once this is over. She'll be fine, Leo. It has to end sometime."

Sooner than I expected, pinpricks of natural light appeared in the distance, marking the bottom of the mountain. Morning sunlight streamed through the entrance of the tunnel, so bright I had to cover my eyes as we stepped onto level ground.

Something soft and furry slammed into me. Rissa's wet nose slid along my arms in her excitement. I laughed and rubbed the backs of her ears, taking note of areas where her fur was singed, but nothing life threatening. Glancing up, I saw both Lark and

Horace smiling faintly at us, the pair of them tired and covered in cinders but alive and well.

"What happened to all of you?" I asked.

"I was keeping watch outside. The fire came out of nowhere," Horace said, crossing his arms. "Smelled it through the tunnels, but couldn't get back to you. It was like a wall blocking me out. I traced a path around the mountain trying to find a way in when these two popped out."

Lark bent down to scratch Rissa's side. "I wouldn't have made it without her. She could smell the way, even through the smoke, and led us right to Horace. What about you and Rose?"

I quickly recounted our tale after we'd left the big cave. As I spoke, I took in our surroundings, surprised to find us not at the forest where we'd entered the mountain, but on what looked like a beach. The rocky path under our feet bled into smaller and smaller pebbles until it became sand, the shoreline meeting blue waves just visible around a curve.

A strange noise punctuated the air. A beating sound that made the wind ripple.

Lark shot me a concerned look. At her side, Rissa growled, a low, ferocious rumble, her ears peeled back to her head.

I strode onto the sandy beach and turned the corner, and was met with the sight of brilliant turquoise waves crashing against white sand and birds squawking above us.

And an enormous dark beast hovering over the ground.

I halted in my tracks.

Vicious horns, a long, curved neck, teeth that shone in the sun. Four sets of claws capable of removing a head from its neck. Navy and silver scales covering a body so massive, so powerful, I had to rake my gaze upward to take it all in.

From its claws dangled a small figure, dark hair streaming in the wind as the creature set her down in the sand.

"Is that..." Lark trailed off and gasped behind me.

I took off at a sprint, Rose's name on the tip of my tongue

before the word fell to ash. In my next breath, the beast—the *dragon*—shifted.

Into Nox Duma.

Horace cursed. "That's impossible."

A moment later, that pit in my chest where I felt my loss of magic suddenly exploded with power. My Shifter instincts erupted so violently I could see every individual grain of sand, could hear Rose and Nox's shaking breaths and heartbeats all the way across the beach, could *taste* her scent on my tongue.

My magic had returned.

Whirling around, I saw Lark's shadows swirling, creeping at our feet as if they couldn't control themselves. My sister launched herself at me and shifted midair back to her human form, then threw her arms around my neck.

"I'm never eating pheasant again," she mumbled.

I let out a laugh as I kissed her forehead. "I'm glad you're back, Rissa." My smile faded when I looked over my shoulder at Nox and Rose. "But we have another problem to deal with."

We stalked toward the two of them, a protective, possessive instinct in me rising and clawing at my skin as I watched Rose scramble away from him. If he so much as *touched* her—

"Leo!" she called out when she saw me, hurtling across the slippery sand and into my arms.

"Are you alright, sweetheart?" I murmured, grasping her face and examining her for any injury or burns.

She nodded. "You?"

"Better now." Aiming a glare at Nox's smug features, I snarled, "A dragon Shifter? What are you playing at?"

"I thought your kind didn't exist anymore," Rissa added, her tone level. She was always better at keeping a cool head than I was, even with her full Shifter blood racing through her, no doubt riling her senses.

Rose looked up at me from her tucked position at my side. "I didn't even know dragons were *real*."

Nox chuckled darkly. "We're very real, but as usual, history has been rewritten."

It made sense now why I'd had such a strong reaction to his magic at the ball. Legend said dragon Shifters were the most powerful, most terrifying beings in the empire, back when the War of Beginnings ended and the magic had been dispersed. But there hadn't been signs of them in over two centuries. Historical accounts claimed they had died out, their nature so volatile that they brutally killed one another out of a desire to be the strongest in the land.

"How is this possible?" I asked.

"You want to do this? Now?" When I held his stare, he sighed. "Your *history*"—the word came out a hiss—"has painted dragon Shifters as violent monsters controlled by their baser instincts. But the truth is that the empire feared them. Feared their strength, their cunning and ambition. Those in power were threatened. They were convinced dragons would destroy the balance of magic and overthrow the throne. Two hundred and fifty years ago, the reigning emperor took matters into his own hand."

Rissa stiffened next to me. "Did he have them all killed?"

The shrewd gleam in Nox's blue eyes left, replaced with a pain I didn't think I would ever understand. He cast his gaze over the rushing waves as he spoke. "In those days, the dragons were *revered*. Celebrated. Not the mockery of a myth they've become. The emperor knew slaughtering them would have only made them martyrs. Caused an uprising, perhaps. He didn't merely want them dead—he wanted them to have never *existed*. To eradicate any chance of their survival. He and his advisors conducted... experiments."

Rose sucked in a breath at my side, but Nox ignored it and continued. "They created a toxin that suppressed a dragon's Shifter half and made it impossible for the same gene to be passed onto offspring. This was during the darkest time of conflict between dragons and the throne. They knew they were on the brink of war, a war they couldn't come back from. And the dragons knew they couldn't protect the rest of the Shifters from it. They allowed the toxin to be used on them in exchange for protection for their loved ones. Their people." He swallowed hard, the column of his throat moving slowly. "They chose their own eventual extinction to ensure the empire never saw such violence again."

The air was still as we took in his words. I struggled to comprehend his story that reshaped the history I'd so long believed. But I could tell he spoke the truth. His features were somber, his eyes hollow, his voice pained. Even after two centuries, he carried this burden of the dragons, this *legacy* that had been tarnished by those in power.

On a much smaller scale, I could understand this burden, too.

"If that's true, then how are you here? Are there more dragon Shifters that survived over the years?" Lark asked.

"If there are more, they've been silent," he said. "I'm the only one of my kind. I don't know how the ability passed to me. Perhaps someone escaped the terms of the treaty, or their bloodline was simply too strong to disappear. When my parents saw the early signs in my childhood and guessed what I was, they tried to hide me away. But young Shifters are...unpredictable. Unstable."

I glanced at Rissa, knowing far too well what that was like. The torment and isolation she'd faced because of her lack of control over her Shifter form had been brutal. And to face that as a *dragon*? With one hundred times the power?

"Word got out," Nox said straightforwardly, not allowing room for questions, then inclined his head toward myself and my sister. "Funnily enough, you and I have something in common. My father is—*was* the governor of Drakorum. Imagine how our people felt when they discovered their leader was illegally housing something so forbidden."

Rose was taken aback. "Your father is the governor of your province?"

"*Was*, darling."

She pressed her lips together. "What happened?"

"The people were afraid. They accused him of experimenting

on his own child to recreate the legend of the dragons and raise an army. He was eventually challenged for his position and lost."

The crease in Rose's brow deepened as she listened. "Where are they now? Your parents?"

A few steps behind us, Lark cleared her throat. "Rose, in Drakorum, a challenge is—it's to the death," she said gently.

Rose sucked in a breath and took a step toward Nox, her hand outstretched. "Nox, I'm—"

"Don't apologize. I don't want your pity. I want your *understanding*. I was taken from my home at fourteen years old and placed in an orphanage, but soon after, the one who'd taken my father's place realized he could *use* me instead of restraining me. He brought me into his home, effectively a prisoner in a gilded cage. Anyone of importance who knew I existed was threatened into silence, and everyone else was...taken care of." Rose winced, but Nox's face remained unmoved. "They kept me hidden, tucked away as their little secret." His lip twitched. "Until now. I told you once, Rose, that I had no choice but to come here. To compete in this tournament. They want me to win. They want me to take back the strength of magic for Drakorum that's been dwindling for far too long."

"There's no competition, not against a *dragon*," Lark said incredulously. "You could win this with your hands behind your back, yet you're tied for third place. It's as if you're not even trying."

"Well, now, I couldn't show my cards too early, could I?" Nox said with a false smirk. His face fell, his tone darkening. "I don't care if I win. I said as much when we first met, Rose. Why would I want more magic, more power, in the hands of the people who did this to me? To my family?"

"Why obey them at all, then?" I asked. "You could surely challenge the current governor. You could probably take on the entire chain of leadership." Something hard settled in my stomach as I spoke, and I quickly added, "What do they have, Duma?"

His eyes met mine. "My sister. They have my sister."

69

ROSE

Silence blanketed the beach. *His sister*. Everything made sense now—how cryptic Nox had been at the briefing before the tournament started, why he'd never wanted to expose his Shifter form, what his dreamscape in the second trial had meant to him. He was a victim here. A puppet. And Drakorum...they'd found the perfect way to keep such a powerful being under their thumb.

"What do you mean, they have her?" Horace asked.

"When my father lost the challenge, they let my mother live but wanted to take my sister away as well." Nox rubbed his jaw, his words stilted. "She was an infant, and they wanted to be sure she wouldn't follow in my footsteps and take the same form as me. My mother nearly lost her mind. She begged them to let her keep her baby, swearing on her life to report signs of her shifting as soon as they emerged. The governor compromised; he let my mother *and* sister join me.

"Vera was raised in the governor's household. Her every step was monitored, every movement watched. I had hoped once her Shifter half showed itself and they could see she wasn't like me, they would let both of them go...but of course, my little sister couldn't let me have all the attention." He shook his head and ran a thumb along his bottom lip. "When she was only eleven, Vera created light."

Rissa cocked her head. "She's a Lightbender? Born to Shifter parents?"

Smiling wistfully, Nox said, "She's *both*."

"That's incredible," I said, my eyes widening as I glanced at Leo. There weren't many people in the Veridian Empire's history to be born with two types of magic. Leo was the only person I'd met who had more than one, and his Shifter abilities were...well, not exactly of natural origins.

But what Nox said next wiped the look of awe from my face.

"And then she wielded shadows." Ice slithered over me as Nox's features darkened. "When Vera cast her first illusion at fifteen...they locked her away."

Nobody said a word. Until—

"How many?" We all knew what Lark was asking. How many types of magic did Vera Duma have?

Another pause.

"All of them."

My stomach bottomed out. The stillness between us and Nox was thick, no longer full of wonder but of disbelief and suspicion. I didn't know what to think. His sister bore *all six*? It wasn't just unheard of, it was *impossible*. Someone with power like that...

They would be unstoppable. Untouchable. A threat to every province, to the entire *empire*.

Or they could be—

"Is Drakorum using her, too?" I asked. "As a weapon?"

Nox didn't answer. Instead, he turned his head to gaze at the water, letting his silence say what words couldn't.

"I haven't seen her or our mother since that day. It's been four years. They give me reports on Vera when I beg, and they've delivered our letters to each other. But my mother...the governor banished her from our province once she began to fight back. When she tried to help us escape." Nox's voice hardened, his jaw clenching. "It was either execution or banishment. A *mercy*, he said."

His neck snapped back to us, eyes blazing. "So I do what he asks. If I don't, my sister pays the price. And there is nothing I won't do to keep her safe in the hell this world has given us."

I took in everyone's expressions, their shock mirroring my own. Leo was the first to speak. "I understand. If it were my sister, I would do the same. I would do anything to protect my family. But how do we know we can trust you?" His question wasn't unkind, merely guarded. A man needing to put the safety of those he loved first, as did Nox.

"You can't. Isn't that the point of all this?" Nox once again fixed his stare back on the ocean. The sight seemed to calm him; his shoulders relaxed slightly as his hands unfurled. "We can't trust one another. *They* don't want us to. But that's why we must. Because if we don't, they win."

"And who are 'they,' exactly?" Rissa asked. Her dark, discerning eyes assessed him. The scrutiny of a leader, of someone many steps ahead with a future in mind.

"Anyone who thrives on the division of this empire. Anyone who lets these injustices continue. These people who revel in tournaments and trials and balls, who lock up innocent children and —" his words came out choked, and Nox paused to compose himself. "People are never stronger than when united against a common enemy. I don't want that enemy to become *each other*. That's why we have to trust."

Rissa didn't respond. Stepping forward, she scanned him, her blonde hair whipping in the wind. Nox held his ground. His gaze was firm, resolute, unwavering.

Then Rissa held out her hand. "I think I know a group you might be interested in."

———

OVER THE NEXT COUPLE HOURS, Rissa, Nox, and Lark were inseparable. Nox's curiosity was boundless once he learned of the Sentinels and their cause, hounding Rissa with question after question about how it began, what their goals were, how their network operated, how he could help in Drakorum.

At first, Leo was hesitant that she should offer any information, worried that Nox may be forced to share their secrets once he went back to his province. But the idea of having someone as powerful as Nox, someone with a similar background as the lost heirs of the empire, and someone just as motivated to make things right...it was an opportunity the Sentinels couldn't pass up.

Horace, ever the dutiful guard, left shortly after to scout the perimeter of the beach and make sure no threats lurked around the corner. Leo and I went off in search of fresh water untainted by the poisonous storm from the night before. With a couple of containers full of water from a stream we'd found—containers I'd enchanted to banish any spell or magic, so the water would be drinkable—we eventually started to make our way back to the beach.

Shoving a vine out of the way, I glanced over and caught Leo's gaze, a hungry look in his eyes that sent heat to my core. I laughed and shook my head, biting my lower lip. "The others will wonder where we are, Leo."

"That sounds like their problem."

The way he looked at me made me feel years younger than I was, sneaking around in the shadows of trees, stealing these brief moments away from the others in the midst of the chaos. But unlike the past, this wasn't some fleeting happiness. This wasn't an excuse or distraction to avoid the demons that plagued me.

This was different. I *loved* him. I trusted him. And I had a feeling I would long after these trials were over.

Before I knew what was happening, his tail snaked out to grab the water containers from my hands and set them on the ground, his hard body pressing into me as he forced me backward. Twigs snapped beneath our feet and my spine hit the bark of a tree trunk.

"Why is there always a tree?" I asked breathlessly.

He chuckled. "Tell me," he said, his voice and stubble rough against the sensitive skin of my neck as he roved over it with his lips. "How it's possible for you to still look this beautiful after the night we've had."

Pushing on his chest, I leaned back to survey him with a smirk. "You know, you're far more charming on this island than at home."

He moved forward and nipped at my lower lip. "Home," he said, his chest rumbling as he drew out the word, letting it flow slowly in the space between us.

"What about it?" I whispered.

"Not the capital. Not Veridia City. You said *home*."

The word settled in me, nestling into my bones.

"Not the capital," I repeated, kissing his cheek. "Not Veridia City." My lips trailed his jaw. "*You.*"

Wrapping my arms around his neck, I kissed him, my body molding to his so effortlessly I had to wonder if it was real. If *any* of this was real. The way my heart threatened to burst out of my chest, the way every inch of me was set ablaze, the way he seemed to want me as much as I wanted him. The way he *loved* me.

I had never known a love like this.

Leo's hands gripped my waist and pulled me closer, his tongue sweeping against mine, a fire building between us that ached to consume. Devour.

A rush of cool wind skimmed my hot cheeks, and he froze and pulled away.

Goosebumps crawled along the back of his neck where my hands rested. Blinking away my haze of thoughts, I asked, "What is it?"

His brow furrowed as his nostrils flared. He sniffed the air, and his head whipped toward the direction of the beach.

Another blast of wind met us, but this one was savage, frenzied. Not the sweet kiss of a breeze I'd felt a moment ago. My hair surged around my face, the end of my torn dress tangling in my legs.

"Something is coming," was all he said before he grabbed my hand and took off.

Wind raced through the forest. Branches creaked with exertion, leaves and dirt and pebbles swirling from the ground and peppering our bodies as we sprinted. Was it another storm? My heart seized at the thought of that poisonous water again, at the void I'd felt when my magic had been erased. But we'd already passed the water challenge. Earth, water, fire—

Air.

We reached the edge of the forest, where soft grass transitioned to rocks which then faded into dirt and sand. I nearly stumbled when I saw what awaited us.

Beyond the shoreline, across the ocean, was an enormous cyclone.

Water and sand twisted and spiraled in the air, forming a funnel high above the surface. Ferocious waves crashed against the shore, water spraying our skin even at the distance we stood. With every passing second it billowed closer, and the noise of the wind and angry swells became deafening.

Rissa, Nox, and Lark dashed toward us. Their feet kicked up sand as they fumbled to keep what meager possessions we'd accumulated from flying away. Along the treeline, Horace lumbered out. His mouth moved, but I couldn't make out a word over the uproar.

"...is it. The air trial," I heard Lark say as they came within earshot. "The final part. We have to get back to the tunnels in the center."

"Then let's go," I said, turning to the forest. "We're getting off this island."

70

ROSE

The cyclone moved from the ocean to land, growing larger by the second as it gathered more and more debris into its revolving grip. It followed us through the woods and back to the clearing the earth trial had spit us out at, creating a barrier that trapped us in.

We weren't the first to arrive.

Magic was heavy in the air, along with dust and leaves the wind caused to spin across the clearing. Callum and Arowyn faced off in the center, the former hurling what looked like small, hand-crafted arrowheads made of sharp rock at the Strider, who disappeared and materialized feet away after every strike. She dipped and twisted to avoid what I assumed were illusions only visible to her, barely having time to stride from his arrowhead attacks.

To my right, Lark let out a loud gasp. When I saw what her eyes had landed on, bile crept up my throat.

Against a tree to the left was a body pinned to the trunk with a roughly hewn spear through his chest. The man's head lolled onto his shoulder and fresh blood dribbled from the hole, pooling at his limp feet.

"Vincent," Lark said, her jaw clenching. The other architect, the one who had been working for Gayl and killed her friend in the tunnels.

One of Callum's arrowheads whizzed past my face, narrowly avoiding my ear. Leo snarled and started to charge toward the center, but I grabbed his arm.

Reaching into Salome's pouch of herbs, I stuck an angelica leaf in my mouth and said, "*Incendar!*"

Two circles of fire appeared around Arowyn and Callum, separating them from each other.

"Why are you fighting?" I shouted and took a few steps forward despite Leo's low growl of warning. "We're supposed to be getting out of this trial. There's no point in killing each other!"

"Tell that to him," Callum said with a sneer as he pointed to the dead architect. "Things changed, Feywood."

"What are you talking about?" Lark asked, stepping to my side. I glanced at Arowyn, whose face remained impassive. But when she met my stare, her brow creased, a momentary glimpse of fear shining through.

"Your *friend* there told me how this works. How we're supposed to get out of here. Only, not all of us will." For once, Callum's haughty expression was nowhere to be found as he spoke. He was outraged. A crazed, furious look gleamed in his dark eyes. "Is this your way of toying with us, architect? Leading us to believe it's all for show, your pretty little tests and trials. Wit, heart, courage. If you wanted to see bloodshed, all you had to do was ask."

Lark looked as confused as the rest of us. "Mr. Orlox, I don't know what you mean. We never intended for any of you to die. I had nothing to do with this—"

"You had *everything* to do with this," he hissed. "You and your emperor. You think we're going to stop now? When we're so close to the end?"

Thick shadows approached Callum's and Arowyn's rings of fire, and I saw Alaric lurking across the clearing. Listening. Waiting. Tension stretched like a bowstring, and I knew one slight movement would make it all snap.

"Callum, listen to me," I said, taking another tentative step forward. "Lark can help us *all* get out. We don't need to fight. We can end this now."

"You don't get it," he responded. He shook his head at the ground with a laugh that was both cruel and woeful at the same time. "Before I killed him, he told me the truth." His eyes lifted to meet mine. "This trial was made for six people. Six challengers." Pausing, he scanned the clearing. "And only six can get out."

I blinked, trying to take in his words. Lark spun on her heels and gripped her head as her lips moved frantically to form numbers. Counting.

Callum, Arowyn, Nox, Alaric. Me.

Lark, Horace, Rissa, Leo.

Nine left. Only six could escape.

"This isn't a trial," Lark murmured. "It's an execution."

Across from me, Callum bared his teeth and lunged over the fire.

71

LEO

The Illusionist leapt over Rose's fire with his sights set on her, and before I could move she was already charging him with her dagger in hand. In the blink of an eye, Arowyn disappeared. Shadows billowed around me, weaving in and around legs and trees.

A burst of darkness pummeled into my chest and sent me staggering backward. A second later, Alaric Rinehart emerged, his tan, wrinkled face grim.

I knew who he was. The entire empire knew of him, the Shadow Wielder who'd had his victory stolen from beneath him in the last Decemvirate. He looked like a man who had aged twenty years in the last ten, just by the desperation in his eyes. Desperate for there to be another way to win, to redeem himself.

None of them had asked for this.

A second spear of shadows hit my shoulder, making me twist with a grunt to absorb the blow. My fingers buzzed from the magic in my henbane and amaranth rings begging to be let loose. Bringing them together with a clang, I whispered a spell for protection. A translucent shield formed in front of me.

"I don't want to fight you, Rinehart," I called out as his

shadows swirled around, unable to touch me. "I'm not even supposed to be here."

"It doesn't matter," he said. "I don't want this, either. But what choice do I have?" A barrage of shadows beat against my protection charm. "Look at what they have reduced me to. Ready to harm a fellow I've never met in my life, willing to kill simply because there's no other option." I grunted as a sharp, dagger-like shard of darkness pierced through the tip of my enchantment, making it ripple.

"It doesn't have to be this way. This should never…have happened," I forced out, digging my heels into the ground to prevent myself from sliding further backward. Fates, he was strong. "What if I told you there was something better on the horizon? Something to hope for?"

He stopped his assault to smile at me sadly. "I would say that's a wonderful dream, boy, but only for six of us. Whatever you did to end up here, I'm truly sorry, but I intend to be one of those six."

My heart sank. He was right. If what Callum said was true, three of us wouldn't be escaping the island.

My sister and Rose *had* to get out.

Taking a leap of faith, I asked, "Do you see that woman over there?" He followed my gaze to Rissa, who was keeping out of the way of a battle between Lark and Arowyn. Even from this distance, I could see my sister's shrewd eyes calculating a plan, determining a way to end this before more lives were stolen. "Her name is Clarissa Aris."

Alaric's mouth parted, recognition dawning on his features. "The Aris heir," he muttered. "How is that possible?"

"She's been forced to hide her entire life because of what Emperor Gayl did to her father. But she doesn't want to live in the shadows, Rinehart." I stepped closer to him, and he didn't attack. "She wants a better future for the empire—one where these dangerous notions of glory and power aren't the only things that matter. And she's here now because Emperor Gayl wants her gone.

Because he's threatened by the past she reminds him of and the future she symbolizes." I took one more step, close enough now to see the wrinkles on his forehead, exacerbated by the anxious thoughts darkening his green eyes.

"This isn't about me," I continued. "If I'm left behind, so be it. But help me get her out of here, Shadow Wielder. She doesn't deserve this any more than you, and the rest of the world deserves *her.*"

He turned his head slowly to gaze at Rissa. My chest tightened with anticipation, my throat too constricted to swallow. I would give my life, my freedom, a thousand times over if it meant keeping my sister safe. If it meant ensuring she made her rightful claim on this empire. I only hoped my words were enough, and that Alaric Rinehart was as despondent as he seemed.

Inch by inch, he lowered his hands.

A high-pitched scream tore through the gusts of wind. Whirling to see where it came from, I spotted the Strider challenger on her knees. Behind her stood Horace with one of the containers Rose and I had made to hold water.

Arowyn's pale hair was dripping wet. Water rolled down her cheeks in rivulets, her features screwed in fury.

"He used...he used that water on her. The one that stole our magic," Alaric said, his shoulders tensing.

I couldn't help but smile. "Horace, you clever man."

Alaric turned on me, arms raised once again. Shadows crept from his skin. "Are you with him? Is this your plan? To lure us in and take away our magic, then leave us here to die?"

I held my hands up. "I don't have anything on me, Rinehart. He was just protecting a friend. We're not trying to hurt you."

His cheek twitched. "I do want a better future, my dear fellow. I hope to one day say that I am a good man. But this tournament..." He shook his head. "This tournament is not for good men."

He caught Callum's eye to my right, and the Illusionist abandoned his fight with Rose. As one, Callum and Alaric both sprinted across the clearing and converged on Horace. Shrouds of shadows enveloped them, so thick I couldn't see what was happening. I charged after them, but Rose was closer.

Shouting Horace's name, she ran straight into the web of darkness.

72

ROSE

arkness surrounded me. Wind and shadows blew against my skin. The second I broke through the haze, I sucked in a breath.

Alaric and Callum had cornered Horace, whose sword did nothing against the surge of shadow magic. He used his blade to block Callum's spinning arrowheads, slashing and weaving it through the air faster than I thought he could move, but it didn't stop all of them. Already, small cuts littered his cheek and neck, blood dripping from the thin red slits. He seemed to be throwing illusions at both the challengers, for Alaric and Callum would occasionally roll to the ground or duck below some invisible force I couldn't see.

Horace saw me enter the fray and lost his concentration for a split second. "Get out of here, girl!" he bellowed, missing a step as he swung. An arrowhead sliced deeply across his neck.

I cried out, and Callum glanced back at me with a wicked smirk. In an instant, he bounded toward Horace who staggered to the ground as blood poured from the wound. Callum's hands circled Horace's throat...and squeezed.

Horror shot through me. Images of both my father and Horace lying flat on their backs, blood spurting from their necks, flashed across my vision, blending together in a fog of red. My heart pounded in my ears as my feet moved of their own accord. Suddenly, I was behind Callum, my dagger in my hand.

"Let go of him, Callum!" I screamed in warning.

"Only six of us get out, Feywood. What about this don't you understand?" His hands remained tight around Horace's throat. The guard's ruddy face turned an alarming shade of purple, his eyes bloodshot as they rolled back into his head. Blood bubbled from his lips.

He was dying.

I didn't think. I shoved the dagger into Callum's back, feeling every inch as the blade tore through skin and muscle with a sickening squelch.

The shadows around us disappeared.

Pulling the dagger out, I stumbled backward, putting a hand to my mouth. *I just killed—*

"Nice try," Callum's voice sounded in my ear. I jumped back with a shriek.

"No, no, no, no, no..." My plea was breathless and shaking as I slowly turned to face my victim, lying face first in the dirt.

Alaric.

"No!" I ran to his side, flipping his heavy body over to find the blade had pierced through his heart, deep red blooming on the left side of his shirt. His eyes were glassy and unmoving.

Horace was nowhere to be found. It was a trick. *Another trick.* One I kept falling for, over and over again.

But this time...I wasn't in a dreamscape, where none of my actions were real. I had *killed* Alaric. He was dead because of me. I'd stabbed him through the heart and taken away any chance he had at getting out of here. At seeing his family again.

And he knew my uncle...Fates, I'd killed Ragnar's *friend.*

I killed a man.

A choked sob left me. I gripped my dagger and spun to face Callum.

This was his fault. It was supposed to have been *him* beneath my blade. Maybe I didn't want to kill him, but he was a poison on this world. The spell Leo and I had found in my father's Grimoire blossomed behind my eyelids. My vision shook with rage, my peripheral going gray as adrenaline and wrath pounded in my skin, my bones, my blood.

Magic swirled within me like it had that day in Gayl's lair. Every cell vibrated with a bloodlust that begged to see this man on his knees, praying for mercy, pleading for my forgiveness.

I stalked toward him and slit my hand on the blade.

I may not take his life, but I could try and take his magic.

"*Phyxie*," I said before he could conjure an illusion. My voice was distant, unfamiliar. Cold. Instantly, the breath left his lungs, his lips already turning ashen with loss of oxygen. My blood made the spell stronger than normal.

Good.

I fisted his shirt and dragged my dagger across his collarbone until a line of blood bloomed to the surface. The siphoning spell only required that I—

"Rose, *stop*," a voice said behind me. Leo's hand wrapped around my upper arm, but my gaze stayed focused on Callum.

"It will have a price, sweetheart," Leo urged.

"You didn't seem to care when we planned to use it on Gayl," I said icily. Callum had precious seconds left.

"If we have to face consequences, let it be against *him*. Not this poor excuse of a challenger. He's not worth it, Rose."

"I'll pay the price."

"But what if it's not *you* that pays it?"

I blinked, his words seeming to break through some of the fog in my mind. Leo handed me a thistle leaf. My fingers shook as I put it to my lips and murmured, "*Finiscere*," and my spell on Callum broke. He sucked in lungful after lungful of air, still disoriented in my grip.

"Think about my father," Leo said. "About Chaz. About the curse. You don't know who will pay this price, Rose." His voice was steady, an odd contrast to the tidal wave rolling through my body. "It could be your aunt. Your cousin. Is that worth it? Is *he* worth it?"

Leo was right. We had no idea what the consequences of such a powerful blood spell would be, if it even worked the way we wanted it to. Branock Aris had been willing to accept the cost...and the entire empire had paid the price.

Would I be able to use it against Gayl? When the time came, would I be willing to accept *any* price? Or would we be starting an entirely new cycle of curses brought about by the hubris of magic?

I let out a breath. My shoulders slumped as my hold on the dagger at Callum's collar loosened.

I was about to back away when he caught his breath and smirked at me.

"Should've gone for the eyes, Feywood."

My blade disappeared, only to be replaced with a stick. I looked down to see my dagger in Callum's hand—he must have taken it from me and cast an illusion. Rissa cried out my name as the tip of the blade lunged for my ribcage.

Snap.

Callum dropped to the ground. Leo stood behind him, dark eyes blazing.

A scream left my lips and I fell backward in shock. Leo was there to catch me, cradling me in his arms.

"You're alright, sweetheart. It's alright. You're safe. He can't hurt you."

I gripped him, letting the feel of his lips on my forehead and his sturdy arms surrounding me keep me grounded. My mind struggled to catch up with what the last few minutes had brought. Every time I blinked, I saw Horace's slit throat, Alaric's dead eyes, my father's spell, the knife at my ribs, the crack of Callum's neck as it twisted on itself.

Looking over, I glimpsed Horace supporting Lark, who limped toward us on an injured leg; a haggard Rissa and Nox; and Arowyn, who leaned against a tree, arms wrapped around her midsection. I noticed distantly that the cyclone had stopped and the forest was now silent.

"The—the portal back to the capital," Lark started, panting slightly. "It's through the entrance to the tunnels. The same one that led us here. It should take us to the palace."

"There's still one extra person." Arowyn strode into the clearing. "Seven. The architect said only six can get through."

Lark nodded. "I know, but there may be a way around that. When we set up the enchantment, it was under the assumption that it would be six magical beings—the six challengers. I think if someone tried to pass through that *didn't* carry magic, the spell wouldn't count them." She gestured to Arowyn, whose magic had been temporarily depleted when Horace threw the poisonous water over her.

"You *think?*" Arowyn asked skeptically.

"That's the best I can offer. Would you rather be the one to kill one of us?" Lark challenged. Arowyn held her stare, her jaw clenching, then looked down. "That's what I thought. Technically, only six of us bear magic at the moment. We should all be able to get through."

"What about them?" Nox asked, pointing to the three dead bodies littering the clearing.

Lark's face fell as she took them in. I wondered if she felt responsible, in a way—this was partially *her* tournament, no matter how many of the strings Gayl was pulling in the background. "We'll come back for them. *I'll* come back for them. Once the rest of you are safe."

She led us across the clearing to the entrance of the underground tunnel system. The terrain became rockier and more uneven as we neared, the ground sloping downward before opening to a wide separation in the earth, tall enough for a person to pass through.

I should have felt relief. Elation, even, knowing the trial was over and we were getting off the island. But I felt...numb. The adrenaline from the last twenty-four hours was fading, leaving me empty. I didn't know how to process what had happened. How to go back to normal life in the palace or Feywood.

Ragnar had been right all those weeks ago. Death wasn't the only outcome for this tournament. These trials, what each of us had been forced to do...they left a permanent mark. One I wasn't sure I was ready to face yet.

"How do we know this won't take us back to the tunnels?" Arowyn asked, looking at Lark as she stood before the dark entrance.

"Once all challengers passed through the first time, the enchantment should have changed course. It leads to the palace now," Lark explained. "Horace, would you like to do us the honor?" she asked, motioning to the burly guard. He grunted and gave a stiff nod before stepping into the portal and disappearing from sight in a faint shimmer.

The remaining six of us stood in silence. Birds whistled through the trees, creatures of the forest returning in the absence of the storm. The peace and brightness of the world around us contrasted with the death and destruction of the clearing.

When nothing happened, Arowyn followed after Horace. The Strider shot a look I couldn't decipher at Nox and me before crossing over.

"You two, go," Leo said, putting his hands at Rissa and Lark's backs and ushering them forward. Rissa looked up and clenched his hand before she and Lark vanished.

"See you on the other side, viper," Nox said, offering a small smile that didn't reach his eyes.

Finally, it was only Leo and me.

He pulled me into him and rested his chin on top of my head. My body sank against him, shoulders dropping and tension unwinding. Just the two of us. For a moment, nothing else mattered.

"Maybe staying wouldn't be so bad," I murmured. I moved to put my chin on the hard planes of his chest, looking up into his eyes. "No expectations or responsibilities. Find a cozy cave to live in. It could be nice."

He smiled and pushed tendrils of hair from my face. "I'll find you a cozy cave once this is all over."

"Promise?"

"I promise." He kissed me gently, with a tenderness that wiped the worries from my mind. My heart felt lighter as we broke apart and I took his hand, leading him to the portal. I stepped into cold, dark nothingness, with the same sensation of ice slipping through my veins. The grassy underbrush of the forest gave way to sleek, dark wood. Leo's hand slipped from mine when my feet planted firmly on the palace floor.

I turned to the wall, waiting for him to appear.

One heartbeat. Two. Three.

The hair on the back of my neck raised.

Placing my hand on the wall, I was met with solid stone. A weight dropped in my stomach.

"Leo?" I called, fist pounding on the hard surface. My pulse stopped then sparked rapidly, roaring in my ears. Where was he? Why wasn't he coming through?

"Did you think," a quiet, steady voice said in my ear, "it would truly be so easy, dear niece?"

73

ROSE

"What did you do to him?" I screamed at Gayl. "Bring him back!"

"What happened?" Rissa asked frantically. I looked around the room for the first time to see my friends each restrained by a guard—in Horace's case, two. We were in a large, dark chamber I didn't recognize, with no windows, a few sconces to light the way, and only one door far across the space.

Rissa struggled against the man pinning her arms behind her back. "Rose, where's Leo?"

"He—he was right behind me—" I whirled around and slammed my hand against the wall. "He's still there. On the island." My breaths came out in shallow spurts as I turned and slumped against the stone.

"And there he will remain until I choose to lift the enchantment," Gayl said smoothly.

"Why are we here, Your Majesty?" Arowyn asked, sneering at the guard behind her. Next to her stood Nox with his hands bound, a look of pure wrath I'd never seen before on his tan features. My brow furrowed. Why wasn't he using his magic? He could shift and take down every single person in this *palace* in a single breath.

My eyes caught on the black metal cuffs surrounding his

wrists. My lips parted. It looked like the cuffs used by the Mysthelm soldiers in my second trial dreamscape. The kind that took away magic.

Could those possibly exist? Is that why none of the others were attempting to fight back?

Gayl regarded Arowyn with his mismatching eyes. "I'm afraid, Miss Garrolas, you were simply in the wrong place at the wrong time." He lifted two fingers, and the guards holding Nox and Arowyn grabbed their charges by the arms and began marching them toward the single door.

Arowyn yanked from the guard's hold. "Where are you taking us?" she demanded.

"You will remain unharmed," Gayl said, his cloak sweeping over the floor as he faced me. He ignored the sounds of the two challengers scuffling against their restraints. A moment later, the chamber door shut behind them with an echoing clang. I glared at him, shoving all of my fury and determination into my features.

His lips thinned. "Do you not believe me? They will be safe. They won't even remember what happened," he said softly, that powerful voice not showing a hint of his emotions.

"How can you expect me to believe you after everything?" I spat. "What about my friends? What about *Leo*?"

"I warned you, Rose. The first night we met. I never promised mercy to those who seek to undermine me, and I have let your *friends* carry on for far too long."

"You've disgraced the integrity of the tournament, Your Majesty," Lark said in a shaking voice, as if still trying to play the part of the dutiful head architect. Her shoulders rolled backward at an awkward angle from the guard holding her. "All we've built, all we've worked for—"

"*I* disgraced it, Miss Everest?" Gayl hissed, striding across the room to stand before her. "You think I didn't know of your betrayal? How you entered my home seeking to trick me?" He brandished an arm. "Tell me what you have built. Tell me what you have worked for, if not to commit treason against your emperor."

When she said nothing, he tilted his head and stalked toward Horace, who thrashed against his two guards. "Imagine my disappointment upon learning one of my trusted guards, of the mightiest in the empire, had fallen to the rebels. Your position was an honor, Horace Banathery. A symbol of the most elite men and women who keep this empire safe." Gayl leaned in closer to Horace, but his quiet voice carried through the room. "Tell me why I should not have you executed for your actions, soldier."

"I can't, Your Majesty," Horace said. "There are some things worth dying for."

Gayl lingered a moment before turning to Rissa, who stood tall, her expression giving away nothing. He took his time appraising her, letting the pressure and anticipation build until it was so thick I could taste it in the air.

"It has been a long time since I've seen you, Clarissa Aris," he finally said, with what almost sounded like reminiscence. "You're not the young girl I remember."

"No, I'm not," she responded.

"You look so much like him." He paused, and I could only see his profile as he stared at her. The lost heir and the man who stole her future. "Tell me if it was worth it, young Aris. Leading your people to their inevitable failure."

She held his gaze, her chin high, eyes flashing. "Every step."

The corner of his lip twitched.

I gritted my teeth. "So this trial, this entire Decemvirate, was your way of what—removing the rebels from the equation?"

"And to teach a lesson." His eyes stayed on Rissa. "Rising to power always comes with consequences. The higher you climb, the farther you have to fall. If you desire to *take* something, you must be willing to lose everything." He faced me again, the wrinkles on his forehead deepening as he truly looked at me for what felt like the first time that night. "You were never meant to be part of this, niece. You were...unexpected."

"Sorry to disappoint," I shot back.

He shook his head, dark hair brushing his shoulders. "You are not a disappointment, Rose. You brought back a past I thought was buried. We are alike, you and I. Have you not realized it?"

Something oily slid along my skin as he stepped toward me. Something toxic and claiming. And, perhaps...true.

"Both outcasts in our lives, both searching for something more," he continued. "Such as freedom from the constraints that this world—this *magic*—has forced on us. Pride in our own abilities, in the extraordinary things we know we're capable of, if only others could see." He was an arms-length away from me now. His dark blue and white eyes delved straight through me, as they always had.

"I *see* you, Rose. And I think, for the first time since your father, I had someone see me, as well. I know how much you care for the people of this empire. I do, too, even if you don't always agree with my ways. But it's because of that, because of your fierce determination, your aim for truth, that I think you could be great."

The world seemed to slow. "What are you saying?"

"I will never have an heir of my own, niece, but you are my blood. Think of what we could do. *Together*." He reached out a gloved hand and, when I didn't stop him, took mine. "Join me. Let me teach you all that I know, and one day this empire could be yours."

I blinked. He wanted me to be his *heir*? To rule in his place once he was gone?

For a single moment, I imagined it.

I imagined life in this grand palace, surrounded by all the magic my heart desired. Learning, growing, *changing*. Living constantly in the unparalleled rush that overtook me every time I practiced my magic. Using our powers to create good.

But this future...it wasn't mine. I didn't know if I could create *good*. And this empire desperately needed someone who would.

"You're right," I said, looking from his hand back to his eyes. "We *are* alike. We both crave a certain type of power, something I hadn't fully realized until you showed me." I swallowed thickly. "But that's a dangerous desire, and even more dangerous when people like us actually *get* it." I slipped my hand from his, lowering my voice. "I don't want to be like you, uncle. My father walked away because he saw the warning signs. Because he saw what this magic and power would do to you. I choose to follow his path."

Gayl's hand clenched into a fist. "And where did that path lead him?" he whispered, his voice deadly. Sinister. "Your father could not handle what I had to offer him. He was weak when it mattered most. And that is why he is *gone.*"

Frozen in place, a thought entered my mind. One too terrible to voice, that I didn't *want* to voice, but the truth swelled inside me.

I sucked in a breath. "Did you—did you kill him?"

He pulled back from me, his eyes shifting across mine. "I killed them *all*, Rose."

74

ROSE

The room went in and out of focus. Magic and blood heated in tandem beneath my skin, like coiling serpents ready to strike.

I killed them all.

He'd had me believe Branock Aris had murdered my father out of revenge, as a way to get back at Gayl by hurting anyone he had been close to. Gayl told me he'd tried to *protect* my father.

Lies. Everything from this man's mouth had been a lie.

And those other men, the ones who had followed Gayl...the Sanguivex, my aunt had called them. All of whom died within a couple years of my father. Once again, I'd blamed Branock Aris, but it had been Gayl the entire time.

"Why?" was all I could force through my clenched teeth, around the cloying, bitter taste of rage.

"They knew too much. After all of our years together, all of the nights spent practicing blood magic and creating such spells, they knew it was I who caused the Somnivae curse twenty-seven years ago. They knew what it could do, what I longed for. And they were beginning to speak. I did what I had to do."

"But...the night my father died, the Illusionist who killed him said 'Branock Aris sends his love.'"

"Hamilton and the others were the very ones who helped me develop the curse. In a way, they were part of the reason for Branock Aris' downfall. That was merely the message I sent. Aris had no idea who Hamilton was, nor the rest of the Sanguivex."

The truth crashed into me. The lie I had believed so wholeheartedly now seared as it warped and twisted at Gayl's words.

He killed my father.

His voice grew fainter against the loud pounding of my heart. That night in his lair when I'd lost control of my magic had felt like an explosion inside my chest, like my very blood had burned, boiling to the surface and releasing in a shattering of energy.

But now I felt…something else entirely.

It wasn't an eruption. There was no sudden burst of magic. It was as if a piece inside of me settled. A silent part clicking into place. A door opening.

"You murdered your own brother," I said, barely a whisper. Looking down, I realized my hands had been balled into fists tight enough to pierce the cut on my palm from when I'd tried to curse Callum. Blood leaked from my flesh and dripped to the floor.

My neck snapped back up to Gayl. "*You murdered my father,*" I growled, louder this time.

Magic swirled angrily in my bones, eager for retribution. Eager to be set free. Taking a step toward him, I raised my blood-stained hand. Gayl's body lifted from the ground, his fingers clawing at his neck as if he was choking.

I uttered no spell, but my magic seemed to have a mind of its own.

"You didn't deserve to call him your brother." With each word, I took another step, his body moving with me. I ignored the gasps from Rissa and Lark and the clambering of Gayl's guards as they hesitated to come to his aid. "You didn't deserve to have him stand by your side. You don't deserve to speak his name *ever* again."

His head slammed into the far wall, but when he opened his eyes, he was grinning.

"Look at you," he said, wheezing. "More power than you have ever dreamed of. But it's still not enough."

With a wave of his hand, he fell to the ground and landed on his feet.

I expected him to retaliate, to execute me on the spot, but instead, he straightened his cloak and rolled his neck along his shoulders. As if this were child's play. As if I was *nothing*. With a simple flick of his wrist, I was suddenly immobilized from the neck down, unable to move my limbs. I thrashed and tugged at the enchantment, desperation clawing at my throat, but it was no use. He had me at his mercy.

"You will never understand the things I had to sacrifice to keep this curse alive, Rose."

My breath left me. "So the Somnivae curse wasn't an accident? You *meant* to cast it?"

"It's not just a curse, is it, Your Majesty?" Lark asked, breaking her silence.

He said nothing, examining us like insects under a magnifying glass. I twisted again within his magical grip, my arms aching to move, but I was stuck.

What did Lark mean? For all my knowledge of spells and herbs and curses, blood magic was a whole new world. A dark realm of possibilities was laid out before us.

"You don't even want to get rid of it, do you?" I asked. Was *that* why he'd let Leo live all these years?

Gayl's focus was solely on me. "Why would I want to get rid of it? The Somnivae curse is the pinnacle of my creations. It has given me *everything*."

"What are you talking about?" I whispered.

He snapped his fingers and the guards dropped their hold on Rissa, Horace, and Lark, unshackling them from their cuffs. I watched in horror as my friends each grabbed a sword from the guards' scabbards and, with foreign expressions of pure rage, turned to face one another.

Horace was the first to move.

He bolted to Rissa, raising his sword and striking hard and fast, leaving her hardly any time to block his attack. Lark came in from the side and brought Rissa to her knees with a swift kick to the hip. Swinging her sword down on Horace's shoulder, Lark let out a battle cry.

Horace spun away just in time, using his momentum to swipe his blade across her stomach. She leapt backward, but not before a splatter of dark blood hit the floor. Stunned, she clutched at her middle.

"Stop!" I screamed. It was like they didn't know what they were doing. They were completely savage, controlled by whatever mind games Gayl was playing. I tried to run toward them, but my legs wouldn't move. A guttural shriek left my throat as I pushed and shoved with all my might, trying to break free of the spell.

"Make them stop, *please!*" I begged as Rissa narrowly avoided having her head cut clean off by Lark's blade. My breaths were broken and wild. I couldn't do this. If I had to watch them kill each other—

In an instant, they stopped moving. Completely frozen, eyes glassy.

"I can do this without even a *thought*, Rose. While I pride myself on innate strength of magic, do you *truly* think there is any way I could be so powerful on my own?" Gayl asked, cocking his head. He was trying to lead me to the answer, guiding me along the way as he had during our lessons.

It had something to do with the curse. He said it had given him everything. How could it have given him his power? The curse didn't affect him. It had taken all those people—

I inhaled sharply. "The people. When they fall to the curse, what...what happens to their magic?" His eyes brightened in triumph at my question, the way they did when he helped me with my magic.

My blood ran cold.

"It—it goes to you, doesn't it?"

He didn't have to say anything. His expression was confirmation enough.

The curse...it was how he had accumulated so much power. Every time someone became cursed, *he* got their power. Or at least, pieces of it.

For twenty-seven years. *Thousands* of people.

He was...invincible. How could he not be, with that much power? I couldn't even begin to wrap my mind around the kind of magic he possessed, all at the expense of his empire. His *people.*

"That's why Leo is still alive," I said, trembling. "Not to protect him. Because you *need* him. If he died, your curse would end." I glanced back at the wall where the portal had been. "Then why trap him there, if not for him to die? What was the point of all this?"

"I told you: to teach them a lesson." His voice was still as quiet, still as captivating as ever, not even a hint of anger or worry that I was uncovering all of his secrets. A constant reminder that this had always been under his control. "To show your Sentinel friends that no matter how large their numbers grow, how pure of heart their goal is, it's all futile. If I wanted to simply detain your Zareleon in my palace, I could have done so. But it's much more meaningful this way, don't you understand?" He took a step toward me. "I do not wish to rule by force alone. I want to see how far you are willing to go, how much you are willing to sacrifice, before I put an end to it."

Gayl brandished an arm and the enchantment over my limbs broke. I stumbled as Horace, Rissa, and Lark fell to the ground at the same time, swords clattering against the hard floor. Lark held a hand to her stomach, her eyes widening when it pulled away red. Rissa rushed to her. Each of them looked confused and terrified, as if they didn't remember what had happened.

This was all for show. He had no intention of letting us go. He had no intention of releasing Leo from his prison on the island.

Another question flashed before me. "How did you get Zareleon and Clarissa into the trial?"

"*I* didn't, niece." Gayl steepled his hands in front of his face. "*You* did."

My mouth fell open. Rissa shot me a look, as if believing, if only for a moment, I'd done something to betray her.

"I don't know what he's talking about, Rissa, I swear," I rushed out. Glaring at Gayl, I said, "I would never do that to them."

With the snap of his finger, a white handkerchief and a small strip of cloth appeared in his grasp. Spots of red stained each of the fabrics.

I blinked. "Those..."

"Are yours. Yes, I know."

The handkerchief was the one I'd used in the dress shop when Rissa cut herself on the pins of my dress. And the cloth...I had accidentally nicked Leo's hand when cutting open the letter from Gayl that same night. The last time I had seen either of them was—

"I asked you to retrieve them for me, and you delivered it the evening of our last lesson. I never did properly thank you," Gayl said, inclining his head toward me in a mockery of a bow.

"How?" I breathed. I didn't remember bringing them that night. I didn't remember him ever asking. I *never* would have agreed to help him, to sneak him their *blood*, of all things.

"Blood is a powerful weapon," was all he said.

It was never a straight answer with him. Always leading, always guiding. He wanted me to figure it out on my own. He reveled in seeing others realize how cunning he was, how he was multiple steps ahead at every turn.

I looked down at my friends, thinking of how he had taken over their minds and controlled their actions without them remembering a single moment. Had he done the same to me? Was that how I'd collected Rissa and Leo's blood for him?

My eyes traveled back to Gayl, narrowing as my thoughts sped up. I was under the impression he needed someone's blood before he could control them. He had access to these three now, of course, but when had he first gotten into *my* head? It must have been when the challengers had their physical exams, or when—

I remembered. Our very first lesson after the second trial, when I cut my hand to cast a fire spell. He'd given me a handkerchief to stop the bleeding.

"You were using me from the beginning," I whispered, hurt seeping into my voice. I didn't *want* to feel hurt by this man. He was a monster, a power-hungry, selfish tyrant.

But for a moment, he had been my uncle.

His gaze flickered across my face, his wrinkled features softening a fraction. "That does not change anything I said. You *could* be great. And I was proud of you. This magic is our birthright, and I only desired to share that with you."

"If that were true, you wouldn't be doing any of this!" I cried. Perhaps there was still a remnant of that sentimental man, the one who told me of adventures with my father, who felt remorse for what he'd done. Some small part of him that could be reached.

Edging forward, I let the rest of the room fall away, hoping, praying, *pleading* that he would see reason. I didn't need him to renounce his magic. I didn't need him to hand the empire over to Rissa. Right now, in this moment, I only needed him to let us go. The rest would come—the Sentinels would regroup and Gayl would get what he deserved. I would do anything to get myself and the ones I loved out of this, even if it meant the world would suffer a bit longer.

"I remember when you told me you weren't the monster I'd always believed. Please, uncle. If even a fraction of that is true, if my father or even I still mean *anything* to you, you'll let the rebels go. Let Leo come back. We want the same thing—for him to stay alive." I stepped closer. "I care about these people. I know they've betrayed you, but even you said you ask for your citizens to prove themselves. To take what's theirs. Isn't that what they've done? Punish them, banish them if you need to, but let them live."

I could feel Rissa's eyes shooting daggers at my back. I was practically handing over their surrender. But she would understand. If this got her brother back, she would forgive me.

Gayl blinked and I thought, for a moment, I had made him pause.

"I have no quarrel with your friends, nor your lover," he said slowly. "But I cannot allow the one person with the ability to take what I have worked for to live."

His right arm shot out to the side, and invisible strings dragged Rissa toward him. Without touching her, she rose straight into the air, flailing and cursing as his hold over her tightened.

A second later, her body went slack.

"No!" I shouted, flinging myself at them. "Please, uncle. I—I'll stay with you," I cried frantically. "I'll be your heir. I'll do whatever you want, but if you care about me at all, please *don't hurt her.*"

His gaze drilled into mine. My heart stuttered as I waited, my promise dragging out between us.

"I do care about you, niece," he said. "But the key to power is knowing what you're willing to leave behind."

His hand squeezed, and a terrifying gurgle escaped from Rissa's throat.

"Now!" Lark yelled. Suddenly, shadows rippled from her in waves, her magic unlocked after Gayl had removed the cuffs earlier. Billowing darkness filled the room. Momentarily distracted, Gayl's head whipped around. His other arm came out to restrain Lark when a flash of silver glinted through the air.

With a strangled cry, Gayl dropped his arms, and Rissa went crashing to the ground. He clutched at his wrist.

A small dagger was embedded in his left hand.

I watched in horror as slowly, painstakingly slowly, the dagger lifted itself from his flesh, controlled entirely by Gayl's magic. Blood rolled down the blade as it rose.

Before I could blink, it twisted midair and fired back the way it came.

Straight into Horace's eye.

75
ROSE

Time froze.

I couldn't breathe, couldn't think, couldn't move.

The hilt of the dagger protruded from Horace's head. His body was suspended, a fierce expression still on his features.

He hadn't even seen it coming. Had no time to prepare.

It happened faster than he could draw his next breath.

Bile crept up my throat, my body realizing the truth before my mind.

He couldn't be dead. It was a trick. My loyal guard, my surly friend…he would be fine. I could *heal* him.

I drew in a sharp breath. *Yes*, I could heal him.

My limbs sprang into action, my feet carrying me across the floor as if I was gliding on air. The buzzing in my ears drowned out the noise of the room; I distantly saw Rissa and Lark's silent screams, their faces red and contorted. I saw Gayl thrust his arm toward me, but whatever spell he cast, I felt nothing.

I felt *nothing*.

All I knew was I had to get to Horace.

I could save him.

Blood poured from his eye, thick and viscous. It covered his cheek, his chin, his neck, pooling on the ground where he lay. His other eye was glassy, unseeing.

I knelt at his side.

My blood thundered in my veins like a drum, harder and faster the closer it got to the surface of the cut in my hand. Begging to be freed.

In the back of my mind, Leo's voice whispered, *"It will have a price, sweetheart."*

I nudged the warning away. It was just an injury. Just a simple healing. There may be a small price, but I could pay it. Nobody else would have to get hurt.

"He's not injured, Rose. He's dead. You can't heal that."

No—no, he wasn't dead. He couldn't be dead. I couldn't lose someone else, not again, not after everything—

"You have to let him go. Don't be like him—*don't do something you can't come back from. Do you remember what happened when Gayl brought back the dead?"*

I choked on a sob, my hands clenching at my side. Yes, I remembered—if Gayl hadn't cast that fateful spell, I wouldn't have Leo. Wasn't that worth it?

I took in Horace's body, the color already draining from his face, the blood flow already beginning to cease. I blinked back against the wave of denial, against the sorrow that sunk its teeth into me and dragged me under the surface.

He was dead.

A shadow approached my side.

"He was your friend, Rose, and for that I am sorry. But Horace—"

I stood, catching Gayl's injured wrist in my hand. He was so close I could see every wrinkle in his skin, every vein in his eyes. "Don't you dare say his name," I hissed, my words like venom as they slithered between us.

"Rose, move!" Lark shouted behind me. Instinctively, I dropped his arm and ducked, right as a long, feline form launched itself over my head and onto Gayl's body. Sharp shards of shadows followed in the fox's wake.

I wanted to scream, to tell them to stop, that Gayl would kill them in a heartbeat—but the two women had converged. Snarls echoed in the chamber as claws dug into Gayl's flesh.

His guards lunged into action, weapons drawn and aimed at their backs. A shield charm was on the tip of my tongue when seconds later, all four guards, Rissa, Lark, and I were blasted off our feet. A sound like a clap of thunder bounced from wall to wall. My head pounded as I hit the stone and crumpled to the floor.

Gayl stood, fury in his eyes and blood dripping from claw marks on his cheeks and neck. His lips moved and the flesh began to knit itself together, the blood disappearing back into his body.

"For that," he panted, glaring at Rissa and Lark, "you will die."

He flicked his hand.

A sickening crunch filled the air.

My two friends fell to the floor. Rissa shifted back to her human form and clutched her ankle. I stifled a gasp when I saw sharp, white bone jutting from the skin. Nearby, Lark's elbow bent at an unnatural angle, her face screwed in agony as finger by finger, the bones in her hand snapped.

Another crack split my eardrums, and Rissa's shoulder hung limp.

Her scream...that scream would haunt my nightmares.

Another crack. And another. They kept coming, over and over. The sound was ingrained in my mind, the sight of their torture overwhelming, blinding.

I remembered the image of my father in front of our fireplace, his choked gurgling, blood gushing. The all-too familiar frenzy shivered up and down my spine, trying to take over—but I couldn't retreat. Not again. Not now.

Everything went numb. My panic receded, and in its place was a steady resolve. I dusted off the cloak that once buried my emotions, the one Leo and my friends had helped me hide, the one that still kept the darkness of my past from view.

I spent too much time covering the depths of my pain. Locking away the trauma of my father, the loss of my mother, the resentment of my province. I'd thought anger and vengeance and pride made me strong. I'd thought getting close to others, letting them see the truth of what was beneath my surface, was weakness.

I took that cloak and shredded it.

Piece by piece, I collected every horrid image from the last month. Every dark memory. Ragnar, the second trial, Callista's death, Chaz, Alaric's body beneath my blade, Leo stuck behind the portal. *Horace.*

Instead of shrouding them under weathered layers, I used them. Molded them. And found that in my pain came courage. In my weakness came strength.

It was with that pain and weakness that I would end this. With my father's help, I would end this.

I rose. Bloodcurdling screams and cracks of bone resounded in the chamber and in my mind as I faced Gayl once again. Each snap brought me a step closer. Each groan narrowed the space between us.

He stood within my grasp, not a single ounce of mercy in his eyes.

"Let them go," I snarled.

With a light scoff, he said, "Ah, you must feel so vindicated. You have seen me as your villain all this time, and now you want to be the brave one, the *good* one, the one who saves them. Have you not learned, Rose, that people like you and me...we're destined for greater things?"

"I never said I was good." My jaw twitched as my fingers dug into the cut on my palm. "I just have to be better than you."

Catching his outstretched hand, I swiftly yanked off his black glove, exposing beads of blood blooming at the end of each of his fingertips. He had installed some sort of sharp needle at the tips of the fabric, something that would allow him fresh blood in an instant. Constant pain, constant blades in his skin, all for the sake of his neverending magic.

"This," I hissed, "is for my father." I crushed his fingers into my bloodied palm, the mixing of our blood sending lightning up my arm.

I uttered the spell Leo and I had found. The one from my father's Grimoire. My last chance, my last hope.

"*Dravenia.*"

Recognition raced across his features at the siphoning spell. "What have you done?" he whispered.

Finally. *Fear.*

"Making sure you and your curse will never hurt anyone again."

A tremor wracked his body. Shockwaves rippled through me, one after another, like something was pulled, sucked, drained from his spirit and set loose. Power hung in the air, so thick I could *see* it swirling around us. Silver and gold whorls pulsing with each breath, carrying with it a strength of magic I couldn't have imagined in my wildest dreams.

Convulsing, he pulled away, his face growing paler by the second. "There is...always a price," he choked, falling to his knees but still holding my gaze. "Can you pay this one, niece?"

He collapsed.

Before my eyes, his skin slowly turned gray and ashen. Wrinkles deepened as his entire body shriveled and shrank, as if the magic siphoned from him had also taken his life.

His head hit the ground. His body was a husk, an empty shell. Dead.

The screams stopped. I spared a quick glance to see Rissa and Lark on their backs, sweat dripping from their foreheads, but alive. Broken and battered, but breathing.

At my feet, something slithered across the dark floor. One small tendril of silver light, as thin as a snake, glided from Gayl's form.

And then came another.

And another.

And *hundreds.*

My breath picked up speed as little silver snakes wormed their way from his body and—and toward *me*.

An instant later, heavy footsteps landed on the ground behind Rissa and Lark.

A weight lifted from my chest. "*Leo.*"

Rissa's cry of shock was drowned out by the pounding of my feet on the wood floor as I flung myself into his outstretched arms.

"Are you alright?" he asked frenziedly, scanning my body while his hands roamed my head and neck. His eyes fell to his sister behind me, and alarm like I'd never seen passed over his features. "What happened? What's going on?" He tried to lurch toward her and Lark, but then saw the writhing mass of silver light still following me. "What is *that*?"

As he asked, the first sliver slipped over my feet and sunk into my skin. It was cool and smooth at first, then searing. I gasped as blinding power tore through me like a savage storm.

But this wasn't natural power. This wasn't *my* power.

There is always a price.

I pushed away from Leo.

"I—I did it, Leo. I used the spell. I took away his magic," I stammered, holding my arms out as the silvery beams surrounded me. My hair stood on its end, every muscle in my body quaking. "*All* of it. And I think this is my price."

At once, the remaining strands dove into my flesh, and I let the darkness take me.

76

LEO

The palace infirmary was white-washed and cold. A long chamber of bleakness, where the shuffling of feet, clinking of glass vials, and potent scent of ointments made my head pound and vision swim.

It had been three days since I came through the portal. Three days since I'd been stuck behind that magical barrier, only to be thrust into chaos.

My best friend, a dagger speared through his skull.

My twin and Lark, bodies broken and skin torn, bones gleaming in the firelight.

The emperor, dead.

The woman I loved...taken. I'd held her in my arms for a mere moment before the magic she'd unearthed had claimed her mind.

She still hadn't come back to me.

I knelt at her bedside, rubbing my thumb against the back of her icy hand. She almost looked as if she were under the Somnivae curse, with her lifeless body and pale features, save for the terrified creases that would mark her forehead every few minutes. The twitch of her fingers, the rapid fluttering of her eyes beneath lids.

My hand balled into a fist at my side. She was suffering—she was being tortured, somewhere deep in her mind, by magic we couldn't see. And there was *nothing* I could do. When those shimmering trails of light had vanished into her three days ago, it was unlike anything I'd ever seen. Cataclysmic power. Her entire body was set alight, silver rays issuing from every surface, her beautiful hair thrown back and wild. She had looked almost... euphoric, for a split second. Her face split into a brilliant beam and her eyes rolled back into her head as if in the throes of passion.

And then she had screamed. A shriek so loud, so powerful it rattled the walls. When she crumpled to the ground, I swear my heart left my body. I thought she was dead. I thought her sacrifice was the price she'd paid to rid the world of Gayl's magic.

But she was still alive. Lying in this infirmary, battling some inner demon or curse or consequence for that siphon spell. The one *we'd* found. One I hadn't been sure would work.

"How is she, brother?" Rissa asked behind me, the tap of her wooden cane following. It was temporary, the Alchemist healer had said. She was fortunate to even be alive. Ninety-eight broken bones. That was what Gayl had done to her. I wished I could bring him back to life, just to shatter every bone in *his* body. Rip every limb from its socket.

Rissa's Shifter blood had healed her broken bones quickly—*too* quickly. They set incorrectly and the healers had to break them again, one by one, and set them before her magic came into effect. She promised me it no longer hurt, that she was only a bit sore. But every time something snapped nearby, she flinched. Every innocent crack had her partially shifting to her fox form in panic. It killed me to watch her, knowing I couldn't help.

"The same. What about Lark?" I responded.

Lark had not been as lucky as my sister. While Gayl hadn't caused her as many injuries as he had Rissa, it had still almost been too much for Lark's body to handle. Several times over the last three days we thought we would lose her. Her Shadow Wielder abilities didn't afford the same speed with healing. The Alchemists of the palace had stayed by her side around the clock, throwing any and every healing spell and potion and charm they could think of at her.

Rissa gave me a smile, a rare sight these days. "She woke up long enough to drink some water this afternoon. The healers say she's turning a corner."

Some good news, at least.

She cleared her throat. "It's time to go, Leo. They're waiting on us to start."

I squeezed Rose's hand, placing a kiss on her knuckles before setting it back on the white sheets. Rissa and I left the infirmary and made our way to the west entrance of the palace. When we stepped outside and passed the gardens, we were greeted by the sight of a long canvas tent, with men and women in the silver uniform of the Royal Guard standing in a line behind a long, wooden box. A handful of others were gathered together before it, the white and gold colors of Iluze so bright I had to squint against it.

Today was Horace's funeral. But unlike the fanfare Rose had described Callista's memorial as, this one was smaller. More intimate. A traditional ceremony of a member of the Guard, with a few friends from his time in the palace and with the Sentinels.

I hated that three of those closest to him couldn't stand here to send him off. Lark, Chaz, and Rose would never get to say their final goodbyes. My sister took my hand as we stood there, silently sharing in our grief.

We said goodbye to our dear friend, the man who had sacrificed everything to keep his chosen family safe. Horace was the bravest man I'd ever known, and the fact that I would never be able to tell him so, that I'd never get to thank him for saving my sister in that chamber...it overwhelmed me, like a pile of bricks pushing on my chest.

I promised myself that when all of the dust had settled, when all of us stood together once again, we would go out to the Drakin's Lair and have a drink in his honor. That disgusting sludge he loved so much. To *celebrate*, not mourn. He would never want that.

Until then, we had work to do. Gayl's death was merely the beginning, and while I wanted nothing more than to sit by Rose's bedside until she woke, my sister needed help.

The empire was in an uproar. In just three days, word had spread about Gayl's demise, leading everyone to question what would happen next. With half of the challengers dead and the third trial left in a state of unknown, the provinces demanded a winner. They demanded their magic. They demanded assurance they would have the power and strength to fight back if this empire fell into ruins. Rumors spread faster than a wildfire, some speaking of provinces rising up against one another, others claiming a false foreign threat waited at our borders.

Gayl's council had been meeting around the clock since the day after the trial trying to find a solution. Something to appease the provinces until they could get their heads on straight. I didn't know what they were expecting in terms of an answer, but it certainly wasn't my sister.

In true Rissa fashion, she had barged into their meeting chamber mere hours after having her bones reset, with her cane reverberating against the floor and fire in her eyes. Begging them to see reason, to put their hysteria aside and work together to bring this empire back to what it was meant to be.

That first moment, that first move, would set the tone for the future. For the path out of this whirlwind of change. And there was nobody else I would trust to pave the way.

She got to work immediately.

The day after Horace's funeral, we sent word to all the governors of the provinces, explaining what had happened and expelling any rumors. We extended an invitation for them to come to Veridia City to let their voices be heard and be part of these decisions. Every one of them came, except for Drakorum. Still, it was a win. That challenge could be faced later. There were more questions than answers when it came to the Shifter province, anyway—such as their determination to hide the existence of dragon Shifters, and what they were truly doing with powerful beings such as Nox and his sister Vera.

Rissa and I thought it would take time to convince the governors of our validity and sincerity, but what we weren't expecting was for some of the members of Gayl's council to have also been on our father's council. They remembered Branock and Evadine Aris, how much they had cared for the people and ruled with both firm strength and compassion. And they remembered *us*. They gave us a chance, which was all we could ask for.

It was a moment my sister and I had dreamed of for years: being able to clear our father's name, to tell what really happened that night twenty-seven years ago and watch as the people who had been forced under Gayl's hold for so long finally saw the truth. At least, part of the truth. I had told my sister the full story of Gayl's curse and the part my life played in ending it, and she was insistent—as Rose had been—that we keep that secret to ourselves. Always trying to keep me safe. We knew we would have to confront the inevitable eventually, but my sister stayed busy with all the other problems brought to the forefront.

Such as our magic.

We decided to divide the wealth of magic evenly between the provinces for the period of a single year. That would allow us time to figure out what we as an empire wanted the Decemvirate to look like going forward—or if there would even *be* a Decemvirate. It was the first step toward peace that was so strongly needed after decades of being pitted against one another.

Not all of the council members were in agreement. There were still several loyal to Gayl and his reign who seemed determined to fight my sister at every step of the way. For now, however, the desire to show a unified front and get back on our feet outweighed any resentment they held for us usurping their former emperor. I feared we would face some obstacles in the future from them, but that was a bridge my sister could cross when she got there.

Two days after the funeral, Lark regained full consciousness and was able to tell the Alchemists of the palace how to reopen the portal to the island so they could retrieve the bodies of the dead: Salome, Vincent, Alaric, and Callum. Their families and provinces were notified, and the four were given proper burials. Even though Rissa and I hated the idea of their deaths being paraded around, Lark asked that we summon scribes and reporters to spread the news and document it for all provinces to see. She said the empire needed closure on this time, a symbol for the end of this brutal, unprecedented tournament. A way for Veridians to unite and draw together.

Over the next few days, something happened that none of us expected.

Spells began to break, and people began to speak.

First, it was the servants of Gayl's household. They whispered of the atrocities they'd seen, of the violent way he and his most faithful guards had handled those they deemed lesser than. Then, the guards. The ones who had never been comfortable with their orders but felt compelled to see them through less their families be punished for their actions. Men and women of the Royal Guard like Horace, who had witnessed scandals and murders and vile persecutions that had been covered up. Lords and ladies of the court, those closest to Gayl, confessed their cowardice and showed letters of Gayl's threats, his blackmail and bribery for their silence.

His death and the death of his magic seemed to have undone the deepest of enchantments he'd cast over the decades. People started convening on palace grounds looking for loved ones who had been captured or killed by Gayl and his men, who'd had the memories of their losses taken away by memory spells. In the last few days, I'd seen countless people fall to their knees in mourning over a lost son or friend or sister or father whom they'd been enchanted to forget years ago, and now relived the trauma fresh in their minds.

With the sorrow came a call for justice. And with that call came the Sentinels.

All over the empire, whispers of the lost Aris heir grew. Planted by members of our ranks hidden in the provinces, the truth of what happened between Theodore Gayl and Branock Aris came to light. Rumors of what Rissa and our people had been trying to do for the last few years spread. Stories of her bravery, her skill, and her conviction rallied hope in a darkened world. It was like a match had been struck, and in a matter of a mere week, the entire land was set ablaze, eager for change. Eager for things to be made right.

Eager for Clarissa Aris, heir to the Veridian Empire.

People lined the streets of the capital to get a glimpse of her. Those old enough to have known our parents came out of the woodwork offering their support, apologizing for believing the lies and slander about our family.

Watching my sister welcomed and celebrated by an empire that had once scorned her brought pride I'd never felt before.

She had done this. She had dreamt and worked for a world better than one she was born into, and perhaps...perhaps that time was coming.

But she hadn't done it alone.

"It's been ten days," Lark said as she wheeled herself into Rose's section of the infirmary. "I would have thought we'd have seen some sign by now." She stopped on the other side of the bed, planting her hands across Rose's arm. The Shadow Wielder despised her limited mobility in the wheelchair, but the healers kept having to remind her she was lucky to even be alive after what she'd been through.

I scratched my chin, still not used to the unkempt beard that had grown over the last week and a half that we'd been living in the palace. Rissa had our mother transported from her sickbed and into a private wing here, along with some of our possessions. The three of us were set up in the guest wings until the imminent future was sorted out.

Morgana and Beau had hardly left the infirmary. Rose's aunt had insisted her niece be placed in a bed near Ragnar so she could spend her days watching over both of them.

I knew what Morgana was waiting for. We'd heard of enchantments being broken, and every day, I could see the hope fading in her eyes that the curse over her husband would be lifted, that her niece would wake from slumber and all would be right in the world.

But still, they slept. And still, we waited.

There was, however, one more surprise Gayl's death brought.

"Leo!" Rissa cried as she scrambled into the infirmary, nearly bringing down the curtain dividing Rose and Ragnar Gregor's beds.

I leapt to my feet, imagining the worst. Some sort of attack or disturbance to disrupt the tentative peace we'd created. My twin's face, however, wasn't scared.

It was joyful.

"It's Mother," she said breathlessly. "She's awake."

77

LEO

"What happened?" I asked Rissa as we strode through the palace to our mother's private wing.

"She spoke to me. When I was checking on her just now, she actually *spoke* to me." I glanced over to see excitement bursting from her features, happiness and hope overflowing. Her lips split into a brilliant beam. "It wasn't a particularly long conversation, but she asked about you. She said she—she loves us." Silver swam in her eyes.

Our mother hadn't uttered a word in longer than I could remember. Always that glassy stare, those lips forever set into a thin line of apathy, no hint as to what was going on in her mind as she aged over the years. Something in my chest fluttered, but I refused to give it attention until I saw for myself. "How is this possible?" I asked.

"I don't know. Maybe Gayl did something to her? Or his magic from the night he saved you and her might have had some sort of residual hold that was broken when he died?"

We burst into her room, and the sight before me stopped me in my tracks.

Pale yellow curtains trimmed with lace fluttered in the breeze from the cracked window. Sunlight splashed across the four-poster bed, highlighting the woman lying there in a golden glow.

No, not lying. *Sitting.*

My mother sat upright, a cup of tea in her steady hands and a kind smile on her face.

"Leo?" she asked softly, her voice hoarse and quiet. The sound nearly made me crumble.

"It's me, Mother," I replied hesitantly, stepping toward her bed. Her free hand trembled as she held it out to me, the corners of her eyes crinkling.

All movement and sound came back to me in a rush. I crossed the room in three steps and knelt on the floor by her bed, clutching her hand in mine. It was warm and soft and full of life, no longer cold and fragile as I had come to know it.

Healed. She was *healing.* Could this be possible? After years of giving up, of us thinking her ever returning to normal was a lost cause, was our mother finally coming back to us?

"I've missed you, my sweet boy," she said. Fates, I had forgotten what her voice sounded like. The backs of my eyes burned as she squeezed my fingers. Rissa moved to the other side of the bed and sat on the edge, taking our mother's teacup and placing it on the bedside table.

"How do you feel, Mother?" my sister asked.

"Like I've been sitting in this bed for far too long," she responded with a weak chuckle.

Rissa laughed and wiped away a tear from her cheek. "Let's take one thing at a time. You need to eat. Let me call for something to be brought up."

Mother placed her other hand on Rissa's leg before she could get up. "Look at you both," she whispered, tears lining her gaze. "So grown up. So beautiful. I—I feel as if I've been a ghost, watching your lives pass through the eyes of someone else."

I swallowed. "You remember? All this time, could you hear us? Could you see us?"

"At times," she admitted, her words still slow. "I remember

bits and pieces. It's all rather...hazy. A different life." She furrowed her brow. "Some parts are darker than others. It feels like entire sections of my life are missing. But I remember *feelings*—warmth when you would hold my hand, joy when I'd hear your voice. I can't explain it, but I *felt* you. I knew you were there. Always there," she finished quietly, a tear dripping off the end of her nose.

"Always," Rissa repeated, bringing her hand to her lips and kissing the knuckles. "We missed you so much, Mother."

"How—how long has it been?"

My sister and I shared a glance. "It's been fifteen years since Father died," I finally said. "And you've been sick for the last ten."

She took in a shuddering breath. I could practically see the shock and denial flashing across her features. Her hazel eyes widened, the wrinkles at her pale forehead deepening. She struggled to swallow as her lips parted.

"Fifteen *years*," she murmured. Looking between the two of us, she took in our faces, scanning us with those eyes that could always see straight through. "My babies," she said in a choked whisper. "Although, you're not babies anymore, are you?"

"I suppose not," Rissa said with a sniffle.

"How did this happen?" Mother asked. "How am I..." She trailed off, releasing her grip on us and glancing down at her hands. "I remember things becoming clearer. Sounds were sharper, colors brighter. I felt as if I had control of myself again. And when I woke up this morning..."

"We don't know," I said. "But we think it may have something to do with Gayl."

Her eyes narrowed. "Theodore? What could he possibly have to do with this?"

Rissa licked her lips. "Well, he's...he's dead, Mother. And when he died, enchantments he cast throughout his entire life started to unravel. Spells he had over people have broken in these last few days. We were wondering if"—she looked at me out of the corner of her eye—"if he had somehow used his magic on you before you became sick, or if it could have been a side effect of what happened the night we were born."

Mother sucked in a breath. "What do you know of that night?"

I paused, silence pressing in on us, until I said, "Everything."

She closed her eyes and leaned her head back on the pillow. Rissa jumped in. "We can let you rest, Mother. We don't have to have this conversation right—"

"No, no, I'm fine." Mother waved her hand. "That night weighed on your father and I for so long, but in the end, we would never have changed a thing. For then we wouldn't have *both* of you," she said, grasping our hands again. "I had always felt...*something* lingering, a piece of Gayl's spell embedded in me, perhaps. I don't think one can go through what I went through and not have consequences. It festered throughout the years, but your father's death..." She let out a long breath and closed her eyes again. "I feared I would never come back from that."

"But you're here now," Rissa said, scooting forward to be closer to her. "Gayl's magic is gone and we're together again. We can start over. Be a *family*."

Mother smiled wistfully, more tears tracking down her cheeks. "I'm here, sweet girl," she repeated. "And I'm so sorry. So sorry we kept things from you, sorry I left you—that I missed so much, and—"

"Don't you dare apologize for that," I interjected. "None of this was your fault."

A sob escaped her. "I only wish we could have that time back."

"We'll *make* time," Rissa said. "We have the entire future ahead of us. So many memories left to make. You're going to be absolutely sick of us," she added, wiping at her nose with the back of her hand.

Mother and I both chuckled. "The two of you will have to fill me in on these past years, I suppose. What have I missed?"

I looked at Rissa, who raised an eyebrow. With that sly grin she got from our mother, my sister asked, "Should you start, or shall I?"

78

ROSE

The darkness was all-consuming. The pain was *everywhere*. But the power...

The power was blinding.

In this rift between consciousness, between time and space, there was nothing separating me from the magic in my veins. From *Gayl's* magic. I understood now what had happened when I cast my father's siphon spell. When my blood had met Gayl's in that tremulous moment and I'd summoned all of my strength into that unfamiliar incantation.

When Leo and I had found it, we thought we could use it to banish Gayl's magic back into whatever crevice the power of this empire was held.

Get rid of the power, get rid of the man.

But that much magic...that unending well stolen from *thousands* of people over almost three decades...it couldn't simply *disappear*.

When that first bead of silver light filled me, I thought I would die from the rapture of it. *Was this what Gayl felt like all the time?* I'd wondered. Like my soul had been covered with this infinite freedom, this bliss I'd never dreamt of.

But then the rest followed.

Thread after thread of Gayl's magic. More than my body could handle. More than my mind could comprehend.

And it *burned*.

It shattered and fractured, forcing itself into me, reshaping the fabric of my very being to find space for its existence. Gayl had accumulated it slowly, inch by inch, like filling an ocean with drops from the sky. But I...I was like a river whose dam had been broken, water spilling over and bursting my seams.

I wanted to die.

I begged for death. Begged for the pain to stop, though I knew it never would.

This was my price.

At times, I thought I could hear a voice. Could feel a warm, strong hand on a body I no longer inhabited. It dispelled the agony, if only for a moment, before it flooded back and tugged me under again.

All I knew was that I couldn't live like this.

I screamed into the void and prayed for my end.

79

ROSE

Muted light slid across my eyelids. Something brushed against my skin. Not the pain I was so used to, but something...light. Soft. Warm.

I was breathing. My chest rose and fell, air tickling my nose as I exhaled. And my heart...it pumped steadily, pounding out a slow rhythm.

One by one, my senses came back to me. The dryness of my mouth, the stiffness of my arms, the soreness of my entire body. Echoes of that pain still vibrated through me, but it was dimmer now. The power wasn't gone, though. It pushed at my skin, no longer excruciating but still relentless, a constant reminder of what lived in me.

It wasn't *mine*.

It wanted out.

My eyes burst open.

It took a moment to work out my surroundings. I was lying on a bed with a blanket tucked around me and a shelf of vials and bandages and other supplies to my right. The palace infirmary, I thought. To the left was a chair, and in that chair sprawled a man, his legs spread out and his head balanced precariously on his shoulder, eyes closed and breaths heavy.

Leo.

I tried to sit up, but the motion made me gasp in discomfort. How long had I been like this? My body was still getting used to the abundance of magic, and it caused even the slightest movement to feel like lifting a bag of weights. I grunted as I gingerly pulled the blanket off my legs.

There was a sharp intake of breath, and suddenly, hands cupped my cheek. "You're awake," Leo said, his voice rough. Those dark eyes were red with exhaustion, but as he looked at me, they filled with relief. His lips parted on a ragged exhale. "I didn't know if you would...if I'd ever..."

My chest tightened. I'd never seen him like this. The scruff on his face had grown into a thicker beard and his hair was unkempt and mussed, as if he'd been constantly running his fingers through it. His hands trembled slightly as they moved to my back and enveloped me in a tight embrace.

The action sent a throb down my body, and I let out a small whimper. He stiffened and pulled away. "What's wrong? Are you hurt?"

I was tired of feeling pain. I'd wished for death in that endless void, and now that I was back, now that Leo was in front of me, I just wanted to feel *him*. To know this was real and not a figment of my imagination conjured to distract me from that torment.

"I'm okay," I said, even as a tear slipped out and dripped down my face. My hands shook when I grabbed his and placed it back on my cheek. Closing my eyes, I inhaled at his touch, at his solid warmth, not the darkness and hurt and agonizing power.

"I thought I'd lost you," he murmured, pressing his forehead to mine.

"How long was I gone?"

A pause. "Twelve days."

I swallowed. *Twelve days.* The memory of those final moments in the chamber with Gayl flooded me. "Rissa and Lark? Are they safe?"

He leaned back and nodded, swiping away a tear with his

thumb. "Rissa healed quickly, and Lark...she'll be alright. She's getting better."

Letting out a breath, I said, "And Gayl? Is he really..."

"He's gone, sweetheart."

My hand gripped the sheets beneath me. He'd killed my father. He'd killed *all* those men who had once followed him. Who had *believed* in him. He started the curse as a way to gain infinite power at the expense of his people. It was *good* that he was dead. My hatred for him burned as hot as a raging fire, simmering in my very blood.

But, for a split second, my heart dropped.

I thought of the young man in that portrait with my father. How happy they'd seemed. Their lives could have been so different.

"The curse?" I asked, daring to hope. "Did Uncle Ragnar wake up? Or Chaz?"

Leo pressed his lips together then shook his head. Disappointment crashed into me. "Other spells Gayl cast have broken, like memory charms he placed on people. But those under the Somnivae curse...they're still asleep."

It hadn't worked. Taking Gayl's life hadn't worked.

"What happened to you?" he asked softly, brushing a strand of hair behind my ear.

"I—I don't know." I struggled to not let myself go back to that place, to not remember the suffering and helplessness. "I siphoned his power and it...it was too much for me to handle. It was like I was in this void. This prison. His magic burned through me, so powerful I thought it was going to rip me in half. I thought I was dead." The pressure at the back of my eyelids and in my chest mounted. "I *wanted* to die. It was too much. It—" I broke off, the words catching in my throat.

Leo carefully sat on the bed next to me and lifted my body, placing me in his lap. My arms circled his neck and I buried my face in his shoulder. I willed my panic to subside as his hand crept under my sweater and rubbed circles on my bare skin, pressing me closer into him.

"What if it's not over?" I whispered faintly, my voice muffled against his shirt. "I—I can still feel it. His magic. What if the pain comes back?"

His hand moved to grip my waist. "We'll figure it out, Rose. We'll siphon it from you, if we have to. I'm not going to let this happen again." When I didn't respond, he pulled me back an inch to look down at my face. "Do you believe me?"

"I want to," I breathed out. I couldn't shake the fear, the ghost of that chasm pulling and searing me whole. His closeness was the only thing holding me together.

As if he could see my distress, he gently asked, "What do you need from me, sweetheart?"

My breath hitched. "Just...just stay here. Don't leave me."

"Leave you?" His brow furrowed. "There is no world, no emperor, no *magic* that could tear me from your side, Rose."

That well inside me rose and crested, and tears sprang to the surface. I clung to him, his body hard and steady beneath mine, and I let him anchor me.

"Can I kiss you?" he asked, the words fluttering over my cheeks. When I nodded, he slowly leaned forward and brushed his lips against mine. Tender and careful, afraid to jostle my sore body or push me too far.

He broke away, still close enough that his eyelashes fanned across my skin when he blinked. "I don't want to hurt you again," he said quietly.

"You won't," I said, bringing my mouth back to his.

He was still hesitant, still careful, his movements controlled as he held my back. But Fates, I didn't want to feel breakable. I didn't want to feel like I could fall apart at the slightest touch, no matter how cracked I truly was. I pinned myself to him and wound my arms around his neck, ignoring the discomfort as the foreign magic still warred beneath my skin. When I bit his lower lip, he groaned into me, finally letting go of his self control.

Gripping my waist, he turned our bodies and pushed my back to the bed, hovering over me with his loose shirt exposing a hint of his chest. Another sharp pang went through me, but my heart was pounding so furiously I barely felt it. He leaned down and ran his lips along my neck, his beard scratching my skin. I gasped when he kissed the spot below my ear, making my pulse race.

A stabbing pain ripped down my spine. My back arched as a cry left my lips.

Next to the bed, a glass vial shattered.

Leo immediately released me. Chest heaving, he scrambled off the bed, searching for some sign of injury.

"I think it—it's the magic," I said, gritting my teeth. "It's trying to get out."

The flash of pain subsided, replaced with the same soreness I'd felt when I woke up. I could still sense the power worming inside of me, though. Urging me.

I flung my legs off the side of the bed and stumbled to my feet.

"Rose, what—" Leo hastily put an arm beneath my shoulder as I almost fell, my legs shaky from disuse. Staggering forward, the magic practically begged me to keep going, to keep putting one foot in front of the other.

The sensation heightened. I ripped aside the curtain hanging near my bed.

Ragnar's still form rested on white sheets, his features frozen in the curse.

Impossible thoughts raced through my mind, twisting with this incessant nagging that pushed and pulled on every inch of my body.

I shoved away from Leo and approached my uncle's bed. My pulse bashed in my neck, my ears, my chest, reaching a crescendo as I stretched out a hand.

My palm touched his cheek.

I felt it instantly. A tiny seed of power flickered, so small compared to the waves embedded within me. Silver light sunk into his skin.

I wasn't sure I was breathing. Eyes wide, I retracted my hand, my gaze never leaving his face.

The air was silent, save for the sounds of Leo's breaths behind me and my own heartbeats.

And then my uncle's eyes flew open.

80

ROSE

Knees buckling, I fell to the floor, my lips parting on an exhale. Familiar eyes locked onto mine—bright gray instead of red shone back at me. Ragnar's face slowly filled with color as he blinked and swallowed.

"Rose?" he said, his voice a scratchy whisper. "Where are we?"

Something heavy hit the floor behind me. "*By the Fates.*"

Twisting my head, I saw Morgana and Beau. Morgana's hands flew to her mouth, a book strewn at her feet where she dropped it. Blood drained from her face as tears filled her eyes. She swayed unsteadily on her feet, and Beau gripped her elbow.

"Is this—is this real?" she asked, reaching out a hand to the bed and teetering forward as if in a trance.

Ragnar tried to straighten, but his arms shook as he lifted himself. "Ana, what's going on?"

At the sound of his voice, a sob ripped through my aunt's throat. Rushing to the other side of the bed, she threw herself at him, tears tracking down her cheeks. I watched with burning eyes as she held him. *He was awake.* My chest felt like it was going to burst. He was as good as dead; we thought we'd never hear his voice, never truly *see* him again.

Beau came up to my side and got to his knees, flinging a gangly arm over my shoulder and gripping Ragnar's free hand with the other. "You were cursed, Pa," my cousin said, his gray eyes glistening. "We thought you were gone."

Ragnar's eyes widened as Morgana backed away to pull a chair up closer to his side. "The Somnivae curse?" he asked. "Wh—how did this happen? How am I awake?"

Leo appeared next to me with a glass of water for my uncle. "It was Rose," he said. His eyes pierced through me, full of wonder. "I saw it. She woke you."

Morgana's gaze slid to mine, as if just now seeing anything beyond her husband. Fresh cries wracked through her. She leaned across the bed to pull me up, trapping me in a fierce embrace over Ragnar's body.

"Rosie, dear girl, you're awake! You're alright!" Wetness coated my shoulder where her tears fell, and my own threatened to rise. "What is he talking about?" she asked, breaking away and wiping her face. "What does he mean, you woke Ragnar?"

"I don't know, it was just a—a feeling," I stammered, my thoughts spinning. I glanced over at Leo. "I thought killing Gayl and getting rid of his magic would break the curse, and when you said nothing happened, I assumed we failed. But we *didn't* get rid of his magic. I *took* it. It's still here, so the curse still lives. But—" I turned back to Ragnar, disbelief coursing through me. "The magic he stole. What if giving it back is what woke you?"

Ragnar's tired eyes creased in confusion. "*Emperor* Gayl? What is this about killing him? Will somebody please tell me what is going on?"

Morgana and I took turns quickly summarizing the events of the last month while my aunt tittered around him, fluffing pillows and refilling water and barely taking her eyes off of him. We explained how he'd fallen under the curse after the attack from the Shifters, how I'd taken his place in the tournament and been informed of his role with the Sentinels. When I told him how I found out I was Gayl's niece, Ragnar shared a look with Morgana.

"Rose," he began cautiously. "We're sorry that we—"

I brushed his apology aside. "You don't have to be sorry. I understand. The Fates know I've kept my share of secrets. I'm just glad you're here," I said, squeezing his hand.

I explained how Leo and I had been searching for ways to stop the curse and were experimenting with using conventional spells in unconventional manners. When I mentioned the siphoning curse we'd found in my father's Grimoire, Ragnar gave me an incredulous look.

"A siphoning spell...and you thought you could use it to siphon one's *magic*?"

I nodded. "It worked. I got close enough to use it on Gayl and it —it took his magic." I swallowed tightly. "It killed him."

"And it almost took you from us too, Rose," Morgana said, clutching Ragnar's hand.

"It was the price I paid."

"The price you..." Ragnar's eyes narrowed. "Have you been using *blood* magic? Is that how you performed this spell?"

Fates, not this again. "You sound like Leo," I said, shooting Leo a dry smile.

"Yes, and *who* exactly is this Leo fellow?" Ragnar asked. He sat up straighter in the bed, already seeming to gain back a little strength. He raised an eyebrow expectantly.

Beau gave a wolfish grin. "Oh, Leo is Rosie's—"

"Are we really doing this right now?" I interrupted, crossing my arms.

Leo held his hand out to Ragnar. "My name is Zareleon Aris, sir, and I'm in love with your niece."

My mouth opened and closed like a fish out of water. Morgana's eyebrows shot high into her forehead.

Ragnar eyed Leo's outstretched hand. "Aris, you say? As in, Branock's son?"

"Yes, sir."

I didn't think I was breathing. My uncle stared at him. "Well, then," he finally said, clearing his throat. "I have a lot to catch up on." He took Leo's hand, and a smile played on the edges of my lips.

"Don't think you're out of the woods for this blood magic business." Ragnar looked back at me.

"Trust me, I've learned my lesson," I said hastily. "But it *worked*. The siphon spell worked. Just...not the way we expected. His magic went into *me*. I can feel it even now, like it's pushing under my skin." I ran a hand along my arm. "And I know it sounds crazy, but I think that's how I woke you up."

I told them about my final conversation with Gayl, about his purpose for creating the curse and how each time someone fell under its power, he gained pieces of their magic.

"By giving back that piece of yours, I was able to break the curse's hold on you," I finished, gesturing to Ragnar.

"Incredible," my uncle said.

"She is," Leo murmured in agreement. His fingers grazed mine, and a blush heated my neck and cheeks.

"Where's Chaz?" I asked Leo. "I want to try again."

"Are you sure you feel alright?"

"Oh, don't go all protective on me now," I teased, then took his hand and softened my voice. "Let's go save your best friend."

Nodding, he led me further into the infirmary, promising my family we'd be back soon. My anticipation built, along with that same urgent force of power, bordering on painful. It was like it knew what I was doing and where I was going. Like it was *sentient*. The magic of thousands of people lived inside me, vying for attention.

We reached the end of the hallway and Leo pulled back the curtain to another section of beds. The first thing I saw was Lark sitting in a wheelchair, reading quietly a few feet from Chaz's bed. Her neck snapped up when we entered, the book falling from her hands and into her lap at the sight of me.

"Rose! What—when did you wake up?"

"Just a little while ago," I assured her. "Look, I'll explain everything, but first I—I think I can bring Chaz back." The sensation was pounding in my bones again, and I didn't have the patience to wait. Lark gaped at me as I ran to the bedside. Clenching my hand, I let out a breath, praying to whatever Fates were listening that this would work.

I carefully took Chaz's hand. A small portion of the magic inside stirred and slithered from me. The same silver glow that had lit my uncle's skin emanated from Chaz's hand. I held my breath and ignored Lark's bewildered expression, waiting.

And waiting.

And then—

Lark cursed. Leo sucked in a breath at my side.

Chaz's dark eyes stared up at me, tired and unfocused but clear. No longer the blood-red of the Somnivae curse.

A beam burst across my face. I whipped around to Leo and gripped his forearms. "This is it," I said. "We *did* it. We can bring everyone back."

He pulled me closer and cupped my cheek, his eyes bright with pride. "*You* did it, sweetheart. You are the most extraordinary woman I've ever met." When he kissed my forehead, a deep voice sounded at my back.

"What, no kiss for me?"

We turned to face Chaz, laughter of relief and excitement bubbling out of me.

"It's good to see you, brother," Leo said, leaning forward and clapping Chaz delicately on the shoulder. "It's been quiet without you."

Once more, we told the story of what had occurred since Chaz had been cursed. When Lark told him what happened to Horace after the third trial, we all went silent. I closed my eyes against the image that punctured my mind, of that dagger flying to his eye, of his cold, lifeless body. I couldn't even *imagine* what Chaz was feeling, learning one of his closest friends was gone and he'd never had the chance to say goodbye.

I sat on the edge of the bed and patted his leg. "He died protecting us. He loved all of you so much."

"Burly idiot. Had to be the hero," Chaz said with a quick sniff, then swiped at his nose.

"Rissa and I never fully understood what happened in those final moments with the emperor," Lark said to me. "How did you kill him?"

I recounted the spell Leo and I had found and my haphazard theory to make it work. I explained how I'd taken Gayl's magic into myself instead of banishing it like I thought I would, and before I could get the words out, Lark gasped.

"So you have his magic. *You* can restore what was stolen. *You* can break the curse."

I simply nodded, letting her and Chaz digest the news.

"We have to tell Rissa," Lark said immediately.

"Oh, I already heard."

Spinning, I saw Rissa leaning against a shelf behind us. Lark cursed again. "You're too quiet for your own good, woman."

Rissa winked. "Some might say I'm as sneaky as a fox." Rushing forward, she wrapped her arms around me and gave me a tight hug. It took me a moment to react to the sudden contact, but then I closed my eyes and squeezed her back, pushing away the slight soreness.

"I'm so glad you're awake, Rose," she said quietly. "We missed you."

Tears stung the backs of my eyes. Fates, I'd cried more today than in my entire life.

Rissa moved to give her brother a quick peck on the cheek and then hugged Chaz. "Well, this is quite the development," she said. "Rose, the curse breaker."

I took a deep breath. I knew what had to come next—had known since the moment my uncle's eyes opened and this well of power within me had purred. "I have to wake everyone up."

Nobody spoke. Rissa crossed her arms and raised an eyebrow. "That's quite an endeavor. There are many people under this curse, Rose. In every province, every town, every corner of the empire. Are you sure you're up for it?"

A sense of purpose swelled in my chest. I'd never had a good picture of my future beyond the Arcane Apothecary back home, and even that had seemed...distant, in a way. As much as I loved that shop, Feywood had never felt like home.

But suddenly, everything was clear. Traveling the empire, using this power to restore the cursed, bringing hope and life to those who thought it was lost. Learning about magic in its entirety —not just the Alchemy I'd seen all my life. Knowing what I was meant to do, where I was meant to be.

How could I refuse this? How could I *not* see this through to the end, after what we'd all been through to get here? I had the chance to right the wrongs of my uncle. To use this magic for *good*.

Determination settled in my chest. Even the power I temporarily held seemed to rest, knowing it would soon find its way home.

"I have to do this, Rissa. I *want* to do this. For myself and for those who have suffered because of Gayl's greed." My voice was steady and my mind was certain for the first time since I'd woken up. "No more. This ends now, and I'm the only one who can do it."

A grin worked its way onto her lips as she studied me. "Then I guess," she said slowly, "you need to start packing."

81

ROSE

Thirty-three. That's how many cursed Veridians dwelled inside the palace walls.

By the end of the week, I had woken every single one.

Children, aged men and women, mothers, fathers. Servants and lords, previous advisors to the throne, members of Gayl's council. Nobody had been safe from the curse when it chose to strike.

I watched a woman reunite with her lover after ten years. An elderly man meet his eighteen-year-old granddaughter for the first time. A child talk with her younger brother who was now several years older than her. Story after story, memory after memory. With every single person, that stolen magic inside of me became less and less erratic. Less painful. Less urgent. Still there, but somehow, it felt...content. Overwhelming emotion crowded me on all sides, with bone-crunching hugs and shouts of relief and more tears than I could count.

And *hope*.

Rissa and Leo had filled me in on what they, the council, and the province governors had been doing during the almost two weeks I'd been trapped in my mind. What we were giving these people was so much more than just their magic back. We were giving them *hope*. To no longer live with the prospect of the curse hanging over them, to not have to worry about their power being based on some ridiculous tournament, to one day be unafraid of crossing their own borders.

The road ahead wouldn't be easy, of course. Plenty of people would be angry, would push back on the direction of leadership. And it would take time—as would my mission.

But it was *exhilarating*, being a part of it. Being a part of *change*.

Rissa had stepped into a role of power in the empire so effortlessly it was as if she was meant for it. After confirming her heritage, the council and governors had elected to name her interim empress while they sorted through affairs. It wasn't unanimous, but enough of them seemed to realize what strength she brought to the table. Within days, she'd organized my journey with the governors, ensuring my safe passage through each province and lining up people to escort me in their regions.

Time was moving faster than I could process. My excitement grew as I thought of the months and months I'd spend exploring new places, something I never thought I'd get to do in my entire life.

With that excitement, however, came a hint of fear. Fear of being away from everything I'd ever known, from my family, from the comfort of my isolated shop. Fear of how I'd be perceived in this new world.

Fear of saying goodbye.

I was leaving Veridia City tomorrow. Ragnar and Morgana had taken turns accompanying me throughout the capital over the last week and a half, visiting all the infirmaries, all the healer's clinics, and all the sickbays on the small island. There weren't as many people here who had fallen prey to the curse as in the provinces, but there were still a couple hundred that needed to be awoken. We'd been up from dawn to dusk traveling and meeting with families. I'd talked to more people in the last ten days than in two decades. Leo, Rissa, and the others had been just as busy working with Gayl's council and the governors on restructuring what they wanted the leadership to look like, and the twins had been spending as much time as they could with their newly restored mother.

I'd barely had more than an hour alone with Leo. It was strange how much I could miss someone I'd only known a handful of weeks. How little by little he'd chipped away at my shell until he was suddenly buried inside my heart. Every scowl, every smirk, every hushed word had spread like seeds, taking root so deeply there was no chance of me ever pulling him out.

Not that I wanted to. I couldn't *begin* to imagine life without him. But...I didn't know what the next months or even *years* looked like. We had no idea how long my task across the empire would take. We could be completely different people by the time it was over.

I didn't know how to say goodbye to him. I didn't know how to *leave* him.

So...in true Rose fashion, I avoided it. It hadn't been too difficult; we were both exhausted and pulled in so many different directions, there wasn't much time for ourselves. And of course, I would have never wanted to take him away from his mother. Any spare moment the two of us had together was also shared with Rissa or Lark or Chaz or my family, limiting the conversation I knew we'd have to have.

But I was good at putting off painful moments.

My eyes drooped as I tucked my last pouch of herbs into my travel bag, buttoning the clasp and placing it beside my bedroom door. I desperately needed sleep before heading off on the first leg of my journey in the morning. The ship Rissa had secured my passage on was leaving for the southern province of Tenebra at eight o'clock sharp. Ragnar had offered to go with me for this first part while Morgana and Beau headed back to Feywood. I'd argued that they needed to stick together, but my aunt and uncle were nothing if not persistent.

A knock sounded on my door. I stifled a yawn as I pulled it open, almost stumbling when I saw who waited on the other side.

"Did you think you could leave without saying goodbye?" Leo asked. He leaned on the doorframe with his arms crossed and his tail flicking the floor. Always a sign of agitation, even when his features remained impassive.

My cheeks flushed. "No, that's not—I was going to say goodbye," I said quickly. "We've both just been so busy."

He raised an eyebrow.

I let out a sigh, then tugged at his arm to pull him inside the room. As the door shut behind him, I circled my arms around his waist, placing my head against his solid chest. "I've missed you so much, Leo," I whispered. Closing my eyes, I listened to the beat of his heart and his steady breaths, tension leaving my body with each passing second.

"I missed you too, sweetheart." Lips pressed into the top of my head. "How are you feeling about tomorrow?"

"Excited. Scared. A little nauseous."

A chuckle rumbled through his chest. "Sounds about right."

"It's Alaric's province," I said in a quieter voice. His features appeared in my mind, the smiling, jovial older man contrasted with his cold body lying on the forest floor, my dagger through his back. "I know you're going to say it wasn't my fault, but I don't know how I can face his family. His *people*. After...what I did."

Leo traced a hand up my back and rested it on my neck beneath my hair, cradling me to him. "And no matter how many times I say it wasn't your fault, I know it won't take away your guilt. I hate that this is going to follow you for the rest of your life, but you're doing so much good, Rose." He leaned back and kissed my temple. "You're bringing *life* back to these families. We can mourn Alaric and honor his memory as you help his people."

I took a deep breath and nodded. "I'm glad Ragnar will be with me, at least."

He licked his lips, pulling further away. "Actually, about that..."

"What? Did something happen to him?" I asked sharply. We didn't know if there were any effects of me waking people from the curse—what if it wasn't permanent? What if it went wrong?

"No, no, your uncle is fine. But he's not going with you to Tenebra."

My brows knit together. "Why not?"

"Because I am."

I froze. "I—I don't understand."

A smile formed on his lips. Slow and shy at first, then a brilliant beam, sending butterflies soaring in my chest. "You're the one who said we should run away together."

"But—but you have a life here," I said. "The Sentinels, your sister, your *mother*. You have so much time to make up for with her. And the empire is getting back on its feet, don't you need to be *here*?"

"I've already talked with Rissa and Mother. My sister is more than capable of handling things without me." He laughed. "And my mother actually told me if I didn't go with you, she'd shear the hair off my tail."

I made a sound in the back of my throat, a cross between a laugh and a sob. "She sounds like Rissa."

"Besides, it's not for forever. This life will be waiting for us when we get back." He took my hands. "What do you say, little wolf? Are you up for an adventure?"

My head spun. That well of power in me sparked, roused by heightened emotions. "You really want to do this?"

"I told you, I would run anywhere with you."

I gazed up at him, searching those dark eyes for any hint of hesitation. All I saw was clear resolve. The hard planes of his face softened as he stared back, his determination shining through.

I threaded my fingers through his and took a breath. "Then let's run."

———

THE DECK of the ship was full of crew members readying for departure. Men shouted instructions, luggage was tightened and stowed, deckhands prepared to hoist the mast. This one was slightly larger than the passenger ship my family and I took from Feywood to Veridia City, and much nicer, with its polished wood and sleek frame.

Leo and I stood at the bottom of the gangway. A deckhand approached to take our bags, then motioned behind us and said, "Sir, ma'am, the empress is waiting for you."

"*Interim* empress," Leo said under his breath, but when I glanced at him, pride shone in his eyes. "It's already going to her head."

"Oh, little brother, you're just jealous," Rissa's voice sounded from a few feet away. She leaned casually against the wooden railing separating the port from the ocean, her arms stretched out across it. Blonde curls blew in the breeze with the backdrop of rolling waves and the rising sun. When her eyes landed on me, she grinned.

Covering the distance in a handful of strides, I threw my arms around her.

"I never did say thank you, Rose," she said into my hair. "For risking so much to help us and for everything you did in that chamber. We couldn't have done this without you."

"That's not true. I may have cast the final spell, but you've been building up to this for *years*. You're incredible, Clarissa Aris." I pulled back and gripped her shoulders. "There's no better person to lead our people."

She smiled. "And there's no better person to *help* our people. No two better people, I should say." Nodding to Leo who was waiting behind me, she said, "I know how much this means to him, getting to be part of the end of the curse. He needs this closure and to see that people don't blame our father anymore. And I'm so glad you're doing it together, because he needs *you*, too."

The idea of someone needing me the way I did them made something crack inside my chest, filling me with sweet warmth. Before I could respond, someone shouted my name, and I turned to see Chaz wheeling Lark toward us along the boarded path.

"You just had to make us get up at the crack of dawn, didn't you?" Chaz said, chuckling. When he reached us, he came out from behind the wheelchair to envelop me in a one-armed hug. "If you ever get tired of life on the go with broody over here, I'll tag in anytime."

I snorted. "It's good to see nothing has changed, Chaz."

When he pulled away, his lighthearted demeanor slipped slightly. "Some things have." His dark eyes slid to the side, as if searching for someone no longer there. Cords wrapped around my heart and tugged, the memory of Horace's last moments branded into my mind.

"You'll be alright," Chaz continued, offering a small smile. "You're good for each other. Just don't forget about us while you're off saving the world, yes?"

"We'll do our best," Leo responded with a smirk, smacking his friend on the back.

As Leo said his goodbyes to Rissa and Chaz, Lark cleared her throat. "I knew I chose well after Ragnar's incident. From the very beginning, I had a feeling about you. You have this fire that can't be quenched, even against all odds." She gave me a thin-lipped smile and wheeled herself to the rail. I followed, taking in the sling around her arm and the fading bruises still visible on her dark skin.

"Thank you for taking a chance on me," I said, and she looked back at me in slight surprise. "Things haven't always been the smoothest between us, but for all the loss this month has brought, I wouldn't take any of it back." Out of the corner of my eye, my gaze lingered on Leo. "My time here...it taught me things about myself. Both good *and* bad. It was twisted and terrible at times, but it made me capable. And in the end, we got what we've been working for, didn't we? A better future."

"A better future," she repeated wistfully, then gave me a once-over. "You two stay safe. We may be heading toward that better future, but we're not there yet. Be careful and watch out for one another."

I reached down and squeezed her hand as Leo approached my

side. "The captain wants to leave soon," he said, then guided me away from the railing. "We only have a few more minutes."

Turning on my heel, I saw Ragnar, Morgana, and Beau walking toward us.

My heart clenched. They were leaving soon after me to head back to Feywood and I wasn't sure when I'd see them again. With a hand at my back, Leo led me to them, stopping far enough away to give us space.

My aunt clutched a handkerchief, her face red and eyes puffy. Beau kept running his fingers through his newly cut hair—he looked so much older without the locks covering his eyes. Flashes of that little gangly boy I used to chase around the gardens crossed my mind, now a vibrant young man with such a soft, tender spirit.

"Don't you dare start crying," he said in warning as I drew closer.

"I wouldn't dream of it." I laughed as I pulled him into a tight hug. "Take care of the shop for me while I'm gone, alright?" I moved back and straightened his collar. "And remember where the foxglove is in case you come across any more Madelines. I won't be there to fend them off," I said, shooting him a wink.

"You'll be back with us in no time, just wait and see." He ruffled my hair the way I always did to him. "Love you, Rosie. I'm gonna miss having my big sister around."

"I thought you told me not to cry!" I exclaimed, my vision blurry with tears threatening to spill. "You can't go saying stuff like that, Beau Beau."

"Well, you can cry with me," my aunt said, hastily suffocating me in her embrace. "Oh, I'm so proud of you, Rose. And I know your parents would be, too. I just wish you didn't have to go." She dabbed at her cheeks, smiling encouragingly through her own sadness. "You are so brave, my dear girl. So strong. The two of you have been our greatest blessings," she added, grabbing her son's hand.

"She's not *dying*, Ana. We'll see her again soon," Ragnar said with a grin, and my aunt swatted his arm.

I looked between the two of them, unsure if I'd be able to get my next words out. Ragnar was right; I *would* see them again, but we had no idea how long this journey around the provinces would take or what dangers we might face. And afterward...well, I no longer knew for certain that my future lay in Feywood. Emotion clogged my throat, a blend of overpowering love and gratitude and heartache that paralyzed me.

"I—I've never been one to show how much you mean to me." I breathed out slowly. "I'm not good at this, at *feelings*"—Ragnar chortled at that—"but I would have *nothing* without you. You took me in without a second thought. You raised me as your own and showed me what love looked like in a world that—that didn't want to love me." My voice broke off. Silent tears streamed down my aunt's face.

I collected myself, instinctively reaching my hand behind me. In an instant, Leo was there, giving me his strength.

"And I don't think I've ever thanked you for that," I continued. "So thank you. For everything."

"You *are* our own," Ragnar responded gruffly. He leaned forward to cup the back of my neck and pull me into his chest. "You may not be my blood, but you're our *daughter*."

Drops of wetness stained his shirt as I leaned back and he said, "Until we see you again, Rose. Bring hope back to this broken world. Have your adventures. Find your freedom. Remember how loved you are." He met Leo's eyes over my shoulder and nodded. "That's the greatest future I could hope for either one of my children."

Morgana and Beau gathered around us. Beau slung an arm across my shoulder while my aunt leaned into Ragnar's side, the four of us sharing one last moment.

For now.

Above us, a horn blew, signaling the ship's imminent departure. The world picked up speed as deckhands began to usher other passengers to the gangplank, leading them up to the main deck. As I waved goodbye to my family, I couldn't help but look over their shoulders for one last person.

"Do you need something?" Leo asked, putting a hand at the small of my back.

I shook my head. "I guess I thought Nox might come, but he's probably heading to Drakorum soon. It's fine." I hadn't seen him or Arowyn since I woke up. Arowyn had evidently journeyed back to Celestria shortly after Gayl's death, and Nox had been in deep discussions with Rissa and her council on behalf of Drakorum, who had never made an appearance in the capital.

From the top of the gangplank, a voice filtered down to us. "I was wondering when you'd ask about me."

My lips broke into a grin. Looking up, I saw that cocky face smirking back at me as Nox leaned against the railing. "Let me guess, you saved the best for last?" I teased.

"Oh, I'm not going anywhere."

Confusion swept over me. "You—you're staying? On the ship?"

"Our dear *empress* has a task for me, it seems." He winked at Rissa.

"We need eyes over in Mysthelm," she jumped in. "An ambassador, of sorts. It's a long road to fix what's been broken between them and us, but it's a step."

"Mysthelm?" My eyes shot to Nox. "How are you getting there?"

"Little detour through Tenebra, then I'll head south down to their border. You're not getting rid of me that quickly."

I could practically feel the glower Leo shot him. Even after their lengthy discussion on the beach during the third trial, Leo still carried a bit of irritation toward the dragon Shifter. I snorted. "This will be interesting."

"Don't worry, I have no intention of interrupting the love birds," Nox crooned. "Strictly business. I am a professional, after all."

Rissa gave Leo and me one last hug. "Stay alert, especially in these first two provinces." We ascended the gangplank and she shouted from below, "Be safe! I'll write to you!"

And with that, they were gone.

I exhaled slowly as I leaned over the deck railing, watching the ship push off from the port. By the end of the day we'd make landfall in Tenebra and start our new journey. A mission of healing and hope. And while it was bittersweet to say goodbye, there was a freedom in this. A freedom I'd never considered but had always yearned for. A beautiful, open landscape ready to be filled.

Leo came up behind me and put his hands on the rails, trapping my back against his solid chest. I turned to nuzzle my cheek against his chin. Before us, waves rippled and gleamed in the sunlight, brushing against the bottom of the boat. Birds sang in the distance as wind skimmed my skin.

"Are you sad to be leaving your home?" I murmured, nodding toward the receding shoreline.

"I'm sad to leave my family for a little while, but Veridia City isn't my only home." He twisted me to face him, and I locked my arms around his neck as he said, "Not anymore."

I smiled. "Are you sure you know what you're getting into with me, monkey boy?"

"I think I have an idea," he said with a chuckle. I lifted up on my toes when he leaned down to kiss me, my lips still grinning against his.

"I love you, Rose," he said quietly. "And I will spend every moment of the time you give me making you as happy as you have made me."

Of the time you give me. "I'll hold you to that," I said, kissing him again as my chest swelled and ached with joy. "Because it will be a very, very long time, Leo Aris."

Our entire lives, our future, our *purpose* lay ahead of us, as clear and full as the day.

This was just the beginning.

EPILOGUE

Dear Rose and Leo,

I'm sorry it's been a while since I've written. Things got a bit hectic here after you left. Once the dust settled from Gayl's death and the Decemvirate, some brave idiots decided perhaps anyone could have a go at the crown. I've been dodging Drakorum inquiries and Iluze appeals like they're daggers. Nothing to worry about—it's being handled, with only a few pissed off governors and one assassination attempt to show for. (Kidding, Leo—I'm fine, I promise. You should see the other guy.)

Rose, your uncle Ragnar has been coming back to the capital often since I lifted the border restrictions. He's been instrumental in helping me deal with some of the bad seeds on this council. There are still a few stubborn remnants from Gayl's time, one of which is that member you woke from the Somnivae curse. Lord Stryker. If I'd known he'd be this difficult, I would've asked you to keep him asleep.

Most of the rest are stodgy lords who have obviously never been told "no" in their lives. And by a woman, no less. They're trying to convince me to take a tour of Mysthelm to strengthen relationships with the new King Grimaldi and secure trade agreements that haven't been around in centuries. It's a good idea, I'll admit. It could unite our territories and start wiping away so much of the stain from our past. The council wants to reconvene later this week with one final proposal.

We'll see. I may be leaving our precious empire sooner than I'd planned.

Hope you're doing well and staying out of trouble. Rose, that is. I'm sure Leo's on his best, most brooding behavior.

All my love,

Empress Clarissa Aris

(maybe you'll have a fancy title one day too, Leo)

ALSO BY V.B. LACEY

The Elementals of Iona:

Long Live

Forever Reign

Wildfire: A Prequel Novella

The Veridian Empire Series:

In the Wake of the Wicked

Of the Curse or the Crown

From the Silence of the Shadows

By the Flames of Her Fury

ACKNOWLEDGEMENTS

First off, thank you so much for giving this book—for giving *me*—a chance. This story has been on my heart and mind for a long time, and it's amazing to watch it come to life and finally be in your hands.

I give all the glory and praise to God for granting me this opportunity and all of the many blessings that come with it.

To Taylor—as always, I'm thankful for the endless support and patience you give me. I wouldn't be able to do any part of this dream if it weren't for you.

To my family—your pride inspires me to keep going, even if I don't often believe in myself.

To my early readers—from alpha to beta to ARCs, your excitement for Rose and Leo's story made me giddy, and I'm so thankful for your boundless encouragement.

To my editor, Kay—thanks for taking a chance on me and helping me become more confident with putting my baby out into the world.

To TLC—thank you for being my safe space. I would go to the ends of the world for you, and I know you would do the same.

To the Bookmasters—Alice, Brit, Cris, Katie, and Melissa. You basically have a permanent spot in my acknowledgements at this point. Going through our journeys together has been one of the most fulfilling parts of this author life, and I'm so proud of each of us.

To my street team—you all are just the best! Thank you for constantly hyping me up and for loving these characters and this world so much. I'd be lost without your support and cheer.

To my readers—you've stuck with me for three books now, and that's three more than I ever expected when I started writing two and a half years ago. Seriously, I can't thank you enough for picking up a little indie's books and helping my lifelong dream come true. You are the reason we do what we do. Please don't ever stop diving into new worlds and escaping to the magic of pages.

Lastly, because why not? Thank you to Stephen Schwartz for writing the musical that inspired this book and that has had such a lasting impact on my creative mind. I hope I made all the *Wicked* fans out there proud.

Till next time, friends. And I think you'll like where we go.

About the Author

V.B. Lacey is an office manager by day and an avid reader-turned-writer by night. She grew up on stories of magic, love, and sarcasm, and equips her writing with all three. She lives in Texas with her supportive husband and two rambunctious dogs. When she's not writing about morally grey characters and far-off kingdoms, you can find her reading (mostly fantasy and contemporary romance), playing board games, or spending time with friends.

Visit her online at www.vblaceybooks.com, or follow her on Instagram and TikTok: @vblacey.books.